A Mortal Mistake

A Mortal Mistake

Book I: Heaven, Hell & Humanity

Vince Seim

iUniverse LLC
Bloomington

A MORTAL MISTAKE
BOOK I: HEAVEN, HELL & HUMANITY

Copyright © 2013 Vince Seim.

All rights reserved. No part of this book may be used or reproduced by any means, graphic, electronic, or mechanical, including photocopying, recording, taping or by any information storage retrieval system without the written permission of the publisher except in the case of brief quotations embodied in critical articles and reviews.

This is a work of fiction. All of the characters, names, incidents, organizations, and dialogue in this novel are either the products of the author's imagination or are used fictitiously.

iUniverse books may be ordered through booksellers or by contacting:

iUniverse
1663 Liberty Drive
Bloomington, IN 47403
www.iuniverse.com
1-800-Authors (1-800-288-4677)

Because of the dynamic nature of the Internet, any web addresses or links contained in this book may have changed since publication and may no longer be valid. The views expressed in this work are solely those of the author and do not necessarily reflect the views of the publisher, and the publisher hereby disclaims any responsibility for them.

Any people depicted in stock imagery provided by Thinkstock are models, and such images are being used for illustrative purposes only.

Certain stock imagery © Thinkstock.

ISBN: 978-1-4759-7066-1 (sc)
ISBN: 978-1-4759-7065-4 (hc)
ISBN: 978-1-4759-7064-7 (e)

Library of Congress Control Number: 2013900455

Printed in the United States of America

iUniverse rev. date: 8/9/2013

For the lost imagination
and sense of wonder....

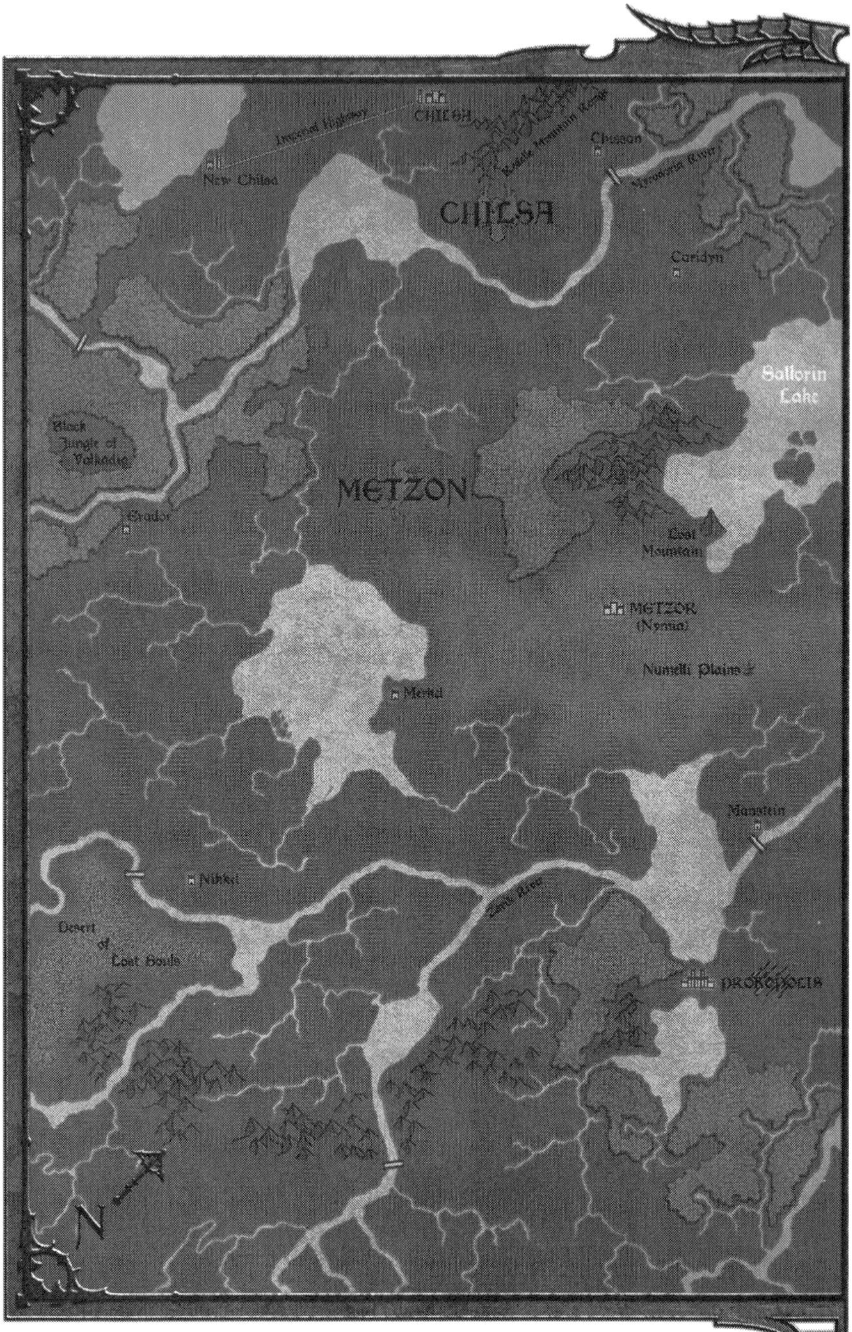
CHILSA
New Chilsa
Chissan
CHILSA
Caridyn
Sallorin
Lake
METZON
Erador
Lost
Mountain
METZOR
(Nymia)
Numelli Plains
Merkel
Manstein
Nikkel
Desert
of
Lost Souls
N

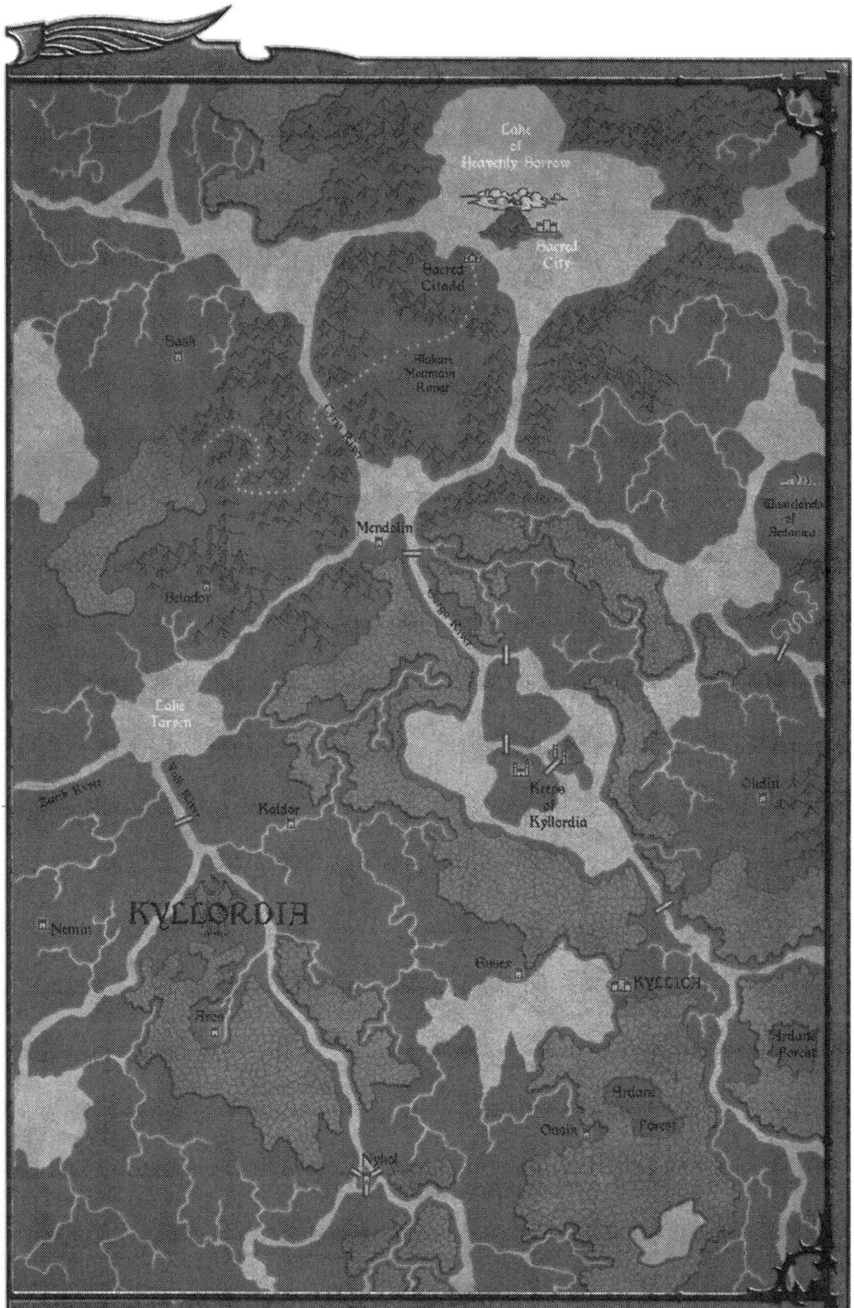
Lake
of
Heavenly Sorrow
Sacred
City
Sacred
Citadel
Mendalin
Lake
Tarpen
Kaldor
Keeps
of
Kyllordia
KYLLORDIA
Nemar
KYLLICH
Ardane
Forest
Oasis

And for our sins, the Lords of Heaven stripped us of our wings and immortality. Cast out from Heaven, never to feel the Light of Heaven's beautiful banner again, we fell disgraced upon this prison world He calls Earth. We all shall live and die by our true beliefs and try to prove ourselves worthy of redemption come the Day of Judgment. Until that day, may our sacrifice not be in vain as the eternal Darkness prepares to consume our souls. Consume all of life upon this world.

Orion,
First to Fall

Chapter 1
Lost Soul

The stinging sand attacked Conrad's eyes as he pushed through the storm raging around him. He had quickly learnt that any who stopped within the voracious sandstorms of the desert would be swallowed whole. The Desert of Lost Souls had many ways to consume mortals, and he was certain he had witnessed them all.

Letting the sand pool around his feet for a moment, he paused to tighten the thin piece of cloth over his dirt-filled nostrils as he tried to peer through the walls of swirling sand. For two days the storm had raged, leaving Conrad few stars for navigation, forcing him to forge on without indication of his direction. At least the storm granted him some relief from the criminals and murderers who called this hellhole home.

A storm lasting two long days was small compared to several others he had encountered in his four-month adventure—now almost five. Conrad had not a clue how his brother could have survived for five years among such constant danger. Was Sven still alive? Conrad had asked himself that multiple times, but he firmly believed that if anyone could do it, it was Sven, without a doubt.

Scanning the barely visible silhouettes of the red rock ridge that was his destination, Conrad took off again. His thoughts became consumed by the events that had landed his brother—and by an extension of events, Conrad himself—in this perilous desert.

Strong-willed and fearless, Sven had always been admired by the citizens of the Metzon nation, none more than his brother. But by disobeying a man even more powerful than himself, Sven had awoken a sleeping titan whose anger refused to be contained. Their father's fury was unlike any other man's Conrad had witnessed; there was no yelling or screaming or violence. A calculatingly calm would overcome his father, somehow making him so forbidding his sons trembled in fear. He punished mind and soul, demoralizing the recipient, who was forced to question his entire belief system. As terrible as the punishments felt, Conrad had found that he eventually came to realize the significance of the lesson. Such lessons improved his life, and his suffering made him a better man.

But his punishment had not involved banishment to the harshest place in the world. A great many would have considered sending a son into the Desert of Lost Souls a death sentence. But his father deemed it appropriate after Sven had sentenced thousands of Metzon's sons to their deaths by leading them into Chilsa.

Conrad had watched him grow smaller and smaller as the army moved out from the blood-soaked plains his brother had created, a look of disbelief upon Sven's face. Forced to march in the dusty cloud created by the army, Sven would eventually disappear completely, not returning home until several months later. Conrad had suspected his father's anger would have abated. He was wrong.

Excitement had filled the air when Sven returned. Conrad had watched his brother march up the cobblestone path of the main road leading to Metzor to find the gates shut before him. The solemn look upon his face as he stared upon the golden gates and the silent viewers who had gathered upon the top of the wall was burnt upon Conrad's memory. Scanning the wall before him, his brother waited. The thundering gates had shaken beneath Conrad's feet.

Conrad watched his father march forward, alone, moving with purpose, his strides long. Sven did not kneel before his father in forgiveness as one would expect of a man who angered his king, even if it was his father. Standing rigidly before the tall walls, the two men of indisputable power met face to face, refusing to flinch. Conrad had only been able to see Sven's face when the hushed argument broke out between them. Despite the muted atmosphere, all the spectators had heard was the blowing breeze of the grassy plains of the Numelli within their ears.

A Mortal Mistake

Conrad watched Sven's face darken, his jaw clenched tightly, as the dispute grew more hostile. Sven drew his sword before him. Conrad had feared it would turn fatal as the sword quivered beside Sven's leg. Conrad's father remained motionless and fearless, inches away from his son.

Reaching to each shoulder, Sven unclasped the flag staffs from his back, letting the black stallion upon his father's golden banners fall to the dusty road. As all those around Conrad watched the blatant display of dishonour, gasps of hushed horror escaped their throats. Conrad watched his brother turn his back on their father and walk away, not seen again after that dark day.

And Sven had still not been found, despite the search Conrad had conducted. Few places remained where he had not looked for Sven.

"Oh, brother, where do you wander? Where among these lost souls do you hide?" Conrad spoke aloud, breaking the incessant whistling of wind. What a question to ask in such a vast place, but at the very least the rocky mountain would provide him with the briefest moments of relief. Trudging down the sandy slope, Conrad's leg struck something solid hidden beneath the sand, sending him tumbling head over heels down the long dune. Pulling himself out of the sand, Conrad turned to observe what object had tripped him.

The rusted knife destined for his left eye missed its mark, cutting him across the cheekbone, only by the swiftness of Conrad's instinctive reaction. As Conrad fought back to his feet, the gauntlet he wore upon his left hand shattered the jaw of the ambusher. He rose from the sand and unsheathed his long sword.

Three new attackers rushed down from the top of the dune toward him carrying crude weapons. Parrying the blow of the foremost attacker, Conrad dipped beneath the attack and thrust his elbow into the throat of the second. He dragged his blade from the parry and sent it into the skull of the third attacker. A crack of steel upon his back alerted him to the final attacker, his blade not penetrating the heavy Metzonian steel. With a low attack, Conrad cut the man's leg off above the knee before running his blade through the attacker to the wide crossguard.

Letting the man slide from his blade, as Conrad turned to scan the dune for more attackers, he twisted directly into their path. Two penetrating blows struck him to the ground, the feathers upon the arrow shafts quivering before his eyes. Five men stood amongst the sandstorm, waving toward three more before pointing to their fallen prey.

Waves of pain washed over Conrad as he tried to crawl through the thick sand toward his dropped sword. Feeling the edge of the pommel beneath his fingertips, Conrad heard hysterical laughter close around him. One man jumped emphatically atop his blade as a second kicked him in the side of the head. Rolling onto his back, Conrad looked at the dirty faces staring down upon him, their dark leathery skin stretched tight over malnourished cheekbones as they smiled black grins upon their prey.

Within their crazed looks, Conrad saw flickers of concern as they inspected him further. Using the long spear shafts, they flipped open the thick cloak to reveal his armour beneath. Eyes lighting up at the shimmer of gold, two of the bandits were animated. The third man's eyes narrowed.

"Dammit, Doober! This ain't him!" the man screamed to those still atop the dune, his shrill scream cutting above the winds howling over them. Conrad pondered who they had set the trap for if not him, but the man in charge looked unpleased.

"What do you mean it ain't him? We've been tracking this prick for months now. Who else would it be! Why the hell am I asking you, anyways? You can't even see your own pecker in broad daylight."

Conrad watched the thicker man trod down the slope to inspect for himself.

"Piss off! Look for yourself—same size, same look, certainly Metzonian, but I'm telling you it ain't him, Doo. Look at his armour, and the gold stallions upon his chest. He still gots the gold emblazin and everything. Still worth a pretty penny … even if he don't survives, I'm supposing." The man staring into Conrad's eyes and flicking at the arrows rammed into his chest was shoved roughly aside as Doober reached Conrad's body.

A Mortal Mistake

"Mother of mine, if I'm not mistaken our fortune's changed, boys! We gots us a bigger prize than we were after! Both of you go call the others down here quickly, before the sand buries him forever." Doober's grimy grin grew wide, showing blackened teeth. "Welcome to the Desert of Lost Souls, son."

Conrad averted his eyes from the greedy beads staring hungrily down upon him. His flesh grew cold as the chills from blood loss seeped into his body. Conrad was furious at himself for having been so easily taken unawares by a band of starving rogues. Conrad felt his soul quiver as he thought about perishing before he was able to find his brother, to tell Sven what he deserved to know, to see his brother one last time. Where was he?

"You're going to die here, kid, where no one will know. No one will come to find you." Doober's laughed to himself as he watched his companions run up the dune ridge. His expression soured as Conrad smiled, understanding at last who they were talking about. "So what in the hell do you have to smile about, boy?"

"I know who you are searching for, the monster you fear. My brother is still out there, isn't he? Lurking amongst the wind and the sand like a ghost. All search for him for different reasons, but now he will have a reason to hunt you. I think you have awakened the wraith."

"Desert of Lost Souls, kid. No one is here but me, you and all my buddies."

"Just you and me, actually."

Doober's eyes went wide as Conrad laughed at him, looking for his hilltop friends but finding only the sandy horizon all around him. Seizing the moment of confusion, Conrad reached out, grabbing the bandit by his greasy ponytail. As he drew the dagger from his thigh, he pulled back and rammed the blade into the neck of the man and twisted it.

Listening to the satisfying crunch, Conrad released the man's body to fall into the sand beside him. Lifting his head to scan the horizon, he also saw nothing; the bodies of the other ambushers mysteriously missing. Leaning his head back, Conrad rested his eyes before he felt a presence looming over top of him.

Feeling a sharp, heavy steel tip press at his naked throat, Conrad opened his eyes to stare at the imposing figure standing above him, both hands resting upon the hilt of a wide broadsword of dark grey; a tattered cloak flapped in the stiff breeze from the storm. Heavy breathing rasped within the confines of the steel helmet hidden in the depths of a heavy cowl that hid the identity of the wraith. Conrad observed the scarred, sharp-edged Metzonian steel, and it left little doubt in his mind about who it was. The sword at his throat caused him to fear he may have been mistaken.

"Hey, brother, long time no see."

The dark void within the cowl did not speak; the head twisted sideways. A pang of fear struck his heart when Conrad realized that his brother did not recognize his face, did not recognize his voice. The desert, with its perpetual sandy wind and blistering heat, had claimed Sven's soul, leaving only a hollow body to wander its dunes. Sven might murder his brother as quickly as he had all others without knowing what he had ever done.

"You need to go home, brother; at least one of us must return home, and it is unlikely to be me now." Conrad gently wrapped his gloved hands around the shafts of the two arrows. Tears stung his eyes, washing away the sand that began to enshroud his motionless body; he had failed to keep his promise to his mother. Knowing how much his mother loved Sven, Conrad had promised her that he would bring her Sven back. No one could have known it would cost him his own life, possibly at the hands of the very brother he was supposed to return. His final words barely audible, Conrad tried one last time to reach his brother.

"Mom's sick, Sven. You need to go home. You need to go home…"

Musty air filled his nostrils as he barked painfully several times, a mixture of sand and blood scrapping the back of his throat. Rolling himself slowly over onto his side, Conrad spit the sandy saliva down onto the floor. He did not know where he was. Whatever he was lying on was hard as a rock and extremely uncomfortable.

Twisting through the pain to lay upon his back once again, he opened and closed his eyes several times, forcing them to adjust to the darkness. Running his hands over the tops of his goose bump–covered arms, he felt chill air upon his naked skin, uncharacteristic of the desert. Turning his head in the opposite direction, he saw a mess of blood-stained rags and pails of dark liquids; two bloody barbed arrows rested against the wall. The glittering arrowheads jogged his memory, revealing pieces of what had occurred.

Conrad remembered little after the ambush except feeling steel grasp the thick armour upon his back as he was forcibly dragged through the desert. Small memories containing nothing more than sand and wind were all he remembered as he slipped in and out of consciousness. He was alive though; somehow and for some reason the world had the grace to let him live.

Reaching down across his chest, he moved his fingertips across the flesh where the arrows had once protruded. A sticky substance lathered at the surface; Conrad could feel the coarse strands of thread holding his gaping wounds tightly sealed. The pain was significant but not nearly as great as he had originally anticipated, allowing him to move to the bottom edge of whatever surface he was upon.

He stood and carefully stretched his limbs, trying not to aggravate his new wounds as he ran his hands over them again. Turning around to look upon his bed, he jumped a little inside as he stared down upon an overly large sacrificial altar, the edges carved deep to capture the life essence of whatever enormous victim it may have once held.

Dressing himself as quickly as any injured man could, he stared upon the walls at the crudely carved demons that lined them and the sporadic language written upon them. Wherever he had been brought, it was a horribly evil and dark place. Conrad refused to linger longer than he absolutely had to, and he hobbled toward the closest exit, pausing at the last second.

Heat rolled out of the exit, washing his flesh with intoxicating moisture that beckoned him forward, enticing him to delve into its depths. Conrad's mind resisted. A warning flashed in the back of his mind as he inspected the exit further. The large staircase climbed down deeper into whatever structure he was within. The heat was not the sweltering dryness of the desert, the place he knew he had to escape to if was to have a chance to leave this horrid nightmare.

He backed slowly away, not allowing his eyes to leave the foul exit or whatever might erupt from its depths to swallow him. Nearing a second exit, he heard the whispering of a single voice within a second room. Looking around the corner, he searched for the speaker, unable to pinpoint the location in the gloomy chamber. He spotted a pair of thick doors that looked significantly more inviting than the first pair; sunlight penetrated the small gaps.

"Countless mercenaries, marauders, murderers have come to hunt me down, and Chilsa assassins with their elaborate murder plots, plus every other gloryhound. Yet your creation, Devotz the Devourer, has slain all who dared such stupidity."

Conrad vaguely spotted the hunched figure, who shifted upon his haunches and paused his whispered speech. A long scraping sound echoed within the corner. "Though never in these years has a member of my family come to return me home. Without her there is little other reason to return home … Why now? Why has he risked his life to return what is gone?"

Conrad hesitated, looking at the door only a quick dash away that would allow his escape. Feeling the pain radiating from his chest, he knew there would be no dash if this individual chose to pursue him. Clutching his sword tightly in the event the encounter turned violent, Conrad decided he had to gamble.

"Sven?" Silence overtook the shadowy second room. A low, rolling chuckle escaped the hunched man's throat. Taking a step closer, Conrad looked into the gloom and saw a demonic face staring back upon him, with sharp white fang and dark eyes that glared menacingly at him. The skull grew blurry, disappearing into the gloom as the figure moved. Conrad rubbed his eyes as he looked twice, realizing he was staring at the crouching figure's back.

"I haven't heard that name in many years." A voice he had not heard in years rang like music in Conrad's ears, offering a slight relief to Conrad's fretting mind. The voice continued. "Sounds so foreign that I hardly recognize it anymore—perhaps I had even forgotten it. The Desert of Lost Souls does not recognize names, nor does it really care who you are or where you came from. All are just souls to be taken."

"Sounds like you have taken your fair share, based on the words spoken within this dark place." Conrad alluded to Sven's hushed conversation with the temple walls, unsure about his brother's sanity. "Or was that the aforementioned Devotz?"

The low scraping along the blade stopped as the whetstone paused. Sven's thick shoulders twitched. Twisting toward Conrad, his brother leaned casually up against the stone wall, facing him for the first time.

His thickly muscled arms, covered in thin scars from countless battles, rested across his chest. Sven's bloodshot golden eyes stared back at Con amidst the gloom. Unknotting the sweat-stained rag wrapped around his large forehead, he immersed the yellow embroidered Metzonian cloth in a small clay bowl beside him. The drops of water splattered on the floor; neither man chose to speak nor broke eye contact.

"Devotz, Devourer of Men, is what the dregs of the desert have taken to calling me. Few flee fast enough to survive such encounters, and none survive the black blade when they choose to fight. One would believe that such legends would cause caution among those who hear it. Unfortunately it does not stop those who relentlessly pursue me for wealth or glory in wave upon wave. Chilsa, Kyllordic, even our own Metzonians, all come to hunt for me. I had figured the whispers of a Metzonian prince wandering the desert were merely another assassin's plot to lure me into their traps. I figured I had become forgotten, never believing it would actually be true after so many years."

"And I thought you had forgotten me and were about to kill your own brother. You were never forgotten, brother, and have always been missed." Conrad paused, feeling more comfortable as Sven spoke with a degree of sanity. Clearing his throat, he continued to probe for answers among the fractured mind. "Why didn't you come home? Why did you not swallow your pride and return where you belong? Why stay in the desert for all these years?"

"You remember Sven, an innocent young man who was wronged

by his father and family. Though I admit that I made my fair share of mistakes, our father did not have to shame me as he did. All was done with only the best of intentions. Do you know what he said to me upon my return to Metzor after my mistake? He said, 'Ten thousand souls now wander the desert because of what you have done. Ten thousand fathers, brothers and sons never to return home to their families. All because of your mistake, so perhaps you should go and try to find your own lost soul among those who will never return home.'"

Conrad had to agree with his brother that their father had dealt with Sven in the harshest of ways, shaming him publicly before the city walls and then banishing him to the desert of lost and forgotten souls until he was ready to admit his wrong. Both men were of course too proud to admit their mistakes, despite how much it pained both father and son.

"The desert changes a man, Con. Every day is a war, every hour a battle, every minute a struggle between life and death. It strips away everything that makes you human, that separates man from animal. To survive in the desert you must lose everything that makes a man noble, all innocence and caring. Only survival matters, which ultimately turns you into a monster. I have done many things that would truly be deserving of death in the land of noble kings and proud peoples. Once upon a time I could have returned, but it is too late. My soul truly belongs among the lost now."

Conrad leaned against one of the large columns in the room, looking high up to the ceiling continuing to feel uneasy within the temple structure. Built with power and purpose, it was a suitable fit for Sven and all he had once embodied, particularly combined with this new darkness he had been forced to embrace in the name of survival.

Desperate not to leave his brother in the desert, Conrad moved toward the doors, trying to discover a way to help his brother return from the dark path, to return him to the proud and noble being he remembered him to be. The Desert of Lost Souls was a corrupt, horrid place to stay, but Conrad was certain that Sven did not have to stay as he believed.

"Leave it all in the past, where such pain and suffering belong. Mistakes are made by all, but one mistake does not dictate the lifetime of suffering you are putting upon yourself. You have punished yourself enough, I think."

"And what does your other brother believe? And our father?" Grabbing his sword by the hilt, Sven moved it to his opposite shoulder, running a finger along the blade.

"You know our father is strong and powerful, like his second-born. But also too full of pride, much like his second-born son." Conrad smiled at Sven, trying to get a positive response out of his brother. "Frederick—I do not know if he is as forgiving after the two of you fell out and the harsh things you said to him. And you know him. He isn't going to say anything that could upset Father."

"Of course he wouldn't, Father's perfect son." Sven picked up the whetstone and began running it along the blade again. "You should really be going. I appreciate that you foolishly risked your life to try and return me home. But I fear returning would be a mistake you would come to regret."

Conrad sadly turned away from his brother, wondering if this would be the last time he ever saw his face again. He scrambled to try and find anything to convince his brother to leave this dreaded place, but he was drawing a blank. Sven's mind was not easily persuaded, and Conrad's fear of this place was growing. "Well, if you ever change your mind ... you know where I live." Conrad smiled and moved toward the entrance, eager to leave the dark temple but not his brother.

"Is it true?" Sven's voice trembled with the words; he refused to look up. "What you said about Mother?"

Conrad waited to respond, collecting his own emotions before broaching the painful subject. "Yeah, it's true. She is sick, Sven. Father has had every practitioner of medicine from across Metzon try to discover what is wrong with her. Even the healers of the holy Order of the Fallen came from Prokopolis, but none have been able to cure whatever it is that ails her."

"Holy, my ass—nothing but a bunch of eccentric kooks who believe they are descendants of Heaven. Damned Order, were they truly who they say they are she would be cured and ten years younger."

Conrad did not comment upon the subject of the Order of the Fallen, knowing how intricately involved they had been within the history of his family and its rise to Lords of Metzon. "My ability to heal flesh and bone far surpasses their own. Look at you—you lay dying on my table for twelve days, but yet here you stand, alive."

Conrad rubbed his face, feeling the slight beard he had grown while unconscious. Despite the magnitude of his wounds, somehow he was still alive. Conrad had seen enough wounds in the conflicts Sven had created to know that his survival was unanticipated. Conrad's brother was known for creating those wounds, not healing them. "Thanks for saving me in the desert, by the way."

Sven did not respond. He dipped his head low to rest upon his hands and knees.

Conrad wanted nothing more than to go over to his brother and embrace him but forced himself to remain where he stood, fighting the pity he felt for the damaged soul.

"Whatever it is, it does not change the course of what will inevitably happen. She wants to see you, Sven, she wants to see her son one last time. No one loved you or understood you more than Mother did. Of the three of us, you were her favourite, so passionate and strong in life." Conrad watched carefully as Sven's thick, ringed fingers wrung his hands tightly. "Come home, Sven. Time grows shorter with every month, so please—come home."

Conrad pitched himself back as quickly as his reflexes allowed, reeling from his brother's speed. Sven's black broadsword flashed through the dim room, smashing against the thick stone columns; rock and steel splinters flew through the air under the impact.

"Look what you cost me!" Sven's screams, rising above the clash of steel and stone, were deafening to his brother's ears. "This was not how it was supposed to go! I should have been home where I could have fixed things! Look at what you cost me! I've lost everything because of one innocent mistake!"

Conrad scrambled backward as Sven approached him, unsure who among the many options his rage was directed toward. Childhood memories reminded him to flee the reach of Sven's wrath.

Sven passed harmlessly overtop, heading toward the exit, leaving his brother where he lay. Grasping between the thick planks, he ripped the doors from their hinges. Conrad was amazed as his brother somehow wrestled their awkward bulk and tossed them to the side. Then he was gone, charging back into the desert.

Hobbling toward the open exit, Conrad struggled to keep up with his enraged brother. Bursting through the doorway, Conrad's new surroundings immediately shocked him, making him feel more uneasy. The great dunes of sand had been replaced by great mountains of thousands of bones, the skeletons bleached a stark white by the blistering sun.

"Don't mind those who hunted me. They discovered the fate they deserved." Sven did not turn around but continued upon his narrow path toward the setting sun. "Come on, we must travel through the night while it is cool and the sandstorms are silent."

Conrad hobbled down the immense steps and followed after his brother, wary of the endless number of skulls mocking him with gaping jaws. Looking at his brother moving powerfully across the desert once again, he wondered if perhaps he himself was about to make a mistake of his own that he would come to regret.

CHAPTER 2
KALLEN

The heat beat down heavily upon the market, the morning warmth rising beneath the sun as it continued along its celestial arc. Looking away from the sun, Kallen turned his attention in the opposite direction, high up at the acropolis that rose from the heart of the largest city east of the Zarik. The bells would soon be announcing the adjournment of another morning meeting of the Elders Council of Prokopolis. Looking at the crowded market around him, he realized he would be pressed for time to reach the gates to meet his foster father.

Waving away a merchant who was adamantly insisting he buy a new woven rug for the home that Kallen did not own, he moved across the narrow path toward a fruit stand. Grabbing a brightly coloured orange from the stand, Kallen tossed a silver coin to the merchant, who smiled at his generosity. The market bustled with great energy as merchants tried to lure customers toward their stalls with flamboyant acts and great speeches.

A group of small children ran before him, playfully screaming for someone to save them from the giant that was coming to eat them. Smiles quickly came to the faces of concerned citizens as they watched Kallen reach out to pick up the children by their shirts and lift them high above everyone. The remaining children gleefully fought back, clinging to his legs as they pretended to wrestle their friends free.

He set their small friends down in defeat, and the children laughed and fled off into the crowd, leaving him to continue on his way. As he gently pushed his way through the crowds, most citizens cleared away from the larger man's path, smiling cheerfully. Complementing the beautiful weather given to them by the grace of the Heavens, the citizens were consistently in good spirits.

Prokopolis was the only city in the land that belonged to the Order of the Fallen. Although the religious order did not own great swaths of land or multiple cities, the Order was one of the most powerful amongst the world powers. The people chose the Order themselves, coming from every corner of the world to share in the holy existence.

The Order had millions of followers, but the shepherds let their sheep choose where they lived and what they did with their lives, asking only that they live righteous and proper lives. In this way, the Order of the Fallen's interests remained in line with those passed down to Humanity through Heaven. A large white banner hung down the side of a stone wall, five silver streaks cut diagonally through the circular emblem, like falling meteorites. The largest in the middle denoted the angel who started it all.

History as dictated by the Order told that the acropolis was where mighty Orion, First to Fall, had crashed as he plummeted from the Heavens. Even as a child, Kallen had been enthralled by the stories he heard about Orion and the Fallen Five. He read every book written about the fallen angel who had established the Order of the Fallen. Kallen could almost have called himself an expert on the illustrious leader.

It was told that during a period of great turmoil in Heaven called the Great Heavenly Purge, a revolt took place between the Lords of the Light and a faction of the angels who served them. Heaven's servants had been powerful, but the Lords were unsurpassable. Punishing the dissidents for their sins, Heaven stripped them of their powers and immortality and cast the fallen angels out. They were sent to prison worlds across the universe as punishment.

Orion and the five who fell with him established the Order of the Fallen for all angels of Heaven who still served the Light. Waves of fallen angels followed. The majority of the dissident angels were well-intentioned souls and over time became stewards for Humanity on Earth. Using their wisdom to teach and nurture Humanity, the society of mortals began to flourish under the Order's caring hands. Until the Sin showed up.

Dark angels known as the Sin had revolted against the Lords of Heaven for their own personal gains and would never serve Heaven or the Lords of the Light again. The Sin had larger plans for the world they found themselves imprisoned upon and its inhabitants. As they began creating their dark paradise, Humanity was to be enslaved to serve the needs of the Sin.

Fortunately for Humanity, Orion rallied his supporters around him and began a holy war to protect the earth from the darkness the Sin envisioned. The War of Beliefs that would span centuries began. Many of the Order's greatest champions rose through the immense darkness. The war lasted until Orion at last struck down the Dark Gods, the Sin leaders, removing the threat from the world.

Not without a cost, Kallen thought. In the beginning, the Order of the Fallen had been completely made up of fallen angels of true descent. The arduous War of Beliefs ravaged both opponents; combined with the incessant passage of time, the result was the continuously decreased purity of the Fallen. Kallen knew that it would not be long before Humanity would be on its own to defend itself from the always-present evils within the universe. Such a day was not one that Kallen looked forward to.

Bells announcing that the sun had crossed its noon point chimed loudly from the two tall white towers that protruded from the acropolis. The palaces beneath the towers of Ori and Bri suddenly bustled with activity as the Elders and their numerous assistants began to leave the tower for the long, winding trek down the rocky slope.

Looking among the throng of people exiting the gate, Kallen easily spotted his foster father's large white beard, which he always parted into two great forks. Militades was the highest-ranked member of the Order's armies and had the power to call every loyal citizen to arms at a moment's notice. Militades remained the only man that Kallen had yet to defeat in mock combat. One tended to develop such skills after a life of real wars, he assumed.

A Mortal Mistake

Militades was a true Fallen who had once served in Heaven, not a descendant. Few who fell ever actually talked about the causes of their being exiled from Heaven. But Militades had always been forthcoming. He had told Kallen he once had a brother in Heaven who had been murdered by one of Militade's former pupils. The grief from the loss sent him spiralling so far that he was eventually exiled; the criminal escaped punishment. Kallen hated to think the lengths he would go if his sister was ever harmed.

Watching Militades approach, he became aware of another person walking closely beside him, whispering in his ear. As they drew closer to the gates, Kallen was able to discern that the blue-robed man was the younger Elder Philotheos who was the Chronicler of the White Elders. As a member of the inner ruling circle of the Order, the Chronicler was in charge of recording current history within and around the Order. Philotheos's largest responsibility was keeping track of the lineage of the Children of the Fallen, as well as discovering those who still remained lost.

As the history and secrets of the Order were bestowed upon him, Kallen's knowledge was growing slowly as he rose through the ranks. He was a Child of the Fallen, the fourth generation of the Fallen family, profoundly more human than angelical beings. He did not have memory of Heaven or the deep senses that could perceive worldly energy that those of the remaining First retained to a small degree. Kallen did not remember who his father was, nor would anyone give him an answer. Militades would only say that he would learn in time and had stubbornly refused to expand beyond that answer, despite Kallen's pleading. His sister had received the same answer from all her foster fathers; all men were equally stern and elusive in their responses. It was a fact that drove his sister mad with rage. She wrote the Chronicler incessantly, demanding answers but receiving none. Kallen was happy to be where he was instead of with the majority of the Children of the Fallen, hidden away within Order's secret sanctuary built within the Alakari mountain range.

Walking through the gates guarding the acropolis, his foster father, the Chronicler behind him, spotted Kallen immediately.

The blue eyes met his; Militades's great white beard swayed in the gentle breeze.

"Young Kallen, a pleasure you see you once again." Philotheos bowed his head toward Kallen. "I believe congratulations are in order in your recent promotion to commander of the Titans. A difficult and hard-earned promotion among the most prestigious of the Fallen's warriors. Earning such a rank at an early age is commendable. Even mighty Militades here did not reach such a lofty post so quickly. You have a very bright future ahead of you."

"Our only desire is to serve the Elders of Orion and protect the followers of the Order wherever they may live." Kallen smiled, returning the proper bow to the Elder of the White, proving his manners. Philotheos clapped him upon the shoulder several times and then looked Kallen in the eye.

"Serve and protect the followers of the Order and the believers of Heaven instead, Kallen. It will serve you much better in the future. We Elders are but old men. There will always be another to replace us. As time will pass, perhaps you shall someday find yourself sitting there."

Kallen did not think he was cut out for joining the Elders. Politics could become a vicious and futile game; he'd watched Militades contend with it for years with great disdain.

"And how does your sister fare in the great city of Metzor? Does she enjoy the chaotic and exciting life of the Metzonians more than the laid-back pace of the Kyllordic? She writes letters to me more consistently than anyone else I know. She is persistent, that one." Philotheos smiled.

"Like brother, like sister—trust me," Militades replied, moving past them, forcing Kallen and Philotheos to follow him. "Alexandra will certainly witness the fervour of the Metzonians within the week. None celebrate like Metzonians, particularly when an event of a magnitude such as this occurs."

Kallen was confused. "I'm sorry, but I don't believe I follow you." Militades and Philotheos stopped in their tracks and looked at one another. Beneath their astonished blank stares Kallen felt stupid,

A Mortal Mistake

"You have not heard the news? After his five-year hiatus, Prince Sven has returned from the Desert of Lost Souls to Metzor."

Kallen remembered hearing about Prince Sven's dishonour and the punishment the king had lain upon his son. He'd never been in a battle of that magnitude, but Kallen still understood the fury and emotion that flowed through the veins in the thick of combat. Granted that Sven's battle rage had resulted in risking the lives of his men to seek revenge, the punishment was harsh. Perhaps the greater risk would have been the breaking out of full war between Metzor and Chilsa. Though it would not have been the first time the two powers clashed.

"The Metzonians cheer and the Elders cringe at the prospect." Militades spoke as he turned off the street and began to climb up a wooden staircase toward a rooftop kitchen he liked to frequent. Kallen allowed Philotheos to proceed first.

As he climbed, he called, "What reasons would the Elders have for fearing Sven's return?"

Militades chose a corner table and leaned over the edge to look down upon the patrons milling about beneath him. Kallen and Philotheos joined him. He ordered a bottle of wine and bread. "You remember your lessons on the history of Metzon and the death of King Mallax?"

"The Cruel King. The mad monarch's title was well-deserved. He had butchered his own people by the tens of thousands for little reason at all. The Order intervened with its armies under General Metz, defeating King Mallax. The Elders placed his brother's daughter on the throne to restore civility and peace. Something like that—am I correct?"

As Militades stared at a group of birds flying above, Philotheos answered his question. Breaking a small loaf of bread with his hands, picking at the thick crispy crust, Philotheos began to explain everything to him.

"Basically, but you need to understand the details and the magnitude of the situation to understand how it connects to the present. Changing his name to match this newfound malice, the newly named Mallax's butchery began with his brother's royal family. He scoured the countryside for every relative until his niece Elia Maxall was the only one left from his brother's lineage. She was the rightful ruler, not Mallax! Forced to flee to her mountainous cousins of the Beladorians, Elia begged and begged the Order of the Fallen to intervene on behalf of her ravaged people. The Elders knew what had to be done but were hesitant to commit until one in their own ranks volunteered and led the invasion."

Laughing at the Chronicler, Kallen refused to believe what the old man was telling him. "Wait … are you telling me Metz was an Elder?"

"Indeed, he once was—and the youngest in history."

Militades looked over, mirthful at Kallen's surprise. "You did not know that, did you? 'The Metz' was a great many things. Very few know how deeply his ties run within the Order. The Elders prefer to let most believe him to be only the brilliant general who slew the Cruel King."

Philotheos quickly took over the conversation and returned back to the story, slightly perturbed at being interrupted so early on. "The Elders knew he was very well suited to the task and were comfortable handing the situation to Metz. Like a ravenous lion he had walked before the walls of Belador. Metz broke the ranks of Mallax's armies despite being heavily outnumbered. However, the Elders had not anticipated the effect Metz had upon those he saved and the loyalty he inspired. With every day, with every victory, he grew swifter and more powerful as all were drawn beneath his banner. Perhaps of greater importance was the unexpected love that resulted between the outcast noble and her new champion.

"As they grew closer, Metz's ties to the Order grew strained as he chose to take complete control of the situation. As he became more obsessive about removing Mallax from the world and restoring the land to his love, the Elders' wisdom fell upon deaf ears. The council had dictated that he restore balance within the conflict and support Elia, not to place the fate of so many upon the support of the Order.

"The Elders were quite furious and almost went as far as issuing orders for Militades to resolve the situation with the use of force.

A Mortal Mistake

Fortunately for all, however, they still saw the opportunity to stabilize one of the remaining Free Nations while weaving their influence into the very fabric of the new nation that was to emerge from the flames. With one last option remaining, they summoned the only person Metz still listened to, hoping he could bring back Metz within the folds of the Order."

"Karl Kallisto," Kallen guessed, having heard the name in both Metzonian histories and the Orders.

"Wise and educated, Kallisto served as advisor, calming both parties back to civility before events got too out of control. He advised the Elders that the only way they would achieve their goals would be to show Metz the loyalty he had always shown them. Kallisto's advice worked. After Metz slew the Cruel King within his keep in Merkel, he regained the calm, allowing the Elders to realize their dreams."

"Leading to the birth of the Order's Metzonian chapter—I know the rest. But what does this have to do with the return of Sven? What has the Elders so worked up over one man?" Kallen turned to Militades, who had not engaged in the conversation. Something within his face showing he was desperately trying to keep himself under wraps.

"The Order has watched Sven closely throughout the years until his disappearance into the desert. Do not mistake a man who survives the deserts, Kallen. Mad Mallax was said to have once been a sane man, a noble and loyal brother within King Maxall's court. Before he went to the desert that is …" Lifting the silver chalice up to his lips, Philotheos let the words hang. Militades continued to drum his fingers upon the table. "Lord Mallax spent significantly less time amongst the sands, and look what he did to the world around him. Coincidence? Or will history repeat itself, as it often does?"

Militades grumbled, leaning into the conversation by resting his elbows on the table. "Sven was always the strongest of all the children of Metz, and by far the most dangerous. On one hand, he carries the strength and charisma of his father; on the other, he carries the spirit of unbridled passion and confidence of his mother. And what happens when you mix those powerful attributes together?"

All were attributes of great strength, a combination of the perfect leader of men this world saw only once every few generations. That was what Kallen wanted to guess, but from the looks of the Chronicler and his foster father the answer was something far different.

"You have a leader of men, a figure who all humanity would march behind. Who would leave all they once knew to be true without hesitation."

Kallen smiled as he slapped his hand on the table, disappointed he hadn't responded.

"Or you have the death of thousands, as we have seen before."

Listening to Militades's dark tone, Kallen changed his mind, glad he hadn't.

"You have heard about the bloody atrocities he unleashed upon the Chilsa, the lives of thousands of men lost because of the anger and hate that flowed through Sven's heart and mind. The Fist of Metzor crushes his enemies, but he also squeezes the blood out of the men he holds within the palms of his hand." Militades's bitterness toward the young man was very clear as he drained his glass.

The men sat silently waiting for the tension surrounding the General to subside. Wondering what the rest of the Elders' thoughts on the situation were, Kallen turned to Philotheos, daring to broach the subject further. "And your thoughts on Sven's return?"

"Life is dictated by the events around a soul, but all it takes is an unexpected, uncontrollable aspect to tip the scales one way or the other. Who knows what may happen. Tell us, Kallen. After five years of enduring howling winds and murderous screams at the hand of your own father, how would you react? Which path do you think that Sven will take?"

"A difficult question … It will be interesting to see the impact such events have had upon his soul," Kallen carefully responded, pondering what mind-set he would choose if Sven's mistakes were his own—an impossible comparison to make. Kallen still felt pity for Sven, despite his mistakes. Certainly the man had made mistakes, but that was a part of being mortal. The prince would not have made those mistakes intentionally, but every event in the world had consequences.

"Don't be damned fools! It will be a question of whether the Fist rips the heart of Metz out! That is what it will be!" Militades slammed his fist upon the table, startling Kallen. "I hope you are both prepared to see blood spilt, because he is coming back from the desert with a vengeance. Heaven help the souls of men who get caught in the conflict."

The outburst startled the patrons sitting around them, and silence overtook the rooftop. Several long seconds passed. Kallen saw everyone return to their private conversations, and Philotheos began to speak softly.

"Your mentor has always been such an optimist, Kallen." Philotheos smiled up at both of them, patting Militades upon the shoulder "I believe it will actually be a question of whether the Metz can regain control over his own Fist. Masen Metz has wisdom beyond his years and is not feared simply because people call him king. Sven will fall in line. He is merely a pup compared to the dire wolf that sired him."

Kallen stopped to contemplate the situation, beginning to understand how large an impact this event could have upon the nation. Would old wounds have healed over time, or festered as mistakes made in the past grew more potent. His sister would indeed be in for a tense spectacle. Ignoring the scowl of his bearded foster father, curiosity got the best of Kallen.

"And if he doesn't?"

The Chronicler leaned back against the wooden railing, taking another sip of wine as he looked up at the sun high overhead beating down upon them. "Well, then the desert winds will ultimately swallow young Sven's soul when his father throws his own son back into the sands of eternal time."

CHAPTER 3
RETURN OF THE FIST

The deep tone of the cathedral bells rang out across the city of Metzor as the bright midday sun rained down upon the beautiful city of gold. Her feet dangling over the edge of the tall bell tower, Alexandra breathed in the intoxicating atmosphere and the beauty that surrounded her.

An air of excitement had filled the city as word spread about the return of the prince. Such buzz was not normal for the return of the ruling royals of Metzon, who tended to come and go frequently. But the Fist of Metzor, the battle hero of wars past, was at last returning with Prince Conrad after years spent alone within the Desert of Lost Souls.

Alexandra knew the basics of Metzonian heritage, but she had not expected the excitement she was seeing. Accepting a new position within the Order, her foster father had moved their family to the Metzon capital city a year ago. She found her new home vastly different from the Kyllordic city of Nykol, with its numerous bridges deep in the Kyllordic countryside.

Unlike all Kyllordic cities, no forests or rivers were visible for dozens of miles here. Built upon the golden plains of the Numelli, Metzor was the largest city Alexandra had visited in her lifetime. Stretching out across the flatland, the size of the city was misleading; a traveller could see it from almost a day's travel away.

She found Metzor society a startling contrast to the relaxed

Kyllordic lifestyle of art and nature. The city had been built upon the principles of deep-seated pride and determination, its structures built to last a thousand years, a notion its citizens believed to be symbolic of how long their kingdom would last.

"I figured I would find you way up here. You and your love for climbing as close to the heavens as possible!" Alexandra jumped slightly when she heard the voice behind her. Her foster father's arrival was masked beneath the toll of the bells. "Getting the best seat in the house for the big event, are you? I believe it will be an epic show if the Fist remains the same man he once was."

Alexandra grew more curious with every person she talked to. She had yet to find anyone who had anything terrible to say about the man; all worshipped the ground he walked upon. Women admired his strength and passion, while men spoke of the war hero's courage with nationalistic pride.

"What kind of man was he?" she asked, rubbing the long scar inside her right forearm.

"Among the best, as I'm sure you have heard on the streets. A man of indisputable fervor who led with his heart in all aspects of life, be it war or politics. Fearless and determined, nothing would stand between him and what he set out to accomplish. The citizens adored him, knowing that he would be in the thickest of the confrontation, shoulder to shoulder with the common man."

Alexandra could not help but smile at her father's description and the strong admiration oozing from his voice as he sat down beside her. "Sounds like a man to be much adored. So if I may ask, what went wrong?"

"Prince Sven came to clash with a man of equal valour and strength, beloved even more than himself. The king." Rubbing his short grey beard with fondness, the man laughed. "Our beloved king rules with a very caring hand and an aura of calmness. As much as the people love Sven, they have a strong and deep respect for King Masen and all he has done for them.

"Disobeying his father's direct and implicit orders upon yet another Chilsa invasion, Sven crossed the border river Myradoria. Hunting down every last invader and putting them to the blade,

Sven succeeded but ended up jeopardizing every man within the advanced force he was leading. Such error ultimately forced the king to take the entire main battle army into Chilsa to rescue his ill-fated son and the few survivors."

"Ouch," Alexandra remarked. "I highly doubt that went over well."

"Invoke the wrath of the Cruel King, and the punishment was a painful death. Invoke the wrath of the Calm King, and the punishment is an emotional toll lasting a lifetime. Sven invoked the wrath of his father in a way that few had seen, not even his most loyal friend Advisor Kallisto was able to restore the calm. Long story short, he sentenced his son to wander the Desert of Lost Souls until he was able to find his own soul amongst the sand and struggles. After five years, the Fist of Metzor returns for the grand encounter."

The Inner City gates opened to the returning princes. Wrapping his arm around her shoulders, her foster father pointed toward the southern gatehouse as an eruption of cheers took to the air. "Listen to them clamour for his return. No one thought it would be this long before his return! All are eager to hear tales of the desert. But perhaps how the reunion between father and son will ultimately unfold is anticipated even more."

The clop of horse hooves was distinct amidst the cheering mob that watched from the streets and the balconies above them. Pedals of golden lilies twirled in great droves around the two men and their escort as they passed through their admirers. Women stretched gracefully from their balconies, trying to touch the men upon their stallions, even if only briefly.

Alexandra smiled, wishing she could be closer to men who held such a power over the people. Her father needlessly reached down to point out Sven in the pair. She had seen Prince Conrad many times throughout the city in the past year, and despite his own potent charisma, she was enthralled by Sven.

Waves of power radiated effortlessly from the confident man sitting tall in the saddle upon a black stallion. Arms the thickness of trees stretched out in both directions as he let the women's fingers graze against his own. He spoke no words; not even a smile crossed his face as he calmly rode through the crowd.

"You find yourself a man like that, and your children shall be angels amongst mortals." Alexandra felt her face flush; her father laughed and gave her a squeeze. "You had better run down and get a closer look. Be careful, though!"

She gave the old man a kiss on the forehead and then ran for the wooden staircase that wound down the tall bell tower. She paused halfway down to open a small side exit that allowed her to sneak out to the cathedral roof. She knew that she could slip across the small roofed bridge and make much better time than by pushing among the throng of people within the streets. Racing across the rooftops, she moved gracefully from one roof to another, hearing the cheering off to her left as the princes continued to move slowly through the winding streets. Looking up, she saw the tall walls of the royal palace, the golden guards marching along the wall ramparts. Only four more buildings remained between her and the palace entrance, and she could already see the beginning of the square crowded with admirers.

She looked across to the last building, which blocked her view of the square—the barracks of the Royal Elite, King Masen's personal guard. The consequences for getting caught up on the roof would be harsh. As she wondered whether she should simply work her way to the front, she looked over toward several long boards piled against one of the walls. She desperately wanted to see and hear what the prince would say, something that would be difficult among the crowd. Looking one more time at the crowd, she picked up one of the boards, thrilled to see it breach the gap. Hoping those below her were too preoccupied, she raced across the makeshift bridge ducking behind the railing to peer through the gap.

"Welcome home, Prince Sven. The citizens of Metzor are thrilled by your safe return," called out a bearded man draped in the robes of the royal advisor high above Sven as he dismounted. "Your journey has been a long and difficult one, but at long last you have returned to where you belong—among friends and family who have all missed you greatly and prayed to the Heavens for your return."

The returning brothers climbed the long staircase toward the palace entrance, and Alexandra watched Sven pause as he scanned the crowd of delegates and family before him. "I came only to see the one who is not standing amongst you. The rest of you mean little to me, so I ask you—where is she?"

The crowd went silent at the aggressive tone of their prince. Tension immediately filled the air. The unexpected hate flowing forth took all by surprise. Inching closer, Alexandra watched Advisor Kallisto for his response, but it was the Sven's oldest brother who broke the silence.

"I beg your pardon, brother? Who do you think you are? You spent the past five years wallowing in the Desert of Lost Souls amongst the criminals of this nation. Yet you return as though you are a hero of the nation? As though you did not abandon your people because of your own stupid selfish pride but instead had championed for the people?"

Clad in brilliant golden armour that glimmered in the sunlight, Prince Frederick was the heir to Metzon's throne and the millions who lived within their kingdom. Alexandra had met him on multiple occasions within the Cathedral of the Fallen and found him likeable, even if he was stern in his manner. The bad blood between brothers was a new aspect she had not foreseen.

"I beg your pardon, brother? Who do you think *you* are? You forget what I have done for this nation, brother! A Metzonian does not forget what the heroes have accomplished for the people in the past. Nor the limit such heroes will go to for them in the future, for there are no such limits. Our father is a hero for fighting for the people, but when I perform such a noble act I am cast as a villain. So do not try to belittle me or my accomplishments for the sake of your petty ego, Frederick."

"Father freed the people from a murderous tyrant! You risked delivering them into the hands of another. Why did you bother bringing him back, Conrad?" Frederick turned to berate the youngest of them. "Life was calmer and simpler when he was lost amongst the sands. How foolish could you be?"

Alexandra corrected herself: *bad blood* was not an accurate description; these brothers hated one another with a passion beyond her comprehension. She made a mental note to ask her foster father about the catalyst that ran deep enough to create a five-year hatred.

"Does a mother not deserve the love of all her children?" Conrad stepped forward to answer his oldest sibling. "Do brothers not deserve to be loved equally?"

"You risked your life for a brother who would not risk his own," Frederick cried out. "Such selfishness does not deserve to be loved, Conrad. It should remain in the desert with other grievous acts, such a murder, robbery and rape."

"The desert taught me more than you could possibly imagine. Step forward and discover it for yourself." Sven suddenly held his sword in his hand, pointed menacingly at his brother. The grey and golden steel shields of the Royal Elite clashed loudly as they were raised, and long spears were lowered before Sven, prepared for any attack that may come.

"I dare you, brother!"

"Enough!"

Alexandra shuddered at the tone of the new voice coming from the highest staircase. King Masen rose from his seat, his voice seething with anger at the bickering brothers. "You will both make amends, or, Heaven help me, I will throw both of you into the Desert of Lost Souls for the rest of time! I will not have a wound from the past continue to fester after five years, not at a time such as this!"

Alexandra waited with great anticipation to see which brother would bend a knee first. Sven stood unflinching, as Frederick looked over at his father. Without another word, the golden prince retreated through the palace gatehouse, leaving a whispering crowd behind him.

"Such harsh words were not truly meant, Sven. Grief-stricken hearts tend to say many a thing in times of great sorrow. Your return is a welcome sight for eyes that have shed many tears, none more than my own. I only wish that your arrival had come sooner …"

Alexandra again shifted closer to the edge. Thousands of eyes fell upon Sven, anticipating his reaction to the grief they had all felt at the passing of their queen. All watched Conrad fall to his knees in anguish, but his brother continued to stand tall, tilting his head back toward the sky. "So all I ever loved within the world is gone then ... Where is she? Where is she?"

The king did not speak. The royal party surrounding the king shifted uncomfortably but did not speak. The crowd who had come for the celebration grew solemn as they looked upon their angry hero.

"Where is she?" Silence dropped to a lower level; all held their collective breath. None dared to speak what was not theirs to tell and incite further anger.

"Damn you all! Tell me where she is!"

"She rests within the Cathedral of the Fallen, my son. You missed her by four days ..."

As the prince's thick fingers flexed in and out, Alexandra breathlessly watched him stare into his hand, trying to calm himself into an emotionless state. Turning away from those above him, Sven descended down the staircase, despite their calls, to the very street that had just hosted his victorious return. The crowd of admirers cleared out of his way immediately. A corridor of shocked and sad citizens was left within Sven's wake.

Watching his steel boots crush the yellow flowers that had only moments before fallen upon him in celebration, Alexandra soon lost sight of the man as he began the long march back on foot. Alexandra pulled back from the ledge, drawing her thighs up to her chest and burying her teary face in her knees. Feeling the emotions of the one who kept his locked within, she wept tears for Sven's loss, for what his heart had to have felt. Despite his tough exterior, she knew he was merely a man, and the pain he felt would be real. Loneliness was a terrible burden for anyone to be forced to bear. She understood what it felt like to be alone and abandoned. The Order of the Fallen had of course taken care of her and her brother, providing them with safety and security by placing them in the homes of foster parents when they were young. But it was not the same.

Her forearm scar was only one of five her body had collected. There was another down her left side, another on the back of her hip, and the final two on the backs of a shoulder and calf. Each held a memory of a different foster family she had joined over the course of her life. She wished one could have reminded her of her true parents.

Both Alexandra and her brother had only the vaguest memories of their parents before their deaths. The only family she had ever really known was her brother. He had been placed with Militades, but Alexandra had been shifted around constantly. As grateful as she was to those who tried, she wanted to know who her family had once been, to understand who she was and who she was expected to become, but the Chronicler had repeatedly declined her requests. Her brother may not have cared, but Alexandra was determined, refusing to stop until she discovered the truth.

"Hey!"

The shout startled Alexandra back to reality. Quickly popping her head back up, she found the face of an equally startled grisly guard. She scrambled quickly and slipped beneath the soldier's grasp, dashing away as he pursued her. She heard him quickly call out for others to join the hunt. She ran across the makeshift bridge she had made and contemplated pushing it over the edge, but seeing the people in the alley beneath, she decided against it.

Casting a glance over her shoulder, she was astonished at the speed of her pursuers. They seemed to move almost as quickly as she did, despite the weight of the steel armour they wore. Increasing her speed, she leapt over a shallow alley to another roof and let herself roll with the impact. She slipped over the edge down onto the sloped roof of a balcony. Leaping onto an adjacent balcony across the narrow street, she looked back just as the guards peered over the edge of the roof she had escaped from.

Picking herself up once more, she leapt across three more balconies before climbing to the roof of a blacksmith shop she was familiar with. Pulling herself up, she knew she was almost home. The tall bell towers and the steep roof of the cathedral remained several blocks away, but she was closer to safety. Behind her she spotted a large squadron scouring the rooftops for her. They had come very close to trapping her within their web.

Crossing over the lower cathedral roof, Alexandra felt relieved to be back in the safety of the Order's compound. The quickness of the Elite guards' reaction was unexpected. Alexandra feared what the consequences would have been had she caught. She felt an unexpected rush of exhilaration as she slipped back into the cathedral.

Light flooded through the open doors of the cathedral. A long black shadow was cast across the marble flooring from the cathedral entrance to the foot of the centre circle beneath the domed ceiling. Hiding behind the corner on the second floor, Alexandra peered down around the edge as heavy footsteps trudged toward her.

As she watched Sven stop before the elaborate setting before him, silence filled the place of worship. The citizens had lain their final gifts around her body adorned in a white gown embroidered in gold. Yellow lilies bloomed all around the sad scene.

Alexandra had heard the story of when the queen and her husband had freed the oppressed citizens from the Cruel King. A young girl, no older than five, had stepped forward, handing the new queen the small yellow flower. "We have nothing golden to give you beyond the sun that grows within this flower." The queen had leaned over, running her fingers through the girl's blonde hair. She placed the flower behind the child's ear, speaking softly. "The smiles of our people are worth more than all the gold trapped within the sun, child."

Gracious and humble, Elia Metz had been the mother to all the citizens of their new nation, looking after them all with loving eyes. *How could you not love a woman such as her?* Alexandra wondered what it must have felt like to be born into a family of such noble values, as Sven had been. She wondered about the enormous pressures placed upon such children to impact the world in as great a way as his parents had.

"Mother …" Sven collapsed to his knees before the bier his beloved mother was set upon, the prince's words as shattered as his heart. "Mother, I do not even know where to begin. I am sorry; I should never have left you for all these years. I am sorry for tearing apart the family as I have; I only wished to make you proud. I had no idea what was going to happen, where my mistakes were going to take me or the things I would be forced to do to survive. The terrible things I have been forced to endure.

"You always told me that my greatest strength was my ability to lead through the power of my heart. That my unbridled passion was my greatest strength, and people would follow me to the ends of the earth because of it. While Father tried to chain my great passion, you were the one who told me it was a gift of gods.

"Please forgive me for what I must do now, dear Mother. I never wanted to bring change to this world, but such responsibility has been forced upon me. All I did was to save those I loved, not for the personal glory or the power. All mistakes I ever made were done for the same reason. Please understand, for if I had realized the cost that such actions would have upon this world, I would have taken death. But even men as fearless as I hesitate when death calls upon our souls."

Alexandra watched Sven's broad shoulders rise and fall as his breathing grew heavier, his thick arms draped over the wide cross guard of the tall sword. His voice became hoarse as his confessions grew deeper. "I was forced to make terrible promises, Mother, promises that I must now keep if I am to protect those few I have left. Rash they undoubtedly were, but I would have made promises of far greater consequences to save you. I could have saved you. I should have been here to save you!" His anguished bellow exploded, and Alexandra jumped back behind the column, hiding from the curses as she waited for the storm to subside.

"The path of my destiny has changed, my dear mother. And the destiny of this world will come to feel the fear I have. The desert did Father's work better than he could ever possibly imagine, tearing apart my soul until nothing remains. Before the end, Father will gaze upon me and realize the monster he has unwittingly created. I fear that even he cannot stop me now."

The cathedral doors opened and shut quickly, and three men walked quietly toward the mourner. Alexandra tried to peer around the corner to see who would tempt Sven's wrath in his moment of mourning. Only the middle man wore thick armour, hiding his identity completely in the darkness; those upon either side hid in loose-fitting cloaks. Stopping well away from the prince, all drew their swords. None spoke until Sven addressed them.

"Monsters and men have come from every corner of this world to murder me. Do you intend to die like those before you? Or have all who are Metzonian forgotten what I am capable of doing?" Wrapping both hands firmly around the hilt of his sword, Sven rose fluidly from his knees. The three interlopers each took a step, dropping to one knee before they stretched down low upon the floor to lay their swords before him.

"Mere mortals such as we are neither worthy nor capable of such a task. We have not forgotten the power the Fist of Metzor wields. We are ready to serve once again, my prince, as is the nation. You have not been forgotten but instead immortalized as your story continues to be told. Heaven or Hell, we shall all follow you along whatever road you desire to travel."

The new speaker's tone scared Alexandra more than the words. Chills crossed her skin as she listened to the words, heavy with darkness. *Whoever these men are, they are not godly men who came to visit the prince.* Listening to Sven's reply, Alexandra realized that he was perhaps not as her father claimed.

"Through the fires and demons of Hell it shall be …"

Chapter 4
A Sinister Storm

The nightmares plaguing Sven's sleep dissipated as the deep boom of reality crashed around him. He rubbed his temples to try and ease the throbbing within his head as the wooden door to his room shook once again with urgency.

"Piss off!" Sven yelled at the door, shifting his palms toward his eye sockets. The knocking continued to bombard the small black room.

"Please make it go away, would you?" A soft female voice woke Sven's other senses. He inhaled the sweet scent of her blonde hair before she pulled the pillow over her head, trying to muffle the relentless sound.

Sitting upright, Sven felt around the bed and found the large wine bottle from last night's activities at his feet. He hurled it in the general direction of the door and heard the satisfying sound of shattering glass. "Piss off! I swear neither Heaven nor Hell will have the power save you from my wrath if you pound upon my door once more!"

Sven paused and waited several seconds for the fools outside his door to test his patience. Satisfied, he lowered himself back into the warmth of his bed. Suddenly the hinges of the doors exploded with a shattering of splinters, and bright light flooded the room.

Sven clawed for the dagger at the head of the bed as the room dimmed. An imposing figure filled the bulk of the doorway and paused. The scrape of steel on steel screeched within Sven's headache-ravaged head more gratingly than the incessant knocking as the armoured figure stepped into the room

"Rise and shine."

"Do my demands fall upon the deaf?" His heart pumping heavily, Sven was relieved to recognize the figure who had stormed his room. "Just what in the name of the Seven Hells do you think you are doing here, Ox?"

The commander of Sven's father's Royal Elite did not acknowledge him or say anything. He just smiled at him. Sven knew his father did not unleash his private contingent of guards into the city for small tasks, certainly not to kick in the doors of brothels.

"Sir Aerox is doing what the king commanded."

A pleasant night ruined by the disastrous dawn, Sven thought, exasperated as the voice of a new speaker crossed the room. The golden-robed Royal Elite guard moved off to the side, letting his father's key advisor into the room. "The demands of the king are all that matter, particularly when his anger is aroused by his children. Your father is a patient man, Sven—you are very fortunate. Even he has his limits, though, something that you of all people should know. One week was understandable, two weeks acceptable, but at three weeks you are starting to push boundaries of reason."

"So why did he send you and the Ox to come and retrieve me? The city guard not up to the task? Figured you would have more success? I suppose a dozen battered and bruised city guards is acceptable, but I certainly cannot hit you, can I?" Sven knew that Karl Kallisto was stronger than he looked, his tall, lean frame hidden beneath loose-fitting cloaks. Despite his old age, the Order's advisor to King Masen remained a worthy adversary. For decades Kallisto had been his father's first commander of the Royal Elite; his duties also included instructing Sven and his brothers in the art of the blade. Despite his mild and peaceful appearance, Kallisto most definitely knew how to take a life if it was required.

Ignoring Sven's veiled threat, the old man continued. "Unlike you, your father is still civil, and he thinks that any being of importance to him deserves some degree of respect. Something you have not returned in kind by ignoring all his other attempts to reach you. You forced him to the last measure he knew."

"Such respect as kicking in my door? What does he want?"

"What do you think? He wants to see his son, whom he has not seen in five damned years! Put your difficulties from the past aside, for the sake of your father. Your mother's illness was difficult for his soul, but knowing she was about to leave him forever was devastating."

"His choice to send me to the desert, not mine." Sven shifted uncomfortably against the elaborate headboard. "I forgot that clearly he was the only one affected by such a mistake, or the passing of my mother."

The old man paused unexpectedly at his sharp retort. Kallisto looked away, inspecting the tanned skin of the woman to Sven's right before glancing to the second companion to his left. "I'm well aware of how the situation unfolded, Sven, and I understand that it affected you far greater than anyone else. I cannot imagine the pain that you endured, nor will I try. Believe me or not, I tried to talk compassion into your father, but he would have none of it.

"However, all men have regrets in their lives, and your father is indeed mortal, is he not? I have watched your father go from controlled excitement at the sight of your face once again, to pain at your rejection, to anger at your ignorance. He only wishes to make amends for his mistakes; you could at least ease the grief and act civil."

"A few years too late for apologies, Kallisto."

The angry tone of his voice took Kallisto back a step; his eyes grew hard at the younger man's coldness toward his father.

Sven turned away, refusing to look at him any further. "Clearly I didn't do a good enough job of lying low. How did you find me?"

"The Desert of Lost Souls does not take the memory of a woman's touch from a man. The women of Metzor have longed for your return, Sven, but I always remembered that you only desired the most beautiful and talented. And while there are many such establishments within Metzor to feed such desires, there are few worthy of the Fist himself."

"All the more of Metzor's finest women left to comfort my brothers, then. Rumor has it that even my stiff-assed brother Frederick himself found a lady."

Kallisto ignored Sven's remark as he gazed over the two women in Sven's bed. A queasy feeling rose within Sven's guts as the old man moved closer to the woman on his right. He pulled the sheet back to expose her naked body. Both women had remained silent during the confrontation, pretending to sleep as they hid beneath the covers.

"Your tastes have certainly grown more exotic … you are a man of dangerous fantasies, Sven."

Sven watched Kallisto pull several strands of blonde hair away from the face of the woman, his eyes narrowing as he inspected her closely. "A whore in the image of your father's greatest enemy's daughter. The resemblance is remarkable. Had I not known the young empress, I would believe she is the beautiful Belle herself."

"I wouldn't get too much closer there, Kallisto. She will strip you of your high morals as quickly as your hidden purse of golden stallions. Trust me; such sick and twisted fantasies do not come cheap." Grinning widely, Sven watched the advisor pull his hand back slowly, not bothering to inspect the other who lay beside him.

"Remember, one can only wine and dine on whores for so long and still remain a reputable royal, Sven. Your father requests your presence in the throne room. Tonight! So clean yourself up and look like a prince, would you?" The king's advisor moved away from the foot of the bed and then paused in the door frame. "If you do not want to end up back in that damned desert, then I strongly suggest you show up!"

The man closest to his father's ear left rapidly, leaving Sven to stare at golden-robed Aerox, who smiled back at the prince. As Aerox set his mask over his face and prepared to leave, Sven yelled at him, "Put my damn door back where it belongs instead of just standing there, would you? And think twice before you decide to kick down my door again!"

A chuckle escaped the thin lips of the man behind the mask, who threw his hand over his chest in salute and walked out the door, leaving the morning light to stream in to Sven's room. Feeling

A Mortal Mistake

the women shift around beneath the sheets, Sven pondered his next move; he was running out of viable options.

He had avoided his father with good reason up to this point, not wanting to weather the upcoming storm. Sven had done everything possible short of returning to the desert to avert the pending disaster, knowing deep down there was no escape for him. Fate was pushing him toward the great clash, and promises and destiny were to become fulfilled.

"Smells like storms are brewing, oh how I love the smell of sweet rain." Sven barely heard the muffled remark from beneath the pillow to the left. Running a hand over her smooth pale skin, he inhaled the scent in the air deeply. As he pulled both women closer to him, the scent of rain disappeared, leaving a horrible taste in his throat.

"I think it smells darker and sinister, like a storm of sins. A storm of my sins …"

After King Mallax was slain within his keep at Merkel, there had been very little left of the nation. The countryside had been ravaged, towns burnt to the ground, and cities left in ruins. What remained of the people had been freed but at a great cost.

Haunted by the endless executions of her family that had occurred within the palaces of Merkel, the queen sought a new beginning. His mother returned to the small city of Nymia, where her family had their summer palaces out upon the golden plains. It had also happened to be the place that the king had first confessed his love for her. And where she went, the people soon followed. Nymia's population exploded. Great hordes of wealth returned to the new nation named after Sven's father. The golden keep rising far above the city was a testament to how far their king had lifted them. The detailed extravagance of the palace was a symbol of how he was loved so dearly by all, the city also soon renamed in his honour.

After Chilsa's Emperor Neurus had delivered his parents a wedding gift of a seven-year war, Masen Metz had returned home to receive two gifts from Sven's mother, the queen. The first was the elaborately designed palace fortress, suitable for a victorious war hero and champion of the people. And the second was a second son, whom she had named Sven. His mother had always told him that she was able to hear the thundering power within his young heart, even when he was a newborn. She saw a strong, relentless spirit within Sven, one that would change worlds.

A crash of lighting shook the roof high overhead. The storm grew more powerful with every hour. The storm that had rolled across the sweltering grass plains had indeed brought the torrent of rain Sven had predicted. The high heat of the desert had crossed past the great rivers, hemming it in, moving northwards to clash with the cool mountain air of the Alakari. The clouds had swirled around Metzor all day, growing ever higher and darker.

By the time Sven had chosen to arrive at the palace, the storm was raging at full climax. The howling wind reminded him of the storms in the desert as the great sheets of rain fell down upon him. Watching great forks of purplish lightning crash across the sky, Sven could feel the power of the storm anticipating the significance tonight would have upon him.

Sven's water-sodden boots echoed loudly off the stone walls as he wound down the endless hallways. Twisting to look behind him, the palace hallways were completely silent, except for the sounds of his own boots. Sven's breath grew shallower as he climbed the wide staircase toward the lofty throne room; he could not stop now.

The burning within the flesh of his back increased the more he thought of what he had to do, the more his conscience tried to fight it. The demons he had been forced to carry upon his back had burrowed beneath his skin. The sins of his past would haunt him forever, whispering their tortuous thoughts to him in the dark.

Within the shadows of his father's grand halls he listened to their whispers, foretelling what was to happen upon the other side of the door.

Wrapping his fingers over the handles, Sven was forced to use all his considerable strength to heave the mighty doors open with an eerie groan. The flickering light of a hundred torches danced within the expectant eyes of the room's occupants.

Surveying the magnificence of his father's throne room once

A Mortal Mistake

again, Sven noticed that it had not changed at all since he had been gone. The tall square columns running around the edges of the room rose thirty feet, unadorned except for a long banner in Metzonian gold with its rearing black stallion. Between each of the pillars stood a member of the Royal Elite, standing as straight as their twelve-foot spears.

In the middle of the room, set atop the higher of two raised platforms interconnected by a single split staircase, sat the golden throne of Metzor. Rising ten feet above the first column that had itself risen ten feet above the floor, the throne was the culmination of the work of the finest goldsmiths in the land. Two rearing gold stallions fighting each other with diamond-encrusted hooves hovered above the two black thrones of the king and queen.

In his throne sat his father.

Looking up at him, Sven felt himself shiver; his size was imposing even from a distance, broader in the shoulders than all his children. Sven could feel the golden eyes of his father stare down upon him as they had all his childhood. A symbol of his father's heritage, they reminded Sven of the large golden cats that preyed upon the wild horses that ran the grassy plains of the Numelli. Never had he been able to escape their calculating gaze; knowing the man behind the gaze had only made his stare ever harder to bear. Silent, emotionless, Sven had always felt the power residing within them that enabled his father to move men and mountain alike. Sven often wondered if his father had ever been forced to speak a single word during his war against the Cruel King.

"Hello, Father," Sven called out with false confidence, striding up the first staircase two steps at a time. "Here I am at last, as per your request. The throne looks lonely without Mother by your side, Father, and I'm surprised to see my brothers are not here to witness my shaming once again." Eyes locked upon his father, Sven climbed the dozen steps, halting at the first column, the so-called "plea platform," where dignitaries, nobles and peasants alike came to plea or bargain, at times with their lives hanging upon his father's words.

"I miss your mother greatly, son. This throne's beauty was always outshined by the beauty that resided within her soul." His father's voice was low. He dipped his gaze away from Sven for the briefest of moments. "As for your brothers, this issue is between you and me. It has been most unfortunate that others have been caught between the crossfire of two great men, but it is often the way of our world. Frederick is not within the city. I told him that perhaps he should spend some time amongst the northern armies to clear his head before an unnecessary conflict arose."

"Ah, yes. I get the desert for half a decade, he gets the northern armies! How soft and lenient you've become with age." Faking a smile, Sven watched the old man stir slightly. He continued to try to provoke his father. Five years away from the city, Sven still knew exactly where to find answers and knew that his father did not speak the truth completely. Frederick did not have the fortitude to confront him, preferring to use the morning light to flee northward, knowing what was to come.

"You led thousands of your followers to their deaths for your own revenge. I think the punishment is hardly upon the same scale, Sven." Masen shifted once again; Sven could sense seething anger beneath the surface as his father twisted the two rings upon his right hand repeatedly. "As for the one who risked his own life to return his brother to where he belongs, he has grown up emulating you to such a point that I would assume he is at the taverns, chasing daughters of Metzonian nobles who made the mistake of not keeping closer tabs upon them. At least they are nobles, not whores."

Sven let his gaze cross over to the left side of the plea platform, staring daggers at the older man. Stroking his bearded jawline, Kallisto looked at him innocently, which Sven found hard to believe. Sven noticed that neither Aerox nor Kallisto were at their usual places at his father's side. The advisor had usually been placed at his father's right, and their protector, Aerox, had always stood at his mother's left.

"Kallisto did not inform me where he found you, nor the company you were keeping. He did not have to, for in my own city I am not blind. You were never one to keep the noblest of company, Sven. I did not care, for even the most foul of men often have noble traits hidden beneath. But nonetheless, that is not a topic we are here to discuss, is it?

"I am one who leads through the mind, unable to understand those who live life completely through their hearts. Kallisto tried to make me understand. Your mother tried to make me understand. But I already knew what it was like to fight a war through mindless passion. And I know the terrible cost one must pay in the end."

"I do not think you do, Father. I was forced to pay the ultimate price, one far more terrible than you could possibly imagine." Pacing atop the plea platform, Sven contemplated all he had been through in the desert, and he let his anger go.

"What had you hoped to accomplish? What exactly was I to learn from the hardship of surviving such horrors?" The fire within his heart began to burn hot and spread throughout his chest. From his heart he poured all the anger he had suppressed over the years. Carrying that grief and anger for all those years had slowly turned his heart black and was finally being released. "I have nothing left! Don't you understand the magnitude of things I was forced to do for the sake of survival? There are no laws to uphold or civility within the desert. It strips you down to the barest of bones of humanity, where there is only survival. Nothing else—no life, hope or dreams, simply life or death. You think I was a monster when I returned from Chilsa? I have done things that shall haunt me for eternity and shall damn me to the fires of Hell! You sent your son to die in the desert, and you succeeded!"

"And yet here he stands before me." His father remained calm, holding both hands out before him. "One must be stripped of absolutely everything that makes up his life to discover the steel of his spine and the power residing within his soul."

"And there were no other ways to get your point across? I had to kill women and children to learn these lessons? Do not hide behind your pride or excuses about a deeper and higher learning. You made a mistake, just like I did! It took the loss of my mother for you to realize the significance of life and how fleeting it can truly be."

Trying to control the anger flowing through his trembling limbs, Sven collapsed to a single knee. An ever-present feeling of rage returned to his blood as the pent-up emotion of all he had endured flooded his body with powerful hate. The darkness held within his heart released in waves; he hunched forward as the great convulsions caused him wretched pain.

"I did indeed—you are most certainly correct. I have not lived without regret since that day, and I doubt you ever will forgive me for such."

Sven was surprised by the touch of two calloused hands that wrapped gently around his neck. Somehow his father had traversed the second staircase without a sound, his son lost within his own painful memories. Looking up slowly, he found he was staring into the golden depths of tear-filled eyes. "But please attempt to forgive me for what I have done to you. I made a mistake, one of many I have made during my lifetime. But one that is unlike the others, as it shall haunt my heart for all of eternity."

Lifting his own hands overtop his father's, Sven squeezed them tightly, feeling the pair of rings beneath his own. Searching within himself, fighting the anger within his own soul, he struggled for words. "Only if you pardon me for all my sins, past, present and future. I did what I had to do, Father. I had no other choice."

"Never have you done anything worthy of requiring forgiveness, my son. Past ... present ... future. All of it." The words fell upon Sven, releasing the rushing pain held within his heart for years. Trembling uncontrollably, Sven concentrated on desperately trying to hold himself together. He knew that releasing the emotions he had wrapped himself in would seal his fate. For all his soul had fought it; there would be no return.

"I fear that your beloved Sven died within the sand, leaving only his black shadow to haunt this world. You must release the last of me, I beg of you." Voice trembling, Sven looked back into his father's eyes, seeing only confusion. Wincing with pain, Sven wished his father had understood and could prevent what his fate would dictate. It was too late; he could feel it already.

The black tendrils twisted within Sven. Sharp pain coursed through his body as the darkness cut deeper into his mind. All the anguish and suffering he had buried within his heart over the years refused to be contained any longer. As his emotions burst from his heart, so too did the demon who coiled itself within him. Sven knew what was to come next: the painful repayment of debt.

The feel of the dark leather wrapped beneath his finger was natural, the scraping of the black steel upon its scabbard as common as the breeze within his ears. The piercing point pressing through flesh as it had a thousand times before was easy; the blood upon his hands as warm as any other mortals.

Looking into his father's calm eyes as he did was not easy.

The sword blade plunged directly through his father's chest, the weak resistance of bone and cartilage transferring through the blade. The weight of his father fell forward upon his torso; his fingers remained clasped firmly around the back of Sven's neck.

As the grip softened, Sven felt Masen's thick fingers slide down the back of his neck, grazing the demonic tattoo. The demon beneath his skin twisted to escape from the fingertips, diving deeper within Sven as though it feared the strength of his father. But as it watched him grow weaker, the darkness rushed back to the surface, bent upon attacking him.

"Tell Mother … I am sorry." Twisting sideways roughly, Sven threw his father off the side of the raised staircase, feeling him slide off the blade. Chaos had consumed the throne room around him. The screams of men grasping the threads of life and death passed throughout the room amongst the din of the raging storm.

Aerox's blade swept instantaneously to his left, cutting down the guard beside him before his backhand took down the man to his right. Kallisto attempted to rally some of his supporters around him, making a futile stand above the dying body of Sven's father.

Lowering himself into the throne, Sven watched without emotion as the two factions began to fight for control of his father's body, like ravaging lions. Sven found himself smiling at how quickly civility was lost when Humanity returned to its basic instincts.

Pathetic mortals.

Chapter 5
A Fallen King

Kallisto watched his king's body plummet to the floor and land with a sickening thud. Red puddles leaked away from the crumpled body lying upon the floor as the golden crown rolled across the room. A bloody hand pulled itself free, slapping the floor; Kallisto watched Masen struggle to move.

Golden cloaks fluttered to the floor as the Royal Elite charged toward the murderer of their lord. The lowered spear of the first guard was almost upon Sven when the soldier directly behind him ran his own through the forerunner's back. Many within the first wave of attackers fell to their own comrades, causing the horror to turn to chaos.

The chaotic murder seemed to have no rhyme or reason. Every man fought for his survival. One guard faced off against another aggressor to be was cut down by another, who himself was attacked. The vicious cycle rotated throughout the room; dozens were cut down within the first fifteen seconds of the battle.

In the midst of it, Kallisto watched as the closest thing he had to a brother struggled upon the stone floor, twisting on his stomach. Sidestepping the numerous battles and leaping over the bodies upon the floor, he reached the wounded man. Pressing his hand over King Masen's chest wound, Kallisto rested his head in his lap. "I'm going to get you out of here!"

"It matters not anymore, Kallisto. My wound is mortal, and it is only a matter of time before I discover if I receive my redemption in the eyes of Heaven." Breath growing more laborious, Masen struggled, weeping in pain. "Look at the ravenous wolves butchering one another, Karl. So much blood and death—it is no wonder Heaven has long abandoned this world. Look at what we do to each other."

Watching many slowly disengage, retreating to where he was, Kallisto searched among them for a sign to distinguish their enemies from the rest. "How are these traitorous bastards able to tell each other apart?"

"It is their hair, Kallisto. It's their hair ... it's black, like death." Masen's voice was barely a whisper. Kallisto looked upon the long blond hair running down the backs of the king's Elite bodyguards. Around them the ground was thick with the bodies of the betrayed, blond hair splayed in their own blood. Those who had coloured their hair dark still remained upon their feet.

"Loyalists of the king to me!" Kallisto cried out to the survivors. He dragged the king deeper into the throne room, away from the worst of the fray. "In the name of the king, only he who wears his hair golden still serves the king! All others are punishable as traitors to the Crown!"

Understanding immediately, the Royal Elite loyalists broke off battle and regrouped before their fallen king and his advisor. Looking at the handful of men before him, Kallisto knew the revelation had come too late; the loyalist numbers were too few to regain control of the throne room. All he could do was try to escape, and he picked up Masen beneath his armpits and scrambled back.

A deep bellow caused Kallisto to look up just as Aerox charged through his defensive lines like a raging bull. Forced to drop Masen to the floor, he barely managed to get his hands up in time to grasp the shaft of the traitor's spear before it smashed his face. A sharp steel elbow slammed into his chest, knocking all air from his lungs, but Kallisto maintained his tight hold upon his enemy's spear. Neither man would relinquish grip of the spear, understanding that a brief second was all that separated them from life and death. Kallisto also understood that Aerox's youth and vigour would far outlast his own.

The Royal Elite commander landed heavily upon Kallisto,

snapping the spear into three pieces. Entwined with his opponent, Kallisto was close enough to hear the heavy breathing echoing within his enemy's faceplate. Heavy fists rained down upon Kallisto, battering him. He watched as Aerox drew the dagger from his sleeve, prepared to finish him off.

"A new era is coming, Kallisto! One that shall usher in a new age of a powerful darkness that has been forgotten. All shall fear it, but none will be able to withstand it." Aerox plunged his long dagger hard toward Kallisto's throat. Forearms locked, he began to push his weight down, inching the blade ever closer.

"Fear not, Fallen, we know where you all hide. The question is, Do you know where your true enemies lurk?" Aerox quickly lifted up and pushed down hard, again trying to use his weight to break through Kallisto's locked arms. Kallisto struggled beneath Aerox's seemingly inhuman strength but refused to give. Something about the Royal Elite commander and the unholy power he suddenly wielded against Kallisto was wrong, and different.

Spotting Kallisto's confusion, Aerox laughed once more. "Not all is as you know it to be, Kallisto. We have waited in the darkness, letting you claim your glory for the moment, but revenge is coming. Soon enough the blood of the Order shall flow freely once more as the Brotherhood returns to take its rightful place …" The whites of Aerox's eyes began to diminish as blood pooled beneath the surface.

The blade was close enough that Kallisto could sense its point mere inches from his throat. Suddenly, the heavy weight of Aerox was thrown off. Another blade had caught the big man across his face. The yellow steel cut through the heavy, full-face helmet, slicing the man from his brow down across his face. Kallisto scarcely believed what he saw, for no living man within the room bore the holy yellow steel.

Gazing over at Masen, Kallisto saw the man upon all fours, his blood-covered arm clutching his wound. Smiling meekly upon Kallisto, he had somehow managed to find the strength to save his friend one last time by hurling his famous sword, the Mirage of

Metzor, which had freed all Masen's people from oppression, adding one more to its total.

Aerox had reeled back, clutching frantically at his face, allowing Kallisto the opportunity to make his escape. Scrambling back, Kallisto avoided the blind swings of Aerox's blades and reached the safety of the last nine loyalists. The battle had at last hit a standstill, as those remaining lined around their respective leaders. Aerox's side still held the distinct advantage as the group reformed around their leader; blood gushed between his fingers.

Kallisto stopped for a moment to witness the destruction that Sven's traitorous dogs had carved amongst the sealed chamber. A hundred of the finest Metzonian soldiers had been within its walls, and fewer than thirty were left.

"Traitorous monsters, I beg there be no mercy upon your souls when the armies of Masen Metz hear of your deceit. They shall tear down Metzor's fine walls and hunt every square inch of the city and countryside until you are all punished with death!"

"The people shall clamour for your head, Kallisto, when they hear what you did. You have foolishly fought yourself into a corner, and the dead do not talk. The only words that shall be spoken will be ours. Kneel and receive a clean death. If not, let us continue this as it was meant to be." Aerox paced before the barricade of spears, looking for the slightest of openings to launch another assault. Kallisto prayed his weakened men could remain vigilant for a few more minutes.

Urging his men to move farther back into the safety of the shadows behind the pillars, Kallisto stared at Aerox's marred face before turning his attention to the one who had orchestrated the treachery. With one last glance toward the throne from the far corner of the room, Kallisto could only see the prince's arm absently twirling his blade between his fingers and the floor of the pedestal. Sitting in his father's throne, Sven appeared to ignore the death around him.

"The entire world will rise up against you when they hear of what you did. One cannot hide the truth forever; they will discover the darkness within your heart. You shall have war upon all fronts as your father's allies and enemies move against you simultaneously, outside your borders as well as within. You will pay for this, Sven, I promise you that."

The spinning blade slowed, but silence was the only response from the murderous son. This had been planned with the utmost care; Kallisto would give the young man credit. Despite the warnings from the Order, both Masen and Kallisto had made the mistake of believing they had control.

Now Sven believed he would eradicate the last who knew the truth. But Kallisto had been a part of his father's realm from the very beginning and knew all of Masen's secrets.

Sliding back into the shadows, Kallisto searched for the key to their escape. Hidden in the shadows, the spears of the last loyalists awaited the final charge of their enemy. Feeling the marked stone beneath his fingertips, Kallisto lifted ever so lightly and pushed in, feeling the stone wall move to reveal the hidden exit.

He dragged Masen's silent body behind him, and one by one they slipped into the darkness. Pushing the door shut, Kallisto's men barred the door with their spears to allow precious moments for their escape. Masen grew heavier within his arms, and Kallisto prayed to Heaven that his friend could hold on for just a little longer. "Keep holding on there, Metz. Keep holding on."

Squeezing through the tight, dark tunnel, the nine men carried the king down the stairs upon their shoulders, anxious to get as far as they could from the throne room. The laborious breathing of their king grew heavier the deeper they moved, but Kallisto knew he could not stop if he was to have any hope of getting his friend help.

"Kallisto my old … friend, it is time. Please put me down. I can go no farther." Pausing in the tunnel, Kallisto turned back, horrified by what he saw. Those who carried their king were slick with his blood. They set their king down upon the ground. Masen grew paler as he continued clutching his chest; Kallisto knew the situation was beyond dire. "Remember, my friend … always protect the innocent and those who follow the Light. Protect my sons, Kallisto. Of greater importance, you need to find the Descendants! Save the Children of the Fallen before my son slays them all."

A Mortal Mistake

"What? Why would Sven want to slay the Children?" Kallisto urged, trying to squeeze the last bit of insight from his far-seeing friend. Tears slipped from the edges of his eyes as Kallisto watched the man try to clear his throat to speak.

"I have seen the demon within his soul, Kallisto. The undying hunger and the hate that wants to consume this world ... The shadows are growing. This time I shall not be here to fight it with you, my friend. The time has come for me to join my beloved wife, although sooner than we expected. You shall not be alone though ..."

Kallisto prepared to ask whom he spoke of, but Masen reached out to clasp his forearm tightly. Another course of torture exploded through the dying man, the bright life within Masen's eyes fading as he winced.

"I would have really liked ... to see the light one last time, Kallisto. Remember to protect the innocent ... good-bye, my friend, we shall meet soon enough. Until that day ..."

Kallisto felt tears well within him as the iron grip softened. Looking up, Kallisto thought upon his friend's endless honour and nobility in life. This dark tunnel was no place for a king to die, let alone a lifelong friend.

The Metzonian king had fallen, and the future of the kingdom lay in peril. The always-watchful and proud Chilsa Empire would prey upon the lands of Metzon once again when word reached the emperor's ears. The Order that had helped Masen into power would undoubtedly turn to Frederick to help maintain the prosperity its decades of work had established.

"Advisor, the longer we wait, the harder it will be to reach our destination. Chaos is soon to run through the city, and for word to reach those who need to know, we cannot remain here." Gesturing toward the next door in the escape tunnel, the soldier urged him to continue. Kallisto took up his king's sword as he stood; he pulled his eyes away from his friend and pushed through the door to continue their perilous journey.

The next portion of the tunnel wound back and forth as it snaked beneath the city, leaving all the men breathing heavily before they finally reached the end of the tunnel. Heaving, the escapees slowly pulled the heavy stone exit back, ducking through a large fireplace and into a sparsely furnished room. A large black banner with the Elite crest hung high above the door, and a thick-bearded man stood beneath it, clutching a tall double-bladed executioner's axe behind him.

"That tunnel has never been used during the command of the last three Elite generals, and yet this uncomfortable stormy night has a particularly horrible feeling. Do you bear the news that will crumble this nation? And what was your role in it?" The burly figure leaned back upon his axe, his dark eyes seeking answers in their faces.

General Brandon Dubryst, built like a bear, had given his entire life to the Elite guard, following his father's footsteps and joining at fourteen, but he'd lived the life even as a child. The scars of past battles riddled the man's massive bare torso; a number of scars marked his bald head. With his two-handed executioner's axe, he had likely slain more enemies of Metzon than any other soldier in its history. He would not hesitate to cleave nine more.

Kallisto pulled the yellow-bladed sword from over his shoulder and presented the blade before the general. Even for a man as tough as he was, the pain was evident across the old man's worn face. King Masen had meant a lot to both men, and having to bear his sword cut deep.

"The late king has been assassinated, General. I fear that corruption in servitude to Prince Sven has woven itself within the Royal Elite, led by Commander Aerox. We must assemble the Elite guard and try to regain authority, or we will have a revolt upon our hands," Kallisto urged, but he noticed the other man's brow furrow as other concerns crossed his mind.

"Vultures seem to have a very keen scent for impending death—such vile beasts. It would seem that many have flocked to Metzor this week." Kallisto waited for him to continue, a bad feeling sinking deep within his stomach. "As you may already be aware, General Hallaken and Lord Baldor's armies are participating in exercises outside the city walls. Both aggressive and bold, they are known for being self-serving and doing anything to end up on top. It is suspicious that the training occurs outside the capital walls at the exact moment such an event occurs, but no longer shocking."

Kallisto rubbed his eyes. He had forgotten about the two armies and their commanding officers. Already knowing whom the men served, such factors would make the retaking of the city all but impossible. "Unfortunately we do not have the time to contemplate or put together the puzzle right now. The puppet master is at work, and I'm sure that all the pieces will show their faces in due time. Until then we must move before we are crushed between the moving blocks. We cannot stop what is coming, only react."

"How do we react to such events? I must confess that I have not thought about such an event truly happening. I know what the Elite are supposed to do technically, by the book, but I do not believe the book applies to such events as an inside assassination." Brandon moved toward the door and peeked outside to ensure no one was eavesdropping.

"No, it does not. It will not be long before the generals both arrive in the city in an effort to 'restore order and balance', as they will claim. All political and military buildings will be under their control before dawn. We do not have much time. I have one last order to obey, and then we must abandon Metzor or become trampled beneath the confusion …"

Several of Dubryst's intermediary commanders pounded upon the door, clamouring for his attention. Opening the door and stepping forward, Dubryst kept his subordinates outside the room. They hurriedly began to address him.

"General, we have heard several startling reports! General Hallaken and Lord General Baldor have entered the city with the First and Sixth Armies. Lord Baldor has taken temporary control of the Royal Palace and all city gates, and General Hallaken is moving to surround the Order of the Fallen's headquarter compound. There are rumours that the king has been slain …"

Kallisto and his followers slowly and silently pulled back into the shadowy corners, not taking any chances. The traitors' plans were moving faster than Kallisto could react; invading a fully manned castle was pure madness.

"The Order has been charged with the slaying of the king, punishable under the penalty of death. We are under orders to relieve Lord Baldor's men and be placed under his command. Why were we not the first to be notified and mobilized?" the second commander queried.

The fresh information gave Kallisto a clue to Sven's dark plan.

"Because things are not as they seem, Commander. Order all our forces on high alert and marshal the entire barracks. If the king has been slain, your primary responsibility is the safety of his heir, young Prince Frederick. He is currently away from the city and must be reached. Be prepared to move on my command, and do not let any others order you until I have allowed it. Dismissed!"

The three commanders rushed off to relay the orders and prepare their men.

Kallisto gave Dubryst credit for being able to quickly think his way out of the carefully laid trap. Both generals were of equal rank but with the Council of Lords behind Baldor, Brandon would have no choice but to relinquish his command and turn over his soldiers to Baldor. But by manipulating Metzonian law, which declared that if the King were slain, the Elite forces were to ensure the safety of the most immediate heir to the throne, Brandon had avoided the threat. None could argue with what he had done, even the Crown Council.

"Hallaken is surrounding the Order. He will move swiftly and relentlessly. I am to guess that your last order lies within that location. We will have better luck if we proceed with only those within this room; it will be quicker and quieter. We will extract the package and quickly return to fight our way out of the city to safety if we have to." Dubryst set about quickly armouring himself for the upcoming mission.

"Surely those who have set upon such a path will have many eyes watching all important aspects closely. You will no doubt be under close watch."

"Do not worry. We will take the bridge exit and then go up to

A Mortal Mistake

the roofs. My men spoke of a girl who moved along the roofs during the celebration for Sven's return, and we have been mapping them over the past month. There will be no going through the front gate anymore, so we shall have to find an alternate entry."

Kallisto knew that with the Metzonian general surrounding the compound, they definitely wouldn't be able to pass through the army unnoticed. He only hoped that the package they were to rescue would be in an appropriate extraction point.

"We should get moving. Every moment we waste is another moment our enemies tighten their grasp."

Mustering their remaining energy to move once again, the group silently and quickly went along through the barracks. Muscles ached and lungs strained for fresh oxygen, though it was only the beginning of the night. Following the Elite's commander, they raced through a covered bridge to an adjoining barracks building and then up to the roof. All hoped that they were not too late and could accomplish the king's last order, but only Kallisto knew what was truly at risk. The future of the Order lay in a precarious balance.

Chapter 6
Fleeing from Fate

Heavy pounding upon the thick wooden courtyard doors startled all within the complex, echoing loudly among the Orders Metzonian chapter's lofty walls. Seated within the open classroom, Alexandra instructed a large group of the younger Children of the Fallen in their nightly lessons. Already distressed by the snapping thunder, the children immediately noticed the heavy knocking.

Drawn by the apparent urgency, Alexandra stepped away from her learning materials and went out onto the fourth-story balcony, leaving Sabrina to settle the children. Many of the Order's other residents were similarly curious to see who was making a commotion in such a storm. Upon the highest floor of the residential wings, Alexandra's viewpoint was the best amongst the spectators, allowing her to catch a glimpse of who beat upon the other side of the walls.

The streets surrounding their Chapter were packed tightly with soldiers, the glint of their steel spears visible in the brief flashes of lightning. Alexandra saw a dozen of the Order's guards pull back the steel doors, allowing the outsiders to enter into the complex. A tall, lanky commander strode into the courtyard in the middle of the complex, followed by several of his captains and their squadrons of infantry. His hand was placed firmly upon his sheathed sword, a rolled document in his other hand.

As the Order's ambassador, her foster father, along with the chapter's high priest and several other members, stepped into the rain, leaving the cathedral to meet the military commander in the courtyard. Halting before the large three-tiered fountain, the

A Mortal Mistake

delegation appeared as confused to Alexandra, but they calmly awaited explanation from the military commander. No one had reason to fear the army; the Order and its members were among the most faithful of the king's close allies.

"The Order of the Fallen is hereby charged with high treason against the Crown of Metzor for the assassination of his Royal Highness King Masen Metz and the attempted murder of his children! All shall be tried by the Lords' Supreme Courts. Any resistance will be punished, and no mercy shall be granted." Screams of horrifying disbelief broke out throughout the compound. "The king can't be dead," Alexandra heard someone whisper from a balcony below. "Even if he is, how could we possibly be charged with such a horrendous crime?"

"What madness is this? The Order has always full-heartedly supported the king. What evidence do you have to support such a preposterous claim?" her father asked with great authority, moving closer, unthreatened by the general. The commanding officer's response ended all thought of further questioning.

Alexandra screamed as she watched as the tip of a silver blade thrust through her father's abdomen. The general shouted commands to all around him, and the soldiers took the cue, killing the Order guards, caught by surprise. Using his forearm, the general shoved her father into the fountain, washing his blade clean in the fresh second tier.

"We need no evidence! All shall be punished for the crimes of their brethren! None shall escape or be able to hide from the justice that will be done upon them."

Soldiers swarmed through the compound, pulling occupants out into the courtyard with the use of brutal force. Alexandra reeled under the swift violence. Her eyes locked upon the fountain, which had grown completely red with the blood of her foster father. Panic was overshadowed by the shock at the death. People she had came to know over the course of calling Metzor home screamed with terror.

Alexandra struggled under the stress, not knowing what to do or where to escape. As a newer arrival, she did not know any escape routes the Order might have designed within the Metzonian Chapter. She looked at her friend Sabrina, who had joined her on the balcony and then past her to the younger students sitting inside. Alexandra hoped with desperation that Sabrina would have a solution, but she saw only fear-filled, teary eyes looking back at her.

"What are we going to do, Alexa?" Her quivering voice spoke softly as the two women looked at the roomful of children. Dozens of small faces stared back, watching the two of them with large confused eyes. The innocence shining within their eyes reminded Alexandra of her own childhood, when others had protected her from danger.

"We need to get the children out of here." Placing her hands upon the younger woman's face, Alexandra quickly wiped away the tears from beneath her friend's eyes. "But we have to keep them as calm and quiet as possible, you hear me? Follow my lead."

Standing tall, Alexandra made sure to maintain her composure, knowing how receptive a child was to distraught emotion. Striding in, she stood smiling at the front of the room. Sabrina came in the back, closing the doors behind her quietly. Alexandra gathered her students' attention.

"Listen up, children! We are going to go up to the library for further study. But we are going to make a game out of it as well. You must be as silent as mice and sneak among the shadows. Make sure that no one sees you. Follow Sabrina quickly and quietly now. If we reach the library without anyone seeing us, then there may be a reward." Alexandra did not want to think that the reward would be to escape death. Innocent children did not deserve the pain and suffering undoubtedly planned for them. If Alexandra could not save them, no one else would come to rescue them in time.

Leading the children outside the classroom, Sabrina moved swiftly through the long empty hallways of the chapter, avoiding the interior where the majority of the fighting would certainly be. Alexandra knew it was the only way to keep the children calm.

Many of the youngest children crept along on the tips of their toes, acting as though it truly was just an innocent game. They were unaware of what was coming for them and what had already

A Mortal Mistake

possibly happened to their parents. Alexandra continued to push them quickly forward. Pausing briefly at each adjoining hallway, Alexandra watched around the corners and waved each child across when she was sure the coast was clear.

The emotional toll of watching her foster father be slain was becoming excruciatingly painful. She tried to concentrate upon the task at hand, but the image continued to run through her mind. All the others who had taken care of her throughout her lifetime had given her up to others, with Alexandra never knowing why. On multiple occasions a couple had become filled with fear, often sending her away with strangers into the darkness. What had scared them, Alexandra did not know, but fear always seemed to follow her in one form or another. But the ambassador had not tossed her away when the danger had appeared. He'd adjusted his life and moved his family so that she could continue to have a semblance of a normal life. He had moved his family away from Nykol for her, not because he wanted to. He was now dead because of her. Why hadn't he listened to her when she told him about the incident within the cathedral? The voice of the general within the courtyard had been perfectly loud and crisp, recognizable as one of the three dark men who met with Sven. She knew it was him who was destroying everything that she knew and loved. Her foster father had idolized the Fist of Metzor, only to become the first of many victims within the Cathedral of the Fallen.

Spotting the staircase just across the final corridor, Alexandra peered around the corner. Despite the apparent safety, Alexandra could hear commotion: shouting muffled by closed doors. Looking back again at the staircase that would lead to their possible escape, she chose to accept the risk.

She urged Sabrina quickly toward the stairwell and the children after her. Caught up watching the children begin climbing the stairs to safety, Alexandra missed seeing the last child freeze in the midst of the hallway. A startled scream broke out down the hallway, followed by loud cursing. Rushing forward, Alexandra picked up the child and dashed forward briefly, catching a glimpse of a half-naked woman fighting off two men who were trying to drag her in the opposite direction. The two swordsmen looked up at the child just as Alexandra dragged the crying girl forward.

She shouted at Sabrina to run, and they fled up the stairs toward the library, hoping there would be no pursuers. The attackers were advancing much quicker than Alexandra anticipated. She realized her window of opportunity was quickly closing. She wondered how many more obstacles would lay in her path as she pushed forward with no other choice.

Reaching the top floor of the cathedral complex without being followed, Alexandra peered cautiously around the corner toward the Ambassador's chamber at the far end of the library. The library was built in three successive rings that grew higher and larger; through a railing she could see the Metzonians running rampant through the first ring of the complex. Fearful members of the Fallen screamed as the soldiers chased them amongst the endless shelves on the second ring before dragging them from the room. The third level remained quiet for the moment, showing no signs of significant force yet.

Peering around the corner, she saw four soldiers outside the door of her father's chambers, blocking their path. She knew that if she could get the children into that room, a small stained-glass window picturing a white angel opened out onto the roof. Freedom would momentarily be theirs, before the larger task of escaping the city itself.

"Sabrina, there are only four guards outside my father's office. I'm going to run across and see if I can distract them away from the door to the other side of the room. You take the children around the other way and hide in the office. I will meet you there." The younger woman nodded, taking the key Alexandra offered before grabbing the hands of the children at the front of the line. All the children's eyes were wide and fear-filled; they had become well aware that their situation was not a game anymore. Watching the two lines of children scurry around the back, Alexandra prepared herself to run, choosing a suitable location far enough back.

Alexandra made a slow dash from behind the bookshelf, ensuring that she was clearly visible to those upon the other side of the circular room. Avoiding eye contact, she dove behind a large shelf, expecting them to come after her immediately. Shouts and the distinct rattling of steel announced her enemy's intentions to pursue her, giving her slight hope. Peering over the books, her hope quickly faltered. She had only managed to provoke a pair of the guards to leave their post. She scrambled for a solution. Seeing the children hugging the wall opposite her, trapped, she understood she would be forced to sacrifice her own safety for the children.

Hearing the first guard close the distance quickly, she pulled the largest book from the shelf and swung it out from her hiding place. Alexandra's aim was dead on. She felt the impact as the book hit the guard in the head, knocking him off his feet. Rushing out, she struck the guard repeatedly to unconsciousness. The second guard grabbed her hair and reeled her back.

Twisting, trying to free herself, she thrust a knee into his groin and tried clawing at the face of the soldier. Feeling the soft flesh of his eyes, Alexandra stabbed her thumbs harder and felt the man's eyes collapse beneath the pressure. Screaming in agony, the soldier struck her down with a heavy fist and quickly pressed his palms on his bleeding eyes. Picking herself back up, Alexandra ran forward, pushing the man over the interior railing and watching him fall atop a bookshelf in the second-story ring.

Hearing the scraping of drawn blades, Alexandra turned to see the final pair proceed toward her with swords drawn, apparently determined not to make the same mistake as their comrades. Her head would be cleaved from her shoulders before she could struggle. Running back amongst the library shelves, she gingerly placed her toes upon the edges of the shelves and climbed slowly, silently up, hoping they would hold her weight. Carefully reaching the top, she saw Sabrina preparing to unlock the door. Then the guards came around both sides of the bookshelf, looking up at her in surprise. Throwing a smile at the guards, she took off across the tops of the bookcases, her life on the line. She leaped from shelf to shelf, only one foot pressed against the wooden top before the second was already landing atop the next, leaving the astonished guards to watch her grand escape.

She jumped down onto the soft carpeting near her foster father's office. Sabrina had just unlocked and opened the door. Smiling in triumph for a second, Alexandra saw a figure move from out of the shadows behind Sabrina. Before Alexandra could warn her, it wrapped one arm around Sabrina's face, quickly stifling any screams. The second arm looped her left elbow and grabbed onto her right triceps with remarkable speed. With a single quick pull, Sabrina, thrashing in terror, was dragged into the shadows.

Alexandra had not come this far to have everything fall apart. Rushing into the darkness, she moved to attack the scarred figure wrestling with Sabrina. Her first step forward was her last. Another opponent grabbed her limbs, trying to disable her by lifting her completely off the ground. She fought hard to break the grip, but it was as if she were already clasped in iron shackles. She tasted heavy leather in her mouth.

Continuing to struggle, she watched the children scream wildly as their teachers were captured. Several other fearsomely armoured warriors holding large torches waited in silence for their counterparts while others rushed forth, grabbing the children Alexandra had been trying to save.

Several children attempted to flee; others sat petrified with fear as the soldiers ran toward them. Several of the fleeing children ran directly into those who had pursued her. One man struck the larger children to the floor with fists or vicious kicks. The other man held several children off the ground by their wrists, leaving them helplessly flailing. The guard smiled widely, as though he'd caught a prized fish.

Witnessing the brutality of the men with the terrified, crying children, Alexandra attempted to scream through the leather glove pressed over her lips. The soldiers dragged several small children at once, three small arms wrapped in one tight fist. Others carried the larger struggling and screaming children out of the library.

Watching the darker, more frightening warriors relieve the guards of the children they had caught, Alexandra finally fell to her knees, giving up, as they carried them past her into her father's office. The pair of guards that had pursued her became confused as they were grabbed by the larger warriors, and they shouted out in

A Mortal Mistake

shock as they were dragged away from the office. Soldiers lifted them under an armpit and by one leg and threw them over the railing, as Alexandra watched them with confusion.

"Burn all of it; ensure that the administrative records and members logs are completely burnt! Hurry up! Others will be here within moments." Alexandra recognized the insignia painted upon the black armour that identified them as members of the Metzonian Royal Elite. She did not understand why the personal bodyguards of the slain king would want to burn all the records. Didn't they want to find all members of the Order, particularly those hidden and most likely to be the culprits in the king's slaying?

Unless the Metzonian generals' claims had been incorrect, these guards now rounding up the Children of the Fallen for slaughter would have been the assassins who had killed the king. She looked outside the door to see that several of the new soldiers had shoved over bookshelves, which then knocked over the next shelf and the next in succession.

"Would you two quit fighting so damn hard already? We have a long enough night ahead of us, and you are not helping things!" The bald man spoke harshly, still fighting with Sabrina. He finally threw her to the ground, rubbing the hand she'd bitten. Another soldier immediately grabbed hold of her, placing his knee upon the back of her neck.

"We are all on the same damned side, for Heaven's sake!" He picked up several books that were on her father's desk, stuffing them into a large brown sack before plucking a torch from the wall and igniting the remaining items. He tossed the torch out the door onto the overturned bookshelves, igniting the books in the dusty haze.

The soldier finally released his grip on Alexandra and set her down on the floor of the burning room; smoke grew thicker as the fire spread through the books. She turned to see who her kidnapper was and recognized the face of King Masen's loyal advisor, Kallisto.

Kallisto looked down at Alexandra and nodded immediately. "She is among the ones we came for, along with the rest of them. At least one thing has gone our way tonight, though the night is still young. Listen closely—we are here to get you all out of the city, but we will not fight with you the whole way. Get the children under control and quiet or else we will have to silence them ourselves. Trust me, you do not want that. Do you understand?"

Alexandra and Sabrina nodded quickly and crawled over to the group of crying children. They tried to comfort the youngest of the bunch, as the others fidgeted in fear. The task was not easy when trapped within a burning library that was quickly filling with smoke.

"Let us escape and get the hell out of this city before there is no hope." The commanding figure of Kallisto spoke as he pushed a younger man toward a small opening that led on to the roof. Several of the other soldiers used their brethren to lift them up through the window before reaching back into the room as others stood atop the thick table and passed the children up to safety. The bald man locked the doors to the office, pushing her father's bookcase that held the entire history of the Order against it.

"Hopefully that will buy us a little time. Let's go!" The thick-bearded bald man she did not know climbed onto the escape route, not wasting any time, leaving only Kallisto and Alexandra in the room. "Remember now; we must keep the children quiet if we are to survive our escape!"

"What about the others? How come we are not saving the rest?" She had known that it would be hopeless to try and save all of the people within the complex, but a life was a life, and each one was worth saving. She looked into the bright blue of Kallisto's eyes; sadness mixed with pain within their depths.

"Because they are all that is left to buy you and the Children of the Fallen the time required to escape. Do not linger on what you cannot change." The group leader picked her up firmly and pushed her toward the open window before grasping the forearms offered to him by the two soldiers and followed behind her.

Reaching the rooftops, the children huddled in a tight circle, shivering in the wet wind. Those who had rescued them crouched around the children, trying to shelter them from the fierce storm. Alexandra felt a thick cloak being wrapped around her shoulders. Kallisto pointed out toward the northeast.

"See the barracks of the Elite over there?"

She gazed out across the rainy night, seeing the silhouette in the brief flashes of lightning. From its black pyramid shape that reminded her of a Chilsa structure, she recognized what it was.

"We have to reach the barracks. General Dubryst and his Elite are the only friends you still have left within Metzor. And it's the only way to smuggle you out that can even be considered somewhat safe."

Alexandra knew that the Elite had their own private gate out of the Inner City to allow King Masen's finest soldiers immediate access to every portion of the city. Looking upon the scarred man, she only hoped that Kallisto knew what he was doing. Upon first glance at the general, one would imagine he was the vilest of men, an executioner who separated spirits from their physical anchors.

"We will get you out of the city, Alexandra, even if we have to fight the entire way. The city guard is not as tough as they like to appear."

Alexandra followed the general across the board bridges the soldiers had used to reach them. Carrying the smallest children upon their backs, the small group made its way toward the Elite barracks.

Weaving across the rooftops, she looked up at the great castle of Metzor standing strong in the midst of the storm. She wondered who else may have been looking upon it and if they perhaps understood the turmoil that swirled within it.

CHAPTER 7
CONFLICTED

Conrad pushed furiously through the endless sea of stern-faced soldiers toward the throne room. He'd been confined to his room for hours by the Royal Elite, and no one had told him a single reason why, no matter how often he had demanded to know. Commanding, bribing, threatening—nothing worked with the guards, and he was forced to sit, fuming, within his chambers. His anger merely masked the fear that grew rapidly in his stomach.

Finally released from his confinement, he headed toward the throne room, knowing the fear was becoming a reality. The halls of his father's golden palace were filled so thickly with Metzonian infantry that moving within its walls was difficult. The closer he advanced, the thicker the soldiers were. He threw open the great doors with trembling hands.

He was sick immediately, vomiting as he collapsed to his knees at the sight before him. Bodies littered the entire floor on both sides of the raised throne, the floor thick with the blood of the fallen. A great number of the fallen guards were clutching their spears in a death grip. Conrad could see the grimaces of pain and the shock of death through the steel masks covering the faces of the men. Undoubtedly most of them had died not understanding what was going on, a feeling Conrad shared with the dead.

High upon his father's throne sat Sven, his elbows upon his knees, his folded hands pressed to his forehead. At the sound of the door hinges swinging shut, Sven looked up for the moment before returning to his previous position. Neither spoke; the silence hung in the air until Conrad sputtered out what words he could.

"What ... what happened?"

"My brother, the Order betrayed our father."

The cold and emotionless words echoed within the dim room. Conrad looked upon his brother with disbelief, struggling to comprehend such a claim. Conrad blinked several times, trying to clear his mind. His next words were barely audible; his tongue felt swollen in his throat. "What? But ... but that doesn't make sense. I don't believe you. Why ... why would they do such a thing? How? What ... what? Why, Sven?"

Rising from the throne of black and gold, Sven slowly began descending the staircase, careful to avoid the blood on the shorter column platform. Reaching the bottom, he beckoned his brother forward with two fingers and stepped over the bodies of Royal Elite guards with little concern.

The shock was too real for Conrad to comprehend what was displayed before him. How was such a massacre possible? His father was protected by the finest of the elite, the greatest warriors this nation had to offer. And yet they lay in mangled heaps upon the floor; no survivors remained within the room.

Following his brother, Conrad was directed toward a corner of the throne room, hidden behind the row of columns that skirted the outer walls. It was the only corner of the room with substantial light. Torches flickered, revealing a wall that had been ripped open, leaving the rubble upon the ground.

Sven bent over, and Conrad caught the stone thrown at him and inspected it closely. Carved upon the face of the stone was a rough but worn stencil of the Order's five falling star crest. Tracing his fingers over it, he looked up at Sven once again as his brother stepped through the hole in the wall and headed down the hidden staircase, silently beckoning Conrad to follow.

Within the small pocket corridor, three dead Royal Elite lay perched against the wall. Conrad found it peculiar that the breastplates of the dead men were removed from their chests, until he saw what Sven had been looking at. Upon their naked chests were scars; the Order's emblem, branded into their chests, once again mocked him.

"This is where we found Father's body, abandoned by Kallisto." Sven pointed to a large bloodstain on the floor, and another wave of nausea threatened to overtake Conrad. Hands upon his knees, he fought it and looked up to see his brother had already continued on without him. Pulling himself upright and wiping his nose, Conrad looked down at the middle of the room one last time.

"I tried to catch Kallisto, but he was too swift. Many souls were sacrificed to provide the precious time he needed to escape," Sven commented as they passed several more bodies along the length of the tunnel. Conrad was able to picture his brother racing through the tunnel after the murders, screams of vengeance echoing within its confined space. The Order certainly had not anticipated the impact his brother had upon their plans.

Climbing up the narrow staircase toward the new light, Conrad exited behind his brother to find Aerox and several Royal Elite within the spacious apartment of the Elite's general. In the middle of the room, a man rested upon his knees, whispering to himself, his arms tied tightly, a thick wooden post pinning his elbows behind his back. Two Royal Elite stood at each side and roughly pulled him back if he started to sway too heavily. Conrad watched the black blood ooze down the prisoner's side from a nasty abdominal wound.

"You did this? You were the one who organized the death of the king?" The man did not respond, continuing what Conrad assumed to be prayers. One of the guards reefed the man upright via the post, causing a hiss to escape the man's lips.

"Prince Conrad asked you a question. You had better answer if you would like to see someday!"

The man's head snapped up, and he scanned the room with eyes swollen completely shut. Despite the abuse upon his face, Conrad was still able to identify the man, as well as notice the slight hope upon his mangled face. "Prince Conrad! Please, my prince, you must tell these men that I had nothing to do with your father's murder! The Order never had a thing to do with his murder. We would not do such a thing. We have been set up."

A Mortal Mistake

"All things seem to say otherwise. The Order's fingerprints are everywhere one looks! Who would have framed you, Ambassador Alessyn? The Chilsa? The Kyllordic?"

"Your brother …" The old man spoke meekly, tensing up in anticipation of further physical abuse. None of the guards moved to strike him. All looked toward Sven, who remained still, flexing his ringed right hand.

"You would like me to believe that, wouldn't you? But why should I believe you? If you are all so innocent, and if it was my brother as you claim, then where is Karl Kallisto? Where is the one who stood beside my father for forty years?" The more he thought about the Fallen, the more he knew Kallisto was behind it all. His proud wisdom and kind heart were merely a mask for when he received the order from his Elders. Conrad wondered if it had been difficult for him to break his father's deepest trust, his only true weakness.

The ambassador dropped his head once again, already knowing that Conrad would not believe his suspicions. His voice was full of fear and doubt as he began trying to explain. "The Order has always been a full supporter of your father! I do not know where Advisor Kallisto is; your brother could have had him buried upon the Numelli or hidden in some wall, along with the father he murdered." The ambassador's brief stint of defiance did not go unpunished the second time. Sven struck the man with terrible quickness.

Conrad looked up at his brother as he turned away from the man, flexing his arms in contained rage as he paced through the room.

The ambassador's chin became red with his own blood as he spit teeth out onto the floor. He attempted to continue through the new pain. "Whoever did it, my prince, there is no possible way to prove Karl committed this atrocity rather than anyone else standing within this room. Advisor Kallisto was your father's best friend from the beginning, Conrad! I, too, was a close friend of your father; we all were. We dined with your family on multiple occasions, as surely you remember. My daughter and I came often, remember?"

Conrad did remember. Multiple times the members of the Order had been invited to dine with them. The ambassador had a very beautiful daughter. She was oblivious to any of his advances, but Conrad had to admit to her beauty.

"I do remember. Alexandra was her name, right? Our father dined with many of you and called you all his friends as well, but how did you reward him in the end? The Elders undermined him constantly, the Metzonian Chapter constantly pressured for its own interests. Everyone wanted something, and look what happened when someone had the courage to say no."

"It is not at all like that, my prince!" The ambassador cried out, struggling against his ropes and the guards in frustration. "I have no clue where Kallisto has gone, or what he has done. Regardless, you cannot judge a people by the actions of a few. I am innocent! My people are innocent! You must free us so we all may discover the truth. Do not make the mistake of washing your hands with the blood of the innocent, my child."

Running his hands through his hair, Conrad tried to decide who to believe, the words and images in a great conflict. He looked at the beaten man with little left to lose, who believed that his people, the descendents of Heaven, were not capable of such an act. Looking at Sven, Conrad saw a man who survived despite losing everything he had known, returning to finally remember what he once had.

Feeling his stare, Sven spoke for the first time in the chamber. "All men have secrets they keep hidden, most of which they take to the grave, Conrad. All men are made of different metal, and all have weaknesses that make them break, be it pain or something else. Torturing is not an easy task, but sometimes it is necessary. I need to find out where Kallisto is hiding. I need to know why he did it. You need to know why."

"No! Your father abolished torture. Oh, no, please! I told you everything already, many times. You can beat me a thousand times more, but I am telling you that what I have said is the truth. My words will be the same until the end. Please, please, please, don't let this happen, my prince."

Hearing the man's voice full of conviction as he pleaded for his life caused Conrad's heart to stir slightly in his dark moment. Pain and anger swelled within him to force away the guilt, his mind producing a black tunnel. As much as he wanted to believe they were innocent, he had seen the signs. He wanted the truth, and he wanted evidence that it was the truth.

Nodding toward his brother, Sven continued to speak. "We shall see, Ambassador. Physical pain is powerless against men of the faith, who absorb their pain within their religious faith. One will never break such strong spirits. But men of true faith often wither beneath love."

Conrad could hear a woman's screams outside the door grow closer. Fear indeed rose within the ambassador as his imagination began to take a hold of him. Trembling upon the stone floor, he shot upright, twisting his head in the direction of the growing screams.

"The love of a daughter perhaps."

The girl was dragged into the room, hands bound before her, a burlap sack placed over her head. Seeing her dirty half-naked body, Conrad looked at Sven, understanding what terrible acts he was planning.

Sven looked straight ahead, showing no emotion as she struggled against the men. Conrad watched with pending horror as his brother unclipped his thick black wolf cloak and hung it up on the wall and then undid the clasps of his shirt near his throat. He began rolling up his sleeves.

"There is no need for both of us to bear this, brother. You should go find yourself a nice bottle of wine and a couple of women to share your woes with for the next few nights. We have the Inner City under control again, but who knows what scum the Order hides outside of them. We shall find out soon enough."

Ambassador Alessyn began crying out for help and forgiveness upon hearing the young woman's screams. Conrad was certain the old man would probably admit anything to stop whatever his brother had planned. Looking at each face within the room left him with a feeling of dread within his guts; he knew what was about to happen was wrong. Seeing where his father had died had momentarily removed the sympathy Conrad knew he should feel.

Slipping past the two guards wrestling with the woman, Conrad took one last look at Sven, who was crouched before the Fallen, raising the man's chin with a single finger. Not looking back at Conrad as he focused upon the whimpering man before him, Sven seemed to add as an afterthought, "Father's funeral will be in five days. Do not forget."

As if he could forget when his father's funeral was.

Conrad's long walk back from the Elite barracks had been surprisingly quick. Struggling to sort out the events of the nights and the role everyone had played left him exhausted. The Elite barracks had been completely abandoned. General Dubryst had exited the city, slaughtering hundreds of Lord Baldor's men who had tried to stop him. His father's death had driven everyone to madness.

Wandering across the palace grounds toward the keep entrance, Conrad had planned to peel his wet clothing off and sleep the next days away. A commotion from within the royal stables drew his attention, piquing his curiosity. Screams of men in great pain and the deep neighing of war horses rumbled throughout the courtyard.

Upon investigating, he discovered the stable hands holding the thick doors closed as men lay in agony on piles of wet straw spread around the entrance. Pushing through them all, Conrad went to peer into stable. He felt two hands land upon his shoulders, pulling him back. Turning to look to see who dared place their hands upon him, he saw the bushy face of the stable master,

"Sire, you cannot enter the barn. Metzotto has gone completely wild and has smashed every stable gate and barricade within the stables! Everyone we have sent in has come out horribly beaten up or hasn't come out at all. Even Cassidus could not get him under control." Wide-eyed, Cassidus sat upon a bale of damp straw, shaking his head, clutching his side painfully where Metzotto had kicked the younger man.

"So we are going to leave him locked within the barn forever?" Pushing past the stable master, Conrad stormed into the stable, smelling the thick air heavy with the musk of sweat from the stallion. Letting his eyes adjust to the gloom, he heard hooves pawing at the very back of the stable. Confidently taking several strides forward, Conrad scanned for his father's prize stallion in the gloom. The great black stallion had run freely across the Numelli plains, untameable and uncatchable; it had only ever responded to his father's call and touch. A symbol of his father's power, the horse and man had shared a supernatural bond, now severed.

Nearly blind in the dim space, he was forced to rely upon his other senses. Conrad held his hands protectively before him and listened to the heavy breathing. A startled cry broke out from Metzotto, deafening Conrad moments before a flash of lightning cut through the window. Rearing back upon its hind legs, the black stallion struck out at Conrad with practiced precision, caving in his breastplate and knocking him across the stable.

Raising himself off the ground, Conrad prepared himself once more. He would not falter where others had failed, not tonight. Screaming into the darkness, he charged in once again. "You think you are the only one who lost someone important to you tonight, Metzotto? Huh, you selfish bastard? What about me?"

Conrad knew the "King of the Numelli" was undoubtedly close before the hot breath upon his outstretched hand caused the hairs on his neck to jump. Swinging its large head around, Metzotto snapped his teeth at Conrad's arm, missing by mere inches. Risking his hand a second time, Conrad jabbed his hand to where he guessed the animal was amongst the darkness. Feeling the snout of the stallion beneath his hand, Conrad rammed his fingers and thumb deeply up the snotty nostrils, pinching in hard until he felt the cartilage flex beneath the force.

Metzotto snorted, jerking its head around, pulling Conrad with ease, but Conrad refused to let go and grabbed a fistful of mane with his right hand. The stallion reared back upon its hind legs in one final hope to be free from the man, and Conrad felt his legs lift off the ground. Knowing if he let go, Metzotto's left hoof would be the last thing he saw in this world, Conrad squeezed tighter, not allowing himself to be denied.

A low, exasperated rumble escaped from Metzotto as he dropped back down, swinging his head back and forth. Feeling the thick nostrils sucking upon his fingers, Conrad focused upon pulling Metzotto closer toward him. Pressing his face against Metzotto's, he released his right hand to stroke the neck of the beast.

"Metzotto, can you carry me away from this pain I feel?" A sadness struck Conrad, a moment of weakness, leaving him empty and not truly caring if Metzotto knocked his head from his body. His father was gone, his mother was gone; one brother was far from home, hating the other brother, who Conrad wasn't sure had ever really returned. "What say you? Should we run as far as we can flee from our pain tonight?"

Removing his left hand from Metzotto's snout, he wrapped his arms around the neck of the great beast, feeling the rush of blood beneath the black coat. Calmness came over both of them as Conrad ran his fingers through the stallion's mane. Pulling back, Conrad looked up at the stallion nodding in agreement, bringing the smallest of smiles to his face.

He called to Cassidus to prepare his father's saddle, and the barn doors opened enough for their heads to poke in. Struggling with Masen's large saddle, Cassidus paused, looking up at the stallion before him. Snorting at Metzotto, he threw the saddle into Conrad's arms, gesturing that he would not be going any further.

Within the hour Conrad felt the thunder beating within the powerful heart of Metzotto. Racing from the city into the darkness of the night, he blindly rode forward, knowing there were few rivers or forests to get tangled in for leagues. Trusting in Metzotto's sure feet, Conrad inhaled the cool moist air rushing over his face as he watched forks of lightning streak across the stormy sky.

Running swiftly through the night, Metzotto effortlessly carried Conrad, who allowed his mind to roam. Conrad had absent-mindedly steered toward the mountains northwest of Metzor, overlooking the grand Sallorin Lake. Leaving the darkness created by the sinister storm at last, Conrad looked around him in the shadowy moonlight. Dread crept into the back of his mind when he discovered where he found himself.

The mighty Lost Mountain stood before him, stretching high into the star-filled sky, just as in his nightmares. Cast off from the rest of the mountain range that ran between the two lakes of Metzon, the Lost Mountain was impressive despite being alone. Tall, craggy and dark, it stood against the midnight sky like a sentinel, overlooking the surrounding land. The grasslands bordering the base of the mountain halted far from the rock, creating an eerie feeling of death. Life refused to grow upon the black soil; rock surrounded larger, darker rock.

Conrad had been unable to sleep a single night since returning from the desert without dreaming about the craggy mountain standing alone at the edge of an oily black lake. Or that was how they had started. As the nights progressed to weeks, the dreams began to get darker and more vivid. The black waters of the lake burst into flames before molten lava flowed out across the bay. The navy sky filled with shimmering stars began to cloud up around the dark mountain, a great storm swirling around the summit, picking up speed and lifting his body toward it. It always ended with Conrad screaming in fear and pain as the mouth of the mountain opened up its jagged stone teeth to swallow him.

Concerned he was going insane, he had confided in Sven and asked whether he had ever received such nightmares before. Remembering the state in which he had found his brother, he was concerned that the desert had done something to his mind. Of greater concern in Conrad's view was the demonic temple he had awoken within. The number of candidates he had to talk with beyond the family was limited; perhaps Cassidus who could not speak his thoughts. Considering the matters of his mind, he preferred to keep his concerns among his family and best friend.

Listening to the question, Sven had initially laughed in his face, telling him that he didn't even remember what it was like to dream. Nightmares were merely a man's fears, he said, and if one confronts his fears then they would subside. The admiration Conrad had for his brother reached beyond that normally held by a sibling; his brother had gone through serious tribulations and had embraced such events to rise above.

Looking upon the dark peak and reflecting upon the tribulations his family had endured, Conrad knew he could not run anymore.

His father had stood strong in the face of all obstacles in his path toward what he wanted. His brother surpassed all the trials that had been forced upon him by those around him. But what had he done? Even now, he fled the death of his father, hoping that it would simply go away, that all the terrible events going around him were not real, just a bad dream.

He patted the stallion on the neck as it slowly grazed beneath him. He stared at the mountain of his nightmares. By confronting the nightmares atop the mountain, perhaps the cloudiness of his confusion would at last abate, and he could concentrate and discover the answers evading him. Fighting fear, Conrad knew he would have to venture forth. But he remained sitting there, waiting for his courage to build up.

Hearing the thundering of hooves behind him, he whirled Metzotto around to face the threat. The stallion's ears twitched forward, and he snorted into the darkness as the silhouette of a lone rider came around the rocky embankment at full speed. Relief was replaced with embarrassment when Conrad recognized the man.

His horse breathing heavily, a livid Cassidus pulled back upon the reins and gestured rudely toward Conrad. Guilt struck Conrad upon remembering that his friend had been following him when they departed the city. Lost within his thoughts and carried by the most powerful horse in Metzon, the shorter man had been left behind despite being the better rider. Smiling weakly and shrugging his shoulders, Conrad patted Metzotto on the shoulder, signifying there had little choice in his speedy departure.

Cassidus shook his head, still angry, before pointing up at the mountain peak. His tongue had been brutally severed by brigands when he was a child, and Conrad would never hear him speak. Using gestures and hand signals, the two men were able to communicate on most levels. His wacky gesturing often created comedic relief, and a strong friendship had formed between the men. Having him nearby, Conrad felt more reassured, knowing he was not alone as he looked up at the mountain.

Metzotto forced Conrad to leave him far from his rocky destination, his hooves firmly planted on the green grass. Preparing to walk the rest of the way, he had grabbed his supplies and noticed Cassidus following behind him. Conrad hesitated; he felt that perhaps this journey was something he should face himself. The look within his friend's eyes caused Conrad to feel more guilt, knowing how deeply hurt and utterly angry his friend had been when he'd sneaked off to the Desert of Lost Souls.

Accepting the companionship, the two men were forced to follow a skinny goat trail zigzagging up the side of the mountain for hours, passing several small empty caves, until they came to the end of the trail. Standing upon a flat crag that jutted out from the mountain, Conrad overlooked the lake upon one side and the flat grasslands leading toward the Alakari Mountains off in the far distance. Looking out over the landscape before him in the rising dawn, Conrad recognized that he had stood here in his dream. He felt heat press against his back, creeping into his skin. Investigating the source of the warm moist heat, Conrad discovered small ruins hidden among a rocky cavern that beckoned for him to enter. The calling grew stronger; the heat invaded his lungs and drew him deeper. The symbols written upon the pillars and walls as he entered were all vaguely similar. Upon entering the main chamber and witnessing the largest symbol on the opposing wall, the memories snapped into place. He was sure none could forget it once they gazed upon it. It was the same one carved on the wall in the temple cavern in which he had found Sven in the Desert of Lost Souls. Large and imposing, just as he remembered it, it had been painted on the wall above a chasm that fell to the depths of the world.

Two red triangles intertwined in a twisting of sharp barbs fought one another like a nest of snakes. Focusing upon any portion of the symbol, the other arms moved, despite being carved into the stone. The symbol appeared to fight with itself in an eternal struggle. Violent darkness invaded his soul as he looked at it.

On their trip back home, Conrad had made the mistake of asking his brother if he had ever ventured down into what lay beneath the sand. He rubbed his jaw in memory of that mistake. Sven's lash had dropped Conrad to the sand, and three successive blows had left him wide-eyed. The sudden burst of violence left Conrad bloodied, but his brother's eyes were wide with fear and his limbs trembled. No other response provided a clearer answer; whatever lay down there had frightened even the unshakable Sven to the core.

"Cass." He turned to his friend, looking him in the eye, and pointed several times toward the mute. "Under no circumstances are you to follow me—you wait here until I return. Do you understand?"

Cassidus looked down into the depths with wide eyes, nodding emphatically toward his master. He slowly backed out of the cave to resume setting his camp upon the rock face. He looked back at Conrad only once.

"What did you face in the depths, Sven?" Conrad asked aloud, his voice echoing down the cavern shaft. The thought of turning back crossed his mind but dissipated quickly as he thought about his sibling, desiring to know and understand what happened to him. Something taunted him from the depths, feeding his inquisitiveness. Picking up the heavy chain wrapped around two scripted columns, he slowly rappelled himself down along the cliff face, disappearing into the darkness.

Chapter 8
Frederick's Concession

The tent door flapped in the stiff breeze, the cold winds coming off the Alakari mountain peaks chilling Frederick to the bone. Squeezing the leather hilt of his sword tightly as he sat within the darkness of the tent, his left hand ached with stiffness. He had refused to let go of his sword for days. His eyes were exhausted from staring at the door, but his nerves refused to grant them sleep.

Damn Sven. Damn him to death for all the terrible things he had done to his family. Frederick knew that it was his brother who had brought chaos to his father's land. Wherever his brother walked, nothing but death and destruction followed. Hearing the cry of his small daughter in the back room of the tent, Frederick thanked all that was holy that his wife and daughter survived the mayhem.

The soldiers of the Northern Armies had split into two very distinct camps upon hearing the news of his father's death. The devout followers of the Order staunchly denied the allegations that the Order would commit such an atrocity. The nonbelievers wanted blood and revenge for what they believed to be the ultimate betrayal.

The commanding officers had tried to regain control of the situation, but with many of them as divided as their army, it was hopeless. Frederick had been forced to place his grief aside to intervene, commanding his men to maintain control of their emotions. He preached patience as they waited for further news, but when he spoke about support for the Order, death ensued.

Without warning, the situation had torn out of control as comrades turned upon one another. A Metzonian swordsman had hacked the head off an Order follower who argued before him, igniting the fire that would swirl through the camp. Chaos ran rampant throughout the northern camp deep into the early morning hours until the last of the Order followers chased their opponents into the darkness.

Upon the cold dawn of the next day, Frederick had witnessed the remnants of the army's winter camp. The charred remains of tents surrounded those splattered with blood from the bodies that filled the laneways of the camp. Survivors huddled around small fires in the midst of the grisly camp, shivering in the stiff breeze, waiting for their enemy to return.

Frederick knew his brother would return too. Sven was never one to worry about getting his hands bloody and always finished the job. He would come because Sven knew Frederick would never stand beside him; it was only a question of when. Or perhaps they would starve or freeze to death before winter truly broke its grip upon them.

The memory of Sven calling him a pathetic coward as Frederick's own soldiers joined Sven's in their march across the bridge into Chilsa would always remain. Frederick had told his father that they should have left Sven to his fate when he charged into Chilsa, should have left Sven to die for what he did. Instead they got to witness the bloody murder he caused as they marched through the fields of death. Surrounded by the Imperial Army, battalion after battalion charged against the undefeatable Sven. Ten thousand Metzonians died. With twice as many Chilsa surrounding him, Sven had simply stood there, drenched in his enemies' blood, as they had rode past to negotiate a peace.

The emperor cursed and screamed and demanded Sven to be turned over. The torture the vile emperor had wanted to unleash upon his brother was terrible, but as Frederick had looked around at the death behind them, he understood why. But their father simply sat there atop Metzotto, looking down upon them all, shaking his head, refusing to give up his son despite what he had done.

And now his father was gone.

The flaps of the tent swung toward him as a figure pushed his way in, startling Frederick from his thoughts. Levelling his sword at the unexpected newcomer as he stood, he noticed how terribly his arm shook. Trying to steady himself, Frederick lowered his voice as he called out across the darkened tent, "Have you come to finish the job?"

The face of the figure remained a shadow beneath the thick grey furs draped over his head as protection from the cold. Raising his hands before him, the figure spoke. "I walked through fields of frozen Metzonian blood that was the Northern Armies. Before that I was forced to wade through the seas of blood that filled your father's golden halls within Metzor. I have seen too much blood spilt this week, my prince."

"Am I mistaken and the rumors of the Order murdering my father are true? How does it work that you live while my father does not! Huh, Karl? You riddle me that one and tell me how it all works!" Frederick moved forward, grabbing the man by the face, pressing the tip of his blade against his throat.

Kallisto did not move, remaining calm as he always had—exactly how Frederick's father had been his whole life. "The Heavens did not call upon my soul yet. My job upon this world is not over, it would seem. I failed in my promise to protect your father; I cannot fail in my last promise to protect his children."

Frederick stood there staring at the old man, holding his life upon the tip of his sword.

Another figure burst through the tent, followed by a second smaller figure rushing in from the cold. The bald, scarred head of Brandon Dubryst rose over the edge of Kallisto's shoulder to observe the situation. "Get a hold of yourself, son. We aren't here to kill you. If we were, do you think we would come in the afternoon and use your front door?"

Placing his thick hands upon the blade and slowly forcing it away from Kallisto's throat, Dubryst patted Frederick several times on the arm. "We come with hearts filled with grief at the loss of your father. Undoubtedly you feel much worse; we all know how close the both of you were. We all loved Masen, and the nation grieves with you."

Frederick took several steps back, grasping his chair as he lowered himself into it, refusing to relinquish his grip upon the sword.

"Breathe, Frederick." Kallisto removed his hood and stepped into the room, leaving the female companion standing at the door. He grabbed a chair from the edge of the room, and Frederick watched him place it not three feet before him. "We are terribly sorry for what has happened to you, Frederick. As Brandon said, our hearts are filled with grief to see you in this position."

"This position? I'm an outcast in my own nation! A thousand miles away from home in some remote village on the run for my life! Why? Because I defended the godforsaken Order. I sided with the religious instead of my own people because it felt like the right decision. Look what it got me.

"But everyone only cares about what Sven did for them! They love him more than me despite everything he has done to them. All I have ever wanted was to be loved like him. Children who pretend to be princes never pick being me. They must be Sven, the Divine Destroyer or the Fist. The men do not talk boldly about me within the taverns over their ales; they talk about the stories of Sven from over five years ago!

"What about me, Karl? I did everything right! I followed my father's beliefs, and now I am the outcast. I make the proper choices, the right decisions, what is best for those around me, but no one cares or notices.

"No one loved my father as much as me, and where am I when they commit his body back to the heavens? My father is to be burnt upon the plains of the Numelli, and I cannot be there to say goodbye! How do you think that makes me feel?"

His daughter's screams replaced the tense quiet after his rant. Hearing her cry caused his anger to grow, and he picked up the chair and smashed it against the ground until only splinters were left. Wiping away a couple tears, his heart pumped hard with uncontrollable anger as he paced throughout the room.

"Alexandra, would you please go help young Lady Metz with her daughter? Perhaps the two of you could take a walk to the inn …"

"No, my wife and daughter stay within this tent, where I can keep an eye on both of them!" Frederick moved across the tent, blocking the doorway to the secondary room. The woman halted in her tracks, looking toward her two companions for a response.

"Relax, Frederick," Dubryst said, leaning against the tent wall, rolling a bottle of wine within his thick hands. "The Elite have this small village completely sealed …"

"Just as the Royal Elite had my father protected?" Frederick snapped, getting no reaction from the Elite general, who set the wine bottle down on the table. Holding his hand up to stop conversation, Kallisto turned toward Alexandra again, restructuring his command.

"Would you please go help Lady Metz? Keep her company if you would, please?"

Frederick watched the thin woman carefully slide around him and slip silently into the second room of the tent. Brandon picked up a second chair in one hand as he kicked the debris of Frederick's shattered chair away before setting it in the exact spot.

"Please. Sit with me. I cannot say that I know how you feel, Frederick. The last month has most certainly been unkind to you, with the passing of both parents. Unfortunately, I have to move beyond those events and look toward your future and the safety of those who continue to follow you, the rightful king."

As there were no other chairs remaining within the tent, Dubryst dragged a large wooden trunk beside them and sat. "While your brother may indeed be the brightest star within the sky, souls like his burn extremely hot and as a result burn up quickly. Your soul is the quieter and softer type that remains constant throughout the turmoil of the universe. The people of Metzor may be drawn to Sven, but when they feel the heat and unpredictability he gives off, they will discover the danger. In time, they will return to their rightful spot before you."

"What we are saying is that you remain true to your beliefs. Do not change without due cause. You have supported the Order because you know such tales of betrayal are not true. Continue to do so. Call Sven out for his deceit and what he has done." Kallisto leaned back in his seat as Frederick contemplated the implications of what the two men asked of him.

"You want me to tell the nation that Sven was the one who slew my father? Tell me, who are they going to believe? This is all Conrad's fault. What was he thinking, going to retrieve him from the desert? How in the hell did Sven survive that long in the desert anyway, Karl?"

Hearing that Conrad had risked his life foolishly in the desert had made both Frederick and their father furious. Hearing that Conrad had, against all odds, actually found Sven still alive filled him with dread, knowing the effect his brother had upon everyone.

"I do not know, Frederick. To be truthful, I am quite scared to think about how, but we may never know." Frederick watched Kallisto shake his head in confusion. "I do, however, believe that I understand what happened in Metzor. And I believe I know roughly what your brother's plan consists of. All his actions hinge upon blaming the Order of the Fallen for the death of your father."

"Why the Order? Why not a known enemy, like the Chilsa?"

"I assume it was simply because the scenario presented itself to him. We had placed Fallen loyalists among the ranks of the Elite, including in your father's personal guard. You must understand that many of them had been with your father from the beginning. Having them amongst the ranks allowed us to protect one of the Order's most valuable assets in maintaining a calm peace. Sven somehow discovered the fact and used it to his benefit."

Kallisto reached into his cloak and pulled out a long bundle of black cloth wrapped tightly with leather cord. Frederick accepted the bundle, feeling the weight within it. As he placed it across the wooden arms of the chair, he already knew what it was. He unfolded the black Elite banner it was wrapped within, and his father's golden sword glittered in the dim light.

"The Mirage of Metzor is a sign of the true ruler of the Metzonian people. Fortune fell upon us when I was able to ensure that Sven's fists will never clench such a weapon. Your father would have wished for you to have it, knowing that you would use it wisely."

Frederick flipped the blade over in the palm of his hand, feeling the sharp edges scrape against his flesh. He had admired his father's sword for as long as he could remember; now he held it within his hands. His father had been so skilled with the blade; witnesses said the blade was a golden blur as his enemies collapsed around him on the battlefield.

"Thousands may not have seen the blade, but I swear that Sven shall see it and feel it. I will avenge our father. If Sven wants a war, I shall give him a war, and people will see their mistake in choosing Sven." Frederick grinned at the thought of engaging his brother on the battlefield. It would be a chance to prove to everyone that he was just as great as his father, and even more so than his brothers.

"You cannot engage Sven on the open field." Dubryst spoke quietly, refusing to meet Frederick's eyes. "You cannot defeat Sven on the open field of battle."

"And why not? I have the Elite and the remains of the Northern Armies at my command. Certainly there are many others out there who would flock to my banner as I reclaim my birthright. Tell me—why am I not allowed to kill my brother on the battlefield for what he has done?"

"You know damn well why!" The general's outburst startled Frederick, jerking him back. "Your brother is his strongest when he is at war. Violence is his fuel, and if you give him the civil war that he desires, there will be no stopping him. You must steal his passion; wear away his great assets by letting him sit upon the throne of Metzor. Dealing with the tedious and boring matters of running a kingdom will unduly wear him down until his people see who he truly is."

"Such a plan could take years, even decades. After such a time people will not be able to do anything about it anyway. My name will not be called when begging for a saviour after I have been in exile for ten years. I refuse to be forgotten or to allow Sven what he wants. How can I run and hide?"

Kallisto nodded, holding up his hands to acknowledge the flaws within his plan. Frederick looked back at the blade. The advisor tried to sway him to look at the problems in a different light.

"Think of it as surviving. Be patient. Show your support for those who your father once served. The Elders of Prokopolis will not simply condone your brother if he continues to persecute members of the Order of the Fallen and their supporters. The silver shields of the Fallen will march against him in full force, an enemy he will regret."

"But do you truly know that he will? Sven may be bold and reckless, but he is far from stupid."

"I do not. How can he sell the idea of peace to the citizens with his father's supposed murderers? How can he confess to the citizens that it was he who killed their beloved king? If you would take my advice, it is this. Do what is right for the future, and protect yourself. Save your strength and that of your followers so you may fight when it best suits you. March your loyal followers into the Alakari with me."

"The Alakari? You tell me that I will die upon the battlefield against my brother, yet you would have me freeze to death in the Alakari? Have you felt how cold it is outside—it's barely spring!" Laughing at the absurd suggestion, Frederick started to get up, but Kallisto grabbed him by the arm, forcing him to sit as he leaned closer.

"The Order has a sanctuary hidden within its heart, a place for us all to regroup and rest. Secrecy is its greatest asset though, only those of the Order may come and go, and even then it is rarely allowed. Because you are all Metzonians, any man who chooses to follow you will never again be allowed to leave its safety until such a time as the Order allows it. Could be years, could be lifetimes. Who is to say what the world will bring? But I believe that when the Order marches to war, and I promise you they will, you will lead your men out from the Sacred City to join them. Until then, survive and be safe."

"Frederick, please." Turning within his chair, Frederick saw his young wife stepping forth with tears in her eyes. Hesitantly his wife clutched his arm as she lowered herself to her knees. "Raise your family within the safety this man is offering you. Your daughter needs a father to raise her; I need a husband to love. Your people need their proper king, but they need him alive."

Staring at the blade within his hands, Frederick could hear his father's words in the back of his mind, reminding him to place his people above his own desires. His father, so calm and strong in his decision making, always seemed to know what to do. Frederick rarely saw him make a mistake, and the one he did make ended up costing him his life. Despite his father's best attempts to teach him how to make those choices, Frederick had never been able to grasp that unbreakable confidence. Fear of making the wrong decision plagued him at every corner. How could he be expected to make a decision of this magnitude? Looking into the tearful eyes of his wife and the steady unblinking eyes of the two men, he could feel the pressure.

"Do I have time to think about it? How would you manage to smuggle what remains of my army into your sanctuary?"

"In six days' time, the moon wanes into darkness. It is in that time when I will lead your men through torchlight. We will only travel the road in the darkness. It is a treacherous trail, but it is the only way I will allow this journey to progress, at least for the first several days.

"If we go down this road, Frederick, there is no turning back. The sleepless rangers control all who move to and fro within the passes. Any who turn back will never see the golden plains again, nor will they see the morning dawn. Do you understand what I am telling you?"

Frederick understood perfectly well. He doubted any deserters would ever see their killers.

Chapter 9
Grief and Rage

A soft breeze rippled through the tall golden grasses of the Numelli plains that stretched out before the city of Metzor. Conrad watched in silence, as did the rest of the crowd, awaiting the arrival of the last member of the funeral gathering.

The arrangements for the funeral were expansive, which was suitable to the significance of the event. Guidelines for the funeral had been issued by Sven; his father would not lay within the cathedral of his murderers. Far from the walls, in the middle of the open fields, the stone masons had erected a twenty-foot-tall stone bier to place their fallen king upon. King Masen would burn upon the golden plains he had spilt his own blood to free.

Conrad walked down the cobblestone road behind the royal guard as they brought his father out from the city. Conrad doubted there was a single citizen left in the city. All were lined upon the east side of the road between gate and bier, awaiting the procession.

Looking across the narrow road away from the citizens, he saw an endless sea of Metzonian soldiery, those who had been held within the city as well as those that had marched to the capital to pay tribute toward their fallen king. The evidence of the power that his father once wielded was stretched across the horizon. Their king may have been murdered, but Conrad believed his people would undoubtedly seek revenge for such actions.

Standing before what remained of his father, the magnitude of the situation was starting to seize him. The death was an unexpected low point within Conrad's life, an event that had arrived far too soon for him. Not a month before he had lost his mother. Being unable to be at her side as she discovered what lay beyond mortality had been a severe blow. Now he was forced to bear the burden of not being there for his father as well.

Many memories had come forth, but in so many he was merely a spectator. His father spent much of his life trying to calm the storms of passion within Sven and nurturing Frederick to someday take his place, and Conrad often felt neglected. Their relationship had never been a bad one; it had been loving and happy. There just never seemed to be enough time left over when it was all said and done. This left him wondering if his father had ever felt such regret as he did.

No one had come forth to console Conrad, nor had he seen his brother for the past two days. Like a wolf on the scent of blood, Sven had stalked through the city, no other thought upon his mind than to find their father's murderers. Much of the city had already been ravaged greatly; the Order of the Fallen took the brunt of Sven's rage.

Gazing into the distance, Conrad was glad that his brother had seen though his blood lust to arrange his father's funeral. Walking along the road between the population, Conrad recognized it as the same road that father and son had confronted each other upon. The road had changed both men implicitly, Sven now walked down it with a greater purpose than before. Confident and strong, he would stand tall for his father's people because their rightful king had abandoned them. Watching him, Conrad realized he had traded one brother for another.

Conrad was unsure whether he completely believed the allegations that had been made against the Order. Despite the word of his brother and the remaining Royal Elite, it was tough for him to accept such a bold and outlandish statement. The Order of the Fallen had repeatedly declared that they had nothing to do with the death of the king, urging patience and clear thinking. Conrad did not believe there was any motive behind such a maneuver without the evidence Sven promised to reveal to him. Perhaps the more startling of recent events was rumour that Frederick appeared to be a prime player amongst the chaos and death. Word had spread across the nation of Metzon that Frederick had thrown his support fully behind the now persecuted Order of the Fallen and balked at all allegations laid against them. Declaring his right to the throne as the first-born, Frederick was prepared to take his place.

Sven declared that he would never allow him to sit upon their father's throne whilst Frederick continued his support for those who had slain their father. Frederick simply declared all of Sven's claims and accusations as wild and outlandish, despite his presence within the throne room when it happened. Frederick would fight for the Order as their father once had, even if it meant war against his brothers.

Conrad knew it would be a mistake to play directly into Sven's hands. Sven was the son of war, and the possibility of a brutal and bloody civil war did not daunt him.

Sven climbed the wooden staircase to the top, having arrived for the funeral before they lit the pyre to reduce their father's body to ash. Draped in his black fur cloak, with his golden chain and Metzonian crest dangling outside it, his eyes were barely visible beneath the large black hood pulled over his head despite the heat.

The two stood side by side, brother to brother, before their fallen father. Masen had been wrapped within his golden cloak, his arms folded across his chest. The Metz lay atop the bier prepared for his final journey, awaiting only flame. No crown or swords, as the kings of old were often buried with, were upon his body. The man who raised them had always said that he would leave this world the way he came into it, naked, with nothing.

"I found the answers I searched for, brother." Conrad did not respond to Sven's whispers. His eyes stared straight ahead as the priests of the old religion began to speak out over the crowds. Believing it hardly the proper time to discuss such thing, Conrad was forced to listen.

"There shall be no more doubt. You know how great a man our father was, do you not?" Conrad had nodded in response to Sven's question, wiping away several tears. "Such greatness among Humanity causes others to fear those who wield it. The Order feared that Metzon had grown too strong and worried about losing their power and influence upon all of Humanity. Fear of that strength was what led to his death, an elimination of someone who had grown too powerful. Even I feared him, having felt the power of his shadow more than any others."

Sven's words made sense to Conrad, knowing how strained the relationship had grown between his father and the Order. Even more so, he understood how strained the relationship between brother and father had been. Surely at this point in time, Sven had finally forgiven his father for what he had done. It had not been done to hurt Sven so deeply; it was a simple mistake.

"I know that the both of you argued all the time, and you did not always see eye to eye with Father, but I hope that you know that he loved you more than you know."

Sven stood, silently staring at the body of their father, no tears or emotion upon his face.

"I overheard him speaking with Mother one night about you. She pled for your case, trying to get him to go and bring you back from the desert himself. I was so hopeful that he would go bring you back, but he couldn't. He told our beloved mother, 'You do not understand. I have made the mistakes of free-flowing emotion, and the end result was my loss of everything I had once held dear. I have no desire to let my children make the same mistakes as I did or being forced to spend a lifetime attempting to make up for those mistakes as I have.' Everything he did was out of love, even if it seemed harsh."

His tears fell freely; Conrad at last understood his father. Every memory of his father had coincided with the fact that it was love that drove his father through life, making him do what he had to. Looking over at his brother, he saw that none of his words had moved him, filling Conrad with rage at his brother's insensitivity.

"How can you stand there like that? We lost our father! The man who only ever sought to protect and prepare us for the world ahead of us and the challenges we would face. Despite the large loss of our father, you now seek the death of our only other brother because he has chosen a side that our father has instilled upon his soul. Yet you stand emotionless, not a single tear for your father. I doubt there will be one for Frederick either. Do you not feel anything anymore?"

Sven remained motionless for several long seconds before he at last turned away from their father, letting Conrad gaze into the depths of his eyes. Emptiness filled their black depths; nothing shone within his brother anymore, leaving an empty soul and his own bleary-eyed reflection within the abyss.

"I lost all feeling a long time ago, Con. I lost much more than just emotion when wandering the Desert of Lost Souls. One who lives with torment and suffering for long enough learns not to feel, for if you feel then death finds you quickly. When you realize that certain tragedies make you stronger, grief is for the past. You turn your grief to anger. Turn that anger upon those who brought this grief into your world. One cannot look upon the past at what was or could have been." Sven's voice sounded distant, drifting off slowly before it came back powerfully. "One cannot change the past, so there is no point in pondering it, little brother. One can only ever move forward."

Conrad had stopped to contemplate the words that his brother spoke, astonished by the wisdom within them. It made him look at his brother once more in the new light of the great strength once embodied by the man who was about to burn before them.

"I have a gift to give to you that I think our father would have wished you to have." Sven stretched his hand forward, dropping two objects into the palm of Conrad's hand. Fondling the two small objects among the lines of his thick hands, he recognized both items with great emotion.

The first was a white steel ring, the Ring of the Order, given to those who serve the Order of the Fallen with great skill and even greater honour. A ring demonstrating loyalty given to those whom served the Order for decades. The second was a plain golden band. He recognized it as his father's wedding band, which he had worn every day since his wedding, past the death of his wife, until his own fate claimed him.

"The first represents where our father started, Conrad, a servant of the Order to which he was forever loyal. The second represents the catalyst that saw him break free of the restraints placed upon his heart, allowing him to see the light of his destiny. The spark that gave our father the courage to pursue his own dreams. They were his greatest possessions; you should have them and wear them proudly."

Sven opened up his brother's right hand and placed the rings on the exact fingers his father used to wear the rings upon: the white upon his forefinger, the gold upon his ring finger. "Upon your knees, with your hands pressed against the dirt in submission, you first see the Ring of the Order. A ring of strict obedience and servitude, your soul serving their purpose and theirs alone. The second represents your heart, which always comes second to the Order and the so-called 'greater purpose' they claim they work for.

"But tell me what happens when you look into the palms of your hands, Con? The palms that hold the power to shape the destiny you desire and carry you ever forward."

Conrad looked into his hands, seeing what his brother was trying to impress upon him. Service and obedience came second to one's own will and desire, secondary to what Conrad wanted his life to represent and become. Conrad stared at his trembling hand as he rotated it from the back to the palm and back again. His hand clad with the rings looked identical to his father's, the same hands that had often carried him, encouraged him and raised his chin so he would look up at him. Raising his chin once more, he blinked back several more tears and took a long breath, letting it whisper out through tight lips.

Two torches were handed to them by Conrad's personal servant, Cassidus. Each took a side and plunged the steel into the bottom of the pile of wood, leaving them to ignite as they returned to their places. Conrad looked upon the face of his father one last time in great pain, knowing that he would no longer be there to protect them or guide them with his wise words and great vision.

"You are going to make them pay for his death, aren't you?"

Sven did not answer him right away. He watched the flames flicker around the base of the pyre underneath their father instead. The flames rose through the piled wood rapidly, the crackling of the flames spreading like the billowing smoke rising high into the clear sky. Watching the orange embers and ash rise up from the pyre as it turned into an inferno, Sven broke his silence.

"I am going to bring about events that will fill their minds with horrors that the Fallen have forgotten exist. There are things I know and have discovered that will tear apart the supposed 'righteous world' the Order has created upon this world. I will teach them the error in the things they have done, as well as how high a Metz can truly rise when unrestrained."

Turning around to face the crowd, Sven climbed atop the small stage, spreading his arms out to address the people of Metzor, speaking with a commanding authority. Conrad listened to his voice carry across the crowd.

"Brothers! Sisters! I thank you all for coming to share our grief with us. Our burden is lighter knowing our family is so large and willing to help lift us back on our feet. You are all sons and daughters of my great father as much as my brother or I are. Reaching down and picking you out of the dirt, he led you and your parents out of the darkness cast over you all by the Cruel King. Caring about your hopes and dreams, he loved your children as much as he loved each and every one of you.

"But now a danger looms near, threatening to take it all away, after all you have suffered to finally receive such freedom. It pains me to think of such a fateful action occurring." Sven paused, the silence filled by the crackling of the flames as the people waited for him to continue his speech.

"The Order of the Fallen claims they are the divine from Heaven itself who have come to show us the way. Claiming to care about our dreams and our fates, they believe they know what is best for Humanity. A responsibility that we did not ask them to take on, nor do we require them to. Their Elders say they are here to show us how to live a proper life with faith and righteousness that will see us delivered to the White Cities of Heaven. A glorious realm, that they themselves were cast out from for sins they will not tell. But look what happens when a mortal rises above what they deem appropriate.

"Metzonians have always been the strongest of Humanity. We are the most powerful and determined of mortals; we are lions among young lambs. None can break the might of our spirits or drag us from our dreams. But now our enemies threaten to try just that, to pull us back as their plan progresses. Even now they wish to brainwash my brother against me, to unleash a great civil war that shall slay our soldiers, fill our children with fear and tear apart everything that my parents had built for all of us. The Fist that has protected you once before shall not let the Order punish you for reaching greatness.

"It is time that we take back our own destiny! It shall not be dictated by those who claim to have fallen from the sky! Who are they to claim that they know what is best for Humanity! My father freed you all from the evil, but he only began what I hope to finish. I ask all of you now to follow me upon my quest to free the rest of Humanity from their oppressive chains. What say you? Let the strength of Humanity break free at last to its rightful place. Humanity shall take its place alongside the eternal kingdoms of Heaven and Hell, and that moment shall be now!"

Chills swept through Conrad's body as he watched Sven scream and pound his fists into his chest, turning his people's grief into anger at those who had brought this upon them. Both groups of the crowd cheered and screamed approval. The front of the crowd began chanting Sven's name, spreading like a wildfire across the plains.

Rousing the spirits of men as Sven had just done astonished Conrad, leaving him wondering where the great orator had come from. Their father had never been a man of great speaking ability; he led through great action and wise words. Sven suddenly had his father's loyal subjects reignited and craving more.

But Sven turned away, returning back to the side of his brother, staring out across the cheering population. Emotion was far from Sven's face as he watched with an eerie calmness, leaving Conrad to ask, "What are you going to do?"

"I'm going to show you." A small smirk and a raised eyebrow unexpectedly crossed Sven's face before he turned away from Conrad and walked back down the steps, leaving him once again alone.

Watching his brother smoothly descend the staircase, Conrad couldn't believe what was happening.

If the Order had not questioned the implications of their actions to remove his father from power initially, they would have certainly soon realized their mistake. Perhaps his father had exceeded beyond what the Order had intended for him, but he was stable, strong and loyal. If Frederick had taken over, as was expected, it would have been a much different fate for the Order: survival and continued prosperity that could have lasted for decades.

Following closely behind his brother, Conrad began the long walk back to Metzor. With all eyes upon Sven, Conrad turned to look back to the flames that carried the ashes high overhead and into the setting sun, marking the passing of an equally golden king. The appearance of a new king coming forth in the pending darkness still left an unshakeable cold feeling within Conrad's heart.

Conflict burnt within Conrad as he mulled the same questions over and over within his head. He did not know what to believe anymore, what was the truth and what was false. Insanity would be his fate if he did not figure out how he felt about what was occurring around him. His unexpected trip to the Lost Mountain had only intensified the emotional battlefield within his mind.

With every passing day, Conrad felt himself swinging ever more under Sven's magnetic shadow. So sure of what he was doing, so fearless, it left little time to ponder if he was at all wrong. What if it had been the Chilsa? What if Kallisto had acted with a small group? Was the world to suffer because of one man?

His doubt had increased since his trip. Amnesia had struck Conrad, leaving him with little recollection of what happened upon the lonely mountain. Had he lost his footing and fallen down the shaft? Had something attacked him within the depths when he was unconscious? Coming forth from the darkness, he had awoken as Cassidus dragged him roughly down the rocky path at a dangerous pace. White with fear, his friend had looked like a ghost in the night, breathing heavily from the exertion of dragging Conrad's limp body behind him.

Casually looking behind him, Conrad noticed that night's

events still hung heavily upon Cassidus's mind; the man was walking several steps farther behind him than usual. His colour had returned, but fear was still running rampant within him. His eyes shifted nervously. Conrad had tried to set him at ease, repeatedly thanking him for saving him, or whatever he had done. Whatever had happened, Conrad was still in one piece, frustrated that his friend couldn't tell him what had actually happened.

When they arrived at the castle, Sven told Conrad to clean himself up before meeting him within his new throne room. Excited to see exactly what his brother had uncovered in his madness, Conrad broke away quickly, with Cassidus closely following. What could his brother possibly have in store for the Order that would bring the most powerful organization to the breaking point? The questions gnawed at him; something within him eagerly wanted to know the answers. Needing to discover if his suspicions about Sven's plans were true or not, Conrad halted his train of thought. What suspicions did he have?

Trying to cut a shorter path by passing through the diplomatic chamber wing of the palace, the diplomatic guard halted Cassidus and him, barring their entry. Pausing at the tall doors, he looked around the corridor at the two dozen men guarding the second inner entrance. Pushing through the men, Conrad thrust the tall doors open to see what was hiding behind them.

Commander Aerox stood before him, surrounded by dozens of his newly formed unit standing around the entrances. His brother had dismantled the Royal Elite for their failure to properly protect their father, implementing a new, more exclusive ranked group of guards to follow him appropriately called the Shadow Guard.

A figure stood in the middle of the room, his tall lanky frame draped in a tight-fitting tunic of royal blue, his white caped shoulder bearing the snow eagle of Chilsa. Dozens more stood silently on the golden carpet set in the middle of the room, eyes upon the new intruder. The white falcon upon the man's shoulder shrieked at the new intruder.

Conrad's felt his stomach contort hard within his guts, nearly causing him to vomit at the sight of the man before him. Staggering back, he moved to draw his sword, but Aerox slammed his hand down upon his hand, holding it firmly.

"You know better than this, my prince. Swords are not drawn within diplomatic chambers. The Chilsa are our guests, and your brother swore an oath of safe passage."

Conrad roughly shoved Aerox back in disgust, leaving his sword within its sheath. Emperor Kristolphe shrugged his shoulders and smirked at Conrad, knowing he was perfectly safe within the heart of Metzor. As long as he remained on the carpet placed in the center of the chamber, Conrad could not touch him without grave consequences.

"Stay here. If this bastard moves an inch from that rug, you cut him down where he stands!" Conrad growled at Cassidus. The smaller man nodded, placing his arms across his chest. "My brother has some explaining to do!"

Storming through the hallways, Conrad moved unnoticed through the castle, working his way ever downward to where Sven had allocated his new throne room. The new king preferred the darkness and drab surroundings to the light and splendour of his father's chambers higher in the keep. Perhaps he fled the memories of that day, but how could he not remember what the Chilsa had done to their people? What they did to Sven himself?

Conrad's emotions raged within him, his nausea turning to anger in the wake of this new information. He was surprised, as he had never felt this confident or certain of himself before, particularly when confronting Sven. Storming through the final hallway and brushing aside the guard who tried to stop him, his mind was set on the heavy door at the end of the hallway.

Hearing laughter through the door, he knocked both doors open with stiff arms. His brother slouched in the oversized throne, looking displeased at the sudden interruption. Clad only in his lower armour, his broad chest was bare except for the heavy medallion he never removed. A young woman draped in the emperor's colours sat on a small stool off to Sven's right, also looking displeased at such a display of rudeness. She quickly turned away, and he watched her readjusting herself and pinning her hair back up.

Conrad was unsurprised by the sight of his brother with the woman he assumed was the emperor's wife. Sven's habit of taking what he wanted with no regard to those around him had consistently landed him and everyone around him in deep trouble. He was powerful enough that few challenged him; it was always the rest of his family that had to bear the brunt of the anger.

He wondered only briefly about how Emperor Kristolphe had not noticed his wife detach herself from him and work through the Metzonian castle back to the throne room. Chilsa nobility within the capital of Metzor was rare, but never had the emperor himself been there. Times had obviously changed in the week since his father's death.

"What in the name of *Hell* do you think you're doing, little brother?" Anger boiled in his brother's voice as Conrad continued forward, prepared to grab his brother by the throat. Instinctively halting just short of Sven's reach, Conrad released his anger by screaming at him.

"What the hell do you think you are doing? Our father is dead not even a week and there are Chilsa running freely around his castle! You tell me what the Hell you're doing before I take your head." Conrad's arms trembled noticeably as he clenched the sword in his right hand, trying to keep himself under control.

"I dare you to try, little brother!" Rising from his seat, Sven pumped his chest forward, daring Conrad to take the first swing, knowing it would be his last. Taking another step back, Conrad looked away from his brother as his false confidence dissipated.

Seeing his brother back down, Sven, not taking his eyes from Conrad, seemed to settle slightly.

"You know me and my beliefs, brother. You have seen what I am capable of doing with the simple power that I wield within my heart and hands." Sven raised his hands up to look in their palms, a grin spreading across his face as he did. His eyes appeared unfocused as he looked up at Conrad, "I intend to change the world. But for what I wish to accomplish, I can no longer simply destroy all of my enemies. And the Chilsa have offered me something special, something that I require."

"Whatever the Chilsa offered to deliver you will be falsely promised, Sven! You should understand this as well as anyone. The Order stabbed us in the back, but the Chilsa will just as quickly slide their blade into your heart as they look you in the eye! I am not going to stand by while you ally us with Neurus," Conrad interjected, kicking the stool across the room, not believing the path his brother was intending to take.

"Old Emperor Neurus has been dead for three years already, Prince Conrad." His brother's female companion spoke from her corner, pulling the strings of her corset tight once again. Looking over her bare shoulder, she remarked, "The empire is vastly different from the way it once was."

"So you claim." Conrad turned away from the woman and stabbed his fingers in Sven's face. "I do not see how your sleeping with Emperor Kristolphe's wife will help improve Chilsa-Metzonian relations."

Sven glanced over his shoulder toward the woman, chuckling low in his throat. "You are the emperor's wife? Marrying your brother always has been a Chilsa thing, hasn't it?"

The blonde gave his brother a sarcastic smirk as Conrad recognized her face as the Empress Belle. "My brother and I wish to express our condolences to your family. Granted, our fathers were two very different men, but the loss is undoubtedly as real for you as it was for us. We only wish to help you extract revenge upon those that did this to you."

"Why?" Conrad screamed in her face before changing his mind. "Actually, no! You shut your mouth. I don't want to hear whatever lies and blasphemy you have to spout!"

"Who do you think murdered our father, Conrad?" the woman whispered, looking at the floor, raising only her eyes to stare at him.

"Dying of old age can hardly be considered murder. Or, and this idea may be ridiculous, perhaps it was the thousands of enemies he acquired over the years while committing his own damned murderous atrocities." Conrad turned away before the urge to hit her overtook him. Sven smiled, lifting the cup of wine to his lips.

"Our interrogation of the ambassador turned up a lot of interesting information. As it turns out, our Ambassador Alessyn was quite a world traveller, with a unique skill set. Living in the bridged city of Nykol deep in the heart of Kyllordia, our friend Alessyn quietly lived a simple life. The death of King Kyllone came within a few years, and mysteriously Alessyn was promoted to an ambassador position within the Order immediately after. His first new assignment was to New Chilsa four years ago; he remained there until the emperor mysteriously fell ill. Returning to his home in Kyllordia, he was offered a position as ambassador of the Order within the Metzonian Chapter exactly two years after the emperor's death. And here we sit."

"You make him sound like a master assassin. He was an old man!" Disgusted with the petty allegations the two were trying to convince him of, Conrad wondered how long the torture went on before the poor soul had confessed to that. How long had it lasted for his innocent daughter?

"Not himself—he was merely the organizer who made sure all the wheels turned perfectly. Kallisto remains the one who drove the dagger. Unfortunately, you pulling me out of the Desert screwed up their plans, forcing them to act sooner than they had planned. Frederick was supposed to sit upon this throne, not me." Sven rubbed the side of the golden throne, tapping his fingers against it.

"But look across the land now, and what do you see? I see three nations that do not have a king or emperor over the age of thirty. Three nations weakened significantly by the sudden loss of their leaders are ready to be swallowed in one decisive fatal war. Or so it would have been had I remained in the desert." Sven tipped back his head as he finished the last drops of wine from the glass.

"Already the Order marshals its armies, as well as your brother's loyalists, and begins to prepare to correct the mistake. With the nation split between two brothers, the Order will use all its influence to place Frederick back upon the Metzon throne. Their plans depend upon it." The empress's voice lowered down to a whisper. "They are coming to kill your brother, Conrad. His knowledge of their secret is all that remains between Humanity and the Fallen."

"Who's secret?"

"Who will lead the fight against the Order before they enslave us all? Is young Prince Raef as swift as his father was? Is your brother Frederick as bold as your father? Is my brother as absolutely ruthless as Neurus was? You will need all three nations beneath a single banner following a single leader who embodies all those traits. Do you know anyone with such qualities within this world?"

Conrad turned to look at Sven, sitting in his throne, holding his empty wine glass in his hands as Belle spoke. Not knowing who Belle was alluding to, Conrad watched his brother in his throne, awaiting his eventual death. Even with the entire Metzonian nation behind him, the strength of the Order's army was unparalleled. The Fallen would crush those who stood behind Sven until none remained.

"Devotz." Conrad did not know why he said it; the words just tumbled out of his mouth. Conrad suddenly felt cold; goose bumps rose on his arms as his vision grew cloudy. Before Conrad knew why, he was speaking once again, his tongue moving without any command from his conscious mind.

"The Sven of the Desert. One who causes *despair* among his enemies moments before he *decimates* and *destroys* them in single, vicious, *deadly* blow. Let us follow the *Devourer* of Souls himself, *Devortez Devitziko*, or, in the human tongue … Devotz. *Slave of Rhimmon*." Emphasis rolled hard off his tongue as his throat struggled to pronounce the unfamiliar language. Sven had frozen completely, not moving at all as Conrad pronounced the unfamiliar name.

In that moment, Conrad realized that he was not the only being within his mind. Something slithered beneath his skin, manipulating his mind and body. Glancing quickly up into Sven's face, their eyes locked upon each other, recognizing something within one another. Both parties reacted quickly, understanding life and death depended upon drastic action. Conrad felt himself thrust his sword toward his brother's bare chest, moving in for the kill.

A Mortal Mistake

The newly named Devotz snapped his torso sideways, letting the sword run through the back of the golden throne. His sharp left elbow smashed Conrad's face, causing Conrad to lose grip on his sword and fall back. A knee struck next, smashing into Conrad's chin, knocking him flat onto his back. His armoured body had hardly clattered to the ground before Sven was upon him, striking blows at Conrad's head. Desperately attempting to block them, Conrad struck out at his attacker. The back of his gauntleted hand struck across Sven's chin, sending the Metzonian ruler rolling back. Using the momentum, Sven rolled back to his feet with supernatural quickness.

"You fool! I thought I made it clear when I saved your life in the Desert of Lost Souls! Are you too stupid to understand what it truly took from me! Where is it?" The anger flowing through Sven's veins was visible to Conrad's new vision; muscles threatened to rip through his skin. Sven's booted foot crashed out high, kicking his brother straight in the chest. The forced slammed Conrad into the stone wall, only to be grabbed and thrown across the chamber into the opposite wall.

Howling curses filled Conrad's ears as his brother picked him up by his back armour plate and started shaking him. Conrad felt his brother strip the armour from his body piece by piece, like a ravenous dog tearing flesh from bone. Conrad struggled to no avail as his brother continued to dominate, stripping the final plate off, revealing what he was looking for.

"*Demousticus Konflixtikus* …" Speaking the demonic words, Sven's golden eyes filled with pain as he stepped back from his sibling. Dark tattoos and brands in ancient demonic scripture ran in lines around Conrad's body. Horror and betrayal were written upon Conrad's brother's face; rage coursed through his body as he realized how he had been betrayed.

As Sven twisted away, Conrad watched the demonic skull tattooed upon his brother's naked back crawl beneath his flesh. The demon's jagged teeth turned into a large grin as it began spreading its tendrils through its host's body; darkness turned Sven's veins black.

Lifting his hands before his face, Conrad let out a scream of horror as he watched darkness creep through his own veins. The darkness reached his fingers and spread beneath his father's wedding ring, halting before the silver ring of the Order. On his other hand, the skin began to turn grey as his veins continued to surge with black.

Memories of the darkness of the caves and the demons that lurked within them oozed to the surface of his mind: the agony as the demon stabbed his claws into the back of his rib cage, the burning as his dark taint seeped into his soul. He remembered how he climbed back up the chain, clinging to the edge of the cliff, screaming at the top of his lungs for Cassidus to help him.

"What have I done, Sven? Help me, please help me! Sven, please tell me what to do." Conrad's vision began to blacken, growing so narrow he could no longer see Sven. Demonic curses and screams of rage could be heard in the background; loose items were thrown against the walls. "Sven!"

Conrad struggled to get up, but his limbs felt numb and heavy, making him all but useless. His head flopped to the floor. He felt the cool stones upon his cheek, and he was able to see both Sven and Belle once again. Sven crouched on his hindquarters, clenched fists pressing hard against the floor as he rocked forward and backward. The darkness within his veins pushed forward several times, fighting against a resistance. Several groggy seconds passed before Conrad realized his brother was using every ounce of free will, trying desperately to not let it take him completely.

Slowly rising, Sven yanked Conrad's silver blade from their father's golden throne and inched closer toward Conrad, prepared to release his brother from his mistake.

Belle dashed quickly from the corner of the room where she had been watching the spectacle and quietly walked up behind Sven to slowly wrap her arms around his shoulders.

Eyeing the sword in Sven's trembling hand, Conrad watched as she wrapped her arms seductively over his brother's skin, seeming to know what the rage within him could do. Placing a hand upon

A Mortal Mistake

the hilt of his sword, Belle helped lower it, stroking Sven's jaw softly with the back of her other hand.

"Konflikt … it is a very powerful and righteous name, don't you think? Even the Devourer could use help from such a powerful ally. Who better than his own brother to help the Dark Prince's plans? Stay your hand. It is a gift—the pieces are coming into place now." She whispered into his ear, running her tongue along his earlobe.

Conrad watched her continue to try to stop Sven from releasing him from the darkness that had consumed him, smiling behind his brother's back. Conrad looked away from Belle to watch his sword clatter to the floor as the last of Sven's veins became overtaken by whatever had corrupted their souls. For the first time, Conrad saw what the desert had done to his brother, what his father's mistake of banishing him had done to his second-born. Conrad cringed to think that he had brought Sven out of the desert, unleashing the Devourer himself upon the world.

Before the darkness completely enveloped Conrad's mind, he spent his last moments questioning whether there was a way he could fix what he had done. Would he even remember what he needed to fix when he awoke, or would another bout of amnesia erase it? Would he wake up at all?

Chapter 10
Marching Orders

"What in the name of the Seven Hells was he thinking?"

"He should be drowned in the Lake of Heavenly Sorrow!"

"The bloody fool! Throw him from the top of the Lifebringer itself!"

The anger expressed during the council meeting was a shock to Militades, who had been forced to attend far too many, though he had never yet heard threats of death shouted within the Tower of Ori. Militades had chosen to stand along the top of the small amphitheatre chambers of the Elders' palace perched high overtop the acropolis. Briefly looking out the window, the old general gazed upon Prokopolis, switching to the western horizon, listening silently.

Slipping into the back corner of the Elder Council meeting, Militades noticed it did not take Kallen long to sense the tension in the air. "The Elders are worked up like a hornets' nest today; you didn't throw a flaming stick at them again, did you? What did I miss?"

"Rest easy—for once it is not this old man in the middle of things. Unfortunately I may soon have to intervene and bring them back to their senses." Militades would once again be forced to get involved. He threw an arm around his foster son, pulling him closer so that he could whisper in his ear.

"Elder Kallisto survived the assassination of Metz and escaped the capital with the Metzonian Elite. He has rescued Prince Frederick, and now they all flee for the Alakari in fear of the Fist. The Elders believe that Kallisto's choice of locations to seek sanctuary was … how you would say … a poor one."

"Have you heard word about the fate of my sister?" Kallen's voice was fraught with anxiety; Militades could understand his concern. Murder, rape, brutal beatings were all tales circulating around the capital upon the news of how the Cathedral of the Fallen had been brutally ransacked. Any who had family within Metzor were worried.

"You will be relieved to hear that I have it on good authority that she managed to escape from the Metzonian Chapter. No harm came to her, and Kallisto has kindly taken her beneath his wing and will look after her now." Patting the man upon the back, Militades smiled to see the relief on the young man's face. There was little other relief to be had considering the state the rest of the city was in.

Prokopolis had become trapped within a storm of anxiety and sadness after learning about the death of King Metz. Upon hearing that young Prince Sven had accused the Order and its loyal subjects of perpetrating the murder, the city had became outraged, full of high-strung tension. The fabrication that the Order wanted to supplant the loyal king with his young son Frederick was completely absurd in Militades's mind. Yet the citizens of Metzon were swaying toward the radical idea and had recently started to call for revenge. Militades was astonished, not knowing how Sven was doing it. The ties between the Order and Metzor existed from the beginning of Metzon's inception. Masen had been one of Prokopolis's brightest and most esteemed citizens, commanding strong respect despite his departure.

The news that Kallisto had survived the assassination attempt was the only welcome news, and the fact that he escaped and was still alive was enormous for the Order's case against the allegations. Yet these old fools refused to see that point; they were already plotting the man's dismal death.

Militades stepped forward, addressing the Elder Council, winking at Kallen as he began descending the staircase. "Perhaps the Elders should perceive the good news in the fact that our brother Kallisto is alive and safe. That he himself did not end up like King

Metz and the rest of the Metzonian Chapter. He's a witness and credible source, with knowledge of what exactly happened within the throne room during the night of the assassination."

"Do not mistake us, we are all relieved to hear that Advisor Kallisto is alive. It does not, however, provide an excuse for such a blatant error in judgement as taking a Metzonian army into Alakari and threatening to expose the Sacred City to the world."

Understanding the angry mood within the tower was quite easy, but its significance was small compared to the events. The Order had gone through great pain to protect its hidden gem from the rest of the world. Natural rocky defences and a difficult route made it all but impossible for the most determined of adventurers, but the Order refused to jeopardize their holiest sanctuary to any inquisitive eyes. And they had done a remarkable job of keeping such an enormous secret.

"He broke Orion's decree! Vows were broken, General! Advisor Kallisto must be brought before the council to explain his actions," a White Elder at the end of the semicircle cried out, empathically slamming his fist down upon the stone chair. Six others seated upon the stage before all the other Elders nodded in agreement.

"You should try retrieving him. Perhaps then you will understand why he did what he has done. Prince Frederick was so far northbound in Sask that there were few reasonable choices but to retreat to the Sacred City. Where else was he supposed to go? Was he to make a dash for Prokopolis with the Elite in tow? To Chilsa, so he could swear fealty to Emperor Kristolphe perhaps?"

"Don't be ridiculous," the Elder growled, awaiting support from others in silencing Militades.

"Then do not be so quick to judge, Elder Khalos!" Pointing his finger directly toward the Elder, Militades let his tone darken several shades. "Prince Sven would have intercepted them and consolidated his power in a single blow. Kallisto is doing what he is supposed to be doing, protecting Prince Frederick, and there is no place better to protect him than in the heart of the Alakari. The Sacred City will not remain hidden for all eternity, and the Children are finally coming of age. How do you expect them to lead this world if they are unable to protect themselves?"

No one else spoke against the grand general, leaving him the only man standing, staring down any opponents. Having the full attention of the hundreds of Elders gathered tightly within the amphitheatre, Militades brought his full opinion to bear.

"The Sacred City is not a concern to a king who has no idea about its existence! For as long as his brother is weakened and does not stand against him, Prince Sven has little to fear from Frederick. The only true forces that stand against him are on either side of his river borders, and the Chilsa did not allegedly slay his kingly father. He is coming for Prokopolis, my Elders. He is coming!

"What should be at the forefront of your minds is the fact that Sven has openly declared war upon the Order of the Fallen. And not simply against the Elders! Sven has aggressively hunted down every citizen who believes in or supports the Fallen. With each passing day, we hear more and more horrifying tales of struggle for survival against this oppression. As Elders of the Fallen, you have an obligation to not just the followers of the Fallen in this province but across the world. You must bring action to bear upon Prince Sven before this escalates beyond Metzon and comes to Prokopolis."

"Prince Sven would not dare cross the mighty Zarik and provoke a full-out war!" An Elder opposite Khalos spoke, waving his hand in disgust at the idea.

"You think that the prospect of war scares him? Might I remind the council that Sven did not hesitate to cross the Myradoria to slay the Chilsa. Look at the chaos and death he managed to create with several thousand infantry. Now, remind me once again, wise Elder—how many does he command now? What makes you believe you are untouchable?"

No one moved. No one dared take another single breath in the silence nor take their eyes off the White Elders who sat upon the stage of the amphitheatre. Moments of silence turned long. The leaders of the Fallen looked upon one another, looking for one who wanted to take the next barrage of words.

"We are growing weary of your sarcasm, Grand General, and

your rude arrogance. If Prince Sven makes the mistake of bringing his armies across the Zarik River, then we shall deal with him like we deal with all aggressors. Until the point when we are forced to act, we shall patiently wait for him to create his own demise."

"You are not going to intervene? Prince Sven and the Lords of Metzor have openly declared war upon you and you are going to sit here and do nothing? Let them ravage everyone who is counting on your help in their time of dire need?"

"We cannot save everyone, General. If Sven comes before our walls to threaten us, our silver shields shall be the last thing he sees in this world."

Militades was shocked to hear these men of the light speak so freely about letting people die. *Orion would turn within his tomb if he heard such blatant disrespect for even a lone soul.*

"Damn you all! If you let Sven march across the Zarik you will pay for it in blood. You must contain him where he stands; there will be no civil war to bleed your enemy this time around as there was with Mallax. Prince Sven will complete his consolidation of power, and when the Metzonian armies start rolling there shall be no stopping them! Since when have the Elders become so self-destructive that they will let their brothers' and sisters' blood run so freely?"

The clenched jaws hidden beneath their thick white beards were clear indicators Militades had struck a chord deep within the Elders. Or perhaps they had simply had enough of trying to defend a position they should not have taken in the first place.

"You are not the only one with an opinion on the situation. We look out for all aspects of the future of the Order. We cannot simply think in militaristic terms. Another outburst such as that and you shall find yourself not only thrown from this chamber but quite possibly from the city itself! Now leave while the choice remains a matter of your own free will!"

Militades turned his back upon the Elders and moved up the stairs toward the exit, feeling everyone's eyes upon his back. "A great suggestion, actually, I think I may go and make a visit to the Sacred City myself. I shall debrief Kallisto on the current situation and make him well aware of the anger he has aroused within all of you. Since it is abundantly clear to all of you that Prince Sven is of no threat to you or the Order, what need for me do you have here?"

"You shall not leave Prokopolis, Grand General."

Militades stopped his hurried exit; the grandmaster's voice was soft yet stern. Militades thought that perhaps the oldest of them had at last came to see the merit in what he had told him. He was just as quickly disappointed.

"In the event that the Fallen are forced into a war, we will not have you a thousand leagues away. Send your beloved Commandant Kallen in your place."

Militades felt his heart drop a little as he looked to the top row to the spot where the young man always sat. Kallen sat wide-eyed in disbelief at what he was hearing, shocked at how he had randomly ended up in the argument. Resuming his pace up the aisle, Militades barked at the man to join him as he exited through the arched doors.

Outside the council chambers, civil servants scrambled to remove themselves from Militades's path. Hearing Kallen's heavy steps behind him as he tried to catch up, Militades slowed down and attempted to regain his composure. "Pack only your most precious belongings for your adventure."

"The Elders weren't serious, were they? My position and oath dictates that I am to remain within Prokopolis for their protection and those they serve. One of the reasons I joined the Titans was to serve. Certainly there is another who is more qualified to debrief Elder Kallisto, a person of higher stature and rank."

The hesitation within his voice was clear, something that Militades had not heard often from the young man. Always a man of honour and selfless servitude, Kallen had traits that were almost unrecognizable amongst the Elders these days.

"The Elders forsake their own vows of protection when they allow the murder of their kinsmen across Metzon. Vows are not perfect promises, Kallen, and sometimes to do the right thing you have to break them. And do not worry; there is no need for you to debrief Kallisto."

"I do not understand. Why then I am being sent to the Sacred City?"

"You are going to take command of the armies for Kallisto so that he can concentrate upon concerns of greater importance. A man of Kallisto's wisdom should be used to discover what is truly happening within this world, not worrying about the menial day-to-day stuff."

"Is that what the Elders want of me?"

Gritting his teeth, Militades was forced to think just how far he was willing to go in defiance of the Elders. Furthermore, he needed to know just how far he was prepared to place Kallen in the heart of the argument. Punishment would be heavy were Militades and Kallen to get caught openly defying the Elders' orders. Then again, he realized, feeling a smile rise to his face, for the moment their commands were implied and not specific, allowing them the slightest room.

"No, that is what I want of you, and more importantly what the Order needs from you right now." Taking a deep breath, Militades went all in, placing his bet that Kallen would ultimately make the correct choice when the time came. "You are to look after both the Metzonian armies and those Fallen soldiers already stationed within the Sacred City. Your primary responsibility will be to train the Children of the Fallen for war. When those who are sworn to protect you abandon you, you must learn how to fight for yourself or perish."

"As much as I am thankful for your support, with all due respect there must certainly be someone more qualified for this task. I command a mere thousand Titans, not entire armies as you are suggesting I do. Why me instead of one of the generals? I am under-qualified for such a task."

"Because you are who you are. In the Orders' moment of most dire need, the world's most dire moment, you will surpass all others and do what is right. You are a Child of the Fallen, and your stake in this world is far greater than any other soldier of the Order. I fear such a heart shall be needed for what is to come." Militades could see that his son was still perplexed by what he was saying.

A Mortal Mistake

"You honestly believe a great war is coming? You speak as though its significance will rival that of the War of Beliefs. That the future of the world hangs upon a precarious balance between life and death."

"If what Kallisto says is true, then indeed it will be equal. Perhaps even greater. We now find ourselves in a serious and very dire situation, Kallen. The death of Masen Metz will spark a war this world has not seen for thousands of years. The Elders are scared; as best they try to hide it, I can see it within their eyes. Sven has them absolutely terrified, and so he *should*!" Militades continued briskly through the halls of the palace and exited into the courtyard.

"But why? Just tell me so I can understand why they fear a mortal so much? Why does he strike fear into you?"

Militades halted, gazing up at the pillared balconies above the courtyard to see if anyone was watching or listening. Slowly turning around, he looked into the young man's confused face, trying to find the words to explain. Would Kallen even understand such significance if he told him what they all feared?

"The Elders do not fear the mortal Metzonians, my son. They fear the immortal darkness that lies buried within the Desert of Lost Souls, fear of what may be coming to destroy what remains of Heaven's touch upon this world. Fear of the forgotten is what keeps the tower lit up at night; they wonder what may still be out there.

"The Order is going to war whether they want to or not, Kallen! Prince Sven shall direct his spears toward the heart of the Order, despite the Elders' ignorance. Fearing the unknown more than Sven is a recipe for disaster, which is why I need to get you out of here."

The look upon Kallen's face confirmed Militades suspicion; the man was too young to understand the significance. Not just too young—too mortal. History of the darkest things within this world did not hold any significance for him and were only mythical stories. Militades's difficult decision was seen as a slight instead of what was right—the evidence was clearly visible within the younger man's eyes.

"You taught me everything I needed to learn about battle! But now when there is a battle to be fought, when the Order requires its followers to stand up and fight, you toss me aside. Left to hide within the shadows when my place is within the sunlight, protecting the innocent lives that have raised me and become a part of who I am! Why, Militades, tell me why!"

Militades listened to his protégé's tirade, quietly knowing he would not understand no matter what he might say.

"There are many things that you will come to understand as to why we do the things we do. This pending battle is a critical point in the timeline of the Order, and we must protect ourselves in the event that it does not go the way we would all like it to. Your importance to this war may come at its most critical point, though I pray it does not come at all."

Kallen scoffed at Militades's remark with arrogant anger. "All battles are critical! You act as though we are already defeated, despite our history. The Metzonians are strong, but they are no match for the silver shields of the Order. Orion! Brianna! Prokop! Titus and Taurus! Heroes of the Order who overcame greater odds than we will ever face in thousands of year. What is my purpose if not to protect the Order from the evils, Militades?"

Names of those whom had a long history of victories but all shared a similar fate, for even the greatest of those heroes fell. All great men, Militades knew, but even Orion did not face such a darkness as he worried was looming upon the horizon. He refused to let his personal feelings and those around him get in the way of what was required of them all, unlike the Elders.

"You will find the purpose of your life is now within the Sacred City, Kallen. You have been prepared to be the one whom the Order depends upon to protect the Children of the Fallen beyond the prophesized Fall of the Old. You must be there to guide the Rise of the Children! As much as I wish to have you by my side in the upcoming battles, this is what the Elders had planned for you since the day you were born. This and so much more, you must understand!"

Kallen was visibly rattled and unsure what to say next; Militades knew how uncomfortable he felt. The feelings were similar to his when his mentor's body had been wheeled back from battle;

Militades had felt the horrid feeling of abandonment. It was the first time Militades himself had felt the sting of their mortality that others had talked so frequently about. Kallen would have others to help him much as he had and would recover, perhaps understanding and forgiving him in time.

"Your place is with the Children as well as your sister, Kallen. I have trained you to the highest of my abilities, and you have surpassed my wildest expectations. I cannot teach you anything more. Hence you must take the next step in your learning with a new teacher. I have taught you everything about war and battle, but let Kallisto teach you about knowledge and life. So much more life lies beyond the battlefield than within it, something I never took the time to understand until now."

Wrapping his arms around Kallen, he squeezed hard, not wanting to release the young man. Kallen had started out as an assigned responsibility and turned into a son he loved beyond all other things in this world. Releasing him from his hug, Militades clasped the taller man on both sides of the neck, his thumbs pressing against the clenched jaw, fighting tears for the first time in his long mortal life.

"It has been the greatest of honours to protect you and raise you as if you were my own. You will forgive me in time, but this is where we must part ways. I cannot see the future, but either we shall meet upon the golden plains of the Numelli, or I shall proudly watch over you from the Heavens. Whatever happens, I will love you forever, my son! I shall meet you at your quarters to see you off. Now go quickly." After watching Kallen take off toward the Titan's barracks to gather his items, Militades walked quickly to his own office to start penning a letter to Kallisto.

Dipping the quill into the ink, Militades hurriedly began writing the letter to inform his friend of what had come to be. Kallisto would share in his anger, but perhaps with the two of them directing pressure from both Prokopolis and the Sacred City they could possibly avert disaster. Though he had never intended to actually debark for the Sacred City, the thought of Kallen leaving him left him feeling lonely already.

All his words rang truer than Militades cared to admit, but the Sacred City would be good for the young man. Close to his sister and the rest of the Children of the Fallen, he could be introduced to life beyond politics and war. Even if only for the briefest of time, it would help remind him what he was truly fighting for.

Unfortunately, Militades had forgotten what that something was a long time ago.

CHAPTER 11
SEDUCTION OF THE EMPRESS

In high summer was the yearly Imperia festival in honour of the glorious beginning of the Chilsa Empire and all its achievements. The weeklong celebration consisted of lavish patriotic festivities in every major city in the empire, an event that its citizens always looked forward to. It had been the last night of the festivities, an extravagant masked party within the palace in Chilsa.

She had been standing off along the farthest wall of the ballroom with several of her expansive extended family members, watching her brother work his way through the crowd of women that continuously flocked to him. It had always been that way; he had an aura that seemed to attract people. Her father had ruled through the power of fear and oppression, and her brother ruled with benevolent love and calm charisma. He caught her glance from across the room; her soul felt a chill as his cold blue eyes locked upon hers for just a brief moment.

Annoyed by the drizzling, uninteresting conversation of the wives, she broke herself away from the group and took a tall crystal glass of burgundy wine from a servant before heading out to an open balcony. The city had seemed abuzz with life, its citizens taking full advantage of the excitement of the last night of festivities before life returned to the dull grind of normal days. The air held an excitement that she was unable to find with royalty.

Discovering an unknown figure standing behind her, she turned, slightly startled, to face the broad-shouldered figure drinking a large flagon of Chissan's best brew. The man's sudden appearance set her guard up immediately; she checked that her hidden twin daggers were still securely within reach.

Taking a deep breath, the masked man filled his lungs with the cool air, arms outstretched, and spoke calmly. "Raw excitement and pure bliss."

"I'm sorry?"

"What you're breathing is the scent of the common folk. Raw unbridled passion and excitement fuelled by emotion pent up for the entire year and suddenly released in one week. It is magnificent to feel and quite contagious. It's very easy to get caught up in after you experience it for the first time. Only after the sun disappears to the other side of the world do the real adventures begin."

She had rarely been allowed outside the citadel but kept within the safety of its high walls, among the courts of the lords and ladies of Chilsa. She had been outside the walls in the carriages and carried through the city but never mingled among the commoners. She had heard only horrible stories of the smells and disgusting habits from lower royal patrons. "I wouldn't know what that thrill is like … Who are you?"

Ignoring her question, the man had continued on, pointing out the flaws of her life. "An unfortunate shame, though I imagine you have little choice in the matter. All the power of the sprawling empire in your hands, yet still trapped within these mighty walls around you." Gesturing to the walls of the vast palace in the distance before continuing, he said, "Perhaps I have overexaggerated it though; it is something that most high-born nobles avoid and never understand or experience. Though in fairness they believe they are above all others and never experience the freedom of releasing themselves from the strain of social stature."

She looked for potential clues that would reveal the identity of the man she was talking to, but he remained an enigma. He did not wear any family crests or rings, preferring anonymity over announcing who he was. Even in a festival that hid one's identity, everyone displayed their rank and family crest. "And what do you believe?"

"There is nothing like the thrill of raw emotion and pleasure flowing through one's veins. The powers of excitement and the unknown are the only things that separate us from death. One must take every opportunity to feel that rush, because it will not last forever."

"Then I am the living dead, devoid of excitement and pleasure. Trapped among the illusion of power and beauty, I must seem to live a weak existence within your eyes."

"Perhaps you merely have to break away from death's slow grip and embrace life as commoners understand it. Perhaps take the first step tonight. Let me break your chains and release you from your cage. Take a chance that I promise you shall never regret."

"And what of the safety of an heiress to an empire? How would I survive against the brutal natures of the commoners?"

"You can rest assured that none shall harm you while I protect you. It will not be a problem, though, as none will know who we are."

She watched him raise a hand past her neck and prepared herself to stab a blade into the base of his skull. As his hands grazed against her neck, she thought she could feel the power in his hands, though they did not feel like noble hands. They were rough and powerful, the hands of a soldier …

"You have great confidence in your abilities, though you are but one man, and susceptible to death from a single blow of an errant blade." Reacting quickly, she flashed her blade from its hiding spot and pressed it against the side of the unknown man's throat. She looked for a reaction and saw a large smile spread across his lips. The man's eyes had changed from mysterious to an impervious, deadly stare. This man was not merely a soldier, he was a relentless killer. Violence and death were mere tools in his extensive arsenal. Her blade did not intimidate him, even pressed against his thin throat.

"How does one such as myself trust that you will not rape and kill me and then toss me aside in the street? Perhaps returning to your household a champion to be greatly rewarded? You realize that an attempt to slay me will result in your family's family being eradicated from this world in a horrific fashion?" She could certainly feel the thrill flowing through her veins now as she tried to control the trembling of her arm.

"Beautiful and deadly—is such a combo a reality? You truly are the treasure I have been searching for, and no doubt the gem of an entire empire!" The man smiled again, pulling his hand back from her throat. "If I had wanted to kill such a thing of beauty I could have easily thrown you over the balcony to your death before slipping off into the darkness. Or perhaps even earlier, as you entered the party alone from the dining hall staircase, unaware of my watchful gaze. You have grazed against my hands, fearing them assassin's hands, only to receive a trickle of the greatness that resides within them."

She glanced toward the sparkling object in his hands, twirling slowly in the remote light. It was her white gold necklace, the Imperial Chilsa cross crest, inlaid with diamonds around its edges, the interior inlaid with light sapphires cut from a single stone.

Her hand quivered, and a single trickle of blood ran down the blade and then down the side of the man's neck.

"You are now merely a beautiful woman, the object of every man's eye tonight, who you truly are left unknown. So I ask again, shall I break the bonds that prevent you from experiencing what your mind has always dreamed of?"

Her emotions switched from mortal fear to a desire to feel the unknown to which this nameless man alluded. A sideways glance into the party showed that her husband among his entourage was already drunk as they chatted up a group of noble women known for their promiscuity and unscrupulous activities. Her husband's friends held him on his feet. Watching them all laugh loudly filled her with anger.

"While you may think that you have thought of everything, it is still an impossible task." Emotional turmoil built within her, as fear started to creep within her, overriding newly felt desire. The repercussions for being caught could prove to be dire, almost to the point that she would prefer death before feeling her father's wrath.

Flashing her a quick smile, he quelled her fears. "There is always a way. The question is, do you dare to take a risk for the rewards you could reap?"

Her excitement became fuelled with brash fearlessness as she had only experienced once before. Passing through the Gates of the Emperor, she watched wide-eyed at their apparent obscurity. None of the guards stopped them, not recognizing who she was among the other nobles. Hidden behind her mask and without the imperial crest at her throat to mark who she was, all around her were unaware of the fact that they were brushing so close to the daughter of Emperor Neurus.

The nightlife she saw among the streets was unimaginably different from that she had glanced down upon during the days. The daylight crowd had been largely depressing, trudging through the streets as the people went about their business. Night was filled with excitement and freedom; they clearly felt liberated from normal life. Women and men alike screamed with glee as they ran with friends to various establishments and street parties.

Together they had immersed themselves deep within the crowd, flowing from one party to the next, their energy levels growing higher and higher as they progressed. Starting off, surrounded by lesser nobles and their wealthy friends, the pace of music had been tame and proper; she quickly found herself primed for the next party on rich wines and tonics. The second party she found substantially larger, as more commoners had joined the party with their untamed behaviour and raging enthusiasm.

Belle could not believe the freedom she felt. Her life had been spent in an oppressive fashion, and she was finally being released from her inhibitions. Her heartbeat and pulse matched the tempo of the music as its speed increased, and the wine continued to feed her recently freed spirit. By the time they reached the final party of the night, the moon was deep within the sky and the air was damp and cool. In the heart of the party, the heat was soaring. Only the most untamed of nobles were found among the hundreds of commoners.

Pressing her hips tight against the unknown man who had rescued her from the citadel, she could feel his heart beating heavily against her own. The smell of alcohol upon his breath mixed with the heavy odour of sweat, filling her nose. The strong hands of the murderer of men ran across her skin, pulling her even closer.

As the party surged later into the night, she no longer noticed the crowd around her. Lost in the centre of the mob, she had been about to become quickly reintroduced to the dangers her mind had forgotten about.

Wavering through the emptying streets, Belle noticed that they were working their way in the direction of the Imperial Inn, a large and imposing building that housed many important dignitaries and wealthy visitors to the capital city. Clinging to his arm, she took a glance back at the Imperial Citadel, standing like a mountain in the city, its black walls absorbing the moonlight to leave only a large shadow. She imagined her husband, who likely had passed out from intoxication by now, as was his norm—likely in the servants' chambers again.

Clutching the strong arm, she did not notice her companion had halted in the middle of the street. She bumped hard into him. She turned to see two rough-looking commoners standing before them. The street behind the couple was blocked off by another three men, who moved in behind them to cut off their retreat.

"A little late for nobles to be walking around without protection, we think. Me thinking that you might come to regret that." A sixth man stepped out from the shadows, his grisly face coming into the moonlight. The large black beard hid his face in the darkness, and several brown teeth protruded in a grim grin as he moved toward them. A large scar ran across his face, leaving his left eye an opaque white. He clenched a large sabre in his hands.

Belle pulled herself behind the soldier's bulky torso, keeping an eye on both the gang and their leader.

"I think you might come to regret stopping these nobles. We

will be continuing to our destination; whether it is over your dead bodies is a question for you to decide."

Hushed laughter broke out among the gang members. "There are seven of us and one of you and a darling little lady. Methinks I am going to save her for myself for tonight's later activities." The leader smiled, moving closer, levelling his blade to throat level. "You will sleep with the fishies like the last fool to threaten me!"

Stepping away from Belle, the man rushed forward, throwing the big leader off balance for a brief moment. Hacking recklessly at the rushing bull, the thief's arm passed harmlessly over him, though his wrist was latched onto with an iron grip. A rigid palm smashed into the man's elbow, and his blade fell from his snapped arm. The blade was plucked from the air by the soldier's striking hand. He rotated behind the bearded man, slicing the blade across the man's throat. The bandit's sudden scream of pain turned to a mere gurgle. The soldier hurled the gang leader's rusty blade, and the bloodied weapon struck the chest of a man hiding on a balcony with a crossbow.

The attack took fewer than ten heartbeats and left her breathless, her mind racing as she stood out in the open. The thugs were as surprised as she was, and it took several seconds for their minds to process what had happened. Her defensive instinct took over, and she pulled free the two blades strapped to her thigh and threw them toward the attackers behind her. Her father's insistence on training her to defend herself paid off. One blade struck one man's throat cleanly, and the other caught the second man in the ribs, puncturing his lower lung. Adrenaline poured into her system. She felt a new sensation of bloodlust fill her mind as she pulled her jewelled dagger and advanced toward the lone man left.

Eyes wide with fear, the man turned to run, but her blade cut through the back of one of his legs, severing his hamstring. Tumbling forward to the stone street and scrambling to one knee, he turned to face the defender-turned-attacker. Jamming her thumb into his eye, she plunged her blade into his heart; hers pounded uncontrollably.

Turning, she found her body pressed immediately against the hard chest of the deadly defender. His lips were instantly against hers. Both were still out of breath. Pulling away with a smile, he handed her the two throwing knives and pulled her hand. "We need to get out of here before the guards arrive!"

On awakening, her green eyes pierced the darkness of the room. Belle slipped out of the large bed; her feet moved silently across the stone floor. The cool breeze crossed her naked skin and made her shiver. She stretched by the window, looking northward. The dream about the defining moment when her life completely changed came to her several times a month. She smirked to herself and peered back to the bed occupied by the man who had opened her eyes to the world.

Sinful living may be frowned upon, but when it feels this good, who really cares? She laughed silently to herself. Those who refrained from what she had experienced over the past hours were fools in her opinion, but the world was full of fools. Now she had been turned from an unknowing fool to a champion of such life. Lust, seduction and pleasure were what made life exciting and worth every moment.

She gazed upon the golden chain between her breasts, shimmering even within the dark room. The horror she had felt when she first gazed upon it in the predawn hours of that fateful morning after the Imperia, her mind placing the monumental significance it held within the free nations.

That last night of the Imperia, she had awoken to the sounds of movement within the room and saw the burly figure already half-dressed. She quietly watched him washing his face in the cold water of the basin.

"Abandoning me already, when we still have so much to explore? You know I could have you put to death for such a minor mistake, but you performed admirably, so I think I will let you live." She smiled to herself, thinking of the previous night's activities. Leaning from the bed, she lit several more candles in the holders beside the bed, watching the shadows disappear.

A Mortal Mistake

Pleasure turned to horror as the man turned around and she looked upon his unmasked face. A thick golden chain hung around his neck, a large rectangular crest of gold swinging in the middle. A black stallion rearing back upon powerful haunches, its eyes and hooves made of glimmering diamonds, pressed upon a gold background. Her stomach churned at the sight of it.

The royal crest of the Metzonian House, her father's eternal sworn enemy and the most hated of the entire empire, shimmered in the dim light. The crest swung from the neck of the man standing before her, who had shared her bed. "Well, you wouldn't be the first of the empire to try, I suppose. Your father has an unhealthy obsession with my death, I believe."

Looking upon his face, she realized it was not the first time she had seen him. He was not just any member of the House; he was the destructive Sven Metz, the Fist of Metzor himself. His hands had been drenched in more Chilsa blood than anyone but his father's. She flashed back to the defiance against the emperor and his Imperial Army ready to bear down upon them. How he had stood there drenched in the blood of her countrymen as his father rode past to negotiate his survival. The rage she had felt around her father during that moment was the greatest she had witnessed within him.

"As much as I would love to stay and explore more, I unfortunately have to escape before the city wakes. The Festival of the Mask is over, and I will no longer be able to walk freely. I suggest you return to the castle. The guard may soon become aware of the princess's absence. I advise you to ask for an escort from the hotel owner. I will not be able to protect you from the street urchins."

She was confused. "You have the heiress to your father's mortal enemy, naked and unarmed in an unknown room, and you're … letting me live?"

Sven froze as her words echoed within the tiny room. Gazing back at her hard, he crossed the room toward her. "You do raise a good point." Kissing her lightly upon the lips, he pulled her hair back to expose her naked throat. "But you performed admirably last night, and I don't usually free beautiful creatures from their cages only to kill them. I came to Chilsa to take your father's head and end the suffering of my people. May they forgive me for my unanticipated distraction. Like I told you last night, if I really wanted to kill you, there would have been ample opportunities."

He finished dressing in tight-fitting dark clothes ideal for shadow skulking. He paused in the doorway and then turned back toward her. He dangled the Imperial crest from his fingers, prepared to toss it to her. "If I am caught, I certainly would not want them to find this upon my body."

"Keep it as a gift from a newly freed soul. I am certain that the other crest upon your chest will land you in more harm than the Cross ever would. Perhaps you could return it during next year's Imperia festival." Emotion rolled within her; she did not know how to react within the turmoil of her new situation or whether to feel trapped.

Smiling again, he backed toward the door. "Perhaps. We will see if your emperor succeeds in killing me first or if I survive the wrath of my own father." He started laughing to himself before opening his arms wide. "Then again, who are we kidding? Until next year!" Then he was gone, disappearing down the dark staircase and out into the streets.

Dawn was soon to break across the dark sky. She followed suit, hurrying to try and get back to the castle before its own party ended.

That morning, her father had been in the foulest mood that she ever remembered. She had suspected that he knew what had happened, because Sven had been the focal point of his rage. Complaining of nightmares during the night involving the hated man, her father swore that he could smell the man within the city walls. His rage boiled over when he heard reports of a large Metzonian banner flying over the southern gatehouse. Several guardsmen felt his wrath and lost their heads as punishment for their negligence.

If there was anything that her father had a deep hatred for it was competition in power. He was to be the sole ruler of everything within his realm and beyond. Assassins were dispatched from every corner of the world to kill the young prince, even sent into the Desert of Lost Souls. None ever returned.

Sven's disappearance into the Desert of Lost Souls had been welcome news to her father but had left her distraught. Clearly Sven's father had as terrible temper as her own, but the desert was an exceptionally harsh punishment that could be considered torture, as death could come at an excruciatingly slow pace.

She should have known that even the desert would not be able to swallow a soul as powerful as his.

Grazing her hand along the cold stone window frame, she peered over the ledge at the marching guards on the platform far below. Her husband had been the first to feel the changing tide, and she really didn't miss him at all. An intoxicated whoremonger who was in the way of what she wanted, she had never truly loved him. After being with a man who exuded power matching her own, she began to crave such prowess. Embracing her new thirst, it was not long before her husband moved her to anger.

Belle was already angry at the news that Sven had been sent into the desert. Caught within the anger she finally refused to take the pain of being with such a fool, who constantly humiliated her among her father's court. His death came in the middle of the night, after yet another round of carousing with his friends among Chilsa's many drinking and gambling establishments. He was drunk from a few too many, and he lost his money on the dog fights for the third night in a row, making him violent and angry. Somewhere in his rage he had forgotten whom he was talking to and how far his true power extended.

The next moment he was free-falling from her tower apartment to his death; she watched to be sure he reached the bottom. Then it was over. She had refused to take another husband during Sven's lost journey in the Desert of Lost Souls, and her father had not brought up the subject again.

She had waited patiently, honing her skills and dealing with other unexpected events that occurred during that tumultuous period of her life. Her patience had paid off when Sven returned to her after five years of being trapped in the sands of time, even stronger and more powerful than he was before.

She looked back at the bed that contained the man who had freed her spirit from the prison she had placed herself within. Opening up a door that could never be closed again, he had led her to become dark and powerful, in a way that even her father had not anticipated, and that was only the beginning.

Sven had arranged to have her and her double smuggled into the city to the high-end brothel that he had called home since returning to Metzor. It was a substantial risk, considering all Sven was planning on doing, but she would be there to ensure he followed through. She refused to have it any other way.

How close it had come to unravelling. Looking to the naked woman in her bed beside Sven, she pondered what would have happened had the royal advisor walked to the other side of the bed. Had the Fallen pulled the sheets back upon her naked flesh instead of her friend, would he truly have been able to recognize her?

It mattered little now. Sven's plan was already in motion, with both parties fully invested now, though it did not concern her. Few remained who were powerful enough to stop them anymore, and their trap was too perfectly laid to fail. The nation would rally around Sven like they had years before, and a beat would not be missed. Now with Conrad joining their side in the most unexpected of ways, the world would soon burn around them.

One final task now remained between them and wielding the promised, almost unfathomable, power. And the world would tremble in their wake.

Chapter 12
Halo and the Valley of Angels

A gentle hand shook Alexandra awake, helping to hold her upright as she regained her bearings. Clutching both sides of the saddle, she looked at her surroundings, noticing they had begun to traverse through a narrow rocky path that cut between two shelves of dark rock.

"My apologies, I did not mean to startle you, but we have reached the final pass." Grave concern rested in his grey-blue eyes as Kallisto pulled his horse away from her own. "You have not been sleeping well, my child?"

"I've had better." Trying to hide how terrible she actually felt, Alexandra decided that horseback was not the most ideal sleeping arrangement. She missed the comfort of her bed, though significantly less than the peaceful sleep that evaded her. "Nothing like being forced to helplessly watch my foster father die on a nightly basis."

Looking over toward Kallisto, she gave him a weak smile and turned away before the tears began again. She'd prayed to the heavens to help her deal with the pain she felt, but Heaven had remained silent, allowing the nightmares to ravage her. She did not believe that anyone could help her, despite Sabrina and many others who tried to help.

"It is painful to lose someone you cared so dearly about. I understand what you are going through, Alexandra. I have not gotten much sleep in the past weeks either. I doubt that fact will change for the next several months, but time is all that will make the pain subside."

Alexandra nodded, wanting to believe Kallisto but unsure of the truth within his words.

"We are almost at the Sacred City. You will grow to love your new home as much as you did the old. May its wonder calm the turmoil within your heart and help ease our pain. I cannot replace the ambassador, but I shall try to do my best to show you the love and care he once did. I promise that you shall not be alone."

She smiled a little at the old man's genuine concern; knowing that someone still cared gave her slight courage. She was not completely alone, a feeling she had started to recognize. Turning back to thank him for his concern, she saw that Kallisto was already staring into the distance as the sunlight streamed across his face. Feeling the warmth upon her own, she turned to look as he spoke with newfound awe.

"Welcome at long last to the Valley of Angels."

Gazing into the bright sunlight streaming through the chasm before them, Alexandra got her first look at the beauty that was the Valley of Angels. Exiting the cold bleak mountain passages she had slowly traversed the past several days, she was astonished to find a green forest spread out before her. On the trail that led down into the valley, the trees towered above, their branches stretching over the trail.

"Behold, Alexandra—the most beautiful place that remains within this world. The mighty Lifebringer rises in the midst of the pure water that is the Lake of Heavenly Sorrow. Legend likes to claim that the angels of Heaven each shed a tear for those lost in the fight against Hell on this world. The battles ravaged Earth so terribly that it took the waters thousands of years to travel out across the land, cleansing the world of its suffering."

Looking further into the forested valley, she saw a great plain open up before the shimmering lake Kallisto had mentioned. Waters the colour of serene turquoise glittered in the brilliant sunlight that danced upon the calm surface. Dwarfing the lake, the steep cliffs of the Lifebringer rose from the centre of the lake; hidden behind sheets of mist swirling around it, the mountain climbed up beyond the clouds.

A bright white reflection shone brightly at the base of the lake and mountain. Alexandra assumed it had to be the Sacred City, standing out like a beacon of hope to those who had recently been forced to endure Hell. Trudging out of the gloom and into the light, a silence of wonder overtook the survivors following behind them.

"It is a marvellous sight to behold, isn't it? Those who make the pilgrimage to the Sacred City claim this first image imprints itself upon your soul. I remember the first time I looked upon its majesty. Believe it or not, I was the first mortal Fallen to ever gaze upon the Valley of Angels."

Alexandra watched the smile blossom upon Kallisto's face as he closed his eyes, remembering the moment.

"You discovered this? How?" As he led Alexandra down into the valley, she refused to believe Kallisto's story. Reaching the shade of the canopy stretching high above them, Alexandra plucked a leaf larger than her entire hand, marvelling, as Kallisto prepared to tell his tale.

"The Golden Age of the Order had just begun after the Sin was defeated by Orion and his followers. A half century earlier I had just fallen at the end of the War of Beliefs and completely missed the dark days so many had talked about. For all the joy and excitement that the future held, the great Orion was still restless and haunted by the blurred visions that awakened lost memories within his mind.

"The most prominent of these visions was of a great throne trapped within the heart of a great mountain temple. Someone spoke to him, telling him that to discover the deliverance Orion so desperately desired, he needed to find the temple before the true evils returned.

"Dispatching teams to every mountainous range that had emerged from the world, his major focus was upon the Alakari. The largest and nastiest of all mountain ranges, all great rivers of the world flowed from within its dark heart. Grandmaster Orion concentrated the majority of his efforts upon the Alakari, sending many teams into it, including mine.

"Fleeing the fifth great storm of the week, its icy wind and heavy snowfall chased our exhausted bodies. We climbed up over the rises of that mountain there."

Alexandra looked toward the peak that Kallisto was pointing out, unsure if she was looking at the proper one. Hidden among the large branches above them she could see very few mountain peaks but doubted it was too important to the story.

Kallisto eagerly continued his story. "Scrambling up the treacherous icy, rocky slope, we had hoped to find safety on its other side. Tied to one another, I had been in the lead as we scrambled up the mountain peak. We had not expected to look down upon this.

"It was the happiest moment of my mortal life; whether it was the thrill of achievement or the mystical powers of the valley itself, I do not know. This valley seemed to cleanse our souls, lifting the weight of our fears and faults from our shoulders. Entering the sacred valley, we immediately felt it illuminate our spirits!"

Inhaling deeply, Alexandra could sense what Kallisto spoke of; the taste of the fresh mountain air was invigorating. Joy swelled within her as they trotted down the path, seeing the light at the end of the tree-created tunnel. Bursting out onto the green plains, the horses threatened to take off through the tall grass rippling in the wind.

"Upon reaching the shore of the lake, several in our expedition believed we should return to Prokopolis to bring Orion word of our discovery. Metz and I could not believe they wanted to turn back after all we had been through. The great storms that encircled us ultimately forced those who opposed to agree there would be no leaving anytime soon. With plenty of time to burn, we set forth to climb the Lifebringer that had never been touched by Humanity. Of course, this wasn't here." Kallisto waved toward the white walls as they crossed the valley floor.

From atop the valley entrance, the Sacred City had looked small to Alexandra, but as they began to traverse the great distance she realized that she had been gravely mistaken. The Sacred City was not small at all, nor was it the Sacred City, but an immense fortress. Dwarfed beneath the mighty Lifebringer, the white stone walls of the outer ring rose a hundred feet into the air, their sentries looking like ants atop their lofty lookout.

As they closed in on the gatehouse, the two thick stone gates groaned loudly as the doors depicting thousands of small angels began to swing toward the new arrivals. They passed into the mouth of the great beast, and the fortress swathed them in darkness as they travelled deeper. The depth of the first wall astounded her when they at last exited into the shadows of the second ring.

"This was all constructed by the Order? How did they ever do such a thing?"

"The Fallen Five turned to a group of Elders who called themselves the Architects to design a way to make this new wonder accessible within the parameters of their new mortality. Over the course of several hundred years, the Architects designed and built the impregnable fortress that you see before you, carved directly from the difficult stone of the Alakari."

Several hundred years! The sheer magnitude of time was astounding to Alexandra. Humanity would have been forced to struggle for entire generations, likely to never be completed. But the Fallen's determination was insurmountable, and she knew they would slave away for generations of their own long, extended lives to see such a dream come to fruition.

"Five concentric walls, each thicker and taller than the previous, make any notion of attack foolish. Those who are granted access to the city must first gain access to the gates and then move to the rear of the fortress to the only access to the first wall. The great bridges you see above you pass directly through the second wall, and so on until you reach the fourth and final wall that leads into the bell tower."

Alexandra couldn't see the tower in the shadows of the large walls, but she remembered seeing its pinnacle in the distance, standing so tall and yet so small beneath the mountain it was built before.

Kallisto's story was interrupted as many messengers and ranking citizens came forth, leaving Alexandra to follow silently behind. She did not mind though; it gave her the time to think and to gaze upon the glory that she had only ever heard whispers about. It was everything she had dreamed about and so much more, and she had not even reached the aforementioned city yet.

"Apparently, the city administrator is extremely ill. Prince Frederick will have to remain outside the walls until we get clearance from the Elders. The Children and Sabrina will stay here, and someone will come to retrieve them. Try not to lose your pass if it pleases you." Kallisto pressed a thin silver tag into her hand. Flipping the small tag over in her hands several times, she saw it was marked by several different symbols that she assumed dictated how far within the Order's sanctuary she was allowed.

"Had to use a little persuasion, but I managed to secure us temporary status to move freely through the city. Apparently I have upset the Elders in Prokopolis greatly. But before I get labelled a convict, shall we continue our tour?"

Alexandra listened to Kallisto laugh, clearly unconcerned at the prospect of the Elders' justice. After seeing the justice his dearest friends had imparted upon his own son, perhaps he figured he had seen the worst. Then again, that justice had ultimately led them all to flee for their lives.

"Come along. The Sacred Citadel may be amazing, but it is by far the least beautiful thing within this valley."

When they exited the bell tower, swirling mist struck her face. She gazed up upon the Lifebringer, displayed before her in its full glory. A thousand waterfalls fell from the heavens, the water fragmenting into a thousand droplets shimmering in the morning sunlight. The streams higher up the mountain carved through great swaths of ice-covered peaks. Craning her neck, Alexandra was still unable to see the peak of the mountain hidden behind the mist and, higher still, clouds.

Shifting her attention down to earth as they continued forward, she looked along the length of the bridge she now stood upon. Alexandra's legs ached as she looked down the length of the bridge crossing the narrow bay. Rising at the gentle slope and growing narrower until it nearly disappeared in the distance, the perspective gave her a rough guess as to how far she still had to go.

Setting forth, Kallisto unexpectedly returned to his story, as though he never quit and still had her full attention.

"And here is possibly the greatest structure the Order has ever constructed, The Bridge of the Bold. It took the Architects just as long to properly build the bridge as it did the fortress. Orion wished to share what he had discovered with his family, his friends, the Fallen and the entire realm of Humanity so that they could see what Heaven could offer this world. An ambitious project considering the scale the project demanded.

"It was not easy, nor was it made without sacrifice. Many times great swaths of the bridge fell to the depths of the lake before the Architects finally got it right. Each time was a sad event, setting back construction, but perhaps of greater consequence were the countless bold builders who fell with their creation."

Alexandra peered over the edge, looked down to the waters that stole the souls of the brave men, all dying willingly to complete one man's dream of bringing what was left of Heaven's grace to the rest of the world. "Who were the bold men who built all of this? I know the Architects designed everything, but it certainly took the manpower of many thousands to build all that is here, even if it took centuries. How did Orion and the Order manage to fund and organize such ambitions?" She was astounded by it all, the significance of what they built overshadowed by everything required to build it.

"Word spread throughout the Order, and all were eager to gaze upon what was once touched by angels. Eager to participate in Orion's ambitious project, the Fallen began a great pilgrimage into the Alakari. Some made yearly trips spanning many months, and others stayed for several years. Many even believed that dedicating their entire lives to the Valley of Angels was their mortal life's sole purpose.

"Unfortunately, Orion never got to see his dream become a reality. Other events forced him to leave the Sacred City in secrecy. One of the many dark moments of his end days, which almost certainly broke his heart."

Alexandra let the silence linger for a moment. "Why did Orion never reveal it to the world? Why not show Humanity what he had desired after so much work? After so great a struggle?"

"A murderous time for Fallen and man alike rose from the shadows; a forgotten evil came to seek revenge, lurking amongst the shadows and luring Humanity back into the darkness. Atrocious crimes were committed against the Order, ending the Golden Age. That dark tale is for another time though. Regardless, knowing that darkness still resided within the hearts of men and this world ultimately forced Orion to avoid that final unveiling."

"What forgotten evil? What reasons did Orion have for not revealing this to the world? What did he find here that was so vital to protect that he chose secrecy? Why can't you just tell me already? I grow tired of the secrets that the Order constantly keeps."

"Patience, my child. All will be told to you, and you will begin to understand in time." Kallisto laughed, wrapping his arm around her shoulders as they reached the halfway point of the long bridge. "Everyone wants to hear the story, and I apologize for boring you, but I am trying to make you understand the significance of the stories, the very reason events that moulded this world happened and the great sacrifices that have been made that changed the course of this world for millennia.

"The history of the Fallen is long and complicated, but it is actually comparable to that of Heaven. I ask you to be patient only a little while longer. The climax of the adventure is most certainly worth the wait. You will soon understand what Orion needed to protect."

Alexandra walked in silence, not understanding Kallisto's thoughts. Frustration was setting in when a peculiar thought popped into her mind.

"Wait? Something is wrong with the timeline. You said that Orion began searching for the Sacred City several centuries after the War of Beliefs. The great wars of the Order started a little under a thousand years ago, and even if you missed the War, how did you know Orion, who has been dead for centuries? That would make you close to seven hundred years old!" Alexandra stopped walking,

A Mortal Mistake

waiting for Kallisto to stop and settle her confusion, but the old man continued to walk off the bridge onto the dais that held the temple entrance. "How is that possible, Kallisto? Who are you?"

Kallisto twisted his neck and looked back at her without missing a stride, raising his eyebrow and giving her a slight grin. Alexandra hurried to try and catch up to him. Alexandra knew all of those who had truly fallen from Heaven had lived long, extended lives. Orion's lifespan was known to have surpassed a thousand years, but such was extremely rare. Few others ever reached close to Kallisto's own age, certainly not without escaping the wear and tear of time, as he appeared to have. She thought of others he had mentioned, and her confusion deepened.

Eight large statues knelt on one stone knee each upon their pedestals, wrapped in stone cloaks, heads bowed low. Great spires protruded in multiple places, as though armour were hidden beneath the cloaks, punching through the stone fabric. Eight stone hands clasped twenty-foot shafts, and the other eight held ornate stone shields. Chills ran up her spine as she looked upon the stone monsters, carved so finely they looked like they could awaken at any moment.

"You didn't answer my questions, Kallisto …" She looked quickly at the doors of the temple, a much larger version of those at the fortress. A display of armour, swords and wings covered the white doors as an army of angels prepared for war. Alexandra quickly noticed the theme of the temple was similar to that carved upon the doors.

"After climbing for about two days, we finally reached this large dais jutting out before the mountain entrance. As we looked upon the statues of angels and the murals depicting the battles between Heaven and Hell, we began to remember. Not everything, I may say, but more than we ever had before. We remembered who we once were, who we had once served. Most of all we remembered being judged in Heaven's Court and being cast out for our sins. We remembered why.

"You see, the Lords of the High Heavens had wiped clean the memories of those who had risen against them, perhaps to protect themselves, perhaps for other reasons we do not know. Orion himself believed that by wiping our memories clean, Heaven could see into the true hearts of those they had created and properly judge our souls by our actions in a new life. Nonetheless, not even the most powerful who fell truly remembered how high they had once soared …"

As she passed a large contingent of Temple Titans, Alexandra thought of her brother, which surprised her. Wondering if he knew that she was safe, she was about to ask Kallisto when he drew her attention back to the temple and the enormous mural to their left.

"This depicts High General Magnius, with his twin blades Havoc and Harm leading the Legionnaires of Hellio into battle against the minions of Hell." Kallisto pointed to a mural of orange-winged angels fighting demons of Hell, a calm and serene look upon their leader's face as he raised a shimmering blade in the air.

"Ancient Lord Siberian and his House of Crux in the last great war waged upon this world between Heaven and Hell as they destroyed the Dark Prince Adramaleck, entrapping his soul. We once had many memories of Heaven; these are the ones of our war."

Alexandra barely glanced at the second mural as she rushed to catch up before Kallisto continued the story out of earshot. She noticed how quickly Kallisto was moving and that some stories she might deem interesting had been skipped. Alexandra assumed he had to be approaching something of great importance to him.

"We split up within this tunnel, which took both parties deep into the mountain. We met up again at the temple exit that led to the Gates of Final Fate and out onto what you know to be the Sacred City with its glorious gardens and the perfect Crystal Cathedral.

"This hallway was not opened for us when we first came through though. When we trekked back through the temple prepared to head home, we unknowingly headed toward what would become the climax of the adventure. It would prove to be the single most significant event to affect the Order in its history. Our party was worn down to the bone, but with so many sets of eyes and all minds locked on the same moment, it was impossible to refute."

As they entered the room, light from above them focused onto a circle centred within the chamber. Alexandra was amazed by the size of the chamber that ran high above them, the peak reaching for the mountain summit until it was a speck of light. Great shimmering trees grew in the chamber, growing out of the strong rock. The silver-leafed trees seemed to feed off the radiance of the light source set perfectly in the middle. Blinding light painfully struck her eyes forcing her to wince.

Using her hand as a shield, she walked closer to the brilliant source of light, trying to let her eyes adjust. In its heart, Alexandra could make the outlines of a gleaming throne larger than any she had seen before. It seemed to be made of the purest material on earth; it had the clarity of diamonds and glittered as trapped white energy swirled within it.

"We were enamoured by the Throne of Creation, where our world was conceived by none other than the Creator himself. Or so it is told. We were filled with excitement, amazement; our emotions were indescribable. Then something even more incredible happened. Our awe-inspiring moment was shattered by a sound we did not anticipate—the laughter of a young child. Shock struck all of us as we watched a small child peer from behind the Throne of Creation. We were amazed to see such a small child in this place where we had seen no sign of Humanity. That was when our lives changed forever …"

"*She is yours to forever protect, and if you do this for her, she will return the favour and protect all who have pure hearts and souls.* The voice had forced itself in our heads. Many screamed out in pain, trying to look for the source. All of us fell upon the hard floor, losing the ability to stand as vertigo knocked all the members of our expedition off balance. Struggling on all fours, we tried to collect ourselves as our minds and bodies reeled uncontrollably. The female voice had continued.

"*She is Heaven's final gift to this world. We sacrificed too much for this world already, but I love my creation of Life too much. And He loves your world more than you can possibly imagine. Love her as your own and protect her from evil,* the voice said.

"I had located the source of the sound that vibrated within my mind just as she stepped into view.

"Walking silently from behind the throne, she turned to face us. Her body radiated light upon our faces. She embodied perfection beneath the tight-fitting veil, her beauty entrapping all men. Walking slowly toward us, her feet did not touch the surface of the stone themselves but hovered inches above it. Nothing shook my soul more than her eyes, piercing orbs of vibrant pink that glowed softly yet with an intensity of great power. I could feel her gaze penetrate my mind and heart; my soul lay bare before her.

"Under this illumination, however, everyone in the party felt the changes stirring within them. Our hearts pumped vigorously; we could feel our blood rushing so fast we thought our veins would explode. The power residing within our spirits became flooded with newfound energy and life. A calm peacefulness overcame our minds. Broken bones and bloody cuts healed, and all stress seemed to evaporate from our souls, removing the age and wear of mortality from our bodies.

"Remember, Fallen. Protect the Child of Angels. Forever love her! With that, her great wings of vibrant white energy hued with the same pink as her eyes snapped open, and in the next instant she was propelled up in a flash of energy, straight to the stars, leaving the entire party in a daze, exhausted and not believing what we had just experienced. All of us collapsed to the floor with no energy to move; the chamber darkened, lit only by the small glow given off by the throne. We could no longer fight the urge to sleep, and we collapsed into the most blissful sleep."

Silence overtook the room as Kallisto finished his tale at last, leaving Alexandra speechless. The man who had saved her life could have been one of the most influential characters of the Fallen since the death of Orion, and yet no one even knew who he was. Always in the background of the largest events, he had gone unnoticed but had shaped the world's future.

Stepping deeper into the light waving around her, Alexandra moved toward the throne, where she found herself surrounded by the white light. Curled in the fetal position, without movement or breath, the child of angels lay upon the seat of the Creator. Alexandra noticed the reflection of a tear rolling down Kallisto's face as he looked down upon the child.

"Did something happen to her? Why is she so small? What happened to her?"

"She is merely sleeping, as all children do, though none more than she does. Such beautiful innocence when children sleep, would you not agree, Kallisto? Minds free from hate, violence and fear—if only Humanity would take lessons from their children, what the world could be." A new voice spoke, and a female figure entered the realm of pure light. She slipped her left arm beneath Kallisto's, patting his forearm.

"Alexandra, I wish to introduce you to Jaina. She has lived within the Sacred City all her life, brought here long after it began as a sanctuary for the Children."

"And this child, Alexandra, is immortal, like Heaven that bore her. Galaxies shall collapse upon themselves and stars burn themselves to dust before she ever ages. She is Halo, the Child of Angels, and the crown jewel of all the Heavens. Or so we believe. Truth be told, we do not know a single thing about her but where she came from. Using the information the Fallen remembered when we come here, we are forced to mostly guess. She has never spoken a word in all these years. Not even to Orion," the dark-haired woman added, smiling down upon the child with the warmth of a mother.

Slowly sliding a foot forward, Alexandra moved one step closer to gaze upon the child's beauty. She froze. Halo's eyes, large pink orbs flecked with shimmering silver strands, flickered open and glowed brightly beneath the reflective sheen, so clear Alexandra could see her own face. Not moving, the eyes stared unwaveringly into Alexandra's soul.

Alexandra felt naked, as though the child shared her subconscious, watching every moment of her life flash before her eyes. Alexandra fell to her knees and tried to regain her balance as she gazed up at the child, wondering what she had done to her.

A soft smile crossed Halo's face, and she closed her eyes to resume her nap as though nothing had happened.

Chapter 13
An Eternal Prison

The two brothers stood silently, tightly holding the reins of the stallions that continued to balk at the structure before them. Staring at the bridge that had been a one-way path to their destinies, neither had crossed as the same person they had initially been. Belle rounded out the trio, although she herself had never before crossed the bridge, as far as Sven knew.

The structure looked more intimidating than either remembered it. Solidly built and wide enough to run five full chariots across, the bridge had been constructed directly into the heavy brown stone of the riverbanks. It seemed to create an eerie feeling as they stood at its base, as if something watched over it silently. Facing east and west, the two rows of stone angels stood tall with wings flared back, connecting at the tips, creating a confined structure.

"So how does one free them from these eternal prisons that they are trapped in exactly?" Conrad questioned. He had not been given the knowledge about how the plan was to proceed but was there merely to support it. Sven looked over at Belle, smiling at her as the simple question was asked. Sven's anger at his younger sibling had slowly subsided over the past month, but he still did not trust his little brother after his escapade.

"After the last great war between Heaven and Hell, the warriors of Heaven hemmed the Dark Princes in their strongholds with their servants. The Dark Princes of Hell, realizing that they could not hope to defeat the heavenly army, decided to release their souls from the physical confines of this world instead of risking capture or an eternal death. They sacrificed their servants to fuel the black magic that would release them from their bodies; such an act allowed them to wait for the next moment of truth," Belle explained to Conrad, returning her gaze to the structure.

"The waters that flow through these rivers have purifying powers that do not allow any spirit of dark power to pass above it. They must cross it physically. This bridge is the only way for them to be released. But their dark spirits are far too powerful for them to be completely contained in any normal mortal body."

Sven joined in on the explanation, pointing toward the members of the Fallen they had taken prisoner during their revolts. "The Fallen are not simply another religious cult, Con; their story goes a lot further and deeper in history. The Fallen happen to be what they worship—angels fallen from the Light. Not all are angels, of course; many are just mortals who wish to bask in the glory, but among them walk beings of former immortality. Having been thrown from the Heavens and stripped of their powers, these beings are still more powerful and spiritually connected than the rest of us. It is why they have been so influential in our world. The Dark Prince needs the energies that still reside in their powerful souls to be reincarnated; it would take thousands upon thousands of Humanity to resurrect such powerful beings."

"How does one know who are the true Fallen versus the false?" Conrad questioned, seeing nothing substantially different from any other citizens.

"Their bodies bear the scars of their shame." Sven turned their attention to the prisoners shackled together in one long line and pointed out the pair of long scars that ran between their shoulders and spine. "For their sins, the Gods of Heaven took their wings from them, along with their immortality, leaving them to wallow in dishonour upon this world."

The soldiers started to move the considerable group of prisoners across the bridge, driving them like cattle into the blowing sands. Immense tornadoes of sand could be seen springing up in the far distance as the first members of the Fallen were forced off the bridge. The land of sand shook and shifted as the Fallen were dragged into the sand, all knowing their fate and unable to escape it.

"How do you know so much about this?"

Sven ignored the question, knowing answers would soon be brought forth and he would not need to explain. Certainly his brother had experienced firsthand what he himself had, but the changes within Conrad only surfaced periodically. Conrad never recollected his sudden outbursts, but Sven saw the great conflict occurring within his brother as two separate people fought for control of his soul. He was brother Conrad one moment and the powerful Konflikt the next. Sven did not wonder *if* evil would win control of his brother's soul, but when.

"You don't know what you're doing! You're releasing something that you will never be able to control or be free of! A terrible darkness!" one of the eldest Fallen members shouted back at Sven. The soldier behind him crosschecked the old man with the wood shaft of his long spear, forcing him to continue forward.

"That is not your concern, Fallen! You will serve the purpose that is intended for you."

Following the last of the prisoners, the three travellers released their horses and drew their blades as they took their first steps back into the desert. Their minds wavered as they felt the massive pressure on their brains again; they heard heavy, raspy breaths among the harsh wind.

"Release meeee … Release meee from my prison … Release meee from my prison and bring upon the Second Coming!"

The voice in the air brought back memories of the sands that Sven had called home for several years. He could feel the power in the wind again and feel its heavy hand beneath the sand as they trudged forward. He looked at the red sandstone mountains in the distance, only a few hours ride from the bridge. Sven knew what lay hidden at the base of the mountainous ring carved deep beneath the sandy dunes.

A Mortal Mistake

Barely surviving the first year of his five spent in the Desert of Lost Souls, Sven had been in more battles for his life than he could recall. Often outnumbered and hungry from days without food, his armour and skill were the only reasons for his continued survival. He let his anger fuel his instinct for survival, but even then he continued struggling. Wounded from several skirmishes with the largest gang of bandits roaming the sands, he had fled to the safety of the mountains while they searched for him among their dead. He had climbed toward the top of the shifting sand dune, the promised safety of the red stone finally within sight, and suddenly he'd sunk deeply among the sand that trapped him. The harder he struggled; the deeper he sank, until he was firmly trapped up to his waist.

This is the way that the Fist of Metzor perishes? Was he to die in the heat of the coming daylight, or were his tracks to be followed by convicts and criminals who sought to slay him and bloody their hands once again? Sven did not have enough energy to struggle further nor to dig himself out; he at last conceded defeat for the night. He wrapped his upper body with his torn black cloak and settled in to sleep in the desert's cool midnight air.

His ears had been finely tuned during the struggle for survival in the desert, and he was awakened by soft steps in the sand. The moon was at its highest point in the sky, reflecting its light down on the shadowy blue sand dunes around him. Without moving, he peered out through his hood.

His enemy had followed his tracks for the last several hours. "Wake up and smell your impending death!" A boot kicked sand into his face but maintained a safe distance from Sven's polished blade. "You have been a thorn in my side since your cursed soul arrived in this desert. For six painful months we have been chasing you among the sand, but now it is finally at an end. Unfortunately for you, there is no place here for your irritating essence among the living."

Sven searched for a response to irritate the large gang's leader. The past six months had been very much a cat-and-mouse adventure, though the mouse had constantly outsmarted and whittled away the cat's strength. It all seemed to be at an end now; Sven was cornered, without anywhere to run or the ability to escape. "Must be humiliating that it took you six months and hundreds of uselessly warm bodies to finally catch up to me."

"Matters not when the end result is that you die a horrible and painful death."

Sven felt his death was finally at hand; he would pay for his reckless abandon in spurring so much anger in his short life.

"Such a strong soul does not deserve death at the hands of weakness. Perhaps another soul as strong as your own could eliminate your enemies in return for the same debt? Release me from my prison, and I will release your soul from its fate. What say you?" The voice crawled through his feet and into his mind; those around him seemed to be unaware of it as they continued to watch him closely.

The leader kicked him in the head, knocking his hood and helmet from his head, and then stepped out of the range of Sven's slow swing.

"Let us look upon the face that has caused so much chaos." When his face was revealed in the moonlight, he heard the murmurs of those who surrounded him. The gang leader took several steps back, having recognized him immediately.

"So it is true. Most believed that it was merely a myth that the great Metzonian Prince Sven had ventured into this desert. Most come in search of treasure, or to flee the law. It was difficult to believe those rumours. Many claimed that it was only a bodyguard, who sacrificed his life in service to his lord and bore his cursed armour upon his back. It does not take long for truth to turn into myth, though. Many who carry the word find death soon after. But this certainly seems to be truth."

"Many myths and legends have been told of me, few of which are not true. What difference does it really make in the end?"

"None," the burly figure answered, staring down upon him. "You may be worth a king's ransom, but for the trouble you have cost me, I will take less to watch you die. Your family will certainly still pay plenty to have your body returned piece by piece. It will be worth it to watch you bleed."

The voice of the desert spoke again. "*I merely await your answer. Let me destroy them and fill you with power beyond imagination!*"

Sven could feel his death coming soon. His mind continued to mull the unknown voice. *What spirit lives within these deserts that could deliver such promises? And what would delivering such a promise require of me?* An arrow pierced the steel shoulder of his sword arm, leaving it useless against the impending blow from the steel war hammer.

Groaning in pain, Sven made the deal presented before him. "Spirit … strike down my enemies … and I shall strike down yours in turn." His hands fell to the sand, cold and bloody, as his sword was carefully pulled away from him with an outstretched spear.

"There is no spirit to save you, Sven of Metzor! Just you and us, though plenty of spirits are ready to watch you suffer in pain! The spirits that watch feed off such pleasure and pain; they thirst for your death and to feed upon your soul. Not to see it survive." The man laughed at Sven's weak plea for help, the dozens around him joining in on the joke.

They were unaware of the changes in the air beyond Sven. The air pressure grew heavier, and the sands shifted beneath them.

Sven tried to pull his legs out of the sand, but they remained trapped, as if encased in stone. Yet the sand rumbled all around him.

Fear rose quickly in those who sought his death as they finally noticed the shifting sands.

Reaching from the sandy depths, a clawed hand composed of stark white bone reached through the sand. Several other hands reached out, together rising to the surface of the desert, pulling hulking skeletons behind them toward the surface. The first head pierced the sand, its demonic skull snapping its jaws. Several large horns protruded from the skull; its gaping mouth was full of long fangs, its eyes orbs of red power. The dark energy held the skeleton together at every joint.

The demons continued to rise from the sand. They struck out at the scrambling men, their rusted armour plating and spiny exoskeletons protruding. Wings of bone and long tails were the last to emerge. Five beasts emerged from beneath their feet to rip apart the dozens of men as they tried to escape. The largest of the five bone demons carved the most destruction. It was covered in large plate steel, and great spires of bone protruded from its shoulders and back. The large rusted blade that one skeletal arm wielded hacked down Sven's enemies around him; the other arm crushed men with its clawed hand.

"*Slay them all! Let their blood sift through the sand and their souls join the Lost!*"

The gang leader fell to his knees in the trembling sand, within reach of Sven, still entrapped. Grabbing the man by the throat, Sven tried to separate the larger man's head from his body, as the two wrestled in a death match.

"*My power and strength become yours to use …*" Pain shot through Sven's feet, arcing up into his body, filling his body with strength. The power hit his torso and then sprung to his arms, giving them strength he had not felt in months. His grip tightened and his muscles bulged as he strained. With a final pop, Sven felt the man's head release from his body and watched it roll down the steep bank. He was the last to die.

Sand continued to slough away around Sven, the dune disappearing around him, but still he was unable to move his feet. The wind howled around him, blowing the sand away to reveal what lay hidden beneath the desert.

Stone buildings protruded as the sand eroded, exposing an old city at the base of the rocky red mountains. Sven stood atop the highest of the buildings; a large, stepped pyramid that he assumed was an ancient temple. Standing beneath him atop the expansive platform stood the demonic skeletons that had slain his enemies. Far beneath them it was a graveyard of bones, clogging the streets and many of the staircases of the surrounding temples.

"Who are you, and where do I stand upon?"

"*I am the Dark Prince Rhimmon, Lord of Hell. You stand upon my burial place and altar. Those around you are my lieutenants, the last to stand among my army.*" As the voice spoke, the red energy holding the skeletons together dissipated, and the skeletons collapsed around the altar. *"We have all waited silently for a champion to release us. Few have come before you, but none with the souls of a true destroyer ever wandered within our realm. I feel your soul and know that will no longer be true."*

Perhaps I have gotten in over my head and promised more than I can deliver. Sven questioned his decision. But he knew his choice kept him from joining the Dark Prince's legion of lost souls. "How am I supposed to release you from your prison and defeat your enemies? I am human, while you are supernatural."

"All in good time, my champion. In time I shall unleash my knowledge upon you and grow you strong once more. The moment of return is soon at hand, but we must wait until it is perfect. Long have we been trapped here, but act too soon and all shall be undone!"

His path had been set in a direction he would learn he could never have imagined. Ancient myths and legends overshadowed his record; history would forever be changed by his promise. And now Sven stood here, at last prepared to fulfill his cursed promise. It had taken years of patience and waiting to move all the pieces into their proper places, the guidance of the demon that had carved a niche within his soul ever-present.

"Release me … Spill the blood of the Fallen into the sand that is my hands!"

The sound reverberated within their heads, and Sven began chanting the demonic rituals he had learned so long ago. Long minutes passed before he finished. Feeling the tension in the air he signalled the go-ahead. The slaughter began silently. The three of them started slitting throats, and the guards cut down those trying to escape from the circle of violence. The massacre became a fifteen-minute bloodbath as bodies crumpled to the ground. The thirsty sand absorbed the blood before it could begin to pool.

Large dunes of sand shifted around them as the desert shook violently. Whirling tornadoes of sand swirled from beneath the sand

and reached for the sky, expanding larger and larger. The beating sun dimmed as the sandstorms pulled the desert higher into the sky. Then as quickly as it had all started, the sand began raining back to the ground around them. The wind turned silent, and not a single sound echoed within the desert. All witnesses looked to the sky or the horizon, waiting for what was to happen next.

Deep heavy laughter from the distant mountains resonated across the vast desert. All continued to wait with silent expectancy, knowing that this is where he would arrive but not knowing what to expect. Anticipation grew as they watched a lone figure fly toward them from within the arid region; it grew larger as it proceeded.

The Dark Prince landed on a high dune directly in front of them. He looked down at himself as he flexed his forearms, remembering his former strength. The dark purple skin covered his rippling arms covered in random spines appeared rough as a mountain, ending with four long clawed fingers. His horned head smiled down upon those who had just released him; he bared his pointed yellow teeth. His black eyes watched them closely as he took deep breaths through his flattened nose. Towering over them all, he stretched his wings out, casting shadows overtop them.

Rhimmon, the Dark Prince of temptation and greed had been returned to his physical form to reenter the world to once again terrorize and bind its occupants to his black will. The Prince of Hell smiled; his final release had finally happened. He was free after millennia trapped within the prison made for him.

"Let the Second Coming begin! My son, you have done well. We can now continue with our glorious plans. It's been too long since my brothers and I walked this world, spreading our terror. You have done well, my young king. You have succeeded quicker than anticipated."

"Our only wish is to serve and please my Prince of Darkness."

"And you shall continue to please with your service. With my reincarnation, we can finally put our ancient plan into action. We must first free my brothers from their prisons, requiring a lot more blood to be spilt."

"We used all those we captured to free you, my lord. We have few prisoners remaining that have blood of the Fallen in their veins." Sven hesitated as he looked at the drained bodies.

"Fear not, Devotz the Devourer. There is enough Fallen blood within this world to resurrect the Dark Armies of the olden glory days. I can sense them far and wide, in one clustered location in particular." The demon looked out toward the horizon, gazing over the mystic rivers that kept his wandering spirit confined within the tomb of sand. Sven watched the demon closely, feeling that the Prince of Hell already knew where he spoke of. *"I also smell blood of another Fallen within this world as well, one that has already turned black."*

"Prokopolis," Belle answered automatically. Sven was more concerned about the "others" Rhimmon mentioned. He knew that Prokopolis was already on the Dark Prince's agenda. The demon had already commanded his servant to begin preparing for the next phase of his master's plan, months before those that led up to this moment.

"Is that the name of it? It matters not to me; there are many powerful souls within its walls. All must be taken to quench the thirst of my brothers' souls. Prepare your army. I have grown impatient imprisoned for so long. It is time to begin."

"My Dark Prince will be requiring further service from us? I believed that you only required us to release you, your powers being far greater than our own." Sven asked hesitantly, staring back at his brother and Belle as he waited for the answer.

"Do you demand answers from he who destroyed your enemies in return for a similar favour? Do you command the Dark Prince, slave?"

Sven hit his knees, shaking his head, holding both hands high in submission.

Rhimmon surprised him, speaking logically as he began to explain. *"My strength is indeed great enough to snuff life from this world. I have many long-awaited tasks that seek my attention more than menial mortals. We must not show our true hand, for it will unite your enemies against you before my brothers are released. Powerful they still remain, but I shall direct you.*

You shall destroy, and in time I shall release your soul of its shackles."

"Yes, my Prince of Hell." There was no turning back now; they could all feel it in the backs of their minds. They were forever on this path until the world ended covered in darkness.

"Let us leave this prison." The demon started walking, not hesitating as he stepped across the bridge that had trapped him for so long. Fists smashed the stone wings off the angelic statues lining the bridge railing, as Rhimmon forced the statues to share in the fate of their Fallen comrades.

Those that released the mighty evil followed behind silently and obediently, their emotions silent as though attached to the monster. The bodies of the slain were left in the Desert of Lost Souls, their bodies slowly covered by sand as the black buzzards quickly swarmed toward their next meals.

Off in the distance five men hid behind the rocky outcropping, watching the Dark Prince of Hell being released from his ancient prison. The watchers had followed the prisoners of the Metzonian prince across Metzon, halting a safe distance from the desert. The spreading violence had made it risky, but the Elder had spoken of its urgency with great animation. Fearful of what he thought may have been happening, the men decided to serve their Order as Heaven intended, even if it required their lives. Their hearts cried out at the sight of all their brethren being slain as they watched helplessly from afar.

"Elder Kallisto was indeed correct in his suspicions. We must warn everyone. Two of you ride to the Sacred City to bring warning of this dark tide that will be spreading. The Fallen must flee, for we have witnessed the dark hate of the Fist of Metzor and the demon he released. Prokopolis will fall next. I and the rest will ride for the Elder Council. Pray for us all." The figure watched the battalion following their demonic leader as they disappeared farther down the trail. Joining his comrades, they scurried for their mounts that were resting down the river. All leapt atop their mounts and rode hard.

Splitting to ride in two separate directions, they took off to spread the dire warning.

A great evil had been released that surpassed all the horrors that had occurred upon the world for thousands of years. Hopeless despair would shake the foundations of the Order upon hearing the fatal words. None were able to defeat the demon's darkness; they would have to flee for their lives.

But where?

Chapter 14
The Oblitoryiat

The ringing of the heavy bells crashed loudly from the steeple of the tall cathedral, echoing out among the structures hiding at the base of the Lifebringer. Sunlight streaming down through the misty waterfalls left endless rainbows crisscrossing the face of the mountain. The loud crash of steel sent many of the large nesting eagles leaping from their cliff-side nests out toward the lake surrounding the small city.

Walking through the wide streets, Kallen watched the majestic creatures soar, their large wings carrying them higher through the sky. He had always dreamed as a child about flying through the air, then plunging, feeling the rush of excitement as gravity pulled you back to Earth. What it must have been like to once fly through the sky.

Pushing forward through the streets, he listened to the babbling streams that flowed through the town, the roar of the mountain waterfalls in the distant background. Kallen had arrived at the Sacred City almost a week ago, arriving in the dead of the night. It had not been Kallen's first trip to the Sacred City, as Militades had forced him to travel there at least once every two years for his three-month leave. Little had changed within the city. However he did not remember the journey being so hazardous; the great dangers had increased exponentially since the last time.

The persecution of innocent citizens because of their religious beliefs was burning across Metzon like wild fire. Multiple times Kallen had come across headless bodies and burnt farmsteads, clearly marking them as former supporters of the king's murderers. Roaming bands scoured the countryside in search of new victims, and the cities were even worse. The border guards in Manstein had pursued him for five hours he managed to escape the city.

Evading the endless patrols, Kallen had reached the Sacred City in record time. Despite his weariness he sought out his sister, surprising her high upon a ladder within the immense temple library. Leaping down to wrap her arms tightly around him, she had cried great sobs of joy upon seeing him once again, drawing few of his own tears. Staying up to watch the sunrise over the cathedral, she told him about the turmoil and pain she had been forced to endure. Seeing her cry left Kallen's heart aching, wishing he could have borne her burden instead.

Passing the cathedral, he still marvelled at the splendour of it. Multitudes of large angelic statues lined the exterior and were placed among the numerous gardens. The large cathedral was a testament to the glory of those that had came before them, overshadowed only by the large temple complex within the mountain. All statues had been handcrafted to match each specific angel and included their name and family. Thousands of statues adorned the Sacred City, creating a historic memoir of all fallen angels who had walked the world. Although they had all lost their wings, the Order's belief dictated that their sacrifice upon Earth would grant them a second chance within Heaven.

For all they had sacrificed for this world, Kallen was not interested in those buried within the Sacred City. He wanted to see the tombs of the Fallen Five, but he would not find them so far down the mountain. For all the beauty within the tall churches and the fragile architecture that spread across his home of Prokopolis, he preferred the pace of life within the Sacred City. In contrast to the hustle and bustle of the Order's capital, the Sacred City offered a different atmosphere, a calming, everlasting peace that slowed one's heart and mind. Life beneath the Lifebringer moved at a slow pace, one that linked his soul to the steady pace of the water trickling down stone, releasing all stress within his body.

As he watched a rigid procession of city guards marching in front of him, he remained impressed. After delivering his many messages to Kallisto and receiving his orders, Kallen took command of the army within the Sacred City, though overseeing was closer to the job description. The Fallen of the Sacred City trained with a religious zeal that he found extremely surprising considering how far they were from any real danger.

The Metzonians were drilled at an incessant rate by their own Elite general, who had graciously accommodated Kallen. Scrutinizing every action by every soldier, Dubryst and Prince Frederick were determined to have their infantry prepared for when the Order marched to war, forcing Kallen to bite his tongue. Having heard the Elders discuss their reluctance to begin a war, Kallen knew that the Metzonians would likely never return home.

With such tight command already established, he had begun to prepare to train the Children. That was not to begin for another week, allowing him time to relax and enjoy the Valley of Angels. Glancing to the other side of the marching guard, he caught the eye of two women. One smiled toward him as her friend continued to whisper in her ear.

"We heard rumours of your anticipated return, but now I see with my own eyes that they are not merely rumours." Her large violet-blue eyes sent quivers down his spine as their eyes briefly met. She was the only person he ever knew with such vibrant eyes inherited through genetics passed down by the rarest of heavenly ancestors. Her large white smile warmed his insides as she playfully harassed him. "Glad to see that you have finally found your way out of your mountain cave though, Kallen."

Compared to his much lighter skin, her bronze skin signified that she spent more time outside. Matched with her long black hair and dazzling eyes, it all combined for a stunning woman in any man's eyes, particularly his. Jaina was an orphan like himself, taken into the care of the fierce gatekeeper after her family perished when she was very young. Under his protection she had flourished and grown, embodying life and its beauty. Her incredible innate ability to nurture and heal combined with her love of life and nature had contributed to her graduation to the Keeper of the Trees of Eternity within the Sacred Temple, as well as looking after the grand gardens within the city. Kallen noticed how much her work had helped to enhance the beauty and glory of the holy city, making her quite popular among its citizens.

"Another beautiful day that the world has bestowed upon us, don't you think? What brings a mighty Titan commander of Prokopolis out into the streets among the common folk instead of rolling around in the dirt with the other boys?" Jaina's companion spoke up, forcing his attention away from Jaina. The innocent question was not as subtle as she played it.

Gatekeeper's actual daughter, Kaylee's beauty was very similar to her foster sister's, though her presence was much closer to her father's. Strong willed and forceful, she spoke what was upon her mind and was not easily deterred by opposition. Her beauty had struck many among the community although none had been able to tame her spirit. Tall, slim and particularly womanly, she wore her bright golden hair long. Her large brown eyes always shone.

"It is indeed a beautiful day. Such a beautiful day that I figured I should escape the shadows and take in the glory of summer. Seeing both of you has only increased its beauty." Attempting to put a smile on their faces, he grinned. A smile broke across Jaina's face before her sister's quick reply broke the small moment.

"Well, that was weak—actually pathetic. Perhaps you should return to your shadows to think up wittier responses so as to not embarrass yourself. That may work upon the pretty and naive girls of Prokopolis, but you will have to try harder to impress women such as us." Kaylee laughed in his face, ridiculing him for even contemplating such a feeble attempt, and then just as quickly changed the subject and pushed past him. "We are supposed to be at the Sabrael Gardens by now and should really get going. Tell your sister to find us there if you see her, would you?"

Kaylee continued past him, her foster sister in tow. Kaylee's abruptness bordered on rudeness but did not diminish Kallen's happiness as he continued on his way through the city. He had been quite thrilled to learn that his sister had become quick friends with the two women, providing him with an excuse to talk to Jaina.

Gazing up at the sun, Kallen could not help but smile as he headed back out toward the shadows of the Lifebringer.

Numerous statues hidden among the thick plant growth overlooked the long, steep path that led toward the rear entrance of the mountain. Four rows of large columns holding the entrance roof up were carved directly out of the dark stone of the mountain. Several lightly clad archers peered down at him from the roof as he walked along, their eyes drawn more to the shimmering lake and misty rainbows the waterfalls projected into the sky. There were few guards at the rear entrance of the temple complex; the Order thought the risk of being attacked ridiculous because of its position at the rear of the mountain. Kallen assumed they were there in the event a problem arose in the city.

The Sacred City was constructed upon a high perch on the backside of the mountain overlooking a large bay. Any enemy who wanted to attack to ravage the city would have to climb several hundred feet of slippery stone through the maze of water working its way down across the mountain. Possible with a small force of mountain sheep, it was impossible for any force that could pose a viable threat.

Kallen started into the temple complex. He quickly walked down the polished stone floors through the protective Doors of Final Fate at the rear entrance, with their ever-present guardians. The gatekeeper's loud laughter could be heard from his headquarters as he joked with several of the other officers.

The Doors of Final Fate were the last line of defence the Sacred City had if their enemies advanced beyond the walls of the great fortress and infiltrated the temple itself. The gatekeeper, Akakios, and his battalion of guardians were in charge of protecting the inhabitants of the Sacred City at any cost. Patrolling the city and maintaining order and security was easy among a population made up of primarily the Children of the Fallen and their caretakers.

Kallen quickly slipped past the entrance, bypassing the older man's attention, to continue to his current destination. He knew that if Gatekeeper Akakios saw him he too would be stuck for many hours laughing with the subordinates.

Without a doubt, Akakios would harass the younger man by mentioning his daughter and her single status. Another smile rose to Kallen's face when he thought of his last conversation with the gatekeeper on the subject of his daughter's disdain for him.

"Kallen, you just have to be persistent to the bitter end! How do you think an old bear such as me came to raise such a daughter of unquestionable beauty? Persistence, persistence, persistence!"

The Titan continued through a conjoining intersection, weaving through a small group of priests and scholars in the middle of a heated debate over a particular Fallen angel from the past and his individual impact upon the Order. It still amazed him how many were within the temple, many with skin ghostly white in comparison to his own.

Finally reaching the library, he pushed open the large doors quietly. A rush of cool air from the vault brushed across his face as he entered as noiselessly as an armoured knight could. Alexandra had told him she had never met a man with a more voracious appetite for knowledge than Kallisto. The old man literally spent days living within the library, so Kallen naturally thought it would be the best place to find his sister. For where Kallisto was, she was usually not too far away. He saw several people silently reading ancient texts of immense size, searching for hidden messages or learning about the epic history the library was full of. Reaching the back of the room, he saw that the doors to Kallisto's private vault were already open.

The old man leisurely flipped the pages as he slowly read through the *Demise of Dev'Azra,* a chronicle of a dark angel who was among the first to be tossed from the Heavens but chose to continue his path of destruction and ruin. Kallisto's eyes followed his large hands across the worn pages, tapping all the important points as they were logged into the man's mind. He paused to look up at Kallen.

"Sorry, Kallisto, I thought that perhaps Alexandra was with you in the library. I did not mean to interrupt you."

"No need to apologize, as it is a pleasant interruption, Kallen." Chuckling to himself, Kallisto leaned back in his chair, beckoning

Kallen forward to take a seat. Kallen refrained for a moment. "Your protector, Militades, does not share my love of reading and knowledge. Hence, why I have been temporarily appointed acting administrator while he commands the armies of the Order. A soldier through to his core, he is, with never a love for history."

Militades was indeed a soldier and not a scholar. He'd taught Kallen everything he required about war. He was a great teacher of the art, though Kallen had never been forced to use his skills in real combat. Kallisto pointed toward the chair once more. "Please, stay a while. I do not very often get to see you or visit with you privately."

Taking the wooden chair at the old man's request, Kallen eased himself into it carefully, ensuring its skinny legs would hold his weight. He leaned back slightly as Kallisto continued the conversation, readjusting some items on the desk before resting his arms upon them and leaning forward.

"How is life outside the Temple, my son? It was a most beautiful morning, so I would assume that it's blossomed into even greater grandeur. I was giving myself a history lesson, rereading about the dark angel Dev'Azra and his witch bride, Xera, who came from the dark side of the world. Fortunately, the Sin's immense army was unable coordinate or combine their terrible powers. Greed and personal ambitions ultimately led to their deaths. Mortality was not a fate they had anticipated.

"What terrible circumstances plagued the Order at its offset and threatened to destroy it before it was able to grow into that which we know today. Glory be that the mighty Orion had the strength and wisdom to withstand such an onslaught." Kallisto shook his head gravely, clearly understanding the story better than Kallen, who nodded in agreement.

"Orion was indeed mighty if the historic records are correct; all should aspire to be as strong and noble as he was." Kallen had heard all about Orion—he was sure there was not a single person who had not. Whoever had the power to throw someone such as Orion from the Heavens must have been truly powerful.

"Indeed, what a beautiful world this could be if all strived to be like him. I've often dreamed about what it would have been like to stand within his shadow and to have witnessed him in person." That was only partially true. Kallen had done nothing but dream about it. "While his physical presence was astounding, they say that his spirit and determination cast shadows upon all around him."

Kallen had spent his life reading the numerous tomes written about the first grandmaster, the one who engineered the Order from the beginning. Every book that had been written about the man, Kallen had absorbed, and he spent many hours listening to scholars debate his impact. Orion was the person Kallen had modelled his life around, the person who he wanted to become—a lofty goal many would claim was foolish, which was why he preferred to keep to himself.

"Alexandra mentioned that you had a fascination with the great Orion. Militades has stood within his immense shadow, but I suppose he never told you that, did he?" Upon seeing Kallen's shocked face, Kallisto smiled and leaned back in his chair. He continued to astonish the adopted son of his dearest friend. "We both did, however so briefly …"

"You both met Orion!" His heart slammed heavily within his ribcage with the excitement of finding these new sources of knowledge who had been fortunate enough to meet him. Kallen's mind spun with thousands of questions, including why his protector had never told him such information. "What was he like in person? Did you get to see him often?"

Kallisto stood up from his seat and readjusted his long robes, pulling them tighter to keep the cool temple air away from his bones. Disappointed that Kallisto refused to answer his questions, Kallen assumed that the subject was going to be another added to the "off-limit" list.

"Your fascination with Orion is like many followers of the Order, but I sense your passion grows deeper than most. Grab that torch and follow me. Let me show you something you will appreciate as I answer a few more of your questions."

Grabbing a torch from the wall sconce, Kallen hurried to follow Kallisto, who had already begun to walk deeper into the vault through a small doorway leading to a narrow spiralling staircase. Deeper in the vault, the air grew moist and stale as the pair spiralled deeper into the depths.

Walking only briefly, Kallen sensed that the vault would not be reached for several minutes when his sister's caretaker began speaking once more. "Orion was everything you have read about and more. Militades and I only met him at the end of his reign, unfortunately. Militades knew him a few years longer than I. Old he may have been, but he still retained all his memory and the mental function that usually decays with time in Humanity. Our new father had taught us all a great many things after we fell from the stars. Where we came from, who we were. He gave us all a purpose in this second life. It was a shame that I was not around to absorb all he would have been able to teach. What he may have known and kept secret from the rest of us makes my heart beat faster."

The staircase continued briefly before coming to a long shadowy hallway. As they walked, Kallisto answered most of Kallen's questions, seeming happy to feed Kallen's younger mind with what knowledge he could. Reaching the entrance, Kallisto stopped suddenly at the stone arch, and Kallen almost knocked into him. Pausing for the briefest of moments, Kallisto spoke, his voice soft. "Gaze upon the grandeur with your eyes, and let you heart fill with wonder."

Kallisto moved aside, letting Kallen's torch cast its light into the darkness. Before him stood a vault that he had never dreamt existed, forcing his imagination to believe it was real for a moment. Carved of stone, a replica of Orion sat in a wide stone throne set in the middle of the room. The grandeur of the statue was diminished only by what surrounded it.

"This is Orion's tomb?" His tongue came untied at last.

"No, this is where the Order has stored all that he owned." Kallen wanted to enter the area but restrained himself. Kallisto continued. "Orion's tomb is near the mountain peak, as is that of his beloved Brianna as they requested on their deathbeds."

Orion's armour glittered in the torch light; Kallen gazed upon the large suit of steel made for a giant, finely detailed and crafted with great care. He marvelled at just how large the first grandmaster had been. Atop the statue's head sat the helmet that was never depicted in the numerous murals of him throughout the temple and beyond.

Unlike the Fallen's single plume of feathers arcing across the crest of the helmet, Orion's crest swept from shoulder to shoulder like a great headdress of white feathers. A mask of matching steel covered the stone face entirely except for the pair of oval eye slits. It chilled Kallen to think of Orion's piercing golden eyes looking through the mask, prepared to tear his enemies' limbs from their bodies. Glancing down, his heart halted and his breath escaped his lungs when he saw the object the fallen angel would have used to perform such actions.

"The *Oblitoryiat*..." escaped his lips. The long white steel of the holy Oblitoryiat lay across the silver armour encasing Orion's stone legs. Kallen couldn't believe that he was gazing upon the sword the Order of the Fallen had been built upon throughout time.

"Forged by Orion himself before he fell, the sharp blade of the Oblitoryiat has seen the death of the most potent of the Order's enemies. Vanquishing enemies such as the Dark Gods of Dev'Azra and Xera, among countless other Sin, the blade was as much a legend as Orion himself. Few holy blades still exist. The knowledge to forge them was lost after the fall of the Golden Age, and none are cast of the heavenly white steel of the Oblitoryiat."

The last item that grabbed Kallen's eye was the great round shield leaned against the arm of the stone throne, the top edge clasped within the fingers of stone. The round shield of Orion did not have the shimmering of the white blade that was cast out of iridescent silver, with the crest of the Order of the Fallen displayed.

The very first Crest of Orion was moulded with silver, five streaks cutting across the face of it depicting the Fallen Five as they streaked across Earth's sky like meteors. The largest along with two other streaks were coloured a glimmering gold; the final two were orange, representing his wife Brianna and another from her house. That crest had now flown upon every white banner of the Order, becoming adopted as a signal that the Order had arrived to continue its noble quest to protect Humanity from its enemies as well as itself.

The ensemble created a terrifying image of indisputable power and strength that threatened the darkness within the world. Kallen felt small before its magnificence, more a human than he had ever felt before. The enemies of Orion must have indeed been fierce to challenge the one who wore this armour into the battle.

"Imagine his strength with the power of the Heavens behind it …" Imagining angelic wings attached to the suit, Kallen knew that it was not the holy armour worn by the warriors of Heaven, but it gave him a sense of the divine powers that once carried Orion across the kingdom of Heaven.

"Imagine one could. Perhaps someday you will wield the Oblitoryiat, much like Orion did in defence of the Order." Kallisto smiled at Kallen, who snorted at the jest of such a thing ever happening. As much as he may dream such a thing, it would never be.

"Unlikely, Kallisto." Backing away from the figure, Kallen made a promise to himself out loud. "I will tell you this though, Kallisto. I am going to do everything in my power to become great like Orion. Someday, with time and patience, I will stand tall before the Order and bring a new light to the world, like he did."

Feeling a hand clasped around his neck, Kallen turned to look into the blue eyes of the old man. A slight smile crossed Kallisto's face as his eye squinted at him, as though in pain. "You will indeed. I have a feeling you will indeed achieve your dreams, and much more."

Chapter 15
Prokopolis

Silence had overtaken the immense city of Prokopolis, the feelings of coming darkness upon many of its eldest citizens. The quiet babbling of the city fountains and the breeze rustling the leaves were the only sounds that penetrated the darkness of predawn. The first streams of light shined upon the tops of the twin towers filling the eastern tower with its rays high atop the acropolis it was built upon.

The Elder Council had convened quietly in the eastern tower of Ori; news had long ago reached them of the atrocities that had befallen their people in Metzor. Their brethren had been attacked, and the Metzonian chapter of the Order of the Fallen had been destroyed. As far as they knew from their spies within the capital, the chapter's followers were still in prison on false charges, being tortured to confession and then dragged off. All Order buildings had been seized by the corrupt crown and turned over to theRoyal Treasury to fund the ever-growing Metzonian military. All attempts to negotiate or question events had proven futile.

As the Elder Council spoke high in their lofty tower, a single chestnut horse rode hard through the sleepy streets toward the government sector of the sprawling buildings. The rider clung hard to the horse, holding on with all his remaining strength, carrying his dark message in his mind. The Metzonian barbed arrow within his left lung forced him to gasp for air as he struggled to maintain consciousness. The horse skidded toward the gatehouse, its path suddenly at a dead end, throwing its rider to the cobblestone street.

Attempting to pick himself up was useless; exhaustion and pain coursed through his body. His leg buckled as he tried to put weight on it. Two tall guards ran up to him, their tall spears pointed toward him, suspicious of anyone who arrived at that hour of the morning. He gasped his intentions and what he required of them; specifying that time was very short. The captain quickly ordered them to assist the man, watching silently as they each locked an arm beneath his armpits and dragged him inside the palace, up the stairs toward the top floor of the tower. A red trail splayed over the white stairs as the guards pulled him higher and higher.

The Elder Council continued to argue over what to do about the state of affairs and what actions to make, but none could guess that everything was worse than believed. An affair that was possibly uncontrollable even to beings who had weathered the events of the world never truly crossed their minds. The tall doors shook the room as they were thrown open by the guards. They dragged their stricken victim down the central aisle and down the staircase. No members of the council spoke or questioned the intrusion, clearly seeing the severity of the man's injuries.

"My brothers … the end is very near for us … and the entire world! We … watched as the Metzonian kin … slayed our brethren in the Desert of Lost … Souls." Struggling, the injured man gasped as he continued to use up the remaining strength that he had tried to save. "My brothers rode … for the Sacred City … The king … He brings with him the demon from the past … the Second Coming. The end has come for us!"

Philotheos exited the tall tower into the morning sunlight, the city now bustling with animation not from excitement but rampant fear and terror. It was difficult to hide anything when all were as emotionally woven together as his people were. The Fallen could sense the fear within individuals of the Elder Council, and their reactions triggered suspicion among those of Humanity who served and built their lives within the Order. The mobilization of the

A Mortal Mistake

army and baggage trains would solidify their greatest suspicions immediately.

Philotheos would have preferred avoiding the citizens walking through the streets by taking back alleys and scurrying across the streets unnoticed, but the citizens of Prokopolis deserved better from their government. Leaving his white gelding within the palace stables, he walked out the front gates to greet a growing crowd of concerned citizens waiting patiently near the gatehouse at the base of the great acropolis the palace was built upon.

Anticipation grew at the sight of his white council robes. Spotting the one who dared to come face the noise, the citizens all cried out to him, curiosity and fear upon the various faces that gathered around the palace walls.

"White Elder Philotheos! What is wrong?"

"Can you tell us anything about the news you have received? Does it have to do with the Fallen of Metzor?"

"Any update on what the Order will do about the rumours of treason against Metzor and their new king?"

"What of last night's rider?"

Listening to the numerous cries, Philotheos knew that he was only going to disappoint them by leaving them in the dark to fret and worry. News of the bloodied rider had spread like the dawn, and all speculated about what news could have been so urgent. Throwing his hands out above the crowd, Philotheos spoke softly, forcing the questioners to silence. All strained to hear him.

"Citizens of Prokopolis. Members of the Fallen. I cannot divulge the details that the Elder Council is currently contemplating. We ask that you remain calm but prepared as the Elders delve into their visions of the future to search for the answers to their own numerous questions.

"The Elder Council will be addressing the Lords of Prokopolis this afternoon and later this evening will be speaking publicly at theatres and public venues throughout the city. I cannot emphasize enough that everyone should stay calm and try not to worry. We will do everything within our power to protect the citizens of Prokopolis, as well as the Order of the Fallen."

Plenty more questions were asked of the youngest member of the White Elders, but he had to ignore them, turning away. A few continued to call out to him; others accepted that they would have to wait until the evening.

Philotheos just wanted to get home; he was already weary despite it only being early morning. Relief washed over him when he reached the gates to his small manor. His guard opened the steel rungs for him and closed the gates behind them as he stared out into the streets. Standing before his house, he took a long look, drinking up the image of his home. The white walls of the building were not large but they were clean. Much of the estate was large gardens, with an orchard of fruit trees and a small garden. It was everything that he ever wanted, more than he truly needed.

Resting upon his bench before a small trout pond, he reached beneath the bench and grabbed a handful of feed for his three fish. Plucking a plump pear from the nearby tree, he then sat back to enjoy the moment of sunlight breaking through the branches upon his skin. He enjoyed the heat of the sunlight, unsure how much longer he would enjoy that feeling upon this world.

Two girls ran out of the whitewashed stone entry into his outstretched arms, embracing him fiercely. Smelling of cinnamon, their noses powdered with flour, each gave Philotheos a kiss upon the cheek. Squirming within his bear hug they pleaded for freedom, his father's heart crying at the thought of letting them go. Freedom and safety were all his little girls desired, and both were on the verge of being taken away.

"We are making hotcakes!" Holly and Emilia declared proudly to their father as they led him inside to witness their handiwork. They skipped along the stone path, their bright red hair dancing in the air, mimicking their glee-filled dance.

"I can most certainly see that." Laughing, he wiped the flour off Holly's nose and followed them into the house. His large-framed household nanny stepped from the door, greeting him with a grin of equal broadness.

"Good morning, Serena—how are you this morning?"

"Better than you are from the looks of the black circles beneath

A Mortal Mistake

your eyes." He never could hide anything from the girls' nanny; she was extremely intuitive at sniffing out the slightest distress in any of them. "You look tired, and the sun did not come up but a few hours ago. Have a seat. I will go and get you a cup of milk."

She disappeared for a moment, leaving him to watch his girls play before him. The faces displaying large smiles had not always been so full of joy. The sisters had come into his arms as sad and lonely children. The guards roaming through the streets had been alerted to their presence in the market in the middle of the night by the shrill scream of a newly born child. The captain of the guards found a young girl, not even four years old, huddled and shivering within a stand of barrels, holding another young child. The market was closed and all patrons and merchants gone home for the night. The moon was waning, and soon the sun would rise, indicating the parent who had forgotten her children had not forgotten at all but abandoned them in the market, lost among the throngs of shoppers and merchants.

Philotheos had gone to the barracks two days later and discovered that the parents of the children had still not been found. His wife being barren, no little children ever passed through his home, leaving a gap within his life. With his beloved wife's passing, the house had grown too quiet and lonely for him for far too many years, so he offered to take them into his home, fulfilling what he had always longed for. He had never regretted the decision, loving the children as if they were his own. Some questioned how he could love and raise children that were not his own; others believed it to be a noble act worthy of the greatest praise. To give a young child opportunity and happiness seemed a great gift to Philotheos; he cared not what any others said about him. He loved both of them so much, he only wished that he would get the opportunity to watch them grow old, find husbands and bear him grandchildren.

That dream is being taken away from me far too soon, he thought to himself once more.

"There is something that we must talk about, girls. Come close to me and sit on your father's lap." Both girls ran toward him and climbed upon his knees. "You're both going on an adventure across the wide land. You're going to run through the grassy hills, over the mighty blue river on a large stone bridge. Through the big forest of the largest green trees you have ever seen in your life, full of colourful birds." Both sets of big brown eye were wide with excitement at what he described to them. "It gets even better! You are going to get to ride a ship down a wild and scary river and then climb up several high mountains to a city of Heaven! Full of the princes, princesses and knights of your bedtime stories."

Excitement grew within them until it was too much for their little bodies to contain. Leaping from his knees, they started to dance before him, giggling happily. "When do we leave and what do we have to bring?"

"Only your clothes and your favourite items, no more." He knew they did not have much more than a few pairs of clothes, but they were happy all the same. "I will not be carrying all your stuff, so you should hurry and pack your clothes. Be packed by the midday lunch bell."

They started to scurry off before halting in midstep and turning around to ask the question that he did not want to have to answer. "You are coming though, right?"

"Your Aunt Serena will be taking you, along with Jakub."

"But not you?" A look of confused fear started to creep into the younger, Emilia. "How come you're not taking us on this adventure? You like adventure!"

She fled back to Philotheos, her sorrowful brown eyes pulling the strings of his heart as she climbed back onto his knees and into the safety of his arms. He held her close. Holly soon followed, tears streaming like her sister.

"I will not be able to protect you from what is coming. Bad people are coming to hurt everyone, but your father is going to make sure they cannot hurt you. I have to stay and help the others who can't escape to the city of princes."

"The princes are supposed to come and save us! Why aren't they coming to save us?"

Philotheos contemplated the simple thinking of the children. So innocent and full of simple understanding, the world of children was clear of hate or pain, preferring the joys of carefree happiness. So simple and so sweet.

Princes were indeed coming to Prokopolis, but not the princes who defeated evil. These princes were filled with anger and violence, the villainous monsters of children's fairytales. He held the two little girls tightly in his arms, trying to comfort them in the only way he knew how.

"I do not know. What I do know is that I have to protect the both of you the only way I can. You are what I love the most in the world."

"Then come with us! If you really love us you would."

"Okay, girls! Enough with the crying. Go to your rooms and pack your things like your father asked of you. You do not question the love of your father or what he does to protect you, only trust in him."

The nanny picked up the children and set them upon the wooden staircase, chasing them upstairs to collect their things.

"We will protect the girls, Philotheos, have no fear. The girls are as large a part of our own family as they are of yours." She smiled at him, giving him a large hug, tightly holding him to comfort the older man who was losing everything dear to him.

"I know, Serena. Thank you for everything. I am eternally grateful for what you are doing."

"Think nothing of it. This is all I have, like you—you are all like family. You know that. Now how would you like a hot cinnamon cake and another cup of goat's milk?" He moved to object but she would have none of it, forcing the food upon him before continuing on in her chores. Tasting the cinnamon, he devoured his cake quickly, letting the sweet goat milk carry the flavour throughout his mouth.

Looking up at the staircase and hearing the stomping of little feet above his head, he knew he could not avoid it any longer. Pulling himself up from his seat, he went to his room to grab a couple of items he had been keeping for a long time that needed to make the journey as well. Carrying the glossy boxes beneath his arm, he began climbing the stairs to help his children begin the sad but necessary task of packing.

Philotheos entered the girls' small room. "Do you think you girls could do one last very important thing for your father?"

"No!" Emilia screamed, not looking back. Watching a small red dress flutter through the air as the youngest threw a fistful of clothes across the room, Philotheos turned to Holly, who ignored his question completely, refusing to make eye contact. Philotheos walked over to pick the little dress up off the floor before lowering himself down upon the small bed and setting the boxes to the side.

"I have a gift for someone. You wouldn't want to deprive someone of a gift that would make them happy, would you?"

"No …" Emilia's face softened at the guilty thought. Holly came over, brushing her tears against her shoulder, running her fingers over a box. "Who is the gift for?"

"You will ask for the one they call the Advisor. The gift is not for him, but when he opens the case he will know who the true recipient is. If not, tell him she carries five scars, and they are not of the Fallen. Take a look at this historic bow." He cracked open the case for the children to look at; their eyes lit up at its beauty. "It actually belongs to a beautiful princess who is tall and lean like the graceful willow tree. She has bright blonde and orange hair like the ancestors she never knew, and this special gift will mean a lot to her."

Careful to avoid pinching their little fingers, Philotheos closed the lid of the top box and slid one into each child's bag. He had sneaked the two boxes out of the large treasure vault beneath the twin towers and hoped they would bring peace to the relationship that had been so rough on both of them.

Rolling the small red dress in his large hands, Philotheos set the item in Emilia's small leather bag. The tears had begun to dry from his daughters' eyes, and small smiles tugged at their cheeks as he tried to make them laugh. On the verge of finishing another joke, he looked out the small round window of their bedroom on an unusual sight, a sight that left him feeling disturbed and unsettled.

Hobbling down the stairs, Philotheos raced out the door and through the gate. Turning around the corner, he tried to follow the marching soldiers who themselves struggled to follow Militades's rapid pace. Militades seemed a man possessed, a scary thought when it pertained to a man who was exceptional with swords. And with a hundred privately trained guards behind him, both blades were within his hands.

Reaching the top of the acropolis, Philotheos watched the last of the Miliatade's personal Defenders of the Orion entering the tall palace doors. Looking out across the city, he wondered if the Order was going to destroy itself even before their enemies reached their doorsteps. He walked briskly toward the doors, able to hear immediate shouting.

"Why is it that a street merchant knows more about an evacuation order than the grand general himself! What in the name of the Heavens have you done?"

Philotheos walked through the door in time to hear Militades shout. The calm, steady voice of the grandmaster replied, despite the armed force presented before him, worrying Philotheos.

"What was required to be done, Militades," Caelestis responded.

Wading his way to the front of the crowd, Philotheos realized why there was no fear from the older man. Two thick lines of Titans stood across the pillared courtyard of the palace, a line of poleaxes lowered before the Militades's swarm of Defenders. If it was a violent encounter Militades had intended, the bloodshed would be immense.

He looked toward the general of all the Order's armies, a man known for his boldness when voicing his opinion, so much that the Elders had implemented a three-month ban from all council meetings, a decision that was about to backfire. Instead of keeping it confined to the chambers in the Ori tower, Philotheos was prepared for the general's violent temper to explode for the entire palace to see.

Looking at his red face, Philotheos knew Militades was more than prepared to step over the line.

"Required to be done! I told you all what was required to be done when Prince Sven first murdered his father! You blithering idiots, why did you not listen to me? I tried to warn you all, but you called me a fool, and now look what your inaction has brought upon us. You all fully knew what was going on, but you chose to imprudently ignore it. What impact could a mortal possibly have upon this world?"

"As such we are prepared to agree that you are right. Prince Sven must be destroyed …"

"It is too late for that now, Caelestis!" Militades cut the grandmaster off, slashing his sword through the air in front of him in frustration. "The Metzonian armies already secured the crossing last night. I assume they followed the rider that arrived in the middle of the night bearing terrible news. Who is the messenger who arrived upon the acropolis to never exit again? What word did he bring to you?"

"Why ask when you already know the answer?"

"Because I want to hear it directly from your lips! I want you to speak the words so you can understand the full extent of what you have brought upon us all, so that everyone who is gathered around us will now know the truth!"

Grandmaster Caelestis crossed his white robe before him, taking a deep breath as he looked up at the arched ceilings. As a member of the White Elders, Philotheos understood what had been spoken and what the remaining Elders had said. The decision to keep it secret had been discussed at great length, and many of the reasons were solidly based. Philotheos watch his elder break the silence.

"Prince Sven took the entire Metzonian Chapter into the Desert of Lost souls. He sacrificed them by spilling their holy blood into the sands of the lost. Butchered everyone down to the last man. How was that for you, Militades. Does that make you feel good to hear me say that? Does it make everything good again?"

"And?"

Philotheos looked over to the grandmaster, waiting for him to answer the question. Hiding his face behind his large white beard, Philotheos could see his refusal to speak within his eyes.

Militades asked him again, refusing to take silence as an answer. He stepped forward. "And?"

A Mortal Mistake

"Rhimmon, the Dark Prince of Hell, has been resurrected from the desert." Philotheos spoke for the first time from the edge of the crowd, and both men looked toward him. Caelestis stared daggers at him as Philotheos stepped out from the crowd, careful not to get directly between the two armed parties. Militades looked away from him to the grandmaster, waiting for his response.

"It is true. But we are already looking toward the survival of the Fallen. Our libraries are being emptied, and many of the Fallen have already begun evacuating. The White Elders refuse to allow genocide of our people to progress further than it already has."

"At the cost of sacrificing over a million Prokopolites to the Dark Prince of Hell!" Militades screamed, raising both his swords toward the Order's grandmaster in outrage. "You would sacrifice all of Humanity to save those who have sinned! You expect Heaven to grant you the Great Return? That they will restore your souls to Heaven knowing you let others die for your own survival? No, Caelestis, it is the Glory Road for us all, just as Orion prophesized."

Philotheos cringed as the commotion drew others into the crowd. All Fallen prayed for the happier of Orion's two prophecies. The Great Return would come after the Judgment, when Heaven at last returned to absolve them of their sins. Seeing that the Fallen had resolved to change their ways, their souls would be lifted back to the Heavens to serve the Light of Heaven once again.

The Glory Road, Orion's second prophecy, was not as its name proclaimed it. The Glory Road was a darker, more painful path: a Fallen would die a mortal's death in this world, but individuals were to attempt to do so in a way that still honoured their commitment to the Light and let their souls rest peacefully, knowing that even in death, they had done the correct thing. It was the prophecy that none had hoped would come true but had now become the more realistic of the two.

"What choice do I have now, Militades? Perhaps you should be grandmaster of the Order and we shall see what you decide to do! We made mistakes. Is that what you wanted to hear? Does that make you feel better now, to know that we admit our errors? The fate of Humanity is now sealed whether we decide to take the Glory Road or not."

Philotheos watched the general lower both his blades slightly, slowing his breathing. Watching the man tremble in anger, the chronicler watched the soldier trying to regain his composure.

"The whole point of the Glory Road prophecy is exactly that, Caelestis. To make the Great Return, you must travel down the Glory Road. It is the selfless act of service lasting your lifetime, even if the ultimate sacrifice must be made. That is what Heaven desires to see. The road to redemption was not meant to be the easy path, it was meant to be the right path."

Silence fell upon the two men, the soldiers on each side cautiously awaiting their respective commander's orders. The Titans guarding the Elder remained like stone, their large poleaxes spaced with perfect precision, matching their body positions. The Defenders calmly remained in their formation behind Militades, hands upon the pommels of their swords. Speaking softly, Philotheos began negotiating the stalemate that had settled between the two men.

"Militades, my friend. We can regret our errors, but we cannot go back in time to fix them. What has been done is done, and we now have to deal with the future. One that looks like it's destined for war. As the grand general of the Armies of the Fallen, what do you recommend we do now?"

"What can we do? Evacuate what remains of the Children of the Fallen along with proper escorts? Perhaps we use the Elder's own Titan guards? After they are safely out of the city, we begin to evacuate those who wish to escape." Militades sheathed his swords and stroked his forked beard, looking dangerously at Caelestis. "Both Fallen and Human."

"Keep in mind, Militades, that the Army of the Fallen will not move beyond the sight of the acropolis palace and the Elders. Destroy them however you see fit, but it shall be visible to the Elders. We will not leave the city undefended for the Dark Prince while you dance with the Metzonians." Caelestis growled, pointing toward Militades. He turned away and retreated into Elder Palace. The secondary line of Titans followed the grandmaster, and the foremost group dispersed among the various hallways and disappeared completely.

Turning back to Militades, Philotheos found the Defenders already beginning to file out of the palace, leaving their commander where he stood. Looking over at him, Militades shook his head. "As though the Army of the Fallen will really make a difference to a Dark Prince of Hell."

Walking his little girls to the main gate as he led his horse behind them, Philotheos saw that many other families were already preparing to disembark; the guard detail was busy organizing everyone around them. Two of the Fallen's carriage trains had left at noon. Philotheos wished he could have sent his children with them. Both had been large trains and heavily defended, but Militades's outrage had changed Philotheos's original plans. Despite the unforeseen circumstances, he was glad to cherish those extra hours as closely as he could.

"Remember who you are supposed to give this gift to?" He tapped the backs of the girl's oversized knapsacks as he handed them over to them.

"The Advisor. And it is for the one who bears scars not of the Fallen," Holly replied, her younger sister echoing her words. Smiling at both of them, he helped them as they struggled to put their backpacks on.

Lifting both girls atop his horse, he hugged them fiercely and kissed both their cheeks and foreheads. His cheeks were wet from his little girls' tears, masking his own. They did not scream or weep loudly, preferring a quiet sorrow, their little fingers digging into his back.

"Listen closely to me, girls. There is a place within the City of Heaven, a mighty cathedral even larger and grander than the one within Prokopolis. If anything happens you stay there, and I will come and find you when this is over, I promise you. Do you understand?"

Both his little orphan girls nodded their heads, understanding a father's promise. A false promise, he forced himself to admit. He had always spoken truthfully to his children and explained everything to them, and he wanted to believe that he would see them again. Deep within, he knew that it was not going to happen. But the love within him made him believe that he would. He had to.

The two girls sat upon his white stallion; two pairs of soft sad brown eyes looking back at him with grey hoods pulled up over their red hair. His armoured guard, Jakub, the young man's brother and the children's nanny led the horse out of the gate. Philotheos stood looking out at them as they made their way out across the sloping plains, both little girls twisted in the saddle to keep him in sight. Both held each other closely until they were gone, out of his life forever, once again abandoned like they had been at the market. He sent up a quick prayer to the heavens to protect the two little girls.

Heaven knew he already missed them dearly.

Chapter 16
The Emperor of Emperors

Emperor Kristolphe climbed down through the monstrosity that was the Emperor's Citadel. The citadel sat upon the highest point in the capital city of Chilsa, but that had not been good enough for the young emperor's father, who ordered the construction to expand the keeps ever higher. He had demanded that he be able to overlook his entire empire, not just its capital.

Quite ridiculous, the blue-eyed emperor thought as he trudged down a continuous stream of stone steps on his way to the ragged lift with its three shady guards. He had spent a good portion of the evening climbing down these ridiculous steps to see his decrepit father, who had once demanded his palace be built to the clouds yet now hid in its black depths. And not just the palace's basement but the very pits of the world, accessed by what Kristolphe assumed to be a primordial mining shaft. Kristolphe had not seen anyone for the last ten minute of his descent, unsurprising considering how many "ghosts" the serving staff claimed they had seen. Smiling to himself, he knew that if only the servants knew what truly moved within the shadows, ghosts would not seem so bad.

Exiting the staircase, he continued out over the wooden bridge toward three black-cloaked guards awaiting him on the decrepit platform, which looked like it could crash into the black depths at any moment. His calf muscles refused to descend anymore stairs, and he really didn't have a choice. Not speaking to the guards, he stepped beneath the partial platform canopy behind them as they began to turn the chain wheel, beginning their long descent.

His father had almost completely retired from the Chilsa Empire when his health began to rapidly deteriorate, leaving his son and daughter to run his empire in his stead. But both brother and sister knew who was still holding all the power; even his enemies did not dare to play their hands. With rumours of his death swirling across the land for years, the boldest did not dare to move, for they feared the reprisal at his hand even beyond the grave.

His sister had taken off to run around with the ever-destructive Metz brothers, who continued to ravage the free lands around them. The thought made him smile; they were undoing all the work that their father had done to keep the peace. From the last reports he had heard, the bastards were threatening to storm upon the Order's stronghold at Prokopolis to complete their revenge. Kristolphe's father would be praying to Heaven, Hell and anyone else who would offer to listen for the success of such an event. Such a blow would effectively destroy the noble Order and its realm of influence, leaving the Brotherhood in the position to spread its own darker influence from the shadows and fill the hole left by their enemy's destruction.

So while his sister was off causing havoc as the figurehead of the Chilsa allied movement, he was left behind to organize the scenes in the background. Everything was coming together quite well, if he were to say so himself, with just a few final pieces to fall into place. Clenching his fists, he swore that he could feel the plans coming together.

The platform reached the bottom of the chasm, chains rattling loudly to announce their arrival. Several darkly robed figures looked up at his arrival, their blood-red eyes meeting his momentarily before they continued on with their designated tasks. Running his hand through his short black hair, he climbed off of the lift toward the torch-lit tunnel, ignoring the numerous guards, until he reached his father's chamber. The image of his father made even his own son cringe, although Kristolphe knew the old man was too stubborn and hateful to relinquish his life.

A Mortal Mistake

Old Emperor Neurus hunched over in the wide stone throne, raising his head slowly to look up his visitor. His bloody eyes had become deeply sunken in his skull, with large black circles beneath both eyes. His skin was as white as bone, wrinkled and scarred. Kristolphe could have sworn that if Death itself showed its face, his father's face would have looked worse.

Raising a boney hand and trying to straighten up, Neurus beckoned him closer. "Kristolphe, my bastard son, I trust the road to imperial glory continues as I have dictated to you?" The raspy voice echoed though the rocky chamber. Despite its shallowness, the voice sustained the harsh and potent tone that had defined Kristolphe's childhood. Kristolphe had found himself on the wrong end of his father's quick anger often, feeling pain both physical and mental.

Looking into Neurus's bloody vile eyes, nightmares flashed briefly through Kristolphe's brain under the sting of hateful resentment. He had only been a small child, unable to control the events in his world. His father's methods of teaching were impossible not to remember. Pain had come in waves as his father lashed him repeatedly, cursing and screaming at him. Kristolphe's young childhood friend watched wide-eyed with horror as the staff around also watched, motionless. His memory flashed between his father's angry red eyes and the teary brown eyes of his friend. It had been a terrifying lesson incurred upon him for making the wrong choice—an innocent mistake any child could have made.

The looks of his best friend were only the end of Kristolphe's most painful memory imprinted upon his brain. They had grown up together all their lives and had planned a great future of friendship. They dreamt they would marry the finest women in Chilsa and their children would grow up to be greatest of friends. They swore they would fight side by side in all future battles, their dead enemies piled beneath their feet like a mountain before moving on to the next adventure together.

Kristolphe had enjoyed that friendship; he did not have many friends, although he did try. When he did make a friend, he would often find out that he and his family had mysteriously disappeared. When he questioned the men around about what happened, the answer was, "Gone." If he asked twice, he got slapped and told the same thing. He learned quickly not to ask his father, for his violence was fiercer than the guards'.

So Kristolphe had tried to keep this new friendship a secret from his father, who told him friendship was a sign of weakness. Not that his father had ever cared anything about him except when it was convenient for him or he required something from the child. Kristolphe was heir to an empire, but his father was going to live for eternity and he was just a random unplanned problem not worth fixing. His growing bond of friendship was a quick fix though.

He did not know how his father had found out, whether someone had specifically mentioned it to him or if he had just glanced out the window one day. Both the boys had been called up the long steps, and Kristolphe had felt fear, knowing that something was wrong. He had wanted to tell his friend to run, to hide, to flee, but they were surrounded by his father's soldiers, and there was no hope of escape. His father had sat in his throne, his grey beard wild and untamed as he whispered quietly to an overweight lord. His son's arrival caused him to look up, and Kristolphe remembered seeing that stare before. He felt sick to his stomach and turned pale as a ghost.

"Is this your new friend, son?" Kristolphe had shaken his head repeatedly, not looking over at the companion beside him. Neurus climbed out of his chair and struck Kristolphe to the ground on the forehand and then his friend on the backhand.

"Are you lying to your father? You know I dislike lying, but I dislike friendship even more," Neurus screamed at him, a deathly calm within his voice despite the volume. "You want to be emperor of this land? Emperors have no friends. We rule and lord over everyone. Do you want friends or do you want to have servants!"

"Please, Father …" Tears were streaming down his face in great rivers as he begged his father, who only grew more infuriated by his son's weakness. He beat Kristolphe flat to the floor with a length of silvery iron chain he kept within his sleeve, continuing even after the child had given up resisting.

Fuelled by his anger, Neurus walked up behind Kristolphe's friend and grabbed the child by his hair, lifting the child to the tips of his toes. The youth refused to scream out or struggle, feeling the rage in the air. He could smell his friend's fear but was unable to help him. Neurus produced his slender blade from behind his back and held it the child's throat. Tilting the blade to catch a stray beam of light, he directed it into Kristolphe's eyes.

"Our world is lonely within the darkness. From within the darkness we gain our strength and our power. Through our power and strength we shall rise to where we began. It is time for you to join us within the shadows, though it is no place for weakness." The reflected light wavered slightly before completely disappearing as the shimmering blade ran red.

"Waste more of my time. I dare you." Outrage shattered Kristolphe's memories as his father slammed his hand down upon the stone throne, leaving a bloody handprint. His old body was trembling as his emotions continued to surge through protruding black veins.

"The road of glory continues exactly as you have laid out for the empire. The Imperial Army is currently assembling from all corners of Chilsa and is already over fifty-five percent of our full armed forces. The draft call has already gone out and is in progress. In the larger scheme, though, it would appear that we are behind schedule …"

Neurus seemed unperturbed by the last sentence, and he never accepted bad news this way, making Kristolphe even more unsettled.

"Ah, the bold Metz brothers continue to skew our timeframes. They continue to drive the world to its end with such reckless abandon that is has become hard to keep up, has it? Not truly knowing or understanding where they push makes me laugh. You are not the only one thrown behind schedule, however." His old man's eyes shifted away from Kristolphe, not returning, alerting the son to additional visitors.

Kristolphe turned back toward the entrance to see three ghastly figures walking silently into the room, clad in the dark robes of the Brotherhood. Judging from how they moved, he gathered they were of higher importance than others who shuffled silently around the floor. Their frayed black robes draped over their worn yet still thick armour; they strode confidently, paying absolutely no attention to those around them.

Clearly he was not the only hound his father had released to do his dirty work. *What tasks were these shades sent upon that they had not been able to complete?* he wondered.

The tallest one towered above his companions, carrying multiple plates of black steel layered upon his shoulder, a partial human skull clipped upon his sternum. His helmet was made of the same black steel. Jagged teeth were cut into the bottom, and two large curved horns rose from his temples, making his almost seven-foot height even more imposing.

Looking over his companions, Kristolphe found them to be exact replicas of each other: same height and stance, though not nearly as tall or impressive as their leader. Kristolphe had to look twice at their faces masked by visors of hammered steel; no bloody red eyes stared back at him like others he had seen. Dark purple threads were weaved in their black cloaks, distinguishing them from others he had seen around the dark caves these banshees called home.

Kristolphe ignored them and began to continue their previous discussions about the next phases of the plan. He was rudely silenced by a raised hand; his father still regarded the new visitors. Attempting to once again bring up his questions, Kristolphe was cut off. His father's hand gestured angrily toward the exit as he addressed the wraith-like creatures.

"Warlord Locan, Krasys and Krysas, you damn well have better news than my incompetent replacement. I swear I will strip all your souls raw if you hand me more bad news."

Kristolphe was outraged and raised his voice high above his father's, drawing his look of ire. "I will not simply leave. We have much more to discuss. It takes me hours of my time to travel down those damn stairs, and I will not have my time wasted! If they have something to tell you, then let them speak and speak quickly. Do not waste my time when we are already behind schedule, as our discussions are vital …"

"We have discussions of other, far more important business than that discussed with you. It does not concern you, Kristolphe. It is a matter that no *half-human* will ever understand. We are done. Leave us!"

Blood boiled within Kristolphe's veins as he stormed past the three wraiths standing by the door. He struggled to keep his emotions under wraps as the bloody eyes of the warlord stared into his own, feelings of contempt and disgust within them.

From the shadows all around, all eyes of the Brotherhood servants were on the young man as he retreated from his father's chambers. A shiver of anger ran through his body as he thought how much he hated the Brotherhood and how his hatred for his father continued to grow every time he saw the man. It was consuming his mind with dark thoughts and painful memories.

Half-human was his father's favourite insult, reminding him of his place in the Brotherhood. His father might be Emperor of Chilsa and all its provinces beyond the curvature of the world, as well as the most powerful member of the Brotherhood, but Kristolphe was simply the weak child of Humanity. He wasn't even a full human in his father's mind, being only the weak son of a concubine. And his father undyingly hated weakness more than Humanity.

Kristolphe hated his father with every ounce of his being. He hated the family that he came from and his half-brothers and half-sisters. He didn't mind Belle; actually, she was the only one he liked and enjoyed. Both shared each other's secrets, keeping many only between them. The consequences would be dire if their father discovered how they spoke of him.

Neurus ruled the Brotherhood of Sin and had ruled with an iron fist for more than a century, controlling every aspect of the empire. His father, Neurik, had expanded the Chilsa Empire five times over before his rule of three hundred years ended; before that was Nuor. All the history books claimed that Nuor was the vilest of all beings to walk the earth in the past millennia. Kristolphe's mind could not imagine how his ancestor could possibly be more evil than his own father.

"Well, that was quick," the lead Brotherhood guard sneered as they clambered back aboard the platform, his companions around him laughing. A grey shadow appeared behind him and lashed out with a single punch that knocked the guard to the stone floor, unconscious. A blade appeared at Kristolphe's throat.

"And terribly easy. You should really get better guards, brother." His face remained hidden beneath the cowl of his cloak, but Kristolphe recognized the voice immediately. *What in the world is he possibly doing here and, a bigger question, why?*

"So the emperor of Chilsa still takes orders? Kristolphe, Kristolphe, I thought you had taken over control of both your father's empire and his ferocious Brotherhood, but I suppose I was misinformed. How about we take a little walk to see who commands the most powerful man in the world, shall we?"

"Surely you are a madman to come into the lion's den this way! How could you possibly anticipate ever surviving this? Using me as a bargaining piece? You will find my expendability quite high, I'm afraid." A faint flicker of concern crossed the face of his attacker, perhaps a half second of self-doubt. If he understood Kristolphe's relationship with his father, they would probably find plenty in common.

"Well, I guess I shall have to improvise along the way. Let's go. Tell Nutsy and Peckerhead here to get the hell out of our way or I will chop them to pieces, two by two." Which two Brotherhood acolytes he was taking about Kristolphe did not know; there were two dozen before them, bare corroded blades held high.

"Move." Kristolphe spoke softly, expecting the acolytes to clear a path for them. All continued to stand, rusted weapons pointed at the two young men, apparently believing that they would be able to stop them. "Move, or I swear your pathetic souls will feel my wrath until the end of time. Do it now!"

Hesitating briefly before responding to his command, the mortal servants created a narrow path for them and then a wider one; Kristolphe started walking toward the throne room he had just left. He wondered how his father would respond to his returning to interrupt him yet again. This new visitor would bring a totally different emotion, and the son did not know how the father would react.

"I thought I told you to get the hell out of here! We have nothing more to discuss," Neurus greeted them, angry, as Kristolphe had known he would be. Kristolphe tried to keep his emotions steady.

"No, but we do." The Metzonian prince raised his head up over Kristolphe's left shoulder to look upon the unexpected face as he whispered in the emperor's ear. "Seriously? I thought your sister told me he was dead. Or are you haunted by your father from beyond the grave? Damn, I really do pity you now, Kristolphe. I am glad my father does not physically haunt me; he would have some *very* harsh things to say to me about my life choices. I'd probably be a miserable asshole like you. I actually feel the need to apologize for the mean things I said to you moments ago."

Crackling laughter echoed high within the stone vault. "My wretched week has been made wonderful again. I was thinking I needed a new piece of artwork for the Black Altar. So convenient for me not to have to go search for it. One has to question your stupidity, or did you come to beg for forgiveness with a quick and easy death?"

"I never beg, Neurus, so perhaps another day. Instead I come with orders. You and your little dark shadowy friends here are going to help me with a particular task I have at hand." Sven started to talk quickly, treating the man much like he would his castle butcher. "Just shut up and listen. We are planning to invade Prokopolis, home to the mighty Order of the Fallen, as I'm sure you are already aware of. Unfortunately, we both know how formidable an opponent the Order can be. I am told that I will need to have equally formidable help, and rumour has it that this is where I can find it. Although I must say, from everything I've seen, my source must be misinformed."

Kristolphe's father's red eye and wrinkled cheek twitched rapidly, his anger barely contained as the Metzonian king continued to chatter, unaware how swiftly he was approaching his death. Kristolphe feared being caught in the storm but with the blade still at his back was unable to move.

"Do not think that you can use us to eliminate your enemy and then just kill us off either. You'll get rid of the Order and be free to go along with your business, or whatever that stuff you guys do is called. What say you, you wrinkled old bag of angel bones?"

Kristolphe leapt as far to his right as he could at the last second, avoiding the torrid bolt of red energy that coursed directly for him. The energy thrust itself into King Sven's chest and spread across every limb, threatening to knock him to one knee. The emperor was impressed that Metz remained somewhat upright; the man was stronger than he gave him credit for.

"You will not dictate terms to me, mortal! It is I who command all who come before me, and those who disobey die. You have granted me great joy by dismantling your father's kingdom and the Order's Metzon Chapter, yet greater misery and constant anger. I do not need your paltry, pathetic human army to destroy Prokopolis or the Order of Orion; my powers are great enough to swallow all in my path."

Fearful of the old decrepit man, Kristolphe was absolutely terrified of the looming figure that stood up from his throne, no longer weak and helpless. Standing tall and strong, Neurus levitated a foot off the ground within a sphere of energy as he moved closer, his Brotherhood guardians forming a loose circle around the incapacitated human kneeling before them. The warlord Locan clenched his large bladed mace in his hands, and his minions both held twin blades, prepared for a sudden attack.

"Your father is not here to protect you now, Sven Metz. I wonder where he is. Oh, that's right—dead. As much as I would love to join the two of you in the afterlife, I plan to make you suffer for eternity and create a glorious display for my viewing pleasure."

"You should fear me like you feared my father, Neurus. You should fear me *more* than you feared my father!" Rising from the attack, Sven pulled himself to his feet, clothing still smouldering from the dark angel's attack. Kristolphe did not understand how the man remained functioning after such a supernatural attack. His golden eyes were glazed over, but he showed no signs of physical pain as he clutched his sword tightly and took one step toward Neurus. "You cannot kill me! I am untouchable, Neurus, and I shall have your brotherhood one way or another. Perhaps I shall conclude our business with your head to show your minions!"

Neurus once again unleashed another torrent of red power, the attacks doing significantly less damage than they did before. The Metzonian pushed forward through the attack, closing the distance. His push never reached the floating man before him, halting quickly as the warlord entered the fight.

Locan stepped heavily into the fight, his mace leaving a red streak of power behind it as it crushed Sven's heavy breastplate, sending the large man flipping through the air. He finally crashed high up the rocky wall above the doorway and plummeted twenty feet back to the ground.

"I am Neurus, overlord of the Sons of the Shadows and the Brotherhood of Sin. I dictate terms within this world. I am the *God* of Earth, and those shall heed my words and worship me! And die for me!" A red crystal blade three feet long appeared in his hand as he moved for the kill and to rid himself of the disobedient Metzonian who had become the focal point of his hate.

Kristolphe had tried to warn the fool away from his own death, but Sven had refused to heed the warning. Kristolphe saw the shadow of death covering him now.

The rock entrance exploded inward, showering Sven's attackers with human-sized boulders and knocking the Brotherhood's lord deep into the chamber. The dust and rock fragments hid Kristolphe's view of the newcomers; he only caught brief glimpses of limbs as the intruder punished those within the chamber who'd threatened the Metzonian.

A fist smashed into Locan's chest, sending the warlord crashing into a crystal statue that exploded into a million shards upon impact. Kristolphe huddled behind the large rocks as far from the entrance as he could get as Krysas and Krasys leaped toward the unseen attacker. One hand wrapped around Krasys, Kristolphe believed, throwing him into the cavern wall as a muscular tail ran his brother into the opposite wall.

"You are not the Gods of this world, Dark Angel! Your powers are weak, diminishing as you slowly rot within this prison. My

servants are untouchable, you should have listened. He would not come into the dungeon of lions without leaving the dragon waiting outside. Do you remember the dragon, Neurus?"

Through the settling dust, Kristolphe saw the great purple demon push farther into the room through the entrance he had created for himself. With his great black wings and clawed hands, he needed no other weapons.

Paying no attention to the swarm of full-ranked Brotherhood angels now surrounding him, the demon's black orb eyes were locked upon Kristolphe's father. There was a long moment of complete silence as the two stared each other down, Neurus finally breaking eye contact, conceding defeat and backing away.

"That's what I thought. With your previous history, I wanted to introduce you properly to my new servant, Devotz, or as you know him, Sven Metz. I do not have time to fight with your pathetic dark angels, so he shall command and you shall listen. You will do everything my young servant of Hell asks of you or face the consequences. I assume you can imagine the consequences.

"The Second Coming has arrived; I suggest you ensure you land upon the right side Sin." The purple demon reached down and scooped up his human servant lightly in his left hand turning to leave. *"Do not force me to return before I see fit, nor think you can hide. And if any harm comes to my precious puppet here—well, I need not say that you should take very good care of him."*

Then it was over. The demon had not been within the lair of the Brotherhood more than five minutes, and he had completely destroyed everything the Sin had worked centuries for. Kristolphe looked at his father, and his form returned to the frail old man, even frailer than before. His father's minions looked at him for guidance about the events that had just unfolded.

"What are we going to do? Who was that?" Kristolphe hesitated to ask, feeling out of breath as he spoke.

"What the *hell* do you think we are going to *do*? Get the hell out of here! We are no longer safe if the Dark Prince of Hell knows where we reside. Until then we are going to do exactly as Dark Prince Rhimmon demands, and his weasel of a pet. I should have known that there was a power far stronger and darker than the Metzonian scum behind everything." Neurus collapsed back within his black throne, melting into its arms. "You are going to continue with what you are doing. The rest is none of your concern! Get out of my sight!"

Kristolphe scurried out of his father's ruined throne room, feeling once again like he was not good enough in his father's eyes. Not that he cared anymore. Seeing his father's fear for the first time in his life left him with mixed emotions. Kristolphe realized the darkest heart upon the world now felt the same emotion Kristolphe had felt his entire life. Fear.

Sven had claimed that he pitied him for being haunted by his father, but Kristolphe could not see how it could be any worse than the situation that the Metzonian was in. Serving a Prince of Hell certainly had to be even worse than a self-proclaimed God of Sin. He wondered if Belle knew how deeply her love was entwined with darkness but decided it was not worth contemplating. Surely she knew; she would undoubtedly be in the depths with him, having hitched her wagon to his a long time ago.

All stepped aboard the platform once again. The tallest guard commanded his companions to begin cranking the wheels. Kristolphe looked coldly at the Brotherhood acolytes, human servants to the Brotherhood who worshipped the dark angels. Fools who did not understand what they were doing, trying to bath in the heat that was the uncontrollable fire. Little did the naive know that once the fuel was finally added to the fire, all would burn in its whirlwind of flames!

Looking up and noticing that they had almost reached the subterranean entrance, he knew he would be glad to reach his palace and escape this emotional torture chamber. He was starting to regain his composure when he looked higher within the tunnel. It was no longer dark; new light and fresh air flowed down from the hole the Dark Prince had created during his ostentatious entrance and escape. His anger reignited from fumes of irritation as he looked toward the guards and their silent captain.

"Perhaps in the next lifetime you will learn to do your *damn job*!"

The lead guard felt a kick in his lower back before free-falling through empty space, his companion soon following over the right edge of the lift. The second guard fell to his knees after a quick blow to the abdomen; Kristolphe lashed out with his knee before grabbing him by the leg and pitching him over the edge. Kristolphe looked calmly over the edge as the two men continued to plunge into the depths, flailing their limbs uselessly. The sight brought a slight smile to his face. He looked over toward the third guard, who was cowering in the far corner, arms raised above his head in terror. They all should have died for letting that Metzonian bastard put a knife to his throat, but he wasn't going to crank the elevator by himself.

His father would kill everyone anyway; no sense getting his hands dirtier than necessary. Walking slowly toward the third guard, he reached down and used the man's cloak to wipe the blood from his steel-clad knee. Feeling the lurch of the lift as it landed, he readjusted his posture to its regal form before walking calmly away. He felt slightly better now, though it did not matter how he felt. He had an empire to run, one on the verge of completing its expansion. His confidence was shaken though—the future was not as certain as he was meant to believe. He wondered what unexpected event was going to happen to him next.

Chapter 17
Fallen Warriors

Feeling the sway of his black stallion beneath him and the thick plate armour pressing down upon his shoulders, Sven felt at home once again. The golden throne in Metzor had never felt correct to the second child, who was always more comfortable in his saddle with sword in hand than upon his father's chair.

Sven was glad to at last be back on the warpath again; the cramped stuffiness of the political dance of the lords and ladies of Metzor around the throne made him weary. The tedious squabbling and begging among the nobles never seemed to have an end. It hurt his head. Sven did not understand why his brother Frederick desired so badly to rule the bickering fools.

Sven was almost prepared for his attack upon his next target, when Rhimmon summoned him with a warning. The Dark Prince's prey—and by extension Sven's—was unexpectedly starting to panic. The Dark Prince was concerned that the souls he coveted might flee from his grasp, reminding Sven of the dire consequences were all the Fallen to escape. Extra time would not be given to scour the countryside for the Fallen. Immediate action was required.

Consulting his scouts, Sven learned there was no evacuation of the glorious city of Prokopolis beyond a small stream that had begun weeks before when his armies had secured the crossing, but it was not a concern in their eyes. The king knew differently, however. The concern and fear within Prokopolis coincided with his last trip to the Desert of Lost Souls, causing concern of his own. Who had betrayed his plans to the Elder Council of the Order?

Those who went with him to the desert all had been carefully selected by him for their personal loyalty to him. No other souls had been seen on the long road to the desert, and the only companion not personally selected was his brother's mute shadow, Cassidus. Perhaps when his brother returned he would have to have a discussion about the young man and his perceived loyalty, though at the moment it was not Sven's primary concern. The Order of the Fallen had forced his hand before he was completely ready to move upon them in his final stroke of so-called revenge.

However the Order had discovered his plans was no longer a concern, and the slow dispersal of Fallen had turned into perpetual panic at the arrival of his army upon their doorstep as the sun rose above the city.

For all Rhimmon's reasoning, Sven still remained confused that a Prince of Hell would require his help when he held the power to destroy cities with a stroke of his arm. How much time or power would it really take for a Dark Prince to destroy Prokopolis? Perhaps Rhimmon feared the Fallen? Perhaps he even feared Humanity? Sven forced the thoughts from his mind. He was sworn to serve, not ask questions.

The Prokopolites had to fall and be destroyed in order for their plans to move forward, and Sven knew that it would be unlike any other war he had fought before. These mortals would not submit to his indisputable strength or his demands. No, he would have to smash down the front door with his boots, slay the dogs guarding the doors and drag the families out one by one, house by house. The people of Prokopolis would not escape their fates. One way or another they would perish.

The itch for another fight had grown within Sven as he had prepared his armies, wondering if the Fallen would truly flee before them, as it sounded like they were prepared to do. The Order was not one to cower when a fight was upon the horizon, having full confidence in their army and its proven track record upon the battlefield.

Marching over the last ridge of hills that blocked his view of Prokopolis, the king was not disappointed. Prokopolis unleashed the

Army of Fallen to the full view of their approaching enemy upon the gentle slopes that surrounded the large city. Sven's enthusiasm for battle rose at the sight of his enemy preparing for war.

The sound of faintly chiming bells was heard as Sven gazed over the city and its surroundings. Perched between two lakes and a southerly forest upon the sides of the city, Sven gazed upon the white walls of the city that protected what lay within. Large aqueducts ran from the distant mountains that surrounded the south, drawing fresh mountain spring waters for the thousands of thirsty mouths living within.

The splendid city of Prokopolis had been built around a large acropolis of rock, upon which the Elders of the Order had constructed their elaborate palace courtyards and the two tall white towers, Ori and Bri. Sven was certain the story had been that the acropolis had been where the first of the fallen angels had crash-landed, marking it as a holy site. He was not sure he bought that story. It did not matter to him anyway. All of the city would burn and its walls turn black in the flames as his warriors tore the lofty towers down. This would be the defining battle that Sven had prepared for his whole life; he was eager to watch it unfold.

Asked if they could set up camp a mile from the city, Sven immediately refused his general's request, citing it as a waste of time. Their persistence eventually forced him to concede. The time required for the army to set up camp could be used for the useless negotiations that Sven would have to go through with the Order. Negotiations were always the frontrunner when it came to the Order and the prospect of going to war. Sven already knew it wouldn't matter.

As he watched the small delegation ride forth from Prokopolis beneath the white banner of the Order, waiting to meet him far from the army upon the open plains, the response of the Order to his army correlated directly with his assumptions. Gathering his Shadow Guard around him and two battalions of his more elite soldiery, Sven rode forth, leaving the main battle armies to set up camp.

"King Sven of Metzor, we are surprised to see you are here. We wish our delegates had returned to us with word of your intent to visit. We would have arranged a preparation more worthy of a king." The tone of the delegate irritated Sven immediately, as did the double meaning of his words. As the second delegate dismounted to join his companion, Sven continued to listen. "Our esteemed Elder Council wishes to know why you ride before the white walls of Prokopolis with such a display of arms for a friendly visit."

"I believe the Elders already know why I am here and also know this is not simply a display of arms strength. Do not waste my time with such foolish questions. I have waited for a proper response and have grown tired of waiting. I would die of old age before you heeded my demands, and my time is too precious to have it wasted any further."

"The Elders ask for patience and understanding, not meaning to waste your time nor force you to take drastic actions. Many believe you press this issue too quickly and have now gone too far, marching your army toward Prokopolis in what could only be called an invasion …"

Sven laughed in the faces of the delegates. "The Elders have forced my hand. I have waited for months for them to hand over those who murdered my father. I have grown tired of waiting, so I have come to collect the murderers myself. It would be a disastrous burden for my men and I to have to sort the guilty from the innocent. Tragic mistakes are bound to be made." He left little room for mistaking the threatening tone of his last remark and watched as the delegates shifted uncomfortably.

"As the Elders have told you repeatedly, the matter had been put under investigation by the Holy Courts, but such matters take time and cooperation from all parties involved. Might I add that the Metzonian Crown has not cooperated, going so far as imprisoning the very men who were sent to resolve the issue."

Forcing himself not to grin, Sven pondered the fate of the countless ambassadors and judiciary investigators sent across the Zarik, never to complete their tasks. Instead they had found themselves within the prisons in Metzor, but they would not stay long in the darkness. As he rode forth to punish the Elders, his brother was wandering through the cellars, dragging the Fallen back to the light.

A Mortal Mistake

"If you would simply allow the investigation to run its course, you would find more than enough evidence that the Order had nothing to do with the death of your father! You have no right to march your army or to bully us into handing over innocent lives …" He let the man continue to talk fervently, his heart rate rising more dangerously the longer the delegate talked.

He stood before their city with an army poised to rip every stone of their glorious city down before them and yet they still tried to dictate his rights to him. Listening to the long, drawn-out excuses, Sven noticed the flag bearer standing erect behind the two delegates. The man was young-looking, as through fresh from training, appearing impressed by the sight of the sinister grey steel of the Metzonian heavy infantry lined up behind him. "I am king and write what is right and wrong! I make the demands, not the Elders. I would assume their paltry demands are the same as previously."

Without missing a beat the delegates immediately began to prattle about the demands of the Elders, the exact conditions that multiple delegates and ambassadors had foolishly brought to Metzor. The demands of a bunch of old men would once again fall upon his deaf ears.

"We ask that those of the Order be released from all Metzonian prisons and given safe passage to Prokopolis. All know that the Order had nothing to do with the murder of your father, as you so vehemently claim. Metz was a son of Prokopolis and an esteemed member of the Order within the noble principles we live by. We do not betray, nor do we slay, our own!

"We also ask that you remove yourself and your army from our city and return to borders previously agreed upon by the free nations. There is no need for conflict of any kind. All issues certainly can be solved through proper diplomatic channels." The second diplomat smiled politely, palms pressed together.

Sven eyed the three members of the delegate team, momentarily pretending to contemplate the already decided outcome. "Certainly, I will meet your conditions." Sven flashed a fake smile of his own. The delegates did not betray the glimmer of hope within their minds.

"But … only if you march the members of the Elder Council and every other Fallen out from the city and turn them over to us."

"Unacceptable."

Sven smiled genuinely at the scowls across both men's faces when they realized he was playing with them. The Metzonian continued, badgering the trio for their beliefs. "Why not? According to the laws of their religion, if they are proven innocent Heaven shall not seek punishment upon their souls, and the Lords of the Light shall fall down to discipline those whom bring harm to the innocent.

"Quit wasting your breath. The time for negotiations is at an end." He raised a hand to stop the second speaker, but the man ignored the king's gesture and spoke rapidly, his voice becoming more animated as the negotiations deteriorated around them. His extra effort only pushed Sven to the edge.

"Shut up!" His blade was in his hand and across the throat of the second delegate, halting his speech midsentence. A forward blow slit the throat of the second delegate, and a backhand blow severed the head of his companion in a shower of blood. "Shut your damned mouths!"

The banner carrier stood splattered in the blood of his companions, watching Sven huff with anger until the rage was expelled from his heart. Pacing back and forth, Sven hurled the sword forward onto the green grass at their feet. "Are you a fool as well?"

The banner carrier shook his head slightly and tried to control the shaking of his knees.

"A Fallen?"

One again the young man shook his head quickly, trying not to look at Sven, who stood within inches of his bloodied face, screaming at him.

"Too stupid to see the real picture that lay before their eyes, but perhaps you can. I know you can; I have shown it to you! It's all here for everyone to see. I am not deceptive or cryptic like your Elders!" The saliva within his mouth was thick as emotion boiled at the smell of blood he had just spilt.

Fearful, the wide-eyed youth shook from the bloody events that took place not thirty seconds before.

"I strongly suggest you carry the words I spoke to the citizens of Prokopolis. Unless you give me what I want, you, your family, your friends and everyone else shall follow the path taken by these blubbering idiots!"

The teen dropped the white banner on the grassy knoll and fled for the armies before the city walls. Sven gave chase for two hundred feet, stopping short when the young man tripped over his own feet several times. As he scrambled forward and then looked back at the man chasing him, the fear within his eyes was unmistakeable.

Looking toward the city, Sven observed the sentries watching him as the walls became filled with citizens as well as soldiers, all watching the spectacle from the safety of the walls. The shrill cries of a pair of hawks circling high in the midmorning sky was the only sound beyond the breeze. Opening his lungs to the crisp morning air, he called out toward the walls and army one last time.

"Do you hear and see me? All outside and inside the walls shall die if I do not have the Elder Council and every other Fallen member marched out the gates to surrender into the custody of my army within the hour! If my army marches through your tall gates, it will be too late to beg forgiveness or ask penance for your foolishness! Such shall decide your fates."

Pointing between his approaching army and the gates, Sven repeated his gesture several times. Even if only the Fallen army heard his original message, the others would hear it shouted through the streets soon enough. It would not matter; loyalty to the religion was beyond even nationalist pride, as he had found out during the religious revolution across Metzon.

Leaving the bloody white bodies of the delegates lying between the two imposing armies, Sven listened to the rumble of approaching armour shake the earth and echo off the white walls at his back. As he walked down the central corridor that ran through his army, the steel lines filled in behind Sven. He worked his way to the back of the army.

"Are you seriously going to give them the hour?" General Hallaken asked with concern. Looking over at the general with a large grin, the large bodied Aerox appeared to already know the answer.

Sven snorted in derision. "Of course not! Let them all burn in Hell. Let us begin this and show them that fear of the Metzonian heavy infantry is not merely a false story like their religion."

His general smiled and wasted no time before shouting his commands to his subordinates, who continued the message down the chain of command. Sven heard the thick faceplace slide down as the Shadow commander covered up his marred face in preparation for the fight. Knowing that Aerox's thirst for Fallen blood almost boiled as strongly as his own, Sven felt the need to reiterate his original commands.

"Remind them of my additional commands if we break through the ranks of the Order's Silver Army and enter Prokopolis. I need the Fallen alive if at all possible!" The general nodded in acknowledgement, and Sven left him.

Turning to his lady standing upon the other side, he cried out with joyous anticipation, "I sense a great victory today, Belle. Can you feel it in your bones like I can?"

Blowing him a kiss, she winked at him. "Shall we see who can kill more Fallen? I have a strong feeling that I will win by a landslide."

Sven smiled and bounced on the balls of his feet, swinging his sword arm in short circles, preparing his body for what was to come. "And what happens if I win?"

"If you win?" She pretended to think, twirling her blonde hair before tossing him a sexy smile. "Well, then you will have anything your heart can possibly desire …"

Sven laughed out loud as the horns of Metzor cried in the air and the rumble of thousands of feet was heard charging forward. Sven sensed he would indeed win today, the reward being far larger than what Belle would grant him.

Today, the Order was going to feel his wrath and crumble beneath his boots as he eradicated their influence upon this world. Without the Order to stand in his way, who could possibly stand up against him?

Chapter 18
A Family of Orphans

Sweat dripped down the bridge of her nose as her heartbeat thrummed heavily within her chest. Her opponent did not look nearly as fazed as she did. The man's strength and endurance were far greater than her own. This was the eleventh time in a row she found herself within the dirt-filled training circle in the barracks of the Temple Titans. Her opponent had only been forced to the ground twice and had recovered too quickly for her to take advantage. And he never made the same mistake twice.

Rising once again, she backed away from her opponent, circling him light-footedly, waiting for the proper moment. Leaping forward, she struck out several times, missing with all but two glancing blows. She could hear her teacher in the background calling out to her.

"Use your primary assets to your advantage, Alexandra! Strike swiftly and precisely before moving back beyond his heavy blows …" Another profound blow struck her shoulder, spinning her around. Unable to recover her footing, she fell a final time to the black dirt, the steel adversary hovering over her as he set his foot upon her stomach in mock triumph.

"Halt." The voice of her trainer called out, ending the battle. Kallisto shook his head, waving her to come toward him and simultaneously filling a silver cup from the cold fountain beside him. Looking around at those who had come to watch the match, the old man searched for the next opponent to face the undefeated champion in the ring. The Titan stood tall, stretching his arms out. The familiar chuckle of her brother escaped through the mask.

"Who is next, Kallisto, or are you at last out of opponents worthy to face me?"

Kallen had drilled the Fallen soldiers and the Children of the Fallen day and night. Multiple times a day they had gathered in the large, arena-like cavern the Temple Titans called home. Any old enough to properly wield the sword were ordered to attend the regimented program Kallen oversaw. Alexandra found her skills had grown exponentially; she even enjoyed the vigorous workouts that left her muscles burning each night. Except for the final hour, when Kallisto came and picked a dozen from the crowd to attempt to take on the Titan commander himself. Perhaps it was because she was his sibling, or perhaps he expected more out of her, but Kallen appeared to hold little back from her. Beyond the group training, he had offered to privately tutor her in fighting in return for her educating him in other matters, such as world history and language.

Kallen had slowly tutored her in the particular style named the Dance of Death. Said to have been perfected by Orion's wife, Brianna, it was intensely fluid in all aspects, requiring swiftness and flexibility to make the first strike the last. She felt it matched her abilities and was not only deadly but as beautiful as any death could be. Unfortunately she had barely gotten to the point in the lesson where the opponent stood more than six feet and was plated in thick steel.

"General Dubryst!" Kallisto pointed to a soldier standing bare-chested in one corner among the dozens of spectators. "Please show Alexandra and the others how to use the advantages of speed and mobility against the largest opponents, particularly those armoured heavily. All of you pay attention; you can all learn from this." Kallisto spoke to all of the spectators, imposing a lesson while drawing attention away from his student. Alexandra felt slightly humiliated about being so handily beaten before so many, but none would have fared much better.

"Gladly." The thick-skinned Metzonian moved into the centre of the circle, hurling his axe overhead into the thick wooden training post. She recognized him as the golden Prince Frederick's fearless protector and the leader of his Elite. The dissident Metzonians tended to keep to themselves, outside the Sacred Citadel walls in their own camp, but Prince Frederick and the bare-chested general had made a routine of arriving to watch the Fallen train, particularly the final battle.

Peering in the Metzonian corner, she spotted the prince watching the spectacle from above the others, not clad in his usual golden armour and smiling mirthfully as his champion strode forward. "Tighten up your chin strap, lad, you're about to go for a little ride."

Alexandra took her seat beside Kallisto, and both watched the warriors prepare for the match. The size differential was substantial between the scarred bald man and the armoured beast that was her brother. Throwing his water cup back into the fountain, Kallen dropped his horned helmet over his mouth; two great spines slanted back from his temples, the single white horn on his forehead stretching straight up.

Despite the dulled edges of the numerous spines on the Temple Titan training armour, there remained many sharp points to impale a body upon. Simpler and less barbed than on true battle armour, the three great clawed forearm spires and the plate extending from the elbows still protruded. Her brother had so far avoided such incidents with great skill, but his new opponent would not hold back, despite the risk.

"Had I a bow, I could easily defeat him, for he moves incredibly slow, and you just have to keep your distance …" Throwing her thick leather corset against the wall with the rest of her belongings, she slumped forward in exhaustion as she wiped the dirt and sweat from her face.

"In the pitch of battle, one is often without a weapon, and it becomes a battle of bare hands. Watch closely, and learn from one who has experienced those moments more than most." Kallisto rubbed her sore shoulders, easing her frustration as the fight began to unfold.

Following Alexandra's own strategy, Dubryst moved within the circle slowly, letting his feet gently cross over in the soft soil. Standing in the middle of the circle, his opponent did not press the attack but turned to remain square to his challenger. As Dubryst increased his speed, closing the circle tighter, Alexandra noticed that the heavy armour began impeding her brother's lateral movement, threatening to topple him.

Kallen felt the impending action and tried to prevent it by pressing his own attack, swinging with his inside arm and twisting sharply in the opposite direction to knock his opponent off his spiralling movement. Dubryst slid harmlessly underneath the arm aimed for his neck, wasting little time in punishing the error. His fist slammed into the exposed armpit before his other hand struck the back of Kallen's leg, dropping the Titan to a knee. Kallen blocked the kick to his head with a steel arm, but the general's second kick caught him in the ribs, sending him rolling.

Racing toward his struggling opponent, Dubryst lifted his right knee high to kick the man in the head with the heel of his boot. That was the moment the Titan struck with quickness belied by his size and heavy armour. Ducking beneath the heel strike, Kallen drove forward and upwards into Dubyst's groin and lifted the thick man off the ground with his shoulder as he rose to his feet. As Kallen threw him off his shoulder, Dubryst reached out with both hands to cushion his fall. Alexandra eyes grew wide watching the strength her brother possessed, realizing now just how easy he had been taking it upon her.

Landing hard upon his chest knocked the wind out of him, and Dubryst grit his dirt-filled teeth in pain. Not allowed the briefest of moments to recover, Kallen latched onto the general's ankles and dragged him back through the dirt like a calf within the claws of the leopard. A mere second later, Kallen had pulled the Metzonian to his knees and wrapped both hands around his neck, pressing his strong thumbs against the base of his skull.

"Halt."

Alexandra watched a large grin cross Kallisto's bearded face at the turn of events; he seemed proud of how it turned out, despite the lesson not being truly fulfilled.

"The mighty Titan commander of Prokopolis remains undefeated in the proving circle for yet another day. We must all train harder, smarter and faster so the title of Champion does not belong to a Prokopolite! You are all dismissed."

Kallen lifted the huge helmet, and the white smile of her twin shone bright. Several of the men cheered their champion; others threw gold and silver coins into the outstretched palms of their jeering comrades. Quickly dispersing from the barracks, the spectators returned to their duties, leaving the two young adults and two old men to themselves.

"You are truly worthy of leading the Titans, young man. King Kyros himself would have been proud to have you fight by his side." Dubryst dusted himself off as he stood up again, grinning widely at his loss as he searched for his lord, who had sneakily vacated the room.

Kallen laughed, shrugging off the compliment as he always did. "You overestimate us both! King Kyros slew demons and their lords for a lifetime; I merely wrestled an old lion to the ground. If only we could have watched them in their moments upon Earth, the things they could have taught us, eh?"

Eight great statues knelt upon their high pedestals overlooking the bridge, stretching from the temple to the fortress across the bay, while their leader Kyros knelt before the Throne of Creation. True Titans, or Throne Guardians, had been created by the Lords of Heavens to encase the dying souls of their comrades, enabling them to continue the fight against Hell. The nine statues were all that remained to mark their existence upon the world, guarding the Sacred Temple and Throne of Creation only symbolically now.

"Indeed, even Kallisto; as old as he is does not remember the Throne Guardians in battle, though the Fallen do not fully remember Heaven either anymore." Looking at her foster father, Alexandra saw that his pain was barely noticeable when he was brought into the discussion he was uncomfortable having, as were most of the

Fallen. Kallisto had been the one to tell them about the guardians, though his knowledge of them had only come from stories and translated scriptures. "How far back to do you remember your old life, Kallisto?" Dubryst asked.

Alexandra and her brother hid their irritation at the Metzonian's insistence on probing the subject that had such an uneasy affect upon the old man. The awkward silence continued for several tense moments before Kallisto surprised them both by answering the Elite general.

"You are correct, my friend. I remember very little of Heaven beyond my sentencing for my sins and the fall of my brethren when we were struck from Heaven's Grace. So perhaps once upon a time I did watch the Throne Guardians fight Hell, and perhaps I even knew Kyros or the Nine personally. Who knows?" Kallisto smiled weakly with raised eyebrows, despite his discomfort.

Alexandra often forgot about the noble man's previous lifetime, that he was once an angel of Heaven before he became an old man. Alexandra hesitated before asking, "If it is not too painful, Kallisto, may I ask what it was like to fall? What was your first feeling or memory upon Earth?"

"Lost." Smiling despite the sadness in his eyes, Kallisto continued to explain his personal past to Alexandra and her brother. "I awoke in the darkness atop a great grassy hill, not knowing how I got there or why I was there. Looking upon the moon and the infinite stars in the sky, I felt great pain with every movement I took, not knowing why. Having no memory, no knowledge of where I was or what to do, I simply began walking.

"For three days I walked before I found another couple who were also walking without a sense of direction. After another three days our group had grown to almost a dozen, all with the same questions and concerns. Then we were found by a wandering ranger. The Order had sent the scout to search for us, having seen falling stars burn through the sky during the two weeks we had all wandered.

"Gathering a greater number of us over a month, the ranger guided us as we started our journey to Prokopolis and began our education among the Order of the Fallen. The great Orion and

Fallen Five were too powerful and regal for Heaven to strip away their memories completely. Orion knew who those that fell from the stars were and who we had once been, so he gathered all the Fallen around him to teach and protect us for millennia. We discovered we were not the first to be found, merely the newest group to arrive from the Heavens; we also happened to be among one of the last as the waves of Fallen grew fewer and fewer."

Glancing between her brother, who just raised his eyebrows in her direction, and the Elite, she did not expect any more questions. Kallisto had already given them plenty to think about. At the last second, Dubryst blurted out a question in the blunt and straightforward manner typical of Metzonians. "So what was your crime?"

"That is between Heaven and me, friend. Perhaps someday I shall receive forgiveness. Until then I shall live alone with my sins." The bald comrade would not get a different answer from the old man. Kallisto looked toward the stunned children. "Good work today, both of you. Each day fills me with great joy to watch both of you grow so strong. We shall meet again this evening for dinner."

Disappearing through the exit toward the library, Kallisto left them contemplating what sins would get such a noble man banished. Alexandra knew the question lay upon all their minds, but none would openly discuss it out of mutual respect for the foster fathers who kept all their secrets close to their hearts.

"You know, I expected my champion to perform better against one of the Titans. Particularly when he has an extra twenty-plus years of warring experience over his opponent." All turned to find the eldest Metzonian prince, who remained trapped in exile, standing behind them. Dressed in his typical gold and black wardrobe, Prince Frederick walked into the chamber with an air of confidence. "Your loss cost me five golden stallions to several very boisterous Titans I had wagered against. The fact that you did not last five minutes cost me double that number! It also did little to help my wounded pride, by the way."

"Sorry, my lord, but these Titans are indeed true to their nature and name. Such beasts are normally chained in dungeons guarding treasure vaults! You would need a dragon to force one from their shell once they dig themselves into their stone den."

The dark-haired man laughed lightly, slapping the bald general and Alexandra's brother upon their shoulders.

"Perhaps we should test them when they are not wedged into a hole then. See how they fare out on the open field against open field tactics against numbers greater than their own."

Both Frederick and Alexandra had been saved by Kallisto, who'd rushed them both off to the Sacred City. Each struggled with painful personal tragedies that had formed an unspoken bond of friendship between them. Both had seen each other in their worst moments, understanding each other without having ever spoken about it.

"I will bet you ten of your precious golden stallions that a squad of Temple Titans could best your top three Elite squadrons. Even on the open fields you do not stand a chance, my friend." Proposing the challenge that he knew Frederick was hinting strongly toward, Kallen sent the first playful jab before the Metzonian could back out. "I have seen how the best of you fight. I am sure that I could take the pupil and his teacher at the same time!"

Frederick laughed heartily, lightly resting his arm upon Alexandra's shoulder, accepting the challenge. "Let us make it twenty golden stallions, though, Kallen. Make my win pay in both gold and glory. Perhaps Alexandra herself will place a bet on the sure winner?" He winked at her.

She gave him a playful jab to his kidney. "Too many times I have learned the hard way about betting against my brother. Perhaps you should begin thinking up an excuse to tell that young wife of yours about how you lost twenty gold pieces in a foolish wager."

"No need! I have total faith that the Metzonian Elite will prove they are the best once again. But perhaps Brandon and I should take our leave and strategize, just in case. Perhaps we can come up with a couple new tricks to spring upon the Titans and humiliate them before all the soldiery of the Fallen, leaving your brother to slink back to Prokopolis."

Waving as they both left, she reflected upon the Metzonian as she knew him. Alexandra had grown to like him, finding he was raised to be very proper and respectful of those around him. At the same time, he had slowly proven himself able to relinquish the strictness and pressure of being born into a royal family to unwind and relax with a commoner's camaraderie. He had struggled through great adversity with a positive attitude, considering his family's internal conflict and leaving everything behind except his wife and child. Kallisto had made sure he was taken care of as much as the Children of the Fallen.

The former royal advisor had gathered all of them together, creating a family of orphans in an attempt to resurrect the feelings and vital family structure that they had all craved. Kallisto was certainly included in her family, now that Alexandra was aware of his beginnings upon this world. She felt more connected with the old fallen angel, now they shared a common feeling of being lost. She did not know if Kallen experienced the same feelings as she did, but moving from location to location with no permanent memories of the past had left her mind spinning with questions.

She had no recollection of her parents herself, and all refused to tell her anything about them. The Order seemed content to let both siblings wallow in the unknown. She had heard all the reasons, which she thought more of as mere excuses. They always told her that the past did not matter because you could not change it. She and her brother were to decide their own fates within a path of personal discovery and enlightenment. With no past, there was only the future to look toward and prepare for. She thought, *Perhaps you cannot change the past, but the past indeed shapes events of the future*, and she would have liked to know. It made her question who she truly was and why the Order refused to tell her, as if it were a dark secret. It sometimes scared her.

"I think that was possibly the most I've ever heard Kallisto talk about himself before. He loves history and can talk about it endlessly, but never about his own." Pulling two sleeves of arrows over her shoulder, Alexandra moved toward the archery range, waiting for her brother's response, receiving none. "Do you think he or Militades will ever tell us about our past?"

"Not this again!" Kallen turned away from her, throwing his

hands into the air in frustration. Slowly unlatching his armour piece by piece, he threw them into a pile, his tone growing angry. "Damn it, sis, when are you just going to let this slide?"

"I will drop it when they tell me what I want to know." She unleashed her arrow at the target; the steel tip struck the dead centre. The tone of her brother's voice irritated her slightly; he knew what it meant to her but refused to join in her crusade to find out the truth about their past.

Alexandra got to see her brother a few times the year before, but now the Metzonian Murder had threatened to take her leagues farther from her brother for good. Only under orders from Militades had he unwillingly travelled to the Sacred City. The chaos and hatred for the Order were making it difficult to traverse across the land, and she truly feared she would not see him again if he left.

Separated since they were extremely young, she had not even known that Kallen was her brother for many of the years that she had actually known him. She hated secrets, like being told that he was her brother but nothing more, no answers about when or why they had been separated. The Elders kept these secrets from those who deserved to know.

Splashing water from the fountain upon his face, Kallen walked down the range to twist the large wooden wheel that moved the targets across the firing range. Shaking his head, Kallen responded as he always did. "The Elders will tell us when they decide it is time for us to know, as they have told you time and time again. You can ask a million times, and they will give you the same answer they always have a million times! It could be tomorrow, it could be a century. Perhaps it will be never. I promise you will be told the exact same thing every time you bring it up."

"Why not right now? Give me a good reason why they should continue to withhold such information. What is it in our past that they fear so much that they cannot tell us? Are we children of the Sin? What?"

Kallen refused to continue the argument and maintained his silence, staring at the stone ceiling.

Alexandra refused to allow him to escape the discussion by

implementing his usual silent strategy. "You can't think of one, can you? And they may think that they have reasons, but that does not make them correct. Everyone has a right to know where they came from; even Kallisto himself was granted that right after he fell by Orion, so why not us?"

The snap of her drawstring as she fired the arrows and the smacking impact when they reached the target were the only sounds within the narrow chamber; neither sibling broke the silence for a long ten minutes. All she wanted was his support in her push to discover answers to questions that they both wanted the answer to. Kallen could hide his curiosity all he wanted, but as his twin she knew that his desire to know was equal to her own, if not greater. But though she tried, he was content to let the answer come in time. And oh, how she had tried.

The time she had spent writing letters to the Chronicler of the Order over the course of years certainly amounted to days. Philip Philotheos was a stubborn old man; his replies, often including endless numbers of excuses, always came in the same soft tone as he tried to let her down easy; her request had been denied again. Writing was a waste of her time, but she refused to quit. She would hound him to old age and beyond! If she ever met the man, he would be in for an earful and lucky if the encounter did not turn violent.

Kallen had begun to juke the targets back and forth, trying to increase the difficulty but to little effect. At this distance she could have struck apples from the top of his head while he danced to the tune of a flute and not have harmed a short hair upon his head. Gazing at him briefly as she pulled back yet another arrow, she contemplated firing it past him in anger, but she held back when he finally spoke to her, grudgingly agreeing to help his sister once more.

"I will bring it up with Kallisto tonight, but do not expect an answer any different those you have already received. I will also try and ask Philotheos personally when we return to Prokopolis."

Alexandra understood that it was about as much help as she would get from Kallen. Although he would not press the issue, Alexandra knew that Kallisto had a particular soft spot for her brother and his questions would weigh more than her own. All she wanted to know was who her parents were and their story. She did not think it was too much to ask. The fact that they refused to tell her increased the fuel within her desire to seek the truth. What were they hiding from them? What fear drove them to keep the past from her and her brother?

"Thank you. When do you think you will return to Prokopolis?"

"I'm not sure if I will ever be going home to Prokopolis. I hope so. The thought of being left hidden within the Sacred City leaves me uncomfortable. As much as I love the Sacred City and everyone who calls it home, there it too much of the world still to explore and experience to remain hidden away."

It hurt her to hear him speak of his desire to leave her and the Sacred City. After what she had experienced within the world she feared that she might never see him again.

"We shall see, though. Maybe another couple weeks. Whenever Militades defeats Prince Sven and his Metzonian army, I would imagine."

Eye upon the last targets, she waited for her targets to line up and released her arrow precisely to watch it strike true and penetrate both targets. Uncovering her secret past would continue to be a top priority, and she would not go away until she knew the answer. But as long as she got to continue seeing her brother, the story of their past could wait.

CHAPTER 19
POISONING OF PROKOPOLIS

Pulling the ends of the white cloth tightly, Belle tied them in a knot. She examined the red that spread beneath as Sven's left arm continued to bleed, despite her efforts. Sven did not even notice, lifting the large mug of ale with his right hand and draining it in a few brief seconds before hurling it across his tent.

Gazing at his multiple wounds, Belle would admit that the Metzonian king had taken a beating today, returning to his tent bloodied and broken. His strong will and stubbornness were possibly the only two things that returned with him to the tent in one piece. That and Aerox dragging him away from the battle when the rest of his army retreated. Belle had done her best to clean and dress the wounds of her love, but of all the damage done, none had been heavier than that done to his pride.

"I think you still won the prize for today's battle. Would you like to claim it now?"

As he shoved her away, the scowl upon his face made it abundantly clear to her that his pride and sense of invincibility were wounded more deeply than she had anticipated.

The Order of the Fallen was the opponent Sven had always wanted to fight, the one he saw as worthy of his skills in battle. The warriors of Prokopolis had proven themselves to be a more than a commendable opponent and had systematically torn the Metzonians to shreds. Refraining from any offensive tactics, they patiently absorbed the endless waves of the king's infantry, holding the stalemate for several long hours of battle.

When the ravenous appetite of the Metzonians for battle had started to slow, the Fallen Army descended upon those who had so eagerly sought the battle. Belle had been too caught up within her personal battles to understand how the rest of the day's battles unfolded. But one moment the Metzonians had held the advantage and the next all were scrambling, on the defensive. The Metzonian lords and their armies had underestimated the superiority of the Fallen in the confines of war. She admitted that she had made the same mistake; history had been more fact than fiction.

The Fallen Army seemed unflappable. Intimidation had zero affect upon their minds; their confidence remained unbroken. Belle thought that the men of the Order must have strongly believed that they were the armies of Heaven. Believed that the Lords of the Light would not let the Order lose this war they fought for the holy ground beneath their feet, the very ground on which they had built their glorious city and raised their families.

Calm had filled the hearts and minds, unaffected by the minimal losses inflicted upon them by the ravenous warriors of the Numelli Plains. As the soldiers of the Order sensed the tide of momentum change, their turn at aggressiveness decimated the Metzonian lines, cutting into them so deeply that they penetrated as far as ten ranks within the formation, successfully obliterating the morale and strength of the Metzonians who fled the battlefield.

For all the confidence the Fallen had going for them, Belle did not know if they were quite able to comprehend the determination and viciousness of the man they faced. So strong and violent had the mind of Sven become that his will was unbreakable, almost to the point of becoming a fault.

"You'll redeem yourself tomorrow."

Her attempt at soothing his wounded pride was once again not received as she expected. His anger burst in her direction. "Redeem? Redeem? They tore me to shreds today and hacked apart my army! I do not even know how we survived at all! If they had pursued us beyond sight of the walls, I'm positive this war would have been over in the first day."

Sven cleared off both side tables with two great sweeps of his arms. Glass shattered and metal dishware clashed. Then silence filled the tent. The armed Shadow Guards outside did not move; they heard the rage of their lord often and did not deem this event any more uncommon or worth investigating.

Belle turned away, scouring her brain for other ideas that would pull the man she loved out of his daze. All attempts to seduce him or approach from a point of vanity were rejected with hostility and violence. Solving the current problems for him was the only way that she believed she could reset Sven back to the man she knew he was. Taking a stab in the dark, she proposed a new solution to their problem.

"You know, Sven, there are other options that you have overlooked."

He sent a dangerous look across the tent toward Belle, his deadly eyes narrowing at her. His thick bloodstained arms latched onto the arms of his chair, and he lifted his battle-ravaged body and crossed the tent in three great strides, quicker than she'd expected from a man suffering from blood loss.

"Tell me! Tell me, Belle—what have I overlooked?" His anger increased, and his hands clenched tightly upon her throat. Belle knew to tread carefully. She felt the power on her throat as she had felt the strength beneath his fingertips the first time she had met him. Rage fuelled this power, though, one that could end her life in the briefest of seconds.

"My father …"

His iron grip tightened at the mention of her father in his presence. Sven lifted her off the ground. Belle refused to panic, knowing her fate was tied to his; her future was with him and no other. If he failed here it would be her failure for not forcing him to see past his own faulty delusions.

"Listen … and you might learn a thing from … your worst enemy." Prying his fingers from her neck as she struggled to breathe, she slapped him hard across the face, trying to snap him back to reality. Golden eyes narrowing as he stared at her and gritting his teeth, Sven finally released her, leaving her staggering sideways as she coughed. "You bastard!"

She rubbed her throat, the dark circles in her vision subsiding, allowing Belle to speak softly as her voice regained its strength. "As I was saying … During my father's expansion of the empire to the far side of the world, he came across a kingdom that proved too much for even the might of the Chilsa Imperial Expansion forces to handle. That angered my father greatly; they stood in the way of what he had dreamt about.

"Their kingdom was perched strategically in an impenetrable mountain pass. There were no other routes except through that particular pass. After months and thousands of lives lost, my father made a personal trip to this bastion that was proving too much for the lords of the Chilsa Empire themselves."

Enjoying the tale she was telling, Belle knew that her father's failure brought Sven slight enjoyment. He did not know that the story ended in a way that, although he would deny it, would prove that that Sven and her father were more alike than either cared to admit.

"My father travelled up into the peaks of the great mountain range to gaze upon the fortress from above, hoping to see something that his commanders had missed. Looking down upon the fortress, he noticed a weakness that would prove to be devastating for his enemies. Stealing a trick his own ancestor Nuor often used, he went to the stream that fed water into the city of fearless barbarians.

"I witnessed the horrors, Sven. Tears of blood soaked the faces of the dead; their mouths locked open in their final scream. Their fingernails had scratched their eyeballs, which turned glossy black. Others had taken to attacking their comrades. Their bodies were heaped before several of the soldiers who had once guarded the gates.

"My brother described the poison that was poured into the stream as a hallucinogen; it makes those who ingest it see demons and monsters. Friend turned into foe, and they slayed each other without ever knowing it. If they didn't kill each other, the poison finished the job.

"A whole city was alive and free in the setting sun; all were dead by dawn. Walking through the city, I lost count of the bodies. Men, women, children—all had died a horrific death to further our father's dream of global domination. This was the dark death my father left in his wake. If you truly want to be as powerful as my father, perhaps even more powerful, then you must have the ruthlessness to do whatever is necessary."

She had been merely sixteen when she witnessed the horrors her father was willing to unleash. It had certainly been a lesson to her brother and her that neither forgot: no matter what stood in the way of what you wanted, there was a way around such obstructions. Sometimes it was simply a matter of how far you were willing to go to make it happen.

As she looked at Sven, she saw a man who fought for what he wanted, but the last strands of his Humanity held him back. He wanted the glorious victories in battle, sword to sword, but the Metzonian would not win this one. Sven needed to overcome the confines of human morals, to step beyond them, if he was to survive what was to come. It was up to Belle to nudge him toward a method that did not offer the glory but contained the victory and fear that would drive them forward.

Sven returned to his seat, pondering silently, not responding to the story immediately. "How convenient for him. However, I do not see any streams that run through the great Prokopolis on my maps."

"Look above the city, like my father did, and you will see that Prokopolis has the same problem that many great cities with large populations have. Their source of fresh water travels a great distance from outside its walls. Prokopolis has many great aqueducts that draw water from the mountains in the south. If done under the cover of darkness, the Prokopolites and their troublesome armies would be weakened, if not eliminated."

"As convenient as it sounds, I require the Fallen alive, remember? I cannot simply kill them all as your father and his ancestor before him did. I require them to be alive, Belle, which also requires me to force myself through that damned army that has humiliated me."

Despite the depths of his failure to crack the spirit of the Prokopolites and the Order, she knew that Sven would stubbornly continue the fight until none were left. If he did not come to understand what she was trying to tell him, she knew he would lay dead upon the battlefield. Belle decided that she could no longer let the man she loved destroy himself.

"Would you shelve your pride for a moment and listen to what I'm saying and perhaps try to make it work? This task has to be completed one way or another; the Dark Prince will have it no other way. Although you wish to win in a great clash of swords, the Fallen are too strong an opponent. We witnessed that today, and unless you have any brilliant battle-changing events planned to turn the tide, we must look to other options. So snap out of it."

Sven ground his clenched teeth, causing her to question whether she had perhaps pushed too hard and was going to lose her own life. He resisted any thought of snapping her neck as he remained seated, allowing her to continue with her account.

"There are many poisons that one can use to kill a human, but the Fallen are not of Humanity, remember? Poisons do not have the same effect upon them, despite their mortality. Do not ask me when; know only that my father tried numerous times but had little of the results he wanted. His desires were opposite our own. He wanted to rule the population, where you only want the Fallen." Belle was starting to see Sven's mood improve, or at least shift to consciously trying to solve his problems instead of moping.

"Such a plan could possibly improve our situation; however, the army is the problem, not the citizens within the city."

Perhaps the king's battle rage had made him blind to the differences of those within the ranks of the Fallen army. From a distance, she was able to see the distinct differences to discover the truth.

"It solves much more than you think. Despite their strength, the majority of the ranks within the Fallen army are filled with the religious fanatics who worship and serve the Order. I have witnessed it from afar; they heavily outnumber their Fallen comrades. You can tell the difference between the warriors of true Fallen descent and those who are of Humanity.

"The Fallen fight better. They are quicker to respond to the changes within the battles around them than their would-be brethren. Stronger and bolder, they are willing to fight multiple enemies instead of hovering behind their shields. Have you not found differences between opponents? How some are easier to slay than others."

Starting to nod in agreement, Sven pulled the cork from a bottle of wine and took a swig of it before passing it to Belle.

Taking a long drink, she continued, not allowing her momentum to slip away. "So we poison the waters of Prokopolis. Because the Fallen armies retreat within their walls every night, the army will become incapacitated along with the population within, leaving only the remaining Fallen able to defend the city. Another benefit would be that it makes selecting those you require from the rest of the rubble that much easier. Those who survive are your true Fallen."

Taking another long pull from the bottle, she let the wine swirl upon her tongue before swallowing. She watched Sven sit motionlessly, seeing the gears turning within his mind as he toyed with her idea. Watching a grin return to his face, she knew she had him.

"I am sure the Fallen would find watching their human brothers' deaths quite pleasant." Belle saw the thrill within Sven as he thought about the agony the servants of the Fallen would endure.

"As for those that will watch the Fallen continue to live while they die, perhaps in the end they will discover that the Fallen are not the protectors and guardians they thought them to be. I'm beginning to like it ... How much poison does it take to murder a city?"

The word *murder* rang particularly loudly in her mind, causing her to pause and smile upon him as the idea grew stronger within his mind. Moving across the tent, she threw a leg over him and sat upon his knees, looking into his eyes.

"It may take a few days, but let me take care of it for you. Consider it a gift." Shimmying closer, she wrapped an arm across his thick shoulders, close enough to smell the ale upon his breath.

"And until then?"

"Continue to engage your enemies upon the battlefields, but be clever about it. And remain alive." Belle did not want Sven performing any glorifying feats upon the battlefield that would result in his death and the defeat of the Metzonians for eternity. His conflicted brother would not be able to pick up the pieces if the king fell.

"Simple enough."

Pressing herself hard against Sven, she switched tactics. As she dug her fingers into his wounds, she felt a grimace cross his lips beneath her own. As his grimace became a grin, she felt his hands tighten around her body, pressing back.

"And you could give me the gift from that wager you made earlier … You don't actually believe that you slew more Fallen than I did today, do you?"

Feeling the power rise back within his body and soul, she let herself relent to the familiar feeling of the formidable strength and power she had fallen in love with. Healing what had been broken, though a dangerous game, was successful. She would allow herself to enjoy her victory. He was back; she could feel it. She wondered if Prokopolis and the innocent multitudes praying within the city could feel it.

Five large enclosed aqueducts moved the fresh mountain spring waters from the mountains, crossing the great rolling hills of the Kyllordic plains to Prokopolis at a steady slope. Belle had been pleasantly surprised to discover her father had stockpiles buried near Prokopolis. Staring at the wooden barrels, she decided she actually wasn't surprised. Watching the wraiths of Sin her father employed for his dirty work dig, they moved at an unnatural speed. Far more efficient than normal Chilsa citizens.

History told that the Chilsa people were spread out across the land of the empire, seeking war against friend and foe alike. Hundreds of powerful clans travelled across the thousands of leagues, each with its own hierarchy of warrior shamans wielding ancient magic. The most powerful of the shamans ruled the clan until he was slain in battle against their enemies or murdered by one of his subordinate shamans. The lands ran red with the blood of its own people as all sought more glory in battle and had since the beginning of time. War covered the countryside until one champion rose up higher than the others and brought the clans together into the modern Chilsa Empire.

That champion had risen from the ashes of the civilization of death, putting the cruelties of all before him to shame. Roaming through the lands destroying entire clans with his dark sorcery, the monster slew all his enemies, creating a reign of terror in a time known for great death and horror. Many bowed before him and swore to serve him for eternity; others put up a futile resistance. In the end all served the ruthless champion.

Nuor.

Once Belle's great-grandfather had established supremacy among the shamans in the lands that were Chilsa, he set out to expand his rule. But he discovered he was not the biggest shark in the pond, as he had first believed. Two other dark angels had been upon crusades of their own, Dev'Azra and his hostile wife, Xera.

Coming from the darkness on the other side of the world, the first Dark God and the Witch Queen came across the Nuor's shamanic army, bringing strength and powers that greatly exceeded Nuor's. To protect everything he had built over time, Nuor swore fealty to the two Dark Gods for the prize of becoming the third Dark God. The trio sought to exact revenge upon those who challenged them for dominion over Humanity. The war did not go as the Dark Gods had intended.

Despite the enormous defeat in the last of the battles fought in the War of Beliefs, Nuor was not one to be deterred. Slowly he began rebuilding, until the proper day came to exact his revenge. Combining together the survivors, he formed the Brotherhood of Sin to influence and control the world, secretly transforming the world to their designs. The Order had become too established and strong for Nuor to exact his revenge, though. His children were left to continue his relentless hate within the shadows.

While the citizens of the empire and its surrounding nations believed all the shamans were extinct or its history all fables and tall tales, they were in truth ruled by Nuor's distant descendant Neurus and his lone remaining son, Kristolphe. The Brotherhood of Sin continued to pull the strings over time to influence the events in their lives, like the insignificant puppets they truly were.

As Belle watched the wraiths spill the dark contents of the great wooden barrels, tainting their purity without visual evidence, she felt she was at last avenging her family. The Sin would soon be able to exact their revenge upon their ancient enemy. All that was now required of her was the patience to wait for the horrible disease to spread throughout the city and infest the population.

She had spent long days watching her love upon the battlefield, always within the thick of the battle that swirled around him, fearing that all would be for naught. Belle had watched with great apprehension as the armies of the Order and Metzor had clashed upon the open fields for three days, waiting for one side to falter or for them to destroy each other once and for all. The empress had anticipated that the Order would realize the strength of their position and try to inflict greater losses upon the forces of that threatened their families. To her surprise, they remained close to their walls, slowly killing off their enemies, waiting for the Metzonians to realize the folly of their quest and return home.

Sven had remained true to his word, not losing his patience as he waited for her to deliver her promise, pressing the attack just enough. She was impressed with him for saving his ravaging nature for his tent the night before renewing his assault upon the dawn, a structured schedule that became routine.

Three days had passed when she had finally received word that things had been prepared as she had asked of her father. Her father's minions had followed her word with precision and purpose, and she watched the servants of the Sin put her plan into action.

It was time to steer her champion in the correct direction and witness the death she had created. Awakening Sven in the darkness of the early morning hours of the fifth night, after yet another

A Mortal Mistake

Metzonian defeat, she whispered in his exhausted ear that it was at last time for him to receive the gift he desired so much.

The chaos could already be heard within the city; only his exhaustion kept Sven from awakening to the uproar of pain and suffering. Shaking him from his sleepy stupor, laughter rose from the bed they shared as his mind slowly awakened to the din. He leaped from his bed, and she looked upon his excited face. A man who had dreamt of nothing but the utter defeat of his enemies had suddenly seen his dream become true overnight. Frenzied with excitement, Sven's loud screams for his armourer to equip him as quickly as possible raised concern within the darkness.

All loyal souls stood around their leader, bewildered by the events of the black night. Shivers ran across the skin of every man outside the walls, whether from the cool breeze or the bone-chilling howls leaping over the walls into their ears. Sven stood silent and unmoving as he patiently waited for his moment, prepared to unleash his final assault upon the walls of Prokopolis. In the gloom of the full moon, Belle and Sven watched as the defenders on the walls came under attack from those they protected within the walls. Swords and screams rang out over the walls as the citizens of Prokopolis attacked all living souls within the city as though they were foes.

The soldiers of the Fallen did not know how to react to the assault by those who they were sworn to protect, but the violence of the poisoned forced the decision upon them. Bells of alarm were raised but rang out only a few short times before they too were overcome when the gatehouses and other defences fell to the humans overcome with insanity.

The tall steel and stone doors shook as the gates of Prokopolis began opening slowly before the shocked Metzonian armies. Citizens with infected minds had seized control of the gates. Worry struck them several times as the Fallen within the gatehouse regained control of the gates several times before at last the final defender fell and the gates opened completely at last. Excitement grew within Belle as she watched their plan finally coming to fruition.

Gates of Prokopolis opened around the city as the Order-worshipping humans ran from the city in panic, screaming hysterically into the black sky. Others fell to their knees, crawling in the dirt before the city walls, screaming for mercy and rolling in the dirt as if their skin was on fire.

Belle watched as the Metzonians, driven from their slumber by the pandemonium, wasted no time in realizing the situation before them. The briefest moments of hesitation spread throughout the army before the dark, steel-clad infantry charged forward. Civilians fell to their knees before the charging ranks, pleading for death and receiving it. Belle could feel the smile cross Sven's face as she watched his back.

"Let us hope that the citizens of Prokopolis do not slay more Fallen than required." Belle looked to General Hallaken as he watched the plan they had spoken of unfold. She watched him clasp his chin strap tight as he entered the circle of the Shadow Guard. Aerox's hulking mass was noticeably missing as his king had sent him and the rest of the guard to the other side of the city to ensure his prey remained properly trapped. Sven responded to the general's comment with slight concern.

"That is what I fear. I wish for the Fallen angels, not those of Humanity that grovel upon their steps and worship at the Order's churches and cathedrals. The weak are of no use to me, so I strongly suggest that we get into the city before there is nothing left of the sinful Fallen." Belle knew if the elusive Fallen were all slain by those who worshipped and depended upon them for guidance, the Prince of Hell would not be rejoicing or rejoined.

Family members of the Fallen were heard screaming as warriors started smashing down home doors and chasing down the stragglers, dragging them from the city. The remaining defenders struck silently, unnoticed among the rooftops, useless as the streets became flooded with Metzonians. Hunting parties began to ravage the city violently; its warriors enjoying the terror they were inspiring. All soldiers were given strict commands to follow; the sacking of Prokopolis was not to be the typical slash-and-burn siege of the Metzonians. The soldiers were to rape, pillage and destroy all they wanted, but the lives of the inhabitants were to remain intact until they could sift out the Fallen hidden among the masses.

A Mortal Mistake

Watching the general leave, Belle remembered her agreement with the Brotherhood in return for their services. She knew she had to reach them before the invasion advanced too quickly. She loved Sven dearly for all his strength, but he would not be able to slay those who guarded the acropolis without help. "I must go now as well, my love. I will meet you at the acropolis. I just have to take care of a few things first."

Belle did not know if he heard her. His attention was too entrapped by the images of his swordsmen charging forward and cutting down the zombies the mortals had all become. The Metzonians mercilessly mutilated the bodies of the Prokopolites; undoubtedly some who had fought for the Metzonians' freedom against Mallax.

Smiling at the irony, Belle slipped back through the ranks swiftly. She felt few eyes upon her as the warriors of Metzon pushed forward like zombies themselves, staggering to avenge the death of King Masen at the apparent hands of the Fallen. Belle wondered how much they even remembered about the event and the circumstances surrounding it, or if they were lost forever in the darkness.

She watched Sven, leading his command staff on foot, reach the gates of the city, letting the screams guide them toward their desired destination. She would have to move swiftly if she was to reach the acropolis before Sven.

Belle felt shivers up her spine as she heard the distant flapping of the heavy, leathery wings of the Metzonian king's master. Booming laughter filled the air as Rhimmon flew high over the city, circling above the army below, inspecting the mayhem created for him. She may have been unable to see him, but she knew he gazed down upon them, slowly flying toward the two towers of Ori and Bri.

CHAPTER 20
The Acropolis of Prokopolis

The bright Metzonian torches flowed like water through the dark streets of Prokopolis. Mimicking the flames of Hell's demons, they came to burn all that remained of the Order and those who still believed in the noble principles of Heaven.

The small satisfaction from knowing the Order had evacuated many of the Fallen to the safety of the Sacred City was a hollow victory for Militades. He was not a fool; he saw the bigger picture, knowing that for every soul they managed to save, multitudes more had already been sacrificed. There were never enough saved. Standing at the edge of the small cobblestone square surrounding the only entrance to the lofty palace and its surrounding walled courtyards atop the acropolis, the general looked down upon the burning city. Militades had fought valiantly to make them believe him, but the Elders had ignored him, and now the impact of those mistakes lay before him.

The evacuation of the city's Fallen had begun the moment the Elders learned about Rhimmon, hours before Militades could reverse it. The majority of his best and brightest soldiers had been sent away in the Elders' panic, too late to recall any, and he could only hope that Kallen would make good use of those forced to flee. By handcuffing him at every opportunity, with the evacuation the Elders had basically handed the keys to King Sven and his Metzonian armies.

"The Metzonians have entered the city, Grand General." The voice of a subordinate hesitantly called out behind him.

"Really..." Militades snorted, having seen the Metzonian torches a mile away before they entered the gates from every direction, "I can see that, thank you."

Militades had been livid with the Elder Council and screamed with a rage he had never felt before. The old angels seemed oblivious and so filled with fear they did not understand what they had done. Somewhere the Elders had lost their will to fight, or perhaps having never destroyed the evil that plagued their world had worn their resolve. *Orion would have been ashamed.*

Looking up at the white circular towers that sprouted from the rock of the acropolis that overlooked the city and surrounding countryside, he knew they would not stand forever. Light continued to glow from the columned peak of the Ori, its sister tower Bri appearing asleep in the darkness.

The Elders continued to converse above, though Militades did not know what they had left to say; their fates were already sealed. Perhaps they were enjoying their last moments of mortality. Judging from the rampant pace of the Metzonian king and his men, the Elders would meet their fates very soon. King Sven's bloodthirsty path to dominance reminded Militades of the child's uncle.

Although the young man had never met his malicious uncle, their styles shared an uncanny similarity. Organizing what remained of the Army of the Order, Militades had led what he believed to be a strong last defence, despite being restrained by the Elders' commands. He could not be prouder of how his infantry fought, making the Metzonians doubt their decision as Fallen blades bled the Metzonians. But watching the dogged determination of their king with amazement, Militades became mesmerized by the young Sven, who fought like his courageous father but with the vile brutality of his uncle, King Mallax.

Militades had not taken a direct role in throwing down the Cruel King as the young man's father had, but Militades had seen plenty of blood during the short reign, starting with the murder of

Mallax's own family. His niece barely escaped, with nothing but the clothes upon her back. Mallax's reign had been nothing but blood.

Mallax's viciousness was the sole reason for maintaining his power. Sven shared his uncle's nastiness, though his mind remained intact, making him the most potent of opponents. As with his quest to rip the power directly from his oldest brother's hands, he had proven himself extremely capable of manipulating people into his way of thinking, a charisma that had been his father's greatest asset.

Militades remained astonished at how cleverly Sven had manipulated an entire nation to seek the destruction of the Order. The deception he created with the murder of his father channelled the anger of his people and convinced his brother to support him as he turned a murder into a war upon religion: Humanity versus the Fallen. Militades would never have believed such a war could happen, let alone that the mortals would win. Even though the Order played a strong part in its own demise, the reality remained beyond comprehension.

The Fallen's situation was harsher than any had originally believed. The return of Rhimmon to the world of mortals was the one factor that the large family of Fallen had feared. The community had feared the figure of darkness when they were ranking angels of Heaven and able to defend themselves against such forces of Hell. Now he was back to finish the job, hiding behind the human King Sven.

Nonetheless, as Militades watched the Metzonian soldiers weave closer through the streets, he understood the young king's reputation was indeed earned and not made of myths. Had Sven's soul not become corrupted by the darkness of his new master, Militades would have admired the man. Kallen came to mind, and he thought about the two men. Similar but so different, the two men were upon opposite scales.

Militades wondered who would come out on top were the two ever to meet.

"Would someone go and inform the grandmaster and the remaining Elders that the Metzonians have breached the city. Arrival is expected before dawn." Although it was already too late for further evacuation, the general forced himself to think about the stubborn angels sitting in their tower waiting for Heaven to lift them to safety and leave the world to its horrendous fate. "Everyone else is ordered to move behind the palace doors and begin preparing to hold the entrances as arranged. It will not be long before they reach the acropolis."

Militades's personally trained Defenders of Orion scrambled around the acropolis defences, trying to form a semblance of oppositions to protect the remaining Elders within the city who'd chosen to remain behind as others evacuated.

The situation left to Militades continued to grow more dire with the passing of each hour, as the Metzonians pushed ever closer toward the acropolis defences. Feelings of desperation that were shared by every commander and soldier on the losing side of the battle rolled in his guts.

The Army of the Order did not have the endless resources required to withstand the Metzonian army, leaving its general with increasingly difficult decisions to make regarding the defences of the city. While evacuating the remainder of the Children to the safety of the Sacred City had been essential, it had not been Militades's decision, nor had he been able to avert the unexpected disaster.

Despite such vital actions required by the Order, their defences, with the support of the citizen army that could be called to arms, should have matched and exceeded the Metzonians that marched against them. Neither Militades nor the Elders had foreseen the sickness that ravaged the city, however. Devastated by disease, men had become so weak they were bedridden, leaving few to protect the city. It was a devastating blow to the even the calmest and most steadfast warrior.

Militades had gone out into the darkness to witness the events for himself, going straight to the barracks of the human commanders. Humanity made up half of his army; with the evacuation of the Fallen, the ratio had quickly skyrocketed to three quarters. The loyalist humans had suddenly become the backbone of their general's defence, leaving him reeling. The Elders' personal healers had been called to the barracks to try and identify what had affected the brave commanders of the Fallen armies.

Entering the barracks, Militades found all the commanders collapsed upon their cots, many having already succumbed to the effects of the sickness. Spotting a close friend among them, Militades discovered that hope was quickly diminishing for all of them.

"General, it is a sickness that has no known cure." The healer had pulled him to a far corner beyond the range of the dying men's hearing. "I have seen these symptoms before, especially among those within the confines of the later conditions. Remember the deadly effects almost three centuries ago when the plague spread throughout Prokopolis?

"Only Humanity was affected by it …"

Militades indeed remembered the sickness from history; it had ravaged the citizens of Prokopolis for almost a decade. Six of ten citizens died in the plague that was traced back to the waters from the lakes the city depended upon. As a result, the great aqueducts were constructed to carry the fresh mountain waters. He looked up above them toward the towering stone structure running deep into the heart of Prokopolis.

"Precisely. This is no coincidence. Our enemies seem to have been testing it and waiting for the proper moment. It appears they have seized such a moment, but there is nothing we can do about it anymore. You must pull those whom remain back to safety before it becomes too violent."

"You believe that it will get more violent?"

The doctor had nodded, confirming Militades suspicion.

"These are only the first symptoms, Militades. As the poisonous disease spreads, so do its victims and their violent outbursts. The infection has warped what good was left within these men. Only the darkness remains within their souls. They are human, not Fallen. Trust me when I say they have darkness within them, as all of Humanity does."

Militades had taken the news to heart, and he had pulled back a large majority of what remained of the Fallen soldiery to charge through the gates and enforce an escape route for the Elders. But he had been unable to formulate even an attempted escape with such chaos devastating the city. Glancing one last time at the towers above him, he thought yet again that the fools had cornered themselves in a self-fulfilling prophecy, and Heaven would not forgive them for it.

Standing at the edge, Militades gazed down upon the Metzonians climbing the long trail; the line had almost reached the top. Moving to the top of the staircase that led to the road, Militades waited in the shadows, awaiting the man who had broke the heavenly minds and spirits of the Order.

As the grand general of the Fallen Armies, Militades had been positive that they could not be bested by a mortal force such as the Metzonians. Overconfidence would be his downfall, a sin for a man who soldiered all his life. He had not accounted for the mortal factor of the majority of his army nor a method that would murder a city. He had at last encountered an enemy without moral boundaries.

Militades assumed that he would never make the same mistake again; there would be no leaving the acropolis alive. Not that it bothered him; he had always known that he would eventually take the Glory Road, as a soldier often did. He would, however, go down it knowing he'd done all he could to gaze upon and understand the enemy who had succeeded in the lofty task.

Coming around the corner, a figure stopped upon the landing, looking up at the lone figure as his entourage of personal guards fanned out before him. Militades gazed down upon King Sven for the first time in years. The black sheep in the herd of golden kings, Sven's armour was not covered in the glittering gold that his brothers and family had always clad themselves in. His plate armour was dark grey, with sharp barbs protruding from every line and corner of the steel plating as though it came straight out of the fiery forge. His full-face helmet was Metzonian-designed, with narrow oval slits for his eyes. Two horned spines protruded from the corners of his forehead, the straight steel hammered directly out and backward, imitating a pair of demonic horns. Militades found it suitable to the stories he heard about the man, more demon than human now.

"I have not looked upon the young Sven since he was a child in his father's noble court. How the young grow to become the very monsters that scared them as children in the dark. I would assume that you are indeed King Sven, come to claim your prize of blood and violence in person, as is the Metzonian way."

The armoured figure showed no recognition of the man before him, though Sven had seen Militades several times in a past lifetime, when he was a teenager.

"My father told me that a true man collects his debts with his own hands. Which of the Fallen are you?" His words spoken were commanding, with great power, but lacked the tone of respect his father's voice once held.

"I am the one who taught your father those exact words, though he took them in the proper context. My name is Militades. I am the Fallen who organized the systematic slaying of your ranks for the past several days and would have continued for weeks more. Poisoning the waters was a clever idea, Metzonian, a method used by those too weak to win war with swords."

"Swords, fire, poison—all destroy my enemies. I do not care which method is used, as long as the end result is death. I warned you all. I told the Elders what would happen if they refused to turn over the Fallen. Now they have the horrific deaths of a million Prokopolites upon their hands!"

"You are insane to blame others for what you have done. The desert destroyed your mind, didn't it? I knew it was a mistake to obey the commands of the Elders and not to press beyond the city walls. It was wrong to hope you would see reason and return home. For my mistake you murdered everyone within the city, filling its perfumed streets with the stench of death and disease."

"Perhaps we do share the stain of all the souls who died within these walls. I, who brought death and destruction, and you, who could have prevented everything, perhaps." Sven paused, his laughter muffled slightly by his helmet. "Your Elders should have listened to me. Perhaps then the innocent would not have had to suffer."

Militades listened to the man talk; speaking of the lives of the innocent meant nothing to him. They were merely meant to be taken, holding no value of any kind. Hearing him speak, he realized

A Mortal Mistake

he was like his uncle and very much mad, too far gone to save. Militades would be left with only one option when the time came.

"So you could butcher thousands of equally innocent Fallen, as you did in the desert?" Militades lifted an eyebrow in Sven's direction and looked out across the burning city, encompassing it within his open arms. "The landscape of blood and fire is that of Mallax reborn! You slayed your father with your own hand and then hunted your oldest brother. Will you also kill your last brother when he discovers what you have done? Thankfully your mother passed before you got to her."

The last comment stopped King Sven in his tracks; Militades could almost hear his teeth crack beneath the pressure of his jaws.

"Does that sting, Sven? I wouldn't worry too much about it; she was already forced to watch one family die. What is another? At least this time she is free from watching her beloved son slip into insanity."

"I would murder Prokopolis a thousand times to see my mother again! I promise you shall pay for that slight, General. But it shall not be death. I do not come to present the Fallen with an immediate death. The Fallen do not fear death because they were never truly alive, but they still fear like Humanity. I have seen it, I have smelt it! I shall give them something far worse than death; they shall become a part of the terror they fear the most."

The time had come; the Glory Road beckoned Militades to step forth. He knew full well what terror the young man spoke of, a continuation of what he had already begun: murdering their souls to fuel Hell's return to this world. He would not be a part of it.

"The flames of Hell shall have fun with your soul, child." Militades reached forward, picking up the burning oiled torch that he'd carried with him from the palace square entrance. Gazing into the dark eyes of the Metzonian lord within his helmet, Militades smiled at him, tossing the torch into the shadows of the cliff edge. "A gift for a new king."

The thin trail of pitch ignited, spreading flames out from the shadows, burning from the edge. Trailing toward the narrow cobblestone trail that twisted up the acropolis to the palace, the gift was one of death. Rocks erupted across the trail as the chain reaction struck out along the edges of the stone mount. Fragments of rock sprayed out over the infantry below as the explosion went off behind their king.

The thick curtain of rock that surrounded the palace walls began giving way from the edge of the acropolis, sliding down upon Sven's soldiers as they worked their way higher up the narrow road. Struggling to maintain his stance, Militades looked back to stare at the slightest sway of the two towers.

The tower closest to the explosion began to sway heavily as the trembling increased. White columns splintered, showering the rooftops with rock fragments. Militades watched with horror as the tower of Bri began leaning in the direction of the Ori that housed the remaining Elders. At the last second, a floor near the middle of the tower gave way, swinging the tower in the opposite direction.

The noise of Bri plummeting over the edge and down upon the road was deafening. The sliding rock of the acropolis gained immediate momentum, carrying what remained of the Metzonians along the trail down the acropolis. A couple thousand went down; only what seemed like a hundred thousand to go. Watching Sven and his followers fall to their hands and knees, Militades saw their fear as they wondered if the thick stone platform beneath their feet would also fall away beneath them.

Looking back as the sliding rock swept away the thousands following him up the road in a thunderous sweep of stone, Sven drew himself back upon his feet as he stared into the cloud of dust. Laughter erupted from Sven as he shook his head, forcing Militades to remember what he had just learnt about the man. Life meant nothing.

Using the brief moment he still had, Militades bolted forward, striking out at the guards surrounding the king. Two guards immediately crumpled back to the ground, and he severed the outstretched arm of a third as the rest advanced upon him in defence of their leader. Militades did not give ground as he drew his second blade, pressing the attack, taking lives at an unrelenting pace. Sven himself joined the fight when number eight of his guards fell. He

A Mortal Mistake

pulled his black blade down in a strong overhand blow meant to cleave the Fallen's leg in two.

"I had anticipated the king of Metzon would wield the sword that carved the nation into being. Tell me, Sven, where does the Mirage of Metzor lie? Does the usurper avoid its touch, knowing it would reject him, or does the blade rest in the hands of the true king?" Militades hacked the end of a spear thrust in his direction, taking the forward hand with it, letting his second blade bring his total to eleven.

Sven charged directly at Militades through the last three guards with great momentum, determined to run his blade through the Fallen's body and beyond. Wrapping his arm around one of the remaining guards, Militades threw the man onto Sven's blade, leaving the two men to tumble down the staircase. As he cut down the two remaining personal guards, Metzonian blood ran down Militades's blade upon the once-white stone.

Treading slowly down the staircase leading to the remains of the road, Militades paused before the bloodied body of the guard Sven had inadvertently slain at its base. There was no sign of the Metzonian king, leaving the older man cautious. Pressing his body against the rock wall, he slid down the last couple steps as he neared the corner.

A black blade penetrated the rock wall at the corner, missing Militades's head by several inches. Reaching around the corner and grabbing the hand that held the hilt, Militades drew himself beneath the trapped blade and around the corner in one swift movement. Feeling his elbow connect with Sven's masked face, Militades watched the man tumble away from the trapped blade down another set of stairs.

The Metzonian king shifted himself onto his elbows as Militades walked down toward him. Militades raised both his swords above his head in an overhand grip, prepared to end the reign of destruction. Looking into the golden eyes, Militades felt a pang of guilt, remembering the fiery golden eyes of his dearly departed friend, Sven's father.

"You betrayed your family and friends, Sven, and worst of all, you betrayed your father! While I believe he still loves you, he must understand that I need to correct the course that has gone astray. May he forgive me for what I'm about to do."

The sound of a whistling arrow reached his ears seconds before it struck, allowing him precious moments to reduce its power. Twisting away, Militades felt the feathers against the back of his neck as it penetrated the back of his shoulder. The pain above his shoulder blade wrenched deeply as he reached over his shoulder to remove the long shaft. Militades was prepared to toss the arrow aside and finish his task, but he paused to inspect the arrow more closely, noticing the foreign details. The fletching of the arrow was not typical of the black Metzonian feathered tip; it consisted of the long white wingtips of the rare Arresian eagle—a marvel of rarity, because the eagles were only found in one place. Gazing into the settling dust against the rising dawn, he watched a lone figure dance gracefully from boulder to boulder up the destroyed trail.

"Chilsa!" Militades hissed, backing out of the way of another arrow as he gazed upon the attacker, catching a glimpse of the blue and silver steel of her weaponry. "How many deals with the Lords of Hell did you make, boy?"

Sven laughed, pulling a long dagger from its scabbard as Militades eyed him and the new archer with an unsettling feeling. As she grew closer, he realized he had heard speculative rumours about her. She was the empress herself. Militades couldn't believe that the two enemies had found common ground.

Pulling his helmet off his head as he twisted onto his knees, Sven smiled at Militades in a way reminiscent of his father's daring grin. "You only need to make one deal when you're dancing with Diabolos himself—just one."

"You are delusional if you think you can control the events you have unleashed. I promise you that you will not survive the end." Militades backed slowly up the wide staircase, barely noticing the arrows bouncing off the stone as he looked into the dusty sky at the looming sunrise. Militades saw but could not comprehend that something else moved within the misty dust swirling around the Chilsa woman.

"Like the Fallen, one mistake landed me where I am. Like the Fallen, I too desire death and release. Until then I serve as all do within this world. Or soon will."

Militades raced up the stairs for the palace doors, fleeing to safety. But the Elders were correct in their beliefs that escape was not an option. His deceased friend's son was not wrong; they were all just servants to powers far greater than themselves.

"What in Hell's name has gotten into the people of this world, sir?" The Defender's commander did not answer his frantic captain as he entered the palace doors; he heard them seal behind him as the guards pulled the locks down across them.

Militades mind was weary; the heavy weight of darkness hovered above them and then began squeezing them from all sides. The high ceilings of the palace trembled and shook with a rumble of laughter; mortar and dust sprinkled down upon the white cloaks of the Fallen protectors as they stared up. There was no doubt in his mind about what had possessed the citizens with such sickness.

"Hell."

Chapter 21
The Sea Dragons

The two Fallen brothers walked side by side as they reached the first staircase of the many that would take them into the royal palace. The Kyllica War Council had been summoned once again, the third time today, as information continued to pour in from the scouts about the war waged upon Prokopolis. Many on the council could scarcely believe that the Order was in a war against Metzon. It was astounding, considering that the Metzonians and the Order had been among the closest of allies. Though that was in the past, clearly all had forgotten that it was the Order that had helped put Masen Metz into power.

The royal palace was surrounded by a high stone wall topped by a tall hedge of columns built more for beauty than for protection. The palace buildings were constructed from round and smooth curves, which when combined with additional buildings gave it a smooth transition. The tower tops were domed in green, overshadowed by the largest central dome, created from a brilliant blue glass. Tall archers casually moved throughout the palace yard as many others stood watch at the entrances.

Kyllica was considered a city of wonder by the world, for generation upon generation had continuously added to its beauty. The city had not seen a war or any major disasters to destroy its buildings or temples, and life grew rampant within it everywhere. Great trees grew within the streets squares, and hanging vines grew both up and down the wooden columns of the buildings. Statues of historic figures ahead of their time and carvings were everywhere, glorifying their proud past. Art was the foundation of the Kyllordic civilization; everything they did had distinct style, and plenty of thought and planning went into everything to create beauty. Art, buildings, cities, all was art, even their own bodies, great tattoos covering their skin.

"Do you think the young prince will listen to common sense this time?" Eli's brother finally spoke, a valid question considering how the previous meetings had gone. Eli doubted it, but he would remain persistent, trying to sway the young man to see logic.

"Probably not, Ethan, but if we can turn the rest of the council to our side, then he will be forced to listen." The two Fallen brothers sat side by side at the war council, taking up two seats at the table of eight; the king's seat at the head created a nine-vote council. Many on the council disagreed with allowing both brothers to cast votes; they had rarely voted against each other. When it came to logic, however, both men were adept at forcing others to see why they voted the way they did. Often they managed to sway others into agreeing with the proper course of action before ever having to use the power of their votes.

Though for all the power their votes had, they only offered their advice and made strong suggestions to the king to make a proper decision. Often the king listened to their advice, seeing reason behind their choices. And sometimes he didn't, preferring to do things in a way he thought best. With the new ruler, both brothers had found their advice carried less and less weight.

"He better hope that he listens to reason, or we may soon drown in Metzonian swords. It still angers me that the entire council voted not to support Prokopolis!" Ethan hissed in Eli's ear, wary of the guards as they reached the palace entrance. Ethan had stormed out of the war room after hurling his papers and cursing the other members. As usual, Eli had been left to calm everyone back down.

Entering the palace entrance, the greatest monument to their civilization loomed above them. A crumbling jade pillar rose from among the great green pools surrounding the path through the entrance hall, breaking sharply and jaggedly. Wrapping around the pillar, the skeleton of a sea dragon rose above the pillar, its large wings flared out from wall to wall. The vertebrae of the beast's long neck curved back in preparation for striking. The tooth-filled skull peered down upon all those who entered the palace to beg for the king's concern.

The dragon's bones were a glossy black that shone blue in the moonlight, including its extensive rows of sword-sized teeth. The display was a testament to the beginning of the glorious golden days of the Kyllordic civilization. The black-boned sea dragon was the largest one ever raised by the Kyllordic kings, as well as the last. No dragon had flown above Kyllica for three generations, their extinction coinciding with the decline of the people who worshipped them.

Every day the Elithane brothers passed beneath that dragon reminded them of the perils within the world and the rise of the great men and the falls of the greatest. Life within this mortal world was uncertain. The pair had served on the war council for almost three generations, serving the current king's grandfather for many long years before serving King Oberon Kyllone for his entire reign, which had been far too short. The new king was not quite king yet, with his coronation date still undecided.

"Behave today, would you, Ethan?" Eli held the door open for his brother, and they stepped into the room, noticing the prince was already seated in his high-backed seat within the war room. Too young to be a king, particularly a Kyllordic one, who's entire society was so heavily weighted in wisdom. The Kyllordic people never had a ruler younger than forty years of age, and the prince's father had been the youngest in history. King Oberon had prepared his people for unfortunate events. As he was an only child, he passed a law that a council of the king's closest advisors would hold power until his eldest son was properly prepared for the weight and responsibilities of a crown.

Taking his seat at the expansive table, Eli ran his hands over the glossy brown that in the dim light shimmered black. The table had been built for the large war maps carefully kept upon the far wall library and could easily have held over a dozen men. The impressive table was minute compared to the woodworking scrolled into the structure supporting the large blue glass ceiling. Centuries of artwork and design had continued to evolve within the royal palace, as in the rest of Kyllica.

"Sorry for our lateness, my prince, but we were trying to collect as much information as we could so we may be as thorough as possible." Eli spoke softly, shuffling through the parchments before him as his brother looked over at him in mild revulsion. He smiled at both at his brother and the prince; Eli had learnt the valuable art of appeasement.

Raef Kyllone was slouched in his chair, eyes wandering freely across the room. Paying little attention to the argument taking place around the dark table, he flipped a large golden coin with the dragon of Kyllordia upon its face across his knuckles. As young as the man may have been, at the age of twenty-five he should have been able to see how serious an issue was and the dire consequences it could have upon his people. Tall and lean, he was a typical Kyllordic, with a lanky look that was often mistaken for awkward instead of stealthy. He sat silently in his deep Kyllordic blue robes, tapping the toe of the dark knee-high leather boot resting across his left knee against the armrest. His white-gold crown was simple: sharp silver leaves encrusted with emeralds and sapphires depicted the Trees of Blue that had once grown across the countryside. Tattoos ran up the back of his neck, revealing only the tips of the artwork tattooed upon his entire body.

"Can we get to the point of this meeting already? I understand the importance of these meetings, but life is short, I remind you." The prince spoke with a voice full of boredom as he stared down upon the council. "Did you drag me here just to inform me that the Order at last defeated the newest Metzonian bastard? I grow bored of hearing about this topic and wish it would just resolve itself already."

"My prince, the courier falcons bring more dire news from the city of Nemin." Eli ignored the prince's snide remark, the message a chilling one. "It would seem that the Metzonians have entered Prokopolis. Calculating how fast the falcon flies, I would assume that Prokopolis could very well have fallen by now. The Order has essentially been defeated."

Silence settled upon the war council as the members contemplated the information. Eli and Ethan had discussed the many possibilities that this development could possibly bring about, the worse being that the Metzonians would continue on through Kyllordia.

"How is that possible?"

"A fair question, my lord, and one that we unfortunately cannot figure out yet. From the scouting reports, the Order battled the Metzonians for the better part of almost an entire week. Multiple times the Army of the Order had King Sven broken and chased them from the battlefield. For whatever reason, he did not continue the pursuit all the way back to their border," Ethan said, not looking over at Eli as he finished the report.

Both brothers saw great concern in how Grand General Militades fought his wars against the Metzonians. The Fallen was a tactical genius when it came to strategy and had commanded more wars than any other mortal. He knew exactly when to crush his opponent, and the fact that he held off meant something was very wrong. The thought worried the Elithane brothers greatly.

"One man's mistake, and the rest always pay the price. I suppose it would seem that the Metzonian revenge is complete then," Raef calmly stated, shifting to the opposite armrest with little concern. "Time for them to go back home now."

Eli disliked the carefree tone of the prince and his lack of concern for the loss of life as well as the strategic importance. "And if they decide to stay?"

"It does not matter what they wish to do; they will go home one way or another. Four days ago after we first heard that the Metzonians engaged Prokopolis, I moved the Seventh Expeditionary Force to Nemin to join with the remaining forces of the border army and the Neminian garrison."

All conversation ceased completely at the words of the prince, and Eli knew it was only the calm before the storm. All considered the implications of the words spoken so boldly yet so foolishly. Eli looked down into his lap as his brother cried out beside him in a tone of disbelief that unsuccessfully masked anger.

"I beg your pardon? You did what?"

An awkward silence filled the room after Ethan's outburst. The eyes of all the members of the war council were on Prince Raef, who seemed nonchalant about what he had done. Staring back at the members of the council, he straightened within his cushioned seat.

Eli moved to calm his brother but it was too late. Ethan's anger burst at the seams as his angry words flew at the young man.

"You fool! What is the point of having a war council if you avoid listening to our discussions and heeding our advice? Instead you just do the first thing that pops into your head! King Sven of Metzor just defeated the most disciplined, professionally trained army within a million leagues; why not just rally the militia and chase them back?"

"I'm king here, and it's my right to command my forces to protect my people. I needed to send a message to Metzor that their actions have not gone unnoticed, that we are watching them and will not hesitate to use force if they move beyond this little revenge of theirs. When they return to Metzon, and they will, our armies will reseal our lands behind them. Do not speak to me as a subordinate, General Ethan!" the royal prince snapped back, unwilling to take heat for his rash decisions, though Eli could see his confidence was shaken.

"You are not king *yet,* boy!" Ethan flew out of his chair, bellowing at the young man and pointing harshly at him.

Eli stood and placed a hand firmly on Ethan's shoulder to force him gently back into his seat. He tried to take a calmer approach than his twin brother and explain to their lord the scenarios that he apparently did not see.

"My brother is merely expressing his concern; I'll agree not in the best of manners. My prince, you must understand Nemin is out in the open, far from the protection of the natural defences we of Kyllordia have always relied upon. The fact that the Order itself, who's military strength is far superior to our own, has been defeated means that the Seventh will be little match against the Metzonians.

If they choose to fight that is. They could as easily move right past Nemin and take the roads across the Valk, the path into the heart of Kyllordia."

"So we move the Third Army out of Essex and recall the Fifth from the Nykol, everything can still work …" Eli watched the young man closely; he shifted uncomfortably in his chair as his confidence faded completely. Raef's glance continuously bounced between Eli and Ethan, who muttered curses in the background as he scribbled.

Ethan kicked his chair back and slammed the sheet of paper before Raef, startling all in the room when his fist hit the small side table. "Oh, you are going to do that and more, but first you are going to rescind your previous commands and pray it is not too late."

Raef did not move. He glared up at Ethan, who grabbed him by the wrist and placed the feather quill in his fingers as he screamed at him. "Do it now, damn it!"

No other council members lent their support to the prince as they found other objects within the room to look upon.

Raef scribbled his signature quickly on the command Ethan presented to him and firmly pressed the royal seal into the paper before it was ripped from his hands and carried to the scout commander outside the doors.

"There is no way to know whether Sven realizes that the East Road is open to him or not. There's also the chance that he could care less. He might have no interest in the east and return to Metzor when his revenge is sated …" An older lord tried to show weak support for the young prince.

"Or he could storm the River Valk whether it is guarded or not. The time to play the 'what if' game is not now, my lords. We must prepare for all contingencies, no matter what result is presented to us." Ethan shouted. His uncontrollable temper was flaring up as others began to question his command, bringing Eli to the realization he should probably end the meeting before Ethan went too far. *To think it has only begun.*

"As our esteemed king has already suggested—" Eli turned to the other six members of the council. "Pull the Fifth from Nykol to replace the Third that should be leaving for Kaldor by dawn to try and support the Kaldor defences. Order the Third scouts to be sent out immediately to get a day's head start on the army's advancement. They must reach the Valk, if they are too late order the immediate retreat of all forces back to Essex. We will leave the rest of the council to issue the orders; we will reconvene tomorrow after the army has left to discuss alternative scenarios for the upcoming events.

"If you will excuse us, we have other matters that need attention. My lord." Eli bowed shallowly toward Prince Raef before slowly backing away. He heard Ethan storming out the doors and doubted his brother had acknowledged the prince. Pressing the thick doors open with his shoulder, he exited the room and heard Ethan cursing loudly in the hallway.

Eli had to jog to catch up with his brother, glad he was not wearing his heavy chainmail. Pulling up beside him, Eli matched his speed for several long quick paces before breaking the silence.

"You do realize that he will probably cut off our heads if he ever reaches thirty and claims the full crown. Perhaps you should apologize and try to make him feel good, even confident, every once in a while. A future king needs to feel confident in his decision making."

"At this rate he won't see next year, Eli, I doubt that we will have to worry too much about the distant future. We may not survive the next month if that Metz continues on his rampage. Amazing how far the acorn can fall from the tree. His father would be irate." Eli did not know which young prince Ethan was referring to, the Kyllordic or the Metzonian.

"King Oberon had several more years of knowledge before he was forced to take the throne. And his father had full knowledge and experience to draw upon for his childhood. Raef has not been as fortunate." Ethan gave no response to Eli's slight defence of the youth. "As for the Metzonian prince, Sven had a father of great renown across the lands. Although the two apparently did not get along, the man could be deemed a very quick study. He picked up far more from his father than he probably gives credit for."

"His brilliance, courage and charisma are his father's, and his fiery temper, willpower and cunning are his mother's. A deadly combination when those aspects combine into one vessel of indisputable darkness and hate." Ethan's pace slowed slightly as they emerged through one of the side courtyards into the gardens. Eli knew they were headed to the babbling streams within the gardens that soothed Ethan's vile temper. Eli had almost lost his brother forever to his anger after he was tossed from Heaven. The brothers remained part of the Order but only remotely these days, preferring to stay among the forests and lakes of Kyllordia.

The Order was well aware of the anger within his brother and had warned Ethan about the perils of the darkness he was dabbling dangerously close to. Calmness was what the Order desired, not fiery passion or violent temper. Those were the traits of the Brotherhood, the black to the Order's white, and as such were punished by death. One could not return to Heaven after embracing the evil traits of Hell, nor had the Order ever allowed any to try. Fearing the loss of his brother, Eli had left the Order's ranks with his brother, planning to move to them to Kyllica, the city of art and ideas and, most of all, peace.

It had not been Eli's preference but more a decision of necessity. Clashing with the Elders and the Order on a rate that bordered on religious consistency, Ethan's temper had boiled too hotly, even if it hadn't been completely his fault. Three members of the Order had mistakenly chosen to pick a fight, not anticipating the violence Ethan was capable of. A mistake they realized quickly. Grievously wounding all three of them, Ethan's lesson had been a cruel one, leaving two of them horribly maimed. The Elders were horrified at Ethan's actions, demanding his permanent banishment from the Order and Prokopolis. When two of the men died of their injuries two days later, Ethan was immediately arrested and given a sentence of death.

Only Eli's staunch defence and the pleas of a brother's love persuaded the Elders to retract their judgement … to a degree. Instead of a quick death, Ethan was to be sent to the dark side of the world to hunt Sin. Wraith hunters rarely lived long, prosperous lives as they scoured the dark side of the world, spending years in small bands or, more often, alone. Becoming a wraith hunter was in essence a very slow, painful death, and the Elders knew it. With little other choice, Ethan had accepted the sentence and dragged Eli with him.

Banishment had somehow prolonged their lives; they'd survived the death sentence and settled down in Kyllica, far from the fields of death outside Prokopolis, but Eli did not know how long it would last now. "Perhaps we shall someday meet this prince. It would be interesting to meet him and to hear how he came to see the world in such a twisted fashion."

"I am sure he would happily tell you his story." Ethan looked over at his brother, a scowl upon his face. "And then I'm sure he would just as happily separate your soul from your body with a steel blade. Have no fear; we will meet him someday, though it will not be under ideal conditions that allow for much analysis of his troubled mind."

Very similar emotions to those that I once knew, Eli thought but did not point out. He noticed his twin's mood relax the farther they moved deeper into the gardens.

"Can the Order really be defeated? Prokopolis is the shining beacon of hope and light within this world. I feel a chilly darkness and quite alone thinking that it could really be gone. Those dead could have been us … probably should have been us."

"I feel much the same, though I try and remember that they are not all gone or completely defeated yet. Militades was, or remains, the best. He should have given the Metzonian boy a ride like he never experienced before. Why he held back concerns me greatly. The scouts noticed a slow and steady stream leave Prokopolis, so we must be missing something. I feel the darkness growing, though; no doubt the Elder Council felt it as well and made the decision to slowly drift into hiding."

"Hiding? We Fallen have been hiding our entire lives. When haven't the Fallen been careful about showing who we truly are, hiding behind the notion that we are an ancient religious cult complete with elaborate rituals and secrets that allow us to be wise and see the future? Look how far we've drifted into obscurity. No wonder the darkness rises."

"Like dusk that fades into the darkness, so too comes the dawn that is the rising light. I know you are not the most patient of people, Ethan, but we must try. Although it may be small, everything we do has an effect on the world and things to come. Impress upon the young prince all your vast knowledge, and he too will make an impact on the events to come, quite possibly astounding and grand, without ever knowing it himself."

"He angers me greatly, Eli—you know that." Ethan's jaws clenched tightly, and he pounded the soft grass as he crossed his legs before him. "Though perhaps I have been too hard upon the kid and expect too much from him. Maybe just a little. I need to relax and unwind. Think about what the future will hold and come up with a way to try and repair the mistakes made today. You can leave me if you want."

Eli lay on the soft grass, flat on his back, staring at the clear blue sky. Such a marvel the world was, hurling through space as dictated by the universal laws of the Creator. The world was dictated by such magnificent powers, it did not notice or care about those who waged war upon its surface. It would just continue spinning as life flourished and perished, none of it mattering over the millions of years it had existed.

Eli smiled, his thoughts returning to his brother. "I think I could use a little unwind time as well. To pray for Militades and the defenders and their safety, and maybe to pray that our message gets across the Valk before it is too late."

"Don't remind me."

CHAPTER 22
Shades of the Shadows

Rhimmon flew over the Citadel Palace in two swooping circles, looking upon the burning city as the Metzonian army scurried through the streets like ants. Landing atop the eastern tower of Ori, he continued to watch and listen to the chaos within the city. Torches marked the trail of the attacking parties, leaving burning paths as they continued to ransack the city.

His senses were buzzing with the surrounding smell of Fallen flesh throughout the city that stretched around the acropolis. The closer he flew to the rocky outcrop that lifted the Elder's Citadel Palace above the city, the thicker the bodies grew. The scent of those beneath him was so thick his mouth watered with an ecstatic thirst. Listening to the screams, the crackling of flames and the crashing of blades, he focused his mind to push out the background noise and listen to the conversation taking place below among the occupants beneath his wings.

Feeling the presence of the one he sought, he flexed his muscles and reached down to rip the top of the tower temple from its high columns; he threw it down on the palace courtyard below and smoothly slipped down into the middle of the assembly of members below. He stood before the Fallen Throne of Order and its occupant, ignoring the others scrambling for safety.

"Indeed it is too late, my old friend; there shall be no escape for you. The Order of the Fallen has fallen and is dying. Perhaps *your former grandmaster should have chosen his protégé more carefully. Letting this noble house die as you have must be such a disappointment.*" Rhimmon taunted the old man sitting upon the white stone throne, feeling the ancient power that beat within his mighty heart. He could sense the others moving around behind him, regaining their composure.

"All things live and die; this is the way of life, Prince of Hell. One cannot change what is encoded in destiny or the methods of creation. You, too, shall one day learn this lesson from which you flee." Caelestis looked emotionlessly upon his opponent, clutching one of the Order's holy blades in one hand. His eyes dropped down to the blade across his lap and scanned the inscriptions on the blade. "I knew that we were nearing our ending when word of your release was spoken in my ear. And while I cannot change destiny, you will find that I have done well to preserve our future."

Rhimmon laughed aloud and, looking at everyone in the chamber, mocked those around him. He withheld his anger. He did not sense fear at his presence, so he pushed upon them his powers of fear and horror. Twisting quickly, he reached with his long arms to lash out at several of the guards, sending several over the edge, while others became broken bodies against the white columns.

"Preserved the Order? You are truly more foolish than I believed, Caelestis. Fallen from Heaven's grace, you and your brethren are shadows of your former selves—weak, powerless … and mortal! You shall all die on this world, never to seek the comfort of Heaven! Darkness is rising within the depths of the world and shall soon cover this world. The Armies of Hell are amassing and shall soon slay all that has been created! You would be a fool to not fear the coming storm!"

The tower trembled, announcing that the assault upon the palace had begun, as the heavy rams smashed against its massive doors. Rhimmon's dark eyes locked hard upon Caelestis's green eyes as he tried to pry into the old man's mind. He was rebuked immediately, drawing his ire at the unforeseen difficulty.

"True we are not wielders of great power anymore, for that has been stripped from us by our lords. But they also took mercy upon

A Mortal Mistake

us, granting us the ability to keep our wisdom and strength of mind. That is why you underestimate the Fallen." The old man rose from his throne, casting aside his tall staff and lifting the round crested shield down from the top of the throne.

The Crest of the Fallen pressed upon the silver shield had been passed down by all the generations of the Order directly from Orion himself. He drew the holy sword the smiths of Prokopolis had forged for him near the end of the Golden Age of the Order; the blade carried the green hue, reminding him of his past life and the road he was about to go down. Gripping the leather handle tightly, Caelestis drew himself to his full height and looked at the beast laughing at him.

"The Earth tells me that it is time. May Heaven come crashing down upon those who slay its children!" The old man moved, charging forward, swinging the holy sword in an upward stroke to begin the fight that he knew that he was going to lose. He did not have the remotest of chances of winning. But what other choice did he have but to go down swinging?

Sven followed in the Metzonian squadrons as they stormed through the breached doors at the palace's main entrance. As he walked in on the turmoil, to say he expected heavy resistance would probably have been an understatement. Violence and death flowed down the ramped floor like a torrential river of red.

Abandoning the city to its fate, the Fallen withdrew all its warriors to defend the acropolis palace. With numbers vastly diminished due to the horrid poison, the remaining soldiers knew defending the city with so few would be hopeless, so they resolved to cause much death among their victims.

Perched above the invaders, the Fallen archers were decimating the incoming attackers, leaving the piles of dead that continued growing. Five rows of infantry kept Sven's heavy assault soldiers contained in the lower sections of the ramp, their heavy shield repelling every assault. A hundred well-positioned Order infantry hemmed his men in the ramp, effectively blocking Sven from the grandmaster of the Order.

Metzonian blood lay thick under Sven's boots as he looked around him at the dead bodies on the ground. All were littered with the barbed Fallen arrows bearing white feathers. Upon the tops of the great walkways that passed between the passages knelt row upon row of white-robed archers, easily plucking off those who ran carelessly forward. Only the heaviest-armoured soldiers had managed to survive the attacks but were unable to move forward.

Shouting commands from high atop the third tiered bridge, Sven recognized the general as he paced back and forth, white cloak tightly wrapped around his bearded chin. Sven wanted nothing more than to ram his blade through the man's blue eyes.

The line of archers upon the third level stood with their white cloaks draped over them, as if curtains were draped over statues. It was an illusion that helped to hide the locations of the majority of his enemy's archers. Even if Sven was able to get around the shield wall, the archers would drop him before he was able to get to Militades.

Charging soldiers around him continued to find death as they attempted to move forward for only the slightest of gains. His own armour and shield already riddled with arrows, Sven realized he would not be able to break through. He would have to ask for help, a thought that infuriated him. Slowly retreating from the palace, Sven left his men to futilely continue funnelling into the death trap. Sven detached himself from the group and continued away from his army toward the large battalion of Sin warriors standing beneath the walls, hiding from the approaching dawn in the shadows. Looking at the Brotherhood warriors, Sven turned toward the largest, recognizing him as Neurus's wraith from Chilsa.

"Warlord, the Fallen have constructed their remaining infantry into a defensive matrix which is too strong for my mortal men to break through. The enemy will run out of arrows before my men breach to a point that we could actually break out. Make this small problem go away, would you?"

The figure did not move much and simply stared over Sven's

A Mortal Mistake

shoulder at the entrance, where the new king's men had at last stopped entering.

The entire group was dark and mysterious. Sven had not seen them in such numbers before, and the sight sent shivers up his spine of steel. Tall and lanky, they all shared the same build and towered over those of Humanity; they were silent as the wind sent their black woven cloaks billowing behind them. They moved like ghosts, silently absorbing all the light around them, despite the heavy armour hidden by the darkness.

Touting the greatness and strength of the Brotherhood of Sin, Belle had sworn that nothing would be able to withstand their heavy-handed approach. Sven knew more about the Brotherhood than he let on, possibly sensing more than the daughter of Chilsa royalty. He could think of one enemy the Sin was powerless against.

The Brotherhood of Sin was mysterious and shady. No one but their illustrious master Neurus knew what they were truly doing. Sven doubted that even Rhimmon knew. Rhimmon's power had been used once already to subdue the Exalted Ruler of the Brotherhood, forcing him to heed Sven's call, but the wraiths still roamed freely. He would have to talk to his master about leashing the hounds closer to home.

The Dark Prince had informed him all about the Brotherhood and the true history behind all the lies and fables they had integrated into their story to hide among Humanity. Sven had become envious of the power they wielded within the darkness. Despite the deep history of Chilsa, they were still no match compared to the Metzonians, a thought that made Sven grin. Facing those before him, Sven wondered if history would have been remade had they fought the true rulers of Chilsa.

"The Fallen threat shall be removed with pleasure …" Locan finally spoke to him, lifting his large two-handed mace to rest atop his shoulder, the black blade the only metal shimmering in the shadow. His lanky form moved soundlessly across the courtyard; his battalion drew their menacing variety of weapons and followed without a word.

Sven glanced over as Belle joined him, grinning widely at the sight of the dark Chilsa warriors. Watching the shady warriors walk past Aerox as he stood beside them, Sven paused to notice the uncanny similarity between his Shadow commander and the Sin. Looking into the depths of Aerox's eyes as he was walking past the soldier, his shadow's eyes were merely bloodshot and not the bloody red of the Sin. Shaking his head, he ignored the uncomfortable thought as they followed the darkness back into the kill zone. The Sin's double crossbows were cocked, and the hunt began.

Caelestis skidded across the slippery floor, spinning in circles, watching his old sword doing the same in the opposite direction. He stared at the bloody streak on the white marble floor that he had created. Completely oblivious to it mere moments ago, he now became aware of the pain in his left side.

He was too tired to continue. His brethren within the city were certainly dead, and Militade's Defenders were probably preparing for their final journey as well. He could sense another dark presence far away at the base of the palace. He could only guess at what evil Rhimmon had brought with him to destroy those who had fallen from Heaven.

"Destroying me will not bring down the Fallen, you know this. Knowing that those who fight for the Light will never stop is a fear inside of you. We knew that darkness would eventually come for us again, and we have been preparing for it since the formation of the Order." Caelestis tried to laugh, but his lungs cried out for every breath of oxygen.

"Prokopolis, our home, has already delivered our victory to us. Most of our Elder Council members were evacuated, along with all treasures and archives, long before your armies rolled over the Zarik. The majority of our population, along with the majority of our army, has escaped. You have been delivered an empty city!"

Rhimmon reached down for the defiant old man, plucking him up by the shield. He threw him hard against the one of the numerous stone pillars. Tossing the round shield aside, he picked Caelestis up in his right hand.

"Fear not, old man, for you are indeed brave, and your self-sacrifice shall be remembered by your people. But as you say, you cannot escape your destiny and fate, as your people shall soon discover. They were not my goal, though ... You were!" The demon grinned widely at the grandmaster, and Rhimmon felt the man's soul turn cold within him. Deafening laughter echoed within what remained of the tower, as wind whistled through the column.

"For all your brilliance at preventing a human victory, you forget that we of Hell work on a completely different scale, Caelestis, with plans that work on a level deeper than Humanity can understand. I wanted you, one of the last and purest of the Fallen, for a special purpose! Foolish to think that you would find your death here like your beloved Militades will ..."

Chapter 23
Death of Militades

Militades's palace defenders had punished the attacking army that was attempting to push through the main doors, even well after the Sin arrived. Militades had watched the shadowy beasts climb the sides of the ramp and engage his men with an unexpected swiftness. Militades had not fought Sin warriors in many centuries, but he was unsurprised in light of the array of enemies pitted against them. If his soldiers were surprised, they did not show it. Their control of the situation had deteriorated as the battle progressed, and his Defender's bodies had begun to forfeit the lives of their master as the effects of exhaustion robbed the men of their strength. All eventually fell to their enemies' blades, but Militades was proud of the tremendous toll his men had exerted upon the reckless and impatient enemy.

Militades shed his long cloak on the golden carpet and swung his blade hard upon his first Sin opponent. All his strength was thrown into the blow, and the resistance his blade met left him unsurprised. He continued his attack, striking the wraith's throat with his free hand, catching him off guard. He then brought his sword up through the attacker's armpit; the wraith dropped with a hiss. Withdrawing his blade, Militades was quickly battling two other masked combatants. Looking around himself as he parried the blows, he realized how they were quickly being outnumbered, although holding their own. His five lines of infantry had been dispersed in full man-to-wraith combat. With the strategic advantage lost, he knew it would not be long now.

Cutting down his assailants, he ran forward to sever another attacker's head as he was about to slay one of his Defenders. He cut down two more wraiths with their backs turned to him. Metzonian infantry were now flooding in behind the last of the Sin attackers. Militades looked upon the white cloaks that lay upon the ground, many stained red with the blood of their owners. Few remained, desperately clinging to life.

"To the Fountains of Benedoria!" His blade flashed quickly as he worked his way among the remaining Fallen warriors, who screamed in unison, releasing their minds from the thoughts of survival and gave in to the Glory Road. Pouring their remaining energy into a renewed assault around their commander, the dying defenders forced the attack upon their enemies, striking down the soldiers of Sin.

Militades continued to battle; the adrenaline pumping through his veins was the only thing keeping his arms swinging. Screams behind him caused him to quickly glance over his shoulder to see a large figure swinging a mace hard and sending two crumpled bodies through the air. He was the last.

Four Sin that got too close to Militades howled in agony as he swung his blades as fast as he could before him, severing limbs. Two more lost more than their limbs and fell to the ground at his feet.

The Sin halted their relentless attack, allowing him to take in the scene around him. Militades watched as the Metzonian army continued to pour into the palace, unaware that it was already empty and they would find few. The remaining forces of evil encircled him, and he stared at the faceless monsters, hidden behind heavy black helmets that in turn were hidden beneath large tattered hoods. He fell to his knees and sat back on his haunches, holding his blades between his legs on the ground.

"So it would seem this is the end. My destiny is upon the golden carpets, watched by the Hundred Statues of the Slain, soon to join their kind." He chuckled silently to himself at the irony of his situation. None of the attackers moved, despite the chaos going on around them. Looking at the crumpled bodies of the dead, he could name every one of the slain, having personally trained each one of them throughout the long years.

He watched the young Metzonian king walk by, following his generals and the Chilsa princess. The young man had no idea what he had done; pity grew within Militades's heart for the man. Looking into his dead eyes, he could still see the glimmer of his great father among the hate. The confidence and unbendable willpower were the trademarks of a man destined for greatness. A family's legacy had turned black. Looking at the slain around him, he knew that those men's legacies would die with him. He'd handpicked the widowed and unmarried, the childless and orphaned from the ranks of volunteers who offered to throw down their lives with him. Guilt tugged at him to think that perhaps they could have had wives or children of their own, but his desire not to rob children of their fathers had been too strong.

"Benedoria is indeed beautiful. Though I would much rather have been able to see Heaven's great Forests of Tyth again myself." Militades looked up toward the commanding figure that spoke the croaking words. He looked curiously upon the figure he had seen cut down many of his finest; the sound of the moving shadow's voice was familiar to him.

"Forest of Tyth is indeed beautiful with its white trees, though I love Benedoria for how it calmed my soul and purified my spirit of the horrors of war. Though such fountains are not to be drunk from …" Militades held his head low, remembering all of his sins that had cast him from Heaven, drinking from Heaven's pure Benedoria being one of the least foul, merely one more added to the list of crimes. Watching the mysterious figure remove his horned helmet, he felt his eyes sting with tears at the distant memories.

"Locan, Legionnaire Captain of Crux IX." He looked into the eyes of his former student, his eyes still a piercing blue, though darkened shadows were cast by his large pupils. The whites had disappeared, having turned bloody red. Locan's appearance both sickened and saddened Militades. His scarred face, hidden from the sun for what looked like an eternity, was a pale, sickly white. His long black hair was matted and mangled, and a large jagged scar ran under his left eye.

"Mighty Militades, Legionnaire Commander of Crux III … a long time it has been. A shame that this is the way we meet. Explain to me why one continues to serve Heaven, even after being thrown from its beauty."

"Son, there are many things that you do not realize. While I may have been cast from Heaven, I am still heavenly. I still believe in the principles on which Heaven is built. Having grown up on those principles and been taught their deeper meanings, one finds it encoded upon their souls, even if they discover such too late. I know what I did was wrong; one must mend his soul and find comfort in the changes he makes. If not, the guilt turns to anger. The anger turns to hate. And the hate turns to horror, until one day he looks back upon his life with shame. I see my own path as one of great strength, though you see it as weakness."

The lanky warlord was not swayed by his speech. Militades knew Locan's escape from Heaven had filled his heart with immediate hate. He became a criminal who taught himself to despise everything he once loved and cherished within his life. Militades understood that it was the only way he could possibly live with himself, knowing what he had done.

"Weakness is within those who serve those lesser than themselves, Militades. You could have been a god … Instead you chose to once again fall upon your knees and serve feeble Humanity. Heaven will not recognize such weakness anymore; it cannot afford to. Heaven is losing the Eternal War, Militades …"

Militades averted his eyes; the last sentence stung his heart. It cried out in pain, feeling Heaven's fear, as he had millennia before.

"From dire need comes unfathomable strength, a lesson that you shall someday discover for yourself, and you shall fear it, Locan. Perhaps not today, but one shall rise to the challenge and bring to light the faults of your path." Militades climbed to his feet, quietly praying for forgiveness and lasting strength. "I only wish it could have been me."

"I have long surpassed you, Militades. Not only upon Earth

but in Heaven as well. The Slayer of Angels has no match on the battlefield. Perhaps I shall remind you of the strength within these arms, something your brother had also forgotten."

Militades felt the brunt of Locan's mental assault; he had never forgotten his brother's loss in Heaven. The death of his brother was the crisis that created the spiral Militades had never been able to recover from. His crimes, his errors in judgement, the loss of his wings all stemmed from the loss of his beloved brother. All the pain he'd ever felt was because of the former Legionnaire captain before him. Militades prepared to take the captain's life, as Locan had his brother's.

"You may believe yourself undefeatable. But for everything within this universe, there is always something more powerful. Something more deadly." Militades raised his swords toward his face, looking upon their blue hue, remembering all those lost to its touch. Taking a deep breath, he tried to calm himself by avoiding further thoughts of his brother. It had been a long road, but soon he would get the opportunity to apologize for every mistake he'd made. Militades would not allow Locan to use the guilt of his brother against him. Tightening his grip upon both swords, he crossed his arms before him in preparation for his final victim.

"'Slayer of Angels' is a name perhaps fit for the Dark Prince of Hell, Locan, not you. You were great in Heaven, Locan—none can deny you that. But fewer have fallen farther than you have. No. You slew the souls that stood beside you in Heaven's battles. You slew the souls that protected you and watched over your own soul. Your name has already been written within the history, and not as you perceived it, but you did not know that, did you? You are *not* the Slayer of Angels. You are only remembered as … the Betrayer of Brothers."

Militades ducked beneath Locan's vengeful swing. His own blade slashed into Locan's armoured side as Militades dropped to his knee. A shower of sparks arced through the air as his holy blade cut into the black armour protecting the Sin's ribs. Locan stumbled back, clutching his ribs, creating some space between the two.

"How does holy steel feel upon your dark flesh, Locan?"

A Mortal Mistake

Militades's wolfish smile greeted his enemy's growl when Locan saw his black blood on his steel fingertips. Locan licked his fingertips clean, eyes locked upon the Fallen commander. Locan stretched his palm out to the side, and a subordinate quickly set the hilt of a long twisted black blade into his hand.

"For the sake of a fair fight to discover the true champion, I shall withhold my darker abilities to offer you a chance at lengthening this fight. I have no doubt that I will stand over your corpse in the end, sending your soul to Hell!"

Bending down lower, Militades dropped his left shoulder to shield his blade low across his body as he prepared himself. Pointing the second blade toward Locan as he lifted his arm high above his crouched body, he grinned. "Heaven shall guide my soul as before, Betrayer! Who guides your soul in the darkness?"

Militades parried the blows of Locan's blade with his own and avoided the heavy strike of the mace as teacher and pupil battled within the tight confines of the circle. Neither was willing to give ground or make the first mistake. The clash of steel blades was the only sound within the palace; all spectators remained silent.

Bellowing with rage, Locan pressed his former master, throwing Militades on the defensive. Straining to keep up with the younger man's speed and strength, Militades's technique saved him. He deflected one of the heavy blows to the side; it hacked deeply into the Sin's forearm. A quick backhand cut into the bigger man's already wounded ribs, and a roar of agony escaped from Locan's fanged mouth. Locan twisted back from the blows to his forearm and ribs, trying to protect his wounded side from his enemy.

Using the weight of the ungainly mace to his advantage, Militades parried the weapon toward his enemy's wounded side, leaving Locan's entire left flank open to attack. Seeing his opportunity to strike, Militades sliced beneath the thick plating covering Locan's shoulders and arm with blue steel, cutting through the top of Locan's shoulder trying to sever his other arm. Grimacing in pain, Locan looked up at Militades with an all-knowing look. His low chuckle quickly grew in volume as Militades realized his sudden vulnerability. Locan plunged his twisted blade up into Militades's chest. The blade ran cleanly through both sides of his breastplate, missing his heart by a mere inch. Locan tried to pull the blade back out, but its twisted steel refused to release from its victim, pulling Militades's bleeding body forward into his arms, face to face.

The fallen angel smashed his forehead into Locan's nose, and a geyser of black blood exploded as he kicked Locan to the ground. Militades watched the shadow burst into smoke and reform again, as though the attack had not happened. Locan's blow, however, remained. Militades put his hand upon the bloody hilt in his chest. He switched his remaining sword to the other hand and beckoned with the other.

Locan charged swiftly, blocking the blue steel with the shaft of his own weapon, pressing the owner's blade back upon him, momentarily reversing Militades's momentum. Militades was caught unaware and lurched forward. Locan smashed the sword from his hands with the head of his mace. As his enemy went for the final blow to his throat, Militades's bloody hands grabbed Locan's own clenched fists, halting the attack just short of final defeat.

Militades was close enough to smell the foulness of Locan; the scent of death filled his nostrils. His muscles trembled and strained beneath the attack, and his strength abandoned him with the blood that poured from his wounds.

"It is slipping, Militades; I can feel your weakness through the calm surface of your mind as you slowly break apart. I will be victorious—another soul of Heaven to add to my collection. But fear not. I will make it quick."

Pressed against one of the numerous white columns within the palace entrance, Militades looked up at the man whom he had once loved as a second brother. Looking in Locan's bloody eyes, he realized that man he cared for was truly dead. There was nothing left in him except the undying hate of one of Hell's minions. Feeling the first rays of sunshine cross his face through the stained-glass windows, the last surviving member of Prokopolis felt his grip slip as the steel shaft of Locan's long mace swiftly crushed his windpipe. He swayed back and forth, suffocating. Locan did not force Militades to suffer long; he fulfilled his promise.

He swung the mighty mace behind him with both hands, releasing a blow that crushed Militades's chest. Stone fragments sprayed when the column cracked under the impact; the final Defender, motionless, was pinned to the column. Reefing the sword from the dead man's chest, his former student hacked Militades's head from his body and let it hit the floor with a sickening thud.

"So the pupil surpasses the teacher." Locan reefed on his mace to pull it free from the body of his teacher, whose body crumpled to the floor. Picking up his teacher's severed head by its forked white beard, the Slayer of Angels turned away from the battle scene to return to his comrades.

A member of the Brotherhood tossed Locan his personal horned helmet as three Sin kicked the helmeted head of a fallen Defender back and forth. The head of the warrior finally escaped its steel confinement and rolled before the other's feet, and a quick chuckle broke out among those playing the game. Looking a final time at their bloody footprints as they exited the battle zone, the Brotherhood of Sin receded back into the shadows.

Chapter 24
Champion of the Light

Kallen walked through the temple that had become his new home when he moved into the apartment complex directly across from his sister. He was growing accustomed to the life and duties in the temple, its pace more relaxed than in Prokopolis, where bustling citizens raced endlessly throughout the city.

Despite how unhappy he was with Militades's decision to leave him out of the great battle, Kallen had tried to accept it and move on. He was a loyal soldier of the Order who strongly believed in the structure and order of the military. A soldier might question the word of a superior if the conflict with the decision was justified or morally wrong, but neither was true in this case.

Militades had cited his responsibility to the Order and the protection of the future, two reasons that Kallen had yet to fully comprehend. But the urgency in the words of his foster father compelled him to keep searching. His love for the man who had raised him was deep; the bond of great respect drove Kallen to trust him instead of pressing to return to Prokopolis. His heart yearned to be part of the battle, but he forced his mind away from the visions and the emotions they fuelled.

Instead he had converted his pent-up anger to energy. He spent a great deal of time with Kallisto and his sister, absorbing the endless knowledge the old man was willing to impart upon him. A new perspective on how to look at all things in this world was slowly developing within him, no matter what the subject.

Kallen's favourite lessons had been about heavenly history that had been based on studying the temple itself. The latest was about High General Magnius, who led a hundred thousand angels into the depths of the world, never to return. Scholars claimed that his great Horn of Hellio remained in the Alakari, perched high upon a cliff. The Order believed the Horn of Hellio had been left behind so that Magnius could find his way home. Or so the story went. Kallen had yet to go out to see it, but he was anticipating the great climb to see another artefact of Heaven with great excitement.

His sister had become a prime source of his learning. He was seeing a new side of her that he had not suspected before. Her knowledge about all subjects was endless, and Kallen became enthralled by how she knew so much. He found her able to hold her own against men many times older who had spent their lives dedicated to whatever subject she discussed. She was not shy about what she knew; he knew she held it with great esteem, knowing that knowledge was essentially power. Many wars had been won by brainpower over brawn.

Kallen had enjoyed the extra time they had at long last been able to spend together. Separated at a young age, both were eager to make up lost time and had an endless supply of topics to talk about. Kallen had worried that with so much time spent apart, their sibling bond would weaken, and he was greatly relieved to discover it had not.

Passing through the peaked doors of the entrance hallway, he was almost at the centre of the mountain. The complex sprawled around this central room that lay within the heart of the mountain. The carved stone murals of fighting angels and demons on both sides never ceased to amaze him, no matter how many times he stepped into the throne room.

The silver-tinged leaves of the Trees of Eternity reflected the light that weaved its way from the peak of the mountain down into its core. Rustling without a breeze, the trees seemed to be talking to one another as he approached. The Trees of Eternity were believed to be as old as the world itself, their roots descending into the core of the mountain, perhaps farther. Fables told that they recorded the history of every detail to happen in the world, from wars to weather; a new leaf grew every century, but Kallen did not know if he quite believed it. Though to discredit such would be far beyond logic with the wonder of Heaven's powers present.

A single large chair was set within the room, its silver and gold back tall, shaped in the form of a hundred feathers, each one taller, until the back of the chair was several feet above the head of the individual who sat within it and the large wooden desks placed before it.

Kallen had seen the chair and many duplicates that were set within the large amphitheatre used by the Elders during meetings when they came to converse within the Sacred City. Why this one had been moved to the throne room, Kallen could only guess. The chair seemed small and insignificant to the one seat in the throne room that commanded all eyes of any audience that entered. The silvery-barked trees and the tall white columns stood tall and pure, supporting the large spiral staircase, but the holy treasures did not command the presence that Heaven's seat did.

Gazing upon the throne, Kallen could not shake the feeling that it watched him, penetrating his thoughts and emotions. The white energy trapped within it crackled and burst as it swirled beneath the thin diamond structure of the throne. Kallen felt the throne was trying to communicate with him, but he was unable to understand. He wondered if it was able to speak with the angels who once fought in this world.

The Throne of Creation placed directly in the centre of the cylindrical chamber that rose forever dominated the room, fit for a mortal man twenty feet tall. Kallen knew that it was not made for a mortal of giant proportions. It was not meant for even the angelical beings who had once protected this world from evil before Humanity. Only one person could sit in the large seat; not even Orion himself. Only the Creator wielded the powerful to control the Throne of Creation.

The great books of the Order proclaimed that the Creator sat upon the Throne of Creation for only seven days and seven nights, using the contained power within the throne to build the Earth around him. Once it was completed, the Throne and its Creator thrust forth from its core, forming the Lifebringer and its steady flow of waters from the heart of the world.

Many scholars had argued about the truth of its existence. Dreams fuelled many ideas, despite a sense of hopelessness at being too insignificant to truly understand how this world and everything beyond it had ever been created. Kallen had often gotten lost thinking about how small his life was compared to that around him. He would grow old and pass on in a lifespan that the mountain would consider a blink of an eye.

Pulling his attention from the glorious items in the majestic throne room, he returned to the single individual sitting within the room. With the passing of the former administrator of the Sacred City due to illness, Kallisto had taken over the position. Kallen figured the man would be perfect for the job, but he appeared exhausted, slumping within the chair, his hands crossed within his lap, his bearded chin resting upon his chest.

"Kallisto, the last of the refugees have been made comfortable, though I do not know how long we can sustain this. We may have to come up with a new strategy because there are simply too many refugees. Hopefully all of us can go home soon."

Kallisto looked up, his eyes bloodshot from shedding too many tears.

"Kallisto?"

"I am one of the last of my friends, Kallen. Those who I fell with, those who protected me, those who put me back together upon this world are almost all gone now." The old man looked down and spoke softly, letting his barely audible words whisper within the cylindrical room.

"Prokopolis has been destroyed by the Metzonians, and all who remained within its white walls have been slain. Fires that burn within the ruins blanket the sky with the black smoke of its victims …"

"What of my foster father?" Kallen moved closer toward the table. Kallisto did not respond to his question. Feeling fear creep into his soul, his imagination began to come to conclusions that were avoided by the administrator. "What of Militades?"

Kallisto dropped his chin to his chest, a new tear rolling down his face as he stared into his cupped hands that caught the grief he shed.

"People think immortality is easy, that it is a gift. That living in the world for eternity is a beautiful thing. But it is not, particularly when you are trapped within a mortal world. Throughout my extended life I have been forced to watch countless friends live and die during this prison term, many very dear to me. Friendships forged not over years but decades. Centuries."

Kallen could not stand it any longer. He restrained himself from picking the old man up with angry hands, slamming them on the desk instead. "Tell me of my father … Tell me!"

"His soul no longer inhabits this world. He's taken the Glory Road back to Heaven after his sacrifice in service to Humanity. Militades died surrounded by his loyal brothers and sisters who had protected all against the darkness. He has fallen for the last time. I do not doubt he took many of his foes with him, but even the mightiest would not be able to survive the odds against him.

"Almost all were slain upon the battlefield, Kallen, or within the acropolis, we assume. The Elders did not anticipate that their army would be defeated or the methods by which it happened. Few survived. They claim that the Metz brothers unleashed a poison into the city that killed all Humanity within its walls and left the Army of the Fallen weak and without numbers. The Fallen left within the city were helpless against what was to come …"

Lifting the desk before Kallisto off the ground, Kallen swung it away from the old man as rage tore apart his heart. He smashed the table against the stone statue of Kyros, letting the debris of wood and papers flutter through the air. The glowing energy within the throne scattered from the hate and anger surrounding it and tried to flee, giving off flashes of blinding light every time a splinter crashed against its surface.

Before the kneeling statue of the Throne Guardian king, Kallen's knees gave out beneath him. He rested his tear-soaked face on the back of his hands as he gripped the edge of the granite pedestal. Grief flowed from every pore of his body; tears and sweat evaporated from his burning body as his heart pumped boiling blood within his veins.

The light of the room diminished with Kallen's emotional collapse; the throne settled, not moving, mimicking the Titan's emotions. A pair of hands rested upon the back of his shoulders, trying to remove the tension and grief that rose within him. Squeezing Kallen's shoulders intermittently, Kallisto waited for the worst of Kallen's grief to subside before speaking again.

"I apologize for my selfishness in this matter. You undoubtedly feel the pain worse than I. Many people will enter and leave your life, Kallen, each having an impact upon you, whether small or large, good or evil. It is you who must take what they gave to you and leave the rest behind. I lost a great friend, one of several within the past few years; each wound was greater than the one before."

Kallen had never experienced grief or loss such as this before; it had always been distant loss that had not held the significance of losing a father. He had not even lost any close friends in his life.

Kallisto continued, pushing him from the grief he was wallowing in to whatever lay beyond. "We must rise to honour their memories and the values they helped to instil in you. Militades was a great man, Kallen; you know that as well as I. He taught you everything he knew to prepare you for the moment when he would no longer be able to stand by your side, preparing you to step seamlessly into the great boots that he wore and continue marching where he left off. Although there are few survivors, we must pick up the sword and continue fighting. You must take his place and defend those who still believe in the Light."

Kallen wiped the back of his hand across his eyes, feeling the pain in his bleeding hands when his shock began to subside. "Me? Why me?"

Kallisto pulled Kallen up from his knees to full height, brushing him clean and rearranging his armour. Noticing that Kallisto's eyes were still red, the younger man looked into their depths to discover that the grief had dissipated from their depths, leaving only a steely resolve behind, despite the tears that continued to flow.

"You were the commander of the Titans of Prokopolis. You are the Champion of Militades. He taught you everything because he decreed that you were to take his place at the head of the Order's defences when his death came, Kallen. He knew who should lead his armies when he moved to the next stage of his journey."

"What about all the others who deserve to command the army?" Kallen's head screamed in pain as his emotions swirled within. Too much was happening too quickly; he was having a difficult time sorting everything out, but Kallisto refused to slacken.

"There are no others, Kallen. Most were slain in Prokopolis. Militades would not have placed you in this position if he did not believe you were ready for it. The rest of us feel you are ready, as is your sister. She has already accepted command of the Rangers as you take command of the Titans. It is time for the both of you to step forth and accept your true place among the Order."

"How?" Kallen paused. "How are we supposed to succeed at what you wish us to do?"

"You become what Militades always wanted you to become! You rise from the death and despair that surrounds you like the champion you are meant to become. You will not be forced to do it alone, Kallen, but the Order requires someone to stand before its banners to reunite those who are now as lost as you are. I am too old, and no others are as prepared and qualified as you."

"Destiny calls upon your soul."

A new voice called out, loudly and clearly; the sound echoed within the chamber and drew Kallen's attention to the new visitors. Four women stood in the entrance of the temple throne room. The two daughters of Akakios, Jaina and Kaylee, stood side by side with solemn faces, carrying a large silver shield of the Order. Alexandra stood beside a woman he recognized as one of the early evacuees who had arrived from Prokopolis. Both carried a white case that stretched the length of their outstretched forearms.

He shivered. Gazing upon the shield, he asked Kallisto for clarification. "Those are the Order's holy artefacts of Orion …"

"They are a sword and shield! Indeed, they are symbols of history, but they were meant for war and battle, for slaying the enemies of the Order and those who seek to destroy everything that Orion and the thousands who followed him fought and died for." The green eyes of the White Elder Vayra burnt with a green flame as she spoke, the death of Militades striking her as deeply, as it had Kallisto and Kallen.

Kallisto pressed Kallen forward. "They require a champion to bear them once more. I know of only one man with the values and strength to wield the responsibility of such a terrifying weapon."

As Kallen took the shield from the Akakios sisters, each gave him a soft kiss upon his cheek, Jaina's lasting a second longer. She hugged him tightly. Whispering her condolences into his ear, she slipped back; two tears rolled out of her violet eyes as she smiled at him.

Alexandra shed a large stream of tears as she witnessed her brother's grief; she attempted to smile brightly for him as she and the historian Vayra held the ends of the great box before him. He gazed upon the blade, and the white steel radiated in the column of bright light showering down upon him.

"Let the Oblitoryiat shine once more, Kallen. Lead the armies of the Order into battle against evil as Militades dreamt you would." Kallisto spoke in his ear, grasping Kallen's wrist and guiding his sword hand into the box. His fingers grazed the thick leather binding, and Kallen wrapped them around the hilt, feeling the weight of the hefty blade beneath his fingers. He pulled the blade from the box. It shone within the light cascading down from above. Feeling the muscles in his arm tremble beneath the weight of the ancient weapon, his grip did not falter. Kallen could feel his spirit rising within him, weaving its power through the holes created by his grief, repairing him from the inside. Its strength grew greater within his chest and spread to mind and limbs. He squeezed the hilt with greater purpose and strength.

Kneeling before Kallisto and Vayra, two of the last Elders he knew to be alive, he set the tip of Orion's old blade upon the floor.

"Elders of the Order. My Oath of Orion now holds a new deeper meaning and responsibility than it ever has before. I accept these new tasks with the greatest of honours. I shall not fail my family until Heaven calls me to what lies beyond. Nor shall a single soul, Fallen or Human, wander in loneliness or fear while the spirit within my heart beats.

"I, Kallen, of the Order of the Fallen, shall forever live by the decrees passed down by the Fallen Five. I shall quote from Orion, First to Fall.

"I shall not fear death knowing what lies beyond, but fear not living with the gift granted.

"I shall not fear the Darkness that surrounds me, but bath in the Light that I march beneath.

"I shall not fear the terrors of Hell, for the courage of Heaven is unbreakable."

Kallen clutched sword and shield tightly as he spoke the great man's words, feeling what Orion must have felt so long before him. His resolve steeled itself within his mind, pushing through the last of his grief, focusing on what was lost but in a new light—a blinding light that Kallen would throw at the Orders' enemies in memory of those who lived and died to preserve it. He would not falter.

"Rise, Champion of Militades, Commander of the Temple Titans. Defend us, Grand General of the Fallen Armies, Protector of the Order of Orion." Vayra spoke loudly, watching him rise. She let Kallisto speak about what was now required of him.

"You are to begin setting up the defence of the Sacred City and our surroundings. Protect those around you as though you are the one you dreamt about becoming in the past. Use him as a guiding light through the darkness that now threatens us! You are in command now."

Pushing the doors open, Kallen looked down the central corridor that ran the length of the temple. The battalion of Temple Titans wearing full battle armour all stood in ranks before him; one by one all began kneeling upon one knee before Kallen, shouting out in unison,

"All hail Orion the Reborn!"

Chapter 25
Memorial of the Lost

The dim light of the new moon cast down upon the Sacred City from the highest point of its long arc through the night sky. Within the dark sky even the dimmest of stars were barely visible beside the narrow sliver of the moons face as it hovered above the streets of the city leaving the multitudes of occupants to rely upon the torchlight.

The population of the Sacred City had grown tenfold since the destruction of Prokopolis. With the collapse of the Fallen's only metropolis within the nations around them, there were few safe havens left for the scrambling citizens of the Order to flee to. The Sacred City remained the only truly safe haven because so few knew of its existence, but with the influx of new citizens Alexandra worried that its biggest asset would not remain intact for long.

Small towns were popping up within the hidden inner Valley of Angels as trees were cut from the virgin forests and soil never before touched by human hands was tilled. Many of the buildings were hastily constructed to provide refuge for the seemingly endless stream of people travelling through the mountain passes. There was simply not enough room for all within the Sacred City, forcing the majority to survive outside the fortress walls.

Tonight was different, though. All had been invited into the Sacred City for companionship and prayer in memory of those lost. Groups large and small had formed throughout the city, singing their sad songs and hymns, creating a gloomy atmosphere. The sense of community was strong; those who were long touched with such losses were coming out to support those who had only recently known such pain.

That was why Alexandra was here instead of enjoying her downtime back in the temple. She could have just as well stayed in her bath chamber and been content with her wine. Jaina and Kaylee had asked her to join them in the noble cause, however, and she could really find no acceptable excuse not to join them. She was not completely at ease about comforting people, perhaps because she had lived in the constant company of men who tried to hide all emotion.

Arriving at the Crystal Cathedral and entering quietly, she left the sad songs echoing outside for the silent solitude within the cathedral. The cathedral was overflowing with refugees who knelt upon the hard floor, offering up prayers for the lost or missing. Some prayed silently; others wailed loudly in great despair. Prayers of forgiveness, prayers for vengeance and prayers of promises were made to any that would listen.

The temple had declared a cycle of mourning for all those who were new to the city, offering a chance to grieve openly and comfort one another. The new moon was to be the first night of grief and the busiest; the grief was to disappear as the moon began its heavenly cycle and the darkness diminished in the full moonlight. After the period of mourning, refugees were expected to pick themselves up and continue on with their lives in memory of their missing, to confront their fears and move on from the past they could not change.

Alexandra had to admit that it was a daunting path to take, but a necessary one. She had never felt what many within the cathedral had felt, having been an orphan and passed from family to family, never growing close enough to truly love any of them until the last that ended in tragedy. All were gone now. The only true family she had left was her brother, and although she knew what it felt like to be separated from him, she'd always felt he was never that far away.

She had always feared losing him, but she had never been forced to face such a reality as those who now surrounded her.

The Crystal Cathedral was alive with dancing streams of light; the dim moonlight absorbed and reflected by its sparkling walls created a sapphire glow, properly setting the mood for those within. As the blue light swirled, the walls danced up and down, looking as though the cathedral itself was attempting to lift the spirits of those in pain.

She noticed her friends near the front of the cathedral, wearing dark colours. In a slim blood-red dress, Kaylee was the first to look up and turn toward her, smiling broadly despite those crying around her. Her long blonde hair was wrapped in a wide red ribbon down to her waist. She silently beckoned Alexandra to join her and her foster sister.

Looking at Jaina as she rested upon her knees, her small, soft lips moving silently as she prayed, she could see what her brother saw in her. She looked so elegant in her slender black gown that Alexandra felt a little self-conscious about her own image. Gazing into the endless depths Jaina's vibrant violet-blue eyes from forgotten angels, Alexandra felt her insides freeze. For as long as they had been close friends, she still was not able to avoid the feeling within her when she looked into them. It must have been pure torture to her brother, who was so madly in love with her.

It was no secret how much he fancied her, and Jaina most certainly knew it more than anyone else, but she never admitted it to anyone. Alexandra saw how much she enjoyed it whenever Kallen came around and wondered if either would ever act upon such feelings. Kallen had sheepishly confessed how Jaina paralyzed him with her icy gaze and all train of thoughts were lost, leaving him thoroughly rattled as he bumbled through conversations.

Alexandra lowered herself onto her knees, silently smiling toward her friends as they returned to prayer. Attempting to quiet her mind to pray, she found it difficult not to listen to the prayers going on around her. One woman mourned the loss of her husband upon the walls of Prokopolis, praying for safe passage of his soul back to Heaven. Another mother begged the Lords of Heaven to help return her missing children to her. Hundreds of voices cried out within the crystal walls, leaving Alexandra to feel the echoes of their grief. Gazing up into the steeple of the great church, she wondered if their prayers reverberated from this world through space and time to the ears they were meant to reach.

Did the angels of Heaven feel the pain as she did, or was it all ignored, as the cries of a prisoner often were?

"Alexandra." Jaina's soft voice whispered in her ear. "We are going outside to help the priests guide other mourners to the upper floors and comfort them."

The Cathedral was overflowing with people, its floors full of kneeling mourners, as were the balconies on both sides. Looking toward the second and third levels, she saw numerous priests consoling families, using their wisdom and kind words to soothe the ache within the grieving hearts. Walking toward the exit, she spotted an oddity hiding in the corner.

A pair of very young sisters sat huddling close to one another in the farthest corner of the cathedral, away from everyone else, their eyes wary of all the strangers around them. Both looked scared and lost, skinny and frail, their red hair dirty and knotted. Alexandra felt shame at the sight. A brief memory of her past came to mind: a small child clinging to her brother's chest tightly as they hid in the damp darkness for hours. Hours had turned into days before white light rained down upon their hiding spot. Then several large men ran frantically around the entrance before a bearded man reached for them with open arms. Fear had struck both children immediately when they were found by those who had not hidden them in the forest cellar. Such fear continued, although the man had not acted with aggression but calmly beckoned them forward.

"Where are your parents? You both look terribly hungry," Alexandra asked the children. They were not merely hungry; a look of complete famine glazed over the children's eyes and their bodies were frail. Alexandra waved for Jaina and Kaylee to continue without her while she waited for the children to answer. They cowered farther into the corner before the older child broke the silence.

"We came with a group from Prokopolis. Our father stayed

behind to defend those who could not leave. He said that he would meet us in the great cathedral when the battle was over. We have to keep waiting here for him to come as he promised."

Alexandra was at a loss for what to do; Prokopolis had been destroyed for weeks. No survivors had arrived from Prokopolis since the Metzonians had entered the city. Only those who managed to leave before the fighting began survived the outcome.

"What is your father's name? I am sure that your father would have wanted you to eat. Do not be scared. Let's find a kitchen and get you both some food to fill your poor stomachs so we have energy to find your father." She held her hand out toward the pair, waiting for them to take it, but neither moved.

"We don't have any more money."

Smiling softly toward the two hungry children, she beckoned them again. "Don't worry about money. I have enough to feed us all. What are your names?"

"I am Holly, and this is my little sister, Emilia."

The children rose from the cold marble floor, and both girls hesitantly followed after her, keeping a safe distance, unsure as to whether they should trust the stranger. Alexandra knew the lure of food must have been strong for them to choose such a risk.

Taking two bowls of steaming stew from a late-night kitchen that remained open for the mourning, she carried them to the table where the two young girls sat, patiently clutching their little satchels of belongings tightly to their chests. Their large eyes followed the bowls. Both satchels were quickly but carefully set aside as the hot bowls were set down. Alexandra felt her heart give a little as both lowered their head and spoke a prayer softly together before eating ravenously. Such preciousness in such a horrible time ... She could remember herself on her knees as a child, praying to the Heavens to help her and her brother.

"Who first taught you to pray, your mother or your father?" she asked, not anticipating that her question would bring both children to silent tears. The response was equally shocking and sad; she had once felt as they did. "Neither. We are the foster children of Phillip Philotheos."

The name shocked Alexandra, for she knew who he was by name. The Chronicler of the Order was a member of the Elders Council, the one she had sent multiple requests to learn of her history, only to be denied time and time again. "He's not our real father. Our mother abandoned us in Prokopolis and never came back for us. We are orphans. Phillip looked after us until he told us we had to leave. He promised that it would be a fun and exciting journey. He lied—it was horrible!" Teardrops began to fall into their stew bowls as the girls described their horrific journey. "They attacked us in the middle of the night. I heard Jakub's brother screaming in the dark. Horrible screams…"

"A man with a black beard and blacker eyes caught us when we were trying to escape. He grabbed Holly and was hurting her. Aunt Serena came from nowhere and grabbed him by his big beard and killed him with her knife.

"She told us that we needed to run as fast as we could without her to Mendolin. She was hugging us tightly. She was all bloody and sweaty. She whispered to us to run and never stop, to run night and day and stay off the roads. So we kept moving for two days, and then I couldn't keep up anymore." The younger child's eyes flashed over to her sister. "And Holly wouldn't stop or slow down for me."

"I stopped for you! And even let you rest, like a fool. When we woke up again we were surrounded by six men again. We thought the bandits had followed us and found us. They were covered in tattoos and green cloaks and asked where we were going …"

Holly's little sister cut her off, adding her own detail to the story. "They were tall like trees."

"They spoke in a weird tongue, but when we said Mendolin their eyes lit up and they nodded. They talked amongst themselves and then pushed us in the direction they pointed. They travelled with us for an entire day, giving us some of their food, and some even carried us upon their backs through the night." Listening closely, Alexandra knew exactly who had found the children, grateful that it had been noble wandering Kyllordic rangers instead of rogue bandits. She did not want to think what such vile men might do to lost children.

"When we woke up, we were hidden at the edge of a big dirt

road. All of them were sleeping high up in the trees, except the one watching over us. When we woke he pointed down the road and said, 'Mendolin, Mendolin', and sent us out toward the Order's checkpoint and onto the big boats. Now we are all alone again."

"You are not alone anymore, though. I shall look after the both of you until Philip comes for you, okay? You can sleep in my bed at night, where it is warm and safe. There are lots of people who feel alone tonight and lots who have lost the people they love. I have lost many parents and important people in my life, too; it just happens sometimes." Carefully rubbing their arms, Alexandra tried to comfort the children.

"You are an orphan too?" The smaller child, Emilia, wiped her eyes and her runny nose on her dirty sleeve.

Alexandra picked up the younger of the sisters, wiping away the moist tears from her freckled cheeks. "Several times now, almost too many to count, my brother and I have been orphans. One family in Nykol, another family in Metzor and two in Prokopolis that I remember."

The little girls relaxed slightly, feeling more comfortable for sharing a common trait with the stranger.

"I have had many mothers, all of them wonderful and loving." There had been many mothers indeed, and all had given up on her to send her away because of their fear. "Shall I tell you about my favourite one of all of them?"

Both girls nodded eagerly, awaiting her tale.

"Let me tell you on the way to my apartment in the temple, okay?"

The journey back to her apartment took longer than she was used to, as short legs traversed a much shorter distance with each weary stride. Alexandra was able to tell the girls about all her various mothers and all the things they had taught her. She believed it helped ease the children's minds, as well as bring back many fond memories that the Child of the Fallen had not thought about forever.

"Do you know who your real parents are? I don't, and my sister can only remember my mom a little bit. She was a merchant's wife.

He died in an argument, and she couldn't take care of us anymore, I guess."

The child's sad little voice echoed loudly through the hallways of the stone apartment. As she used the key to unlock the heavy wooden door, the extra time gave Alexandra more time to think up a response to the child's difficult question.

"No one has ever told us who they were, only that we would meet them again someday before the glory of Heaven. That even though we do not remember them, they loved us more than anything and had to give us up so we could have a better, safer life.

"I wish I knew what happened to my parents and why they abandoned us," Emilia said. Opening the door to the small but adequate quarters Alexandra had called home for the past months, she gently pushed the children into the room.

Taking their worn shoes off, the children once again surprised her with their politeness. Both stood off to the side until she asked them to sit upon the small cushioned bench while she called for warm water to be brought. Returning quickly, she stood for a moment, watching the two children on the bench wagging their legs back and forth and clutching their satchels close to their chests. She smiled to cover up her uncertainty as to what to do next; she'd never had visitors to entertain before, particularly such small ones.

"Is that your bow?" The little finger pointed toward her arched bow hanging above the mantle of her small fireplace to keep it dry from the damp air of the stone walls.

"Indeed it is. It was a gift for me from my last foster father. I have a good memory of him teaching me how to use it properly." She looked upon the smoothly crafted white wood with fondness, remembering the hours spent with her father scraping the layers of the wood back piece by piece after the family had moved their home in the bridged city of Nykol deep in the Kyllordic Kingdom.

"We have one too ..." The younger child was silenced when her older sister elbowed her fiercely in the ribs, shushing her harshly. Holly was clearly unimpressed with her little sister for spilling the beans of their little secret.

"You do?" Alexandra was confused. Neither child was large

enough to properly use such a weapon, and she could see no place that the children could hide such an item. "Where is it? Do you think I could I see it?"

Holly shook her head no, brow furrowed tightly. "We were supposed to keep it a secret until we find the right person to give it to."

"Look at her hair!" Emilia squawked loudly, pointing to Alexandra's brightly coloured copper-blonde hair.

Her older sister refused to budge. "That doesn't mean anything!"

"Well, who are you searching for? Perhaps I could help you find the person you are supposed to give it to."

Holly eyed her closely, cautious of the level of generosity proposed to them by one who was still a stranger in her eyes. Emilia looked at her sister, waiting for her response, nudging her slightly forward.

"If our father did not arrive at the city in time, we were supposed to ask for an old man called the Advisor who lived within the mountain. He would know what to do with the bow and who to give it to."

"But it's not really for him. Our foster father said that she would look like her ancestor, hair yellow but also orange. She's a princess. You look like a princess with bright hair."

Alexandra grasped a lock of her hair, rubbing it through her thumb and forefinger. Suspicion crossed her mind with the little girl's description. She had a strong feeling that perhaps she was the one they searched for. "I happen to know the Advisor. However, the description fits me somewhat, and I did write to your foster father many times this year and in ones before."

The expression of the oldest girl remained unchanged; Holly continued to look wide-eyed at Alexandra, who seemed to claim to be the rightful recipient of the package. Noticing her vulnerable situation—being in Alexandra's apartment without a route of escape—the girl grew frightened. If Alexandra had wanted, she could easily force the children to tell where they'd hidden it.

Treading carefully Alexandra relaxed and backed up a couple steps from the exit, trying to think how she would be able to solve the situation. "You don't believe me, though, do you? Is there any other way to prove it to you?"

"The scars! Ask her about scars." Alexandra overheard the younger Emilia hiss in her sister's ear.

Alexandra was a child of the Fallen, born of this earth; she did not have the scars where once-great wings had been clipped like the true fallen angels, and she reversed her inital thoughts and quickly doubted she was the proper recipient.

"She does not bear the scars of the Fallen Five, but she carries five of her own."

Hearing the words, Alexandra smiled and pulled her right sleeve up to display the thin scar across the inside of her right forearm, moving closer so the girls could inspect and touch it. Twisting the left side of her dress she displayed the one on the side of her ribs and a second on the back of her upper hip. Then she revealed the last two on the backs of her shoulder and calf; she waited to see the reaction of the children.

Emilia's eyes widened at the sight of the multiple scars that riddled Alexandra's body and ran her small fingers across the lengths of all of them in some amazement. Not completely convinced, her sister reluctantly admitted that Alexandra met the qualifications that Philotheos had told them to look for in their quest to return the item. Alexandra became slightly uncomfortable, having never met the man who had such a vivid recollection of her.

Both rummaged around in their cloth bags. Holly pulled forth a glossy white case wrapped in thick pieces of fur to protect it and set it carefully upon the bench before helping her struggling sister. Moving closer, Alexandra opened the silver clasps of the short case that was supposed to hold a bow. She was surprised when she cracked open the fine box.

A finely crafted blade lay within the carefully made case, secured by the moulded orange velvet wrapped around it. The leather-wrapped handle was bound around the white steel of a slim, curved blade two feet long. The white steel blade looked fragile and delicate but she recognized where the weapon had come, although she'd only seen anything like it once before, when her brother received the Oblitoryiat. The highest-tempered steel would not be able to stop the metal of the gods. "Who knew such pretty little girls held such a rare item?"

"Our father gave it to us and told us that we were to take it with us to the Sacred City. He said it would be needed again to defend the Order. Only the true owner can wield it …" Emilia handed her unmarked case that mimicked the first to Alexandra. The blade inside was identical to its sibling in the other case.

"Did your father ever tell you what this truly is? These are short blades crafted within the armour forges of Heaven! The white steel is not of our world. I have only seen it once before in the library vault. It is extremely rare and powerful. It is not a bow, however."

"He said it was! Maybe you just have to put it together," Emilia interrupted her with surprising abruptness. Alexandra stopped to look closer at the identical blades and then held both of them together in the form of a bow. Holly reached forward and twisted the handle of one of the blades loose, leaving Alexandra to screw it off to expose the spiralling white steel encasing a bright orange crystal within the centre bore.

Carefully placing the two hilts together, Alexandra began to gently screw the blades together, careful not to touch the honed edge. The blades glided with such a smoothness that with a single flick the blade twisted quickly snapped into place with uncanny preciseness.

Emilia turned the case upside down, cramming her little fingers along the edges of the soft case. "We lost the string!"

"I'm telling you girls that this is not a bow. This area right here is where the string would go." Alexandra passed her hand through the space the string would have been quickly. The girls looked extremely disappointed, almost heartbroken, "It is still very beautiful though!"

Standing up and holding the weapon like a bow, she practiced as though it were a bow to humour the girls. She bent her middle finger and pulled back. She felt a slight resistance for a brief second before her hand passed directly through it. She paused, wondering what she had just felt.

Trying a second time, she paused when she barely felt the invisible resistance, and she wrapped her finger around it to pull it back. The bright orange string burst into existence, a narrow strand of energy swirling from the tips of the bladed bow. Meeting at her fingertip and letting her draw it back, Alexandra was surprised to find it required every ounce of strength she had.

The children's eyes opened wide as they watched the bowstring glowing in the gloom of the room. All doubt removed from their small minds, they watched with amazement as Alexandra pulled the string several times; the orange string burst forth every time it was drawn, disappearing when released in a show of magic.

"Wow!" The girls giggled loudly, and Emilia shouted out exuberantly, "I told you it was a bow!"

Alexandra was mesmerized by the holy weapon and its magical construction. The weight of a feather, the bow, having no mass to focus her strength upon, felt awkward in her hands. And yet it took every muscle in her body to use it; the white steel was unyielding. The holy weapon drew upon unknown powers to do its deadly work.

Gazing at the bow one final time, she disassembled the heavenly weapon, setting it back in its case with great care. Turning to look at the children again, she noticed large tears welling up in Emilia's large, round brown eyes, surprising her.

"Are you going to kick us out now?"

"Of course not!" Alexandra was horrified at how quickly joy fled from the self-conscious orphans at the thought of their uncertain future. She was uncertain why their imaginations would choose such a dark idea. "Why would I want to do that?"

"Because we don't have anything else of value to give you anymore …" Looking balefully down at the grey stone flooring, Emilia clung to her older sister's arm once more.

"Never would I think of such a thing. Look how much joy and happiness you have brought me in just one night." Hugging both girls tightly, she squeezed, feeling their small hearts beating within their chests. "Thank you so much. It is the most precious gift that I have ever received from anyone. I will take very good care of it and put it to good use in honour of your father, a friend I did not know I had."

She immediately decided to look after the children until she found a more permanent place for them where she could watch over them from afar. Too many had been forced to look after her as a child and protect her with their lives. She felt that perhaps it was her turn to continue the tradition with these two, who needed the safety and happiness she had been blessed to receive so often.

Hearing the knock at the door that announced the arrival of the warm water, she let go of them, rubbing their noses with her thumb. "Time to clean you both up. Our warm water is finally here."

"Bath time!" screamed little Emilia, running for the opposite room and bringing a smile to Alexandra's face. She only wished that she could make them a more permanent part of her life. Such innocence and happiness was becoming rarer with each passing day.

Chapter 26
Storms of Hell

For three excruciating days they had pushed through the Black Jungles that lay at the southern edges of the Chilsa Empire. Immense dark and damp storm clouds had rained acidic waters upon them the entire time. Metzotto trudged forward as Conrad hacked wildly at the gloomy vegetation, frustrated after not seeing the sun for three stinking days. Travelling during the day felt like moving during the night as the storm blocked all light from the land below, leaving it in eternal darkness.

The insistent howling of the massive black wolves that prowled endlessly through the jungle gave him the chills. Already they had lost over a dozen men and sixty of their Fallen prisoners to the constant assaults. With many more deaths, this trip would be for nothing, Conrad thought, though the attacks had nearly subsided since Rhimmon had joined them. Conrad had noticed the demon carrying a particular prisoner with his clawed hands at all times.

The unfortunate prisoner appeared to be an old decrepit man; his once-white cloak was tattered and covered in dirt and blood. The Dark Prince conversed with the mortal on a regular basis, whispering and laughing in his booming tone; Rhimmon appeared to be torturing the old soul. Overhearing pieces of their conversation, Conrad had deduced the man had once been the grandmaster of the Order. His brother clearly had been successful in his march upon the Order's capital, leaving Conrad far from the glory.

Instead, Conrad had been forced to march west into the land of the Chilsa with the prisoners. Conrad had been angry at the prospect of missing the battle against the Fallen and argued fiercely to avoid doing so. As always, the will of the Dark Prince was higher than Sven's, and by extension Conrad's, and he was forced to move in the opposing direction for almost three weeks.

Marching through the borders of Chilsa had left Conrad uncomfortable. He spotted the scouts of the Chilsa armies, who were keeping a close eye on the black banner of Metzon that flew over their heads. They had not forgotten its shape nor who bore it through their lands once before. But Emperor Kristolphe's word had been good, and none moved against them as they travelled upon the direct path laid out by the emperor's sister. It had been a wonderful little trek; crossing the open plains might have even been called enjoyable.

Unlike this damn rotten jungle forest. They trudged forward without knowing where they were going for days, both stars and sunlight blocked out by the incessant rain, leaving them with no markers to judge their directions. Conrad was sure they went in endless circles before Rhimmon had at last returned to guide the group to where the soul of his doomed brother resided.

"I'm sick of this damn jungle, Cassidus!"

His friend beside him said nothing, in his typical style, and simply looked at him blankly, nodding in agreement. Although they had been together since childhood, there were no events more tumultuous during their entire history to test their friendship than those in the past year. Conrad wondered what his tongueless companion's opinions of the recent events and how they reflected upon him were. Was he seen as just a monster, or did the younger man understand everything? He had witnessed everything Conrad had done for years, so he must have drawn his own conclusions. What they were, Conrad would never know.

Conrad had begun noticing small changes within the mute, an uncomfortable air of caution and concern at the actions of his master. In the Desert of Lost Souls, Cassidus had stood back, watching the carnage with wide-eyed disbelief. Yet Cassidus still rode beside him, even into the jungles, aware of what was to come. His loyalty helped to ease the concern from Conrad's mind; it was a relief to have such a friend.

"Cassidus, can I confess something to you?" The trot of Cassidus's brown mount increased as he pulled alongside him. Cassidus eagerly awaited his confession, but Conrad wondered whether he should really express his concerns to the younger man.

"I do not know if you've noticed, but my bouts of amnesia have grown more rampant. Several times a day now they come and take over. I don't even know for how long. I fear that soon I won't remember anything. I have no idea what is causing them. I don't know what is happening to me, but to be truthful, I'm getting a little worried."

Looking at him for several long seconds, Cassidus raised his hands to his temples, his index fingers raised, symbolizing horns. Pulling back his lips in a toothy grin, Conrad understood what he was indicating as he looked toward the head of the caravan. The Dark Prince of Hell pushed through the jungles, snapping limb-sized branches off before tossing them aside with ease.

"A strong possibility. The instances do tend to grow worse whenever his presence is around. But they started even before Sven released the Dark Prince. After my father was murdered, when we somehow ended up at the Lost Mountain …" Conrad tried to think about that night, knowing that it had been horrifying, but he could not conjure up the images. Every time he tried to visualize the fleeting image it blurred instantly as pain sliced sharply through the left side of his forehead.

Cassidus nodded aggressively, performing the same gesture, except he held down the index finger of his right hand, nodding several times before pointing at Rhimmon and performing it again with the same distinction. Raising four fingers, he pointed to Rhimmon and back to the first finger and then ran down the sequence until he got to the fourth. He wiggled it furiously.

"Impossible. Sven said there are only three Dark Princes of Hell who fought in this world. Prince Rhimmon, Prince of Greed and Temptation. Prince Mammon, Dark Prince of Storms. And Prince Adramaleck, Prince of the Flame. Heaven killed them all and their

A Mortal Mistake

minions before they burned this world. Three is all there were, no more." Conrad held up three fingers. His friend's expression soured and he held up four fingers fiercely.

"Just keep an eye on me, would you?"

Cassidus nodded sternly several times, accepting the new responsibility. He placed his fist over his heart in salute and slapped Conrad on the shoulder to let him know he had his back. Slapping him back, Conrad smiled at him and turned within his saddle as the party finally exited the dank jungles.

"We are here!" The heavy voice of Rhimmon echoed through the dense jungle as they crashed through the edge of the undergrowth toward the clearing that held the city of Valkadia. The city lay in ruins, temples crumbling, demonic statues toppled, the bones of slain demons littered everywhere. No vegetation flourished within the city, refusing to grow in a place of such pulsating dark power.

Conrad could envision the battle that had taken place in the city as if it had happened yesterday. This was a place frozen in time, old armour and weapons strewn where their masters had fallen. It seemed quite one-sided; they did not find any of the fabled Legionnaires of Heaven among the dead. But perhaps the victors had taken their dead away from this horrid place.

"The Legionnaires of Orion are of terrifying power, young Konflikt, but do not think their lives were not forfeited in this battle. My brother had been stalwartly holding his stronghold against the House of Orion ... until their Ancient Lord himself entered the battle. Ancient Lord Oron. Slayer of Hell's Sons. Father of the First to Fall. My brother's fate was all but sealed. Let me show you so you can truly understand!" Rhimmon clasped a large hand around his torso as he lifted him from the saddle. Using his power to take Conrad back in time, the Dark Prince allowed him to witness the battle through his own eyes.

Seeing the Legionnaires for the first time as they battled the demons among the temples and buildings, Conrad watched blood and energy run down temple stairs and splatter upon the walls. The Legionnaires of Orion moved with an efficiency he had never seen before, not even among the finest soldiers of Humanity. Even outnumbered they overcame their enemies with stunningly smooth attacks against the demon horde, resplendent in white armour laced in silver and yellow, their high-crested helmets hiding their faces as their massive wings of yellow energy surrounded them in bright light. The Legionnaires moved slowly through Valkadia as the noose tightened. Suffering few losses, the Legionnaires of Orion continued forward with a single, divine purpose.

Mammon, the Dark Prince of Storms, stood atop the highest temple in the city centre, watching as his army slowly collapsed within his city of power. His army commanders continued to try to resist, reorganizing the army to continue to try to take as many lives as possible. Mammon unleashed a powerful dark storm down upon the invaders; orange lightning crashed to the earth as thunder echoed among the black clouds.

Rhimmon's brother seemed strong of mind, unfazed by the invaders, despite their decimation of his forces—until he heard the beating wings of his true enemy. Conrad could see that even a Dark Prince feared those wing beats. The Ancient Lord of Orion landed atop a tall temple directly across from him.

Father of the First to Fall, Oron stood tall, his white wings closing silently behind him, glowing orbs of yellow locked upon his enemy. Bloodshed and slaughter continued silently, all sound dissipated by his mere presence. The storm lost all fury, turning from howling winds to the slightest breeze that blew his long yellow hair behind him.

Mammon, Dark Prince of Hell's Storms. By Decree of the House of Orion and its Legion, you've been tried for your crimes against the Dominion of Heaven. Guilty of all charges, you are to be executed for all that you have done. Oron pushed his cloak behind his white wings, slowly reaching behind his neck and drawing his long two-handed sword from between his white wings.

The gold blade of Orytheosykius shone brightly, as did the splendid armour hidden beneath the robes. In a blur the mighty wings flashed the Ancient forward, leaving his blurred figure behind him. Mammon's great spear deflected the golden blade but was unable to stop the attacker; Oron's shoulder crushed into his giant grey chest. Conrad watched as the Dark Prince was slammed full force into the top of the temple, shaking the very foundations. He also noticed that the Legionnaires resumed their precise assault, seeming to draw unseen power from their master standing above them, fluidly dodging all attacks and retaliating in terrifying fashion. The strongest of the demon commanders could not hold them back any longer.

Orange tattooing began to burn to the surface as Mammon quickly regained his composure, escaping the Ancient's blade and raining heavy fists down upon his enemy. The drive forced Oron back onto his heels. Quickly pivoting out of the way of a high blow, he retaliated with a terrible left fist to Mammon's midsection. The punch lifted the demon from his feet, and Oron's right hand stabbed deeply from above. Black blood covered the mighty blade as it plunged into the demon's shoulder. Grabbing Mammon by the large horn protruding from his head, Oron smashed his opponent's skull into the stone temple altar, shattering the black rock.

A blast wave ripped through the city when Mammon's scream pierced the chaos. Debris and dust clouded the view of the battle below the powerful beings; the storm above erupted in anger. Clouds boiled furiously, rumbling from within as tornados began spiralling down into the city.

Mammon cursed ferociously, ejecting the blade from within his body, and unleashed a powerful burst of energy, forcing Oron back. Clenching his fists, his massive grey wings unfurling from behind him, his body stretched fully out as he kicked off hard to race toward the growing storm. Feeding from its power, he attempted to heal himself from the sacred wound created by golden Orytheosykius. Consuming the orange electricity from the growing storm, Mammon started to swell in size as he flew closer to the eye of the storm and the sanctuary he sought within its heart.

Among the ruins of the city only the Legionnaires stood, all their enemies either vanquished or lying lifeless as their souls became consumed by their lord. All watched the Dark Prince flee toward the sky growing ever larger. Upon the command of their leader, a general named Hektorius flew off to the sky, toward the battleground in the air.

Justice shall be done upon you, Mammon! No storm shall protect you from my wrath!

Oron blasted past the demon, raking his mighty sword along Mammon's flank. The Ancient ripped through the sky, burning holes through the clouds, his wings swept behind him. Conrad could feel the Legion of Orion amassing beneath Mammon. Thousands of Legionnaires took to the air, slowly gaining upon him as they dodged the storm's electrical weapons.

Their flight was hopeless, as none but their fearless commander was within reach of Mammon. The biggest question on Conrad's mind was how Mammon could survive the next attack from the Ancient, who seemed to have disappeared. The demon prince continued onward and upward, reaching frantically for the power within the eye of the storm. He could not reach it; the storm was ever so slightly out of his reach.

Mammon paused as he watched the storm slowly weaken, its power fleeing within the clouds. The violent lightning slowly vanished; the powerful wind turned weak and silent. Looking above him, he saw Oron hovering silently above the clouds, his hands outstretched, pulling the power from the storm into his open palms.

This is the end, Mammon. The quest for endless power shall once again end here, as it did millennia before. This is the end, Mammon. Can you feel it? Oron's piercing yellow orbs cut through his enemy, both realizing destiny was closing fast upon both of them. Hektorius had caught up to them. His blade tore into Mammon's wings, sending the giant demon spiralling out of control.

Oron's white wings laced in yellow snapped quickly behind him as he shot up in a big circle, the sonic boom far behind him when he dove straight down, aiming directly for Mammon. His hands reached toward the demon, and blinding yellow energy crackled between his hands as he collided with the demon. The descent quickened as the Ancient's energy pierced his enemy's heart, increasing their speed.

Legionnaires' blades sliced into every inch of Mammon's skin as he fell through the thousands who had taken to the air and cut him as he fell through their ranks. The glowing blade of Orytheosykius burned in his chest, as Oron's white hand reached for the demon king's heart. Conrad could feel Mammon's horror as the fingers of the Ancient Lord of Heaven tightened around his black heart, pulling it from his chest as they struck the earth.

As the impact shook the earth beneath them, buildings crumbled to their foundations, leaving only the largest and strongest standing. The world continued to groan long after the crash, as if a giant had been rudely awakened beneath the city. Earthquakes rippled through the jungles, large sinkholes and chasms opening from below, swallowing anything that rested above them.

"And this is where my brother of great storms lies, awaiting his return to this world." Rhimmon removed his hand, letting his puppet see with his own eyes again as he set Conrad down. Atop the centre temple, he looked upon the remains of the centre square, decimated into a deep crater; Mammon's ancient skeleton lay at the bottom. The demonic bones were large and white, showing through where the heavy, rock-like armoured exoskeleton had been bare.

On Mammon's chest plate, Conrad could see where the Ancient had poured his raw power into the prince, drilling an opening through his chest and destroying the heart of his enemy. The Ancient Oron of Heaven had bored a hole through six inches of solid demonic bone. Peering into the hole, Conrad swore he could actually hear the heart still beating within, envisioning it as it pumped black blood.

The Metzonian guard started to shove their prisoners down into the crater, closer to the demon prince than they ever thought they would be. Rhimmon had fed off the lost souls of the desert after he was cast down by Heaven, but for centuries none had dared walk within the black jungles.

The number of prisoners they had brought with them was far greater than Rhimmon had required. Rhimmon marched down into the crater, the Fallen prisoners scrambling away from him, only to be kicked back down by the leather and steel boots of the men above them. All fled, except for the oldest among them, clothed in the tattered robes of the Elder Council of the Fallen, who stood tall and defiant.

"Still no fear of your death, mighty Caelestis? Even at the end you are strong and will not allow your spirit to break. It does not anger me, though, for that is exactly the spirit that I require. The Heavens have forsaken you by giving you a cruel and unjust destiny after all your centuries of service. All your efforts trying to regain your place among the sparkling White Cities again are for nothing!" Rhimmon hissed at the withered old man, who stood silently listening. The Fallen members all looked toward him, stunned by their leader's unwavering faith.

Unable to invoke a response, the silence grew to astonishment as Rhimmon appeared to grasp onto their grandmaster with the powers of his mind, lifting him off the ground. The archers at the top of the fissure started firing down upon the entrapped prisoners. *"Instead you shall be the one who revives our lost brother and his armies! Forever shall you fuel the enemy you spent your life fighting!"*

Rhimmon raised a single clawed hand above them all, pointing at the floating Fallen with his index finger. Caelestis screamed out in agony as he watched a bloody red line slowly tear across his chest. Conrad watched with controlled horror as Rhimmon ripped out the Fallen's still-beating heart for them all to witness. Chanting a ritual from the old tongues of the wicked, the Dark Prince waved his arms, writing ancient scripts in the air as Conrad watched the crater twist in darkness. Caelestis's beating heart was still quivering, wrapped with the black power, growing to ten times its size. Rhimmon reached out to grab it and placed the heart in the ancient chest cavity of his deceased brother.

Conrad felt the trembling deep within the earth as heavy black mist started to seep out of the ground, swirling around the bodies of the fallen and the white bones of the old demon. The city around him began trembling as the clouds above them started to twirl menacingly.

A large charred wing stretched out of the black haze that had filled the chasm, followed by a second, and then a long tail whipped hard into Rhimmon, almost knocking him back. The storm's

A Mortal Mistake

rumbling increased steadily as orange lightning flashed within the black clouds once again. The Metzonian peered cautiously toward the sky, diving out of the way as a large bolt blitzed down at the crater. The lightning struck into the opening through the black haze, followed by a steady stream of energy that rained down, pulling the old Prince of Hell from his resting place.

Orange electrical power crackled loudly as it raced along Mammon's resurrected body, repairing his wounds and fixing the damage done long ago. Mammon's eyes flared open, looking out upon those below him; his mind reached out upon those around him as he tried to fill his dormant mind with the events of the world.

"I breathe in the stench of this world again, that which had been taken away from me! A growing fear I can smell within the world—chaos … and conflict." Mammon brought himself down in front of Conrad, towering above him as he leaned forward, looking into his soul. *"I sense the touch of the mighty Abaddon upon his soul and the imprint of Konflikt. Are you watching me, Abaddon? Coward who fled, abandoning me in my time of need! I shall have my revenge, and it shall start with your slave!"*

Conrad smelled Mammon's breath as he looked into the mighty orange eyes, but he felt no fear. Mammon stepped forward, reaching out toward the human, trying to wrap his hands around him. Conrad watched Mammon angrily trying to get through the invisible barrier that surrounded the servant of Abaddon. Hate flaring through his mind, Mammon used all his power to compress the barrier.

He felt his breath grow shallow, and Conrad's heart pumped quickly as the space around him grew smaller. His vision grew dark. Mammon smiled sharply, watching the pathetic human succumbing slowly. Slowly suffocating, Conrad struggled to move, as though he was buried in clay. Sensing his doom nearing, his mind began to grow black as he felt the black taint begin pumping through his veins. Looking down upon the Ring of the Order, Conrad understood that his survival hinged upon completing Abaddon's demonic taint.

Barely able to feel the steel ring, he struggled, slowly wiggling it off his index finger. When the steel clattered upon the stone floor of the temple, the darkness poured completely though his veins.

Konflikt looked up, threw Mammon's strangling hands off, and moved to the offensive. Konflikt's sharp right hook knocked the demon back; Mammon fell off the edge of the temple into the cratered temple square.

"Do not question my loyalty, Mammon! Do not blame me for your futile and pathetic attempt at destroying those in your way! We each have our destiny, and mine was a different course than to save you from your fate! I have released Konflikt back into this world—you shall not destroy him! I see your remain as stupid and selfish as you were back then. Have you learned nothing?" Konflikt bellowed down to his victim, his vocal cords struggling with the power of the voice commanding them.

Mammon collected himself and charged back up the stairs, slamming his opponent into the temple wall. Smashing the human body many times against the surface, he tried to destroy the puppet Konflikt, with no result.

The human pawn grabbed Mammon by his dark horn, twisting the demon's head with such force it flipped Mammon onto his back. Climbing atop of the Dark Prince, Konflikt slammed the demon's head into the ground several times. Konflikt deflected defensive strikes before he plunged his hand into the outraged demon's chest, wrapping his hands around Caelestis's heart.

"Remember who you serve, Mammon!" were the final words in the feud, words far more venomous and dark than the voice of Abaddon. A new speaker had taken over Konflikt's tainted soul. Both Rhimmon and Mammon froze at the sound that rumbled from the mortal's throat, and terror quickly seeped into their souls at the voice of one from the Halls of Hell.

"I beg forgiveness … Dark Lord Cayn."

Konflikt collapsed upon Mammon, his bloody fingers releasing the submitting demon's heart.

CHAPTER 27
CHILDREN OF THE FALLEN

Alexandra was surprised she still had energy after spending two hours cleaning the dirt and grime caked on the children's tiny bodies. Scrubbing ears and greasy hair, she had forgotten that children had the ability to get dirt on every square inch of their bodies, and she gladly accepted the help of the chambermaid who brought them warm water.

The children beamed brightly after their hard work paid off. Brilliant red hair shone brightly in the torchlight. Alexandra noticed they had far more visible freckles on their face than before. In the safety of a comforting bed for the first time in weeks, both children fell asleep almost immediately. Alexandra was filled with joy at such a sight.

Slipping out the door to go and see how Jaina and Kaylee had made out with their own quest to console the lost, she was surprised to find she was not the only one awake so late. She was shocked to find the door of Kallisto's apartment wide open and the old man himself sitting upon the stone steps looking at the administrator's medallion in his hands. Looking up at her, he did not smile. "Seek out your brother. The both of you will join me in my chambers."

Seated behind the large desk at the entrance of the Temple Titans barracks, her brother had been genuinely surprised to see Alexandra in the dark night. Kallen wasted little time when she told him that their new foster father requested their immediate presence. Rarely did their protector ever request their attendance; Alexandra told Kallen that his character was anything but normal. As they knocked upon the white door emblazoned with the administrator's seal, it seamlessly opened to allow them into the apartment. Kallisto had only recently moved into the apartment when he was unexpectedly forced to take on the administrator role. He beckoned for them to seat themselves in the large living chamber. A bottle of red wine was already open on the table between the chairs meant for them.

Alexandra poured wine into a tall stemmed glass for Kallisto and then poured herself one before asking Kallen, who declined.

"You, too, Kallen. I know that you are on duty but I will allow a slip in discipline for this occasion."

Kallen continued to hesitate before finally reaching for the bottle. He eyed the distraught old man closely and looked at Alexandra, who did not hold the answer he searched for.

"It is time that you both learn a couple of the great secrets kept within the Order of the Fallen's hierarchy. While there are enough secrets within the Order to fill a library, one has the utmost significance for the both of you."

Their anticipation increased substantially, but they allowed the old man to prepare himself to tell the two Children of the Fallen his secret. Excitement filled Alexandra as she waited for the mystery to reveal itself, praying it was what she had always hoped for.

"It is the story of your parents and what happened to them."

Lifting the cup to her lips, Alexandra felt unsure whether Kallisto was truly going to release information they had begged of him and the Elders for years. Excitement flowed through her body with increased anticipation. Pondering Kallisto's sudden change of heart, Alexandra asked, "But why now?"

"A tiny echoing voice was heard throughout the temple corridors several hours ago, filling an old man with guilt and shame. She spoke with genuine sincerity, wishing she knew her parents. And why they had done the things they had done. It had made me rethink many things and reconsider decisions I made in the past that perhaps were wrong. I do not know if the new choices are better; I only pray for the mercy of those about to hear these secrets locked within my heart for so long."

"You will find these minds open and no forgiveness required. We understand that you would have good reasons for keeping such information from us." Kallen spoke as he resumed pouring the wine, watching carefully within his peripheral vision.

"Good reasons are not always proper. Trying to protect you from those who would wish you harm is justifiable. Though when you do not know who you are or where you came from, such information can wear upon you and fill you with resentment. The Elders had decided that it was best for you to become your own people, unaffected by the past, which is not always pleasant. Having seen how you both have grown, I doubt such news shall be as devastating as was originally feared."

Her heart racing at the dark tone of Kallisto's voice, Alexandra slowly sipped the fine wine. As he paced back and forth before them, visibly struggling with what he was about to say, her imagination pulled out from the back of her mind all the horrific reasons she had come up with as to why they were never told. Fear overtook her, but the deep desire to know the truth kept her seated.

"I do not know where one even starts with such information, though I suppose the beginning would be ideal. The lineage of your family goes back to the very first generation of the Children of the Fallen. Your great-grandparents were both born during the Order's golden days, when peace and prosperity reigned for almost a century. The great wars had been fought and won; Humanity was flourishing under the guidance and wisdom of the fallen angels of Heaven.

"Grandmaster Orion foresaw a bright future for the Order and all its children, claiming they would rise even beyond the Golden Age. The Children would raise Earth to rival that of other worlds within Heaven's kingdom. It would stand out as a testament of the Fallen's loyalty to Heaven and be presented as a gift of forgiveness to the Lords of Heaven on the Day of Judgment."

Pausing for another drink of wine, Kallisto's eyes went dark. Alexandra watched his mind dig into the library of knowledge within his head, flipping through the pages and pages he had read over the years. Alexandra could feel him coming to the point where his happy story turned disastrous.

"Orion and the First Fallen had made a single mistake that would cause vast misfortune to fall upon them. The Order had forgotten their old enemies of the past, presuming the Sin would never regroup or return. An error all would soon regret when the Sin returned with a bloody revenge.

"The Brotherhood had not wallowed in the darkness of their defeat, using it instead to further their hate for all things good and just. Delving into the black mysteries of Hell, they continued to try to rebuild themselves and become more deadly. The Sin had somehow discovered a way to bend themselves between the physical world and the nether world, becoming what we call wraiths. With this new power, Nuor, last of the Dark Gods, returned with the Sin with a vengeance carefully planned out within their black souls, almost befitting the Dark Lords of Hell.

"The Sin did not prey upon those who defeated them in the past, however. Nuor knew that he could not defeat Orion and the Order's warriors, forced to let mortality do what he could not. But knowing his enemies would eventually die of old age was not enough for Nuor. His enemies had to be tormented and tortured every day until they died to sate his own anger."

Kallen asked, not waiting for Kallisto to continue with the story, "How do you inflict pain upon an enemy you cannot defeat? What sort of action can cause pain that lasts forever?"

Kallisto turned away from them for a long moment.

Alexandra felt horror rise within her heart as the answer to Kallen's question slipped from her lips. "You slay their children ..."

Kallisto nodded quietly as he stared into the flames of the fire. "The bond of parent and child is eternal. While we do not have the Creator's infinite knowledge of the universe and its workings, a soul of Heaven exists for eternity within the universe; it is guessed that a soul of Humanity may not. The Children of the Fallen are not of Heaven; nor are they of Humanity. One does not truly know what happens to the souls of Fallen children. Nuor decided to take away his enemies' children, knowing that their parents would likely never receive the opportunity to see them again …

"The Brotherhood attacked the Children of the Fallen, finding them easier targets than those once connected to the Heavens. The assassins of Sin swept through the lands and slaughtered children numbering in the tens of thousands within the first week. Orion commanded the Children be protected both by secrecy as well as under arms as he waged a new war against the Sin: the War of Shadows.

"Orion's crusade slowed the pace of the attacks, but they did not truly end until there were so few children remaining that none could be found, and the Sin returned to the shadows to wait until the Order diminished to extinction. The Order was in tatters, their golden future now a black abyss."

Alexandra was stunned. The horrors that the Fallen would have felt at the loss of their children was beyond her comprehension, although she'd never had children of her own. She knew only a few Children of the Fallen within the Sacred City but wondered how many others within the city or among those who had recently arrived from Prokopolis were Children without knowing it? Extinction would indeed be the course of Heaven's influence upon the world, a snuffing out of the light.

"And our parents?"

"Your great-grandparents, as well as your grandparents, were murdered whilst in protection, surrounded by dozens of Orion's handpicked guards within Orion's personal citadel in Prokopolis, along with all their guards. Being among the holiest bloodlines within the Order, your family was at the top of Nuor's kill list, and the story claims that he took a personal hand in their deaths. Few others would have been able to reach them and succeed."

History was becoming all too real for Alexandra as she realized how greatly the past had affected their lives and those around them. The monsters and dark angels were supposed to be of the past, defeated by others within the world. She could not comprehend that they slew her entire family and ruined the life she could have had.

To learn that their lives had cost others their own was tormenting and almost too much to bear.

Kallen stole his sister's questions, handling the history lesson much better than she. "How did our parents survive?"

"The Children of the Fallen were ordered to go into hiding. Orion also commanded the Children of the Children be hidden. As youths, your parents were hidden among Humanity as their own, far from the Fallen or any association with the Order. You must understand the Order was desperate as they struggled to hunt down their elusive enemy. And the War of Shadows has never ended.

"Your parents were pursued by the Sin for many long years. The Elders tried desperately to do everything they could, but the power of the Fallen waned after the Fallen Five moved on. Some of the Orders' remaining wraith hunters were dispatched to try and save your parents, and none returned. Numerous times the Order tried sneaking your parents into the Sacred City, but their pursuers followed at a relentless pace.

"With the Sin closing in rapidly and refusing to put other Children at risk, your parents realized only one option remained to them. As once was done to protect them, they hid you both amongst Humanity and fled into the sunset. After several years passed, we secretly arranged for you to move in with Fallen families, though the danger has never truly faded, as Alexandra has felt many times in her young life."

Using her fingers, Alexandra wiped away her tears, which were immediately replaced with fresh ones. Kallisto looked up at her briefly from his chair, his shoulders slung low, looking exhausted from telling the emotionally difficult story. He rubbed the knuckle of his left ring finger as he spoke once again.

"The Sin still hunts the Children of the Fallen; like ravenous hounds they scour the world. Of all the hidden Children's Children in the world, those now within the temple have been the only ones the Order has ever found before the Sin. Some surely were hidden beyond even our ability to find them, but we will likely never know. You are among the last, and if you are slain then it is only a matter of time before Heaven's footprint upon this world dwindles and dies. And Nuor has his ultimate victory."

Kallen sat brooding silently, his nostrils twitching as he kept his emotions under wraps. Alexandra looked at her brother and saw the turmoil that stirred beneath the surface. He cleared his throat. Alexandra listened as he plunged into the question that his sister knew he had been desperately trying not to ask.

"So who is our family then? What line of Fallen do we descend from?"

Kallisto did not respond. He turning slightly and waved his hand in a single sweep before the mural upon the wall.

The image of Orion stood ten feet tall upon the wall before them, displayed in his glorious victory during the Battles of the Beliefs. Looking into the golden eyes, Alexandra saw the spirit that reflected within her brother's eyes. Looking back at her brother quickly before returning to the mural, her attention turned to the second figure within the mural.

Her bare back pressed closely against the First to Fall, Orion's bride, Brianna, was painted in a flowing white cloth that danced to her movements. Orange forearm guards scripted in ornate white runes covered her forearms, matching the tall greaves wrapping around her bare legs. Long flowing orange hair danced in the imaginary wind; her eyes cast sideways over Orion's shoulder sent a chill down to Alexandra's soul. And there was the great bow within her elegant hands, its string drawn back against the light skin of her cheek, prepared to unleash death upon her enemies.

Alexandra leapt from her feet, looking hard at Kallisto for signs of a hoax, feeling he had gone too far over the top. There was no way that it was possibly true. Disbelief rippled through her mind at the prospect of being the distant grandchild of the First to Fall. How was it possible?

Her brother did not stand but remained perfectly still, his eyes locked upon the greatest figure in the Order's history. Staring at her brother, Alexandra wondered how he felt in the shadow of Orion. Her brother, who adored Orion and had dreamed of the greatness within the man, now found himself a descendant. How was he supposed to live up to the expectations now set before him?

"You are the last surviving descendants of Orion and Brianna. The death of Orion's family absolutely crushed him. Nuor was successful in the end at destroying everything the First to Fall ever loved in this world. He spent his last couple of years watching your father grow from a painful distance, knowing he could never be part of their lives without jeopardizing them. I suppose one could say that it did not matter in the end, but I think it delayed it long enough for your parents to enjoy some of the small joys of life."

Kallisto walked from the room into the back, returning with two large leather-bound books. Very carefully, he handed one to each of them. Alexandra took the volume from his shaking hands, running her fingers over the smooth cover. Kallisto's shoulders remained slumped despite the removal of the burden of his secret. Alexandra watched the haggard man stoke the fire for the tenth time that hour.

"These are the only two books in the world that recorded the events of the Children of the Fallen. I have kept them upon my desk in my room. I searched one out from the library and requested the other from Prokopolis. They go into far greater depth than I have, as well as containing recorded family trees of the First Fallen."

"The woman bearing the bow …"

"She is the mother of the family you so desperately desired to know about and the sole reason for Orion's disastrous fall from Heaven. Their love was forbidden by the Ancient Kings of Heaven because of the rift it caused between the Houses of Hellio and Orion. As I'm sure you figured out, Orion did not agree and went as far as challenging the Creator himself. A fight he did not win." Kallisto wearily smiled at the outrageousness of the tale, looking back up at the mural.

"It is Brianna in her prime, wielding her famous bow, named the Bane Bow by the Sin who feared its touch, only ever feeling its sting once. I must assume that you have seen such a weapon once before, if not recently?"

Alexandra looked at Kallisto, wondering if he had known the weapon had just come into her possession.

"I went down to the Cathedral to find the children our dearly departed Chronicler had sent to the city, and I happened to pass you as you took them to the kitchens. Philotheos had written to me about your last request and mentioned that the time was soon coming when we would no longer be able to hide you from the world. Your frustration with the man was great, I know. But you must know his own frustration at keeping such a secret was just as great; he wanted nothing more than to come here and tell you what you desired.

"We were preparing an expedition that would have taken the both of you before the Elders to end the age of secrecy. It was merely fate that had you safe within the Sacred City when Prokopolis fell to the malice of the Metzonians, leaving you alive instead of lying among the slain. Knowing his fate, Philip would not leave you to be lost forever though, and he sent the Bow with his daughters. Wonderful it is that you discovered the children sent to deliver you the truth on your own."

Moving closer to the large mural, she looked at the bow within her grandmother's hands; its orange string blazed as brightly as her fiery orange hair flowing behind her. Alexandra wiped away tears from beneath her eyes. She had learned what she had longed for, although it came to her in a way she had never anticipated. As of the previous morning she'd had no idea who she was, and by the early hours of the next, she had received all she had ever asked for, and more, in such a mysterious way.

Because of two little red-haired children, their new mentor changed his mind and broke open the history of their lives. The man she had written hundreds of letters to had not been the dishonourable man she once believed him to be. He was a caring individual who had taken orphans like herself under his wings and looked after them to the best of his ability. He was the holder of a secret that he feared to release for her safety because it would bring the Sin from the shadows to attack the weakened Order once again.

Sending his twice-orphaned daughters to safety, knowing that he would never see them again, he knew of her sympathy toward lost and lonely children. The connection of their past would bond their future together so she could carry forward what he had started. Sending the bow had been his peace offering to her before his death. He knew she would not be able to accept it without also accepting the burden that the bow brought.

Her grandmother's bow filled a hole within her heart created by her unknown past and origins. The orphan sisters resonated with her past but also surrounded her heart with the thought of the future. She would not dwell upon the past anymore.

"Aeden and Alleera …" Kallen said. He'd opened the book and was flipping through, discovering the page he was searching for had already been bookmarked by the administrator for his ease.

"The names of your parents, as you never knew them. I did not know them personally, though from what I heard they were indeed wonderful people. Aedan was the child who represented the values of the Orion family well, and Alleera was another beautiful child of the Fallen Five. A perfect representation of everything Orion and Brianna had dreamed for their children and this world."

The twins were speechless, having a million questions but not knowing which ones to ask first. Words became stuck within their throats, causing a jam within their minds. Alexandra collapsed to the bench beside the wall.

"Any more dark secrets that you want to bestow upon us tonight, Kallisto?" Alexandra asked lightly, trying to raise the spirits of both men, as well as her own.

Kallen continued to sit in silence, not shedding tears or words.

"Dark? What you heard is a torchlight compared to the dark secrets this mind has been forced to hold and endure." A slight smile crossed the bearded man's face. "I will wait to reveal any further history lessons, as I am sure you already have enough on your minds. My own is quite exhausted, and I ask that you could perhaps let an old man get some sleep. We shall talk more tomorrow."

Showing themselves out the door, both siblings knew there would be little sleep tonight. Both would be awake many nights, trying to read a very large book and find answers to a million questions.

"Well, now you've got the answers you always wanted, sister. Make you feel any better?"

"Truthfully?" Alexandra tried to sort out the emotions whirling in her head, the magnitude of them hard to comprehend in such a short time. "Pretty good, actually. I'm relieved to know the truth after so many long years of waiting."

"Hmm … Well, at least one of us is relieved." Kallen, once again the Titan commander on duty, started down the hallway to leave the Sacred Temple apartment complex. "Night, sis. Sleep if you can. Heaven knows I will never receive another restful night's sleep for the rest of my days as I try to find a way to live up to these new expectations."

CHAPTER 28
FOREST OF FIRE

Listening to the Metzonian swordsmen around him, Conrad watched from atop Metzotto as his men systematically kicked down every household door as they proceeded through the lakeside city of Essex. Much as it had been during his entire journey through Kyllordia, there was no resistance to be found within the land. Sven had laughed as he told Conrad that loyalty was easy to come by in this land of the weak; none ever choose the blade.

The Metzonian war machine had become an unstoppable force of malice as it continued to roll through the countryside. No resistance was found within the realm of Kyllordia other than what had been the futile resistance in Kaldor. Whoever had organized the soft defence of the nation, it had quickly become a catastrophe. Upon hearing Sven's tales of Prokopolis, Conrad ached for a battle of true proportions so he could be a part of it.

The behemoth representing their army continued to grow daily as countryside was conquered and the remaining folks either swore fealty to them or were cut down by the blade. The Metzonian army now swelled so large that it had become too immense for any successful resistance to be pitted against it. The Kyllordic had given up their futile guerrilla warfare tactics and simply fled into their beloved forests and across their lakes and rivers, but Conrad knew they would not find safety.

Manpower of the size his brother had gathered moved at an incredibly slow pace, allowing their enemy significant time to vacate the land. The message of death had been taken seriously by the civilians, and during the entire seven-day journey his armies were finding the countryside and towns completely devoid of any type of life. Even now at their first key destination they found little signs of life.

Essex had been the great gateway to the Kyllordic capital city, protected by the lake and the large Ardane forests that expanded for leagues around Kyllica in all directions. The lakeshore harboured the small flotilla of craft used to cross the lake, the blue sails of the lake guardians barely visible in the distance against the clear afternoon sky. At least he was finally here and would not miss the next battle.

Knowing Sven would drive his force at an unrelenting pace, Conrad had ridden back as swiftly as possible from the Black Jungles. A deep-seated fear within his soul urged him to flee as quickly as he could, his mind not knowing why, but he knew he should not linger to ask questions.

Looking back at the adventure his brother had sent him on, he could not remember anything beyond entering the jungles. Questions about his extended amnesia went unanswered by all he asked; none knew how they traversed back out of the cursed jungle, but all felt a deep-seated relief nonetheless.

His sudden bouts of amnesia were becoming a larger problem, coming more frequently and lasting longer with each successive spell. Looking at his gauntlet, he had discovered one thing for certain; his father's rings and his memory loss were most definitely linked.

After every bout of memory loss, his father's Ring of Order was missing from his hand. He'd find it in his pocket or step on it in his boot; the ring was everywhere but where it was supposed to be. And wearing the ring was the one thing he did remember. Trying to solve the problem, he had decided to wear his gauntlet over his hand so that the ring could not be taken off. Conrad had been surprised and relieved when his extended periods of amnesia seemed to decline.

Maintaining consciousness, however, left Conrad with plenty of time to think. And to worry. Cassidus had not left the jungles with the rest of them, and Conrad was incredibly uneasy at the disappearance of his lifelong friend somewhere within the Black

Jungles. The Metzonian prince had not noticed the true impact of his absence until they began the long trek back to Metzor.

The mute had never spoken a word to him in his life, but it was his constant presence and companionship that Conrad now missed. For over twenty years they had been inseparable, despite Cassidus's growing distance from him since the release of Rhimmon. Conrad feared what he may have done within the blackness of the jungles. Had he become so trapped within the hateful anger toward those who murdered his father that he inadvertently killed his friend in the storm? Did Cassidus's body lie among the rest in the rotting jungle, never to return? The thought tormented Conrad every waking moment. He struggled to let such fears slide. Was this Konflikt, a name Rhimmon had taken to calling him, the monster who ran wild within his unconscious?

Looking up toward the walled port, he saw the green and blue flags flying in the stiff breeze coming off the lake, giving him the uneasy feeling that they were being watched. He spurred Metzotto forward, and as Conrad grew closer to the harbour his suspicions proved true. He saw a lone, tall figure step on the highest point of the wall above the gatehouse, chewing on a bright green apple. Wearing richly coloured clothes over his light chain mail, the young man did not speak as the soldiers reached the base of the steel doors. Longbow strung across his back, he did not appear concerned by their presence.

"Well, boys, time to turn around. There is no way that you will reach my capital, for it lies across this fine lake here, and these magnificent doors were crafted over five hundred years ago by the Smiths of the Haldoric, a gift to my great-great … great … great-grandfather." Hitting his chest several times to dislodge the piece of apple he was choking on, the man continued. "They have withstood the test of time, as well as the brute forces of previous invasions. All you will find here is a frustrating disappointment."

"Do not be so sure, for we have ridden over much bigger and impressive gates than these. They will not protect your pretty, fragile city anymore than others have." General Hallaken spoke loudly

A Mortal Mistake

to the figure foolish enough to show himself before the numerous crossbowmen awaiting Conrad's command.

"Bigger is not always better, you know," he quipped, polishing another apple against his green cloak, keeping a wary eye on those below him.

"I bet the Kyllordic queen would beg to differ!" Conrad tossed the insult quickly, laughing as the thin prince scowled harshly down upon him. In a quick fit of rage, he threw the green apple, splattering it against Conrad's breastplate and sending Metzotto twisting in circles.

"Clearly a little too close to the truth ..." Conrad pulled his stallion back under his control and grinned as the men continued to laugh at the young Kyllordic's expense. Conrad could see the young prince's temper was starting to wear thin. The two glared at each other.

"You can either come down here and kiss my metal boots, or I can come up there and kick you with them. Your choice, Prince Raef. Save your city and its people or watch them all burn!" Conrad was thrilled to see the man's anger intensify.

"You shall never walk down the streets of our beautiful capital—your continuous conquest and reach for power ends here!" The young prince was now joined by two much older men, easily recognizable as commanders of the Kyllordic armies by their dazzling blue armour.

Conrad looked to Hallaken as they heard footsteps run along the ramparts of the tall port defences. The ramparts quickly filled up with green-clad archers, who drew their bows, awaiting the command to unleash their arrows.

General Hallaken's commanders quickly pulled their men back slightly, hiding behind their own shields or finding coverage among the surrounding wooden structures. They could hear distant battles erupting in the distance. Prince Raef watched from the top, a smile creeping across his face as he used his higher vantage point to look out across the city toward the northern Ardane forest, where the remainder of the Metzonian army had been setting up camp outside the city's wooden walls.

"And from the great forests of this nation, death shall fall upon you!" Raef smiled down on Conrad, feeling it his turn to laugh. "Looks like you've underestimated your enemy again."

"As you have underestimated the nastiness of Metzor." Conrad pulled back on the reins to back himself out of range of the arrows as he gave his men the go-ahead. "Your forests and lakes won't save you from our steel Prince Raef. Nothing ever does …"

His servants had finished heating his bathing water, and Sven submersed himself into the warm water to relax. The small soft hands of the serving girls had already relieved plenty of the tight knots in his back from the endless march to Essex. Upon finding the city completely abandoned, he had released the army to his younger brother to provide himself a release for his sore body.

High from his conquest of the Fallen, Sven had marched the army past the Kyllordic forces jammed within the city of Nemin, smelling the fear in the city as he rode toward the Valk. The Metzonians shouted out jeers and taunted their enemies, eager to continue after the sacking of Prokopolis.

The army perched upon the stone bridge, four chariots wide, across the Valk had been comprised of poorly trained recruits and fat garrison soldiery from the nearby city of Kaldor. The thick smell of sweat and urine had filled Sven's nostrils as he led a thousand charging cavalry into the mass.

Leading the charge, Sven, sword in one hand, spear in the other, had swept down upon the Kyllordic, leaping over their weak shield wall as he rode Destructico through the ranks. Armour steel cracked against the broad steel plating covering his stallion's breast as he punched through the centre of the barricading troops. Sven's sword sliced the commander's shocked head from his torso. Kyllordic men were kicked into the river as Destructico's hooves lashed out, crushing ribcages and skulls, his temper as fierce as the warrior riding upon his black back.

He had driven the column forward, not stopping to allow his enemy the opportunity to prepare against his charge. His Shadow

Guard followed their king through the mass, cleaning up those left alive. The riders struggled to keep up with their lord. Many of the Kyllordic garrison leaped into the Valk, taking their chances of drowning in the rapids rather than face certain death by Metzonian steel.

Kaldor also fell quickly and hard; the small army within its walls was slain down to the last man but one. The last man was given a prized horse and sent as quickly as he could travel to the capital city of Kyllica, bringing word that they were soon to be next. The army had planned to rest for two weeks outside the city walls before beginning the final direct march toward the capital.

The unanticipated arrival of Conrad with further reinforcements was exciting, particularly upon hearing how he crushed the armies of Nemin. Catching the Kyllordic army moving back toward the Valk, Conrad had overrun the force from the rear, routing the army quickly and leaving the survivors to throw their weapons aside and flee across the rolling hills. The men had cheered Conrad's name upon hearing him tell the story, but Sven felt something wrong within his brother. Conrad did not display the emotions Sven would expect so soon after his first victory.

The condition of his brother concerned Sven as to what had actually happened within the Black Jungles. Sven decided against broaching the subject with Conrad, knowing that when he was prepared to talk about it Conrad would come to him. Perhaps he wouldn't. Some things in a man's life were best left forgotten in the past.

If I could only truly forget the past and the horrible things I have done.

Screams of dying men and battle cries, sounding like part of his numerous reoccurring nightmares, brought Sven's mind stampeding out of its dreamy state. The sounds of battle continued even when he opened his eyes, and he realized they were too close to have been coming from within the city. Their camp had been set up before the tall wooden walls of the Essex's northern defences, upon the pristine plains spread between the forest, lake and city. Leaping from the tub, he quickly searched the royal pavilion for his sword.

"Make it quick, would you, Sven …?" Belle slipped deeper into her tub, showing little sense of alarm at the riot outside the large tent. Eyes still closed, she tipped her head back and disappeared beneath the steaming water.

Pushing the yellow sheet door aside, he strode out into the afternoon sunlight, squinting to observe the chaos that had erupted within the camp. Aerox and a dozen Shadow Guards were already stationed at the entrance to his tent, blades drawn, shielding him. Beyond them, the encampment was in complete disarray as several groups of Kyllordic attackers engaged his soldiers. The unprepared were quickly singled out as they scrambled for their misplaced weapons. The Kyllordic made a strong push for Sven's tent, appearing determined to slay the king in one swift strike.

Sven grabbed another sword resting by the door and, heading directly into the centre of the fray, led a charge toward the assailants. His Shadow Guard followed closely behind, rallying defenders to join the push. Sven's hatred flowed through his veins at the thought of his enemy being so deep in his camp. Quickly cutting down several attackers racing toward him, Sven charged forward, pushing into the thick of the skirmish.

The Kyllordic ambushers were quick to realize that their attack was losing the element of surprise that initially made it so deadly. Momentum slipping, many started to swiftly retreat into the forest. The lighter-footed warriors and archers continued the attack with a quickness the heavier soldiers could not match. Sven watched as, before long, they too started to retreat into the brush and tall trees of the great Ardane.

Rage and embarrassment fuelled the Metzonians as they chased their enemies into the forests, unaware of their mistake until another ambush sprang upon them. As they pursued their fleeing enemies, silent attacks from unseen enemies cut down the sons of Metzor. Kyllordic scouts watched as their prey ran along the trails beneath their hideaways in the trees above. Silently picking off many from above, their light footed brethren slipped from their hiding places, plunging their blades into ribs before disappearing once more in the gloomy undergrowth.

A Mortal Mistake

One of Sven's Shadow Guards noticed an attacker seconds before it became too late. He leapt ahead of Sven to intercept the arrow meant for his naked king. The arrow struck the man in the throat, and another arrow was quickly notched and aimed at the king. A second guard stepped forward, taking the arrow in the shoulder, before Aerox swung his large shield around Sven's chest and pulled him backward. Additional guards stepped up to protect their unequipped king and began a slow retreat out of the forest.

Sven tried to halt the slaughter by ordering a retreat for those still within the forest, as others rushed in behind their comrades, turning around as Sven screamed above the chaos raging around him. The Metzonians retreated to the open ground, leaving the forests to the Kyllordic rangers slinking in the shadows, laughing and tormenting them with their foreign jeers about being afraid of shadows.

Coming from beneath the canopy of the Ardane, Sven found his younger brother looking down on him from atop his steed. A smile crossed the young Metz's face as he looked away, keeping himself from breaking out into laughter.

"Well!" Sven yelled at him, trying to hold his anger in check as he wiped the blood from his body. Following Conrad's gaze, he watched two long boats working their way back across the lake slowly, the green flags at its bow fluttering quietly. The oars slowly dipped and rose out of the water, the chain spanning the lake keeping them firmly upon the safe course. Sven knew what his brother was going to tell him as he saw the smoke in the protected harbour. Kyllordia's capital lay barely visible across the lake, shimmering in the light shining on its buildings and towers, staring them down defiantly.

"The young prince was indeed correct. The gates held against anything that we could throw at them. But just to be sure, he lit the harbour on fire and sank the remaining boats. You do realize you are completely naked?"

"What the Hell do you think?" Sven scowled at his brother's joke, knowing full well his clothing situation. Although they could climb the walls and reach the other side, he knew there would not be any craft left within the harbour. The attack itself would be impossible to initiate from the sea anyway. Metzonians were soldiers of the wide flat plains of the Numelli, not of the sea. Sven knew traversing through the forests would be suicide, leaving their enemy with a horrific advantage.

"Perhaps our dark masters could crack it open for us?" Conrad suggested, turning his attention away from the boats. Rhimmon and Mammon had not been seen since the Black Jungles of Valkadia; they were apparently doing whatever they deemed fit and merely showing up to order the next phase of whatever they were planning. Sven thought about the latest command, having nothing to do with the Kyllordic nation at all, it was simply in the way.

Reach the Wastelands of Aedanica on the other side of Kyllordia. Burn all in your path.

A smile crossed his face as he looked back at the forest filled with Kyllordic infantry. Observing the great expanse of forest that ringed the large lake, he wondered how long it would take them to burn their way through that many trees. A shame that the Dark Prince of Fire was so far away; he could have cleared the forest for them with his flames in under a day. Unfortunately they would have to do it the hard way.

"Prepare the siege engines… we will burn our way through!" Throwing the bloody cloth to the ground, Sven strode back into the tent. Cursing extensively as he lowered himself into the cold water, Sven let the thoughts of the fiery flames burning the flesh off the Kyllordic attackers as their precious forests burnt around them warm him.

"Let it burn, boys. Let it burn …"

CHAPTER 29
Raef

Lapping waves and the wind were the only sounds in the middle of the lake as the Kyllordic vessels pressed for home. Rowing forward, the boat remained on course, connected to the long Chain of Connection. Stretching above the lake linking Essex and Kyllica, it defined the only "road" reaching the capital city in a land of forbidding forests.

The prince noticed the forlorn looks that his men wore as the oars splashed in the cold lake waters. They shared in his bitter mood as he replayed the day's events: the threats that had no backing, the small victories overshadowed by their impending doom. He was distraught with sheer hopelessness, not knowing where to go from here.

Quiet murmuring caused him to look up from the wooden floorboards in time to see the Metzonian siege engines begin their attack on the tall trees of the Ardane. Tall trebuchets hurled flammable clay pots through the air, smashing deep in the forest and spreading their fiery payloads through the leafy branches. Raef could hear the flames burn away the forest; he envisioned the trees screaming as they burned. He turned away from the sight, looking instead toward the port, hiding his tears from his men.

The giant statue at the port entrance looked across the lake, his mighty arms holding the Chain tight. Bulkier and more muscular than normal Kyllordic statues, it looked like his father and grandfather, strong men, built for power over agility. He did not share their attributes, following instead his mother's tall and thin lineage. Unable to wield his father's mighty axe effectively, Raef preferred the light and precise bows favoured by the stealthy Assassins of Aros. He ran a finger along the length of his grandfather's bow; the white wood contained a sparkling blue hue, making it as beautiful as it was deadly. The stiffness of the wood made it extremely difficult to pull, but the power it contained would have ripped through the arrogant Metzonian prince's armour with ease. He wished he had done so instead of taking his verbal abuse but Ethan and Eli refused, as they always did.

Within the safety of the harbour, the crew unlinked the longboat from the Chain, drifting to the right of the bearded statue of his grandfather. He looked back toward the other boats behind them, looking for the twins, who were locked in a deep conversation. Wondering what argument they were upon this time, he was glad that he could not read lips. He already felt his ears burning, knowing they were talking about him. They always were, and he had been through enough confrontations with the both of them to know they were not words of praise.

"There is madness within the Metz brothers, hate and horror that will not be contained. They will not be stopped. Every breath they take, they grow stronger, connected deeper with the evil that has entrapped their souls." Ethan grumbled. He watched smoke billow profusely as crackling flames spread through the forest. Large trebuchets spread a blazing fire deep into forest as shorter-ranged weapons started burning a swath through the greenery at the edge. Ethan hoped most of the rangers had realized what the invaders were up to and had begun to work their way back through the forest to safety.

"I felt it too; their souls are dark, like the demons of past. Humanity is crumbling in on itself, and all opposition is nearly defeated. Soon there will be nothing left but servants to the darkness. It is only the beginning, Ethan. How can we hope to avert it, let alone save those who would flee its grasp?" Eli rubbed his face, looking toward the horizon and the city upon the shores. The city was thick with refugees who had fled from the countryside, trying to find a safe haven from the marauding invaders.

"It's not just the Metz brothers who drive Humanity to its end. The few escapees of Prokopolis massacre claim that there is another group behind it all, influencing everything that has happened. Any who wield the power to slay Militades are formidable; my bet would be the Sin again. There has been an increase in the number of Fallen members who have disappeared without any trace. I think it is time to leave our positions and retreat back home. What remains of the Fallen will have to begin regrouping and stand as one against the coming evil. I believe that includes us as well." Ethan looked deep into the water, watching his reflection ripple as the boat pushed forward.

"You are suggesting we leave our positions and retreat to the Sacred City? Abandon those whom we have defended for so long? We have an oath to the Kyllordic people, yet we also have an oath to the Order. With so many conflicting promises, how can we possibly keep them all?" Eli looked toward the boat ahead of them carrying the prince. Dark times had fallen upon the child with the loss of his father, leaving him often moody and at times depressed. Yet the young man had continued to push forward and continue to fight against the struggle. It was an unforeseen strength in Eli's mind but not Ethan's.

"He's emotional and reckless, too often following his heart over his mind. It could very well lead to his downfall."

"He is still young, Ethan, he will learn. Even if it has to be forced upon him, he will learn." Eli pulled down upon the small chain, opening the clasp that released their boat into the harbour. They rowed to the left, around the corner, and saw those waiting on the stone wharf.

"And there is the reason for his constant emotional instability …"

The queen-to-be, Cleos stood waiting for the return of her prince. Tall and thin, she wore a dark green dress trimmed in the royal blue silk. Her long blonde hair ran down her back in a single braid. Her prince leapt from the boat and came down the wharf, and she gave him a shallow hug before turning to lead him away.

Ethan caught up with the pair and clutched at the young man's elbow. "My prince, I think that we need to begin the evacuation. Their tactic of burning the forest will take several days at the minimum, but it is inevitable that they will march their armies through the capital within the week …"

"Excuse me, General, but an enemy has *never* walked the streets of Kyllica. It will continue to stay that way, or we *all* shall die defending it!" replied the prince's quick-tempered fiancée. Her eyes burned into Ethan's with such intensity that even Eli could feel the heat. Neither broke their stare.

"My Lady, our defences will be no match against the ferocity of these beasts that burn down our beloved forests. Long have our kings defended this land, but they have not faced an enemy like this before. Even the Order fell to their—" Eli said, trying to lend support, but he was quickly cut off by her quick temper.

"We are not the Order! We shall be strong while they were weak, and we shall win where they lost! My prince has great strength and will not cower from the fight as they did. Our great nation will continue to prosper where other nations have failed." She quickly silenced their responses, cutting her arm across in front of them.

"Do not worry, we will defend the capital. We shall find a way to defeat these enemies. Let us regroup later tonight with the council and formulate the next phase. Until then, Generals, I bid you farewell." Raef took his lady's arm and continued off the docks, leaving the conversation unresolved.

Left to look at each other incredulously neither could believe what they had heard. They had just witnessed the evil that had come to destroy them, and to believe that they had a remote chance was ridiculous.

"How many lives will be taken to satisfy my future sister-in-law's dreams of grandeur? Only in the end will he discover the truth of everything, and it will utterly destroy him from the inside."

Eli and Ethan turned to find who had so eloquently predicted the future.

Shorter than her brother, her long, straight black hair, blue eyes and high cheekbones defined her as the young prince's sibling. King Oberon's second-born child, the quiet Sylvanna, sat upon a bench in the shadow of her grandfather's statue. She slowly moved out from the shadows, looking past them with distaste at the couple moving up the stairs into the city.

"Much like our father, he has a weakness for those of the fairer sex, and it will control him and slowly consume him. He will find out too late when the fires within him burn out of control and all that he has ever loved is turned to ash. She, on the other hand, would not blink an eye over the countless thousands who would bleed on the battlefield." She stared up at them, her vibrant eyes making her words shine with truth.

"My lady." Both brothers quickly bowed their heads to her, and then Eli continued. "Your words speak great truth as to what is to come. We unfortunately cannot go against the wishes of the crown completely, not without bringing heavy punishment upon our heads."

"And while we would gladly sacrifice our own lives in return for saving thousands upon thousands, truth be spoken they would be sacrificed in vain. As long as Cleos owns his heart, he will not abandon the palace, nor will any lives be spared." Thoughts of their own deaths had crossed their minds, but the thought of an entire nation being slain because of the stubbornness and selfishness of one shook their souls. Cleos would not care about anyone, most likely not even her future husband, at the cost of her own future.

"Great friends of my father, I'm going to say only this. The council sees the burning of our sacred forests, and with it they see a destiny of death coming upon us all. Unlike those of the Fallen … they fear it." She ran her tattooed hands upon both sides of Ethan bearded face before walking back toward the wharf entrance. They watched her closely, contemplating her words; the royal blue dress dragged silently along the stone. She paused in the sunlight and stared into the deep blue waters.

"Sometimes sacrifice has to be made to preserve the future. Remember … my brother is not king yet …" She turned and continued on her way, disappearing among the milling crowd.

In their chambers within the royal palace, Raef watched silently as Cleos slowly continued to dress, enamoured by her beauty and grace. He loved every way that she moved, how she spoke, the way that she dreamed; he would not be able to break her love spell on him if he tried. But then he really couldn't think why he would want to in the first place.

Switching to a different dress in preparation for the council meeting about the next plan for the Kyllordic people, she spoke her mind, continuing the same conversations that they already had several times before.

"Why haven't you been crowned already so that we could just make the decisions? Like it's supposed to be, without theses stupid council meetings. I don't understand why your father did this to you, leaving you in the wake of a bunch of cowards and greedy men trying to save their own skin and power." Cleos ranted to him, venting her anger as she combed her hair slowly.

"All that most of them talk about these past weeks is the safety of your grandfather's stupid little island and the Keeps of Kyllordia! Stand and fight for what is yours, you cowering fools! My child is going to be a *king*, not some petty lord of an island."

Raef's thoughts stopped at that last sentence, mulling over the idea. It was a kingdom secret, not known to anyone but the two of them. Unfortunately it was a secret that they would not be able to hide much longer.

She had confessed it to him one night. Her feelings had been mixed, but he had been elated by the news. Promising her the world, he filled himself with dreams of their future together. He imagined a bright-eyed boy, one who would grow up in the royal gardens playing with the servants as he had done in his own childhood.

"Don't worry, we will find a way to defeat this army, and our children will grow large within our lands. Nothing will stop that," he promised her, his mind trapped within dreams of the future and not on the present dire situation only miles from their home. He placed his arm around her waist, pulling her close.

A stiff knock came at their door.

Growling in disappointment, Raef moved her reluctantly aside to answer the door. Pulling the doors open, he saw both Elithane generals, who were surrounded by a complement of palace guards. Ethan smiled widely at him, setting off alarms within the prince's head.

"What the hell do you want? I told you that I would see you at the council meeting tonight."

"The council has already sat. The council has already voted," Eli answered as his brother pushed through the room. "It is time to pack up, my prince. We are leaving Kyllica for the Keeps."

Struggling to grasp the words, Raef was momentarily confused. How had the Council of Lords sat and voted without his being there? Why had they not included his opinion in the discussion? Watching the solemn looks of the palace guards who followed Ethan into the room, Raef's stomach turned when Cleos's harsh tone filled the room.

"How have you come to believe you have the power to do this? Your liege told you that we were going to stay within the city and fight our enemy. What authority gives you the right to overrule a king's command?"

"When you do not care about the costs of your actions, the responsibility to make the correct decisions will not be yours. In order to preserve the future and ensure the survival of our people, we have taken control for the crown and issued orders to abandon the city. We leave before dusk and travel under the moonlight."

Raef was shocked. He looked at Ethan, who looked back at him with a smug smile as the palace guards encircled them.

Eli entered the room last, speaking in his usual proper tone. "By the order of King Oberon Kyllone the First, we are sworn to defend the people of Kyllordia and to preserve the future until the next king is crowned and of an age to make the proper decision! Our decision is in the best interest of everyone, including the both of you. We tried to reason with you, to make you see the logic. But once again you have both failed to see logically, appearing willing to sacrifice those around you. A true and worthy king refuses to let his people be butchered out of personal pride."

Cleos jumped out of her seat. "This is high treason against the crown! You cannot do this! Such an act carries a penalty of death! We rule the kingdom, not you or the council. You have sworn to defend the crown and to sacrifice your lives for its defence. You all shall have your heads upon the block for this!" she screamed at the generals. She threw her cup at Eli, who barely had time to block it.

"I ask that you be civil throughout this ordeal so we can avoid any damaging or humiliating scenes. Or are we going to have to resort to unfortunate measures?" Standing before them, Ethan held up two long pieces of blue silk that draped from his fingertips to the floor.

"Raef and I are not going anywhere!" Cleos, inches from Ethan's face, growled in a menacing tone that Raef had never heard before. It sent chills down his spine. He watched Ethan laugh in her face.

"Captain! May I receive your assistance in restraining the young lady?"

Cleos screamed in protest. Raef tried to intercept the captain of the watch, before his wrist was jerked back. Without looking behind him, he swung at the figure holding him. He turned to see Eli a second before he knocked the old man to the ground. Rough hands grabbed him by the neck as his feet were kicked out from beneath him, sending him plummeting to the ground. He felt excruciating pain from a steel knee crushing into his spine, and he watched Cleos continue to fight valiantly against her opponents. "Your lives are forfeit, and you will not last through the winter! Such a betrayal is unforgivable by both the crown as well as the Heavens."

Raef's stomach contorted at what was happening within the chamber. Additional traitors entered their room, ripping open drawers and throwing their belongings into open chests. Raef watched Eli pluck up the crown from its cushioned position and placed it upon his forearm, wiping blood from his lip.

"Forfeit our lives may be, but at the cost of saving several hundred thousand lives, we accept that. Had we left you to make the decision, our lives would have been lost for nothing, as well as costing needless deaths. Perhaps you will learn in time," Ethan snapped at Cleos, his built-up anger toward her finally released without fear of consequence.

Dragged to their feet by the guards, Raef and Cleos were forced toward the doorway. Raef met the generals' eyes; Ethan's eyes were cold, and Eli's showed little sign of resentment over how things had come to this. Perhaps if his anger had not been quite so intense he would have felt a little shame, knowing he would have to put both to death when the proper time came.

As he was marched down the long spiral staircase, Raef was greeted by the provincial lords of Kyllordia, who were lined up on either side of the blue carpeted hallway. Staring at all of them as he passed, he realized all had conspired against him. Hate rose within him as he committed the faces of all those who had allowed his disposal to memory.

"You are all cowards!" Cleos screamed at the spectators, fury burning in her eyes. "Cowards! You should not call yourselves men, for you are unworthy of it. True men push their fear aside and are willing to follow their king into battle, to die gloriously by his side if needed."

Cleos spit in the general's face as she fought with the guards. Ethan ignored it, grabbing her by her bound wrists and dragging her behind him as he entered the armoured wagon they had prepared. Drawn behind six white mares, the large wagon was beautifully crafted with the finest details; Raef knew it had been strongly built for great swiftness.

Eli carefully placed a hand on Raef's head, forcing him to duck as he was gently forced into the carriage seat beside Cleos. Raef reached out and squeezed her bound hands, and she turned away, tears rolling down her face. Both generals settled in across from them, showing no emotion at what they had just done, or the consequences it would bring.

"I'm going to remember this," Raef warned.

Ethan ignored him and peeked out the edge of the covered

window as they exited the palace and began the journey into the city. Holding the Kyllordic crown within his lap and slowly turning it within his hands, Eli did not look up as he responded, "I pray that you do."

Snorting with contempt, Raef looked out the wagon as they flew through the streets that were already packed with fleeing citizens, filled with fear and forced from their homes, all because of the cowardice of the men before him. Had he not been surrounded by cowards, he would have led a war that would have crushed the Metzonians. Because of them, his kingdom had collapsed, but he would have his revenge.

All in good time, he thought to himself. He was their true king, and he would rise to claim his birthright against those who denied it to him. He could already see himself raising his blade over his head, all those who doubted him on their knees in the dirt.

Bloody righteousness would indeed be his.

CHAPTER 30
Ashes of the Past

An army of ghosts marched through the swirling storm of ashes that surrounded them. The dark steel armour of the Metzonians slowly turned a ghostly white as they trudged toward Kyllica. The tall trees that once stretched out high to the sky were black, the red embers at their cores still burning hot.

The trio of hate rode their steeds silently through the forest of ash, feeling the waves of heat radiating from beneath and all around them. It reminded Conrad of his descent into the depths of the world, the dark hot places that he had encountered. The dark stain upon his heart continued to grow as he fought to feel any emotion over what they had done or the destructive path of death that they were carving across the countryside. He looked over at his companions. Belle's eyes were upon the city far in the distance, soon to be within their grasp. Emotionless atop Destructico, Sven gazed at the swirling ashes blowing around them that painted his dark armour white. Looking at those behind them marching through the cloud of ash, Conrad saw an intimidating force of ghosts, as if the souls of all those they had slain followed them to war.

Sven's promise of vengeance reached far beyond the comprehension of all: the release of two Dark Princes of Hell, the destruction of the Order's crown jewel city of Prokopolis and the vengeful slaying of tens of thousands of the Fallen servants. The naive Conrad had expected his brother to find and punish those who slew his father, not rip the world apart completely. Perhaps that was what haunted his brother, the spirits of those of his past eating away at him. It seemed extremely unlikely; his brother had never been one for emotion or living in the past. Conrad was not as strong; he saw one spirit in particular following him constantly. He could not shake the image, seeing it every time he closed his eyes.

The thought of Cassidus not returning from the Black Jungles continuously arose within his mind. Because of his increasingly dreadful bouts of amnesia, Conrad's memory had become so fragmented that he did not know what a real memory was anymore. He had confessed his fears to Cassidus, fearing what was happening to him. Was his death a result of Conrad telling the man his fears about what rested within him? Did the demon slowly devouring his soul kill Cassidus because he knew his secrets? Did it fear that Cassidus would betray him and kill him?

Conrad's most haunting memory had occurred during his brother's release of Rhimmon. Cassidus stood amongst the blood and death as they butchered the Fallen, a look of pure horror upon his young face. He did not participate in the bloodshed, which had for some reason filled Conrad with rage. In his bloodthirsty state, he'd raised his sword to strike down his friend. By chance a Fallen prisoner crashed into him, sparing Cassidus.

Replaying the image, Conrad realized the monster he had become. He was rapidly losing control of himself. He had begun to fear what he had done and what he might do in the future, the terrors he might inflict. Looking at his brother, he wondered how Sven could look so calm, knowing what they had done to this world. Conrad had not signed up for all of this, and yet he remained, unable to escape and falling deeper and deeper. He feared soon there would be little left.

"Something has been bothering me of late, and I can't get it out of my head, Sven."

"I already told you, Conrad, it's the called the jungle itch. It

A Mortal Mistake

will pass if you do as I instructed. Either that or you picked a bad brothel."

Belle laughed loudly at Sven's joke, bringing a burning to Conrad's face.

"It's not about that!" Scowling at both of them, Conrad ignored the humiliation, returning to his original concern. "It's about Cassidus. I fear that I may have inadvertently been the cause of his death. I worry that I killed my best friend from within my darkness." Conrad smiled despite the dark thought, as if it was a small victory against the taint within his veins. Cassidus would never have defended himself against Conrad, but his brother would not hesitate for a heartbeat to strike him down.

Riding silently for a brief moment, Sven replied with a tone showing little concern for Conrad's question, as though fully believing he knew the answer. "No, you didn't."

"How do you know?" Eyes narrowing, he waited for Sven to answer the question. His brother's reassuring words were what he needed in this moment, yet they didn't help. The sinking feeling within his stomach refused to go away, growing worse as Sven's eyes met his.

"Because I killed him," Sven said back to him, his face showing no concern for what he just admitted. "Cassidus had to go, Conrad. His family were Fallen, he was loyal to the Order and he almost cost us Prokopolis, among other reasons."

"Our family is Fallen!" Conrad protested, not understanding how his brother could have done such a thing. Awkwardly reaching across Metzotto's back, Conrad grasped for his brother's throat, wanting to strangle the life from him. "One only has to look into your golden eyes to know we are Fallen! Cassidus was loyal to me! How could you murder him?"

Metzotto and Destructico fought against the commotion between their riders, but Conrad refused to relinquish his grip. Feeling his legs slide from Metzotto's back, he hooked his fingers onto Sven's breastplate and pulled him down with him. In a cloud of ash, Conrad fell beneath his brother.

"Our family is Metzonian! Our family has risen far above all things Fallen." Sven's tone remained calm as he slammed Conrad's shoulders repeatedly into the bed of warm ash. "I have watched the Fallen destroy our family. I lost everything I once loved because of them; I have no desire to lose what is left because of perceived loyalty. They murdered our father, turned our brother against us and left our mother to die, Conrad!"

"You cannot possibly blame the Fallen for our mother's death …"

"I can, Con! It was the first step to weaken and isolate our father. It has turned us brothers against one another. All was done for reason. Cassidus and Kallisto are two in the same, Conrad. Fallen, not Metzonian, as we always believed them to be."

"You are delusional, Sven! This obsession with the Fallen will soon kill the rest of your family! Look at the path we have marched down. You deceived us all with tales of revenge, but that was not your plan at all. The Order murdering our father was just the catalyst you needed. When will this all end, brother? How many more innocent people will have to die to sate your thirst?"

Did the entire world really need to suffer for the actions of a few? Their desire for power and greatness had ultimately led them into servitude to the Dark Princes that would last an eternity. How was this any better than what his father had been to the Order? What had he done? As his mind tried to contemplate everything, his heartbeat increased within his chest, sending his psyche reeling. His mind started to flash between black and bright white, blotting out his vision, flickering back and forth in a vomit-inducing seizure. The emotions within Conrad's body fought a great battle within him; his stomach rolled and he sweated profusely he struggled to maintain control of his body.

"Until this world is cleansed of the Fallen!" Sven growled at him, leaving Conrad to question whose words his brother spoke.

"Is that you speaking or Rhimmon?" Conrad snarled, and he tried to push Sven off him. "Look at what you have done to us!"

"What I have done?" Slamming Conrad back into the ashes, Sven shifted his weight. "Blame me all you want, but you remained at my side the whole time. What we did, we did together. It's as much your fault as it is mine."

Conrad paused, realizing his own path had run parallel with Sven's. In all the terrible things his brother had done, Conrad had played a role. He had found him within the desert and dragged him back to Metzor, unexpectedly forcing the hand of the Fallen to act against his father and his family. All stemmed from his mistake of loving his brother and believing he was the same man Conrad had remembered. Looking at Sven, he understood he had been painfully wrong.

"I am not like you, Sven! I cannot continue following the same path as you. It is slowly destroying my soul and devouring me from the inside out. You may not be haunted by the terrible things you have done in the past, or by the army of ghosts, but I am." Conrad craned his neck to look behind them at the motionless, ash-sodden soldiers.

"Not like me?" Sven chuckled, leaning forward as he whispered in his ear. "You are more like me than you possibly know, little brother. You are exactly like me!"

Sven grabbed his right arm and leaned back, and Conrad knew his wrist would have broken beneath Sven's pressure had it not been for the black power already within it. As he pried the gauntlet from Conrad's hand finger by finger, blood ran between Sven's knuckles from the sharp edges cutting his flesh.

Spotting the white ring upon his hand, surrounded by the darkness that pumped beneath the surface, Conrad understood what his brother intended to do. Fighting to free his right hand, Conrad struggled beneath Sven's weight as his brother pinned his left beneath a steel knee.

"No, Sven! Please don't do this to me. Please. I beg of you!" He was barely able to concentrate as his vision began to narrow.

Slowly inching the ring off his finger, Sven's dark eyes watched Conrad's pupils as they began to grow with the spreading darkness. Pulling the ring free and holding it before his eyes, Sven rapped his knuckles on Conrad's breastplate.

"We are exactly the same, little bro. Two souls entwined in destiny to bring this world to its knees!"

Reaching the walls of the Kyllordic capital city was a different experience than Conrad had anticipated. Almost the entire city had been created from the tall forests that surrounded them, stone a commodity the Kyllordic did not have a ready supply of. The lack of stone that the Metzonians found so common gave the city a mystical magical feel, as though they were transported to a different world.

The outer walls were built out of great rows of oak logs wider than a man could stretch his arms, planed smooth and covered in some sort of lacquer that refused to burn. Each great vertical log was carved into in a series of animals stacked upon one another. A great bear, a sitting wolf, a perched eagle, a mountain lion, a great fish, and an antlered stag were upon each pole of the wall in different combinations; no two same animals were side by side. A row of serpentine dragons with wings locked together ran along the ramparts, the tips of the wings and long necks providing cover for the archers that should have been there. But there was no one within the city. The Kyllordic had fled, leaving the Metzonians to once again collect a hollow treasure.

"Kyllica, ancient capital of the secretive people of Kyllordia. Few foreigners have walked your streets, none bearing arms. Oh, how the mighty have fallen before the fear of our swords." Conrad smiled, arms open wide before the decorative city as if bathing in its radiance. Several battalions rushed around them, entering the city through the open, unguarded gates. Conrad and his brother had been told that the young prince was weak and easily manipulated and would not have the strength to abandon his home. The nation of Kyllordia was to die within its capital with all its people and royalty. Their master had foretold of a decisive blow to mankind's last free nation, not of an empty, abandoned city. He feared something about Rhimmon's misplaced prophecy and the ability of even the most powerful to be wrong.

Belle looked upon the walls for signs of any enemies as a misty rain started to fall down upon them. "We were told of the great battle and victory that was to be ours, Sven. This is wrong and unexpected—it changes everything. An undefeated nation leaves an enemy at our backs, a dangerous proposition for the final battle we seek." Uncertainty was within her eyes as they moved past gates and into the city.

The hooves clopped loudly as the stallions continued down the wide main street toward the distant domed palace that lay in the city centre. A squadron of swordsmen marched down a side street as another group crossed several streets ahead, crisscrossing through the city in search of any sign of resistance. The echoes of the empty city haunted Conrad; he could imagine the tall and elegant, vibrantly dressed Kyllordic with their tattooed bodies walking through the streets, worshipping at their temples and selling their wares. The ghostly images continued to swirl around Conrad. Most of the illusions seemed to be headed in the same direction as him, to the beautiful palace that overlooked the city.

The royal palace, so round and curved, had a beautiful flow to its large expanse, an appearance that it was not built but had been grown. Ghostly guards marched through the palace yard; many stood watch at the entrances. A single black figure stood in the shadows of the great arched entrance, hidden from the rain. The figure looked up, his eyes a hateful red, startling Conrad as the apparitions disappeared from his mind, leaving only one.

The tall being did not disappear but stood in their way, his eyes peering at them behind his mask and hood. Behind him, cloaked men were dragging dead men dressed in tight-fitting green and grey clothing and throwing them upon a burning pile. Conrad knew that the dead men were Kyllordic, most likely from the secret guild of assassins that trained in Aros.

"Warlord Locan, you seem to arrive before us yet again." Sven addressed the tall figure. He did not move, forcing them to stop before him. Conrad looked upon the Brotherhood of Sin for the first time; he had heard about them in the battle for Prokopolis when he was returning from the horrid Black Jungles. Looking at the wraiths, he now understood the terror they could inspire.

"These assassins were not prepared for true wraiths of the night. Your men will not find any resistance. We now know that they abandoned the city five days ago as you burned their holy forests."

Sven did not ask how the Brotherhood had discovered this fact; he very well knew that one of the tortured souls in the burning pile of corpses was undoubtedly the source.

Conrad noticed one man who was possibly still alive, his body stretched out between four poles set at each corner of the pile of burning men. The man looked down at the faces of all those who were slain, forced to feel the heat off their burning bodies. Conrad felt a slight pang of pity for the man and dared to ask the warlord about the particular assassin.

"That one was far more skilled and deadly than the rest of his kind we faced. He was able to slay ten of the Brotherhood, and he fled through the city for almost a night before I myself was forced to intervene, catching him almost at the gates. I offered him a quick death, but he refuses still and shall watch his brothers burn and die a painfully slow death among the flames."

"And what of the rest of their kind?" Belle asked, looking around the palace and the city. Her eyes had seen the same torture performed before several times before. "Where do they flee to?"

"The Kyllordic run for the Keeps, their impenetrable sanctuary, which is safe from defeat and death. With them they take a precious object of the Brotherhood's." The trio had all heard about the Keeps, but most believed them to be a myth. Of the few who had found the general location, none had ever been able to get to the actual Keeps themselves, hidden away on several islands surrounded by the fast-flowing bodies of water that originated in the high Alakari. A mighty drawbridge expanded across the river, held up by mighty chains. At any sign of trouble, the chains would be released from both sides, letting the bridge sink to the depths of the river. It was the same technique that was used to reach the second and the third islands, on which the Keeps were actually built. Construction had begun with the royal family three generations earlier and was never truly completed. Regardless, the warlord was correct in stating that they had bigger things to worry about.

"Nothing is impenetrable, Warlord, we have certainly proven that," Belle announced defiantly.

Conrad waited for the Sin's answer, watching the flames rise higher and start to burn the man above them. Protecting his mind within a warrior's meditation, the man did not scream or shout for mercy. His eyes closed and his muscles became rigid, absorbing the pain as his flesh began to turn black.

"True enough, Empress, but the amount of effort and time that it would require are negligible to the true timeframe of our masters. Your lords shall arrive in six days to lead you into the Wastelands of the Aedonica. You have five days to meet them at the entrance with the required pieces to move forward. I suggest not disappointing them. Hurry forth. My brothers and I must leave you once again on an assignment of our own. We shall meet again soon, though. Until then …" The figure had been joined by the rest of the Brothers of Sin, who stood silently behind him, done with their task. Locan's body slowly disintegrated into a wispy cloud of black smoke and took off through the darkness; the others did the same. Soon all had completely disappeared.

"Perhaps we have scared these Easterners enough that they will not dare come out of their protective hole in the woods. If they choose to, there will not be much hope for them."

Sven turned to peer toward the northeast, looking over the city and its walls from the height of the royal palace. "It matters not. We have one final prince to release; then our power will be complete. Soon enough nothing will be able to resist us. Go and release the army into the city to do as they please until we return. Order the Shadow Guard to organize the final prisoners for the march to the Wasteland."

Conrad set off to do his brother's bidding, a smile upon his face as he too stared toward the northeast and the rising thunderheads.

"Adramaleck, Burner of Worlds, do you sense your release?"

Chapter 31
The Stairway to Heaven

The ambassadorial chamber was erupting in pandemonium as members from all sides of the world screamed at one another. Arguments were flaring up everywhere between almost every member in the room. The guards too seemed to be feeling the emotion within the room, becoming slightly unsettled as arguments heightened and threatened to become violent.

Kallisto held his hands to his temples, massaging his throbbing head. He swore that the world was falling apart and he was powerless to help hold it together any longer. Where had this rush of anarchy come from? Along with the senseless violence and hatred that ran rampant through the immediate countryside, had the rest of the world gone mad as well? The first of the Order's Elder Council meetings in the months since Prokopolis's fall was quickly becoming a disaster. While a couple members of the White Elders had already made it to the city, several others were said to be scattered across the countryside, but no one had heard from them. The voids that needed to be filled amongst the White Elders were small in comparison to the rest of the Elder Council.

Looking upon the young faces surrounding him, he was proud to see many survivors attempt to step up in the wake of the disaster. As they screamed at one another, he knew they all had a lot to learn.

Kallisto worried that the Order would not receive the time necessary for recovery. Reorganization took time, and with Rhimmon and the Metz brothers' relentless pace, the flow of refugees travelling in from Mendolin had not slowed. The number continued to increase quicker than builders could construct appropriate structures, and time was running out.

Winter was closing quickly upon the Alakari and would soon make travel dangerous, on top of putting pressure on food supplies now that the bulk of the Order refugees had arrived from their journey through the pass. The logistics of relocating a population had not been something the administrator thought he would be forced to take on. It made life much more complicated.

Ending the meeting, Kallisto was once again forced to ask for everyone to reflect on knowledge that was present and ponder what was to come next. Perhaps with some time the anger would clear from the minds of his fellow members and a solution would present itself. The discussion about what course the Order would chose to take was an endless one. Too many unknowns remained within the situations; everyone was overwhelmed with problems, leading to panic. Pandemonium was not a quality that suited the Fallen. Their enemies were a breed that fed off fear, consuming those who were unable to fight such emotion.

"How do we ever recover from such an event? Prokopolis was not only the home of our Elder Council but a symbol of everything the Order has done through the history of the world. It was built upon countless centuries of work and worldly events," Kallen said, joining his sister. They followed Kallisto out of the chamber and into the long corridors of the Sacred Temple.

"Unite. If those around us continue to bicker and fight over events that cannot be changed, such mayhem will be the death of us all," Kallisto answered. He only had the first step. Collecting what remained would be easy compared to the second step of defeating such evil.

"How do we combat such a thing? Our leadership is scattered and defeated, with few to take control of what remains. Everyone is fractured with fear—and for good reason. Their lives have been torn apart." Alexandra observed, letting a trio of scholars pass them by before moving to Kallisto's left.

"As we have experienced before, when turmoil brought the end of the Metzor Chapter."

"I disagree. Not to this level. We lost many important and distinguished figures with the loss of Metzor, but they were merely an arm compared to the crowned head of Prokopolis. The loss of Caelestis is monumental! He guided the Order through many ordeals through the free kingdoms."

Kallisto was unsurprised that Kallen did not agree with his interpretation of the loss. In many minds, young Kallen's included, the destruction of Prokopolis left the Order in its most vulnerable position in a hundred years.

"Monumental as such a loss is, Caelestis was a mortal man, wise as he may have been. We have lost grandmasters before, and there has always been a strong soul to take his place. Tell me, children, what happens to the fallen acorns when a fire blazes through an old oak forest?" Kallisto looked up at both of them, not breaking stride, avoiding collisions with other members moving through the halls.

"The seeds crack and grow to replace it, feeding off the fertile ashes of their predecessors," Alexandra was quick to answer, but perhaps without fully understanding the cryptic question.

"Exactly, and long have seedlings rested within the safety of the Order's tall shadows and its fertile learning environment. It is time for the Children of the Fallen to rise from the ashes to lift the Order back into the sunlight of this world."

"Such an event takes a lifetime, Karl; we do not have a lifetime to rebuild. The farmers who burnt down the forest are planning on tilling the soil so that it never rises again," Kallen exclaimed, using his arms to mimic a farmer grinding his plow into the soil.

"Hence why it is best to start growing now. Remember that hope always remains. Try as he might, that farmer will also grow old and weak, and the determination of the seedlings is unending. The farmer will die and the forest will grow again in time. There are more powerful forces within this world and the universe, and they are what are truly eternal. Remember that.

A Mortal Mistake

"Now I must go and talk to Vayra and discuss what the future holds. As you have pointed out, such a disaster needs to be controlled and calm returned after the storm. Contemplate what I have told you both; find the strengths that we old men and women see within you. No longer are you hidden from the sunlight within shadows of the old and dying. Stretch and grow, as is your destiny." Kallisto turned off to their left toward the temple quarters.

They were so caught up in their conversation that Kallen realized they had traversed from one end of the temple to the other. Breathing in deeply to reset himself, he realized that he was included among those perturbed by their emotions. Kallen watched Kallisto walk toward his usual hideaway in the library, leaving Kallen alone with his sister.

Alexandra remarked, "I'm going to the cathedral to clear my mind and think. A reset will feel good in the sunlight, I hope; we have a lot to think about. Kallisto is correct; we cannot be children anymore, and we desperately need to find some sort of solutions. I will see you tonight at supper, brother." She walked off down the opposite hallway toward the doors that led into the city, leaving Kallen alone.

Taking note of his own need to calm his own spirit, Kallen walked toward the temple throne room and then halted quickly. Jaina slowly moved across the room, carrying a wooden bucket of sloshing water toward one of the large Trees of Eternity. A small girl followed her, carrying her own bucket of water, helping out with chores. The small girl had usually been found within the throne room, rarely being seen outside the temple except upon the sunniest days. Kallen had asked Kallisto about her and was referred to his sister, who told him all about the great quest and the surprise. Yet another orphan, the Order had taken to calling her Halo, believing her innocence and pure heart to be among the crown jewels of Heaven. All protected her as though she were another member of their family of orphans.

Watching her slowly tip her bucket into the base of the tall tree adjacent to the one Jaina was watering. Kallen felt himself smile as he watched the joy upon her face as she finished emptying her bucket. She hugged the holy tree before skipping off to grab another bucket of water. Such joy and innocence in tumultuous and terrifying times were reminders of why Kallen had to step forward. He had to defend those too small to protect themselves.

Taking a few steps back he began to turn away, leaving them to continue with their tasks. His movement caught Jaina's eye. He quickly considered continuing with his escape, not wanting others to catch his depressive mood, particular Jaina. But he had little choice but to continue forward, which grew easier when she smiled toward him and straightened up.

"What honour do we have with the rare company of the mighty Titan? Come to collect all our water for us?" Jaina threw her pail toward him, forcing him to catch it and fill it from one of the small spouts pouring into pools at the edge of the room.

"Actually, I was just looking for a place to relax and calm myself down, but since a bucket has magically appeared in my hands, I suppose I could help the two of you out. Though why water them when their roots extend throughout the mountain to the Lakes of Forgotten Souls and beyond?" Dipping the edge of the bucket beneath the fountain of pouring water, he inspected the sparkling water as it rippled in the bucket.

"True, but these waters are from the Pools of Purification, the purest of the holy waters. It is a symbol of our love to the Trees of Eternal Life. The waters help to heal the ailments and pains given to them over the course of time. We like to believe that it also removes the terrors that they have been forced to witness at the hands of Humanity." She dipped her fingertips into the bucket as it overfilled, and Kallen watched her swirl and splash the water, making it dance.

"However, I doubt you find this topic interesting, being such a strong man of war and death. What has gotten you so perturbed? I thought that Titans did not have emotions and were made of stone and steel." Her quick wink warmed his heart, as did the slight jab at the Temple Titans. Staring into the pools of violet, he saw a sparkle of life that lifted his spirit. He always became lost within her eyes, taking all his strength not to stare. Jaina playfully pulled the pail from his hands, bringing him back to reality.

"A stone heart wears and chips from the constant turmoil of the world and is not completely impervious to breaking." Many within the Order had joked that the Titans were not human, forged from the mountains themselves. They rarely showed any heart or emotion. Kallen knew that it was more a matter of strict mental training meant to prepare them for the horrors of war than being supernatural beings.

"Oh, you poor man. Perhaps we should cast your cracked heart back into one of the numerous volcanoes of the Aedanica so it can spit you out a new one." Jaina paused when she did not receive a comeback.

Kallen remained lost in his thoughts.

"You are seriously shaken by these events, aren't you? You realize that you have no control of anything within this world, right?"

Kallen held his silence, for he felt within his heart a different philosophy. He believed he had the power to influence and shape events that were to come. He had a responsibility to protect the innocent and defeat those that threatened them. She was proposing an age-old debate between the uncontrollable destinies that had already been written by the Heavens versus the belief that each individual had the power of free will. Kallen believed the smallest drop impacted everything around it, creating ripples throughout the world. Both had strong points of merit, but no one knew which one was the correct answer.

"Okay. Well, let me take you to a place that will relieve you from all dark emotions and reconnect you to what is justly important and beautiful. It is well worth the effort if you take the chance; trust me. You can come, too, if you want, Halo." She turned to the small girl who stood silently watching as Jaina moved toward the wide staircase behind the large diamond throne.

Kallen did not know if she was truly serious. The Staircase of Seventeen Thousand Steps was among the holiest of the relics within the temple—a paradox considering that the entire temple complex was the holiest of the relics, with exception of the Throne of Creation. The Staircase had felt the footsteps of the Heavens when thousands of Legionnaires marched down from Heaven to defeat the forces of Hell. Not to mention that with how many steps there were it would take all day to travel to the top.

Kallen felt a chill shake through his body when he let his imagination take over so he could picture the power. He looked over toward the throne; a regal, winged angel sat upon the throne, looking down the temple's main corridor. He imagined rattling armour echoing within the open cavern as Legionnaires marched down the staircase, splitting around the throne and marching out in perfect harmonious unison toward the war beyond.

"Umm … are you coming?" Jaina interrupted his vision, and another chill crept down his spine as he turned and took the first couple steps of what would be a long journey. No one had actually counted the steps, but those who climbed it claimed their legs felt as though they had marched seventeen thousand steps. Looking back, he saw that Halo did not share Jaina's enthusiasm; her big eyes, wet with the beginnings of tiny tears, were wide with fear of the stairs. She picked up her bucket and returned to watering the trees.

Together the two of them climbed the stairs, making their way to their destination slowly. It was a long climb, but one that he did not notice or mind as they conversed. She did not broach the subject of his emotional distress, instead distracting his thoughts. Carefully listening more than talking, he found her small talk relieving and enjoyable. The cool air became more difficult to breathe the higher they rose, and the light grew ever brighter upon their eyes.

"So you have come here before? Defiling one of the Order's holiest of places with your human presence, as some would claim, all for calm and serenity. Such an action carries great risk, even for the foster daughter of the terrifying gatekeeper." The growing soreness in his calves from the hours of climbing was starting to overtake him. He looked over the edge of the staircase to see just how far they had climbed.

"Some risks are worth taking in life, Kallen."

The sunlight was harsh upon their faces as they broke out of the mountain peak, their eyes slowly adjusting to the brilliance that shone down upon them. Breaching through to the mountaintop, he understood what she was talking about. For years he had visited the temple and the Sacred City, astounded by their articulate beauty and the art with which they were constructed. This view, however, put all else to shame. His mind spun in awe. He looked down upon the snow-capped peaks of the marvellous Alakari mountain range that surrounded them far beneath. He could see the perpetual Four Falls as they carried the waters that surrounded the mountain out into the range, the water's life-giving powers sent out into the remainder of the world. Following his companion, he continued away from the staircase, walking across the flat peak and taking in the panoramic view around them.

Beneath their feet, Kallen believed he should have felt the thunderous waters of the mountain falls, or at least heard them. Looking over the edge of the platform, he watched the endless volume of water plummet back toward Earth, shattering upon the ice and mountain rock below. Far beneath, Kallen could barely see the five white circular walls of the fortress perched upon the lake shore.

"This is the beauty that the angels perceived of our world. Quite amazing, is it not?"

No response came from Jaina as she stood opposite him, silently gazing down upon the pristine waters. Joining her, he took in the view that had her captivated.

Protected between the two mountain ring walls, the Sacred City nestled within their protective arms high above the lake. The cathedral and the numerous bell towers and high arched bridges stuck out among the numerous gardens and foliage. The high viewpoint gave him a different perspective of its beauty but stirred his emotions away from the calm.

Within the magnificent city lived thousands of Fallen citizens, the population growing larger with the influx of refugees into the Valley of Angels. People's lives would soon be threatened by the chaos and death that was ready to ravage what remained of their worlds. He was supposed to protect and save such lives from the threat that loomed on the horizon. Looking back over his shoulder to the opposite horizon, he stared toward where such violence and chaos resided. The evil hunted them night and day, growing stronger with each passing day. The deep mountain range would not protect them from the violent kingdom of Metzon or its bloodthirsty monarch. He closed his eyes, trying without any success to reset his mind.

"So tell me how someone can still look so unhappy when a view such as this lies before your feet? When you can reach up and touch the glory of Heaven?"

Kallen mentally regained his composure, realizing he was carrying his emotions physically. Reopening his eyes, he saw that Jaina's eyes looked into his, where she could easily see his turmoil.

"How can one not be unhappy when such news overhangs us all? My mind already grows weary from all the bad news, and the tough times have not yet come to knock on my door. So many refugees and sad tales of lost love and fear make it difficult to enjoy what small joys are found in everyday life."

"And beneath all the sad tales and that horrendous fear lies the true joy of life. It is the invigorating cool air within ever deep breath that a person takes, the warmth of the sunlight upon our skin. Every day is a gift in the beauty of small things often forgotten. Live in the moment, Kallen, not in an unknown future or the past that you cannot change. You may die tomorrow; you may die a century from now, which is why every day should not be wasted." Reaching for his hand, Jaina squeezed it several times, seemingly trying to pump his spirit back up.

"I do not fear my own death; I fear my failure to protect those who deserve life. How can such darkness spread unchecked? Is there no balance within this world? How can mere mortals fight such an endless and immortal darkness?"

Jaina did not respond, letting Kallen continue venting, listening closely to his words as she contemplated her own response. Kallen let his emotions flow, the fears and worries that kept him up for nights with no reprieve because they had no answers. Such events were not within his control; he wished he had the power of Heaven to alter the trials to come with a single thought.

"What about those around me, those whom I love and care deeply about? What about them and their unknown future? What does one do when their unknown futures may lie in these hands? People's lives are in my hands, and I feel them slipping through my fingers, unable to grasp them to save anyone. I'm responsible, and I fear for the fates of those who can fight as well as those who cannot."

"As all great leaders of men do."

Kallen listened to her words, their softness penetrating his heart and mind, trying to rouse the courage hidden within the depths. "Through great responsibility comes even greater strength, particularly in the heart of a hero, such as that which beats in your chest. You cannot control everything in your world; it is how the Heavens created the universe. Do not fear not knowing what is not meant to be known to you. Nor what you cannot control. Fear not living with what time you have instead." Placing a hand upon his chest, she tried to quell the fear of uncertainty within his chest.

"You are the grandson of Orion! First to Fall! The same blood flows through your veins as the man who built the Order of the Fallen to protect all from the evils of this world. Who stood before the Dark Gods and their hordes unafraid of what was to come, throwing the challenge before him against an even larger challenge. He did not challenge himself to defeat the enemy but challenged the enemy to try and break his powerful spirit and those of his loyal followers."

Kallen felt her fingertips wrap within his.

She did not present him with any time to reply or doubt himself and his abilities. "Orion did not rise up against his enemies alone, remember. I am the distant granddaughter of his best friend, one of many who perished in the great War of Beliefs. Like the first grandmaster of the Order, you have many strong and noble followers who will put their lives upon the line as quickly as you would. Some you have met and some are yet to come. It will not be an easy road, and plenty of sacrifice will be made, as it was by our grandparents.

"Our great-grandparents did not hold the answers or see perfectly into the future, Kallen. Losing much of their powers in the Great

Purge, they rose from the despair and took their new lives one day at a time. Not deterred by their sudden mortality, they followed the beliefs within their hearts and souls. One day at a time. One problem at a time. Approach the events to come the same way your great ancestor did."

Kallen remained silent. The more he thought about how he felt, the more confused he became. Every thought presented itself with ten more questions. The knowledge of being of Orion's lineage had not presented him with a clearer conscious or confidence. Now he felt the full pressure of following in footsteps far greater than his own with a new degree of responsibility. "I only wish that I was truly worthy of such a family."

She wrapped her arms around his neck, and Kallen found her violet eyes staring into his own. "You fear you are not worthy to be of the blood of one of Heaven's champions? Those around you do not believe such a worry is warranted, and I do not see many differences. Two great men stand upon this world, as darkness and despair rage around them. Both have a great love for this world and desire to protect everything within it. Both men do not stand alone but surrounded by their friends and allies. Both men shall stand in the gloom of the impending war, and both men shall rise from the remains to bask in the light once more, victorious."

Jaina had drawn herself tightly against Kallen's body while speaking; the scent of her perfume filled his nostrils as her fingers pulled his face toward her own. Her soft lips pressed gently against his, his mind going blank as her sweet taste surged through his veins.

"Everything happens for a reason; every thought of every living organism is connected within the web of life. One must feel the growing darkness to remember how fragile yet beautiful the light is. So tell me, Kallen." She stopped to smile at him. "Will you remember being within the light even in your darkest moments, knowing now what life has to offer you?"

Chapter 32
Sinful Brides

Watching the moon slowly creep across the sky, Brigade Commander Ferris moved through the guards on shift, conversing with them in an attempt to keep them alert at the end of their shift; he understood it was the most dangerous time, as sleep was on the minds of all men, his included.

Red speckled the small valley for miles along the road they had taken earlier in the day. Within it slept what remained of the homeless Kyllordic people, fleeing not only for their lives but for the preservation of the fundamentals they based their entire society on. Extinction loomed upon the horizon; how any slept when the future was so grim he did not know. Restful sleep had not come to him for weeks, far before setting out on their venture, which had too many problems they were ignorant of. No longer did he feel the safety and guidance of the Order; the presence of righteous confidence was slipping. Did they still know the right thing to do? Or would it even matter in the end?

He felt a moist warmth creep around his ankles and noticed a thick fog roll across the ground, continuing past him through the royal camp. He watched it move quickly, growing denser. He was soon enveloped in the thick mist up to his waist. The fog swirled back and forth through the camp despite the absence of a breeze. The warm fog encouraged his body to embrace the sleep he desired. Several drops of sweat fell from his brow, alerting him fully to the changes taking place around him. The humid fog had limited his visibility beyond an arm's length. The heavy heat was stinging his eyes in addition to making it hard to breath. Raspy breathing reverberated through the heavy fog closing in all around him. He set off in what he believed was the direction of the royal tent but tripped over a heavy object at his feet.

He stared down at the bloody head of his young captain, the dark sockets looking blankly back at him. Screaming at the top of his lungs, a louder, more sinister scream responded as a wraith raised its blade, its smouldering red eyes the last thing Ferris saw.

Ethan and Eli rose from their restless sleep when the shriek pierced the darkness; shouting and screaming filled the royal camp as everyone woke. The staff within the tent scattered quickly, reacting with confusion and fear. Ethan quickly made his way to the young prince's sleeping chambers to retrieve the prince, and Eli quickly stepped out the door of the tent.

The chaos within the camp was reaching its peak; all its members ran around without a sense of direction. The fog swirled fiercely within the commotion, with several columns reforming into the ghastly appearance of wraiths. One column swirled around the feet of a circle of soldiers and rose high inside the defensive circle, cutting down the unsuspecting with a flurry of savage swipes.

Several more wraiths swirled into the encampment, attacking a pair of spearman on one side of the camp and disappearing in a puff of smoke, only to reappear against new enemies on the other side. Soldiers lay everywhere. Those fleeing tripped over the bodies of the dead and did not receive the opportunity to rise again.

Within the confusion, one figure was not panicking, remaining calm as if completely immune to the death and despair. Eli could not believe her indifference to what occurred around her, seeing no sense of shock or panic. Eli took several steps in her direction without distancing himself from the prince's private tent, calling out Cleos's name. Watching her continue to drift farther away, Eli thought perhaps she was walking in her sleep, and he called out to her again, to no avail.

A new rush of smoky fog raced into the centre of the camp,

reforming into a tall column that blocked his view of the prince's fiancée. Eli gritted his teeth at the thought of letting the girl go, knowing how irate the young prince would be.

The palace stable master and his sons rushed in behind Eli leading a train of frightened horses they had been pasturing at the edges of the creek. The broad-shouldered man and his four sons struggled to maintain the horses, wild with fear and panic, as they reared, pawing at the air. Clasping Eli by the back of his neck in old friendship, the stable master yelled into his ear over the chaos.

"General, get the royal family to safety! We will try and buy you as much time as we can. May our lives not be in vain …" The five men charged into the fray with nothing more than daggers and shoeing hammers. Other soldiers had taken up burning torches, trying to burn the wraiths after having no luck with their steel. Several of the wraiths did indeed burn, but not enough to turn the tide.

A commotion drew Eli closer to the tent. He feared the worst at hearing a struggle taking place within the tent itself. He pulled the heavy flap aside, and the Prince Raef and Ethan tumbled out onto the grass, wrestling with one another.

"Where is Cleos? Where is she!" the prince screamed, trying to break Ethan's grip as Ethan dragged Raef from the tent, shoving him violently. Despite his valiant struggle, the prince was unable to fight the strength of the old general.

"We don't have time! We will find her later. Now let's get out of here before you end up dead along with everyone else! Don't be a fool, dammit …" Raef continued to fight Ethan, who was unable to get him onto his mount. Eli grabbed the prince by the throat, squeezing his fingers hard to settle the man.

"She's gone! Gone! Gone! Gone! I saw it with my own eyes, so pull yourself together."

"We don't have time to put up with any more childish emotions! Grow up already and become the leader to our people that you're supposed to be," his sharp-tongued sister screamed, trying to maintain control of the wild mare she was clinging to with desperation.

"You shut your mouth!" The prince leapt to his knees, snarling toward his sister. Then he resumed his brawl with those around him. "I'm not leaving without her!"

"Oh, I beg to differ."

Raef's limp body fell back into Ethan's arms as the man released his grip on pressure points on his throat. Throwing him atop the stallion, the brothers bound his hands and legs, ensuring that his slumped body would not fall off. "Now let's make our escape before it's too late." Mounting their own horses, Ethan and Eli glanced over their shoulders as they rode away from the camp. The small family of stable keepers huddled tightly together with the remaining survivors, cowering amongst the burning chaos.

The figure appearing from the shadows caused both brothers to pull back on the reins. Towering above its minions, the new wraith attacked with a fury of flames and steel, decimating those bold enough to challenge the giant. The wraiths started to push the survivors into a tight group, circling them like a pack of wolves searching for the weakest link.

"No! Ride, Ethan … ride, Ethan!" Grabbing hold of his brother's horse's bridle, Eli started pulling both his brother and his horse away from the scene. The horse followed eagerly, trying to keep up with Eli's mount, driven by fear as the stunned rider watched behind him. Eli did not know what was to come, but he knew enough history to know that he did not want to be anywhere near the king wraith.

"How is he still alive …? It's him, Eli. It's him …" Ethan's voice quivered slightly, whether from disbelief or from fear his brother did not know. Eli did not care.

The figure raised mighty arms, and a circle of flames ignited around the survivors, trapping them within the wall of fire. The figure lifted its arms high into the air in great circles, the flames mimicking his action, turning the ring of fire into a cyclone that grew tighter and taller. The victims within the fire found themselves slowly incinerated as they were lifted into the sky.

"Locan," Ethan stuttered as he looked away from the carnage, eyes wide with shock. "It's Locan, Eli!"

Locan's long strides passed over the numerous bodies and the debris throughout the camp, working toward the exterior where the defensive lines of watchmen had once stood. While perhaps ample against a weak mortal enemy, they were no match for the Brotherhood's supernatural abilities. How many deaths had fallen to that rolling fog tactic over time, Locan had not bothered to keep track.

Purple threads were woven into the black cloaks of the two wraiths that came before him, waiting patiently for him to acknowledge their existence. Locan let them wait a moment longer, already knowing what they were going to report. Looking out at the main camp far down in the valley satisfied him that their human enemies had made it easy for them. Separating themselves from the main camp had been a crucial mistake that allowed Locan to spring his trap with minimal effort.

The warlord turned to finally acknowledge his subordinates.

Both were identical in all physical aspects, from their size and posturing to the way they walked. Locan would not have been able to tell them apart except for the masks shielding their faces. Neither had ocular holes; the thick steel plates followed the general contour of their faces. One mask featured a smile, the other a frown.

"Krysas. Krasys. The Blind Brothers of the Sin come to greet me, bearing disappointing news, I imagine?" Both blind from previous plights within their lives, Krysas and Krasys were quite remarkable in their unique abilities that allowed them to be deadly even without their eyesight. They heard and smelled their prey before they killed them. Although Humanity was easy to kill, blind or not, their skills were particularly useful when fighting others who had fallen from Heaven, who were far more subtle and dangerous.

"The royal family has escaped, Warlord ... I do not know how they escaped, but their bodies are not among the dead." A low hiss escaped around the steel plate as the frowning Krysas spoke, hands held firmly on two daggers attached to his hips.

"Did you see them run away with your own eyes?" Locan mocked them for his own amusement. The purple thread upon their black cloaks marked them as survivors of the War of Beliefs, from the clans of first Dark Gods, Dev'Azra and Xera. They were two of only a very few who had survived the great final battle. Locan's own cloak was threaded with the red of Nuor's former clan. United under the Brotherhood, they were as one, though all the dark angels of the past kept their clan colours. But Locan had no love for the Dark God or his witch wife because of their mark upon his past. However, that was not the blind brothers' fault.

"Of course you did not see them because they know how to remain shielded from our eyes. I thought that perhaps you could have smelt them as they escaped, but I suppose not. The young prince does not ride alone, though I doubt that even he knows with whom he rides." Even now the widespread influence of the Order continued to surprise him. Commanding and significant as an exterior body, the group also seemed to have infiltrated and influenced the surrounding kingdoms themselves, maintaining complete control over all facets.

"Do we pursue?"

Locan didn't respond. Whoever the prince rode with, the man's history was one very few who were still alive shared. Select few within the Fallen had chosen to join the ranks of the wraith hunters who hunted the Sin; it was a quick path to death. Locan had sent hundreds of the hunters to their deaths and thought their unique skill set had become all but extinct.

"No. We will not be able to find them if we cannot see them. These will be far more cunning, beyond the human mind. We accomplished our primary task. All else was merely for enjoyment." His lieutenants nodded, suddenly realizing what his lord was referring to. Few things within this world were able to hide from the eyes of Sin, which narrowed their list of suspects.

"Though we should not let them escape so easily. We may not be able to track them well, but there are others who can." Locan followed the trail with his eyes, peering off into the distance in the general direction they'd fled, to the Keeps. Now that he knew who his foes were, it would not go as they originally planned. His

A Mortal Mistake

foes would not allow themselves to become cornered without the ability to put up a significant fight. Locan would not give them the chance to catch their breath and reorganize. His lieutenants understood what his orders consisted of and set off quickly to issue commands.

"I am beginning to doubt the power of Lord Locan, Slayer of the Angels." A woman's voice spoke behind him, chiding him for failure. "You slay mighty champions among angels, yet weak and feeble humans escape your cunning thirst for blood."

The shrill voice grated and irritated him, her rudeness creating a fantasy of him snapping her thin neck. Looking like a thing of beauty, her soft skin and luscious pink lips beneath the large eyes were a farce. Cleos, queen-to-be of Kyllordic was not as she pretended to be. Locan had dealt with her kind for a lifetime, and despite the disguises they wore, he knew the truth was that they were ugly and vile creatures.

"Silence, witch. Do not try to insult what you do not understand."

"Oh, I understand more than you think, dark angel. I am not the fool you perceive me to be, nor blind to the world as you seem to be, much like the blind brothers."

"Perhaps I should make you so!" Locan wrapped his long fingers around her throat, lifting the witch high off the ground. "Your use does not require your eyesight. Perhaps you should live in the world of darkness in both senses of the word."

Caught off guard by Locan's sudden movement, she clawed weakly at his immovable grip, fear spreading within her black eyes.

"You know whose daughter I am, and you know who owns me. Doing harm to me would bring the death that you have so desperately fled."

Locan laughed at her paltry threat and continued to squeeze her throat, watching her writhe back and forth. Her face grew old and haggard as she continued her futile struggle, the pockmarks and wrinkles on her face becoming apparent as her beautiful visage started to fade.

"Death has tried to find me for a long, long time, witch. I could slit your throat to watch you bleed out; death would still steer clear of me, for it fears me. I know your purpose. I have known brides of darkness who came before you. I have known many brides of Neurus and how far his love for them truly goes. I could rip your limbs from your body, remove your voice and tear away all your senses. As long as you have a heartbeat you will suffice for your purpose."

Throwing the witch roughly to the ground, Locan watched her tumble among the dirt and blood. Locan hated witches almost as much as he hated angels. Remembering the first witch, Xera, her black eyes and the tendrils of witchcraft creeping from her hands as she ran them over his skin still gave him a slight chill, even though she'd died a thousand years ago.

He was looking into similar black eyes. Stepping forward, he kicked Cleos hard in the gut and watched her writhe in pain.

"Now let us leave this place. It is time for me to send you back home."

The small group of escapees looked across the wide plains toward the bridge crossing the Gorga River that flowed rapidly and protected the Keeps. A small segment of the Kyllordic army had already reached the gates and set up camp in preparation for the arrival of the main population. Several small groups of civilians were winding along the dirt path, choosing speed over the safety of travelling with the army.

Constructed over three large islands surrounded by the fast-swirling currents of the Gorga, the Keeps of Kyllordia had been King Oberon's father's idea to provide a safe refuge for his people in the event that their borders fell. He had felt the strength of his neighbours' armies firsthand.

Eli looked up at the first bridge of the three. On the far shore its stone pillars rose high into the sky. The first bridge was the largest, wide enough for six wagons to simultaneously cross the light brown stone causeway. The banks of the first island were sheer cliffs rising twenty feet above the swirling waters below, requiring a large earthen ramp be built on the shore side to level the bridge. At the first sign of trouble, the gatekeepers on the island would release the chains and lower the bridge into the depths of the river, thus isolating the island.

Ethan and Eli had toured Oberon's Obsession, the nickname the sanctuary had earned, several decades before it had ever been completed. The first isle was the largest, containing the farmland required to sustain the population. The second isle rose thirty feet above the first and housed the cities and villages of the displaced population; the third island contained the palaces of the royal families and the army barracks. The Keeps had been built in a non-Kyllordic style, its buildings constructed of stone and displaying more functionality than artistic design. King Oberon had commanded that everything be built quickly and solidly, with the art to be completed once all other features were complete. But the king never got to see his creation finished; his heart stopped in the darkness of night far too soon. The Royal Council broke apart quickly after, and the Keeps were forgotten, and resources were shifted to other projects. Without the artistic Kyllordic touches, the Keeps felt cold and impersonal to the Elithane brothers. Perhaps they would finish the Keeps now; they would have little else to do if the bridges sank beneath the waters ahead of the Metzonians.

"Lady Kyllone. This is where we part ways. Ride hard for the gates, and do not slow down until you reach the Keeps." Ethan squeezed Oberon's daughter's gloved hand and smiled kindly toward her. "Those of you sharing mounts, ride with her down to the camp, recruit fresh horses of your own and rejoin us."

Sylvanna did not move. Her eyes were wide. "You're not staying at the Keeps?"

"No. We pray that the last ship has not left yet, and we must ride to Mendolin with all haste. We have come to a fork in the road, and we must now take separate paths. Hopefully we will meet again, but we cannot know for sure. You must lead and protect the Kyllordic people until their king returns to them. Beware of all things, and stand strong in this time of peril."

Her fear was visible as she fought back tears. Eli rode upon to her other side. He wrapped her in a tight hug, rubbing her back with one arm. "You can do this, Sylvanna. We will not forget or abandon you within your father's Keeps, but there are several things we must do first. Perhaps you can finish your father's vision for his Keeps. He would have liked that. Keep busy, remain vigilant and heed the advice of those around you whom you have known all your life."

Sylvanna nodded silently, tears escaping. "What of my brother?" She watched her brother, who seemed to be asleep atop his war horse. He had not woken since the attack, which clearly worried her deeply.

"We will protect him and return him to you at some time. He has much to learn and realize about his life, and we'll need a careful eye on him. Meanwhile we must bring word to the remnants of the Order about the elusive force that has been hunting us. Quickly now; time is not on our side anymore. Do not fear, though; we will find a way to right things. Now ride and protect your people." Eli watched the group set off toward the tall bridges.

He hoped that he would see the glorious bridges again in the future, but as he looked upon them, he saw visions of billowing smoke and crumbling supports. Was it the future or merely his mind running away with her fears? Eli led the group away, turning his back upon what remained of his home. He no longer had a choice about what needed to be done and could not risk the greater good for what he had grown to love.

Chapter 33
Black Prince of the Flame

Five days they had marched through the Wasteland of Aedanica, forever looking upon the distant mountain that lay ahead in the distance. As they neared the peak, they realized they had not been scaling a mountain for the past two days but a dreadfully active volcano.

The mountain shook beneath their feet, expelling ash and rock around them. The poisonous gases had already caused massive headaches while they had trudged through the Wasteland for the past week. Trying to avoid the worst of it, they had taken an old road known as the Weesic's Ridge Road that wound back and forth through the land, high above the gaseous land beneath them by a couple hundred feet. They could not avoid the gases completely; the fumes wafted up though the air as the land rumbled far below.

"Wish we were out of this putrid-smelling land already." Belle rubbed her eyes, trying to relieve them of the ash and smoke. Listening to her complain reminded Conrad of the stench-filled jungles of Valkedia. Conrad would rather live in the wastelands for years in comparison to the soaking wet Black Jungles.

"We are almost on the summit; be patient. The pieces have nearly fallen into place, with only a couple more to fall. We have sent the majority of the Kyllordic forces scurrying, and the Order of the Fallen has been decimated and is unable to turn the tide now." Sven twisted in his saddle, looking at the steady procession of the group behind them. "With this final piece in place we will be able to begin our invasion of the Alakari and find what remains of the Order to complete our revenge."

"I'm guessing that our scouts have managed to follow the path of the refugees to this 'hidden' city?" Belle asked. They continued to ride up the steep path, seeing the structure entrance above them.

"It's hidden within the Alakari mountain range—high up within them would be my guess. Scouting parties that have gone in particular directions have seemed to disappear off the face of the world." Sven spoke but did not look at either Belle or Conrad, continuing to ride behind the Dark Princes, who had joined them as anticipated.

"Well, that is a rather vague description; it could mean a week of travel or three months. I would think for as long as they have been working on it they should have found it. Clearly someone is protecting it. Wouldn't happen to be your long-lost brother, now would it?"

The only response was a snort from Sven.

"Frederick's time will come." Conrad chose to look forward when he felt Sven's stare on the side of his face as he spoke. He would not be dragged into another argument about his brother's loyalties. Conrad had refused to think about what Sven would do to their remaining brother. "He will have plenty of opportunity to forsake the Fallen and rightfully join his brothers. I would like him at our side, but if he does not … I will not hesitate to strike him down."

Reaching the peak, Conrad stared into the abyss and observed the temple that stretched out far over the tops of volcanic Aedonica, the ancient altar that sat on an open platform in the middle of the volcano. Seven great chains the thickness of a fully grown man stretched out across the abyss, securing the temple, which otherwise would have plunged into the rivers of molten rock below.

Both Dark Princes of Hell opened their great wings and glided over the volcano above the spitting globs of molten lava, leaving the

A Mortal Mistake

humans to take the lone rickety suspension bridge to the hanging temple.

The riders dismounted as they prepared to cross and join their demon lords. Peering down into the throat of the volcano, Conrad panicked, clutching the chain as his brother shoved him from behind, much to his amusement and that of the men around them. Conrad shoved his brother back with one arm; the only response he got was a wide grin. Belle smiled and sent Conrad a wink as they followed the king toward the altar.

The last of the Fallen prisoners were dragged out onto the suspended bridge by their guards; the scraping of their chains against the rock planks echoing within the crater. These were the last of the Fallen; unable to escape Prokopolis, they had been dragged across Kyllordia behind the marching armies. All prisons within Metzon were empty; the Order's presence was completely silenced throughout the free nations.

The forlorn faces of the prisoners showed they had at last accepted their fate. In the beginning, the Fallen Prokopolites had resisted at every opportunity imaginable. They had used every conceivable weapon—rocks, tree branches, teeth and nails—to try and kill their captors, succeeding countless times and raising the wrath of Conrad's brother. The Fallen had paid for each act of violence as one by one their limbs were chopped off. One could likely follow the path from Prokopolis through Kyllica to the Aedonica by the lost limbs alone. Even that did not halt the Fallen. Conrad and Sven were forced to sift through the masses to find those who initiated the majority of the violence. Since the last cull, the remaining Fallen had been unusually quiet as they returned to their silent prayers, seeking not the help that they knew would not be arriving but one last chance at forgiveness.

Philotheos stood silently at the back, watching those he called family wait patiently for the end. Managing to avoid the major culling of the revolt leaders, he had saved himself for the last act of defiance. Awaiting his final moments had given him the time to think about his life as a mortal, a life that none of them ever imagined they would have experienced. He could not say that he had regrets about it; mortality had been almost a gift for him. Mortality had given him a deeper and stronger love of life. Life was short, but its moments could be most beautiful. One could not compare its beauty to the kingdom of Heaven, but it could be more readily felt. Time was not infinite, making him realize how to enjoy the moment he was in and the beauty around him, for it would flee at the slightest change of the wind. He used to be able to fly for days and not have to worry about what tomorrow would bring.

When he began fearing death for the first time, he did miss all of what he used to have. He knew that death was his release from this world and he shouldn't be worried; he merely wondered if he would get the second chance in Heaven he dreamed of—that all the Fallen dreamed of.

Staring down the length of the bridge, he watched the Metz brothers climb onto the large temple perched precariously over the lava flow. Philotheos had heard all about the rift between the two brothers, including the murder of Conrad's best friend—yet another body added to the pile of Fallen corpses that Sven created. Philotheos wished he could sever the temple chains and send them all to the bottom of the world with him. He signalled those ahead of him that it was nearing their final time and watched as they silently sent the message forward. Without attracting the attention of the guards, as the prisoners filled the black platform each looked back at him to signal that they were ready to accept the plan and to attempt to do their part.

"The Balance shall always find a way to right itself. May the Heavens have mercy on all your souls, and shall your Father forgive his sons!" Philotheos called out to the Metz brothers, who stopped in their tracks as the words settled down upon the group. A guard stepped forward, the hilt of his sword raised to silence the Chronicler.

"NO!" Rhimmon cried out, his arms outstretched, but it was too late.

Philotheos threw his arms forward, his manacles hitting the

large guard across his head; he grabbed on to the man's breastplate and pushed him toward the edge. The remaining prisoners forced themselves upon their captors, using their abused bodies with every last bit of strength for a last battle of defiance. Eluding their guards for a moment, all of the prisoners raced forward to follow their leader over the temple edge to their doom below.

Watching Fallen leap over the edge by the dozens, Philotheos continued fighting alongside the dozen men his ankles were chained to. As the last groups of prisoners leaped off, he knew his time had at last come. Shuffling as far as the lengths of chain between his legs would allow, he leaped over the edge toward the rolling lava far below that could grant him freedom.

The chains snapped taunt, the resistance working its way down the line until it at last reached Philotheos and broke his spine as the extreme force reefed through his ankles. Coughing and screaming in pain, he twisted his neck to look, knowing his plan had somehow faltered. His arms wrapped through a huge link, Conrad held on to one of the guard's chains. The massive weight of the string of prisoners tore at his shoulders and slowly weakened his grip.

Philotheos's skin seared as he looked down upon the sea of red and orange, the heat threatening to cook him alive. He could not see Rhimmon and Mammon, but he heard them reciting the dark rituals required to release the last of their evil poisoned hierarchy; the demonic words filled the crater. He looked upon the grimacing face of the youngest Metz, feeling shame for him, for he knew not what was truly happening in his own world. Even for the older brother Philotheos felt some pity, knowing how both had been manipulated and controlled till they were unable to turn away from the path.

"Conrad, mighty Metzonian prince … it is true what they say about the strength of your spirit … Your father would have been proud of you, and still is. I bet that he has … not forgotten you … as you have forgotten him … and all he once stood for." Philotheos struggled to maintain his gaze on the youngest prince. Next his eyes found the Chilsa empress, and then they rested on Sven.

"If only your brother … had loved him as much as you … and perhaps stayed his blade a moment longer. Certainly you can finally see … the truth now. Look at … all Sven has done … Frederick … Cassidus … your father!" he gasped. He felt his skin turning liquid and his blood starting to boil. The heat threatening to steal his last breaths, Philotheos managed his final remark upon Earth. "See through your love for him. See the monster inside. Good-bye … Child of the Fallen!"

Tears evaporating on his cheeks, he locked eyes with the man holding his fate, watching the poor soul try to piece the puzzle together and realize the full picture. Conrad's shoulder joint dislocated, and his last effort to hold on to the Fallen faltered as his grip gave way.

Rhimmon and Mammon watched silently from the end of the platform as their captives tumbled into the lava.

Tremors rippled from deep within the bowels of the volcano, with lava and volcanic ash erupting into the air. Ash billowed from beneath the temple platform as the lake of lava rose rapidly within the dome. The Temple of Adramaleck shook, the massive chains holding it in place and absorbing the shock. It continued to float over the superheated air.

Sven quickly looked away from his brother, not knowing how to explain his actions. He could feel his brother's presence behind him as he stared into the rising flames beneath them. As he looked up to speak, he was hit by Conrad's left fist, which knocked him to his knees. Sven watched his brother swell in size as anger and rage filled his heart; Konflikt threatened to burst through once more. Conrad rained blows down upon his brother with his one good arm, and Sven watched his brother struggle emotionally. Conrad screamed violently as his mind ruptured.

Sven felt the tendrils of darkness creep back through his veins, but he resisted, knowing if he gave in his brother would die. His temper flaring, he took one final blow from Conrad and then kicked out at Conrad's knees to knock him on all fours. Rolling to his feet, Sven lashed out, kneeing his brother in the head, steel greaves deeply slicing Conrad's forehead. They wrestled back and forth on the platform. Sven struggled with his brother's immense size before letting the darkness within his heart flow to his limbs, granting him renewed and indisputable power. He yanked at his brother's dislocated arm, and Conrad screamed out in physical pain, adding to his emotional pain. Sven rolled on top of him and then picked Konflikt off the ground. Hand clenched tightly around his brother's throat, Sven held him over the chasm that was filling quickly as the volcano continued to gain steam. Sven stared hard into the blue eyes, tightening his grip. Blood streaked down across Conrad's right eye; his legs dangled over the edge.

"You murdered a million Prokopolites! You murdered Cassidus! You murdered our father! For what, Sven, you tell me for what! You traded our father's life for what? Power? Immortality? Glory? What did the Dark Princes of Hell promise you? You tell me what our father's life was worth!" Conrad kicked out wildly, his hand wrapped around Sven's wrist that gripped his throat as his brother continued to hold him out of striking distance.

Jaws clenched tightly, Sven continued to feel the hatred through Conrad's eyes that were locked upon him. Pain struck at Sven as he saw his mother within his brother's blue eyes, remembering why he did what he had done.

"His life was worth your life! I did what I did *for you* ... Your foolishness in following me to the Deserts of Lost Souls changed the course of my destiny. *For you* ... I embraced the darkness completely to save a life, *your life*! For you ... Everything that I have sacrificed has been for you! *I gave up everything for you*!" Sven's body shook as he spoke loudly, forcefully, on the verge of tears that tore at his heart for the first time in years.

"If I hadn't killed our father, you would have *died*. If I hadn't released Rhimmon, you would have *died*! I was granted a choice, Conrad! It was your life or his, so I made the difficult choice ... and I picked *you*! For my sacrifice and that of our father's, *you* walked out of the Desert of Lost Souls alive ..." Sven watched Conrad's eyes glance over to where the two Dark Princes stood around the altar, their backs turned from them, knowing they listened to the heated argument behind them.

"You should have let me die, Sven …"

Sven watched the rage subside within his little brother as great tears streamed down his bloodied face. Trapped within his emotional agony, his soul had somehow temporarily broken free from the evil grip. Sven was astonished as he watched his brother regress back to humanity, something he had never accomplished.

Conrad struggled with the last few words. "Do what you should have done in the Desert. What you should have done in the throne room. Release me from this suffering. Just let go."

The teary blue eyes staring at Sven moved him as he felt the powerful pulse of his brother beneath his grip. Flexing his fingers, Sven slowly felt himself loosening his grip, giving in. His brother smiled at him weakly. As his grip was just about to release, Sven felt it retighten. Looking at his bare wrist, he saw the black taint surge into his hand, refusing to release his brother. Catching a brief glimpse of Rhimmon smiling over his shoulder, Sven pulled his younger brother back onto the platform and dropped him onto the temple floor again. Conrad collapsed on all fours, tears running out of one eye, blood from the other.

Reaching into his pocket, Sven pulled out the Ring of the Order and dropped it upon the platform before his brother.

Conrad reached for the spinning ring, the darkness descending down his arms the closer he got to the ring. Sven watched him pause, flexing his fingers before it. "I don't want to remember the mistakes of our past anymore, Sven. And I certainly do not want to remember the future horrors we are undoubtedly bringing to this world."

Sven watched Conrad send their father's white ring over the edge with a single flick. His brother had given in to the darkness, the burden of knowing what they had done too great for him to bear. Hoping that the amnesia would last forever, Sven knew the truth of it all. The beauty that once was amnesia turned into the horrible nightmares that would never end until the release of death.

All joined Rhimmon and Mammon on the altar platform; they watched silently as the eruption quickened, the volcano's contents spilling out through vents cut below the level of the temple base. A violent crash shook the temple, followed by consistent, systematic tremors of something stirring beneath them.

"Who summons me from the depths of the world, trapped within my prison? Through the fire and the flames shall I, Adramaleck, Dark Prince of the Flame, rise! And from me shall the world burn within the flames of Hell." A molten hand slammed at the edge of the altar. The tips of the wings stretched out above, burning off any lasting residue of magma. Adramaleck pulled himself up onto the altar to face those before him, his red skin continuing to burn with flames as molten rock dripped off his body.

Booming laughter roared from his massive head. He bared his sharp yellow fangs as he howled. Three clawed fingers hit the floor as the demon continued to laugh, the curved horns on each side of his head cooling to a glossy black. Molten red skin splotched with great streaks of black covered his armoured exoskeleton. Grand black wings with burning edges speared high overtop them.

"My brothers! What took you so long? I have only been stuck in this prison for ten thousand years; it is about time someone came to visit!" The demon's mouthful of fangs grinned at his own joke, casting only one glance over the humans that surrounded his hellish brothers.

"I am going to assume that greater events are already in motion."

CHAPTER 34

BLUE TREE OF MENDOLIN

Dawn broke out over the wide forested valley, bringing life back to the silent road that the company travelled. On the hill, Ethan and Eli looked down upon the small town tucked away in the valley's midst, the stone bell tower in the centre of the town marking it clearly from the wooded forest. A short winding road could be seen leading toward a long riverside harbour; a small convoy of loaded wagons was already heading out of town. Two wide riverboats sat in the harbour, already piled high with cargo, masts raised as the crew prepared to debark.

"Well, let's hurry. Looks like they are preparing for the last departure. We certainly want to be on those ships before they set sail or we will never make the Sacred City." Ethan reached into his saddlebag and pulled out his silver and white banner, replacing the Kyllordic green on his pole. Several of the guards followed suit.

"So you finally show your true colours, you traitorous bastards!" Raef glared upon the men around him, realizing all were hidden members of the Order. His arms remained bound to the saddle, but he had been awakened from his dreamy state, in which he had heard everything but was unable to interact.

The lives of his nation had been tossed into his sister's hands when he was forced to accompany the generals on their quest to some unknown town. Despite the mutinous command of his father's generals, his mind was trapped within his memories. As his mind repeated the events of the night he lost his love, he felt he was on the verge of madness.

Over and over he dreamed of the attack, his imagination taking control for portions that he did not recall or had not been a part of. In one vision, he saw Cleos being carried off by the brigands that had attacked the camp. Another had her falling to the blade of enemy soldiers as they rolled through the camp. Of all the visions, one portion had been crystal clear every time: the beginning, when he was dragged away from the fray by Ethan and Eli. It was not his fault, it was theirs. The two of them had taken his kingdom away from him, and now they had taken his love away from him. Not even the sacrifice of their firstborn children would be enough to win his forgiveness.

The procession rode quickly and hard, the heavy thundering hooves echoing off the road among the forested trees. The trees blurred behind them as they raced down the road, the high bell tower growing closer as they surged toward the town of Mendolin. The surroundings seemed to fly behind him, and yet Raef swore something moved equally fast in the same direction. He only caught fleeting glimpses though and could not confirm if he saw anything. At their current speed, nothing would have been able to keep up, especially through the heavy forest brush.

A wooden barricade was now visible across the narrow road before them. Two dozen infantry quickly readied themselves at the sudden sight and sounds of the force moving swiftly toward them. The commander strode forward, raising his hands high toward the visitors. The horsemen slowed slightly from their breakneck speed.

Raef leaned forward to look past the soldier riding beside him, trying to see if he could see anything in the forest moving at a slightly slower pace. He peered closely but saw nothing. The guard partially blocking his view suddenly disappeared. His horse collapsed to the ground, throwing its rider. Looking quickly behind him, Raef saw dozens of large wolves racing toward them, snapping viciously at the rear riders' horses' legs, dropping them to the ground. Several small packs of wolves appeared along the banks and jumped over the embankments to land among the company, knocking riders off their mounts.

Bracing himself for impact, Raef felt his horse lurch as its hind legs were caught in the sharp teeth of its attacker. His horse skidded wildly as it ploughed through the soft, dark soil, kicking out with all limbs at the large wolves. Commotion overtook all of them as men and horse screamed together, growls and tearing of flesh filling the gaps.

Fear filled his heart as he watched one soldier hack down one large wolf, only to be taken down by another and dragged away by his neck. More wolves continued to run out of the forest around them, joining their brethren in the frenzy. Raef's hands were still bound to his saddle; he was unable to free himself to escape the wolves or defend himself. Even growing up in the great forests of Kyllordia, Raef had never seen wolves such as these before. They stood tall and feral, with coats as black as night and bloody eyes. The wolves stood higher than a man's waist. Despite their lanky appearance, the thickly muscled beasts were vicious and wild in mind. He caught the eye of a newly arrived pack member as it began a quick dash toward him.

Helpless against what was to come, Raef once again prepared himself for death. He was temporarily spared when an Order soldier threw his spear from the other side of the road, dropping the wolf in its tracks. Raef watched as the soldier who saved his life quickly gave his up to a pair of wolves that pulled his legs out from under him. The attacking wolf's companion leapt over its dead body, continuing on its course toward him, its razor sharp teeth already bloodied.

A steel boot kicked the beast in the head, sending the creature tumbling to the side before Eli's large spear pierced its throat. Spear in one hand and sword in the other, he slew several other wolves before being joined by Ethan, who cut Raef's bonds, releasing him.

"Come on, son; let us send these beasts back to Hell."

Raef picked up the spear of a fallen soldier and moved forward, Ethan and Eli on each side of him. Barrages of arrows flew through the air as the guards at the gate attained a distance where they were able to help out the defenders. Their attackers bared their teeth before quickly retreating back to the bush when their numbers started dwindling.

"What was with those feral beasts? I apologize that we could not help you sooner, nor save more lives." The barricade commander looked sullenly at the bodies around them among the numerous dead.

"No one has come down these roads for more than a month, so you are rather a large surprise. Fortunately the last river ship has not yet debarked, though you are cutting it close. We are expected to leave before high noon and are merely awaiting the runner. As unnecessary as it may seem, we must ask you for your names."

"My name is Eli Elithane, and this is my brother, Ethan. Both of us are of the Order of the Fallen, and this is Prince Raef, Lord of Kyllordic people. We are pledged to his protection and well-being and seek the safety of the fortifications of the Forgotten. Sounds like we are not the only ones who have sought its safety."

"Unfortunately not. Since the Fall of Prokopolis, chaos has reigned through the land. We have been trying to collect the remnants of the Order for months, with very limited success. I have been told the majority of the vital members arrived safely and unharmed before Prokopolis fell. Since the fall of Kyllordia, survivors have dwindled even further."

"The majority of the members arrived safely? You mean the Elder Council escaped?" Ethan seemed astonished at the confirmation of the information they had heard. Raef had overheard the brothers discuss the grandmaster, saying how wise and far-seeing the man was. If he had been able to foresee what was to come, it still confused Raef to as to why he not rallied the Order in a defiant stand against their enemy. If they had, perhaps Raef would not be in the terrible situation he currently was in. At least his hands were free once more.

"I merely guard the road. It is not my place to say who survived and who did not, nor would I know truly know who is important and who is not. I do know, however, that one arrived with a large guard of steel giants. I assume he would have the answers you seek."

"We should hurry then; we bring word that must reach the

remains of the Elder Council and the grandmaster." Listening to Eli, Raef watched the distant riders race quickly toward them, the gates runner having summoned reinforcements. His attention returned to the roads commander, who refused to meet anyone's eyes. The rest of the group stared into the dark earth or high into the sky.

The knights pulled back hard on the reins, their massive white warhorses spinning tight circles. Eli and Ethan were surprised at the massive steel warriors that peered down upon them, their faces hidden behind steel. Raef had only seen the Titans once in the Elder Palaces of Prokopolis; he recognized them as the elite guards to the members of the Elder Council.

"If you seek the safety we all do, then come quickly. We are ready to leave." The largest knight of the group gestured toward the town as he looked around at the death surrounding him. Eli stepped toward the knight, pointing toward the numerous bodies.

"What of the dead? Certainly we have time to bury them."

"If only all our brethren were lucky enough to receive such an honour …" The lead knight started to ride away and then paused in his tracks, looking up at the sun. The Titan was lost in his thoughts for a few moments, and then guilt forced him to change his mind. "Bring them to the church. We must be quick, though, or we may miss our ride."

Helping the Fallen carry the dead to the cemetery behind the large stone church near the edge of town, Raef saw that the rear of the town overlooked the edges of a large rocky river mouth flowing from the lake in the distance. He wondered where they were going to bury the remaining soldiers who had fallen in the wolf attack. The graveyard appeared to be already quite full of headstones and tombs, despite its large size. A vast number of the headstones were greatly aged. In the midst of the cemetery a great tree grew over the tombstones beneath its outstretched branches. The leaves dancing in the breeze were every shade of light blue and shaped like tear drops prepared to fall to the earth.

"Surely you know that tree?" Eli saw Raef staring upon the great tree. Raef was still angry at both brothers, but Eli was relentless in his attempt to make Raef realise that they were only trying to protect him. For all it had cost him, he didn't care.

"I do, but I have never seen one alive before, only in books and the tales told by my father and grandfather. The Blue Tree of the Dragon. There isn't one within the Gardens of Kyllica or the Keeps anymore. At least not one that is alive." Raef looked at the branches stretching out over the large cemetery, reminiscent of the wings of the blue-leafed tree's namesake. The white trunk and branches were smooth and as hard as bare bone; blue sap wept from the smallest cracks on its surface.

"One seed every century. They were as rare back then as they are now. Their seeds were reserved for the greatest of heroes. I wonder what this particular individual did in the past that earned him the right to be buried with such an honour. You know your father had always dreamed of seeing one in bloom but never got the opportunity."

"How can you tell that it is blooming?"

Eli stopped to rest upon the handle of his shovel, pointing up at the leaves. "This one has already blossomed, and it is in its final stages of life. The leaves are changing colour. Look how light they are. Before long they will turn white and shed, and the tree will leave its skeleton in its place, much like we do. They say that all the blue trees in the world blossom at the same time. Can you believe that? Your children are likely to never to see one bloom in their lives."

"So it's dying?" A pang of regret stirred within Raef's stomach.

"Everything dies eventually, even the great trees. But the circle of life continues. Its seed will grow within the shell of its mother and eventually break through to take her place for another century. How do you think your grandfather got that magnificent bow upon your back?"

A blue hue still remained within the bow from its former life; his grandfather had his fletchers bend the branch into its bow form while it dried for two years. Deadly beauty was the end result of their hard work, a duplicate never being produced. It took great strength to draw the cord back, but the arrows flew with great force and much farther than from any normal bow. His head ranger had spent months building Raef's strength to use the weapon efficiently.

His grandfather had told him stories of his ancestors seeking the blue trees in the fiercest storms because they were immobile against the strong wind and provided a large protective umbrella. Raef picked up the bow that his grandfather had taken from a great branch of such a tree. Using a jagged rock, the man had spent months scraping the stone-like surface of a dead branch before reaching the living core to cut a blue bough from within the tree to make his bow.

"Shame that more are not around for everyone to see; people could remember the glory days."

"Indeed, they are like the sea dragons, so rare that few believe in the stories anymore. Perhaps in the deepest of unknown forests where even the Kyllordic rangers have not delved they survive. Who knows? Kyllordic kings of the past granted their seeds to their heroes as gifts for great deeds of valour in their service. When they perished, the seed would grow over the body to mark the spot they died for all to see."

Raef had read about how the sea dragons used to lick the sap of the trees, flying or swimming for hundreds of miles between trees. As the trees disappeared, so did the dragons. He mentioned the story to Eli, and the older man nodded thoughtfully, mentioning that the dragons would rise again with the trees and the cycle would continue endlessly.

"And what of the dragons when the trees go dormant?"

Eli looked at him mirthfully. "Well. Then they turn miserably hungry and eat the local cuisine instead."

Ethan looked up at both men, finally joining the conversation, a scowl upon his face. "Let's hurry up, guys. The last ship is almost loaded, and soon we will be leaving. Let us remember the solemn task at hand here."

The white flag bearing the crest of the Order caught the breeze that blew through the steep rocky cliffs stretching high above the swiftly

A Mortal Mistake

flowing river. A lone ship waited for departure, heavy ropes securing it as if it were a wild creature struggling for freedom. The bottom of the hull was flat and wide to avoid perils hidden beneath the frothy surface, and the sides were built high to keep the river from sinking it to the rocky depths.

Raef watched as the final preparations were being made, the final horses and supplies tied tightly, soldiers still clad in their heavy armour finding their places among the remaining spaces.

"Are they completely foolish? If our ship runs afoul, they will all sink to the bottom like a rock."

"Boy, if we crash on this river, all will die regardless. We are in Heaven's hands now, Raef. Find faith, and hope for the best. We cannot read the future because we would never truly experience life." Eli patted the younger man on the back, grinning at him, not at all easing his concerns. Raef could feel his stomach churn, but Eli turned away from him before he could protest and climbed the ladder to the small second deck at the rear of the vessel.

Following his father's friends to the second deck, Raef found it was a flurry of activity. Several of the helmsmen made final preparations; another man climbed the rope ladder to the small box beneath the large flag. Turning back to the group of men his protectors were heading toward, Raef was surprised that Eli recognized the man before seeing his face.

"Elder Damocles."

"Gentlemen, we are glad to see that you have arrived alive. There has been far too much death this past year within our ranks. So much death …" The new speaker did not turn around to address them, his eyes locked onto a heavy book. He was flanked by four of the large guardian knights, their armour painted a stark white in memory of their purity in service to the Heavens. It also symbolized their higher rank and position as personal guards of the high ranking Elder Council leader. They had sworn death debts to protect their leader, and they would not hesitate a moment to do so in deadly fashion.

"Listen to this passage. 'And fear reigned throughout the Heavens, as the Ancients purged their ranks, declaring that only the purest champions of the Light shall stand beneath their banners in their war against the darkness of Hell.'" He closed the book slowly, wrapping the lock around it as the man pulled it to his chest.

"Long have I wished to be hidden within the safety of that banner. To feel the warmth of its light, to feel its power run through my veins again—how I miss it. Perhaps then we could free this world from the death and destruction that is consuming it. I feel so hopeless against the darkness …" The robed figure shuddered slightly, the ripples flowing through his silver cloak down his back to his feet. Pulling himself upright, he finally turned to address them, pulling his hood back.

"Please forgive me for my moment of weakness. I feel more and more human with every setting sun, it would seem." The older man wiped a lone tear away from his right eye, pulling himself back together after his sudden lapse in emotion.

"Perhaps once we are all reunited we can turn the tide. Reorganize, reflect and return to the glory and good. Fight this darkness with a fury that will remind them of Heaven's Legionnaires, striking fear back in our enemies." Ethan offered his hand to the old man.

"We believe we have discovered who is spreading the darkness and chaos, which is why we have come to Mendolin in hopes of catching a ride to the Sacred City. We have news that must be discussed with the grandmaster and Elder Council. Our enemies have unknowingly shown themselves; no longer can they hide within the shadows." Joining his brother, Eli moved closer, embracing the man briefly under the watchful eyes of his guardians.

"That is indeed good news, although we already know who it is. Unfortunately they have struck so ferociously from the shadows that they no longer need to hide. They have thrown blows that the Order shall never be able to recover from. The Order has fallen," Elder Damocles continued in his soft tones.

Raef smiled upon hearing that the Order already knew who their enemies were, making their trip of little significance. No longer having a reason to travel to the Sacred City, they could quit the dangerous journey and return back to safety of the Keeps.

But hearing the despair within the Elder's voice brought Eli to anger. Raef knew the Elders were supposed to inspire and bring courage to the members of the Fallen.

"These are very pessimistic words coming from the Order's Architect! Perhaps you have forgotten all that we have all gone through, and yet we still stand. Through all our troubles, we have engineered a strategy to overcome them. We need you to help build the next plan, to rebuild the Order!"

"Do not give up on us yet, for we are not yet done fighting! We, as well as the rest of our brothers and sisters, refuse to give up and will not quit until the end of time. Stand with us; help us in our quest to right what has been wronged. Help us convince the grandmaster to reignite the fire within the Order's heart," Ethan argued.

Raef watched both men attempt to sway the Elder Council member, trying to inflate his spirit and mind. The depressed man refused to give any ground, having clearly thought out the situation and chosen his words wisely. Raef did not realize how quickly the old man's next words would deflate his generals' spirits.

"The Grandmaster has been slain, my brothers. I've waited months for him to ride down that road. Your arrival gave me hope, but once again my hopes grew too high with all that has passed. The Order has been shattered. Too many key pieces are missing within the structure to rebuild correctly. Too much knowledge and strength has been lost to engineer and rebuild anything that can stand against this impending darkness. Fear not, I have not given up on those around me. The task before us is simply of unimaginable proportions."

The heavy bells within Mendolin rang out one last time, chiming loud and clear, echoing into the rocking harbour. "Let us wait until we reach safety to further discuss matters such as these. Perhaps other survivors can provide additional information, as well as clearer thoughts than our own."

The four men who rang the bell one last time ran out onto the docks and leaped into the boat. Several others produced large ship axes and severed the vessel free from its moorings, releasing it into the mighty river, which wasted no time carrying the ship downstream.

CHAPTER 35
Merger of Darkness

The cool waters of the largest lake of Metzon chilled the night air as the trio sat between it and the base of the mountain. The waning moon cast few shadows upon the hills surrounding them, allowing them clear view of any encroaching visitors. All they had seen was a small herd of deer and a couple of lone coyotes that were traversing through the night.

Sven sat impatiently within the shadow of the Lost Mountain, the exact spot where they had been waiting for several days. He had been losing his calm three days before, and yet here they were, still waiting! Belle was sleeping silently among the craggy rocks where they had made their camp, while his brother skipped stones into the lake. Rhimmon had commanded them to await their arrival on the full moon, but apparently the dark demons followed a different moon than his own.

Perching beside Belle, he leaned his head back, listening to the stillness, disrupted only by his brother's annoying child's game. Conrad had not recovered after the confrontation of the Aedonica, leaving him distant from his brother. Quiet and lifeless, Conrad hadn't spoken a hundred words the whole trip back, leaving Sven to understand that Konflikt was here to stay.

"Cut it out before I knock your head off!" He hurled a rock through the darkness, dissatisfied that he missed his mark. Fortunately it seemed to stop his brother from what he was doing.

Sven reached for the bottle of wine to pass the time. Closing his eyes, he savoured the taste of the wine and the silence of the night. The brief silence was quickly shattered by the pattering of a large rock skipping across the water. Sven pulled himself to his feet, ready to pummel his younger brother to a bloody mess. Belle clutched his arm, pulling him back to her with a look in her eyes that made him lose all previous thoughts.

"My father's here …" She looked quickly around the camp, trying to distinguish where she felt his presence. Sven felt the chill cut through his layers, indicating without doubt the presence of her father. His angry heart pulsated against the coldness within his body.

"Show yourself rather than clinging to the night for safety. You continue to display how pathetic and feeble you are becoming, dwindling from power to weakness." Sven taunted the shadows, feeling the breeze quickly increase around the camp, as if infuriated.

"Stay your tongue, human, before it brings the end of your life! Foolish are those who believe that they are mightier than Brotherhood." Neurus spoke through the darkness as the smoky forms of two individuals materialized within the camp.

"Your mortal strength cannot match that of the immortal! We possess powers that will burn your souls and crush your bodies!" Locan's hand clutched Sven's neck, slowly tightening as his raspy voice slithered through the air.

Locan fell back as Konflikt entered the fray, throwing a heavy right hand into Locan and knocking him among the rocks. Konflikt stood tall beside his brother, fists clenched, ready for Locan to come at him. "And yet you too are mortal, except you fear death, where we do not!"

An axe appeared in Locan's hand, his eyes wide with rage that a human would dare strike him. He charged toward the young man, and Sven watched the wraith swing, prepared to cleave Conrad's head from the rest of his body for a trophy.

The clash of metal on metal caught them all by surprise, and the blade of Locan's axe shattered into hundreds of splinters. The collision sent Locan back where he started to look on the new situation forming before them.

A massive blade had been plunged in front of Conrad, protecting him, the black blade thick and broad, more ten feet long and a foot wide at its narrowest point. A large red hand clutched the hilt, causing the blade to blaze into an inferno of molten steel.

"Petty dark angels!" Booming laughter echoed among the mountain rocks, joined by a pair of equally intimidating laughs.

"Petty and weak they are indeed. They may still have their uses, however small." A large spear poked Locan, knocking him from his feet again. Mammon walked heavily behind the two fallen angels, herding them closer together.

"You foolish and pathetic angels. You call yourself strong and above Humanity! For ten thousand years we have been trapped within our eternal prisons, forced to observe with disgust the feeble attempts of the Brotherhood to take our rightful title. Ten thousand!"

"So we had to take matters into more capable hands; fortunately, your weakness led them to us. Had your 'mighty' empire been able to defeat him, we might never have had such champions. And you would have been able to continue your pathetic campaign to rule the world." Rhimmon showed himself, closing the group off completely from any escape routes and backing them into the mountain crags. Their large winged bodies cast vast shadows in the moonlight, their eyes shining in the darkness.

"Our plans are more sophisticated than they seem and have been moving like clockwork for centuries. Your sudden appearance has certainly changed things, but not everything. Do not dismiss us so easily, for we are more powerful than you may believe." Neurus spoke calmly, trying to control the fear Sven knew he felt. Sven sensed that the Dark Princes were enjoying the scent of fear and feeding off it.

The dark angel's shoulders began to smoke as his physical body began to slowly disappear. Locan followed immediately, joining him in twisting his form into whispery fog and then disappearing from sight.

Laughing loudly after the humorous escape attempt, the demons howled into the night. Mammon cast currents of electricity within the disappearing cloud, the currents passing between the particles, drawing them back together, reforming the smoke into its original forms. Mammon continued to torture the dark angels as they crouched upon the ground, their bodies convulsing, unable to escape.

"*Apparently our absence for so many years has turned you foolish. Have your forgotten our power, the fear that we inspire around the universe? Legions tremble at our sight, and yet you believe you can control your own destiny.*" Adramaleck threw both hands forward, and red flames licked their bodies, crawling along their white skin, inflicting further pain.

Rhimmon raised his hand, ceasing all torture as quickly as it started.

Staring at the charred and smoking bodies of the Brotherhood's leader and his faithful hound, Sven smiled at his enemies' pain.

"*Now you may rule, but in turn you will be ruled. It is a bargain that you will take, or you will find a slow and agonizing death, handed out over the course of what remains of your mortal lives.*"

"What exactly do you propose? Explain to us *petty angels* how we can be useful in comparison to such power? Why require us when you have the power to cleanse the world quicker without?" Neurus wheezed, slapping the flames off his burning flesh, barely clinging to life.

"*This world and its inhabitants are even more pathetic and weak than those of you who have fallen. We have grander ploys that stretch beyond this world, and powerful foes to wreak revenge upon. We would leave you to rule this world as part of the Realms of Hell, answerable to its rulers and lords to continue our dark designs for this world.*"

"*What!*" Sven shouted furiously. He turned his attention away from the Sin to confront the Dark Princes, letting them know of his anger despite their display of power only moments before. "What about us! We have succeeded where the weak Brotherhood *failed* …

and now we are thrown aside! We have not risen to the top to merely become puppets and servants to the Brotherhood!"

"Your purpose has almost come to an end. You may have the dark spirit of a demon, but your weakness lies in your physical abilities and mortality and will never become anything more."

Sven drew his sword, moving forward to attack Rhimmon, who had betrayed him for the last time. The demonic markings on his back stung as he wrestled Rhimmon for his mind. His knees suddenly gave out; he dropped among the stones. His vision started to blur as he attempted to regain his footing, struggling for every breath.

"I have let you keep the last bits of your souls so that you could continue to function and maintain control of your nation, a lesson I learned long ago from your uncle's weak mind when he snapped too soon. Now that it is insignificant, it is time that you give up the last bit of humanity that you've been holding on to. You shall be a servant of the darkness until the end of your time!"

Around him Sven saw the demons staring at him, stone faced; his brother and Belle stretched out on the ground screaming out in agony, as the remnants of their souls were consumed by the dark powers that flowed within their veins. Feeling the darkness start to consume him from the inside, he thought back to the beginning of this journey and where it had taken him.

Feeling the demon crawling through his veins for the final time, he looked back at his brother, lying motionless beside Belle. This was not what was promised to him; this was not how it was to end. Sven had accomplished everything the Dark Princes could have possibly desired, yet he still found Rhimmon's betrayal unsurprising.

Glaring into Rhimmon's black eyes, Sven knew in this final moment his hate bore the level of a true servant of Hell. Rhimmon underestimated both Humanity and Sven, or Devotz; his eternal soul was his and his alone. And he would return from the darkness for revenge.

Locan watched the pleasure spread across Neurus's face as his enemy succumbed to the darkness, filled with unbridled joy despite his own dire situation. Years of hate had haunted him whenever he thought about the Metzonian and what he had done to him. Neurus had hated the power that had grown within the defiant young man, who was fearless against anything the Dark God had set against him, to the point where Locan began to think that Neurus was fearful of what the monster might do next. But now the prince was no longer a threat. Locan knew his master's thoughts did not spread to the other members of the group: not to the incapacitated beast of a brother, not to the loss of his daughter.

"So what say you, Neurus? Rule and be ruled, or embrace the cold touch of eternal death?" Locan watched Neurus ignore the stares of the demons watching him calmly. A sense of panic began to form within Locan as he awaited Neurus's response.

"What is to be demanded of the Brotherhood and its warriors? What do you request of me?"

"You already know of the Metzonians' plans. They will proceed as planned, to begin as soon as you return. We will use our servant's army to crush those who have escaped its touch once before. We must remove the remaining Order members and the remaining servants of the Light." Mammon explained the beginnings of their plans, much of which Neurus had already known as he followed Sven's progress very carefully. Locan understood that they would never discover what the princes of Hell truly had planned for the Sin.

"The Brotherhood's warriors should also be there to help with more 'resistant' enemies, should the need arise. Assemble your army. We shall utilize it if we require. That includes your loyal lapdog as well." Adramaleck raised a large red finger, gesturing directly toward Locan.

His brother issued the next part of the orders to the warlord. "Succeed, and we may yet come to an understanding that may prove beneficial to you. What will be your decision?"

A Mortal Mistake

Neurus's attention returned to Rhimmon as Locan pondered what the Dark God would say. Was it the right choice? Did he really have much control over the choice? Neurus slowly looked back at his mortal enemy, still motionless among the rocks. Locan contemplated how the young man's choices had taken him the completely opposite direction he had likely intended. The Dark Princes could not be trusted; evidence of their betrayal lay before his master's eyes, but Locan knew that they would have little hope of winning this fight.

"I have one small request … the Metzonian. He is mine … forever." Muscles tensed as Locan heard Neurus's demand, unable believe his lord's mindset. His hate for the the son of Masen Metz continued to remain strong enought that he was willing to risk both their lives over some petty fued.

"Succeed and he and his companions are yours—only if he lives through this final test."

Limping forward, Locan watched Neurus stand between the three Dark Princes, staring up into their menacing faces. Their horned heads were full of sharpened smiles, eyes seething with malice, all waiting in anticipation for his next move. His master's old worn-out knees hit the rocky surface painfully as he slowly lowered his weakening body to the soil. Locan knew that Neurus's body was deteriorating at an insatiatble pace. As Locan's fate was connected to Neurus's, it was a problem they were desperately trying to resolve before death found him. All they needed was more time.

"Neurus is yours to command, as the Brotherhood of Sin is. Command as you will, and we shall obey for all eternity. To the glory of the Dark Princes of Hell and all whom serve you within your glorious domain." Locan shuddered as he listened to the words, lowering his foreheard to the cold ground as the Sin waited for a reply; he received none. No dark laughter came, or further taunts; there was no movement from any of them.

"A smart decision. You are free to put the plans into motion and await our messengers."

Picking himself from the rocky dirt, Neurus bowed slowly before turning his back upon the demons. The scowl upon the Dark God's face displayed his disgust at what he had done as he refused to meet Locan's gaze.

"*One last thing, Neurus …*"

Neurus paused to turn his head slightly to hear Rhimmon better. Locan took a step back as Neurus rose off the ground, struggling futiling as he became trapped within an invisible grasp. Rhimmon remained silent, a horrific scream bursting from Neurus as the demon began tracing an ancient symbol within the air before him. Locan watched the brand seared through his lord's flesh as the dark symbol burnt deeper to imprint itself upon his soul.

"*Just so that you never forget who you gave your soul to …*" Rhimmon released him, letting him plummet back to the ground. Neurus did not pull himself from the soil but winced in great pain as his bloody red eyes stared into Locan's. Both disappeared into the wind as Locan followed Neurus's lead as he disappeared back into the shadows in a whisp of smoke, leaving the princes and their puppets alone. Tonight's torture may have been over, but Locan knew the storm of torment was only beginning for the Sin.

"*I have a feeling that they will be more trouble than use, Brother. Despite their dark ways, they were still once members of the Heavens. Resistance against Hell is permanently imprinted within them.*"

"*Let us hope that we get most of their usefulness out of them before they can become trouble. And once they cross the threshold of useful to being a problem, we will kill what remains of them. A simple solution, though we still need them for the time being.*" Rhimmon acknowledged Mammon's concern, knowing that it would not be an issue that could not be quickly solved if need be.

"*No need to ruin useful resources. Use the disposable Brotherhood to slay their former friends and save your armies for the true enemy.*"

None of the Dark Princes spoke these words, and all became silent when a fourth figure appeared among them, shocking the demonic brothers Mammon and Adramaleck.

"Abaddon." The eldest of the demon brothers was not surprised to see Abaddon arrive from beneath the Lost Mountain. Rhimmon had always been aware of the taint upon Conrad's soul but had never known who was watching them through the mortal's eyes until Mammon's confrontation in the Black Jungles. Abaddon had placed himself in the midst of their grand plans through a deviously clever method.

"You do not seem thrilled to see me in the flesh once again, brothers."

Slightly smaller than all of them, the demon's skin matched the dark blue of the sky, making him invisible against the night sky. The demon's pale yellow eyes gave him away as he approached them. He looked much different from when the Dark Princes had last laid eyes upon him.

"You certainly look as weak as you have been in the past. I should have guessed that you would hide within the dungeons of the Lost Mountain instead of fighting. Though it appears that some heavenly whelp gave you a beating. You always were soft, Abaddon," Mammon growled at the newcomer, remembering their past. Mammon had long blamed Abaddon for abandoning him instead of saving him from his demise at the hands of the Legionnaires of Orion, though his enemy seemed in far rougher shape than himself.

"Taunt those who actually survived the last Great War of this world if you may, Mammon. But I did not spend the last ten thousand years within spiritual prisons." Abaddon had plenty of battle scars as a result of the last great battle he was in. His black wings had been shredded in several spots, likely impairing flight, and he was missing his left horn from an Ancient's blade that was aimed several inches lower.

"The past is insignificant, for we have more important objectives now. During your little sleep, I have been continuing our ancient plan and have been busy building our armies beneath this world. We are only now finally reaching the strength of the past. We are almost ready to unleash a new war, but we must eliminate the Fallen forces quickly and without alarm."

The prospect of their demonic armies being rebuilt, a task that was tedious and difficult, was welcome news to Rhimmon. Since their resurrection, the brothers had regained much of their powers but not to the point of regenerating their armies. Rhimmon was glad the survivor had undertaken such an immense task on his own but had an underlying feeling that he was missing the important information hidden within his words. His brothers also sensed something unsaid was underlying this conversation.

"All shall be slain, rest assured, but why without alarm? Who is possibly going to raise the alarm, as Heaven has not walked upon this world since they designated it as their prison world for sinful angels?"

"Not completely true, Adramaleck. Several centuries ago, a tremendously powerful heavenly presence was felt in their stronghold. Even within the depths of the world it was felt, though it did not linger long. None have been within the Ancients' mighty citadel, but a few of our scouts have reported feeling a small heavenly presence still residing within it. It is shrouded within the Light, though, and we cannot discover what it is. Eliminate it, or we fear our plans will encounter greater difficulty."

"Yet we are not overflowing with our enemies' numerous champions of the Light? Why?" Rhimmon stepped forward, trying to threaten Abaddon into revealing information he was withholding.

With a big grin, Abaddon began to fade into the shadows once again. *"We do not know. What Heaven placed within to watch over the world we can only guess. But I cannot spend any more time here. I do not believe I have to remind you ... but do not forget the last time the Legionnaires of Heaven came down upon you. The Ancient Lords of Light will not let your souls survive a second time!"* Abaddon disappeared into the shadows, swiftly climbing back up the mountain from which he came down. Pausing halfway up, Abaddon halted his ascension to speak one last time.

"While I warn you about Heaven, consider my next warning a gift. The price of failure could be deemed worse than death. Your actions are being closely watched by those who once sat

impatiently amongst the Halls of Hell. Your father's wrath will be unstoppable in both Heaven and Hell if he be forced to intervene ..."

They watched the crippled demon lumber back up the cliff, thoughts of both the past and the future swirling within their minds. None had any desire to return to their prisons of solitude to spend the next millennia in a spiritual cage. All of them feared the Ancients and what they represented, but there were few that did not.

Knowing that those fearless against the Ancient Lords of the Light watched their actions, Rhimmon shivered, feeling the gazes of the Dark Lords upon them. Already discovering that the Dark Lord of Hell Cayn was upon this world was enough terror, but if their father truly conspired once again in this world? Rhimmon would take a million years within Heaven's prison before desiring the feel of his father's wrath.

Though Abaddon had been correct ... there would be no future prisons.

Chapter 36

Reunion

Kallisto had never witnessed as great a gathering of the Order of the Fallen, though he'd heard about the great rally Orion had called at the beginning of the War of Beliefs. The darkest angel to walk upon this world, Dev'Azra the Nightmare, and his newly recruited companion Nuor had rallied their dark allies to challenge the Order for supremacy of Earth. Believing that Earth was their prison, they viewed it as a stepping stone to their rightful place among the powers of the universe. Earth was to be turned into a weapon to combat Heaven for the injustice done upon them. There was little doubt in Kallisto's mind they would have succeeded had it not been for the First to Fall.

Gathering the fallen angels, Orion collected those around him who did not forsake the Heavens for their punishment. Those who wished forgiveness for their actions and sought a way back into the grace of their lords were recruited to create an army to combat Dev'Azra and his terrifying minions. As they had then, the Fallen would be forced to unite once again.

Peering around the room, Kallisto knew that not one of those present had actually participated in the battle but had arrived after the great victory. He remembered many of the faces of those who had participated in the War of Beliefs, though, making him realize just how many fine people the Order had lost over the course of time. Those who remained now would have been perceived as ancient men by Humanity. Although the wings of prestige had been pulled from their backs, losing them immortality, they lived for centuries. He caught the eye of Damocles, one of the few remaining men whom he had shared his descent with and risen to the top with. Among the rest of the Order, though, he felt a very human feeling—he felt old.

"Kallisto, my old friend, it seems like forever since I last saw you."

"Old is indeed how I'm feeling, my friend. Time has passed us by, and now we stand where those who led us did, trying to rouse those around us to greater purpose. I fear that we will not be as strong as those who stand against us. We are not the Fallen Five, nor do we have a Champion of the Ancients to lead us."

Damocles replied, "How can we possibly defeat the powers against us, when the Five did not even fight against those who wage war upon us? We have gathered to wage the great war; that is an impossible situation, yet no one realizes how hopeless this fight we are in is."

Kallisto felt the pain within his comrade's words, his sense of defeat and willingness to give in. Damocles had always been one to see the bitter side in situations, but despite his pessimistic views Kallisto had seen his great strength and knew of his great feats of ingenuity. There was something inside of him that refused to quit, despite his contrary surface.

"Damocles, your words carry such depression and sorrow. We gather to fight the invincible simply because we have no other choice. We shall stand as one, and we shall die as one. Perhaps Heaven will show mercy on those who fight for the Light, even in the darkest of shadows. We can only pray and defy the demons seeking to destroy us."

"You aren't going to tell them what lurks in the darkness for us, are you? Such words will draw all hope from their breath; it will unravel our cause faster than it already progresses!"

"Telling them will prepare them for what is to come. Going into the battlefield unknowingly will cause more harm than knowing what is coming and properly preparing to fight it. We must stand as one in mind, body and spirit!"

"Administrator Kallisto, Architect Damocles, everyone is taking their places. We are almost prepared for your address."

Kallisto nodded in acknowledgement, waited for the young man to walk away before turning back to speak to his friend.

"Damocles, I understand your concerns, but we must rise to our calling and follow the path laid before us by others. While the future looks bleak, we must cling to it, because it is all we have left. Our brethren have been taken from us, our prestige and glory in the Heavens lost and now the encroaching darkness threatens to take our life away. We only have hope, but I cannot do it alone. I ask for your help. Help me reignite the spirit within the Order. Please."

"I apologize for my lack of heart. You know that I would never turn my back on a brother who fell with me, nor those around me. We shall stand together to the end and send these foul demons back to the dark realm whence they came from or perish down the Glory Road in a last act of defiance. Let us go and reignite the burning hearts of the Fallen." Damocles put his arm around Kallisto's shoulder, and they turned toward the amphitheatre that housed the council and its leaders. A mighty task lay ahead of them, but even Kallisto doubted the outcome would really matter. Was Heaven watching what was about to come?

Hundreds of the highest-ranking Order members sat patiently in their seats. Their positions varied among the various groups within the Order, from commanders of the army to high priests and civil servants. All came to hear and discuss the situation that affected them all, leaving many with no choice but to abandon their former lives for safety.

"Brothers and Sisters of the Order, it is a pleasure to be standing among you all once again. It has been a very long time since we have all gathered, and in that time there have been many drastic and devastating changes. Many empty seats lay before us, reminding of the darkness that continues to pursue us. May their spirits rest with our Fallen Father or find their way back to Heaven.

"Despite everything that has wreaked havoc and destruction

upon our Order, we have never turned our backs to this world or ever will. During these uncertain times, we must not panic or waver under the pressure. Perhaps with this gathering we can bring our minds together to understand the full extent of events that are going on around us. Let us discuss and share our information and thoughts on these matters.

"Our first speakers are servants of the Kyllordic Kingdom and their young prince, Raef Kyllone. They have rediscovered a threat that has previously been hidden from our eyes. Let us listen to their tales and think upon how this elusive force maybe be influencing current events. General Eli Elithane and General Ethan Elithane, the floor is yours."

The two brothers rose from their seats in the back, standing tall and proud, wearing their white cloaks trimmed in a royal blue. Their long greyish-black hair billowed with their cloaks as they hurried toward the stone podium in front of their brethren.

Kallisto had not seen either Ethan or Eli in decades, if not a century, after they settled among the forested havens of Kyllordia. Faithfully serving the Kyllordic kings, they were well respected within the civilization that rarely accepted outsiders and preferred to keep to themselves. Bearded Ethan could be violent and rash if provoked and was much remembered for the clashes he had with the Order and its members, almost at the cost of his life.

When he'd desperately pleaded before the Elders, Eli's smooth and soft tongue was able to win the pardon. He cited a brother's love and reminded them that even the Holy Throne of Heaven reserved the harsh punishment of death for only the vilest of crimes. Crying out in his brother's defence, he demanded to know whether the Elders were disciples of Heaven and its Creator or if they were like the Lords of Hell who slayed those who failed to observe their will. As Kallisto remembered Eli's defence of his silent and stoic brother, the memory stirred up old shivers. Would the gift of inspiring speech come from Eli's throat to help rally the spirits of his ancient cousins?

"Hello, Brothers and Sisters of the Order. We are glad to see all of you who managed to reach safety, and we pray for the safety of the souls not as fortunate as we have been." Eli spoke softly. All had friends who had not survived the recent events, but all understood they could not dwell upon such memories any longer.

"In our quest to reach safety after our lands were invaded by the Metzonians, we were assaulted by an enemy who has unknowingly shown his hand. We believe that this enemy has been granting the Metz brothers a supernatural force against their enemies. We believe that the former fallen angel Locan, who as history dictates was against the Lords of Heaven, has supported these young princes. We saw him during our escape from the royal camp and there is no mistaking he has returned."

Locan, Slayer of Angels, was the title he had been dubbed throughout Heaven. He was in the top tiers of the most wanted fallen angels in Heaven and had evaded capture for millennia. He had slain several angels in anger, as well as several of the hunters who had found him on several worlds throughout the kingdom of Heaven. In desperation, Locan had fled to the only place among the stars they would not think to look for him: Earth, Heaven's prison world. Here he was able to hide among the other fallen angels who had angered Heaven.

The news of Locan's appearance did not surprise Kallisto. He had already heard the Elithane twins speak about their tribulations and observations. Kallisto had discovered that both Eli and Ethan were initially under the impression that the Elder Council was aware who the enemy was. Locan and the Brotherhood was indeed a deadly combination, but he was not the enemy the White Elders knew of. They were just another enemy to add to the growing list of foes who had united against the Fallen.

"Locan, as powerful and dangerous as he may have been, is not a strategist of these proportions. We are talking about the complete dismantling of our Order, which has been carefully crafted by generations of Fallen. Our roots run extremely deep and are hidden from the rest of the world. How would Locan uncover so much without alerting us? The Order has very carefully covered our footprints on this world since the resurrection of the Sin and the Slaying of Children."

"Uncovering a single root can eventually lead back to the tree that sprouts it. I don't believe that they found us from our roots, but perhaps our branches extended a little too far? The majority of our remaining members have been hidden among the roots of our structure. Those slain were members of highly visible positions. This storm may have broken several few branches, but we still stand." Vayra spoke softly, her voice having a calming effect on those gathered within the room.

"Regardless, there must be a larger power beyond Locan behind all of this. Who else supported his revolution? Who were cast out with him or before him; who influenced him?" A member of the audience stood up, voicing his opinion to the council members who sat upon the stage. He looked among the crowd and raised his arms.

"What about his old master, Nuor? We all know that he was one of the original groups taken before the High Courts of Heaven. Elusive and cunning, with intelligence that outranked many of his peers, he is one who would be able to uncover our secrets." Eli tossed out the suggestion, his mind stuck on the formulated Sin theory.

"Impossible. Nuor was defeated by our Fallen father, Orion, as has been recorded in the ancient records. The battle declares that Orion defeated Nuor and his lieutenants, as he did Dev'Azra and Xera. While it does not confirm his death, those battles were before the end of the reign of Orion. Nuor himself was at the end of his own lifespan upon Earth; he would have perished too long ago from age alone," Vayra answered.

"Why would the Metzonian princes be in league with Black Angel Locan? What use would Locan and his mysterious lord, if there is one, have with Humanity and its armies; even their champions are not able to withstand the strengths of the Fallen?" Kallisto raised his eyebrows at the statement, thinking of the recent fall of Prokopolis.

"The thirst for power and glory is strong within Humanity. Metzonians are well known for their strong will, strength and pride, which built them into the powerful nation that represents their ideals. It runs particularly deeply in the king's second son, Sven. Coveting a strong and powerful nation enabled them to provide distraction from their true plans, as well as eliminate any human aspect that might resist them," a high priest from the Metzonian Chapter answered. He had been fortunate enough to have been away on errand during the revolution and avoided the massacre.

"Locan also creates a diversion that draws our attention away from activities the Sin are conducting. Clearly someone is pushing their carefully crafted plan in the correct direction and has certainly timed it to perfection." Ethan spoke for the first time.

"Locan and his mysterious puppeteer may well be the least of our problems. Word has reached my ears of far graver concerns, as it did the late Grandmaster Caelestis. It regards the greatest fears of the Order and this world's future …" Kallisto used his words wisely, shifting the conversation to his more pressing concerns to silence negligible questions of a weaker enemy. Silence clung to the walls, and he could smell the fear seep from their pores and radiate from their eyes as their minds clutched at very old memories; many slowly realized what he hinted toward.

"A Dark Prince of Hell has been released from his prison in the Desert. He was reincarnated by the holy blood of our brethren who were captured from our chapter in Metzor. There are too many questions that come with this statement to address them all. We all know this much: Rhimmon will or has undoubtedly sought the release of his brothers, and once they are united they will resume their crusade to bring this world to its knees and add it to the realm that is Hell."

"How in the Heavens are we to defeat them?"

Panic was spreading through the gathering quickly, cries of fear raging from some, while others sat in simple shock. Without their holy armour and divine commanders, they indeed faced an impossible task, with little hope of defeating their ancient adversary.

"We can fight and defeat the Metzonian brothers; we can even defeat Locan and his dark angels. We *cannot,* however hard we try, defeat a Dark Prince of Hell. Add his brothers of ancient times and there is *zero* hope for us. *Zero*! It took the powers that created the universe to defeat the Princes of Darkness; even they failed to destroy them."

A Mortal Mistake

"Perhaps if we all gather in the Crystal Cathedral and pray to Heaven they will hear our desire for penance and come to save us," a high priest called out, offering the only solution his peaceful mind could come up with.

"We are *Fallen*!" an older man with a heavily wrinkled face cried, his eyes full of fear. "Heaven's gates are closed to us, as are their ears! They have not listened to our prayers of penance and forgiveness in the past and will not now. No divine messengers have ventured to this world since the Wardens of Justice cast the last Fallen angel down in the Great Purge! Are we to hope that the Archangels of Heaven just happen to appear to throw another lost soul down to us, only to discover the carnage within this world? Our fates and that of this world are sealed. No rescue for us shall come; they left us here to die for our crimes."

Chaos once again overtook the leaders in the large chamber. Frightened conversations about all the enemies that were coming out of the darkness to ruin them and the lives they had built erupted all over the chamber. A former ally and an elusive, shadowy enemy had transformed into three strong powers they were helpless against, one so ancient and powerful all others no longer mattered.

"We understand how all of you feel. Know that we feel the same. Unfortunately, such events have been thrown into the paths of our destinies. We have no choice in the matter and must confront those that press our destruction upon us. We must stand united against such a formidable enemy if we are to survive. Stand with us as brothers and in memory of those who passed before us!" Damocles the Architect called out among the crowd, his hands held stretched out above them, trying to cast a calming spell upon them.

Conversations turned to murmurs and quieted; others kept their thoughts to themselves. Kallisto certainly felt their concerns; he had been struggling with them for such a long time that he only wished that he could rest his weary mind. He knew that the Fallen would come around and join him, for reasons of pride and glory, maybe hope. Though whatever reasons they would come up with would not matter, for they really had no choice left.

Rhimmon and his brothers were coming for them. The members

of the Order's memories were long, and they could remember most things, but the Dark Princes had perfect memories, and this place was burnt upon their souls. They would never rest until the Sacred City was destroyed, along with all its inhabitants. The darkness within their hearts was colder than the black holes of Hell. And like a black hole, they would absorb and destroy everything within their grasp, never to see the light of Heaven again.

Chapter 37
Darkness Rising

The Chilsa emperor marched quickly up the blue carpeted staircase of the Imperial Citadel's tallest spire, his steps light due to the news he had just received. Belle had written to him again to inform him that the Metzonian war nation was soon to be on the move once more. In five day's time, they would be leaving Metzor for the north, marching at long last for the Alakari mountain range to seek out the fabled Sacred City of the Fallen. Although she wrote that her love did not know the exact location, their scouts had found major resistance deep within the passage, and the Fist of Metzor had lost all patience and planned to seek it out himself. It had been the news Kristolphe had been waiting a long time for.

Kristolphe's Imperial guards stood upon every tenth step all the way up the circular staircase, remaining perfectly still. Nothing would ever enter his personal chambers except for him, not without facing the entire garrison of the palace guard and then sneaking along a bare hallway posted with a hundred personal bodyguards sworn to die for the emperor. No, it was a task too great for any human.

Kristolphe could have run up the stairs, powered by the excitement and anticipation in his chest, but he forced himself to maintain his regal composure before the guards. Sealing the black doors behind him, he tapped his fingers joyfully upon the wood, containing his excitement.

At this moment, the Chilsa Imperial army, over a million infantry marshalled from every corner of the empire itself, were being issued their marching orders by the lord generals. Months and months of preparation and logistics to arrange for the manpower to travel great distances in anticipation of this battle were not to be wasted after all. Kristolphe had not known whether King Sven would actually succeed with his great war upon the last of the free nations. Neurus had unknowingly helped his enemy by keeping the last two nations on the rocks with his siege of covert attacks for the last few years. The biggest surprise was that the Order had not thrown Sven down immediately after he assassinated his father and picked up the reins of the Metzonian army. Often seeing the dire consequences of particular actions before they happened, the Order missed its opportunity this time, and the man grew too strong to control or steer in the proper direction.

But then again, the king was the servant of a Dark Prince, so perhaps he was shielded from such foresight. It did not matter now; those events were in the past, and the future was swiftly to be brought closer. And Chilsa was going to take everything one step further.

Grabbing a bottle from the wine rack in his chambers, Kristolphe felt a sudden cold enter his body. He ran his hands over the outside of the bottle of wine and noticed it was not chilled. The fireplace had been blazing when he had entered the chamber. Pouring the wine to the brim of his cup, he set the bottle down, listening carefully. Feeling the chill again creep up his spine, Kristolphe's pleasant mood turned sour.

"Ah, Father, I had not thought that you would ever return to the Imperial Citadel." Turning to the centre of the room, he noticed the bundle of ratty black rags seated in one of two large blue chairs before the fireplace. "Such a … wonderful surprise."

"You thought I would leave my empire in hands as weak and fragile as yours and then simply forget about it?" Neurus snorted loudly, laughing at his son, but Kristolphe hardly heard. Chilsa had always been Neurus's empire and would always be Neurus's empire. "Your stupidity continues to astound me. No, I am here to ensure that the main directives of this vital phase are understood and to tell you what you are going to do."

A Mortal Mistake

Kristolphe had forgotten that he had not yet received the final commands of the Brotherhood yet, nor spoken to his father since Rhimmon had destroyed their basement lair beneath the Imperial Citadel. Kristolphe had enjoyed the months of pleasant peacefulness.

"I already have plans of my own that I believe will amaze you and accomplish all your dreams and more," Kristolphe responded proudly, trying to keep his confidence up.

His father quickly scoffed at yet another of his son's attempts to impress him, clearly anticipating another failure.

"I have seen your plans in design and execution before, and never have I been anything more than disgusted. I shall allow it though, as it has indeed been a while since I last received the opportunity to punish you for your foolishness."

Kristolphe watched as the swollen knuckles of his father's hands opened, revealing the silver serpent of iron rings his father had been so fond of using upon his children. Kristolphe took his seat before the large fireplace, watching the logs crackle and calming his nerves as he second-guessed himself. Looking at the grotesque, white, wrinkled face of his father, he began describing his upcoming plan and how he had been nurturing this plan forever. After carefully laying each layer and filling other pieces in, his plan had now evolved to the point of becoming what his father would call a beautiful thing. Dark and deceitful, loaded with treachery and betrayal, it was a culmination of everything his father loved, blood flooding the ending.

Kristolphe had used his sister to forge a connection with the Metzonians, to infiltrate and keep him informed of all their plans. Using Belle to nurture Sven's plan to start a religious war against the Order, he used his father's enemy to destroy the Brotherhood's sole opponent. The fact that Sven had unexpectedly destroyed the weak Kyllordic Kingdom as well had been wonderful news. Now, Kristolphe would march his army on their final war path in a show of support for the Metzonians and finish the Order off. Crushing the remains of both enemies within the Alakari, the Chilsa Empire would at long last be complete, with the known world completely beneath their blue banner.

Surprisingly, Neurus did not interrupt him once, waiting until he completely finished. "You arranged for all this?"

"Arranged and choreographed as though it was a play in the Chilsa Theatre Grandeur. All shall dance to the tune of the flute at the exact places I have designed for them. If any portion fails, which it shall not, I assure you that I have no qualms about resorting to the plan you desired."

Kristolphe eyed the swinging silver chain in his father's right hand carefully, fearing the lash that he expected. He was surprised to watch the chain retract back up his father's sleeve.

"Everything is in place," Kristolphe continued. "But it looks as though you have more important things to worry about, such as that nasty-looking stamp upon your soul? It looks horribly infected and growing."

His father scowled at him, reaching his hand over his shoulder and working his fingers over the face of the brand burned through his cloak. Kristolphe could see the pain it inflicted upon him and the fear it wrought within his eyes. It worried Neurus; and he was perhaps lost for the first time in his life, unaware of what to do.

"Speaking of that fine brand upon your back brings up another question of some importance. You do realize that when I have eliminated all the empire's mortal enemies, only the immortal ones will remain, and I will be of little use to you. I would not want to see my father's work completed at long last only to suddenly be undone by demons from the past. I assume you have a plan to eliminate threats that we mortals cannot?"

Neurus did not reply; the Sin simmered in his own thoughts. Before Kristolphe could ask again, his father cut him off. "It will be taken care of."

Kristolphe waited for the old man to elaborate, but his bloody red eyes barely blinked. The subject was closed before it was broached. Pouring himself another glass of the fine red wine, Kristolphe turned away from his father and looked back at the flames. The crackling and splitting of the logs in the fire were the only sounds in the room shared by father and son.

Moving to break the silence, Kristolphe turned to find the chair his father had sat in empty. Smiling to himself, he drained the last of the wine and reached to refill his glass. There were plenty of reasons for him to celebrate and reward himself, and he planned on enjoying it.

His carefully laid plan had actually been accepted by his father. He hadn't been beaten mercilessly or his soul tortured for perceived failure. The Metzonian nation was on the move, about to wipe out the Order of the Fallen, his grandfather's hated enemy of the past, by which he was then going to destroy his father's current hated enemies. Now if only Kristolphe had been able to discover a method for eliminating all of his future enemies.

Three victories were considered decent-enough success to satisfy him tonight.

From the top of the great gatehouse of Metzor's formidable walls, the Metzonian king watched his forces march out. The gates of gold were inlaid with the images of the sixteen states that made up the kingdom and their crests. The slight breeze rolling off the great yellow plains that were prepared for the winter seemed to breathe an air of things to come. Within its cool touch, Devotz could smell blood and fear.

Watching his creation move out from its lair to devour his enemies filled him with great pride. The Metzonian nation had rallied around their new king with renewed vigour and with him at the helm, achieved greatness. A rematch against the remains of the Order and his quest for power was almost complete.

"How high the Metzonians have risen beneath the black banner of the Fist of Metzor." The gravelly voice behind him avowed, stealing the thought straight from his mind. *"Soon none will remain. What does a king of war do once all his enemies are slain?"*

Devotz had not contemplated what he was to do once the next

glorious battle was won; he had known nothing else in his life but the struggles of war. His father had turned from civil war to build a new civilization, restoring Metzon's glorious cities and culture, neither of which Devotz had interest in. His legacy was to be built upon blood and sweat; perhaps he would find new peoples to conquer.

"A king of war never seeks an end to the violence he creates, nor can he control such carnage. One battle at a time, it will spread. I can see the battle already, the bodies beneath my feet and upon my blade as the full might of the Metzonians is at last felt by those who sought to escape its touch."

Devotz looked up to where the demon stood, feet upon the thick stone edges of the high lookout, his winged back before Devotz's great black banner strung high over the walls. No one else seemed to notice Rhimmon among them; all eyes remained focused upon those marching beneath them, their ears oblivious to the conversation between the dark master and his eternal servant.

"You will lead your army as far north as the pass—that is all. You will then turn over your command. I have a more important task that you must do for me."

Pausing at his master's words used so nonchalantly, Devotz knew the demon was undoubtedly able to feel the anger rise within his human heart. Jaws clenched tightly and heart beating furiously; he slapped his hands against the stone ledge, turning back to the one who owned his soul and pointing his finger menacingly up at the Dark Prince.

"No! Everything I have done leading up to this point has been for the glory that shall be mine on the famous battlefield. To face an opponent against whom I can test my true strength in the splendour of battle. Not once have I come across an opponent that did not weaken or flee before my blades. I have waited and yearned for this battle! That glory should be mine!"

"Do not make us repeat the Lost Mountain." Rhimmon's tone quickly turned darker, and Devotz could feel the demon run his invisible black fingers through his body, prodding his mind toward the unpleasant memory. *"If glory is what you seek, then listen to what I am willing to grant you. Even greater glory shall be yours.*

Such a glory that no mortal has ever been able to receive it or will be able to replicate. A battle that will test you to the very limits of your abilities. Most likely it will result in your death."

Devotz, struck with the prospect of not being allowed to lead his soldiers to their glory, did not have to wait long for the explanation. What could possibly be greater than full-out war with his last numerous enemies preparing for one final battle against him?

"The Order of the Fallen have retreated to protect their greatest treasure. Information has surfaced that the Fallen serve an angel of Heaven. Full born and still retaining all his or her powers of the Houses of Heaven, this being hides within the Temple Mountain, protecting all against the Dark Powers and refuelling the Fallen for their next battle. This angel must be removed from this world."

Devotz was stunned. He listened closely as his dark lord continued explaining to him the new situation he had never expected or dreamed possible.

"Your forces will never breach the great walls while the powers of Heaven protect and command those who fell. I would leave the Brotherhood to this task, but as you have proclaimed so often before, they have failed where you have succeeded in every aspect set before you. What greater way to achieve eternal glory than to slay an immortal?"

To slay an angel? He looked at the dark lavender-skinned demon closely, not sure whether to believe what he was speaking of. "How is one to do such a thing?"

"You are to infiltrate the Temple Mountain as your men fling themselves upon the enemies relentlessly. Distracted by the battle, your path should not be difficult, for they will need every man to bear weapons against the strength of those you march toward them."

"How will I know where to find them?"

Rhimmon's response was less pleasant, the black tendrils of his powers dancing to life once again through Devotz's veins in response. The sensation made Devotz's stomach churn on as a wave of naseau threatened to overtake him, but the demon released him from the torment quickly.

"Follow the light, my slave. Through the light and the stench of purity that radiate from such beings, I shall help guide you to your prize. When your army breaches the doors, they shall find their king over the winged beast, holding its head within your fingers. All shall witness and worship you for eternity!"

Rhimmon's black beady eyes gazed into the distance, away from Devotz, putting an end to the conversation. Pondering the change of events, the young mortal no longer felt as much anger as he watched his men exit the city.

Growing up with his father's stories of angels, he would never have believed that the Fallen were protecting a true angel within their midst. His mind became preoccupied with wonder at the powers the being would possess and how he would defeat such a creature. Would his mortal blows be able to penetrate the holy armour of Heaven? He had seen the powers his father's blade had upon hammered steel before. But it was only holy, not heavenly.

"But beware. If you hear the singing of the Ancients, the painful journey of your soul will have already begun. For it is the tongue of the Hounds of Heaven, created by the very souls of wretched angels slain before them. Pray they do not still reside within the Temple Mount! Now quiet your mind. We have an unexpected visitor, soon to arrive." Rhimmon's command shocked him from his questions, and Devotz searched for the new visitor. He saw no one for miles from the wall; Devotz looked to the sky for one of his master's brothers, finding nothing.

Three guards removed themselves from their positions, walking around their king. Stunned by their sudden return to life, Devotz watched them wake from that statue-like state and walk past him without acknowledging his presence. Turning back he discovered a black figure writhing in pain upon the brown stone before him. The ragged cloak of the white-skinned figure wore gave away the dark angel's identity.

"You did not think that you could pass through the city of Metzor unnoticed, did you, my dark angel? You forgot that you

serve me, and I know where you roam through this world. When I summon you, you obey from your own free will or through the pain of my own."

Devotz watched the demon torture the mind and body of the dark angel without a single visible movement. The overwhelming power of Rhimmon's mind inflicted great pain and suffering impossible to resist. Devotz had felt its terror before.

"Perhaps with enough pain and suffering you dark angels will at last realize your place within this world. Fallen and disgraced, you are below even Hell in Heaven's eyes! We give you the opportunity that you would not receive from your own kind. All we ask is that you obey, but even that evades your simple mind."

Neurus refused to scream despite the pain, accepting the agony instead of begging for mercy through foolish pride. Rhimmon did not let up as he waited for the angel's spirit to break. He casually gazed toward Devotz, who stood motionless before his enemy, watching him suffer in silence.

"You will provide three dozen of your best warriors for a separate mission of great importance to your continued survival upon this world. They will camp beneath the Alakari mountains that lie within your northern borders until required by my servant here. The rest will follow the Metzonian army into battle against the Fallen to provide support when commanded, as we had previously discussed.

"Do you understand? All shall arrive and serve me, angel, or all shall suffer. My anger has no limits!"

Released from the demon's mental grasp, Neurus melted upon the floor and fled as quickly as he arrived, without a single word. His bloody eyes glared at Devotz, for the briefest of moments, as if he were to blame. Devotz watched the smoke race through the tall golden wheat fields surrounding the city.

"Join your army for their march to glory, one of my brothers shall come for you to provide transport to where you will launch your attack. Prepare yourself, your brother and the other for the

battle to come. I do not exaggerate the power within the hands of Heaven."

Leaping from the lookout, Rhimmon flew back over the city, weaving through the towers and steeples of the large churches erected by the Order of the Fallen. As he passed into the gloomy distance, sunlight broke back through the clouds, shining down upon those atop the gatehouse once more.

The guards around him looked upon him with their own eyes once more, grinning brightly as they pointed toward their comrades exiting the city. None noticed the change within their king. No longer enthralled by his army that was going to crush his enemies; he could not remove the image of the angel he was to be pitted against.

The quest of a nation had turned to a personal pursuit of immortal glory. But only if he could discover a way to slay the immortal …

Locan sat upon the remains of a stone column, running his whetstone over his bladed mace, honing the fine edges. Gazing up briefly to look upon the other Sin preparing for war, he regarded their new surroundings. The black bones of deceased dragons littered the ruins of the great altar devoted to worshipping the sea dragons of Kyllordia. Hundreds of dragons that once roamed the countryside now filled the niches within the great cavern; all had come there to die with their ancestors' remains.

The Brotherhood's new lair within the dragon's graveyard certainly looked fierce, but the walls did not ooze the dark powers as the lair beneath Chilsa did. The three Dark Gods Dev'Azra, Xera and Nuor had conspired within those dark walls, conjuring new spells to use against their enemies in future wars. Absorbing the fallen angels' powers over time, the porous rocks still held their energy centuries after their deaths. It had been home with the comforting feeling of the power within the walls.

Until Rhimmon ruined everything.

Now everything they had done in the past had been for nothing. Ruined by the Dark Princes when they returned to this world, the

A Mortal Mistake

Brotherhood now found themselves in servitude to Hell. Locan had been upset with Neurus's pact with the Dark Princes, but his master had told him patience and silence was all he required from the warlord. Locan wondered how Neurus would break the news to the rest of his servants.

The witch queen Cleos sat off to the side, glaring at him from her seat at the foot of the altar staircase. Belly swollen with the spawn of Neurus, she hissed at him. Locan wondered why she had not remained in the birthing den she had constructed out of the old Kyllica throne room. *Damned witch.* Locan would be thrilled when her purpose was at an end and he could dispose of her.

A swirl of smoke wove through the rock columns holding up the roof of the cavern, reforming on the top of the shattered altar and settling upon the dragon bone throne constructed upon its peak. The soldiers of the Sin quickly rose to their feet at the sight of their lord, who had returned from his excursion.

"Come forth, Sons of Sin!"

Thousands moved silently to look down upon the leader, waiting for him to speak, knowing a war was at last upon the horizon. Locan stared at the thousands in the shadows, knowing Neurus would leave out the fact that they all now fought and served Hell.

"Children of Sin, Brothers of the Broken, and the Disgraced!" Neurus beckoned more from the shadows as he continued.

"The time has finally come for the Brotherhood to take our rightful place within this world once more. Gods, that was the vision once brought forth by those who were wrongfully purged from Heaven. Dev'Azra, Xera and Nuor united all of us in this great vision, leading us into many great battles against our noble enemy, the Order of the Fallen.

"Defeated and destroyed in the War of Beliefs, we were forced to return to the shadows. But no longer, as our eternal enemy has grown weak over time, while we have not. Humanity has at last turned its back upon the Order of the Fallen, seeing their own potential if they release themselves from the restraints of morality. All march toward the Order's last sanctuary, eager to slay all!

"As the last of the Order fall beneath the blades before them, for our patience we shall receive our vision. I will not leave this opportunity to chance! The Brotherhood shall march behind Humanity and ensure our victory. We will witness a new era!"

A cheer went up from the thousands, who bashed steel against steel and rock, stirring up the dust of the bones around them. The screams of thousands echoed into the cries of a million, fuelling Locan's eagerness for real war against the Order at long last.

"The end of the Light is near, and we shall usher in a new age of darkness and glory this world has not seen!" The cries continued, Neurus's final words stabbing through the din around him as he threw his arms over his head. "Now go and prepare yourself for the greatest glory the Brotherhood will ever achieve. Sharpen your steel, hone your skills and stir the rage within head and heart for the battles to come!"

Locan listened to the cheer quiet as the Sin started to slip back into the shadows, leaving the air abuzz with anticipation. The Brotherhood and its members had been waiting for this war forever, but not long enough to forget their desire to bleed their enemy dry.

"Warlord Locan!"

His name echoing around the cavern, Locan walked off the ledge, floating down into the blue light before his master's feet. Neurus did not gaze upon him but looked into the surrounding alcoves until all peering eyes slid back into the shadows to resume preparing for war.

"The Dark Princes demand three dozen of your best for a special mission. They are to meet upon the Alakari mountain peaks that lie at the very north of the Chilsa borders. The Metzonian brothers are to meet them there to proceed with this unusual mission."

"The Metzonian is not leading his own armies?"

"No, but apparently they will not notice his absence. Rhimmon's power is deeper in this world than I had hoped it to be. I have a surprise in store for them via my son, but it does not matter. The primary objectives remain the same and of most importance."

"Those being the defeat of the Order?"

"The primary objective is to ensure that the Order is not only defeated but utterly destroyed, never to rise again! But in the chaos of such events, certain new allies must, must, *must* be slain. As my child pointed out, I do not want to have our moment of triumph ruined due to someone else stealing our crown. The Princes of Hell must die! All the princes must die!"

Locan had been eager to learn how his master had planned on getting out of this new bind, and at last he was about to find out. "How does my master believe that we are to do that? The Lords of Heaven were unable to completely remove their stain from this world."

"Deceptively, before they realize what has happened. If my history serves me correctly, the Ancients were not able to get close enough without them releasing themselves from the physical bonds of this world. We, on the other hand, have the ability to get very close.

"We must strike them swiftly in the midst of the battle, when their minds are upon the war and not us. One shot is all we shall have—failure is not an option! If one escapes then we will never be able to rest easily as lords of this world.

"We must isolate them, one at a time. Together they will be able to feed off one another. Rhimmon's power is the most potent, and all the black souls of the Sin will not be able to defeat him with his brothers alive within this world."

"We should have slain him and the Metzonian when they were within our lair," Locan growled, as he remembered the extremely brief encounter.

"His sudden appearance was a great surprise. Had I known then what I know now, it would have been a gamble that I would have taken. Speaking of his Metzonian puppet, I hope in the end to have him alive even after his master is dead." Even now, with the Brotherhood on the cusp of eternal slavery, the Metzonian continued to afflict his master.

"Angels have the ability to slay demons, Locan. And you are a Slayer of Angels, are you not? I am sure that you will discover a way."

Locan did not voice his own thoughts. He could slay the front ranks of the demonic hordes for days, as the Legionnaires of the past had before him. But they were not the target. Heaven had long ago lost track of the number of angels slain by the Dark Princes, many far greater than Locan himself. Defeated in mock combat by many of the angels who fell to the Dark Princes, it caused Locan to fear his new order.

"If we do not do this, you will die at the hands of the Dark Princes, Locan. Like those of Heaven you slew, it is you or them. I would imagine you would prefer to take the battle to them at your own free will and kill them according to your own plans. Do what you must!"

CHAPTER 38
Defending the Pass

Kallen stood among the rocky, snow-capped peaks, gentle snow dropping thickly around him. His breath was visible in the cold winter air; he breathed through his nose to leave his vision of the mountain pass stretched out beneath him clear. From Metzon, this was the closest high observation point to the passage that led into the Alakari mountains. Kallen and a few others knew of the goat trail that cut across the mountains from the river pass. Kallisto had directed Kallen how to find the secret path, citing it as one of the passages that the adventurers had taken when they had explored the mountain ranges. From this point he could watch over the large horseshoe pass that all armed forces had to take to enter the Alakari.

A thousand feet below, he observed what both his mentor and he had hoped would never occur. An enemy army was slowly trudging through the snowy pass, certain of the path they were to take. He knew their scouts had reached as far as the holy waters of the River Tyris that ran deep through the Alakari.

Young as he was, Kallen doubted that even the last fight of the War of Beliefs had included so many men. Kallen had watched the movements of their enemy all day long; the stream of Metzonians below had stretched from the pass entrance and through the long horseshoe path before disappearing around another mountain. The Order now knew how the princes had gathered such an army to their banner, but he had not seen any dark demon lords among the army. Had he really expected to?

The tail end of the supporting baggage train had almost disappeared from Kallen's view, announcing to the unseen spy that it was time to leave for the defensive points to prepare to ambush them to try and hold back the inevitable, if only briefly. "All damage inflicted upon the enemy is necessary for our survival" were Kallisto's words as he had commanded Kallen's sister when she geared up to organize her rangers.

Taking one last look across the snowy mountain peaks, he saw several riders softly working through the pass. Kallen's curiosity stopped him for another ten minutes as he watched the scouting party, waiting for something to happen. The men were clearly scouts, but Kallen had no clue why they were following the densely packed trail. After another ten minutes, he almost left his post. Then he saw the force on the horizon.

Light blue and white banners of the Chilsa Imperial Army entered the passage that the horsemen of the Numelli had cut through the forest surrounding the mountains, following their sworn enemies into battle. Why would the Metzonians allow a far larger, well-organized enemy at their rear, Kallen wondered. Had they pulled every available man in their quest for revenge, leaving their borders open for invasion? Did they know they were being followed by their mortal enemy? He had no logical answers, but the new threat before him concerned Kallen.

He waited and watched the stream of cavalry enter into the valley first, a hundred horses across. The ranks were so thick and long that Kallen lost all ability to estimate the number—certainly five times as large as their already formidable Metzonian adversary.

Attacked by the Chilsa to their rear, the Metzonians would be trapped within the mountains, only able to flee deeper into the snowy winter mountains. The Chilsa now had both the Metzonians and the Order trapped within the mountain range. There would be no escape for either side; it seemed to Kallen that young Emperor Kristolphe had trapped them perfectly.

Darkness enshrouded the rangers waiting within the cover of the rocks for the opportunity they required to spring their trap. Darkness was always dangerous for armoured soldiery trying to manoeuvre. Darkness combined with the ice-covered slopes of the rocky crags the rangers scrambled upon was close to suicide.

The rangers had been in position for hours, awaiting the Metzonian vanguard units. Alexandra shivered to think how much longer they might be there. Looking upon the other side of the valley cliffs, she searched for the rangers waiting on the edges. The falling snow made it difficult to see anything, and those of her unit she thought she could spot among the snowy rocks were as perfectly still as the boulders and snow they imitated.

Alexandra's patience was wearing thin. She had expected their enemy to set camp for the night, yet they could hear the troops continue marching through the mountain pass. The snow may have helped silence their footsteps, but the rattle of thousands of infantry echoed throughout the mountains loudly. They had all heard them when they turned around the final curve that led to the long pass that went almost directly north. For hours they were forced to listen to the coming force, growing louder as they neared but leaving no visible signs.

The long trilling hoot of a night owl cried out in the darkness, announcing that her commander of the eastern wall could at last see them climbing up the slope. The long, straight northern pass rose at a steep incline to ever-higher elevations through the mountains. Over the course of multiple leagues, the soldiers would traverse a winding, steep climb that would carry them ten thousand feet above the great plains of Metzor. When the enemy armies at last came to rest before the walls of the Sacred Citadel, they would be utterly exhausted. If they did not die before they reached the Valley of Angels, a likely scenario if they continued to climb with such recklessness.

The first of the Metzonian scouts, well ahead of the vanguard, rode quickly through, giving a quick glance up to the rock walls. The dry streambed the army travelled upon always flooded in spring, when the violent rivers of the Alakari broke free from their banks to flood the mountain range for months. Looking at the snow-covered peaks above her, Alexandra knew that spring would come months too late to wash their enemies away.

As casual as the riders appeared, the lightly armoured scouts had eyes of eagles, able to spot the slightest disturbance within the terrain. The slight disadvantage of falling snow in the darkness combined with the obsessive training of the rangers proved to be enough to conceal the ambushers. The scouts rode in silence, the echo of hooves clopping upon rock muffled by the snow as the scouts faded once more into the darkness.

Painful cramps coursed through her legs, but she could not risk moving. The vanguard battalion commanders were now within view as they continued to trudge through the knee-deep snow. The dark grey steel was easy to see against the white snow, even in the growing darkness surrounding the shadows cast among the faint moonlight. Continuing to let them pass, she counted their ranks, which formed a single column of seventy infantry across and seemingly forever deep. The lightly armoured men forced their way through the thick snow, their more heavily armoured comrades following behind. The front five ranks alternated opening the trail; the snow overworked the muscles of their legs, forcing the Metzonians to slow.

Alexandra's place was near the end of the western cliff; behind her lay the escape path that waited to take them back around the last mountain peak before the river pass. Eight hundred rangers watched for her signal to begin the attack, eyes upon the vanguard commander riding atop his black steed. Notching her snow-covered arrow, she slowly rose from her hiding position to peer through the darkness, searching for the whites of her target's eyes.

The stretched string motionless against her face, she steadied her breathing, lining up the Metzonian in her sights. She had not brought her grandmother's Bane Bow with her, knowing the holy weapon's bright string would have immediately revealed her position in the dark. Forced to use her foster father's ordinary bow, she recalculated the distance one last time.

The whistling arrow's higher pitch cut over the dense marching armour beneath it and tore the vanguard captain from his mount. No scream was uttered as the arrow pierced the man's throat, his armour crashing loudly into the rocky snow. The moment of silent peace lasted only a heartbeat before the silent attack of the rangers exploded down upon the ranked men below. Screams broke out among those under attack within the trough, as the least-armoured men were turned to pincushions among the massed firing from both sides of the ravine cliffs.

The supreme advantage of Alexandra's ranger attack was evident among the outer ranks of lightly clad soldiers, who were cut down by the dozens. The Metzonian heavy infantry were unexpectedly quick to reduce the rangers' advantage as they pushed through their comrades violently to the edges of the columns, hiding behind their elaborate tall shields. No one tried to advance up the steep embankments, though; they waited for their comrades to join them behind a shield wall, stacking them one high, then two, before a third tier was added.

The thick steel of the stacked shields sheltered the army beneath it; arrows skittered harmlessly across the steel or punctured but refused to completely penetrate. A few of her rangers took pot shots at gaps within the shielding with little effect. Bolts of sporadic crossbow fire erupted at the elusive attackers from within the tortoiseshell of steel. The centre fifty ranks from the cover of shields began flowing up the mountain pass, moving at a double pace.

Alexandra understood that the men beneath the floating shields were pushing as quickly as they could through the snow, trying to move from the ambush point and reach an elevation that would provide the ability to cross onto the cliff sides. Such a move would eliminate future attacks, as well as provide them the option to trap her rangers within the mountain passes.

Whistling down the line, Alexandra called for the retreat to the mountain pass. Hopefully the eastern slope rangers were already withdrawing quickly; if they did not reach the river pass before their enemy, they would become trapped among the rock and water of the mountains. No one would be able to mount any sort of rescue to break them free. The Metzonian scouts would already be on the return path, slowing their retreat enough as it was.

Rangers in their long white cloaks raced past her, moving swiftly up the rock-strewn slope and down the other side toward the next ambush point. "To the river pass, everyone—move quickly now." Alexandra urged her warriors on, slapping each on the shoulder after a mission of limited success; the Metzonians' response was quicker than she had anticipated. Perhaps having been at war so long, the sons of Metzon instinctively knew how to save themselves from death. Even with such factors, something still did not sit right with her and how quickly and fluidly their enemy was moving. Calculating the time to travel the remaining distance, Alexandra figured they should still have enough time to set themselves up again. Certainly the pursuing soldiers would not be able to continue their pace through the thick snow.

A pair of rangers carried the bleeding body of a wounded comrade up the slope, headed for safety. Another thousand rangers waited for the enemy in the next pass defence, but after looking upon the numbers of their enemies, Alexandra knew it would not be enough to halt the advance. She was already losing men, and she needed everyone she could muster.

Looking back down the pass, Alexandra noticed the outer edges of the shield wall were still intact in the event the ambushers returned. The centre column had changed substantially though. A stream of heavily armoured cavalry thundered through the clear central column, riding swiftly through the opening, past their brethren in hasty pursuit. Alexandra watched them move hard toward the escaping ambushers as she flung herself down the snowy path. She had not anticipated the cavalry would reach the front vanguard so quickly, and she cursed herself for a miscalculation that would likely result in the deaths of many. She feared the cavalry would come around the pass to cut off her retreat. Her aggressive recklessness with the lives of her rangers would have angered her brother.

Alexandra wished she had the extensive training experience of her brother, but she would prove to him that she was a quick study. She would eliminate the advantage the cavalry depended so heavily upon.

A Mortal Mistake

Frederick felt his eyes strain as he watched the dizzying curtain of water coming down before him. Hiding within the narrow cavern beneath the rushing waters, the rangers watched and waited. Despite the water thundering down around him, he could hear the stampeding of hooves echoing through the canyon pass.

He had been raised upon the sound of wild horses running across the open plains as most young Metzonian boys were. Trained to ride from the youngest age, the elite horsemen of the Numelli rode swiftly through the pass. At such a reckless speed, a single slip upon the icy rock could be disastrous. But Frederick knew these riders would not falter.

Watching the dark shadows running pass the concealed entrance, he hoped they continued down the marked trail. Frederick had marched his Elite up and down the pass to create a false trail to lure their enemy deeper into the mountains. Cursing the bitter cold, his soldiers had been the first to realize the purpose of his madness. The winter winds of the Alakari could do more damage to an invading army than every blade in the Sacred Citadel.

As he struggled to see through the falling water, he noticed one shadow moving slower than all the others. A single rider pulled back on the reins before the shallow pool of fast flowing water. The stallion snorted loudly, shaking its head as it fought the rider upon its back. The stallion wanted to continue to run with the rest of the group but the knight had wandering eyes.

Spurring his charger into the cold waters of the pools before them, Alexandra and Frederick watched the knight tread slowly towards them. Frederick heard the creak of Alexandra's bow as she prepared to cut down the inquisitive knight. He could sense the anxiety rise within her as she held her breath, seeing a second knight pause upon the shore followed by a third. Slashing his sword into the waterfall, the blade cut harmlessly through the water.

The arrow from Alexandra's bow did not.

Nerves coming undone, Alexandra fired up to strike the knight through the chest. The stallion panicked as the knight was thrown over its back, charging forwards into the cavern. Frederick threw himself forwards to knock Alexandra out of the horse's way as it crashed into the palisade.

The chilling cries of the dying horse trapped upon the wooden stakes echoed amongst the rocky walls as he pushed Alexandra deeper into the cavern. Slipping upon the wet stone as they fumbled through the dark, Frederick heard the sounds of additional horses and their riders crashing into the wooden palisade. It would not be long before the splintering of wooden and the cry of dying horses turned to the screams of dying men.

Few torches remained lit as they passed through the water, and those that did were quickly extinguished. The rangers immediately fired towards any source of light that made it through the falls. The rangers knew their advantage lay within the darkness and were eager to use it. Their enemy hacked at anything they sensed in the darkness, Fallen or not.

Torches inevitably began entering the passage, flooding the passage with brightness, making the carnage visible to those fighting within. The Metzonian heavy cavalry charged forward on foot, the once-icy waters swirling red around their feet, warm with the blood of their slain comrades. The Fallen rangers fled the light, fading to the darkness with elusive quickness, unburdened by the heavy steel plating of the Metzonians.

Leaving Alexandra and the rangers to continue their elusive fight, Frederick retreated back up the long staircase to prepare his Elite. Long ago the Architects had carved the long staircase through the dark tunnel of the cavern to allow easier passage for the women and children of the Fallen. Listening to the battle cries of his brother's soldiers behind him, Frederick had a feeling the Fallen would regret that decision.

The sight of his loyal warriors standing shoulder to shoulder before him filled him with pride. Frederick had commanded each squadron spaced upon every flat landing to allow the retreating rangers room to regroup upon the staircase behind them. But as he watched the torchlight grow brighter and the mass of dark steel chasing the rest of the rangers, Frederick wished he had brought more men.

Arrows burst in both directions as the Fallen rangers holding the high ground attacked the shield wall of Metzonians. The boldest of the enemy passed through the protective barrier, charging recklessly up the staircase. More followed the first; emboldened by their courage, unaware that they ran over the bodies of the first who had charged so bravely.

"For the Metz!" Frederick shouted, the loyalists flooding down to engage those beneath them. Frederick was finally receiving the fight he had been waiting for. Throwing his shoulder into one of the first challengers, he had always expected it to have been one of his brothers. But yet neither was to be found, a thought that bothered him.

The battle ebbed and flowed as the factions fought back and forth but Frederick's Elite were not enough as they were continuously forced up the long staircase. He knew it was only a matter of time before the dam holding back the sea of swords burst. Once his brother's infantry broke through there would be little hope for the remaining rangers as all would become completely overwhelmed. Only one final catalyst would be added to signal the end. From the depths of the cavern, Frederick saw it coming.

Among the endless mass of Metzonian steel forcing its way through the river pass, Frederick noticed an anomaly within the shadows. A single figure that stood taller and broader than the rest. Pushing through the mass as though he were wading through water, it did not take long for him to recognize the man.

"The commander of the King's Royal Elite, once sworn to protect me, now hunts me through the Alakari, pursuing my death." His voice echoed within the cavern, loud above the violence around Aerox. The large man paused as he looked up from the grey mass around him to the golden warrior high above him.

Aerox didn't reply with any words. He lurched forwards, knocking aside those in front of him as he bulled his way through the cavern, rushing up the staircase towards Frederick. Three steps at a time, his father's bodyguard moved through the dark tunnel, his mind focused upon one man of the hundreds above him.

The riders of the Numelli followed the momentum of Aerox as he smashed his way through the front ranks of the Elite. Clawing his way through those who stepped forward to challenge him, Aerox was ruthless in the dispatching of those before him. His perilous gaze never left Frederick.

Slowly backing himself up the second last stretch of staircase, he raised his father's sword high as Aerox grew closer. The arrows of the rangers behind him filled the air above him as the Elite finally collapsed before them. He could sense the end was nearing. Watching Aerox step within his range, Frederick swung his father's sword with everything he had.

Aerox's blade clashed with the yellow-hued steel of the Mirage, a shower of light erupting as the blades collided. Frederick had witnessed the holy power within his father's sword enough to realize something strange. Aerox grinned as his weapon held firmly against the Fallen steel.

"The Mirage of Metzor is not the only holy blade around, my prince. The Brotherhood of the Sin had long ago been forced to counter the Order's special blades. Those of its acolytes who serve them well are delivered such secret treasures." Swinging several times, the acolyte of the Sin went upon the offensive, seizing the moment.

Deflecting the attacks as they came, Frederick realized how they were all just pawns within a dangerous game. His father had sat with the Order whispering in one ear as the Sin listened from the other. Sven would have known every detail of his father's life and every conversation he had ever had. His father hadn't received a chance in Hell.

Frederick surprised himself as he managed to hold his ground against Aerox. Feeling his confidence rise as he realized dedication to training had actually paid off, he let it fuel him as he went upon the offensive. The Mirage of Metzor hacked away at the dark armour of Aerox, but Frederick was unable to deal any significant damage.

A Mortal Mistake

Swinging harder as the frustration rose, he realized he was about to pay for his mistake in pain.

The momentum of the glancing blow twisted Frederick out of position and his enemy wasted little time. Aerox swung his axe just as Frederick was attempting to bring his shield to defend his open flank. Feeling the edge of his shield jam into the shaft of the axe, it was not enough. Crying out in agony as the axe cut through the side of his golden armour, a gauntleted fist knocked him off his feet.

"Your skill has improved, Frederick. But you are still a far cry from matching your brothers skill." Aerox reached down to grab onto Frederick, slamming him against the rough stone wall. Lifting his axe behind his back, Aerox grinned at him as he taunted him with his failure. "Sven will be furious when he hears you were killed by my hand. Not because he ever loved you, but because I will have denied him the thrill of doing it himself."

An unexpected shove sent Aerox's swing off course, axe smashing into the rock face in a shower of sparks as the Shadow guard plunged face-first into the rock wall. Frederick turned to watch his saviour continue to dance throughout the cavern from battle to battle. Her smooth movement mesmerizing as Alexandra engaged her enemies with a deadly dance of blades, leaving the Metzonian knights in a sleep they would not wake from as they crumbled to the ground.

Watching Aerox clutch the rock wall in front of him, Frederick noticed his other hand was pressed tightly against the side of his neck. Pulling it away to look at the dark blood dripping down his fingers, a dangerous look crossed Aerox's face. Watching blood fill the whites of his dark eyes, Frederick fled for the cavern exit.

Feeling the fear within his soul come alive, Frederick realized he was not alone. Dozens of surviving rangers ran before him, stepping over the bodies of the hundreds that littered the staircase. A struggle between life and death continued around him by those unable to escape. Hundreds of bloody footprints led the way.

The morning light shimmered among the second curtain of water as Frederick watched several of the Fallen disappear through the other side. Others charged back through, the guilt of abandoning their brethren foolishly forcing them back into the fight. As Frederick turned to watch the brave charge back into the fight he stumbled upon the icy rocks. Twisting to look behind him, Frederick barely had enough time to raise his hand to protect himself.

Aerox pounced upon Frederick's chest, the forward momentum carrying both men forward into the pools of water. His face tingled beneath the icy waters as Frederick struggled against the thick forearms threatening to drown him. Watching oxygen bubbling from his nose as Aerox's knees pinned him to the bottom of the pool.

Having trouble distinguishing the features of Aerox's face through the water and his narrowing vision, Frederick had no difficulty seeing the smile upon the Royal Elite's face. Laughing as he watched Frederick slowly drown. Feeling a shadow pass over him, Aerox quickly looked up before he was thrown from his chest as a flash of silver crashed into the large man.

A bare hand plunged down into the water, grabbing onto his golden breastplate and hoisting him from his watery grave. Frederick collapsed upon the stone, coughing up all the water Aerox had force-fed him. Opening his eyes to stare at the large steel boots before him, his gaze carried higher towards the broad shouldered figure carrying a large curved sword in his right hand. A round silver shield upon his left arm, the five-falling-star emblem of the Order emblazoned upon it, already red with Aerox's blood.

The thick armour hidden within the thick fur cloak of solid white, the figure within the full-faced mask of silver steel looked over his left shoulder at him. As the shining golden eyes that reminded Frederick of his father looked down upon him, the Mirage of Metzor was kicked towards him.

Bellowing in anger as his prey escaped again, the bloodied Aerox charged towards the newest competitor. Kallen charged forward in kind, not intimidated at the size of his opponent. Tucking his shoulder into the curve of his own shield as he dug low, Frederick watched the terrible collision of two titans.

The mass of Aerox appeared weightless before gravity regained it grasp upon him. Tumbling backwards as he fell, the rattle of steel echoed particularly loud within Frederick's ears. Rising to his feet one more, he began to walk through the battles towards the two giants who continued to fight. Bending over to pick up the Mirage, he watched Kallen hammer Aerox back down to his knees.

Swinging his axe as he pivoted, Aerox hacked at the advancing Titan but Kallen easily knocked the attack aside before slicing Aerox's arm clean off. Clutching the remains of his arm as he rested upon his knees, Aerox looked up towards the man waiting for him to finish the job. Yet the Titan just stood there.

Kallen looked over his left shoulder at Frederick once again, slowly turning and walked away as he left Aerox's final fate to him. Calmly walking towards his father's personal guard, Fredericks grip grew tighter as he leveled his father's sword.

"My father treated you like a member of his own family, Aerox!"

Chuckling laughter erupted from Aerox's lungs as his tongue reached out to taste his own blood that dripped onto his lips. "Indeed he did, and I treated him just like your brothers treated family! At least I was at his side when he died. Where were you, my prince?"

Screaming out in agony as he released his pent up anger, Frederick plunged the Mirage of Metzor into the chest of his father's betrayer. Tears of release began to flow as his lips trembled as he tried to control his emotions. The bloody red eyes of Aerox blinked several times as his mouth opened and closed several time but no words escaped.

Feeling a hand clasp onto his shoulder that began dragging him out of the tunnel, Frederick could not look away from the large body of black armour. Vengeance had finally been done upon one of many who had conspired to take away everything from him. Knowing he would never find peace until justice was done upon his father's murders, Frederick understood what it would require of him.

Even it if meant slaying his own brother.

The icy waters made Kallen shiver as he passed through them a second time, dragging his companion through the mountain waters. The Fallen rangers were quickly losing ground to the Metzonians, their thick armour and aggressiveness too much for lightly armoured rangers to handle. Frederick had not brought enough of his own heavy armour to hold any longer. Several continued to fight on, sacrificing their lives to hold back the tide so others could escape. Other refused to abandon their brothers to death, charging back into the fight already bloodied.

Line upon line of horses was tied outside the rear waterfall entrance, and many of the rangers were already grasping at reins to make their escape. Horror struck Kallen to witness the number of mounts waiting for masters that would never return.

"Quick! Get the hell out of here, Metzonian!"

"What about you? What of your sister?" Pain wheezed in Frederick's voice as he continued his laboured breathing. The predawn sky was awaking to the world of blood, sweat and grief, the chilly morning air fresh compared to that within the confinements of the cavern.

Alexandra burst through the waters in response to Frederick's question as he pulled himself wearily atop his mount. Kallen's sister was covered in blood, hot tears streaming down her face as her body trembled uncontrollably. Grasping both her arms tightly in his hands, Kallen looked into her eyes to ensure she understood his vital words.

"Get what remains of your rangers through the Final Pass. Our numbers are too thin to defend it anymore, so get to the gates and alert the Elders about the passes and what has happened. They will be arriving upon the walls within days." Kallen helped her mount the white mare beside Frederick's golden palomino stallion and worried about her. Looking to the brightening sky above the mountain range to his left, at the snow-covered peaks high above the valley, he searched for his last chance to halt the invasion.

"Where are my brothers?" Kallen was surprised by the sudden change in topic and did not know how to answer the question. Frederick had told them everything about his brothers. Both the men enjoyed leading their warriors into battle personally, savouring war and carnage with a personal touch; to not see them in the forefront was unusual.

A Mortal Mistake

"We shall see them before the Gates of the Sacred Citadel. Now go!" Slapping the stallion upon the rump, Kallen sent the horse with its rider down the narrow trail that would ultimately cut through the large valley toward the distant Final Pass. Cutting several lines of horses free, Kallen slipped through them, plunging into the snow, letting several of them follow him to cover his tracks as he raced for the cover of the pine trees at the mountains edge.

Bloodlust continued to ravage the Metzonians who overpowered the last of the fleeing Fallen, hacking men down and savagely mutilating their corpses. Kallen climbed higher up the rocky slope, several times having to climb in short vertical bursts. None of the advancing troops noticed him, their vision narrowed to those who were riding as fast as they could to make their escape.

Bloody fingers dug into the rock and ice as he made his ascent with the sunlight upon his back, clinging to the rock as he pulled himself at last to the shelf he had been aiming toward, a pile of snow cooled his weary and sweaty body. He stopped to remove his steel mask, the cold winter air rushing in to freeze against his perspiring face. His plan to scale a mountain wearing his armour was a ridiculous idea, but Kallen had few options. Climbing up was the easy part. It mattered not as he stood in the late afternoon sun. He had made it at last, several hours behind schedule and completely exhausted, but he made it. Reaching the ledge, Kallen grew worried when he did not see what he was hoping to see in the deep snow, nor any sign of where it might lay.

Digging through the heavy snowfall, he used his wide shield to shovel the snow over the cliff edge. The Elders would be horrified to see him using the holy relic of Orion as a common shovel, a thought that made him chuckle to himself. Numb fingers burrowing through the deep snow, he desperately hoped to soon find what he was looking for. The snow had fallen heavily within the mountain interior, burying the surrounding mountain peaks in a thick cap of snow, making his difficult task a nightmare.

Feeling the scrape of steel on steel, Kallen paused; digging through the snow with his bare hands, he uncovered the white steel of Heaven. An ancient language scribed in dull orange encircled the length of the horn. Like a coiled white snake, the horn might have been ten feet long uncoiled. The head of the horn, several inches in diameter, sprang upwards and out toward the valley before it.

Grinning widely in triumph, Kallen used all his strength to try to lift the horn, yet it refused to budge. Resisting his strength, the heavy white steel and the ice encasing it refused to move the slightest. Kallen peered down into the steepest portions of the Three Passes, monitoring the progress of his enemies and his allies.

The valley between the River Pass and the Final Pass was full of Metzonian soldiers, surging from the river passage like ants. A large group of the cavalry had secured the horses left behind to carry the slain rangers. Some were chasing after the few rangers who were barely visible from his vantage point. A large gap was widening through the steepest potion of the pass, the rangers expertly navigating the path they had ridden hundreds of times before.

Heavy cavalry was riding equally hard in pursuit, with much less success. The rage of battle had evaporated, and self-doubt crept back in their minds. Behind them, the first of the vanguard had successfully navigated through the tunnels and emerged. With a quickened pace the infantry had reformed in the open space into the perfect lines not allowed by the tight tunnel.

Kallen had pleaded with the Elders to allow him to take the entire army into the mountain passes, to try to blockade their impending doom. He had been denied several times, despite the support of many of the other commanders. The remaining Elders' fear of the Dark Powers was too great for them to be left beneath the shadow of the Lifebringer without protection. They refused to leave the Sacred City and the temple undefended and demanded the army remain within the walls, despite the strategic opportunity afforded to them by the Alakari and the narrow river pass. Kallen had thought they would have learned better after their mistake with Prokopolis. Perhaps they believed that it was their destiny to die within the walls, surrounded by everything that was sacred to the Order of the Fallen. But they forgot it was no longer just the Fallen within the walls. Metzonians, Kyllordic, Prokopolites—all were huddled within the walls and had more to sacrifice than simply the sanctity of the surrounding walls: wives, children, and the future. It had become about more than a struggle between good and evil. It was about the struggle for survival of Humanity.

And now the end would begin soon.

The vanguard was completely through the river pass, and their soldiers were on their way to gain control of the final bottleneck that protected the Sacred City and its inhabitants. Even though it was a still a day's march away, it was inevitable now that the army would reach it. From his vantage point Kallen could see over the inner mountains to the crown of the world, the tallest peak among the Alakari shrouded in a misty cover against the backdrop of the afternoon sun. If his dangerous gamble did not pay off, he would never look upon the Sacred City again. The remnants of the Order could certainly have defeated or at least withstood the Metzonian army now marching far beneath him. Were the Chilsa army to reach the walls, they would stand against impossible odds, but there was still a chance.

"Well, here goes nothing." Kallen looked at the peaks around him one last time.

Tightening his cloak around him and ensuring that all his equipment was firmly attached to his person, he knelt on one knee. Expanding his lungs with the cool mountain air, he blew into the long coiled horn, bellowing out heavily among the mountain peaks, a sound not heard in thousands of years.

The marching Metzonians instinctively stopped, looking toward the sky and mountain peaks surrounding them. The low, heavy rumble of Hellio reverberated upon the snowy peaks again, and small rocks trembled. Panic broke out within the ranks of disciplined Metzonian regulars following the vanguard as the distinct cracking of snow joined the bellowing horn sounding above them.

Tucking himself between the heavy horn and the cliff, Kallen wrapped his thick snow tiger fur around him again and sat back to watch the tumbling snow slide from its lofty height. He could not hear the cries of the men far beneath the mountain. Roaring snow shook the mountain before encasing him and the horn.

Chapter 39
Death's Dark Destiny

Rhimmon monitored the army as they pushed into the final mountain passage and gazed upon the farthest point Hell's armies had ever reached. The resistance along the long, winding mountain pass had been futile against the monstrosity that he'd helped the Metz brothers create. Strong by Humanity's standards, it was weakly pathetic by Hell's.

The Dark Prince could not believe his luck when he felt the powerful soul of the second son of Metz pass the bridges into his realm. Testing the prince against those in the Desert of Lost Souls, he knew he had found the soul that would not fail him as others had before.

King Mallax had been the first true puppet of the Dark Prince and a thrilling opportunity. But it had been a disastrous affair, the pathetic human mind snapping under the pressure the demon placed upon it. It had been a learning experience for the Prince of Greed, one that he was glad he had learned before the truly powerful soul of Sven had entered the desert decades later. His brother coming to the desert had been the final catalyst required to seal Sven's fate.

Eagerly trading his father's life in exchange for that of his little brothers, Sven's debt had grown steeper. Not realizing the seed of darkness Rhimmon planted within his brother, Sven's rage at being betrayed had been comical. Once released, Rhimmon spread his dark influence to every corner of Metzon, filling the hearts of all its citizens with an unquenchable thirst for power. No real power had to be expended upon them; the nationalistic population only needed a light nudge in the right direction.

Now bound to one another by a single demonic bond, Rhimmon's mortal army was complete and prepared to crush his final opponents. Provided the Fallen did not come up with any more clever ideas, such as the one that buried the front of his army beneath an avalanche. The demon clenched his fists at the unforeseen action brought on by the Fallen. He would concede the small stroke of brilliance that cost him time and soldiers, but it would not halt what was coming to those waiting within the walls before him.

The first battalions pushed into the Final Pass opening and would soon spill out onto the expansive field, glimpsing the city they would soon die within. This was where Rhimmon and his brothers wanted them, trapped among the lakes and mountains, where one final act would eliminate all their opponents. The Mortal Army of Darkness continued to funnel into the final pass toward their true target. Soon the war would begin and test the will of the last remaining good men to their limits.

"I must say that they look impressive for being weak and clueless humans. Too bad that they are of little use. Small and weak as they stand alone, it requires such a large population to accomplish anything of significance. There is such weakness within this world; it should not have been as troublesome as it has been."

Rhimmon listened to Adramaleck's words of truth. It really should not have been as difficult as it had been to subdue this world, but it had not been Humanity that had prevented it last time.

"They will serve the purpose that is demanded of them. And while there is little other use for them battlewise, I think that we will find other uses for them somewhere within the plans."

"Even as slave labour they are weak and useless. I suppose we could feed them to ..."

Rhimmon halted the Prince of Flames comment, already fully understanding the limitations of Humanity. *"Let us stay with the* task at hand, Adramaleck. I trust the remainder of the plans continue?"

"*Your puppet and his crew are in place and likely preparing for their mission. Those petty dark angels showed up as well, but not as many as I would have preferred for the task required. Far too much of our success lies within the Sin's hands for my liking, Brother. They could ruin everything! Will the rest of their disgusting kind show up?*"

Mammon asked a fair question, especially for righteous angels. Darker than their cousins, the Sin were not dark enough to even serve as chambermaids in Hell's halls. No time could be spent chasing around such dissidents, who would have to be dealt with after all else was taken care of.

"*If they do not, I will hunt them all down and ensure their spirits will burn for eternity. I have an insurance policy for such an event. I do not think it shall be needed.*" Rhimmon had arranged with Abaddon to part with several battalions of his growing demonic army. Extremely agitated and resistive to such an action, Abbadon feared upsetting a plan of grandeur beyond even the Dark Princes themselves and refused be held accountable for such failure.

"*Of the human whom released us—you put a very risky prospect on the fates of our plans by believing the Metzonian and his brother will be able to defeat a heavenly being …*" Both his brothers looked at him after the remark rolled off Adramaleck's forked tongue.

Rhimmon took a break from watching his mortals march toward their impending deaths. "*What would you suggest, Adramaleck? A personal intervention?*" Rhimmon snorted, shaking his head, turning back to his brothers. "*You both know how rattled Abaddon was in regard to the situation. Whomever Heaven has left within the Temple Mountain, they would undoubtedly sense you the moment you stepped onto that rock. You would not reach the front door without Heaven raining down upon you. We shall only intervene if absolutely necessary!*"

"*Abaddon is as weak and fearful as he has always been. A

dread lord who is unworthy of death itself, he should be cast from the hierarchy for the shame upon his black soul," Mammon hissed angrily, refusing to let Abaddon's slight against him abide.

*"Perhaps, but whomever this angel of Heaven may be, it will not sense the humans to be our assassins. **The corruption of the Metz brothers' souls are complete; the only ties to Humanity are their own physical abilities. He and his companions will succeed. Soon enough the Temple Mountain will be in our hands.*** The rewards for such a task would be glorious and renowned greatly in the realm of Hell. Such had been dreamed about by many demon lords, but they were going to succeed where others had failed. Rhimmon and his brothers had no doubts about their plans. And with the Order's defeat, their accession to the higher halls of Hell would soon follow.

The fortress was in a dead calm. A skeleton crew was commanded to man the walls simply to maintain a watchful eye on the pass. All knew what lay beyond the protective mountain ridge, even if they could not see it. All eyes waited for the threat to come boiling toward them.

Everything was prepared, as it had been for years as they waited for the Order's enemies to return from the shadows and rear their ugly faces. The armouries were stocked, blades sharpened, armour shined—all waiting to be bloodied in the final struggle.

The bulk of the Fallen's army resided in the Sacred City, enjoying the last few days with family or relaxing beside its streams to calm their minds before the storm. All knew what they were about to sacrifice their lives for, and reminders surrounded them at every turn. All were ready to be taken away whether they fought for those ideals or not, but for the moment they were able to savour such things.

Kallen stood looking out from the central bell tower down upon the layers of ramparts and bridges. The defences had been set and prepared as the war council had decided. Kallen found himself the first mortal to defend the Heaven's ancient stronghold upon Earth, a feat the even his grandfather never claimed.

Hearing the others regrouping around the table, Kallen reconvened the council to discuss the final aspects of the battle plan and to see if anyone had anything else to add or bold new ideas to propose. Walking into the room and feeling the overwhelming tension, he noticed that the Kyllordic prince and his two generals sat at the far end of the table, eyeing the Metzonian prince, flanked by several of his own commanders who ignored the stares completely.

Raising an eyebrow toward his sister at the situation, he let the Fallen military leaders file in last and take their proper places around the circular chamber. All stood silently waiting for him to begin, allowing him to turn the attention away from past feuds toward the looming disaster moving ever closer to them.

"Okay, let us begin, gentlemen. As we all know, holding the first wall will be the key to the defence of the castle. While the largest wall to maintain, it is the only one that will see the attack on a single front. Once our enemies are over the first wall and gain full control of it, we will be completely surrounded, and fighting will spread to all fronts." Kallen looked at the model of the fortress that stood in the middle of the war room, one half of the outer walls standing upon land and the other surrounded by the cold mountain waters of the Lake of Heavenly Sorrow.

"Remember that if you feel that you are losing a section, do not risk becoming entrapped. Pull your men back across the bridges and reset on the next wall. We must hold each wall as long as possible to have any chance of weathering this storm, but it will do us no good if we unnecessarily lose all our soldier strength defending one wall.

"The outer ring wall and the gatehouse must hold out the longest, which our enemy no doubt understands. Our granite walls are almost impenetrable; forcing the majority of their strategy to focus on getting over our walls. We must try to repel as many attacks as possible and eliminate their options. Our biggest worries will be the siege towers and ladders, as those are the only ways they can get significant enough numbers up top." Unable to dig trenches into the rocky ground to halt the rolling siege towers, Kallen had ordered the

A Mortal Mistake

large stones within the Alakari be placed before the walls, providing immovable obstacles. But the fortress wall was too long and there was simply not enough time to effectively deploy the tactic.

"The gatehouse is fortunately very strong and will withstand an external attack, but it will still be the primary target for those who reach the walls. To flood the fortress with the full extent of their army, they will have to seize and maintain control. Going over the walls will be time consuming, and cost many lives at the start, and that is where our only advantage against them lies. Holding the gates will allow us to rearrange the odds significantly."

Alexandra looked at her brother. They both knew that such odds would still be far from being in their favour. An entire nation was preparing to march upon one castle, and formidable as the fortifications might be, they were the underdog in this battle.

"I do not think it will matter either way. They have a force large enough that they will simply swarm over us. Like ants, they will climb the walls, squeeze through the holes and cut us down. We can burn off the first few waves, but soon enough we shall be overrun," young Prince Raef added sourly, his stare and comment directed to the Metzonian prince in exile.

The Kyllordic leader remained upset over the losses they sustained while being overrun by the neighbouring kingdom of Metzon, and he refused to resolve the grudge. Corruption did not seem to run rampant through his kingdom as it had through its neighbour. It had not mattered in the end though; Kallen had tried to explain to the young man that the Metzonians within this citadel were as angry about the situation as he was. The stubbornness of the prince was not to be released though, irritating Kallen. The pending battle could afford no unrest.

"Unfortunately for us, we do not have any other option than to try. Hopefully we can hold our own against such impossible odds. If that doesn't work, you better start praying for a miracle, because you don't have any other choice in the matter." Clutching his injured ribs closely, Frederick gruffly spoke as his short temper started to flare.

"You are holding your own against mortal enemies, as though that really matters. Those are not the enemies that are really coming for you. It's the Dark Princes of Hell and probably those damn Sin soldiers I keep hearing about. A miracle is the only thing we really have left now. All you Metzonians are too stupid to see such truth, aren't you?"

"Ah, well. Let's take the Kyllordic route and just flee. We'll run and run and run. At least some of us are making an attempt to solve it, to find a solution, while others just hide and cower from the problems around them." Frederick slammed his hand down upon the table, staring fiercely at the younger man, prepared to throw down at the next remark.

"Relax …"

Nerves were flaring between the respective leaders. Kallen knew that he had to keep everyone tight and controlled if they were to have any chance. If the Metzonians got any more riled up, the meeting would end in blows and a lot of wounded pride. "We all know about the situation and how bleak it is. Every one of us just has to hold it together, take a breath and continue on. We are all soldiers, the best leading the best from our nations. We are against overwhelming odds, and even the best cannot withstand forever. But if they want to take this fortress, then they are going to have to do it down to the last beating heart."

Prince Frederick replied, "My apologies, General Kallen, as well as to those of the Kyllordic nation. I too have been forced to flee when the situation did not present more … likable terms before the same enemy, and it was uncalled for to point that out."

Alexandra looked at Kallen, as surprised as he, caught off guard by the sudden apology. Perhaps seeing the final struggle and possible death made the man understand he already had too much hate to carry more needlessly.

Kallen waited for the Kyllordic prince to follow but continued on when he realized the younger man was not prepared to put the rift behind him. "Once we lose control of the outer wall, everyone is to use the bridges to the second wall. The only forces that will remain on the outer wall will be those holding the sea wall and preventing complete loss of the wall. As much as I would like to avoid heavy man-to-man conflict with the Metzonians, I want to avoid fighting the three hundred sixty degree war I mentioned earlier. We can funnel reinforcements up to the second wall if needed. If the gates open or the possibility of losing the second wall appears, then all units will abandon the first wall and funnel into the third and fourth."

Alexandra took over. "Use as many of the fortress defences as possible to stall the assault. The longer we can stall the full use of their army, the heavier their losses. We want to make this place even more of a nightmare to attack than already it is. Fortunately for us, the Architects understood battle as well as construction and understood how to defend against their enemies.

"If it gets to the point where we have lost all walls besides the tower, the bridge defence will begin. And that will be a head-to-head battle for life and death. For every foot we give up, we're going to take as many attackers as we can. Can everyone agree with this battle plan?" Alexandra asked the war council. Royalty, generals and commanders all nodded their heads, looking for someone to disagree. All had fought multiple wars with their own strategies, but none argued against the simple and efficient plan.

The deep bellow of distant horns signalled that they were out of time. The army was upon them, and there was no way out. The army that believed in life and all things that are good was about to duel for the world against all that was evil.

Council members pushed themselves up from their seats and stepped outside onto the bell tower balcony, looking out across the walls toward the southern horizon. Infantry wearing the dark armour of the Metzonian armies marched across the open field before them, flattening the flowery fields beneath their boots. On the wide open plains, they moved quickly and with incredible fluidity into perfect formations. They all watched for an hour as the Metzonian army grew ever closer, leaving them speechless at the sight.

"So my brothers bring the full might of the Metzonian nation to bear against us. This will indeed be a battle to the death. Perhaps I will receive the opportunity to slay my traitorous family and reclaim what was mine." Frederick clutched his father's sword to his chest tightly, memories flooding his mind.

"I fear that the Metzonian nation is not the only force that we face. And small in comparison …" the Kyllordic General Ethan announced, his eyes keener than many of those around him. Alexandra looked into the distance, trying to see what he was talking about. Faint sounds gave the first hints of what he was talking.

Kallen knew who was now arriving, for he had seen the soldiers when he was upon the cliffs of the Alakari. It would seem they had almost caught up with their enemy. The heavy sound of thousands of drums could be heard echoing within the mountain pass as a pinpoint of shimmering silver shined into the valley. The reflection grew brighter and larger as time passed slowly, hiding what came behind it. The beating drums grew louder, and then the fortress defenders caught the first sight of the renowned blue and white banners. The Chilsa Empire had also arrived upon the grassy plains.

"What the hell are the Chilsa doing here?" the Kyllordic prince asked aloud, confused about the situation.

"The emperor has come to destroy the Metzonian Army and complete their empire. Upon the defeat what remains of my people, I would guess they will continue to destroy the Order, leaving none to oppose them."

Frederick watched his father's citizen's march toward one enemy and away from another, feeling a pang of guilt and anger. In response to the Metzonian movement, the Chilsa army systematically adjusted the forces already in the valley. The survivors within the bell tower were stunned when the two forces prepared to link up in perfect unison and continued to march toward the imposing fortress walls. Two mortal enemies had seemingly set aside their differences to bring the end of the Order of the Fallen.

"You have got to be kidding me …"

All hope evaporated from the war council. Their defiant attitudes melted as men lost their tempers and others doubled over with hopelessness. Prince Raef cursed loudly at his generals for leading him to his death, as the Metzonian prince smashed the model fortress to pieces.

Kallen quickly took command of the group, reasserting himself. "Fate has arrived at our doorstep, men; let us find out what it has in

A Mortal Mistake

store with us. Our battle plan remains the same. Let us go out there and show them steel. Ring the tower bells to bring the fortress to full battle stations, and start praying."

Kallen and the rest of the command staff started to descend toward the impending battle, the heavy bells ringing out across the valley drowning out all other sound. All walked with heavy feet to the overwhelming task at hand. Demons would not be required; Humanity would destroy one another, leaving few left to witness the horrors of Hell. Perhaps that was a positive thing.

The young emperor sat upon his large blue and white travelling throne, marvelling at the sight before him. The high walls were glorious and seemed to shine even in the evening light. Although Kristolphe was not well educated in the history of the world before Humanity truly prospered, he had to admit that those of the Order knew how to build a fortress. His imagination doubted itself at the prospect, wondering what the Sacred City must look like. This was a bastion that put even his father's own Imperial Citadel to shame. Though perhaps not as tall as the Imperial Citadel, height would not have mattered in the shadow of the great mountain and its thousand waterfalls. The sheer size and the magnitude of the space that the fortress encompassed was astonishing, even without its stunning architecture adding to the glory.

"Wow!"

The emperor's generals stood before him, not sharing in his awe of the fortress. Great concern was written upon their faces. The large task of somehow finding a way of defeating the enemies upon the city's magnificent walls landed squarely upon their shoulders, and they were to do it as efficiently as possible given the other parameters of their orders.

"Well, generals. Go ahead and tell me how you plan to bring down the mighty fortress of the Order. I'm excited to hear how you plan to write one of the greatest moments in history."

No siege in Chilsa's history of sacking cities and subsuming entire populations had ever been waged on a level such as this.

Thousands of cities and hundreds of great castles had felt the touch of their trebuchets as their population trembled at the distinctive swoosh of the swinging arm and crashing rocks. Looking upon the thick, seamless rock walls, the emperor did not feel as confident, knowing its population would not fear them or beg for servitude. One wall at a time, this battle would not be won until every enemy within the fortress had been slain.

"We are finishing our plan for the attack formation, my emperor. Our siege engineers are already starting on the construction of the large siege equipment. The gates seem to be one of the strongest points of the castle and are made of what appears to be thick stone. We will test it regardless." The man stood tall, letting his comrade take over and expand upon the siege engineers' plan.

"It must be noted that construction may take slightly longer than anticipated. The walls are … higher than we had expected, my emperor. Our siege towers must be expanded substantially simply to reach the top of the first wall. However, once the siege equipment is complete we shall start to systematically test the walls for weakness with the throwers before proceeding with a manned assault involving the towers. I must warn his highness that losses will be incredibly heavy as we try to get a foothold upon the fortress. The defences, as you can see, are most … impressive."

"Yes, I do see that, General, and the solution is quite simple." Kristolphe rose from his throne and looked out across the army spread before him, spotting the black and golden banners at the forefront. "Use the Metzonians. That is what they are there for, remember. Everyone knows they like fighting impossible battles to prove their prowess, so make them feel good."

All nodded in agreement with the emperor's assessment, several smiling at the thought of being able to command their lifelong enemies to pursue their own deaths.

"I fear to ask, my emperor, but would it not be easier to starve the army and the entire people? We understand the population within its walls is impossible to feed for very long. There is nowhere for them to escape, and a Chilsa life would not be spent."

"Has Chilsa in its long, proud history ever wasted its time,

A Mortal Mistake

waiting to starve our enemies into submission? Or have we broken down the doors to remind our enemies of our indisputable power?" His father would never have allowed his army to wait outside the doors of an enemy until they submitted to his will. Kristolphe had no qualms about the general's suggestions, but he had the entire Metzonian nation to use as an expendable force and would not let such an opportunity go to waste.

"By tomorrow night I want those white walls red with the blood of our enemies. You will find that I can lack even my father's patience. Do not let me down! Dismissed." Sitting back in his throne, he watched his army arrayed before him as the command staff hurried from the makeshift room.

Even as emperor and the chief commander of every invading soul in the inner valley, he did not exactly have free will or control of their timetable. Control of his first true battle was not actually his at all; he was merely the figurehead trapped under the command of the impatient. His father could be considered patient by the true commanders of this battle. The Dark Princes would not wait for the mortal army to take the fight to the enemy. Kristolphe knew that, having waited thousands of years for this revenge, they refused to allow their plan to expand a day longer than absolutely necessary. The punishment for failure from his father had always been dark and cruel, often inflicting both physical and mental pain. But to discover the torture a Prince of Hell would unleash from his black heart?

That was a road that Kristolphe had no intention of travelling down.

The dark silhouette of the temple entrance was barely visible in the darkness, lit only by the light from the full moon. The small boats made their way across the Lake of Heavenly Tears, or Sorrow, or whatever Mammon had called it. Devotz sat motionless as the small force slowly reached their destination, paddling in slow silence as they glided toward the mountain sprouting from the middle of the lake. No words were spoken; any noise held the possibility of sinking them to the bottom.

They had waited impatiently for the sun to set, listening to the rumble that seemed to be taking place across the lake as the armies preparing to shed blood tried to intimidate one another. Both brothers wanted to be there right now, in the midst of the largest mortal conflict on the earth. They should have been leading their armies over the walls, all the way to the temple entrance, but instead that honour had been given to Belle's brother Kristolphe. Devotz doubted the man would even draw a sword for fear of blisters on his soft, manicured hands.

Devotz paddled carefully, ensuring that he did not touch the water, which one of the Brotherhood had discovered was quite dangerous. He looked over to the empty spot in the other boat where the missing Brotherhood member would have sat. Hearing shrieking from across the camp, Devotz had stormed over, pushing the dark angels aside to see what caused the commotion. Devotz realized the fool who clutched the stump of his arm before him had dipped his hand into the icy waters, not realizing its purity would burn corrupted souls. Raging at such stupidity and putting the secrecy of their mission at risk, Devotz stepped forward and lifted his leg high. He forcefully kicked the Sin back into the water. The Sin thrashed around in the holy water while the flesh burned from his bones. His screams soon came to a halt, leaving no trace of what happened.

The remaining Brotherhood members had been furious, which created great tension between the two groups. Devotz did not care at all for the Brotherhood and would have thrown them all into the cursed lake if he had his way. But Rhimmon had commanded that they create chaos within the temple and provide him with the opportunity to succeed with his primary objective.

The thought of the Dark Prince's primary objective sent tendrils of anticipation through Devotz. He was barely able to contain himself. The moment could not come soon enough for him. He barely caught a glimpse of the large bridge expanding across the strait. It was not lit but hid in the darkness like the rest. *They prefer to sit in the cold as well as the dark*, Devotz thought as he looked at the temple entrance, which was also without torch light. The entire complex was without any form of light except from the moon.

A Mortal Mistake

Tonight they had to reach the rocky base of the Lifebringer and start their ascent. His master's armies were no doubt surrounding the fortress, preparing for the assault on the grand fortifications. He did not think that it was possible to organize such a terrifying army of unbelievable size, but few others knew the extent of what Hell's power could do, let alone witnessed it as he had.

Belle's small craft was widening the gap as she tried to scout the best route. Without the moonlight, the task would have been impossible. It was still proving extremely difficult, especially without attracting unwanted notice. Continuing to cling to the shadow the mountain cast across the lake, her craft pushed toward the niche that she'd spotted.

So it began! Devotz motioned toward the location silently, preparing his gear for the climb.

The rocky outcropping was large enough for the attack party and their supplies. All prepared for the next part of the difficult plan. A complex and deadly plan usually meant rewarding results, especially with unsuspecting guards. But to get even remotely close, they would have to traverse up the rock of the Fountain of Life and over its endless streams of holy water.

Konflikt started up the mountainside first, heavily muscled arms pulling his mass up. His brother noticed how much the younger sibling had grown, the dark corruption of his soul expanding him into a beast of reckoning. He'd doubled in size, and Devotz was eager to witness his brother's true power in battle now. Konflikt would lead the way and show the rest of the party up to the next rest point and then into the temple.

Devotz looked at the long climb up the slippery mountain; he'd long anticipated this glorious fight. Somewhere within the mountain awaited a true test for his battle expertise, which none in this world could best. He would prove the Princes of Darkness wrong and show them the true might of the Metz family.

Chapter 40
Raining Blood

The Dark Princes of Hell looked down upon the soaring walls before Heaven's ancient stronghold at long last. The demon lords had led hundreds of Hell's army into the Alakari against Heaven in countless epic struggles but had never before been able to penetrate the imposing mountain range that had long protected the fabled Lifebringer.

The misty purity that spread out from the Lifebringer through the mountains shielded everything from their unholy eyes with a burning brightness that struck the Dark Princes eyes from afar, abating only when they moved through the rocky passes. That had once been a treacherous proposition when Heaven's holy blades hid amongst their misty peaks to dive down upon the demons below. But times had changed, and Heaven no longer defended the Lifebringer; only the disgraced shadows of the Fallen remained.

"Here we are, brothers! Look at it in its magnificence in the shadows of the Mountain of Endless Life. Hidden from us for the ages, it has now at last been revealed and finally stands before us, the last bastion of Heaven's hopes and dreams for this world. With its destruction we shall permanently remove Heaven's foothold from this world."

Rhimmon gazed upon the Lifebringer, from which Heaven's high generals had coordinated the attacks of their holy blades against the Lords of Hell. Beyond the Lifebringer, he saw the Fallen had been busy within the Valley of Angels, building many great structures, including the great fortress and bridge. He could smell their fear and despair as they huddled within their weak mortal structures.

"I have waited too long in this world to see this moment with my own eyes, although my vision of this final battle had a darker and more sinister appearance. Perhaps we should provide a proper atmosphere for the Fallen's impending doom. One more suitable to the forthcoming death and destruction?" Wings stretched out wide as Mammom flew his hefty mass toward the peak above their mountain perch. Shouting his ancient curses into the cold morning breeze, he raised his fists over his head, letting his forgotten powers flow to the sky.

"As the storm bleeds, so shall those who stand against us." The armies below searched among the mountain peaks, trying to pinpoint who spoke, but the voice came from all around them. The wind grew fiercely warm, swirling around the men, blowing the dust and leaves around them as grey clouds boiled higher and darker. Swirling around the mountains as the clear sky grew smaller with every fleeting moment, brief orange flashes of lightning spread within the storm.

Mammom opened the storm up, letting a bloody rain fall from the sky. Rhimmon's army beneath the storm revelled in the hot rains from his dark brother, feeding off the power of the storm, drawing blades already running with red. Sending out his dark influence among those within the valley, Rhimmon let himself creep into the hearts of the Chilsa, igniting their souls in a blaze of rage as they looked around the events upon them with confusion.

Humanity was feeble compared to their power, unable to resist the forces residing in their dark hearts as they corrupted and deformed the souls of men to their will and designs. Their minds hungered for worthy opponents to test their powers and strength against. The Princes of Hell's thirst for heavenly blood had expanded as they wandered the world; they were now reunited in the full extent of their universal power.

Rhimmon shouted out to the bloodthirsty army, his dark influence flowing out over all his minions. *"It has been far too long since we waged true war against our enemies. Too long this world has sat without knowing true fear and terror. Reunited we shall remind this world of its long-forgotten fears and tear open the wounds of old. Let us not waste any more time and throw the first punch in this war."* The dark army went into frenzy, screaming savagely, jabbing swords in the air, as hearts thirsted for blood and the beginning of the assault. Siege weapons unleashed the first artillery strike, and boulders smashed into the wall as the endless siege towers rolled forward. The hordes charged the walls, each eager to be the first to reach the wall, eager to be the first to die.

Listening to the screams of a million men calling for their blood, the defending army huddled below their defences, holding on to the shaking walls. The end war had finally arrived at their doorstep.

The ancient walls refused to let loose, mocking the assault as though it were dirt blown on the face of a rhino. The punishing assault continued without pause, the attackers determined to smash through the walls. Kallen did not worry yet; the Order had carved the walls of the fortress from the granite formation that it rested upon. Solid, seamless stone from outside to inside, it would withstand any brute force thrown at it.

The forces of evil were not completely oblivious to the fact that their assault upon the walls had left little damage. The majority of the long-armed catapults were adjusted to assault the battlements, pinning down the defenders as the siege towers and short catapults rumbled toward the soaring walls. Those remaining continued firing upon the gatehouse, determined to wear down the walls holding the thick gates.

Tall siege towers slowly progressed toward the white walls, foot by foot. The men beneath them struggled, pushing and pulling the towering wooden structures. The defenders had watched from the safety of the walls throughout the night as the towers were constructed section by section at a frenetic pace. Archers from atop and below fired upon the defenders hiding behind the crenels of the fortress walls, trying to protect the vulnerable crews. The castle defences still remained silent, waiting for a lull in the attack that many thought would not come.

Kallen stared down at the great strength pitted against them. From the bell tower, he could see both armies in their entirety; the enemy army was arrayed from shore to shore, a full hundred and eighty degrees before him. The dissident armies of Metzon and the Order that fought for freedom matched their opponents within the walls, positioned within the first two rings, facing their opponents and waiting for the opportune time to attack.

"So much hope rides upon us holding the gatehouse and the first wall. Look at all of them …" The black flags snapped in the stiff wind as the Metzonian Elite stood huddled atop the gatehouse awaiting their attacking brethren.

The oldest Metzonian brother had demanded that he and his men be charged with defending the fortress gates. Alexandra believed that the proud man had wanted to restore honour to his father's name and restore the glory that it had once been renowned for. Kallen, however, knew the truth; Frederick sought one soul among the million before him. He waited for the one who had taken everything from him. The exile was itching to return the favour.

Kallisto had come down from the Sacred Temple to join Kallen and Alexandra on the bell tower when he heard the chilling demonic words carried on the furious wind. He arrived in time to witness the storm seal off the fortress from daylight. He did not speak a word, his eyes sad to witness the charging mass of men who were soon to die.

"Hard to believe that there are this many people in this world, and all are here to participate in the end. The fate of Humanity rests upon the results of this battle; I suppose I would want to participate in it as well. I wonder how many lives will be lost during this battle." Kallen observed the swells of Humanity that stood outside the walls.

"So much hate and misunderstanding will cause such a massacre. All shall perish, Kallen. In the darkness, they are blind, rushing toward their death one way or another." Kallisto spoke softly, leaning on the edge of the bell tower and gazing at their warriors and the army beyond the walls.

"Perhaps in another, more peaceful lifetime we will have enough time to ponder such questions. Until such a time, we have to fight for ideals that are slowly dying, fight for the lives around us, as well as our own. We are returning fire." Alexandra called returning Kallen's attention to the battle, watching their enemy's army finally passing within range of the defenders.

Realizing that they could wait no longer, the Order's army on the walls opened fire. The wind carried the sounds of whizzing arrows and screaming men, mixed with the crashing of catapults, up to their ears. The spectacle before their eyes turned bloody as both sides engaged, killing without thought.

Siege towers reached the edges of the walls and prepared to drop their doors down upon the ramparts to unleash the tide of warm bodies within. Plumes of black smoke climbed into the air as hot pitch was thrown upon the tall wooden structures and ignited; their sister structures pulled up beside them to quash any small victory.

From the high vantage point on the central bell tower, the battle upon the ramparts looked to be fought by ants. The surge from the attackers and the counter surge of its defenders ebbed and flowed across all segments of the walls under siege.

"I am going down to the walls to join the fight."

"Remember a general's responsibility to his men, Kallen. You must direct those upon the walls to ensure the most successful defence. Your presence upon the wall will undoubtedly be welcomed, but the fortress is too large for one man's influence to truly be felt. Always remember the larger picture and the true goals over your own desires to help your friends and comrades."

Kallen stopped at the doorway, turned around and returned, unhappy at the necessity of his position. Kallisto certainly knew the desire that burned within his heart, as had his grandfather's and so many other heroes that had crossed this world. "Too many heroes have I watched seek their own deaths before their appointed time, Kallen. There will be ample opportunity to feel the heat of the battle;

A Mortal Mistake

I only ask that you pick your fights wisely. Life is not to be thrown away so carelessly, though it would seem our enemies disagree."

Squeezing both children upon the shoulders in a possible final farewell, Kallisto turned away from the carnage to start his way back slowly across the bridge toward the temple. "May we survive to see the end …"

The first rings of defences were swarmed by the enemy when the Order's defenders became unable to force back the tide. For half a day the warriors had bravely held the walls, cycling with their brothers on the inner walls so the exhausted could rest. The endless supply of soldiers was finally too overwhelming to resist, and in sections that had fallen to the enemy the Order called a reluctant retreat.

Frederick was forced to watch as the section of wall on the gatehouse's left flank had at last been overrun, leaving him vulnerable for the first time. Frederick had monitored what he could, watching beside the gatehouse for hours as both sides pressed hard to gain and regain lost ground. Fighting valiantly, the enemy on the left flank would now try to climb the narrow, enclosed staircases toward the gatehouse roof. And Frederick knew the thick doors would not hold forever.

The gate complex still remained strong despite the onslaught. The Metzonian Elite refused to give at all, following the lead of their fallen king's son. The first wall became black with the dark steel sea of infantry pouring out from remaining siege towers, not noticing the bodies they clambered over.

The siege weapons changed targets and honed in on the second wall, trying to protect the advancing soldiers from the Fallen archers, who braved the conditions to fire furiously upon the invaders trapped in the open. Frederick knew that they could fire every arrow available and it would not be enough. The Chilsa support troops worked to near perfection with the heavy Metzonian armour, which continued to push forward despite all efforts to resist. The majority of the army waited outside the walls, cheering and taunting as they eagerly waited to join their comrades. The colossal gates still remained sealed, much to the ire of the invading lords.

The Metzonian Elite stood tall, holding back any attempts to take control of the gatehouse, but their defiance was beginning to be noticed by more potent eyes. The black and yellow banners stood defiantly as the heavy shouts of men cried out in unison, marking the end of each successful resistance by the old nation's survivors. Multitudes of spears prickled in every direction, leaving those who reached the walls with nowhere to go. The frenzied soldiers had the choice of throwing themselves upon the wall of spears or tumbling the great distance to the rocky base. The ruthless Elite and their prince forced the decision upon them as they stabbed relentlessly and sent their corpses down to the red rocks beneath.

Fashioned after the ancient Doors of Final Fate, the front gates had been constructed of a single slab of Alakari mountain rock. It had required years to carve the walls and months to simply erect it. The great gates had not let the Elite down yet and still remained closed, despite the momentous effort exerted by Frederick's enemies.

Three siege towers burned out of control, halting the largest threat to the gatehouse. The breeze carried the heavy smoke into the Order's fortress. Many commanders within the army redirected several of the siege towers destined for the gates toward the walls, where they had proven more effective. The heavy stone doors remained standing against the attempts of the Metzonian and Chilsa battering rams, refusing to turn crumble, only leaving their crews exhausted and unable to move.

"Stand tall, soldiers of Metzon, followers of the noble Masen Metz and defenders of the True Crown! None shall take what we protect until death parts our souls from our bodies. Our legend shall stand for a thousand years. Great ballads about the might of our resolve and the sharpness of our spears will be sung!" Prince Frederick called to his troops, successfully defending their position against another onslaught of the coalition's new siege towers. Cheers and fists rose into the air, the resolve of his men untarnished by the events around them.

The battle had progressed remarkably well for the Fallen and

Metzonian Elite, but Frederick knew that would not last long. Despite anticipating a quick defeat, his men had fought valiantly on, refusing to give in.

"My Lord, the Grand General Kallen commends your staunch defence of the gatehouse. However, he grows concerned. Larger portions of the walls are starting to fall quickly now, my lord. By nightfall the first wall will be completely overtaken, and we will be abandoned to fend for ourselves." His comrades on the walls had taken the majority of the onslaught and were at last being forced to retreat along the stone bridges into the secondary defence ring, sealing the heavy stone doors behind them.

"As long as the gates remain sealed, we shall stand guard over them. The gatehouse must stand if we are to have any hope of continuing this fight. Our gates are all that keeps us from becoming overrun by the monstrosity pitted against us. The sooner they fall, the sooner we will be overwhelmed by sheer numbers. All shall perish then. We shall stand until the end!" Frederick gazed around his forces, engaged in the heat of battle around him, their enemies now trying to fight their way onto the roof of the gatehouse from the rear. The narrow winding staircases would mean a long and deadly fight before his enemies reached him. The costs would be dear indeed if that was the way the enemy hoped to open the gates.

"The stairways are of no concern; we will fight on all sides and from above if we have to." Grabbing one of his captains by the arm as he ran by, Frederick pointed toward the stairway. "Captain, go down to the stairwells and begin reinforcing the barricades. Triple the soldiers guarding them. Are you content? Now get out of here!"

The Fallen subordinate shook his head, continuing to shout over the battle noise, his polite tone lacking the fire Frederick expected of men within the heart of war. "General Kallen strongly suggests that you begin pulling back your men so that we can destroy the Keep Bridge ..."

Frederick looked over at the bridge that rose from the rear of the gatehouse roof; the bridge extended out and across toward the second wall. It was the only bridge within the entire fortress that reached the ramparts of the second wall directly; all other bridges forced passage through the solid rock ring walls. A vital reason why Frederick's Elite had to hold the gatehouse and its imperative control of the second wall. He understood why Kallen wanted to destroy it.

But Frederick knew if he pulled back he would never receive the opportunity to avenge his father. The black stallion on the golden banner on either side of the bridge would draw his brothers in to him, provided they survived the initial few waves. Frederick knew they were coming to try and take his life. He needed more time.

"You tell General Kallen that if he chooses to destroy the bridge and abandon us to our fate, then so be it. I will understand. However, this is where my brother will be, and this is where we stay! The Metzonian Elite shall fight until we are all slain. I shall have my revenge upon my brothers, and nothing shall remove us from here until then!" Frederick screamed at the Fallen subordinate, forcing the young man to back off, his hands raised before him.

"My Lord! My Lord! Look!" All his soldiers were screaming for his attention as controlled panic spread along the front wall of the gates. All pointed toward the figure working its way through the ranks of savage men, crushing any that got in his way. Fear struck the pit of Frederick's heart as he watched the red monstrosity paw his way forward, large burning black wings casting shadows over his subjects beneath clawed feet. The beast of Hell presented itself openly for all to witness, all battles slowing as both allies and enemies cast their gaze upon the demon slowly working toward the gates. Flames snorted from his black nostrils as Frederick watched the demon tower over the humans around him, fire flickering upon his burning skin.

"Dark Prince Adramaleck … death shall fall upon all of us! I must warn the commanders, and I strongly advise you to evacuate your men. Immediately!" The Order subordinate took off immediately, fleeing toward the large staircase to the bridge stretching from the middle of the gatehouse to the tops of the second wall tier.

Pressing his way closer to the front of the wall to look upon the long-forgotten demon of ages, Frederick pulled back as the red eyes locked upon his. Everyone held their breath collectively as they watched the towering demon move through the ranks, leaving a blazing trail in his wake. All eyes were upon the fiery sword in his clawed hand, as wide as a man and three times as long. With a single effortless swipe, the blade cleared the battering rams from his path, along with their mortal crews.

Adramaleck stopped his charge before the doors, smouldering molten eyes staring up and down the gates before him. Frederick held his breath as he waited for the Dark Prince to unleash whatever foul powers his place in Hell had granted him.

Inhaling deeply, the Dark Prince of Fire filled his lungs, his red chest visibly expanding, all mortal eyes upon his next course of action. An eruption of flames bellowed from his fanged mouth, and the flames crawled across the stone doors, engulfing them. The white stone gate doors glowed red immediately as the flaming demon's breath pushed the extremes of their limits.

The flames ceased, leaving all holding their breath as they watched the doors. Crackling and hissing erupted from the stone as the doors cooled from the extreme temperature change forced upon them. Expecting the doors to melt under the breath of the Dark Prince, euphoric cheers erupted from the defenders on seeing their mighty gates still standing. Archers renewed their onslaught, spirits restored to new heights. The earthly arrows bounced off Adramaleck's unholy armoured skin, irritating him as he stared at those mocking him from above.

Listening to the jeers and cheers from the defenders of the light, Adramaleck gazed upon the fortress. His laughter sucked the enthusiasm from the Elite, attention returning to him once more. Clutching the dark steel of his blade's hilt, the fiery blade turned molten red, reforming his heavy blade into an equally forbidding war hammer. Letting out a bloodcurdling bellow, the demon swung the hammer with both heavy hands into one of the doors. The gate structure shook, knocking those stationed upon its roof to the floor, and fear crept back into their hearts. All cringed as they heard the heavy crack of falling stone. Dust rolled out to surround the fiery beast, turning the cloud red. Another heavy swing saw the fall of the second door, followed by more demonic laughter.

The Gates of the Citadel were strong enough to halt Humanity, forcing their enemy to realize they would have to show their hands. But within the hands containing the infinite strength of Hell, the thousand carved angels that once adorned the gates fell in a shower of dust.

Cheers filled the air above the invading army, mimicking that the defenders had shouted earlier, as their onslaught was renewed with vigour. Adramaleck moved farther into the gatehouse and proceeded with the destruction of the other gates and portcullis within it, the booming laughter echoing inside as the minion army followed behind him. The smell of death and taste of blood was close, feeding their dark frenzy.

The Slayer of Angels watched the battle for the majority of the day. Dusk was now upon them, its approach hidden behind the mountains and Mammon's thunderous storm. The warriors of the Brotherhood stood behind him, all expecting to be in the heart of the battle but forced to view the battle from a far.

Despite the forces against them, Locan admitted the defenders had done a remarkable job of defence against the army of death. The Fallen had ridden out the numerous assaults that had been thrown at them, though the tide was quickly turning against them. Despite their strong defence, the fall was predictable. Waves continued forward, wearing down their opponents by outnumbering them multiple times over. Murmurs had rippled through his army as they watched a very old enemy of fire burn his way through his own army to smash down the front door of the Order's mighty fortress. Hell was growing impatient to show its hand, but Locan doubted it mattered. As valiantly as his enemies fought, all would die in the end. It was inevitable.

Defending catapults were firing from the walls at a relentless pace, pelting the swarm that was amassed against the walls below them. Boulders ripped through the ranks of infantry below, but the assault ceased to have any impact; the soldiers simply continued shoving forward. The sea of men swarmed in through the open gates like black water flooding into the wide streets.

A Mortal Mistake

Orange lightning flashed, its great forks of energy striking the ramparts of the wall, incinerating the enemies in the vicinity as their companions careened over the walls. Locan looked around the near mountaintops, trying to spot the demon casting the bolts down on their unsuspecting victims. Several more catapults exploded as Locan finally spotted Mammon calling upon his damaging storm from a nearby mountaintop, barely visible on its peak.

Locan had located two of the Dark Princes, but where was the third?

"Bring back old memories, Locan? Feel strange watching those who did you wrong perish into the fires of Hell to burn for eternity? Vengeance is a very sweet taste that lasts forever. It's satisfying to know your enemies died horrible deaths. It appears you have fallen upon the victorious side, unlike the rest of your ill-advised brethren. Soon enough you will witness what your Brotherhood has sought since its wretched birth." Rhimmon floated silently to the ground behind him, his eyes upon the death and destruction he was creating.

There was no mistaking the double meaning of Rhimmon's words, a menacing and taunting tone within his voice. Rhimmon was correct; watching the events unfold, Locan felt strange and conflicted, bothering him more than he ever thought it would. It was wrong, but Neurus was correct when he stated it was the only option for survival. For as much as he hated the Order and the Heavens, he hated Hell and its servants with an undying passion. To be allies with Hell's princes burned him with conflict, despite that it meant his enemies' certain death.

"As much as we enjoy watching the demise of our enemies, we prefer to deal such pain and death with our own blades, to taste their blood upon our blades and hear them scream. Yet you leave such a useful asset sitting useless upon the edge of the battlefield." Locan looked away from Rhimmon, still feeling the dark, beady eyes upon him as the demon contemplated what he had just said. The former angel could feel the demon prince try to probe his thoughts and steal them away from him. Locan wanted only to escape from his presence and to join the battle.

"*Useful as you may think you are, dark angel, you are merely a puppet among strings, and I am your master! You are mine to command as I wish—your life is mine! The Brotherhood is mine to command, as are all of its servants and lords.*" Rhimmon moved swiftly, seizing Locan around his chest, squeezing the life from his lungs.

Gasping for oxygen, Locan quickly surrendered to the will of the demon. "My apologies. My life is yours to command. What do you wish to do with it? Perhaps you have a task to prove our undying loyalty to your throne?"

Rhimmon continued to squeeze, his mind ripping into the dark angel's as his composure was lost.

"*Fear and hate cloud your judgement, Locan! Let such emotion fuel your soul instead of clouding your mind over things you do not control. You are my puppet. No thought is necessary on your part anymore, nor are your feelings. Do not make such a mistake again, or fear the consequences.*" He threw Locan upon the soil hard; no movement came from the ranks of dark angels who all stood silently witnessing the spectacle. Watching his helmet bounce into the feet of his warriors, Locan dared to wonder if the thousands he brought with him could slay Rhimmon right here and end it all. Yet the fortress still stood, and dark mortal armies still required Rhimmon's dark desires.

"*The gatehouse controls both the gates of the fortress and the only bridge to the tops of the second wall. It would seem that our Metzonian's oldest brother and his Elite warriors defend it and defend it well. The young emperor's forces have been unable to gain vital control to proceed with the plans. And Mammon and his mighty storms I fear will destroy the entire gatehouse, let alone the bridge.*" Rhimmon looked to the fortress where the black and yellow banners continued to fly over the gatehouse in the distance, lightning crashing down around them as explosions sent white rock flying.

"*Eliminate them all and open access for the rest of our forces to the second wall. Use your limited powers to ensure that all the inner gates are open as well. This is your first and only priority.*"

Once it is complete, then you can slay Fallen to your heart's content."

"Yes, my lord." Locan remained on all fours, not moving as he slowly oxygenated his black blood to normal levels. Surely Rhimmon would leave them alone now that he had his orders. He hoped he would but knew that the prince would haunt him forever. Pausing for one last second, Locan watched the winged monster turn toward him.

"To ensure that you do not forget your place ..." An axe blade sliced down, imbedding itself into the rock that Locan lay upon. Upon the other side of the blade lay his left hand, severed from the rest of his body. He shrieked in pain. The black blade burned his skin with an intensity that he had never felt before. Clutching his wrist, Locan pulled his arm back to his chest. His attacker crouched down before him and Locan watched his severed hand float up before his eyes. Wrapped within the powers of Rhimmon's mind, the bloody hand hovered between them.

"See how much your soul is worth to me, angel? I do not care if you die in this battle. You are of no consequence to me. I will win this war with or without you. You are merely a tool, a slave, a blade. Show me that you are a useful tool, and perhaps some distant day you will receive this back as a gift. Remember who put you here, and use the rage that I feel building inside of you against our enemies." Rhimmon slapped Locan across the face with his own severed hand and then spread his massive wings and flew off into the darkness above them.

Chapter 41
Beginning of the End

A pair of armoured Fallen guards stood watching the battle far below them from their temple perch. The first ring of the fortress had been completely overtaken by the Metzonian and Chilsa armies, pushing the defenders to the secondary defences. Trying to place another barrier between life and death, the defenders had retreated to the packed inner rings of the fortress.

With the battle now unfolding all around them, there would be no escape from death, only delay. The noose was slowly tightening around those who stood in the path of destruction; it would not be long before their lives would become suffocated in violence.

The black haze flowed through the remainder of the army outside the walls, swirling around the men and machines as it continued its path toward the gate. Colliding with the remains of the gatehouse, the mist's pace did not slow. It climbed directly up the face of the fortification, spilling over the barricades among the Metzonian Elite.

Far above the battle, Devotz clung to the rock, knowing exactly what was contained within the rolling fog. Devotz was familiar with the form that the dark angels used to move throughout this world, noticing the impressive number of Sin old Neurus actually had at his command. Excluding the thirty-five Devotz had in his small band, the cloud of Sin stretched deep into the battlefield as they charged forward. The Brotherhood of Sin was on the warpath after several hundred years of sulking through the shadows.

The perilous climb up the mountainside took far longer than anticipated, though that was not a problem. Devotz regarded the sight of the Brotherhood as an effort to quell a resistance stronger than anticipated. The climb also had numerous unforeseen difficulties; the holy water of the falls caused extensive and arduous detours that took all night and day. Damned mist continued to irritate their eyes and burn their exposed skin until their small entrance point was at last reached.

Belle drew her bow back, aiming toward the enemy, an arrow notched, ready to silence the first cry of alarm. Konflikt signalled toward the two unaware guards below them, holding out his arm. Devotz clasped his forearm, letting his sibling lower him silently to the flat ground below their perch. Overhearing the two guards arguing heatedly, Devotz looked down the small stone corridor, ensuring no others were hiding within it.

The scouts never noticed their attacker. Devotz's attack was swift and violent. He smashed their heads several successive times against the rock ledge of the observation deck, and both fell, bloodied, to his feet.

Konflikt lowered himself behind Devotz, catching Belle as she followed. Peering over the ledge at the pandemonium below, they saw that the defiant gatehouse was fragmenting. Dark angels could barely be seen amid the Elite forces, carving death among the human defenders. All those who had once sworn to serve his father to the death were at last being released of their oath. The lone golden banner in the midst of the Elite banners representing the last of the old kingdom would soon burn as the rest of them had. Devotz was positive that it would bring Warlord Locan himself crashing down upon the victims fighting around it. Devotz contemplated his feelings, knowing his own brother was about to die, surprisingly finding nothing.

His attention shifted from the gatehouse battle to the war that was taking place within the Sacred Citadel, one of his master's main objectives, following the long bridge from the central tower of the fortress as it stretched across the crystal waters toward a platform near the base of the mountain. The platform was cut between sheer rock faces on both sides of it and housed the primary entrance to the temple complex. Among the eight statues perched along the edge of the platform rested several contingents of heavily armed knights, guarding it and the lengthy bridge.

"Gather up and listen closely to what I have to say. Prince Rhimmon has demanded that the Temple Mountain doors be closed …"

"Why close them before his army? That is …" The Sin paused as Konflikt moved across the circle, confronting him, weapon in hand.

"Do you wish to share the fate of your ill-gotten brothers in the lake of holy water?" The dark angel was taken aback by Konflikt's immediate response, backing away from the double-edged axe at his throat, hissing at his aggressor.

Devotz was annoyed that one of the Brotherhood members would question a member of Hell's hierarchy plan. "Shut your mouth and keep it shut before I lose patience and cut out your black tongue! Prince Rhimmon wishes to have his army completely defeat the army before it reaches the temple. In the event that they decide to abandon the fortress for the temple, he wants them to have nowhere to escape to. Once the entrance doors are sealed, he will crush what remains against them, bringing the end swiftly, after which they shall be reopened for the sacking of the temple and Sacred City.

"My companions and I have a more pressing matter to take care of within this temple. I will leave the Brotherhood to the glory. Now let us weave our ways silently through their fabled temple and find our way down to the main floors. And one last reminder—try not to awaken anything that may remain sleeping with your stench. Now, let's move!"

The wispy fog towering over its human opponents and engulfing the gatehouse twisted and reconfigured into its original form. Locan's black spirit reconnected with the physical manifestation that was his body. Gripping his bladed mace with his right gauntlet, he squeezed his fingers, feeling the steel shaft, ensuring his reconfiguration was complete. Looking toward his missing left hand, he still felt infuriated at its loss to the demon.

The Brotherhood members had already started the violent attack upon the unnerved army Elite who watched the shadows reform into dark, sword-wielding shades in the midst of their impregnable defences. Screams cut through the clashes of steel on steel as blood sprayed out among the wounds inflicted. With the element of surprise, the Sin attacked with gusto, testing the seasoned veterans of mortal conflict.

A lone Metzonian confronted the warlord, his spear held firmly in both hands, the mortal careful not to get tripped up in the conflict of those around him. Locan stepped over a fallen body to move within striking distance, not taking his eyes from his opponent. The spear strike came quickly and forcefully, the Elite using the power of his legs to strike forward, aiming toward the large target of his enemy's chest. Locan quickly reached out to grasp the man's spear and tear the weapon from his adversary.

Locan felt a pang of physical pain from the mortal weapon. Looking down at the source of pain, he was surprised to see the base of the weapon penetrating beneath his collarbone. Following the shaft he stared at where his hand should have been attached to the spear. The stub of his forearm ignited rage within his mind and heart.

The Dark Angel's mace swung over his shoulder, crashing into the top of the soldier's head. The weapon crushed the human's skull into his body, the flattened helmet clattering to the bloody floor below. The body still holding the spear fell back, pulling the spear from Locan's body. Black blood spilt from the open wound. Locan swore violently upon every lord of Heaven and Hell that he would have his revenge upon Rhimmon.

Calling upon the dark arts to heal his wound, he swung the mighty mace several more times, knocking several of his enemy over the edge of the walls as he stormed across the top of the gatehouse.

The call for retreat rang out from the centre of the gatehouse, and many Elite soldiers retreated up the tall staircase and across the bridge toward the safety of other defences. Others courageously stood their ground, using every ounce of energy left within their broken bodies to defend the retreat of their comrades. At the base of the staircase, Locan saw a soldier decorated in the golden armour of a Metzonian royal son cut down a Sin soldier and cry out for the retreat. Over him flew the golden banner of old King Masen's flag, the crest wavering defiantly.

"Do not think that you will escape the wrath, young fool," Locan growled as he looked around him. All the Sin warriors remained engaged with enemies or lay slain, surrounded by dozens of opponents. The blind brothers Krasys and Krysas had cornered a large group and were hacking away at the humans, covered in the hot blood of the dying. The Dark Princes' army was now moving up the stairs and onto the gatehouse roof, their opponents finally defeated and without support.

Locan saw Prince Frederick start to retreat, pushing his soldiers with both tongue and hand. An arrow of the advancing dark army caught a soldier Frederick was pushing toward the staircase in his thigh, dropping him. Locan watched Prince Frederick turn back for the man, grabbing and dragging him toward the second walls, trying to use a discarded shield for cover.

"Your soul is mine!" Locan ran toward the edge of the gatehouse, leaping off its edge as he disintegrated into his wraith form, swirling around one of the large columns that held the bridge up over the crowded streets beneath it. Clinging to the stone, Locan swirled up the column, squeezing between the column railings on the side. He reformed between the fleeing royal and his retreating army. He shoved Frederick, who tumbled forward as Locan stomped down upon the head of the man Frederick was dragging, crushing him beneath his steel heel.

"Look upon Death, for I am he, come to take you from this world like the rest of your family." Locan smashed his mace mightily against the ground, but the human rolled out of the way, avoiding the blow. Several arrows hit Locan's heavily armoured backside, forcing him to avoid the attacks, as the Elite warriors charged back across the bridge in defence of their lord. Swinging his mace in a wide forward arc, the warlord knocked the first three over the edge of the bridge, taking another two as he swung with a second backhand blow. Wispy smoke shot around his ankles and reformed into the blind Sin brothers, who defended Locan's flanks, attacking the charging forces savagely.

A burning pain coursed through the right side of Locan's lower ribcage, ravaging his chest and sending his body into spasms as his nerves burned. Pulling his elbow back sharply, he sent his attacker skidding back across the bridge, his amputated arm pressing the wound that continued to burn. Screaming in his pain, the high-pitched squeal caused the humans around him to clutch their ears as Locan searched for the source of his intense pain.

Turning back to face the golden man, he spotted the blazing yellow sword that caused him so much pain. The blade radiated as the runes blazoned upon its blade darkened with the dark angel's blood. Locan tried healing himself. Cut by a holy weapon of the Fallen, his wound would become a permanent one, matching Militades's upon his opposite side. After hundreds of years, the blade remained effective against his dark powers, remembering the taste of their black souls. He wondered where in Hells' wide realms had the young man found such a weapon.

The golden prince had recovered from the blow. Blood dripped down upon his golden armour from beneath his mask as he held the blade in a two-handed stance.

Locan could sense the Dark Princes of Hell's patience wearing even thinner. Their enemy's armies were still on the second walls despite the gatehouse being in their hands now, which forced the warlord to bring this battle to swift conclusion. The human continued to duck and roll out of the way of his swinging his mace, keeping close to Locan's weaponless side. Noticing this tactic, Locan feinted one attack with a midsection arc, waiting for the man to roll before he kicked the man hard across the chest with his armoured boot, sending him skidding into the stone railing.

Barely believing that the man was still alive, Locan could hear raspy breath and the spitting of blood from within the enclosed crested helmet. Locan moved closer, preparing for the final blow to the Metzonian crown.

The Kyllordic prince notched another arrow in his long bow and took precise aim, releasing the taunt string to send the arrow into the throat armour of a Metzonian heavy unit. The armoured soldier thrashed among others behind him before falling over the wall. Raef had situated himself above the third wall within the shadowy confines of one of the numerous carved niches along the wall. It was perfect pickings; he had numerous targets who were unable to see him. It was a tactic perfected by the Assassins of Aros, and while assassins were not used to seeing all-out war, it was proving very successful.

The first wall had all but collapsed and was now crowded with enemies firing upon the second and working their way toward the single bridge rising from the top of the gatehouse. Raef doubted that it would take long before the call would be made to abandon the second wall. The burning remains of the fortress's catapults still smouldered from the storm strikes, which meant they no longer had the ability to destroy the bridge. Now with the gatehouse taken, all knew it would cost more lives to defend it than the army could possibly spare.

Lining up an archer this time, he pulled back, adjusting for the distance and wind before releasing. Tracking the arrow, he watched it strike home, piercing the man's heart. Curious how the enemy responded to wounded soldiers, Raef had struck one attacker purposely in the lung, only to watch his brethren push him off the wall because he was blocking the flow of soldiers. *Not even a second look, just off you go!*

Scanning for his next target, he looked around the gatehouse. He spotted one of the dark monsters mercilessly hacking up an Elite soldier. Drawing his string, Raef lined up the attack and was about to release his arrow when another arrow struck out and pierced the neck of the beast, dropping him in his bloody feeding frenzy. Lining up another target of similar stature, he saw that it also fell. This time he had barely tracked the orange arrow streaking above him.

Another arrow sliced overhead and down upon a Chilsa knight following a group of knights toward the gatehouse. Risking losing his cover, Raef slowly stood up from his niche, peering over the edge of the third wall he was perched upon and looked up. Another long white arrow fired past, allowing him to track the source to a lone figure that stood upon the fourth wall, towering way above his vantage point. Another arrow, another mark found. *Well, aren't you a treasure!* he thought, watching the stunning feat.

Squinting to see in the darkness and distance, he was unable to see her face but watched the string of her bow flare bright orange every time she pulled back. Recognized her by her movements, he knew she was indeed a treasure, and not for just her archery skills. The tall woman was fluid and smooth in her actions as she notched another arrow and fired mere seconds later. He stood taller, and his hiding place was discovered. A pair of arms reached over the wall, beckoning him up angrily. "Two sets of walls! I told you two sets of walls between you and the battle!"

"Damn it!" Raef batted the outstretched arms away, looking into the angry glare of Eli's eyes. The general was encircled by four battle-worn guards soaked in blood and sweat.

Both generals had commanded divisions of Metzonian regulars and Fallen soldiery upon the first walls as they lent their experience to the defenders. The general himself looked quite battered and bloody although the anger within his eyes proved otherwise. He clearly still had enough energy to verbally reprimand the younger man fiercely.

"Don't look at me like that! We had an agreement, and we both know your abilities with a bow. Two walls shots are easy for you but make a big difference for your safety against the enemy fire. And stay where we can damn well see you!"

"As I already told you, quit treating me like a child. I know when to retreat and when to stand! It certainly doesn't look like any of us are going to survive this damn war, so what difference does it make to you if I die now or later! Where are your saviours of Earth?

The Heavens have left us here to die, so you should just accept it already!"

A broad hand lashed out, slapping Raef to the ground.

Raef's jaw ached as he rubbed a gloved hand across it. The general stared him down hard, clenching his jaw tightly in recognition of what he'd just done. "Do not disrespect the Heavens. And smarten up and have a little respect for the lives around you, as well as your own. Survival goes to those who fight the hardest for life, not always he who is bigger and stronger."

Raef held his tongue and let the anger simmer instead of starting a useless argument. Both had strong and valid points, but there were larger and more important issues to worry about. Raef was not about to spend the last moments of his life in another argument that he would never win. Soon enough he would be free of Ethan and Eli and the rest of the traitors, though a lot of good it would do him then.

Commotion whirled through the ranks of archers and their commanders, who turned toward the upheaval taking place along the second wall. Cries of fear broke out among the ranks as they all witnessed a new battle breaking out that looked to have dire consequences for the emotions of the survivors.

Raef's attention turned toward the turmoil that was taking place upon the bridge extending from the gatehouse. He watched the golden figure trapped upon its expansive stretch of white stone briefly turn to a pale orange whenever lightning streaked across the sky. He recognized the figure, not that he cared for the man very much: the strong-headed Metzonian who believed that he was the true king to a lost throne, a man who still seemed to command great respect merely because of who his father had been. Raef himself had never received that respect, though he deserved it just as much as anyone else. The Metzonian's glorious gold armour was merely an opulent symbol of his nonexistent power and glory. But he was just a man like Raef was, mortal, with flaws, and certainly no king, yet they worshipped him as though he were a god.

The golden knight rolled as the opponent he faced smashed a mace the size of the man's torso down upon the spot where he had stood. His Elite guards raced back across to help their leader, realizing their mistake at leaving their leader behind in the retreat. Raef did not know how they had; the man was dressed in golden armour, for Heaven's sake!

The monster pitted against the Metzonian was imposing. Almost appearing twice the size of his opponent, the creature towered over other dark angels, draped in their dark and shadowy robes. His black helmet with its large bloody horns made him look even taller and larger. The black armour extended to the spiny gauntlet carrying the mace, which packed plenty of power as demonstrated by the men flying through the air. So this was Locan, the king of the dark angels he had heard rumours about.

Two additional dark angels appeared between Locan and the pressing defenders, creating space for their commander to move in for the kill. The battle continued between Frederick and the black monster, few blows struck against the latter. Frederick's lone attack inflicted great pain, based upon the shriek Raef heard, but it did not last long. The next blow appeared to end the battle.

The golden warrior was clinging desperately to the railing on the edge of the bridge, stunned by the last attack. The defenders fired arrows that bounced harmlessly off the thick armour as the beast moved closer for the kill, his weapon preparing the final blow. Death seemed imminent for the man, making Raef rethink his opinion briefly. Guilt was entering his heart for the man whom he may not have liked, but he certainly did not deserve death by this monster.

Notching an arrow into his bow, Raef pulled back, aiming at the dark angel as a double-bladed axe was hurled from behind the line of Elite trying to push the dark angels back in one last desperate attempt. The large axe spun through the air, and a lone man broke through the barricade to race after the blade. Raef watched both the trajectories of blade and man carefully as they raced against time.

The bladed axe found its mark in the leader of the dark angels, lodging itself into Locan's thigh. Using its handle as a stepping stone, the bald man leapt upon the back of his master's attacker, clinging to the back armour plate. Trying to shake the new attacker, the giant monster swung his torso, trying to knock him off with his arm. His attacker reached out, raking his fingers into the face of his helmet, the other wrapped around one of the large horns and reefing the helmet back as far as he could. The golden warrior was still dazed and coughing up blood, unable to retreat to safety despite the distraction.

Rage overtook the Sin. He could not grasp the soldier upon his back. He'd dropped his weapon and tried to reach behind with his other hand, to no avail. Continuing to twist and shake his upper body, Locan finally burst into flames as he called upon his dark sorcery to eliminate the opponent once and for all. Pain from the flames loosened the attacker's grip, and Locan finally forced his attacker over his shoulder. He reached out to grab him.

Raef's arrow bounced off the thick shoulder plates of Locan, unnoticed. Raef felt pity for the man making a valiant attempt to sacrifice his life, all for naught. Raef watched the bald man fight heroically. The dark angel grabbed the burning man by his leg, throwing General Dubryst against the stone bridge. Dislodging the two-handed axe from his burning armour, Locan moved to finish the original target: Prince Frederick.

In one last act of heroics, Dubryst, whose skin continued to burn, reached out to push the Metzonian prince off the bridge, sending the gold warrior spinning over the edge toward the buildings far beneath him. Watching his commander fall, the general never got to see the man meet the ground, as his own bladed weapon sliced through the back of his neck, slamming into the marble barricade and pinning his body to the railing, where it clung.

Locan turned toward the forces in full retreat with the loss of their lord and general. None were left to challenge him. With his primary task complete, the warlord turned his full attention to the second and third walls standing before him. "Forward!"

The Mortal Army of Darkness flowed across the bridge with a renewed thirst for death. The servants of Locan flew toward the retreating soldiers, eager to beat the defenders' retreat to the next gate. Raef had no doubts they would succeed and leave the wall he was upon all but lost. Moving across another bridge away from the third wall as quickly as he could, Raef fled swiftly among the throng that fought between their orders and their fear. Perhaps he could shoot a few arrows with the vixen he spotted before. Not that it mattered; they were all doomed to death.

But he could not think of a better way to go out.

CHAPTER 42
FINAL FAILURE

Kallisto walked through the temple library, working his way through the large shelves of texts from when angels roamed this temple. Something as magnificent as this portion of the temple didn't deserve the desecration it was likely to receive. The world's history was stored in these shelves, as were books on all subjects of life. Knowledge that had taken Humanity generations upon generations of work to discover was soon to disappear forever.

At the far end of the library chamber, one of his most precious and sacred items lay within his beloved vault: a giant two-handed sword, inscribed in the ancient language of the Heavens. A remnant from a ancient battle between a Legionnaire and some elements of the Dark, it had been recovered and brought to the temple by mountaineers who had found it and then smuggled it out of the Redelle Mountains in Chilsa. Kallisto had seen many holy swords, including his best friend's Mirage of Metzor with its golden hue, but they had all been created upon Earth and enchanted with only the remnants of a Fallen's touch.

This blade was truly holy and blessed beyond all others. Hammered by the smiths of Heaven, its white steel remained keen and clean even after being left among the other holy relics within the library's vault for years. Many had claimed to have heard the old sword whisper to itself, unable to understand what may have been said. The silvery white metal continued to glow from within, ensuring the room was never dark, a slight blue tinge visible only in the darkest of nights.

A Mortal Mistake

"Angel of Heaven, the world is in peril, and once again is in need of assistance from those who dwell above us. Please help me in wielding your mighty weapon in the defence of the Light, as I try to protect the innocent and free." He rose from the ground, plucking the weapon from the wall and placing it in the scabbard that had been made for it when it had been brought here.

The sword over his shoulder, he took one last look at his favourite place and slowly pulled both sets of doors shut. One last prayer whispered, he continued toward the temple entrance. The highest-ranked Titan commander was already waiting for him at the temple crossroads.

"Our defence is faltering; we cannot hold back an army of this magnitude. We are starting to take heavier losses as men grow weak from the nonstop assault …" Kallen reported, both hands upon his knees in exhaustion. He could feel Alexandra's fright when he looked into her eyes, knowing that she worried about those around her.

"The gatehouse has finally been taken by the enemy. It has been reported that … Warlord Locan led the assault, followed by his army of dark angels. The Elite, while performing nobly and successfully, held it for an impressive time, but they had to finally pull back in retreat. There has also been an unfortunate tragedy during the retreat …"

Kallisto waited for the news, both siblings unable to look him in the eye. Faces flipped through his mind and settled on one in particular, his stomach immediately dropping and his head throbbing.

"No …" He clutched both by their collars, knowing within his heart that it was too late.

"General Dubryst and Prince Frederick did not reach the second walls …"

Kallen confirmed what he had believed. If the general had breath and blood pumped within him, he would do whatever was required of him to protect his lord. Kallisto looked back upon his promise made to his old friend, having botched his last task to protect his sons. Another failed promise.

"Unfortunately, the bad news continues to grow. The Princes of

Hell have shown their reborn hands in this quest to rid all Fallen from this world. Adramaleck with his fiery fire has smashed through the gates and opened our first line. Mammon conjured a storm that casts deadly lightning down upon us with unrelenting rage, as blood and fire rain from the sky. We can only guess that Rhimmon is out there somewhere, motivating this massive army. We cannot defeat such darkness, Kallisto … it simply cannot be done."

"You two must go to the Doors of Final Fate. Tell the gatekeeper that all is soon to be lost and to seal the mighty doors to protect the city. It is then up to you two as to whether you want to stay on the other side, hidden within the Sacred City, or come back to fight with the last of your brethren. The Doors should hold even against the Dark Princes, though Hell has never had the opportunity to try cracking them open. Nor do I believe it will matter in the end." He solemnly watched them start down the corridor, praying that they would choose to stay with the gatekeepers on the other side but knowing deep down that the protectors of the children had trained them too well in the true meaning of life.

Getting down on his knees, Kallisto waited for the humans who chose chaos and death as their path to arrive.

Hairs upon the back of Konflikt's neck rose; he felt something odd at the emptiness of the temple. For being the home of the Order of the Fallen, it was starkly undefended. He concluded that most must be dying or already dead upon the walls.

Descending several spiral staircases toward the main level, Konflikt watched his brother as he weaved his way silently. Looking like a hound sniffing along the trail of a rogue fox, Devotz acted like he knew he was on the correct trail of what they hunted. The Brotherhood had split from them earlier, floating toward the entrance as the trio worked their way deeper. After sneaking down one final staircase they could see the main hallway that Devotz was certain they were searching for.

The stone floor looked slick with the blood of the wounded defenders dragged through the temple. A waste of energy and resources in his opinion, as they were all going to die in the end, but he had forgotten how the weak valued life and felt the need to protect the hopeless and even the dying.

Belle took a look outside in both directions, huddling close to the shadows and using her slim profile to her advantage. She signalled to them that she had spotted a lone armoured guard coming toward them from the direction of their destination.

Konflikt and Devotz tucked themselves in the shadows of the corners at each side of the door, their weapons ready to rain heavy blows upon the man if he entered the room. Belle fled light-footedly up the staircase, peering around the centre column as the heavy footsteps neared.

Konflikt's senses were heightened to battle standards; he heard every heavy footstep as he visualized the soldier unknowingly treading toward his impending death. The rattle of armour continued forward as the sentinel finally stopped his slow march. He passed the doorway in an uncomfortable silence. Peering around the corner for a mere second, Konflikt saw the figure they were pitted against, and he felt his pulse increase in anticipation.

The sentinel was robed from neck to floor in a thick white cloak that hid his body. It reminded Konflikt of the Royal Elite in his father's chambers. Even through the figure was cloaked, Konflikt could see that the man was large and powerful-looking, a juggernaut who would not stop them but still posed a slight inconvenience.

Konflikt went to take a second peek around the corner; the guard was gone. He had not heard the man walk away or the rattle from his armour. His eyes went wide with surprise when he moved farther out and found himself looking down the barrels of two imposing crossbows. Both fired simultaneously, one bolt streaking past his face as he pulled back to avoid its steel tip, the second aimed for the stairway. Belle took cover. Devotz ran around the corner toward the knight and was knocked unexpectedly sideways when he stepped on one of the crossbows on the ground. He deflected the second that was thrown at him. No cry of alarm came from the lone guard, whose back was against the other side of the wall. Calmly undoing his cloak, the knight reached up and hung the white fabric from the wingtip of a large angelic statue.

Who does this guy think he is? Konflikt snorted to himself, preparing his muscles to rip the overconfident guard apart. The trio moved closer, spreading out to give themselves ample room for combat.

The warrior reached over his head and dislodged the two large curved blades attached to his armour. Pulling the blades from his back released something from within the silver armour. Plates of steel that previously lay flat snapped into vertical positions, turning the soldier's armour into a defensive matrix that eliminated many of his weak points. Steel plates covering his large shoulders snapped upright, protecting sides of his neck and head. How the man walked with that much steel on his frame, Konflikt could not understand. Fortunately the beast would be slow, and the trio could dismantle him piece by piece.

"You have defiled this temple with your existence. May the Lords of the Heaven have mercy upon your souls, demons! You shall find none from the Titans. Prepare for a merciless death!" the warrior rumbled from within his large helmet, lowering himself into a battle-ready stance. Konflikt noticed the heavy metal boots on the figure's feet and how wide and solid they were, enabling the man to support so much armour without tipping over. Large claw-like protrusions stuck out from all sides of the boots.

Belle fired an arrow destined for the beast's armoured throat, but the warrior pulled his chin into his throat as he advanced. Swinging forward simultaneously, Konflikt and Devotz moved together against the lumbering beast's first blows. Belle circled them all, her armour-piercing arrows fired at precise moments, though few stuck and none did damage. The Titan was quicker than anticipated. He blocked Devotz's blades and dipped his shoulder down, allowing Konflikt's axe to carve harmlessly through thin air.

Overswinging, Konflikt left his right side open, and he felt the dropped shoulder of the Titan crush into him, lifting his feet off the ground before he tumbled. As he fell toward the stone floor, he reached out with his left forearm to brace against the impact and rolled with his forward momentum. Rolling away, he heard the vicious curved blade slam upon the stone floor where he should have fallen.

Devotz bellowed from the opposite side of the hallway, distracting the Titan as his younger sibling continued to roll out of striking distance. The Titan continued to block the strike with one blade before turning to bring the second blade to bear upon Devotz. The second blade sliced underneath Devotz's guard position, blocking him from defending his midsection. The blade scraped across his breastplate in a shower of sparks; it peeled through the metal as though it were cloth. Blood leaked from the armour, but Devotz looked unfazed by the wound.

The Titan kicked out with his steel foot, knocking the enraged Devotz down. Belle fired more rapidly as the Titan advanced upon the fallen man, blocking the arrows with his second blade. The Titan sent a long swipe toward Belle to force her back slightly, and as he did, Konflikt swung his axe from high overhead, burying the blade in the Titan's thigh.

The beast roared out in pain and fell to one knee, halting the Titan's attack on the susceptible king. Devotz let out a howl of rage and moved against the Titan, bashing at the crippled armoured figure. The Titan continued to attempt to defend himself, swinging hard and quickly as his breathing grew heavy with exhaustion. Devotz's blade shattered across the top of the Titan's helmet just as Konflikt's axe cut into the man's bicep. The Titan's second blade tumbled to the floor. Dazed, the Titan pulled himself up to swing at the defenceless Devotz. Fear struck Konflikt's heart momentarily, though only rage could be seen in his brother's eyes. Lashing out with his left fist upon the helmeted head multiple times, Devotz temporarily prevented the Titan's deadly backhand blow.

Knowing he had to act fast or lose his brother forever, Konflikt grasped the back of the steel cuirass, hauling the enemy away from his brother. Fuelled by the rage within his heart, his muscles trembled with the strain as he picked the suited man high above his head. Bellowing loudly, Konflikt gave a final heave and sent the Titan into a stone angel; the statue shattered as it fell on their enemy.

Konflikt and Devotz halted to catch their breath, relieved that the battle was finally over. Devotz picked up the finely crafted spear that had been part of the tall statue, testing its strength against the floor. "Those damn dark angels are going to have one hell of a time sealing the front gates if these 'Titans' are upon the gates in any significant number."

"Damn demons …" The Titan coughed violently among the rubble, pushing away what was left of the rock torso.

Konflikt looked incredulously from the pile of rubble toward his companions. *Is he serious? How did the man possibly survive?* "Some just don't know when to die, do they?"

Axe in hand, he walked over toward the struggling man. He placed a heavy steel boot against his chest. The Titan's helmet had three large spires, and Konflikt wrapped his hand around the largest that ran from his chin to high above his forehead. He pushed back the dying man's head, exposing his throat. Aiming at the proper angle, Konflikt swung down, severing the armoured man's head from the rest of the body. The thrill of battle continued to flow through his veins, making him feel stronger than ever as he pulled back his axe.

Heavy shouting and the chime of alarm bells announced the conflict at the temple gates had begun. The trio looked over toward the entrance and heard shouts of battle and the screams of the wraiths attacking. It was time to leave, and quickly.

They were unaware of the dark demon taint silently surging through their blood. Rhimmon listened, keeping aware of their movements within the temple. He could sense that they were nearing their objective, but he still could not get a clear picture of who they hunted for. He had a long list of heavenly beings it could be, but he still did not know. *Who hides within the temple,* he wondered. *Who …?*

Kallisto knelt in the middle of the corridor, watching the trio of demonic warriors stride toward him. He did not know how they had gotten this far this quickly, but he could guess at their purpose—to reach the massive Doors of Final Fate before they sealed shut to protect the Sacred City. Fortunately he had already foreseen this and had sent the Descendants of Orion to ensure they were sealed. The fate of the army would have to be sacrificed to protect its unarmed citizens.

"Ah. And they finally arrive. I've been waiting for you. A very long time, actually, but clearly the nightmares have come home to stay." The dark shadows started to enter the light, revealing their very human forms. The commanding form of one stirred strong emotions within Kallisto's core: the sole reason for his suffering, as well as that of those Kallisto once cared about.

Sven mashed his teeth into a grin as he saw Kallisto. Deliberately dragging his large spear along the floor, letting the eerie sounds fill the chamber as he circled Kallisto once. The darkness that coursed through his body had taken its toll on him. Kallisto saw his eyes had turned bloody, his teeth were pointed and yellowing, and his hands were becoming more like great talons, though Dark Prince Rhimmon had likely never allowed the trio to notice their true appearance.

"Kallisto! It would appear that destiny demands you die at my hand, and mine alone. You know, I remember you told me that the world was going to make me pay for what I did. Yet here I stand, in the heart of your holy temple. So many broken promises you made. Are you finally prepared to meet those who never protected you, Karl? To be reunited with Heaven that watches you suffer as the Earth becomes swallowed in the darkness that is Hell?"

"I am ready to die at last, Sven. But first I ask you to let a dying old man have a reprieve to tell you a quick story. It is about my closest friend, your father."

All three paused, unsure of what to do. Kallisto saw that Conrad's interest was piqued, and he spoke before he looked over at his brother. "Let me tell you why your father was cast out during the Great Purge. Do not worry. I will make it a very swift story."

Kallisto cleared his throat to begin his story, somewhat surprised the trio allowed him this moment and knowing their patience would wear out quickly. He could not defeat all three himself, but if Kallen and Alexandra hurried, then hope remained.

"Your father had been leading a detachment of Legionnaires against an Army of Darkness that had attempted to seed itself upon a world within the Dominion of Heaven that fell under the protection of the Light. He was not the first to be dispatched, however; another group had been sent to scout out the world. On his arrival there, he found them all slain, but not by demons of Hell. The species on that world had slain them all, attacking the unarmed and unprepared Legionnaires. After Heaven had protected them for so long, the beings of that world slew the angels sent to defend them from demons. Metz found no demons.

"In a bout of great passion and misplaced anger, your father annihilated those who had betrayed his brothers and sisters. He destroyed every ounce of life upon the small world … including the demoness he found in deep hiding that had influenced all the events that occurred. A horrific crime of passion was executed, which would result in dire consequences influencing the rest of his life.

"You see, your father had the same passion and fire within his spirit as the both of you do. But knowing the devastation that it could cause, every ounce of his mortality was required to contain that passion. It almost escaped him during the crusade against the Cruel King, a constant reminder of its power and influence upon him. Masen did not want to see the cycle continue and feared it greatly when he saw it within his children.

"Like the demoness influencing those upon that world, so does darkness influence this one. I see within your soul that it is too late for you, Sven. The darkness is all that is left of your spirit. But perhaps there is hope left. One never knows. At least now when you fall upon your knees before the Creator of Heaven, you will feel a bonding connection with your father like none have ever experienced before."

Kallisto looked into the dead eyes of the mortal Sven, seeing no changes at all. His soul was completely gone, a shadow for Rhimmon to manipulate. The young empress looked uncertainly toward Sven prepared to follow whatever decision he made without question.

Conrad's blue eyes twitched with the great conflict within as spirit and darkness fought within his body.

Come forth, child, and see through the darkness. Come forth!

Sven stepped before Kallisto, blocking his view, looking down upon the old royal advisor with a large grin. "A shame he did not tell me that story earlier himself. I almost respect him more now that I know he was as powerful and deadly as I always dreamed he could have been. Too bad he switched back to weakness and servitude. A disgrace ... To think what we could have accomplished with all of us alive and united. If that is the end of story time, we really have pressing matters farther within this temple, more important than clearing up unfinished business."

"You may have reached our coveted temple, but the doors to the city are closing as we speak. Soon enough I shall avenge all my brethren whom you slew. Forever they have haunted me, Sven, but I shall finish what they have been asking from me." Kallisto raised himself to a single knee and reached over his shoulder, withdrawing the ancient sword. Scanning the ancient runes along its length, he drew strength from inside himself for the upcoming battle; the battle he knew would be his last. He had done all he possibly could upon this world. It was time to go back home.

Devotz's impatience led to the first attack. He swung his spear over his head in a wide arc, bringing it down violently as he leaped forward. He carried forward, slashing and stabbing, his attacks quickly deflected.

Surprised by his own agility, Kallisto became aware of the supernatural powers remaining within the sword that revitalized him. Kallisto was grateful for the sustaining powers but knew Sven was able to draw from vast dark energies were he to call upon them. Kallisto felt that this battle superseded any previous battles, the winner being the better mortal Metzonian.

The two former Elite members continued to strike at each other, although neither gained the edge. Damage was taken by both parties, but, unrelenting, both continued to press the other side hard. Devotz's anger and violence could not overwhelm the quiet calmness within Kallisto and his mighty sword.

Kallisto deflected the last string of attacks and began a counterassault. Swinging the massive sword, he pushed Devotz back. He felt a calm strength that he had not felt for decades; he moved with fluidity. He felt energy flow from the sword, swimming through his veins. He lashed out hard. The sword made a large arc, catching Devotz slightly across the top of the shoulder. The older man rotated his body sharply, bringing a free elbow down across the side of his enemy's head. Devotz hissed in pain. Kallisto joined his hands on the hilt and pulled back hard, smashing the sword's hilt into Devotz's chest. The member of the Order repositioned himself in his guard stance, preparing for an attack from the other two demons.

Neither attacked nor moved from their current positions except to look back at the sprawled form of their leader. Recovering and rising on all four of his limbs, Devotz's body was shaking with pent-up anger. "You are not the only one with sacred powers, Kallisto. My master also gave me extra strength for my quest to eliminate all those who protect this temple. He tells me … that I no longer have time to spare." He curled a fist, throwing it toward his enemy. Kallisto screamed out as every nerve in his body burned molten hot. He collapsed to the stone floor.

As Devotz watched his father's old counterpart struggle to regain composure; he continued to assault Kallisto. The demon smashed his old commander against the floor and walls, dishing out abuse. "Die, old man! You could never save those around you that you cared for! Are you ready to receive the same horrible death?" The demon screamed into his face, spit streaming from his lips, his mind a storm of rage.

Kallisto's hand slammed out, cutting the ties of the dark energy, letting his memory fuel his soul with the painful memories of the past. His arms burned as he threw Devotz down. Spasms and fire tormented him as he crawled to pick up his weapon. Grasping the sword, he spun toward his enemy in a last twisting attack. As his attack started, his life ended.

Devotz leaped through the air in a perfect Metzonian spear strike, like he had practiced thousands of times with his father's own Royal Elite. It was the move Kallisto had taken the time to teach

A Mortal Mistake

Sven since he was old enough to lift a spear. The tip of the spear drove through Kallisto's heart, ending the master of the manoeuvre. Kallisto's weapon caught Devotz's knee, injuring the king's murderer slightly but failing to deliver his revenge.

The temple administrator fell to the floor. The light began to take his soul as he spoke his last words. "Run, my child. May Heaven feel your fear and save us all."

Devotz could barely hear Kallisto's last words. They made little sense to him, as they were no last insult or words of wisdom that would have been typical of the man. He looked up at his brethren, searching for answers, noticing that both stared past him into the distance.

A small girl was at the foot of the staircase within the temple. Despite the incredible distance, he could see her large pink eyes, laced with silver, shimmering within the gloom. The child quickly turned to flee up the staircase, escaping the demons' sight and moving with a swiftness that astonished them all.

"Isn't she supposed to be a myth among mortal men?" Konflikt whispered, enthralled by the child's eyes, as they all had been. "I remember the stories about the child with the silver and pink eyes. Don't you remember, Devotz? Father used to tell us the story of a child of Heaven forgotten upon Earth. Halo of Heaven! I always thought it was a myth. Do you think Heaven can hear her prayers among all others?" He looked away from the empty staircase toward the distraught looks around him, realizing the implication if the myth were true.

"I have no desire to find out the consequences if she can! How about we get her before she has the opportunity to test that theory?" Belle growled as she started to lead the rush after the child. Devotz had known the truth but had not shared it with his companions. Rhimmon had commanded him to find the heavenly creature hidden within the mighty temple.

None of the Dark Princes would have believed that it was a simple child, an ancient story told to him and his brothers by their father. Devotz had prepared himself for a glorious battle with a benevolent angel of universal power that his masters had fought in the past. But a child?

Devotz felt robbed of the glory he had been promised. How could he kill a child? Feeling the tendrils of Rhimmon's grasp tighten upon his soul, he knew it mattered little as the demon took control of his limbs, sending him in swift pursuit. The task before him now was going to be easier than he originally anticipated, though his glorious victory would once again be hollow.

Rhimmon never delivered on his promises.

Chapter 43
The Final Fate

The Doors of Final Fate were not small; they were more than a dozen men thick. Made from the mountain when the temple was first created, each solid rock door displayed the most elaborate carvings within the temple, depicting six great angels that commanded the hundreds behind them. No manmade mechanisms would ever be able to smash through the gates once they were closed. To close them was to accept fate. Originally thought to simply have been two narrowing walls before the exit to the Sacred City, the doors required the original architect himself to come up with a way to allow mortals to move the stones to their sealing point.

The gatekeeper might have been joked about being a thousand years old, but neither Kallen nor Alexandra would ever want to wrestle with the old man. It was a running joke throughout the temple that he actually built the great gates and was created from the mountain itself. A giant of a man with a beard as white as the mountaintops, he was plated in thick armour and always carried the largest war hammer Kallen had seen in his life.

"Children!" His voice boomed through the hall toward them as they hurried toward him. He did not smile or offer jokes of any kind, untypical of his personality, as he knew that their presence was not a good omen. As the other members of the gate battalion continued with their tasks, all ears were tuned closely to see what information the newcomers might bring.

"The battle from outside the mountain … it does not fare well, I fear?" He tried to lower his booming voice, without much result.

Akakios dropped the question, already having a feeling that he knew the answer. He had been standing as a guardian to the gate for ages, hoping that he would never have to perform his final duties. "I have not seen any of the army that marched out return. Is it truly that bad?"

"The defences are breached, and the army cannot hold off the assault. There doesn't seem to be another way, and we can't risk moving any men back in without risking a complete collapse. We will not risk leaving the Sacred City open and lose it all. We must close the Doors and pray for a miracle."

"Once the Doors close, my son, they are closed forever. You will not be able to open them again without the hands of Heaven to help you. If it is required of us, we shall seal them, but please be sure of your decision."

"Seal the doors to the city … and pray for us," Alexandra ordered, her voice conveying the sadness that they felt. Both turned to leave, taking a last look down the shining path that led to all the families waiting for the return of their loved ones—the loved ones who were about to unknowingly sacrifice their lives to protect their families from the terrors they bravely fought against.

"There is no need to sacrifice more lives than necessary. You can stay on this side of the Doors and feel no shame …" The gatekeeper stepped slowly backward toward the gate, attempting in vain to save a couple more lives. It was to no avail. Both smiled at him as they watched him cross back through the threshold. They were indeed the children of Orion's lineage, refusing to save themselves when others continued to die. "Maybe we will see each other again. I shall pray for all of us!"

The two temple commanders watched from the corridor as the massive doors slowly sealed shut. The angels depicted on the carved mural seemed to come alive, sliding as the stone hands clutching their weapons shifted, thrusting into the rock beneath them. The heaving sound of rock sealed the door shut forever. Kallen prayed that myths were true and that the doors would withstand the coming assault.

"We better hurry; something keeps urging me to rush back."

Running toward the main corridor, Alexandra urged her twin brother to do the same. Kallen looked back at the doors one last time, knowing that Jaina knelt upon the shimmering floors of the Crystal Cathedral, soft hands folded before her, eyes closed as lips carried her prayers to Heaven over and over again.

Kallen and Alexandra caught a glance of a trio standing in the middle of the central corridor intersection that led to the throne room. Two muscular figures armoured in black steel were followed by a smaller figure that lurked among their shadows. Kallen wondered how the trio had managed to infiltrate through the Titan patrols he had set to wander the temple hallways.

Preparing their weapons, the siblings rapidly increased their speed toward the suspected assassins in an attempt to catch them before they escaped into the numerous corridors. In an unexpected response, the trio took off toward the Throne of Creation, seeming oblivious to those who pursued them. As the three fled, their figures disappeared in a black streak into the darkness, allowing Kallen to notice the white-cloaked body that had lain upon the floor among them.

Alexandra screamed at the sight of the bloodied form of Kallisto sprawled before them. Falling to her knees, she slid toward the man who had protected her for the past year. Kallen shook with rage at his death, knowing that when he had lost the only father he had ever known, Kallisto had been there to lift him back to life.

Hot tears streamed down Alexandra's face as she watched her brother shudder, breaking under the stress of his emotions as he joined her in grief. The moment she thought he would fall apart once more, he stopped, going completely still as he pressed his forehead down upon the hilt of his sword.

Like a bellowing bull, her brother charged down the hallway, accelerating swiftly from his crouched position over Kallisto's dead body down the hall after the killers. All subtlety was lost from Kallen as he rumbled down the long corridor with a roar and the rattle of his steel plating that announced his pain to all, echoing upon the stone within the tunnel. The Titan sounded as though he had ascended to Heaven and returned as a Throne Guardian, thundering down upon the demons of ancient history.

Alexandra readied her bow to support her brother's brash charge in hot pursuit of the unknown attackers. She sent several high-flying arrows silently twisting through the air. The middle man was knocked to the floor as the arrow struck through the back of his calf. She faintly recognized the face that had taken everything from her. The other two leaped instantaneously, without a second of hesitation, for cover behind the Trees of Eternity closest to the Stairway. Sven scrambled behind the Throne of Creation, tearing the arrow out and throwing it across the floor.

"So Kallisto did manage to save those Children of Orion, did he? Guess the ambassador was speaking the truth after all. What a pity the Sin failed in that quest as well! Unfortunately for the both of you, the outcome will be the same that it was for both Kallisto and him so long ago. Failure that was twice theirs is now to be shared with you," Sven snapped, clutching his wounds.

"The filth of your presence in these halls shall be cleansed," Kallen screamed out, slowing his charge into the Throne room. His circular shield effortlessly deflected a couple arrows as Belle fired from her hiding place, slowing his rampant rage.

"How very noble of you. Unfortunately, that will be more difficult for you than you realize. Your protector also thought that he would cleanse us, but he too is no longer around to breathe this fresh mountain air. I would love to stay and chat, but I think I shall leave that to Belle and my brother Konflikt. As for myself, there is a little girl I have to catch and kill!"

Painful rage grew within Alexandra's heart at hearing Sven announce his intentions. Horror filled her to think that Halo had somehow slipped back through the Gates of Final Fate. She fired two arrows as he fled up the staircase. She knew they had to save Halo, but little hope remained while the two remaining evils blocked their way.

Belle and Konflikt unleashed their attacks upon their unwanted guests, covering Devotz's retreat up the stairs. The larger Metzonian attacked from behind one of the white-skinned trees as his partner sent arrows to cover his attack. Konflikt's heavy axe smashed hard into Kallen's shield, knocking him back. The axe continued to rain blows upon the shield, forcing him closer to the wall with every swing.

Kallen defended himself against the barrage, his brain desperately trying to regain control of emotions that raged within his body. His mind struggled with the realization that Kallisto was actually gone, joining Militades and numerous others who had fought to the end. Kallen was angry that he had been forced to die alone, not receiving any help from those he protected, a feeling that he had learned to suppress for his entire life. Screaming at the top of his lungs, Kallen let the rage take control of him. When the next attack came at him, he twisted his shield to send the blow glancing harmlessly past. His enemy off balance, Kallen struck out with the Oblitoryiat, pushing the large beast back and striking wildly at him several times, using rage-fuelled power over precision.

Alexandra continued to try to pin Belle down, but she proved extremely elusive. Alexandra continually lost track of where the Chilsa had moved to, several times almost leading to her own demise when the poisoned arrows barely missed their mark. Looking out from her cover behind the large tree, once again Alexandra did not know where the demoness had disappeared to. She thought she noticed movement off to her left, and she twisted, firing an arrow off in that direction. The arrow grazed Belle's leg, her shrieking curse ringing within the chamber as she resumed hiding among the great Trees of Eternity.

A shout of rage caused both women to turn their attention to the corner where the second battle was going on. Kallen screamed as he pushed onto the attack. Cursing and swinging with rage, the two battled around the ancient statue standing before the great throne. Kallen lashed out, knocking the giant Konflikt to his knees. He raised his grandfather's white sword high above his head.

His raging assault ended when a pair of arrows pounded into his chest, both powering directly through the thick breast plates protecting his heart. Konflikt shoved the top of his axe forward, the force crashing into the seam joining Kallen's leg and hip. The impact shattered Kallen's left hip and sent him crumpling to the ground in a roar of pain.

Alexandra watched her brother fall to the floor in a motionless heap. The chamber filled with screams as she felt her heart wrench. Arrows flew from her bow toward Konflikt, who quickly tucked his head and dove behind the large statue of Kyros as the Bane Bow unleashed its deadly power.

Belle stepped around the tree between them, stabbing wildly with her short blades, attempting to use the distraction to her advantage. Deflecting the attack with the blades of her bow, Alexandra forced the offensive, finally able to engage her elusive enemy face to face. Belle danced around with a light-footedness that made her difficult to pin, but Alexandra was not deterred.

The sharp edges of her bow sliced through the skin of her enemy each time before the empress was able to escape. Sensing she was close to finishing off the darker-skinned woman, Alexandra pressed to end the battle.

Konflikt lashed out with excessive force, punching directly into her spine with the spiked knuckles of his gauntleted fist. Alexandra shouted out in pain as she was crushed between the silver trunk of a tree and his armoured arm. Thick hands wrapped around the back of her neck, and she felt her feet lift from the stone floor, kicking freely in the air.

She felt a calmness overtake her before her world went black. A sickening crack came from within her neck as her lifeless body was thrown effortlessly through the air.

Pursuing the fleet-footed child, Devotz cursed his leg. He continued to push himself up the mountain despite his blood loss. Drawing on his master's dark powers, he had taken the stairs at a fast pace but was still unable to overtake his fleeing victim. She indeed had the immortal endurance to outpace him, and the gash across his knee was throbbing. The wound continued to bleed profusely, as did the back of his calf. Hate and dark determination continued to push him forward though at a slower pace; the sounds of battle far beneath him had grown faint. Listening closely, he could hear the sobbing of a little girl not too far above him. He knew that she was starting to get tired and slow down. Soon he would overcome her, but he was starting to run out of time.

Approaching the peak of the mountain far above the black clouds of Mammon's dark storm, the light of the temple exit shined in the moonlight. Catching a glimpse of the fleeing child looking back down upon him from atop the staircase, tears rolling down her face, as he moved closer, he smiled. The little immortal would finally be trapped so he could finish the task that would see the world drown in eternal darkness.

The blue moonlight lit up the white stone and ice of the mountain peak. Reaching the top of the endless staircase at last, Devotz's sweaty skin steamed in the crisp breeze as it ran across his boiling skin.

Tiny whimpers drew his eyes toward the child kneeling upon the cold stone across the peak. Clutching his spear tightly, Devotz began to cross toward his final target, listening to her sobs of fear echo within the chilly air. Soft and sweet, her prayers between short sobs begged for salvation as she sang out to the starry heavens so clear in the sky above the peak. Picturing the great tears rolling down her face as her body shivered with cold fear caused the demonic Metzonian to smile. Sven's heart would have perhaps caused him to pause to comprehend his impending actions, but the black heart and soul of Devotz would not.

His hands had been covered with the blood of millions over the course of his life; thousands felt their strength directly. A child was worth no more than another man simply because of its innocence. His soul had been innocent and pure of sin once, but life changes all things, those two aspects more than any other. He had experienced it all first-hand.

Grasping his spear over his head with both hands, preparing for the final downward thrust aimed for the little heart he could see beating within her chest. A single blow was all that was required of him to launch him into history as the only mortal to slay an immortal angel of Heaven. The time was finally at hand to collect his glory. Preparing to finish the task, Devotz did not realize that he was hearing the first words she had ever spoken, but he knew they would be the last she was ever to speak within this world. Like a sorrowful song, her last musical words tumbled out of her throat.

"Our Lords in Heaven, Creators of Life, please save me, I beg of you …"

Chapter 44
Return of the Light

Kallen felt cold. He had been cold plenty of times during his life while travelling and staying in the mountains. But this cold had a different grip on him as it slowly tightened around his soul. He struggled to move, the pool of red slippery against the shimmering white floors. His vision narrowed and blurred as he watched his sister trying to defend herself from the two remaining demons. The searing pain shot through his chest again as the barbed arrow twisted deeply when his heavy armour shifted.

He let himself fall back to the floor and stared up at the roof of the mountain. He could barely see the exit of the Staircase of Seventeen Thousand Steps, the small speck of light raining down upon him as he neared death. *Angels help us.* He thought about how the Light had once ruled over this world. His attention moved to the gargantuan throne sitting in the heart of the mountain. His eyes remembered its purity as the sunlight once hit it, though it had also glowed even in the darkest of nights, such as this one.

His body shook violently; he coughed hard into his hand, which filled with the blood of his fading life. A scream broke into the serenity that he had slipped into without noticing. Alexandra's cry echoed around the temple several times, piercing the sounds of battle. He watched as his sister was thrown against the Throne of the Creation. Her blood splattered against the gleaming diamond structure. He cringed, forgetting his own pain for a second.

"Alexandra …" His throat wouldn't cooperate; blood and bile filled it. He reached for her motionless body, the pool of blood growing ever larger. His world was being torn apart, and yet there wasn't a thing that he could do about it. Evil was crushing the last little bit of good that was left in the world. The temple boomed with dark laughter, mocking everything that Kallen had believed in his life, what his grandfather and every member of the Order had believed in. But everything he had been taught, everything imprinted upon his soul, all the stories told over and over again by their protectors seemed to have been for naught.

The diamond throne before him grew dimmer as Kallen felt the last of life seep from him. Surrounded by such evil, the trapped power within the throne also seemed to feel that its life was also at an end. How long had it waited for the touch of the heavenly again? Never again …

Kallen watched the throne slowly fade, waiting for his last dying breath to turn it dark. He continued to wait, fighting the darkness that was consuming him and his vision. The Throne of Creation also seemed to fight the darkness surrounding it, refusing to give in. It was fighting the darkness like a true Fallen, pushing back, slowly glowing brighter, and finally flaring out, unleashing a flash of startling energy.

The demonic humans took a step back, startled by the unexpected light, not knowing what to think or do. This was not what was supposed to happen. Their lords had shown them how events would unfold, and this was not part of it. Their masters peered upon the throne through the eyes of their puppets to see what drew their concern.

In a flash of light, the Metzonian and Chilsa felt the mountain shake; the very foundations of the world were shaking, alive with fear. The world was trembling in fear of whatever was coming. The Earth shook violently, as though it were being torn apart by the very forces that put it together. The atmosphere carried the thunderous bang around Earth until it crashed into its own echo. The entire world moaned like an animal dying in extreme pain as it shook from the core to the surface. All that had stood upon the earth were knocked from their feet in a heartbeat. They clung to the ground, trying to regain their thoughts and balance.

The soldiers of the mortal army swirled around him as they charged through the open gates of the final wall and rushed towards the tall bell tower. Listening to the heavy tones of the bells ring out as the Order of the Fallen signalled for a final retreat, the Sacred Citadel had at last fallen.

Looking above them at the large bridge that stretched out across the Lake of Heavenly Sorrow, his battle against the Fallen was finished. Victory against the Order was all but ensured leaving one last enemy in the way of the Sin's long awaited destiny. Searching among the mountain peaks for Mammon and his terrifying brother, Locan turned back to the inner walls of the Citadel for the weakest brother of the dark trio.

Perched above the mortal army with wings folded behind him, the Dark Prince Adramaleck watched the mortal scurrying around him. The warlord signalled towards the Sin warriors that stood patiently beside the gates they had cracked opened for the Metzonian and Chilsa. Swirling back into the shadows, the Sin once again began to slink towards their next enemy.

Reforming behind the demon before him, he watched the tip of the flaming tail waving back and forth absentmindedly. Pondering whether he would actually be able to sneak up behind the demon and end the fight in a single strike, his thought was immediately revealed for how foolish it truly was.

"Betray the Lords of Hell, and the suffering shall be eternal." Adramaleck spoke as he paused, noticing the shadowy forms of the Sin that had began to collect around him. Walking out of the shadows towards the demon, Locan did not respond as the Sin tightened the noose and began the silent attack.

The red flesh of Adramaleck burst into flames as the demon called upon the powers of darkness. Swinging his long sword in four swipes hacking down those before him as Locan and the other Sin charged through the wall of flames. The first attackers were followed by dozens more as Sin warriors from throughout the fortress joined their brethren.

Locan charged forwards to lead the assault as the Sin followed behind him. Ducking beneath the black wing and leaping over the tail that attempted to cut his feet out from beneath him, Locan penetrated the demon's inner defenses and aimed his attacks low to knock the demon from his feet.

The prince of Hell's eternal flames fell at his hands as Adramaleck's lower body spun around beneath the force of Locan's first strike. Swirling into a cloud of smoke to avoid the demon's backhand, Locan reformed upon the opposing side to drive the head of his mace into the exposed face of the demon. Seeing his opportunity to make the crucial blow he required to allow the Sin the advantage.

Aiming for the wide jaw of Adramaleck's horned head, the underhand blow sailed wide as his enemy pitched backwards to avoid Locan. The demon let his momentum continue as he rolled through a dozen Sin to rise back to his feet with back to the courtyard wall.

Stretching his wings wide above the Sin before him, Adramaleck's black blade liquefied into long strand of molten steel. The string of flames snapped as the whip sliced through the air as it stuck down several Sin as their warlord resumed his attack. Spewing a wall of flames across the courtyard, Locan pushed through Adramaleck's wall of flames, unaware of what lay upon the other side.

Leaping through the smoke and flames, Locan opened his eyes in time to see the tip of the lashing whip reach for him. Knowing it was too late to become the wraith, Locan braced himself as the whip struck him across the chest. All forward momentum was reversed as he felt the steel tip tear slice into his chest and he tumbled back through the wall of flames.

Locan's chest burnt as he looked down to stare at the gaping wound created by Adramaleck's fiery whip. Locan was unsure how he had survived the attack believing the whip should have cut directly through him. Looking back at the battle continuing on, the Sin were beginning to pull back as arcs of flame circled around the Dark Prince.

The ground beneath them shook as the atmosphere began to change, a pressure forming within Locan's ears and upon his mind. The crackling of the flames and the snapping of the fiery whip turned silent as time began to slow. Both opponents took a pause to re-evaluate the situation around them. Locan stared into the burning eyes of Adramaleck before following their gaze back towards the Lifebringer that loomed behind them.

The peak remained hidden by the raging storm that swirled beneath it, but neither had to see to know who stood high atop.

"Heaven has at last returned to this prison world of sinners. They shall destroy this world and all its inhabitants when they discover the truth." Locan spoke quietly, letting his flesh slowly begin to smoke as he began the retreat.

"This is not over, dark angel. Such treachery shall not be forgotten."

Rhimmon looked across the battlefield for his brothers as the battle continued to rage, most of its combatants too caught up in their personal struggles to notice the changes around them. The demon princes had experienced such cosmic events before. As dark and evil as their hearts were, balls of fear now formed in their souls. *Very few beings make such an entrance. But it cannot be …*

The Dark Princes watched a fast-moving smoke form and flee across the open fields within the heart of the Alakari, heading in the opposite direction from the burning fortress. The warlord Locan also sensed the coming danger and rallied his dark angels to flee from the Light.

Fools! Weak and petty fools! thought Rhimmon. If they united they could slay their common enemies before they once again established a foothold upon this world. The Princes of Hell knew what happened when the forces of Heaven had managed such a feat before; they had expanded at a consistent and methodical rate until the world was covered in the blasted light and all Hell's minions were dead.

Adramaleck, still within the walls of the fortress, noticed

the rumbling within the earth and atmosphere. His fiery wings soon spread wide as he took to the sky to join Rhimmon atop his mountain perch. Mammon abandoned the mountaintop he had held and landed upon all fours loudly behind his brothers.

Concentrating on the minds of his assault force, he could feel two of them within the heart of the mountain, feeling content and strong at the defeat of their enemies. Rhimmon had not relinquished control of his prize champion and focused deeper to peer though his soul, finding him atop the mountain.

Dread overtook him as their fears became true. The Lord of the Earth had returned.

Hot tears continued to roll down her small cheeks. Emotions of every type had filled her small head, but it was mostly dominated by fear. But now her mind was completely blank, her world covered in a blinding white light. She could no longer remember the monster that chased her to the top of the mountain or what he may have looked like. Was this Heaven, the blinding white light, the coolness that surrounded her, the pure serenity? She looked up, staring into the magnificent image that filled her vision. A massive silhouette towered over her in the blinding light. Barely visible amongst the light, the hooded figure stood bare-chested, enormous wings of white energy flaring out behind him, looking out over the landscape from the highest point on Earth. Halo could see the deep breath of mountain air he inhaled, as though reacquainting himself with something from a very distant past.

The being took one stride toward her, covering distance between them effortlessly. Leaning toward her, the being reached down with a single hand.

"Fear not anymore, my child. I am here to protect you."

The hand was large enough to pick her up and crush her within its palm. And although her tears continued to fall, Halo no longer felt threatened. A single large finger wiped the tears from her cheek. The voice had spoken softly, yet the sound reverberated within her head. The touch was cool but carried emotional warmth beneath it.

The blinding light behind the authoritative figure softened, barely revealing the finer details. Stunning beauty seemed to radiate, as if it were the perfect being. An angel. White of the purest she had witnessed within her life covered the wings, luminous white eyes that could pierce clouds as well as souls at the slightest glance radiated brightly. Heavy heavenly steel clad the immortal below the waist, shining bright white yet articulated with the finest detailing upon its divine steel. The hood hid most of the soft facial features, but she could barely see in the bright light reflecting within the covering that they were chiselled to perfection. She could not tear her eyes away from him.

Without warning, the angel pivoted on the heel of his bare foot, swinging himself in the opposite direction above of her. She remained unharmed despite her close vicinity to the movement sweeping over her in a flash of light. She caught a glimpse of the demon that had pursued her up the stairs regaining his composure at the sudden change of events.

The demonic human's true form came clear before the blinding light the angel cast, his flesh sinking beneath the bone protrusions no longer hidden under the illusion the Princes of Hell had empowered. Devotz hissed and snapped at the being, his long spear pointed at its throat, waiting for the proper moment to strike. The heavenly being strode forward unflinchingly.

"Those who misuse the gift of life shall be purged from this world!"

Devotz thrust his spear forward with all the quickness of his demonic ability. The spear halted before the chest of the motionless Creator. The white orbs narrowed. The demon felt the cold air beneath his feet. The invisible grasp of the Creator was unbreakable, and the demon screamed out in agonizing pain as his joints snapped rigid. The Creator raised curled hands before his body, lifting Devotz into the sky.

The demon struggled, fighting with every ounce of strength as the life was being slowly drawn from his body and absorbed in the outstretched hand. Halo could feel the demon's limbs grow heavy and watched as they turned stiff as a stone. The demon continued to howl, curse and shriek until there was no life left in his lungs, leaving an eerie silence in its wake. Even the breeze did not dare blow. The angel picked up Devotz's body in one arm as it peered through the raging storm below. After a last second of silence, it hurled the demon's body down through the atmosphere toward the depths from which he had been born.

The young girl pulled her cloak around her against the sudden chill on the mountain peak, watching her saviour stand upon the edge and gaze down upon the clouds surrounding the peak.

"Angels of Heaven shall descend upon those who wrought evil within my Creation!"

She felt an air of calmness surround him from within, despite the chaos and death in the world he had created, as though he had seen it all before. With a single glance toward Halo, the Creator leapt over the edge of mountaintop, white wings of energy folded back like an eagle bent on vengeance.

Chapter 45
Wrath of the Creator

Devotz's body plunged through the dark storm created by the demon lords. Lifeless, it smashed into the earth at the feet of the three demon princes, the empty black eyes staring. The slave of Rhimmon was no more, and although Rhimmon had many to replace him with, the symbolism pierced him. His puppet's reign of terror was over, and soon Rhimmon's would also be jeopardized. He would be cast down to the depths, as the Metzonian had been.

"*Brother, what do we do now? He has returned and puts everything in jeopardy. Without a doubt, he has brought the Heavens with him to repeat what he started ten thousand years ago. Not repeat ... finish!*" Rhimmon did not acknowledge Adramaleck's trepidation. As dumb as Adramaleck could be, he pointed out a very dangerous thought, obvious as it was. Rhimmon's mind raced for answers and solutions as he watched the storming sky, black as night, continuing to strike the ground with horrific orange lightning. He looked upon a diminutive portion, where the clouds were boiling and tearing apart in a wide white gash. Blinding white light poured through the tear, and a figure burnt into their memories slashed forth.

The entire mortal army was looking to the sky now, their attention caught by a sonic boom before they became mesmerized by the brilliant light flying forth. Most did not realize how this event would affect them.

The white wings snapped out, slowing his descent slightly before he crashed into the centre of the demon's mortal army. The impact dropped the entire army to the ground. White lightning shot out of his hands, arcing across thousands of infantry at a time, claiming the life from their souls. The wings beat heavily, forcefully picking up men and blowing them across the valley as if their bodies were merely dust in a storm.

A crack of lightning blistered from the eye of the storm still hovering overhead, destined for the angel. Mammon cut his hand across the air, his open fist guiding the bolt to where it was meant to hit. It missed at the last second as the heavenly being sidestepped the attack, casting his white eyes not to the sky above but toward the one who directed it.

Anger flowed through Mammon as he watched the bolt pass the angel's wings and crash into their own army. Eyes locking across the plain that had become stained in blood, loathing flowed through both at the simple sight of each other. Rhimmon felt even more of the angel's calm distaste rise as he noticed that Mammon was standing among his brothers. Three demon princes, all united, their powers combined. Three evil minds bent as one, with Earth and all its inhabitants to be trapped beneath the banner of the Princes of Hell for eternity.

In a single bound, the angel cut the distance by half, standing tall as he confronted the three. If the sight of three princes in one location bothered him, the angel didn't let it show in the least. While his power was limitless, three demonic princes could pose a slight challenge, but the Creator refused to be fazed by them.

"Three forgotten Princes of Hell united in a crusade of darkness and terror. You picked the wrong place to desecrate with your mere presence once again. The Throne of Creation is for the Pure and the Pure alone! Three princes can't sit on one Throne, I remind you all."

"You small-minded angels are all the same. When this is over, I'm destroying your throne, and I'll spread the remaining dust across this pathetic world. We are in the process of wiping Heaven's footprint from this world, down to the last child!" Mammon snarled, letting the dark powers flow through him, clenching his large black spear tightly. Rhimmon and Adramaleck also tightened up, preparing themselves for the inevitable battle that was soon to be unleashed upon the world. *"You saved her once, but we have others to finish the task! You will not intervene this time; none are left within the temple to save her."*

Awaken!

Kallen's eyes snapped open, fluttering to adjust to the light. He gasped for air, filling his lungs as deeply as he could. *Is this the next stage of life? Is this Heaven, as we often talked about as children?* The air was cold and crisp, as if he was a child climbing the mountain peaks again. The floor that he lay on was hard as stone, and yet he didn't feel pain anymore. He rolled over, staring into the marble floors of the … temple floor? His head snapped up as he focused on the room around him, seeing the two demonic humans of the princes of evil. They too were collecting their thoughts, on their knees.

Flee from the grasp of death.

"What …?" Kallen pulled himself upright, stretching as he tried to loosen his rigid muscles. His body felt like it had been asleep for eternity, stiff and tight. He reached down to pick up his sword, his gaze falling upon his fallen sister. He saw her fingers twitch and flex before she began coughing. Kallen watched with amazement as she rolled over onto her stomach, consciously looking up at him again. Feeling tears well, he smiled at the miracle before his eyes. Something or someone had simply given them back their lives: a second chance.

Rise once more. Cleanse this evil.

The demonic humans Konflikt and Belle were startled by the strange change of events and fully believed that other forces were at work in this temple. Both had known what their masters were able to do with their terrible powers, from ripping people's souls right from their hearts to wiping out towns with a single breath.

Belle locked several arrows into her bow and seconds after the first let loose a second draw. Konflikt plucked his axe from the floor and charged toward the twins, swinging wildly, letting his rage once more fuel his strength. The descendants of Orion dove apart, separating as Konflikt burst between them. Alexandra let loose two arrows, but both passed harmlessly over his shoulder as he ducked behind the throne. Reversing direction and coming at her from the other side, he swung his axe hard around the corner, the tip grazing her greaves as Alexandra did her best to avoid the attack.

Kallen tried to get within striking distance of Belle. But no matter how he moved, what direction he took, she sensed every plan of attack. She pinned him down with a barrage of arrows and just as quickly fired a couple in support of her partner.

"You may have been granted another chance by the Light, but we shall continue to strike you down, over and over and over again! Good is losing its foothold on this world and soon shall be wiped clean. Your army is collapsing; soon even the temple will be overrun." Demonic laughter echoed within the temple.

A chill ran up his spine as Kallen thought about the fierce fighting that was getting ever closer to the temple. He imagined the cries of mortal men as they were at last overtaken, their brethren slowly being pushed back toward the temple's large outer gates as they began collapsing. The shouts of leaders bent on fighting to the end urged them on, even if they knew their end was inevitable. Once over the bridge, past the statues in memory of the Nine, the invaders would pass through the temple to try and break down the Door and reach the Sacred City and its trapped inhabitants.

The sound of wood splitting quickly reminded him of the danger that was at his back. He watched as his sister worked her way around the circle of large trees, firing as she darted back and forth, finally taking cover behind a tree near him. Konflikt charged from behind the throne at full speed, smashing his large body into a Tree of Life, sending splinters spinning in all directions as the tree collapsed beneath the massive force.

Alexandra attempted to roll away from the falling tree but to no avail. She felt her right elbow snap as a thick branch landed on her forearm. Her shoulder smashed into the floor, followed by her face, leaving her struggling to maintain consciousness. She gave her arm a quick pull; the slightest movement occurred, but not enough to free

A Mortal Mistake

her. She glanced behind her and saw the gleam in Konflikt's eyes. The monster crushed her left arm as he stomped forcefully on it with his steel boot. She could smell the stench of his breath as he leaned over and grabbed her by her hair. He pulled back hard, snapping her head back as he gazed into her eyes. Thrill was upon his face, as though he couldn't believe his luck. "How blessed I am to get to kill you twice in one afternoon," he roared in enjoyment, raising the axe over his head. "Headless it is!"

A gauntleted hand slammed hard down on Konflikt's thick wrist, and Kallen tried to pull Konflikt over backward. Konflikt resisted and pulled forward, trying to use his brute strength to overpower Kallen. His axe remained cocked over his shoulder. As Kallen kicked the larger man in the side of the knee, a hiss of pain escaped Konflikt's tight lips. The knee buckled. Belle unleashed an arrow that flew through the Titan's shoulder.

His cry of pain was music to Konflikt's ears as he swung his arm forward, but Kallen refused to relinquish his grip. Konflikt swung the axe into the thick skin of the tree. Drawing his dagger from his belt, Kallen stabbed the thick forearms repeatedly, desperately trying to force him to release the axe. Konflikt roared out in pain, swinging his massive torso to face his attacker, knowing Kallen's sister remained helpless. An armoured elbow smashed into the side of Kallen's helmeted head as yet another arrow pierced his bicep.

In one last-ditch effort, Kallen pivoted to throw himself in front of Konflikt and protect himself from the arrows. Pushing back with all his might, he heaved the large demon backward until he fell against the throne. Konflikt tumbled backward, smacking his head against the armrest. Another arrow soared past Kallen's waist, grazing his armour. He pulled his shield in front of him to block the second.

Alexandra continued to struggle, ever so slowly freeing her arm inch by inch. Her brother was trying to continue the fight on his own, and she could sense that Belle was quickly moving into killing position. If she could just get out she could help him. She needed to get out.

Twisting herself around so she was able to place both feet against the white trunk of the tree, she pushed with all her might several times. She only made the slightest of gains and knew time was running out. The thick whack of arrows puncturing steel within the air filled her with worry. She had to get free now or lose her brother once more. Closing her eyes, she focused every ounce of strength, screaming at the top of her lungs.

The vambrace protecting her forearm shifted slightly, giving her a taste of freedom. Alexandra felt the strain in her legs as she pushed the last time. Scraping against the thick bark, her arm came free, sending her careening across the room. *Freedom!* She scrambled for her holy bow, hearing the enemy's arrows cutting through the air. The heavy thump when one hit the mark made her despair. Her brother's curses rang out as Belle continued to evade him. She could not lose Kallen another time!

Alexandra leaped for her bow. Swinging around to face the threat, she drew the orange string back. Unleashing an assault of arrows toward Belle, she fired as many arrows as she could, no longer caring how accurate she was. She wanted Belle pinned down, unable to move.

Belle fell to her knees as an arrow pierced her upper thigh, tearing deeply. Another caught her below the ribs as the final one landed several inches higher. All three arrows cut through their victim, stopping only when they struck the thick bark of the Eternity Trees. Belle's cursed as she collapsed, clutching her wounds.

Consciousness returned to Konflikt just in time to watch Belle collapse beneath the blows from the Bane Bow; blood oozed from her lips. He watched her pull her hand away from her chest to find it covered in blood, the realization within her eyes that she knew what was next. Konflikt knew his brother had promised her a different situation than the one she found herself in. Death had never been within the realm of what Devotz had expected, not for them. Looking at him, Belle's once beautiful complexion had changed; her eyes were dark and hollow as her skin paled when death came for her.

He watched her succumb to the last of her injuries. He wondered if perhaps he was the last; Devotz had not returned from the mountaintop. Certainly his brother's soldiers should have crushed the last of the Order's defenders by now and, provided the Sin were successful, be entering the temple soon. He needed to continue to survive. Konflikt reached with his uninjured arm, trying to find a handhold to pull himself up to his feet. All he could seem to find was the damned throne he had cracked his head upon. Rolling to his knees, he reached for the seat of the throne. His hands burned as he tightened his grip to pull himself up.

"Only the Purest among Angels shall sit on the Throne of Creation!"

Konflikt instantly tensed up. A new voice, deep and booming … dark enough to send shivers through the highest-ranking demons. He heard the faint singing of hymns, of glorious tales of great battles, great victories combined with verses of extreme sadness, spoken in ancient tongue. A very ancient tongue. Perhaps it was not all just a legend. Konflikt twisted, shocked, and for the first time in his life outside the experiences of his father and brother, deathly frightened.

The lone statue within the Circle of Life before the throne was not kneeling anymore. The creature was standing straight as an arrow, pointing a large arm straight at him. The purple orbs burned fiercely, never leaving his eyes.

"Only the Purest among Angels shall sit on the Throne of Creation!"

The Throne Guardian stepped off his large pedestal within the throne room, moving toward Konflikt at a steady, intimidating pace. His heart pumped faster and faster as the guardian approached. He sensed his brother's Mortal Army of Darkness was almost across the bridge, the final elements of the Light being pushed back into the temple. He had accomplished everything that the princes had asked of him and more, and now they were abandoning him. Looking into the depths of the horrible purple visor, every moment and every thought was torn from his mind, replaced with images of the future, where the blood of Devotz's warriors ran like a river, countering his own hopes. The singing of an ancient hymn in a forgotten tongue reverberated in the back of his mind. As it grew louder within his mind, he remembered the ancient song Rhimmon had forewarned them about. He stared deeper into the glowing spirit within the suit of armour, and it spoke to him and beyond.

"Let the Light shine down on this world once again! Let the Nine of Creation once again cleanse this world of evil darkness!"

The Darkness pressed heavily within their minds as the last surviving defenders of the Order gave more ground. The dark legions relentlessly pressed forward upon the bridge. The sounds of battle and the smell of death fuelled their souls and body, as exhaustion and hopelessness fell upon the Order. The destruction of this last bastion of the light appeared to finally be at hand.

Protected by Ethan on his left and Eli on his right, Raef participated to the end. After the collapse of the third wall the prince had grown a second shadow created by the two men. Alternating back and forth, one led the forces at the front of the army while the other rested at Raef's side until his turn once again came to return to the bloody front.

The twin generals of Kyllordia urged the last of the Order's followers forward in yet another counter push. Bottlenecked upon the bridge, the Fallen had managed to slow the torrid pace of defeat. How anyone managed to continue lifting their swords at all was beyond Raef's belief. The tips of his fingers bled from his bowstring. Battle exhaustion had started to become devastating as the days of straight battle wore them down.

Raef watched the Metzonian and Chilsa infantry who had pressed the survivors tirelessly for two days move ever closer to their target. The Temple Titans had helped to stem the assault momentarily when they joined the battle on the bridge. The fact that the guardians were engaging the enemy proved to Raef what he had anticipated. The Army of the Fallen had failed to halt their enemy despite the defences provided to them, which proved how dire the situation was. If not the treason of his generals, he would be safe within the Keeps instead of dying at the foot of the flowing mountain.

Leaving Ethan to command the bell tower defence, Eli and Raef had pulled back to the bridge with the reorganized battalions recovering from battle. Devastation was written upon Eli's face as they left the tower for the bridge and the sight across the bay of blue water. The tall stone doors of the temple entrance were sealed, trapping the army upon the platform. Wading through the ranks of the Titans surrounding the sealed doors, Eli had pressed himself against the doors, screaming in agonized frustration as the heaviness of their situation finally collapsed the man. The forlorn looks upon the Titans faces were hidden by their helmets, but their voices shook with shame.

"The Sin attacked us from inside the temple entrance, catching our men off guard. We were not expecting an attack from inside or the strength we were forced to face. We slew most of their brothers, but a few managed to lock themselves within the gate control house. Those still within the temple have been unable get into it."

And now their fate was sealed as the army was pinned against the Sacred Temple doors, no escape possible. Gazing down the length of the bridge from his higher vantage point, Raef looked upon the opposing enemy as it packed the bridge with every man possible. Their comrades did not wait for the soldiers before them to defeat their opponents; all simply shoved forward as those behind them pressed upon their own backs in a steady unrelenting push. Looking beyond the bridge itself, he could see that the walls of the fortress—and, to his disbelief, even beyond the walls—crawled with the soldiery of Chilsa. They might as well have thrown their swords to the ground and accepted fate rather than continue this futile battle.

A rumble from within the temple made Raef jump. Another thud hammered at the doors, rattling the thick stone, as though a great beast trapped within the mountain was attempting escape.

"Cleanse this evil! Let none escape!"

Hearing the voice boom from within the temple, both Ethan and Eli turned around. The angel-adorned doors shook with a deep rumble as Fallen warriors were forced forward by their shifting mass. The eyes of the Fallen were directed toward the black maw; all waited for what would appear from within.

A grey silhouette emerged from the darkness, marked by glowing purple specks that grew brighter as it hurtled toward them. The men before the doors ducked for cover as the massive figure leapt out of the temple over them. Kyros, ancient leader of the Nine Temple Throne Guardians, was no longer a stone statue that watched the Throne, awaiting his master's return.

Before the Titans, Kyros leaped over the shocked Fallen faces, landing among their enemies. The swarm of dark men collapsed under his powerful swing, each swipe of his bladed spear clearing five ranks.

"Brothers! Sisters! Holy blood stains our walls once more. The Creator himself has returned! Awaken and come forth once more! Awaken!"

Stone skin cracked and turned to dust as the remaining Nine woke from the slumber that had surpassed ten thousand years. Years of dust mixed with the mists of the falls had settled upon their dark armour, camouflaging the once-powerful Throne Guardians as stone statues even the Fallen were unaware of.

Standing upon their great podiums, they looked down upon the darkness of Humanity thrusting forward with bloodthirsty hate. The guardians did not have to feel the souls of men; their actions spoke loud enough. Without hesitating a second more, the Throne Guardians fell upon those under the influence of Hell.

Raef and his generals watched the mayhem nine single creations of Heaven carved upon mortal flesh. Trapped upon the bridge, the wholesale slaughter before their eyes was conducted without thought or feeling: emotionless. Thousands lay dead within minutes, the white bridge stained red as blood flowed down the sloped stone. Moving at a constant pace of death, the steel arms did not hesitate or slow as they waded through the mass of humans.

Raef was surprised by the tenacity their enemy presented against this new threat. Like waves of water crashing upon a stone shore, the soldiers of the dark powers threw themselves at the Throne Guardians and were repelled, bloodied limbs soon flying in the air.

Evil refused to be shaken. The men continued to attack, retreating only as their lives were being taken. They continued to swing and barge forward despite the futility, not fully understanding that it was out of their control. Smaller demons of true form started to push forward through the ranks, followed by larger ones. It was no longer a battle of men anymore. Forces of pure darkness and light were about to do battle once again upon Earth, for the first time in thousands of years.

The eight Throne Guardians followed their leader down the bridge, leaving a wake of death in their paths. The bridge was reclaimed, leaving a stunned Fallen army beneath the shadows of the Lifebringer in the dawning light. Led by the remnants of Kallen's Temple Titans, a small number of survivors followed the charge back into the fortress, leaving the remainder to collapse in astonished exhaustion. None could believe they were still intact when so many had fallen.

CHAPTER 46
AN ANCIENT BATTLE

The Princes of Hell cringed at hearing the songs of the Ancients that burned their ears, reminding them of their own defeats. Rage and hate burned hot within their chest as the Nine Throne Guardians sang their return to the world. The appearance of the Nine on the temple ramp infuriated Rhimmon.

Rhimmon had been told that they had been taken far from this world when the Creator left, and they would not be forced to contend with their strength. Instead they had remained dormant for thousands of years, waiting for his return to awaken them from slumber. Even so, he doubted that they would turn the tide of this war. The Creator of Heaven, on the other hand, could possibly ruin everything the Lords of Hell had planned for this world. Returned once again, the Almighty Lord of the Light would purge evil from this world if it meant taking it apart to the very core and rebuilding it from the very atoms he'd used to build it. He would not stop this time.

Rhimmon and his brothers found themselves trapped in a dire situation. They must defeat the Creator himself or suffer the wrath of the Dark Lords themselves. Retreat would result in their immediate death. Only one true option remained.

The three Dark Princes lashed into the offensive against the

Creator. Flames shot toward the angel; dark lightning crackled from the sky; the earth heaved and broke apart. The demons continued to punish the angel relentlessly as they cursed and swore, calling upon all the dark spells from their past to create a unified attack.

"This is our world now! Nothing shall stop us; we have twisted this world into our own image! It shall stay as such." Mammon continued to make his storm boil violently. The black clouds rumbled as a constant stream of lighting blazed from their depths. The brothers could not see the angel behind the wall of flames and dust but could sense him, could smell the purity of his presence.

"You have grown very strong indeed in my absence. But you still do not know many things. You can twist and contort what I have created. But I am the Creator!"

The flames dissipated instantly. The burning lightning halted, and Earth became silent. Before them, as pristine as ever, was the Creator. His white eyes remained calm and emotionless as he waited to see if his opponents decided to continue their futile battle with him.

Rhimmon watched as his brother took the challenge and unleashed his storm once more. Orange electricity coursed through the clouds toward the central focal point at the eye of the storm, swirling quicker and quicker. Eyes cast up at the force collecting above him, the Creator raised his hand over his head and waited for the impending strike, challenging the Dark Princes once more.

Mammon released the power of the storms directly down upon the heavenly being, striking the raised arm. Rhimmon and Adramaleck watched as the energy coursed down the arm, disappearing into the wings and body of the angel. Then the black clouds grew lighter, beginning to fade, letting the first rays of sunlight break through to look down upon the carnage from the two-day battle.

The Creator turned his attention back to the demons, throwing his arms toward his enemies. Pure energy shot from his hands; the massive electrical force knocked the trio backward. As they struggled to dodge the attack, the angel glided forward. The unrelenting assault continued against the princes of evil. Attempts to strike back were brushed off and immediately punished with blasts of cold white energy thrown by the Creator.

The battle of light and darkness raged on as the Dark Princes continued to struggle against their enemy. Their powerful sorcery did not phase the heavenly being, so there was little choice but to take it to the personal physical level. The princes of evil could feel the battle slipping through their fingers like it had centuries before. They lifted their dark steel blades in their clenched fists.

Rhimmon led the charge, taking the brunt of the force, hammered with white flames that burned his skin, which flickered and flared. He rolled out of the way of the second attack and continued forward, drawing his venomous blades and lashing out over his shoulder. He watched helplessly as his heavy attack grazed the Creator harmlessly, leaving his flank open. The angel's punishment was quick. A grave heavenly blow smashed at the back of Rhimmon's shoulder as an armoured leg crashed into his knees and spun him in the air. His expected descent back to the earth was delayed.

Both Adramaleck and Mammon moved quickly into the fray as their black brother was plucked up. The angel lifted him several feet in the air, the gigantic wings beating only once, and then he threw Rhimmon hard onto the rocky surface with the force of a meteor. The impact shattered the hard Alakari stone, creating a crater in a clash of dust and rock, Rhimmon's bulk in the centre.

Tumbling over the debilitated body of his brother, Mammon thrust his spear toward the back of the Creator's neck. It was quickly defected by an immense white wing. Adramaleck was shoved beneath the angel and smashed through the rocky ground.

Mammon brought his spear down fiercely on the angel's back, dropping his opponent to one knee. The small victory sent adrenaline and black blood pumping through his veins as he quickly attempted to pin the angel down. The heavenly being grabbed onto the shaft, ripping it from Mammon's hands as he drove for the final blow. As it sliced harmlessly under his arm, the Creator pulled it through and smashed his shoulder into the prince. Then he kicked Mammon's torso, sending his body skidding through the rock to join his brothers.

A Mortal Mistake

"*There shall be no more death and destruction at your hands! I grow tired of these futile attempts to spread darkness. Too many times I have been forced to intervene in these affairs—there shall be no more!*"

The fiery white eyes flashed as he raised all three princes off the ground and felt the anger and hatred flowing through their bodies, full of evil and pumping with pure destruction. The Creator could barely sense the pain he had inflicted beneath it.

He could feel darkness, destruction and hatred from all of them. But an even deeper underlying evil coursed through them. He felt it grow within them as if it fed its power back into their hearts once more. They grew stronger again, resisting his hold upon them, a force of terrible evil, of which there were only a few sources in the entire universe. Hurling the Dark Princes deep into the Alakari stone once more, he focused upon the new feeling.

"*I can smell you and feel your presence within this world. You can never truly hide. I should have guessed that a Lord of Hell created this destruction!*"

Through the darkness a blurry figure crept forward, swallowing the light around the shadow. Not stopping long enough to create a solid figure, it continued to shape-shift within the vague darkness. He reeked of death, and his figure represented carnage. Bloody red orbs appeared out of the gloom as darkness grew around the lone angel. It started to compress around him, turning the space around him black, slowly cutting him off from the world and the empowering sunlight.

"*It cannot be …*" He lifted an arm and pointed toward the shadowy winged demon, disbelief filling his mind as a memory emerged. "*I watched you die! I destroyed the darkness that was your soul. I watched your lifeless body tumble through the universe and fade into darkness …*"

"**Darkness cannot die nor be destroyed. You should know this.**" The bone-chilling laughter rippled forth from the shadow as the unblinking red eyes continued to stare into his. The whispery wings of pitch black shadows stretched out casting the darkness overtop of them. "**Your irritating Light may make the darkness** disappear, but it is always there. Lurking silently, waiting for you to turn your back upon the shadows.

"You should never have returned. This is not your world anymore. Not your creation. This world is mine! From here, the Lords of Hell shall launch the campaign of darkness that will swallow everything. And now, with you here, and Humanity thoroughly in our control … the end has come at last for Heaven!"

The Creator pushed back the darkness around him, revealing two similar monsters that were hidden behind its veil. He leaped off the ground, taking flight for the Heavens, but he was too late. The ground beneath where he had stood only moments before erupted. A massive chasm started to form as the earth split and fell to the depths. A great swirling black maw opened, trying to absorb him. A figure of black shot out from the centre of the dark magical storm in pursuit after him.

Dark Lord Cayn ripped through the centre of the vortex beneath the Creator, reaching for his feet and latching on to them with all four arms. Dark Lord Asmodeus attacked from the rear, leaping over the chasm, adding his own weight to the battle. He wrapped his clawed arms around the angel's waist, and both Lords of Hell began dragging him slowly back toward the dark pit.

Sheets of energy poured from the Creator as he lashed out at the Lords of Hell, desperate to escape. Their grips refused to loosen at all even as pain rippled through their black bodies. The Creator used every weapon available to him but was unable to escape the grasps of the two Lords of Hell and their infinite darkness.

As Diabolos's shadowy weight crashed between the white wings, all four began the endless plunge into the swirling blackness, destined for the hells of Earth. The vortex within the crater sealed itself behind them, disappearing into the oblivion.

CHAPTER 47
Houses of Heaven

Dragging himself out of the crater his impact created, the Dark Prince of Temptation and Greed let the loose stones tumble harmlessly across his purple muscles. Grasping the stones, he felt whole and strong again as he crushed the rock between his thick fingers.

Within the death grasp of the Creator, the demon once buried in the Desert of Lost Souls had truly believed he was about to become one. He had not expected to awaken in the cavern created by his body. Climbing from his berth, he found Adramaleck's body upside down in the grey stone and Mammon's body in much the same position.

All were alive, and Rhimmon could feel the darkness return to his heart and veins that only one could infuse. He had little doubt of the powers that had somehow returned him to the Halls of Hell to continue his purpose. Grasping the edge of the crater's rock ledge, he gave one final heave and knelt on its edge. Looking up from the bloody rock, he gazed at the dreadful sight before him. Bright streaks of light fell from the sky upon the remains of his human army. The Legionnaires of the Houses of Heaven had arrived at last upon Earth. His brothers dragged themselves from the crater to look upon the nine figures standing before them.

"You are too late and have failed, as you always do." Rhimmon's booming laughter did not faze those standing emotionlessly before them, weapons casually prepared. While they were no longer angels, the Heaven's Throne Guardians remained potent headaches for the Dark Princes. But it did not matter. ***"Our masters have defeated***

your own and dragged Him to the depths of this world. Their wrathful grasp shall never be released from Heaven's fate now that they have its Creator. You failed once again but at no time greater than this one, Kyros."

Looking up at the Temple Throne Guardian standing in the middle, Rhimmon was unsure whether the abomination, the largest and most dangerous of the guardians, had any emotions. The purple soul of Kyros watched him from within the mechanized visor that still contained his ancient spirit. Kyros rushed forward with spear in hand, as Rhimmon jumped backward. Stretching their wings over the crater behind them, the Dark Princes watched the creature of steel skid to the edge.

"Remember who you are, Titan, not who you once were." His brothers joined his laughter as they flapped their leathery wings before the flightless warriors of Heaven. *"You are not angels anymore, nor can you fly like you once did. You are all abominations; even Heaven denied you the grace of flight."*

A silver spear cut through the air, spiralling from Kyros's fist toward the demon's heart. The spear slowed as Rhimmon grasped it with his mind, and it stopped inches from its mark. Reading the scriptures upon it as it continued to spin, Rhimmon shook his head at his immortal enemy.

"I do not think so, Kyros, not this time. We are no longer weak like Humanity and all other life on this world. Our strength has been at last completely restored to us by our father. A father's disappointment we may be, but we feel him quite proud of us for bringing the Creator himself down from Heaven into his waiting grasp."

Rhimmon reversed the motion of Kyros's spear, firing the bolt back at its owner. Disappointed when Kyros caught it as easily as he had released it, Rhimmon was not wholly surprised by such an action; he remembered the powers the Creator had granted his demon hunters. Damnable murderous machines was what they were, constantly sniffing out even the most powerful of demons from their hiding places. He would not leave them helpless.

"I see that your Father has not forgotten to replenish the

power of his abominations either. I would like to stay and converse longer, Kyros ..." He looked toward the sky, full of angels streaking through the air, growing more numerous with every passing moment. *"But it's starting to rain a little heavy for my liking. We will meet again soon ... I promise it!"*

Knowing Heaven's strength grew stronger with every moment, Rhimmon took his leave from the battle. Grinning toward the Nine, he turned away and flew to safety. As he passed, he surveyed the carnage below. The white steel of Heaven fell amongst the army, hacking and slaying the army the Dark Princes had spent the last year manipulating into creation.

The horned demons Prince Abaddon had lent him became the primary targets for the swords of Heaven. Abaddon would not be pleased at all, but despite the unexpected defeat of their original plans, the Lords of Hell had come away with a much larger victory than they had ever hoped for.

Provided they could contain the Creator. Rhimmon was curious to see how the Lords of Hell planned to keep him in such a helpless state. He had no desire to feel that touch more than once.

The water that poured from the mountaintop looked alive, shimmering and roaring heavily. Sunlight rained down upon the mountain and the land surrounding it. The life within the Valley of Angels visible as it had become the bloody graveyard of Humanity.

Armoured angels continued to scour around the mountain range. The beautiful view was hard for the humans who recovered below to believe. Magnificent as they were, they had a more deadly purpose, as the Heavens continued to search out hidden evil in the Alakari. Their brethren continued to fall in great waves from the sky.

Much of the dark army had fled at the arrival of the Legionnaires and the rest of Heaven's army. But heavy losses were inflicted upon them, and many battles still raged. All those of the Mortal Dark Army trapped within the city walls were decimated; none left alive. The battle continued to rage as remnants of the army retreated back through the mountain pass to reach the safety of open land. Mountains were proving to be exceptionally deadly. The heavenly legions would fly hard through the mountains and dive down upon the retreating soldiers

The Ancients stood upon the peak of the Lifebringer, high above the lands, looking down upon them, unable to believe the destruction Humanity had wrought upon itself. A slaughter without question as to why or of the motive had almost wiped Humanity to extinction.

"Such violence and hate this world is capable of. The mountain continues to reek of death even after it has been washed. Sadly, the greatest violence is only about to begin." The soft voice of the Ancient Rhia spoke first. Her wings hung low, relaying her feelings physically. Her heart was heavy with the pain of seeing life thrown away so easily. The burning orange eyes turned away to look up into the sky as her House of Hellio began to arrive.

"War like this is devastating. The next war will be a complete atrocity, one that Humanity will not survive. Knowing that the Dark Lords are at work here, it is very possible that this world will not survive. The human Dark Army is hardly as deadly as the Dark Ones' real army that assuredly hides below the surface.

"Prepare for the battle of time. Without He Who Created Us, we may lose this battle against the darkness. We could lose the Eternal War we have been waging since the beginning of time. Such events could result in the end of the Light. Heaven's time could be nearing its end …"

Glowing orbs of yellow looked over the carnage surrounding the Lifebringer, filling the air with the stench of death. The Ancient Lord Oron looked back into his past to the last time he had come to this world, observing that little had changed. This world was nothing but a cesspool of death and despair, and yet their Creator refused to give up on it or its inhabitants.

They were correct; this war would stretch the world and all those who inhabited it to the brink. Most would not survive, and those who did would be left with nothing. And without Him, the world would be covered in darkness forever.

A Mortal Mistake

The Dungeons of Andagrron deep beneath Earth's surface lay hidden from the light and wind. The demon fortress had been created with the darkest of energies, its black walls pulsing with the dark energy of Hell. It had been created many millennia before Heaven and Hell had first fought for control of the Earth. And with the darkest of intent. Angels, the archenemies of the demons, who found themselves behind the black gates never left.

He found himself deep within the bowels of the Dungeon. He would have been able to feel the molten flow just beneath him had he not been trapped within a blindfold of darkness that blocked most of his senses. Three Lords of Evil—he could not believe it.

Without access to his creation, he would be forced to sit within the darkness unless help arrived. Help would arrive, he was sure. The Ancient Lords would not be able to survive the coming storm without him. Conserving the power within his heart, the Creator could only hope that help would not arrive too late for him to correct all that had gone wrong in the world.

All of it began with the single soul he had removed from this world on the Temple Mount. Flipping through that soul's memory, he was able to witness exactly how the events unfolded. A single mortal was responsible for the release of all three Dark Princes, for the murder of entire nations in a great purge of Humanity, as well as for reigniting the ancient war between Heaven and Hell on Earth.

The single mistake of a mortal had unleashed an immortal war in this world that could destroy everything that He had spent eternity creating.

Everything …

Excerpt from Book II:
An Immortal War

White light surrounded the tunnel that pulled him through time, which sped up the farther he progressed. It was a strange feeling to shoot through time, watching the images speed by a rate that only his mind could comprehend. Every defining moment of his life flashed quickly through his mind

Images of his mother playing with him in the courtyards of Metzor passed first. He splashed her with water from the fountain and heard the purity of her laughter. Her funeral and the week of mourning were the first time he saw his father emotionally break down. He remembered his brother Sven when he was ten, holding him on the ground and punching him violently before his oldest brother, Frederick, flew into him and wrestled him to the ground, allowing Conrad to escape.

His older brother, Frederick, giving him advice on how to wield a blade against the wooden practice dummies in the courtyard. In another image, Frederick pushed him into a large fountain, much to the amusement of his friends and the girls in the courtyard, leaving Conrad feeling flustered. In another memory, Frederick rode beside his father, tall and proud, the king of Metzon reaching over and patting Frederick on the back for his just and proper rulings after a day in Merkel.

There was an image of his father, a stern look upon his face, before his hand came out and cuffed Conrad across the side of the head for breaking several of the vases in the palace. Another image of his father showed his soft side as he threw his little boy into the air and caught him, laughing. The memory of another argument between his father and Sven that raged throughout the night, as his mother rubbed his tears away from his cheek by while hers ran freely.

An image of him lying in the sand floated by, his brother standing above him in worn black armour cutting down unnamed men who tried to drag him away. Arrows stuck out of his armour, and black blood ran from his wounds, but Sven never relented. In another, Sven embraced him tightly after his first victory after Conrad told him about charging the rear of the Kyllordic garrison. The last image of Sven was when he'd held Conrad over the fires of the Aedonica volcano, pain and anger within his eyes as he tried to tell his little brother why he did what he did.

Thousands of images from his life passed before him; he relived everything as he passed through the white space. Some were of great joy, lots were of anger, and several of sadness. The last images were of him before his death as he grabbed the armoured girl by her hair, his foot upon her back, his axe raised to remove her head. Then falling against the Throne of Creation, reaching for it to pull himself back up, and the awaking of the monster who pierced his heart with a thick spear.

Conrad looked through the white tunnel and for the first time in what seemed to be an eternity he saw an object within the white, growing ever so slowly. This was the end for him; his journey was finally completed.

"Sorry, *my child, perhaps another distant* day *you may make the final journey. You have unfinished business. This cannot be the end for you.*"

Conrad suddenly stopped, everything frozen in time. The ball of blue and white energy did not crackle or flare wildly as it had before. He was almost there; the blinding white tunnel around him had started to turn to colour. A grasping hand wrapped tightly around his ankle, pulling him backward in time.

"What are you doing? And who are you?"

"I am Azrael, Archangel of Death and the Final Journey. You are

not allowed to finish the Final Journey, for you did not complete the path set before you. Your destiny does not lead you to this point yet."

"What do you mean? I did finish the path before me. I was slain within the temple of the Ancients by some type of guardian. I have seen my mistakes, where I went wrong and the horrible things that led me there. I deserved death, to be taken from the world, for through me Konflikt was once again born into the world.

"You were not Konflikt, young Conrad Metz. You were The Konflikted—the one torn between the love of a brother and the love of your father, torn between what was right and what was wrong: a conflict between Light and Darkness. In the end the decision was made for you by the Dark Princes of Hell, not by you. The truth has been brought forward to the Lords of Heaven for their decision."

"So a decision made by Hell drove me to my death, and now Heaven is making a decision to pull me back from death? It would appear that I have little true power over my own destiny, whether for good or evil. I wish to see my family again, to hold my father and mother, to joke and play with my brothers. And now Heaven is going to deny me what I really want."

His response garnered a few moments of silence from the Angel of Death. *"Truth your words speak, but under false understanding. This is a gift from Heaven for you to take or discard. The decision is your own. You will not find your father in your Heaven, as he is Fallen, nor has your older brother yet made the final journey. This is an opportunity to redeem your brother, Sven, and repair the destruction he wrought upon Earth and Humanity. His soul was also taken from him, but it may not be given back in the same way that yours can be. You have eternity to spend with your family in the expanse of Earth's Heaven, but only a short time with the gift of mortality and the fragility of life. The choice is yours."*

Looking between the beauty of Heaven and the Archangel Azrael, Conrad closed his eyes to try and think. He saw his brother Frederick sleeping silently on a cot, a young woman of great beauty watching over him. He saw his father in full armour surrounded by several other young men as they swung their swords against vile-looking monsters, calling for a charge forward. Another image of a crying child in the arms of an unidentified person racing through crowded streets. Another of a demon and a large black sphere crackling with energy. An image of him pushing a man out of the way, the blade plunging into his own chest. The last image was of Sven chained around the ankles, standing on a giant pyramid-shaped structure, his muscles straining to pull himself loose.

"What am I seeing?"

"They are the future. They are the present. They are the past. They are what could have been. They are what could be. And they are what may never be." Azrael stared at him, not blinking. Conrad wondered what the angel was thinking, or if he could read Conrad's own thoughts.

"Well, thanks for clearing that up for me," he replied sarcastically. He really was conflicted now; he did not know which way to go ... or perhaps he did know. Something pulled him backward through the white space, toward the images that he had seen. His stomach churned with guilt at leaving his brother and father to fight alone. Curiosity pulled at his mind about the images of the unknown; he wondered what such events would lead to. Terror struck him at the sight of Sven struggling upon the altar with the skies burning around him.

"So what is your choice? Do you accept the gift of a second chance? Or do I let go of you forever, leaving your true destiny unfulfilled?"

CIVILIZATIONS OF HUMANITY

Metzon

Metzor	Political Capital of Metzon, Formerly Nymia
Merkel	Military Capital of Metzon
Caridyn	City of the West, Armies of the West
Manstein	City of the East, Armies of the East
Sask	City of the North, Armies of the North
Masen Metz	King of Metzon, Slayer of the Cruel King, "The Metz"
Elia Metz	Queen of Metzon, Daughter of Former King Maxxal
Frederick Metz	First Son of Metz, Heir to the Metzonian Throne
Sven Metz	Second Son of Metz, "The Fist of Metzor"
Conrad Metz	Third Son of Metz

Vince Seim

Cassidus Caspius	Personal Servant to Conrad Metz
Aurik Aerox	Commander of the Royal Elite, Personal Guard to Metzonian King
Brandon Dubryst	General of the Elite Army
Werner Hallaken	General of the Sixth Army of Metzon
Jorhan Baldor	General of the First Army of Metzon, Council of Lords
Mallax	The Cruel King, Brother to King Maxxal
Maxxal	First King of the Middle Kingdom, Father of Elia Metz

Kyllordia

Kyllica	City of Wonders, Political Capital of Kyllordia
Nykol	City of Bridges
Essex	City of Chains, Gateway City to Kyllica
Kaldor	City of Knowledge
Nemin	City of Thieves
Aros	City of Assassins, Home of the Assassins of Aros
Raef Kyllone	First-Born Son of King Oberon, Heir to the Kyllordic Throne
Cleos	Wife of Raef, Queen-to-Be of the Kyllordic Throne

Sylvanna Kyllone	Second-Born Daughter of King Oberon
Eli Elithane	General of Kyllordia, Kyllordic War Council, Order of the Fallen
Ethan Elithane	General of Kyllordia, Kyllordic War Council, Order of the Fallen
Oberon Kyllone	Past King of Kyllordia, Father of Raef and Sylvanna

Chilsa

Chilsa	Political Capital of the Chilsa Empire
New Chilsa	Military Capital of the Chilsa Empire
Chissan	Imperial Border Protector of Chilsa Empire
Kristolphe	Emperor of Chilsa, Son of Neurus
Belle	Empress of Chilsa, Daughter of Neurus
Neurus	True Emperor of Chilsa, Son of Neurik
Neurik	Second Emperor of Chilsa, Son of Nuor
Nuor	First Emperor of Chilsa, Dark God of the Three Black Powers

ORDER OF THE FALLEN

Prokopolis	Political and Military Capital of the Order
Sacred Citadel	Hidden Fortress of the Alakari, Gateway of the Temple and Sacred City
Sacred City	Hidden City of the Alakari, City of the Fallen, Sanctuary of the Children
Cale Caelestis	Grandmaster of the Order, Council of White Elders
Damon Damocles	Architect of the Order, Council of White Elders
Vana Vayra	Historian of the Order, Council of White Elders
Kaleb Khalos	Treasurer of the Order, Council of White Elders
Philip Philotheos	Chronicler of the Order, Council of White Elders
Militades	Defender of the Order, Council of White Elders, Grand General of the Fallen Armies
Karl Kallisto	Administrator of the Sacred City, Royal Advisor to the Metzon Throne

Alek Akakios	Keeper to the Doors of Final Fate and the Sacred City
Kallen	Child of the Fallen, Commander of the Titans, Alexandra's Twin Brother
Alexandra	Child of the Fallen, Teacher of Children, Kallen's Twin Sister
Jaina	Child of the Fallen, Keeper of the Eternal Trees
Kaylee Akakios	Child of the Fallen, Caretaker of the Fountains of Life
Orion	First to Fall, Father of the Order of the Fallen, Son of Ancient Lord Oron
Brianna	Second to Fall, Orion's Bride, Daughter of Ancient Lady Bria

BROTHERHOOD OF THE SIN

Neurus	Dark God of the Brotherhood, Overlord of the Sons of Shadows
Locan	Warlord of the Brotherhood's Armies, "Slayer of Angels"
Krysas	Lieutenant of Locan, Blind Brother
Krasys	Lieutenant of Locan, Blind Brother
Cleos	Bride of Neurus, Witch Mother
Dev'Azra	Dark God of the Dark Angel Army
Xera	Dark Goddess of the Dark Angel Army
Nuor	Dark God of the Dark Angel Army

ACKNOWLEDGEMENTS

First and foremost I would like to acknowledge the painstaking work done by my oldest brother, Jordan. While certainly considered one of my harshest critics, he willingly read the painful first few drafts and the book would not have evolved to this point without his advice and suggestions.

Thanks to my close friends, the real Conrad Metz (whose full name was not originally intended for use!) and Kylle Bosch, who listened to my babbling about this project for many long years. To Nicole Rubin and Angela Leer who offered endless encouragement to pursue this crazy dream, as well as to not give up on it. Thanks to the rest of my family—Sam, Heather, and Jarrett—who put up with the tired, frustrated and grumpy Vin during the entire process.

Second acknowledgements go to staff at iUniverse and its editors for their great patience as I worked tirelessly to repair errors or problems to the best of my ability. A lot of the hard work is put into a book from others whose names are not on the cover.

I also like to acknowledge, Chance Clark, of C3 Creations for his skill and amazing artwork. An incredible cover is a truly important aspect of the book and setting first impressions. He took my crude ideas and with his great skills brought to life many of my ideas in a way that I could only dream.

Lastly and more importantly, I would like to thank all of you who took the time to read my first book. I truly poured heart and soul into this book for many long years and hope that it paid off for a thrilling and epic read for all of you. I am beyond excited for the rest of this powerful story I have created and have only begun to tell you all.

Vince Seim

Once again, thanks to all those mentioned above as well as those I missed. And I certainly missed many. I hope that you enjoyed A *Mortal Mistake* as much as I enjoyed creating and writing it. Now let *An Immortal War* begin!

Vincent Seim

Edwards Brothers Malloy
Oxnard, CA USA
September 9, 2013